D0495991

THE BEAR AND THE DRAGON
VOLUME 2

Newly elected, Jack Ryan has found that being President isn't easy: domestic pitfalls await him at every turn; the Asian economy is crashing; and now, in Moscow, someone may have tried to take out the chairman of the SVR—the former KGB—with a rocket-propelled grenade. Things are unstable enough in Russia without high-level assassination, but more disturbing may be the identities of the potential assassins. Were they political enemies, the Russian Mafia, disaffected former KGB? Or, Ryan wonders, is something far more dangerous at work here? Ryan is right to wonder. For even while Russian investigators pursue the case, and some of his most trusted eyes and ears, including antiterrorism specialist John Clark, head to Moscow, forces in China are moving ahead with a plan of truly audacious proportions. Tired of what they view as the presumption of the West, eager to fulfil their destiny, they are taking matters into their own hands. If they succeed, the world as we know it will never look the same. If they fail . . . the consequences may be unspeakable.

THE BEAR AND THE DRAGON
VOLUME 2

Tom Clancy

PARAGON

CHIVERS PRESS
BATH

First published 2000
by
Michael Joseph
This Large Print edition published by
Chivers Press
by arrangement with
Michael Joseph
2001

ISBN 0 7540 2463 6

British Library Cataloguing in Publication Data available

Printed and bound in Great Britain by
BOOKCRAFT, Midsomer Norton, Somerset

CHAPTER THIRTY-ONE

THE PROTECTION OF RIGHTS

CNN transmits its news coverage twenty-four hours a day to satellite dishes all over the world, and so the report from the streets of Beijing was noted not only by the American intelligence services, but by accountants, housewives, and insomniacs. Of the last group, a goodly number had access to personal computers, and being insomniacs, many of them also knew the e-mail address for the White House. E-mail had almost overnight replaced telegrams as the method of choice for telling the U.S. government what you thought, and was a medium which they appeared to heed, or at least to read, count, and catalog. The latter was done in a basement office in the Old Executive Office Building, the OEOB, the Victorian monstrosity immediately to the west of The House. The people who ran this particular office reported directly to Arnold van Damm, and it was actually rather a thorough and well-organized measure of American public opinion, since they also had electronic access to every polling organization in the country—and, indeed, the entire world. It saved money for the White House not to conduct its own polling, which was useful, since this White House didn't really have a political office per se, somewhat to the despair of the Chief of Staff. Nevertheless, he ran that part of White House operations himself, and largely uncompensated. Arnie didn't mind. For him, politics was as natural as breathing, and he'd decided to serve this President faithfully long before, especially since serving him so often meant protecting him from himself and his frequently stunning political ineptitude.

The data which started arriving just after midnight, however, didn't require a political genius to understand it. Quite a few of the e-mails had actual names attached—not mere electronic 'handles'—and a lot of them were DEMANDING!!! action. Arnie would remark later in the day that he hadn't known that so many Baptists were computer-literate, something he reproached himself for even thinking.

In the same building, the White House Office of Signals duly made a high-quality tape of the report and had it walked to the Oval Office. Elsewhere in the world, the CNN report from Beijing arrived at breakfast time, causing more than a few people to set their coffee (or tea) cups down immediately before a groan of anger. *That* occasioned brief dispatches from American embassies around the world, informing the Department of State that various foreign governments had reacted adversely to the story on CNN, and that various PRC embassies had found demonstrators outside their gates, some of them quite vociferous. This information rapidly found its way to the Diplomatic Protection Service, the State Department agency tasked with the job of securing foreign diplomats and their embassies. Calls went out from there to the D.C. police to increase the uniformed presence near the PRC's various missions to America, and to arrange a rapid backup should any similar problems develop right here in Washington.

By the time Ben Goodley awoke and drove over to Langley for his morning briefing, the American intelligence community had pretty well diagnosed the problem. As Ryan had so colorfully said it himself, the PRC had stepped very hard on the old crank with the golf shoes, and even they would soon feel the pain. This would prove to be a gross understatement.

*   *   *

The good news for Goodley, if you could call it that, was that Ryan invariably had his breakfast-room TV tuned to CNN, and was fully aware of the new crisis before putting on his starched white button-down shirt and striped tie. Even kissing his wife and kids on their way out of The House that morning couldn't do much to assuage his anger at the incomprehensible stupidity of those people on the other side of the world.

'God damn it, Ben!' POTUS snarled when Goodley came into the Oval Office.

'Hey, Boss, *I* didn't do it!' the National Security Adviser protested, surprised at the President's vehemence.

'What do we know?'

'Essentially, you've seen it all. The widow of the poor bastard who got his brains blown out the other day came to Beijing hoping to bring his body back to Taiwan for burial. She found out that the body had been cremated, and the ashes disposed of. The local cops would not let her back into her house, and when some members of the parish came by to hold a prayer service, the local cops decided to break it up.' He didn't have to say that the attack on the widow had been caught with particular excellence by the CNN cameraman, to the point that Cathy Ryan had commented upstairs that the woman definitely had a broken nose, and possibly worse, and would probably need a good maxillary surgeon to put her face back together. Then she'd asked her husband why the cops would hate anyone so much.

'She believes in God, I suppose,' Ryan had replied in the breakfast room.

'Jack, this is like something out of Nazi Germany, something from that History Channel stuff you like to watch.' And doctor or not, she'd cringed at the tape of the attacks on Chinese citizens armed only with Bibles.

'I've seen it, too,' van Damm said, arriving in the Oval Office. 'And we're getting a flood of responses from the public.'

'Fuckin' barbarians,' Ryan swore, as Robby Jackson came in to complete the morning's intelligence-briefing audience.

'You can hang a big roger on that one, Jack. Damn, I know Pap's going to see this, too, and today's the day for him to do the memorial service at Gerry Patterson's church. It's going to be epic, Jack. Epic,' the Vice President promised.

'And CNN's going to be there?'

'Bet your bippy My Lord President,' Robby confirmed.

Ryan turned to his Chief of Staff. 'Okay, Arnie, I'm listening.'

'No, *I'm* the one listening, Jack,' van Damm replied. 'What are you thinking?'

'I'm thinking I have to talk to the public about this. Press conference, maybe. As far as action

4

goes, I'll start by saying that we have a huge violation of human rights, all the more so that they had the fucking arrogance to do it in front of world opinion. I'll say that America has trouble doing business with people who act in this way, that commercial ties do not justify or cancel out gross violations of the principles on which our country is founded, that we have to reconsider all of our relations with the PRC.'

'Not bad,' the Chief of Staff observed, with a teacher's smile to a bright pupil. 'Check with Scott for other options and ideas.'

'Yeah.' Jack nodded. 'Okay, broader question, how will the country react to this?'

'The initial response will be outrage,' Arnie replied. 'It looks bad on TV, and that's how most people will respond, from the gut. If the Chinese have the good sense to make some kind of amends, then it'll settle down. If not'—Arnie frowned importantly—'I have a bad feeling. The church groups are going to raise hell. They've offended the Italian and German governments—so our NATO allies are also pissed off at this—and smashing that poor woman's face isn't going to win them any friends in the women's rights movement. This whole business is a colossal loser for them, but I'm not sure they understand the implications of their actions.'

'Then they're going to learn, the easy way or the hard way,' Goodley suggested to the group.

*   *   *

Dr. Alan Gregory always seemed to stay at the same Marriott overlooking the Potomac, under the air approach to Reagan National Airport. He'd again taken the red-eye in from Los Angeles, a flight which hadn't exactly improved with practice over the years. Arriving, he took a cab to the hotel for a shower and a change of clothes, which would enable him to feel and look vaguely human for his 10:15 with the SecDef. For this at least, he would not need a taxi. Dr. Bretano was sending a car for him. The car duly arrived with an Army staff sergeant driving, and Gregory hopped in the back, to find a newspaper. It took only ten minutes to pull up to the River Entrance, where an Army major waited to escort him through the metal detector and onto the E-ring.

'You know the Secretary?' the officer asked on the way in.

'Oh, yeah, from a short distance, anyway.'

He had to wait half a minute in an anteroom, but only half a minute.

'Al, grab a seat. Coffee?'

'Yes, thank you, Dr. Bretano.'

'Tony,' the SecDef corrected. He wasn't a formal man most of the time, and he knew the sort of work Gregory was capable of. A Navy steward got coffee for both men, along with croissants and jam, then withdrew. 'How was the flight?'

'The red-eye never changes, sir—Tony. If you get off alive, they haven't done it right.'

'Yeah, well, one nice thing about this job, I have a G waiting for me all the time. I don't have to walk or drive very much, and you saw the security detail outside.'

'The guys with the knuckles dragging on the floor?' Gregory asked.

'Be nice. One of them went to Princeton before

6

he became a SEAL.'

That must be the one who reads the comic books to the others, Al didn't observe out loud. 'So, Tony, what did you want me here for?'

'You used to work downstairs in SDIO, as I recall.'

'Seven years down there, working in the dark with the rest of the mushrooms, and it never really worked out. I was in the free-electron-laser project. It went pretty well, except the damned lasers never scaled up the way we expected, even after we stole what the Russians were doing. They had the best laser guy in the world, by the way. Poor bastard got killed in a rock-climbing accident back in 1990, or that's what we heard in SDIO. He was bashing his head against the same wall our guys were. The 'wiggle chamber,' we called it, where you lase the hot gasses to extract the energy for your beam. We could never get a stable magnetic containment. They tried everything. I helped for nineteen months. There were some really smart guys working that problem, but we all struck out. I think the guys at Princeton will solve the fusion-containment problem before this one. We looked at that, too, but the problems were too different to copy the theoretical solutions. We ended up giving them a lot of our ideas, and they've been putting it to good use. Anyway, the Army made me a lieutenant colonel, and three weeks later, they offered me an early out because they didn't have any more use for me, and so I took the job at TRW that Dr. Flynn offered, and I've been working for you ever since.' And so Gregory was getting eighty percent of his twenty-year Army pension, plus half a million a year from TRW as a section leader, with

7

stock options, and one hell of a retirement package.

'Well, Gerry Flynn sings your praises about once a week.'

'He's a good man to work for,' Gregory replied, with a smile and a nod.

'He says you can do software better than anyone in Sunnyvale.'

'For some things. I didn't do the code for "Doom," unfortunately, but I'm still your man for adaptive optics.'

'How about SAMs?'

Gregory nodded. 'I did some of that when I was new in the Army. Then later they had me in to play with Patriot Block-4, you know, intercepting Scuds. I helped out on the warhead software.' It had been three days too late to be used in the Persian Gulf War, he didn't add, but his software was now standard on all Patriot missiles in the field.

'Excellent. I want you to look over something for me. It'll be a direct contract for the Office of the Secretary of Defense—me—and Gerry Flynn won't gripe about it.'

'What's that, Tony?'

'Find out if the Navy's Aegis system can intercept a ballistic inbound.'

'It can. It'll stop a Scud, but that's only Mach three or so. You mean a *real* ballistic inbound?'

The SecDef nodded. 'Yeah, an ICBM.'

'There's been talk about that for years . . .' Gregory sipped his coffee. 'The radar system is up to it. May be a slight software issue there, but it would not be a hard one, because you'll be getting raid-warning from other assets, and the SPY radar can see a good five hundred miles, and you can do all sorts of things with it electronically, like blast out seven million watts of RF down half a degree of bearing. That'll fry electronic components out to, oh, seven or eight thousand meters. You'll end up having two-headed kids, and have to buy a new watch.

'Okay,' he went on, a slightly spacey look in his eyes. 'The way Aegis works, the big SPY radar gives you a rough location for your target-interception, so you can loft your SAMs into a box. That's why Aegis missiles get such great range. They go out on autopilot and only do actual maneuvering for the last few seconds. For that, you have the SPG radars on the ships, and the seeker-head on the missile tracks in on the reflected RF energy off the target. It's a killer system against airplanes, because you don't know you're being illuminated until the last couple of seconds, and it's hard to eyeball the missile and evade in so short a time.

'Okay, but for an ICBM, the terminal velocity is way the hell up there, like twenty-five thousand feet per second, like Mach eleven. That means your targeting window is very small . . . in all dimensions, but especially depth. Also you're talking a fairly hard, robust target. The RV off an ICBM is fairly sturdy, not tissue paper like the boosters are. I'll have to see if the warhead off a SAM will really hurt one of those.' The eyes cleared and he looked directly into Bretano's eyes. 'Okay, when do I start?'

'Commander Matthews,' THUNDER said into his intercom phone. 'Dr. Gregory is ready to talk to the Aegis people. Keep me posted, Al.' was Bretano's final order.

9

'You bet.'

*　　　*　　　*

The Reverend Doctor Hosiah Jackson donned his best robe of black silk, a gift handmade by the ladies of his congregation, the three stripes on the upper arms designating his academic rank. He was in Gerry Patterson's study, and a nice one it was. Outside the white wooden door was his congregation, all of them well-dressed and fairly prosperous white folks, some of whom would be slightly uncomfortable with having a black minister talk to them—Jesus was white, after all (or Jewish, which was almost the same thing). This was a little different, though, because this day they were remembering the life of someone only Gerry Patterson had ever met, a Chinese Baptist named Yu Fa An, whom their minister had called Skip, and whose congregation they had supported and supported generously for years. And so to commemorate the life of a yellow minister, they would sit through the sermon of a black one while their own pastor preached the gospel in a black church. *It was a fine gesture on Gerry's part*, Hosiah Jackson thought, hoping it wouldn't get him into any trouble with this congregation. *There'd be a few out there, their bigoted thoughts invisible behind their self-righteous faces, but*, the Reverend Jackson admitted to himself, *they'd be tortured souls because of it*. Those times had passed. He remembered them better than white Mississippians did because he'd been the one walking in the streets—he'd been arrested seven times during his work with the Southern Christian Leadership Conference—and

10

getting his parishioners registered to vote. That had been the real problem with the rednecks. Riding in a municipal bus was no big deal, but voting meant power, real civic power, the ability to elect the people who made the laws which would be enforced on black and white citizens alike, and the rednecks hadn't liked that at all. But times had changed, and now they accepted the inevitable— *after* it had come to pass—and they'd learned to deal with it, and they'd also learned to vote Republican instead of Democrat, and the amusing part of *that* to Hosiah Jackson was that his own son Robert was more conservative than these well-dressed rednecks were, and *he'd* gone pretty far for the son of a colored preacherman in central Mississippi. But it was time. Patterson, like Jackson, had a large mirror on the back of the door so that he could check his appearance on the way out. Yes, he was ready. He looked solemn and authoritative, as the Voice of God was supposed to look.

The congregation was already singing. They had a fine organ here, a real hundred-horsepower one, not the electronic kind he had at his church, but the singing . . . they couldn't help it. They sang white, and there was no getting around it. The singing had all the proper devotion, but not the exuberant passion that he was accustomed to . . . but he'd love to have that organ, Hosiah decided. The pulpit was finely appointed, with a bottle of ice water, and a microphone provided by the CNN crew, who were discreetly in both back corners of the church and not making any trouble, *which was unusual for news crews*, Reverend Jackson thought. His last thought before beginning was that the only

11

other black man to stand in this pulpit before this moment was the man who'd painted the woodwork.

'Ladies and gentlemen, good morning. I am Hosiah Jackson. You all probably know where my church is. I am here today at the invitation of my good friend and colleague, your pastor, Gerry Patterson.

'Gerry has the advantage over me today, because, unlike me, and I gather unlike any person in the church, he actually knew the man whom we are here to remember.

'To me, Yu Fa An was just a pen pal. Some years ago, Gerry and I had occasion to talk about the ministry. We met in the chapel at the local hospital. It'd been a bad day for both of us. We'd both lost good people that day, at about the same time, and to the same disease, cancer, and both of us needed to sit in the hospital chapel. I guess we both needed to ask God the same question. It's the question all of us have asked—why is there such cruelty in the world, why does a loving and merciful God permit it?

'Well, the answer to that question is found in Scripture, and in many places. Jesus Himself lamented the loss of innocent life, and one of his miracles was the raising of Lazarus from the dead, both to show that He was indeed the Son of God, and also to show His humanity, to show how much He cared about the loss of a good man.

'But Lazarus, like our two parishioners that day in the hospital, had died from disease, and when God made the world, He made it in such a way that there were, and there still are, things that need fixing. The Lord God told us to take dominion over the world, and part of that was God's desire for us

12

to cure disease, to fix *all* the broken parts and so to bring perfection to the world, even as, by following God's Holy Word, we can bring perfection to ourselves.

'Gerry and I had a good talk that day, and that was the beginning of our friendship, as all ministers of the Gospel ought to be friends, because we preach the same Gospel from the same God.

'The next week we were talking again, and Gerry told me about his friend Skip. A man from the other side of the world, a man from a place where the religious traditions do not know Jesus. Well, Skip learned about all that at Oral Roberts University in Oklahoma, the same as many others, and he learned it so well that he thought long and hard and decided to join the ministry and preach the Gospel of Jesus Christ . . .'

*   *   *

'Skip's skin was a different color than mine,' Gerry Patterson was saying in another pulpit less than two miles away. 'But in God's eyes, we are all the same, because the Lord Jesus looks through our skin into our hearts and our souls, and He always knows what's in there.'

'That's right,' a man's voice agreed in the congregation.

'And so, Skip became a minister of the Gospel. Instead of returning to his native land, where freedom of religion is something their government protects, Skip decided to keep flying west, into communist China. Why there?' Patterson asked. 'Why there indeed! The other China does not have freedom of religion. The other China refuses to

13

admit that there is such a thing as God. The other China is like the Philistines of the Old Testament, the people who persecuted the Jews of Moses and Joshua, the enemies of God Himself. Why did Skip do this? Because he knew that no other place needed to hear the Word of God more than those people, and that Jesus wants us to preach to the heathen, to bring His Holy Word to those whose souls cry out for it, and this he did. No United States Marine storming the shores of Iwo Jima showed more courage than Skip did, carrying his Bible into Red China and starting to preach the Gospel in a land where religion is a crime.'

*   *   *

'And we must not forget that there was another man there, a Catholic cardinal, an old unmarried man from a rich and important family who long ago decided on his own to join the clergy of his church,' Jackson reminded those before him. 'His name was Renato, a name as foreign to us as Fa An, but despite that, he was a man of God who also took the Word of Jesus to the land of the heathen.

'When the government of that country found out about Reverend Yu, they took Skip's job away. They hoped to *starve* him out, but the people who made that decision didn't know Skip. They didn't know Jesus, and they didn't know about the faithful, did they?'

'Hell, no!' replied a white male voice from the pews, and that's when Hosiah knew he had them.

'No, sir! That's when your Pastor Gerry found out and that's when you good people started sending help to Skip Yu, to support the man his

14

godless government was trying to destroy, because they didn't know that people of faith share a *commitment* to justice!'

*   *   *

Patterson's arm shot out. 'And Jesus pointed and said, see that woman there, she gives from her *need*, not from her riches. It takes more for a poor man or a poor woman to give than it does for a rich man to do it. *That* was when you good people began helping my congregation to support my friend Skip. And Jesus also said "that which you do for the least of My brethren you do also unto Me". And so your church and my church helped this man, this lonely minister of the Gospel in the land of the pagans, those people who *deny* the Name and Word of God, those people who worship the corpse of a monster named Mao, who put his embalmed body on display as though it were the body of a saint! He was no saint. He was no man of God. He was hardly a man at all. He was a mass murderer worse than anything our country has ever seen. He was like the Hitler that our fathers fought to destroy sixty years ago. But to the people who run that country, that killer, that murderer, that destroyer of life and freedom is the new god. That 'god' is *false*, Patterson told them, with passion entering his voice. 'That "god" is the voice of Satan. That "god" is the mouthpiece for the fires of Hell. That "god" was the incarnation of evil—and that "god" is dead, and now he's a stuffed animal, like the dead bird you might see over the bar in a saloon, or the deer head a lot of you have in your den—and they still worship him. They *still* honor

15

his word, and they *still* revere his beliefs—the beliefs that *killed* millions of people just because their false god didn't like them.' Patterson stood erect and brushed his hair back.

'There are those who say that what evil we see in the world is just the absence of good. But we know better than that. There is a devil in creation, and that devil has agents among us, and some of those agents run countries! Some of those agents start wars. Some of those agents take innocent people from their homes and put them in camps and murder them there like cattle in a slaughterhouse. Those are the agents of Satan! Those are the devotees of the Prince of Darkness. They are those among us who take the lives of the innocent, even the lives of innocent little babies . . .'

*   *   *

'And so, those three men of God went to the hospital. One of them, our friend Skip, went to assist his parishioner in her time of need. The other two, the Catholics, went because they, too, were men of God, and they, too, stood for the same things that we do, *because the Word of Jesus IS THE SAME FOR ALL OF US!'* Hosiah Jackson's voice boomed out.

'Yes, sir,' the same white voice agreed, and there were nods in the congregation.

'And so those three men of God went to the hospital to save the life of a little baby, a little baby that the government of that heathen land wanted to kill—and why? They wanted to kill it because its mother and father believe in God—and, oh, no, they couldn't allow people like *that* to bring a child

16

into the world! Oh, no, they couldn't allow people of faith to bring a child into their country, because that was like inviting in a spy. That was a *danger* to their godless government. And why is it a danger?

'It's a *danger* because they *know* that they are godless pagans! It's a *danger* because they *know* that God's Holy Word is the most powerful force in the world! And their only response to that kind of danger is to kill, to take the life that God Himself gives to each of us, because in denying God, they can also deny life, and you know, those pagans, those unbelievers, those killers *love* to have that kind of power. They *love* pretending that *they* are gods. They love their power, and they love using it in the service of Satan! They know they are destined to spend eternity in Hell, and they want to share their Hell with us here on earth, and they want to deny to us the only thing that can liberate us from the destiny they have chosen for themselves. *That* is why they condemned that innocent little baby to death.

'And when those three men went to the hospital to preserve the life of that innocent baby, they stood in God's own place. They took God's place, but they did so in humility and in the strength of their faith. They stood in *God's* place to fulfill *God's* will, not to get power for themselves, not to be false heroes. They went there to serve, not to rule. To serve, as the Lord Jesus Himself served. As his apostles served. They went there to protect an innocent life. They went there to do the Lord God's work!'

*   *   *

17

'You people probably don't know this, but when I was first ordained I spent three years in the United States Navy, and I served as a chaplain to the Marines. I was assigned to the Second Marine Division at Camp Lejeune, North Carolina. When I was there, I got to know people we call heroes, and for sure a lot of Marines fall into that category. I was there to minister to the dead and dying after a terrible helicopter crash, and it was one of the great honors of my life to be there and to comfort dying young Marines—because I *knew* they were going to see God. I remember one, a sergeant, the man had just gotten married a month before, and he died while he was saying a prayer to God for his wife. He was a veteran of Vietnam, that sergeant, and he had lots of decorations. He was what we call a tough guy,' Patterson told the black congregation, 'but the toughest thing about that Marine was that when he knew he was going to die, he prayed not for himself, but for his young wife, that God would comfort her. That Marine died as a Christian man, and he went from this world to stand proud before his God as a man who did his duty in every way he could.

'Well, so did Skip, and so did Renato. They sacrificed their lives to save a baby. God sent them. God gave those men their orders. And they heard the orders, and they followed them without flinching, without hesitating, without thinking except to be sure that they were doing the right thing.

'And today, eight thousand miles from here there is a new life, a new little baby, probably asleep now. That baby will never know all the hubbub that came just before she was born, but with parents

18

like that, that baby will know the Word of God. And all that happened because three brave men of God went to that hospital, and two of them died there to do the Lord's Work.'

'Skip was a Baptist. Renato was a Catholic.'

'Skip was yellow. I'm white. You people are black.

'But Jesus doesn't care about any of that. We have all heard His words. We have all accepted Him as our Savior. So did Skip. So did Renato. Those two brave men sacrificed their lives for The Right. The Catholic's last words—he asked if the baby was okay, and the other Catholic, the German priest, said "yes," and Renato said, *"Bene."* That's Italian. It means, "That's good, that's all right." He died knowing that he did the right thing, And that's not a bad thing, is it?'

'That's right!' three voices called out.

*   *   *

'There is so much to learn from their example,' Hosiah Jackson told his borrowed congregation.

'We must learn, first of all, that God's Word is the same for all of us. I'm a black man. You folks are white. Skip was Chinese. In that we are all different, but in God's Holy Word we are all the same. Of all the things we have to learn, of all the things we have to keep in our hearts every day we live, that is the most important. Jesus is Savior to us all, if only we accept Him, if only we take Him into our hearts, if only we listen when He talks to us. That is the first lesson we need to learn from the death of those two brave men.

'The next lesson we need to learn is that Satan is

19

still alive out there, and while we must listen to the words of God, there are those out there who prefer to listen to the words of Lucifer. We need to recognize those people for what they are.

'Forty years ago, we had some of those people among us. I remember it, and probably you do, too. We got over all that. The reason we got over it is that we have all heard the Word of God. We've all remembered that our God is a God of Mercy. Our God is a God of Justice. If we remember that, we remember a lot more besides. God does not measure us by what we are against. Jesus looks into our hearts and measures us by what we are *for*.

'But we cannot be *for* justice except by being against *in*justice. We must remember Skip and Renato. We must remember Mr. and Mrs. Yang, and all like them, those people in China who've been denied the chance to hear the Word of God. The sons of Lucifer are *afraid* of God's Holy Word. The sons of Lucifer are *afraid* of us. The sons of Satan are *afraid* of God's Will, because in God's Love and in the Way of the Lord lies their destruction. They may hate God. They may hate God's word—but they *fear*, they *FEAR* the consequences of their own actions. They fear the damnation that awaits them. They may *deny* God, but they know the *righteousness* of God, and they know that every human soul cries out for knowledge of our Lord.

'*That's* why they feared Reverend Yu Fa An. That's why they feared Cardinal DiMilo, and that's why they fear us. Me and you good people. Those sons of Satan are *afraid* of us because they know that their words and their false beliefs can no more stand up to the Word of God than a house trailer

20

can stand before a springtime tornado! And they know that all men are born with some knowledge of God's Holy Word. That's why they fear us.

'Good!' Reverend Hosiah Jackson exclaimed. 'Then let's give them another reason to fear us! Let God's faithful show them the power and the conviction of our faith!'

*   *   *

'But we can be sure that God was there with Skip, and with Cardinal DiMilo. God directed their brave hands, and through them God saved that innocent little child,' Patterson told his black congregation. 'And God welcomed to his bosom the two men He sent there to do His work, and today our friend Skip and Cardinal DiMilo stand proudly before the Lord God, those good and faithful servants of His Holy Word.

'My friends, they did their job. They did the Lord's work that day. They saved the life of an innocent child. They showed the whole world what the power of faith can be.'

'But what of our job?' Patterson asked.

*   *   *

'It is *not* the job of the faithful to encourage Satan,' Hosiah Jackson told the people before him. He'd captured their attention as surely as Lord Olivier on his best day—and why not? These were not the words of Shakespeare. These were the words of one of God's ministers. 'When Jesus looks into our hearts, will He see people who support the sons of Lucifer? Will Jesus see people who give their money to support the godless killers of the innocent? Will Jesus see people who give their money to the new *Hitler*?'

'No!' A female voice shouted in reply. *'No!'*

'What is it that we, we the people of God, the people of faith—what is it that we stand for? When the sons of Lucifer kill the faithful, where do you stand? Will you stand for justice? Will you stand for your faith? Will you stand with the holy martyrs? Will you stand with Jesus?' Jackson demanded of his borrowed white congregation.

And as one voice, they answered him: *'Yes!'*

*   *   *

'Jesus H. Christ,' Ryan said. He'd walked over to the Vice President's office to catch the TV coverage.

'Told you my Pap was good at this stuff. Hell, I grew up with it over the dinner table, and he still gets inside my head,' said Robby Jackson, wondering if he'd allow himself a drink tonight. 'Patterson is probably doing okay, too. Pap says he's an okay guy, but my Pap is the champ.'

'Did he ever think of becoming a Jesuit?' Jack asked with a grin.

'Pap's a preacherman, but he ain't quite a saint. The celibacy would be kinda hard on him,' Robby answered.

Then the scene changed to Leonardo di Vinci International Airport outside Rome, where the Alitalia 747 had just landed and was now pulling up to the jetway. Below it was a truck, and next to the truck some cars belonging to the Vatican. It had already been announced that Renato Cardinal

22

DiMilo would be getting his own full state funeral at St. Peter's Basilica, and CNN would be there to cover all of it, joined by SkyNews, Fox, and all the major networks. They'd been late getting onto the story at the beginning, but that only made this part of the coverage more full.

*   *   *

Back in Mississippi, Hosiah Jackson walked slowly down from the pulpit as the last hymn ended. He walked with grace and dignity to the front door, so as to greet all of the congregation members on the way out.

That took much longer than he'd expected. It seemed that every single one of them wanted to take his hand and thank him for coming—the degree of hospitality was well in excess of his most optimistic expectations. And there was no doubting their sincerity. Some insisted on talking for a few moments, until the press of the departing crowd forced them down the steps and onto the parking lot. Hosiah counted six invitations to dinner, and ten inquiries about his church, and if it needed any special work. Finally, there was just one man left, pushing seventy, with scraggly gray hair and a hooked nose that had seen its share of whiskey bottles. He looked like a man who'd topped out as assistant foreman at the sawmill.

'Hello,' Jackson said agreeably.

'Pastor,' the man replied, uneasily, as though wanting to say more.

It was a look Hosiah had seen often enough. 'Can I help you, sir?'

'Pastor . . . years ago . . .' And his voice choked

23

up again. 'Pastor,' he began again. 'Pastor, I sinned.'

'My friend, we all sin. God knows that. That's why he sent His Son to be with us and conquer our sins.' The minister grabbed the man's shoulder to steady him.

'I was in the Klan, Pastor, I did . . . sinful things . . . I . . . hurt nigras just cuz I hated them, and I—'

'What's your name?' Hosiah asked gently.

'Charlie Picket,' the man replied. And then Hosiah knew. He had a good memory for names. Charles Worthington Picket had been the Grand Kleegle of the local Klavern. He'd never been convicted of a major crime, but his name was one that came up much of the time.

'Mr. Picket, those things all happened many years ago,' he reminded the man.

'I ain't never—I mean, I ain't never *killed* nobody. Honest, Pastor, I ain't never done that,' Picket insisted, with real desperation in his voice. 'But I know'd thems that did, and I never told the cops. I never told them not to do it . . . sweet Jesus, I don't know what I was back then, Pastor. I was . . . it was . . .'

'Mr. Picket, are you sorry for your sins?'

'Oh, yes, oh Jesus, yes, Pastor. I've prayed for forgiveness, but—'

'There is no "but", Mr. Picket. God has forgiven you your sins,' Jackson told him in his gentlest voice.

'Are you sure?'

A smile and a nod. 'Yes, I'm sure.'

'Pastor, you need help at your church, roofing and stuff, you call me, y'hear? That's the house of God, too. Maybe I didn't always know it, but by

24

damn I know it now, sir.'

He'd probably never called a black man 'sir' in his life, unless there'd been a gun to his head. So, the minister thought, at least one person had listened to his sermon, and learned something from it. And that wasn't bad for a man in his line of work.

'Pastor, I gots to apologize for all the evil words and thoughts I had. Ain't never done that, but I gots to do it now.' He seized Hosiah's hand. 'Pastor, I am sorry, sorry as a man can be for all the things I done back then, and I beg your forgiveness.'

'And the Lord Jesus said, "Go forth and sin no more." Mr. Picket, that's all of scripture in one sentence. God came to forgive our sins. God has already forgiven you.'

Finally, their eyes met. 'Thank you, Pastor. And God bless you, sir.'

'And may the Lord bless you, too.' Hosiah Jackson watched the man walk off to his pickup truck, wondering if a soul had just been saved. If so, Skip would be pleased with the black friend he'd never met.

CHAPTER THIRTY-TWO

COALITION COLLISION

It was a long drive from the airport to the Vatican, every yard of it covered by cameras in the high-speed motorcade, until finally the vehicles entered the Piazza San Pietro, St. Peter's Square. There, waiting, was a squad of Swiss Guards wearing the purple-and-gold uniforms designed by Michelangelo. Some of the Guards pulled the casket containing a Prince of the Church, martyred far away, and carried it through the towering bronze doors into the cavernous interior of the church, where the next day a Requiem Mass would be celebrated by the Pope himself.

But it wasn't about religion now, except to the public. For the President of the United States, it was about matters of state. It turned out that Tom Jefferson had been right after all. The power of government devolved directly from the people, and Ryan had to act now, in a way that the people would approve, because when you got down to it, the nation wasn't his. It was theirs.

And one thing made it worse. SORGE had coughed up another report that morning, and it was late coming in only because Mary Patricia Foley wanted to be doubly sure that the translation was right.

Also in the Oval Office were Ben Goodley, Arnie van Damm, and the Vice President. 'Well?' Ryan asked them.

'Cocksuckers,' Robby said, first of all. 'If they really think this way, we shouldn't sell them shit in a paper bag. Even at Top Gun after a long night of boilermakers, even Navy fighter pilots don't talk like this.'

'It is callous,' Ben Goodley agreed.

'They don't issue consciences to the political leaders, I guess,' van Damm said, making it unanimous.

'How would your father react to information like this, Robby?' Ryan asked.

26

'His immediate response will be the same as mine: Nuke the bastards. Then he'll remember what happens in a real war and settle down some. Jack, we have to punish them.'

Ryan nodded. 'Okay, but if we shut down trade to the PRC, the first people hurt are the poor schlubs in the factories, aren't they?'

'Sure, Jack, but who's holding them hostage, the good guys or the bad guys? Somebody can *always* say that, and if fear of hurting them prevents you from taking any action, then you're only making sure that things *never* get better for them. So, you can't allow yourself to be limited that way,' TOMCAT concluded, 'or *you* become the hostage.'

Then the phone rang. Ryan got it, grumbling at the interruption.

'Secretary Adler for you, Mr. President. He says it's important.'

Jack leaned across his desk and punched the blinking button. 'Yeah, Scott.'

'I got the download. It's not unexpected, and people talk differently inside the office than outside, remember.'

'That's great to hear, Scott, and if they talk about taking a few thousand Jews on a train excursion to Auschwitz, is that supposed to be funny, too?'

'Jack, I'm the Jew here, remember?'

Ryan let out a long breath and pushed another button. 'Okay, Scott, you're on speaker now. Talk,' POTUS ordered.

'This is just the way the bastards talk. Yes, they're arrogant, but we already knew that. Jack, if other countries knew how *we* talk inside the White House, we'd have a lot fewer allies and a lot more wars. Sometimes intelligence can be too good.'

Adler really was a good SecState, Ryan thought. His job was to look for simple and safe ways out of problems, and he worked damned hard at it.

'Okay, suggestions?'

'I have Carl Hitch lay a note on them. We demand a statement of apology for this fuckup.'

'And if they tell us to shove it?'

'Then we pull Rutledge and Hitch back for "consultations," and let them simmer for a while.'

'The note, Scott?'

'Yes, Mr. President.'

'Write it on asbestos paper and sign it in blood,' Jack told him coldly.

'Yes, sir,' SecState acknowledged, and the line went dead.

*   *   *

It was a lot later in the day in Moscow when Pavel Yefremov and Oleg Provalov came into Sergey Golovko's office.

'I'm sorry I couldn't have you in sooner,' the SVR chairman told his guests. 'We've been busy with problems—the Chinese and that shooting in Beijing.' He'd been looking into it just like every other person in the world.

'Then you have another problem with them, Comrade Chairman.

'Oh?'

Yefremov handed over the decrypt. Golovko took it, thanking the man with his accustomed good manners, then settled back in his chair and started reading. In less than five seconds, his eyes widened.

'This is not possible,' his voice whispered.

'Perhaps so, but it is difficult to explain otherwise.'

'*I* was the target?'

'So it would appear,' Provalov answered.

'But *why*?'

'That we do not know,' Yefremov said, 'and probably nobody in the city of Moscow knows. If the order was given through a Chinese intelligence officer, the order originated in Beijing, and the man who forwarded it probably doesn't know the reasoning behind it. Moreover, the operation is set up to be somewhat deniable, since we cannot even prove that this man is an intelligence officer, and not an assistant or what the Americans call a "stringer." In fact, their man was identified for us by an American,' the FSS officer concluded.

Golovko's eyes came up. 'How the hell did *that* happen?'

Provalov explained. 'A Chinese intelligence officer in Moscow is unlikely to be concerned by the presence of an American national, whereas any Russian citizen is a potential counterintelligence officer. Mishka was there and offered to help, and I permitted it. Which leads me to a question.'

'What do you tell this American?' Golovko asked for him.

The lieutenant nodded. 'Yes, Comrade Chairman. He knows a good deal about the murder investigation because I confided in him and he offered some helpful suggestions. He is a gifted police investigator. And he is no fool. When he asks how this case is going, what can I say?'

Golovko's initial response was as predictable as it was automatic: *Say nothing.* But he restrained himself. If Provalov said nothing, then the

29

American would have to be a fool not to see the lie, and, as he said, the American was no fool. On the other hand, did it serve Golovko's—or Russia's—purposes for America to know that his life was in danger? That question was deep and confusing. While he pondered it, he'd have his bodyguard come in. He beeped his secretary.

'Yes, Comrade Chairman,' Major Shelepin said, coming in the door.

'Something new for you to worry about, Anatoliy Ivan'ch,' Golovko told him. It was more than that. The first sentence turned Shelepin pale.

*   *   *

It started in America with the unions. These affiliations of working people, which had lost power in the preceding decades, were in their way the most conservative organizations in America, for the simple reason that their loss of power had made them mindful of the importance of what power they retained. To hold on to that, they resisted any change that threatened the smallest entitlement of their humblest member.

China had long been a *bête noir* for the labor movement, for the simple reason that Chinese workers made less in a day than American union automobile workers made during their morning coffee break. That tilted the playing field in favor of the Asians, and *that* was something the AFL/CIO was not prepared to approve.

So much the better that the government that ruled those underpaid workers disregarded human rights. That just made them easier to oppose.

American labor unions are nothing if not

30

organized, and so every single member of Congress started getting telephone calls. Most of them were taken by staffers, but those from senior union officials in a member's state or district usually made it all the way through, regardless of which side the individual member stood on. Attention was called to the barbaric action of that godless state which also, by the way, shit on its workers *and* took American jobs through its unfair labor practices. The size of the trade surplus came up in every single telephone call, which would have made the members of Congress think that it was a carefully orchestrated phone campaign (which it was) had they compared notes on the telephone calls with one another (which they didn't).

Later in the day, demonstrations were held, and though they were about as spontaneous as those held in the People's Republic of China, they were covered by the local and/or national media, because it was a place to send cameras, and the newsies belonged to a union, too.

Behind the telephone calls and in front of the TV coverage of the demonstrations came the letters and e-mails, all of which were counted and cataloged by the members' staffers.

Some of them called the White House to let the President know what was happening on the Hill. Those calls *all* went to the office of Arnold van Damm, whose own staff kept a careful count of the calls, their position, and their degree of passion, which was running pretty high.

On top of that came the notices from the religious communities, virtually all of which China had managed to offend at once.

The one unexpected but shrewd development of

the day didn't involve a call or letter to anyone in the government. Chinese manufacturers located on the island of Taiwan all had lobbying and public-relations agencies in America. One of these came up with an idea that caught on as rapidly as the powder inside a rifle cartridge. By midday, three separate printers were turning out peel-off stickers with the flag of the Republic of China and the caption 'We're the good guys.' By the following morning, clerks at retail outlets all over America were affixing them to items of Taiwanese manufacture. The news media found out about it even before the process had begun, and thus aided the Republic of China industrialists by letting the public know of their 'them not us' campaign even before it had properly begun.

The result was that the American public was reacquainted with the fact that there were indeed *two* countries called China, and that only one of them killed people of the clergy and then beat up on those who tried to say a few prayers on a public street. The other one even played Little League baseball.

It wasn't often that union leaders and the clergy both cried out so vociferously, and together they were being heard. Polling organizations scrambled to catch up, and were soon framing their questions in such a way that the answers were defined even before they were given.

*   *   *

The draft note arrived in the Beijing Embassy early in the morning. When decrypted by an NS employee, it was shown to the embassy's senior

32

watch officer, who managed not to throw up and decided to awaken Ambassador Hitch at once. Half an hour later, Hitch was in the office, sleepy and crabby at being awakened two hours before his accustomed time. The content of the note wasn't contrived to brighten his day. He was soon on the phone to Foggy Bottom.

'Yes, that's what we want you to say,' Scott Adler told him on the secure phone.

'They're not going to like it.'

'That doesn't surprise me, Carl.'

'Okay, just so you know,' Hitch told the SecState.

'Carl, we do think about these things, but the President is seriously pissed about—'

'Scott, I live here, y'know? I *know* what happened.'

'What are they going to do?' EAGLE asked.

'Before or after they take my head off?' Hitch asked in return. 'They'll tell me where to stick this note—a little more formally, of course.'

'Well, make it clear to them that the American people demand some sort of amends. And that killing diplomats cannot be done with impunity.'

'Okay, Scott. I know how to handle it. I'll get back to you later.'

'I'll be awake,' Adler promised, thinking of the long day in the office he was stuck with.

'See ya.' Hitch broke the connection.

CHAPTER THIRTY-THREE

SQUARE ONE

'You may not talk to us this way,' Shen Tang observed.

'Minister, my country has principles which we do not violate. Some of those are respect for human rights, the right of free assembly, the right to worship God as one wishes, the right to speak freely. The government of the People's Republic has seen fit to violate those principles, hence America's response. Every other great power in the world recognizes those rights. China must as well.'

'Must? You tell us what we *must* do?'

'Minister, if China wishes to be a member of the community of nations, then, yes.'

'America will *not* dictate to us. You are not the rulers of the world!'

'We do not claim to be. But we can choose those nations with whom we have normal relations, and we would prefer them to recognize human rights as do all other civilized nations.'

'Now you say we are uncivilized?' Shen demanded.

'I did not say that, Minister,' Hitch responded, wishing he'd not let his tongue slip.

'America does not have the right to impose its wishes on us or any other nation. You come here and dictate trade terms to us, and now also you demand that we conduct our internal affairs so as to suit you. Enough! We will not kowtow to you. We are not your servants. I reject this note.' Shen

34

even tossed it back in Hitch's direction to give further emphasis to his words.

'That is your reply, then?' Hitch asked.

'That is the reply of the People's Republic of China,' Shen answered imperiously.

'Very well, Minister. Thank you for the audience.' Hitch bowed politely and withdrew. Remarkable, he thought, that normal—if not exactly friendly—relations could come unglued this fast. Only six weeks before, Shen had been over to the embassy for a cordial working dinner, and they'd toasted each other's country in the friendliest manner possible. But Kissinger had said it: Countries do not have friends; they have interests. And the PRC had just shit on some of America's most closely felt principles. And that was that. He walked back out to his car for the drive to the embassy.

Cliff Rutledge was waiting there. Hitch waved him into his private office.

'Well?'

'Well, he told me to shove it up my ass—in diplospeak,' Hitch told his visitor. 'You might have a lively session this morning.'

Rutledge had seen the note already, of course. 'I'm surprised Scott let it go out that way.'

'I gather things at home have gotten a little firm. We've seen CNN and all, but maybe it's even worse than it appears.'

'Look, I don't condone anything the Chinese did, but all this over a couple of shot clergymen . . .'

'One was a diplomat, Cliff,' Hitch reminded him. 'If you got your ass shot off, you'd want them to take it seriously in Washington, wouldn't you?'

The reprimand made Rutledge's eyes flare a

35

little. 'It's President Ryan who's driving this. He just doesn't understand how diplomacy works.'

'Maybe, maybe not, but he *is* the President, and it's our job to represent him, remember?'

'Hard to forget it,' Rutledge groused. He'd never be Undersecretary of State while that yahoo sat in the White House, and Undersecretary was the job he'd had his eye on for the last fifteen years. But neither would he get the job if he allowed his private feelings, however justified, to cloud his professional judgment. 'We're going to be called home or sent home,' he estimated.

'Probably,' Hitch agreed. 'Be nice to catch some baseball. How do the Sox look this season?'

'Forget it. A rebuilding year. Once again.'

'Sorry about that.' Hitch shook his head and checked his desk for new dispatches, but there were none. Now he had to let Washington know what the Chinese Foreign Minister had said. Scott Adler was probably sitting in his seventh-floor office waiting for the secure direct line to ring.

'Good luck, Cliff.'

'Thanks a bunch,' Rutledge said on his way out the door.

Hitch wondered if he should call home and tell his wife to start packing for home, but no, not yet. First he had to call Foggy Bottom.

*   *   *

'So, what's going to happen?' Ryan asked Adler from his bed. He'd left orders to be called as soon as they got word. Now, listening to Adler's reply, he was surprised. He'd thought the wording of the note rather wimpy, but evidently diplomatic

36

exchange had even stricter rules than he'd appreciated. 'Okay, now what, Scott?'

'Well, we'll wait and see what happens with the trade delegation, but even money we call them and Carl Hitch home for consultations.'

'Don't the Chinese realize they could take a trade hit from all this?'

'They don't expect that to happen. Maybe if it does, it'll make them think over the error of their ways.'

'I wouldn't bet much on that card, Scott.'

'Sooner or later, common sense has to break out. A hit in the wallet usually gets a guy's attention,' SecState said.

'I'll believe that when I see it,' POTUS replied. " 'Night, Scott.'

" 'Night, Jack.'

'So what did they say?' Cathy Ryan asked.

'They told us to stick it up our ass.'

'Really?'

'Really,' Jack replied, flipping the light off.

The Chinese thought they were invincible. It must be nice to believe that. Nice, but dangerous.

*   *   *

The 265th Motor Rifle Division was composed of three regiments of conscripts—Russians who hadn't chosen to avoid military service, which made them patriotic, or stupid, or apathetic, or sufficiently bored with life that the prospect of two years in uniform, poorly fed and largely unpaid, didn't seem that much of a sacrifice. Each regiment was composed of about fifteen hundred soldiers, about five hundred fewer than full authorized strength. The good news was that each regiment had an organic tank battalion, and that all of the mechanized equipment was, if not new, then at least recently manufactured, and reasonably well maintained. The division lacked its organic tank regiment, however, the fist which gave a motor-rifle division its offensive capabilities. Also missing was the divisional antitank battalion, with its Rapier antitank cannons. These were anachronistic weapons which Bondarenko nonetheless liked because he'd played with them as an officer cadet nearly forty years before. The new model of the BMP infantry carrier had been modified to carry the AT-6 antitank missile, the one NATO called 'Spiral,' actually a Russian version of the NATO Milan, courtesy of some nameless KGB spy of the 1980s. The Russian troops called it the Hammer for its ease of use, despite a relatively small warhead. Every BMP had ten of these, which more than made up for the missing battalion of towed guns.

What worried Bondarenko and Aliyev most was the lack of artillery. Historically the best trained and best drilled part of the Russian army, the artillery was only half present in the Far East's maneuver forces, battalions taking the place of regiments. The rationale for this was the fixed defense line on the Chinese border, which had a goodly supply of fixed and fortified artillery positions, albeit of obsolete designs, though with trained crews and massive stocks of shells to pour into predetermined positions.

The general scowled in the confines of his staff car. It was what he got for being smart and energetic. A properly prepared and trained military district didn't *need* a man like him, did it? No, his talents were needed by a shithole like this one. Just once, he thought, might a good officer get a reward for good performance instead of another 'challenge,' as they called it? He grunted. Not in this lifetime. The dunces and dolts drew the comfortable districts with no threats and lots of equipment to deal with them.

His worst worry was the air situation. Of all the Russian military arms, the air forces had suffered the most from the fall of the Soviet Union. Once Far East had had its own fleets of tactical fighters, poised to deal with a threat from American aircraft based in Japan or on aircraft carriers of their Pacific Fleet, that plus what was needed to face off the Chinese. No more. Now he had perhaps fifty usable aircraft in theater, and the pilots for those got perhaps seventy flight hours per year, barely enough to make sure they could take off and land safely. Fifty modern fighter-class aircraft, mainly for air-to-air combat, not air-to-ground. There were several hundred more, rotting at their bases, mainly in hardened shelters to keep them dry, their tires dry-rotted and internal seals cracked from lack of use because of the spare-parts shortage that grounded nearly the entire Russian air force.

'You know, Andrey, I can remember when the world shook with fear of our country's army. Now, they shake with laughter, those who bother to take note of us.' Bondarenko took a sip of vodka from a flask. It had been a long time since he'd drunk alcohol on duty, but it was cold—the heater in the car was broken—and he needed the solace.

'Gennady Iosifovich, it is not as bad as it appears—'

'I agree! It is worse!' CINC–FAR EAST growled. 'If the Chinks come north, I shall learn to eat with chopsticks. I've always wondered how they do that,' he added with a wry smile. Bondarenko was always one to see the humor in a situation.

'But to others we appear strong. We have thousands of tanks, Comrade General.'

Which was true. They'd spent the morning inspecting monstrous sheds containing of all things T-34/85 tanks manufactured at Chelyabinsk in 1946. Some had virgin guns, never fired. The Germans had shaken in their jackboots to see these tanks storm over the horizon, but that's what they were, World War II tanks, over nine hundred of them, three complete division sets. And there were even troops to maintain them! The engines still turned over, serviced as they were by the *grand*children of the men who'd used them in combat operations against the *fascisti*. And in the same sheds were shells, some made as recently as 1986, for the 85-mm guns. The world was mad, and surely the Soviet Union had been mad, first to store such antiques, then to spend money and effort maintaining them. And even now, more than ten years after the demise of that nation-state, the sheer force of bureaucratic inertia *still* sent conscripts into the sheds to maintain the antique collection. For what purpose? No one knew. It would take an archivist to find the documents, and while that might be of interest to some historian of a humorous bent, Bondarenko had better things to do.

'Andrey, I appreciate your willingness to see the lighter side of every situation, but we do face a practical reality here.'

'Comrade General, it will take months to get permission to terminate this operation.'

'That is probably true, Andruska, but I remember a story about Napoleon. He wished to plant trees by the side of the French roads to shade his marching troops. A staff officer said, but, Marshal, it will take twenty years for the trees to grow enough to accomplish that. And Napoleon said, yes, indeed, so we must start at once! And so, Colonel, we will start with that at once.'

'As you say, Comrade General.' Colonel Aliyev knew that it was a worthwhile idea. He only wondered if he would have enough time to pursue all of the ideas that needed accomplishing. Besides, the troops at the tank sheds seemed happy enough. Some even took the tanks out into the open to play with them, drive them about the nearby test range, even shoot the guns occasionally. One young sergeant had commented to him that it was good to use them, because it made the war movies he'd seen as a child seem even more real. Now *that*, Colonel Aliyev thought, was something to hear from a soldier. It made the movies better. Damn.

*   *   *

'Who does that slant-eyed motherfucker think he is?' Gant demanded out in the garden.

'Mark, we laid a rather firm note on them this morning, and they're just reacting to it.'

'Cliff, explain to me why it's okay for other people to talk like that to us, but it's not okay for us to talk that way to them, will you?'

'It's called diplomacy,' Rutledge explained.

'It's called horseshit, Cliff,' Gant hissed back.

41

'Where I come from, if somebody disses you like that, you punch him right in the face.'

'But we don't do that.'

'Why not?'

'Because we're above it, Mark,' Rutledge tried to explain. 'It's the little dogs that yap at you. The big powerful dogs don't bother. They know they can rip your head off. And we know we can handle these people if we have to.'

'Somebody needs to tell *them* that, Cliffy,' Gant observed. 'Because I don't think they got the word yet. They're talking like they own the world, and they think they can play tough-guy with us, Cliff, and until they find out they can't, we're going to have a lot more of their shit to deal with.'

'Mark, this is how it's done, that's all. It's just how the game is played at this level.'

'Oh, yeah?' Gant countered. 'Cliff, it's not a game to them. I see that, but you don't. After this break, we're going back in there, and they're going to threaten us. What do we do then?'

'We brush it off. How can they threaten us?'

'The Boeing order.'

'Well, Boeing will have to sell its airplanes to somebody else this year,' Rutledge said.

'Really? What about the interests of all those workers we're supposed to represent?'

'Mark, at this level, we deal with the big picture, not the little one, okay?' Rutledge was actually getting angry with this stock trader.

'Cliffy, the big picture is made up of a lot of little ones. You ought to go back in there and ask if they like selling things to us. Because if they do, then they have to play ball. Because they need us a fucking lot more than we need them.'

'You don't talk that way to a great power.'

'Are we a great power?'

'The biggest,' Rutledge confirmed.

'Then how come they talk that way to us?'

'Mark, this is my job. You're here to advise me, but this is your first time to this sort of ball game, okay? I know how to play the game. It's my job.'

'Fine.' Gant let out a long breath. 'But when we play by the rules and they don't, the game gets a little tedious.' Gant wandered off on his own for a moment. The garden was pretty enough. He hadn't done this sort of thing enough to know that there was usually a garden of some sort for diplomats to wander in after two or three hours of talking at each other in a conference room, but he had learned that the garden was where a lot of the real work got done.

'Mr. Gant?' He turned to see Xue Ma, the diplomat/spook he'd chatted with before.

'Mr. Xue,' TELESCOPE said in his own greeting.

'What do you think of the progress of the talks?' the Chinese diplomat asked.

Mark was still trying to understand this guy's use of language. 'If this is progress, I'd hate to see what you call an adverse development.'

Xue smiled. 'A lively exchange is often more interesting than a dull one.

'Really? I'm surprised by all this. I always thought that diplomatic exchange was more polite.'

'You think this impolite?'

Gant again wondered if he was being baited or not, but decided *the hell with it*. He didn't really need his government job anyway, did he? And taking it had involved a considerable personal sacrifice, hadn't it? Like a few million bucks. Didn't

43

that entitle him to say what the hell he thought?

'Xue, you accuse us of threatening your national identity because we object to the murders your government—or its agents, I suppose—committed in front of cameras. Americans don't like it when people commit murder.'

'Those people were breaking our laws,' Xue reminded him.

'Maybe so,' Gant conceded. 'But in America when people break the law, we arrest them and give them a trial in front of a judge and jury, with a defense lawyer to make sure the trial is fair, and we damned sure don't shoot people in the head when they're holding a goddamned newborn infant!'

'That was unfortunate,' Xue almost admitted, 'but as I said, those men *were* breaking the law.'

'And so your cops did the judge/jury/executioner number on them. Xue, to Americans that was the act of a barbarian.'

The 'B' word finally got through. 'America cannot talk to China in that way, Mr. Gant.'

'Look, Mr. Xue, it's your country, and you can run your country as you wish. We're not going to declare war on you for what you do inside your own borders. But there's no law that says we have to do business with you either, and so we *can* stop buying your goods—and I have news for you: The American people *will* stop buying your stuff if you continue to do stuff like that.'

'Your people? Or your government?' Xue asked, with a knowing smile.

'Are you really *that* stupid, Mr. Xue?' Gant fired back.

'What do you mean?' The last insult had actually cracked through the shell, Gant saw.

44

'I mean America is a democracy. Americans make a lot of decisions entirely on their own, and one of them is what they spend their money on, and the average American will not buy something from a fucking barbarian.' Gant paused. 'Look, I'm a Jew, okay? Sixty-some years ago, America fucked up. We saw what Hitler and the Nazis were doing in Germany, and we didn't act in time to stop it. We really blew the call and a lot of people got killed unnecessarily, and we've been seeing things on TV about that since I was in short pants, and it ain't *never* going to happen again on our watch, and when people like you do stuff like what we just saw, it just sets off the Holocaust light in American heads. Do you get it now?'

'You cannot talk to us in that way.'

Again with the broken record! The doors were opening. It was time to head back inside for the next round of confrontational diplo-speak.

'And if you persist in attacking our national sovereignty, we will buy elsewhere,' Xue told him with some satisfaction.

'Fine, and we can do the same. And you need our cash a lot more than we need your trade goods, Mr. Xue.' He must have finally understood, Gant thought. His face actually showed some emotion now. So did his words:

'We will never kowtow to American attacks on our country.'

'We're not attacking your country, Xue.'

'But you threaten our economy,' Xue said, as they got to the door.

'We threaten nothing. I am telling you that my fellow citizens will not buy goods from a country that commits barbarities. That is not a threat. It is a

45

statement of fact.' Which was an even greater insult, Gant did not fully appreciate.

'If America punishes us, we will punish America.'

Enough was goddamned enough. Gant pulled the door open halfway and stopped to face the diplomat/spook:

'Xue, your dicks aren't big enough to get in a pissing contest with us.' And with that, he walked on inside. A half-hour later, he was on his way out again. The words had been sharp and heated, and neither side had seen any purpose in continuing that day—though Gant strongly suspected that once Washington heard about that morning's exchanges, there wouldn't *be* any other day.

In two days, he'd be totally jet-lagged but back at his office on 15th Street. He was surprised that he was looking forward to *that*.

*   *   *

'Anything from WestPac?' Mancuso asked.

'They just put three submarines to sea, a Song and two of the Kilos the Russians sold them,' BG Lahr answered. 'We're keeping an eye on them. *La Jolla* and *Helena* are close by. *Tennessee* is heading back to Pearl as of midday.' The former boomer had been on patrol for fifty days, and that was about enough. 'Our surface assets are all back to sea. Nobody's scheduled to get back into Taipei for twelve days.'

'So, the Taipei hookers get two weeks off?' CINCPAC asked with a chuckle.

'And the bartenders. If your sailors are like my soldiers, they may need the relaxation,' the J-2 replied, with a smile of his own.

'Oh, to be young and single again,' Bart observed. 'Anything else out there?'

'Routine training on their side, some combined air and ground stuff, but that's up north by the Russian border.'

'How good do they look?'

Lahr shrugged. 'Good enough to give the Russians something to think about, sir. On the whole, the PLA is trained up as good as I've ever known them to be, but they've been working hard for the past three or four years.'

'How many of them?' Bart asked, looking at his wall map, which was a lot more useful for a sailor than a soldier. China was just a beige shape on the left border.

'Depends on where. Like, if they go north into Russia, it'd be like cockroaches in some ghetto apartment in New York. You'd need a lot o' Raid to deal with it.'

'And you said the Russians are thin in their East?'

Lahr nodded. 'Yep. Admiral, if I was that Bondarenko guy, I'd sweat it some. I mean, it's all theoretical as a threat and all, but as theoretical threats go, that's one that might keep me awake at night.'

'And what about reports of gold and oil in eastern Siberia?'

Lahr nodded. 'Makes the threat less theoretical. China's a net importer of oil, and they're going to need a lot more to expand their economy the way they plan to—and on the gold side, hell, everybody's wanted that for the last three thousand years. It's negotiable and fungible.'

47

'Fungible?' That was a new word for Mancuso.

'Your wedding band might have been part of Pharaoh Ramses II's double-crown once,' Lahr explained. 'Or Caligula's necklace, or Napoleon's royal scepter. You take it, hammer it, and it's just raw material again, and it's *valuable* raw material. If the Russian strike's as big as our intel says, it'll be sold all over the world. Everybody'll use it for all sorts of purposes, from jewelry to electronics.'

'How big's the strike supposed to be?'

Lahr shrugged. 'Enough to buy you a new Pacific Fleet, and then some.

Mancuso whistled. That was real money.

*　　　*　　　*

It was late in Washington, and Adler was up late, again, working in his office. SecState was usually a busy post, and lately it had been busier than usual, and Scott Adler was getting accustomed to fourteen-hour days. He was reading over post reports at the moment, waiting for the other shoe to drop in Beijing. On his desk was a STU-6 secure telephone. The 'secure telephone unit' was a sophisticated encryption device grafted onto an AT&T-made digital telephone. This one worked on a satellite-communications channel, and though its signal therefore sprinkled down all over the world from its Defense Department communications satellite, all the casual listener would get was raspy static, like the sound of water running out of a bathroom faucet. It had a randomized 512-bit scrambling system that the best computers at Fort Meade could break about a third of the time after several days of directed effort. And that was about as secure as things got. They were trying to make the TAPDANCE encryption system link into the STU units to generate a totally random and hence unbreakable signal, but that was proving difficult, for technical reasons that nobody had explained to the Secretary of State, and that was just as well. He was a diplomat, not a mathematician. Finally, the STU rang in its odd trilling warble. It took eleven seconds for the two STU units on opposite sides of the world to synchronize.

'Adler.'

'Rutledge here, Scott,' the voice said on the other side of the world. 'It didn't go well,' he informed SecState at once. 'And they're canceling the 777 order with Boeing, as we thought they would.'

Adler frowned powerfully into the phone. 'Super. No concessions at all on the shootings?'

'Zip.'

'Anything to be optimistic about?'

'Nothing, Scott, not a damned thing. They're stonewalling like we're the Mongols and they're the Chin Dynasty.'

Somebody needs to remind them that the Great Wall ultimately turned out to be a waste of bricks, EAGLE didn't bother saying aloud. 'Okay, I need to discuss this with the President, but you're probably going to be flying home soon. Maybe Carl Hitch, too.'

'I'll tell him. Any chance that we can make some concession, just to get things going?'

'Cliff, the likelihood that Congress will roll over on the trade issue is right up there with Tufts making the Final Four. Maybe less.' Tufts University *did* have a basketball team, after all.

49

'There's nothing we can give them that they would accept. If there's going to be a break, they're the ones who'll have to bend this time. Any chance of that?'

'Zero' was the reply from Beijing.

'Well, then, they'll just have to learn the hard way.' The good news, Adler thought, was that the hard lessons were the ones that really did teach you something. Maybe even the Chinese.

*   *   *

'*What* did that capitalist *diao ren* say?' Zhang asked. Shen told him what Xue had relayed, word-for-word. 'And what does he represent?'

'He is personal assistant to the American Treasury Minister. Therefore we think he has the ear of both his minister and the American President,' Shen explained. 'He has not taken an active part in the talks, but after every session he speaks privately with Vice Minister Rutledge. Exactly what their relationship is, we do not know for certain, and clearly he is not an experienced diplomat. He talks like an arrogant capitalist, to insult us in so crude a way, but I fear he represents the American position more forthrightly than Rutledge does. I think he gives Rutledge the policy he must follow. Rutledge is an experienced diplomat, and the positions he takes are not his own, obviously. He wants to give us some concessions. I am sure of that, but Washington is dictating his words, and this Gant fellow is probably the conduit to Washington.'

'Then you were right to adjourn the talks. We will give them a chance to reconsider their position.

50

If they think they can dictate to us, then they are mistaken. You canceled the airplane order?'

'Of course, as we agreed last week.'

'Then *that* will give them something to think about,' Zhang observed smugly.

'If they do not walk out of the talks.'

'They wouldn't dare.' *Walk away from the Middle Kingdom? Absurd.*

'There is one other thing that Gant man said. He said, not in so many words, that we need them—their money, that is—more than they need us. And he is not entirely wrong in that, is he?'

'We do not need their dollars more than we need our sovereignty. Do they really think they can dictate our domestic laws to us?'

'Yes, Zhang, they do. They apply an astounding degree of importance to this incident.'

'Those two policemen ought to be shot for what they did, but we cannot allow the Americans to dictate that sort of thing to us.' The embarrassment of the incident was one thing—and embarrassing the state was often a capital offense in the People's Republic—but China had to make such a decision on its own, not at the order of an outsider.

'They call it barbaric,' Shen added.

'*Barbaric?* They say *that* to *us*?'

'You know that Americans have tender sensibilities. We often forget that. And their religious leaders have some influence in their country. Our ambassador in Washington has cabled some warnings to us about this. It would be better if we had some time to let things settle down, and truly it would be better to punish those two policemen just to assuage American sensibilities, but I agree we cannot allow them to dictate domestic policy to us.'

'And this Gant man says his *ji* is bigger than ours, does he?'

'So Xue tells me. Our file on him says that he's a stock trader, that he's worked closely with Minister Winston for many years. He's a Jew, like lots of them are—'

'Their Foreign Minister is also a Jew, isn't he?'

'Minister Adler? Yes, he is,' Shen confirmed after a moment's thought.

'So, this Gant really does tell us their position, then?'

'Probably,' Foreign Minister Shen said.

Zhang leaned forward in his chair. 'Then you will make them clear on ours. The next time you see this Gant, tell him *chou ni ma de bi.*' Which was rather a strong imprecation, best said to someone in China if you had a gun already in your hand.

'I understand,' Shen replied, knowing that he'd never say anything like that except to a particularly humble underling in his own office.

Zhang left. He had to talk this one over with his friend Fang Gan.

CHAPTER THIRTY-FOUR

HITS

Over the last week Ryan had come to expect bad news upon waking up, and as a result so had his family. He knew that he was taking it too seriously when his children started asking him about it over breakfast.

'What's happening with China, Dad?' Sally asked, giving Ryan one more thing to lament. Sally didn't say 'daddy' anymore, and that was a title far more precious to Jack than 'Mr. President'. You expected it from your sons, but not from your daughter. He'd discussed it with Cathy, but she'd told him that he just had to roll with the punch.

'We don't know, Sally.'

'But you're supposed to know everything!' And besides, her friends asked her about it at school.

'Sally, the President doesn't know everything. At least I don't,' he explained, looking up from the morning *Early Bird*. 'And if you never noticed, the TVs in my office are tuned to CNN and the other news networks because they frequently tell me more than CIA does.'

'Really?' Sally observed. She watched too many movies. In Hollywood, CIA was a dangerous, lawbreaking, antidemocratic, fascist, and thoroughly evil government agency that nonetheless knew everything about everybody, and had really killed President Kennedy for its own purposes, whatever they were (Hollywood never quite got around to that). But it didn't matter, because whoever the star was always managed to thwart the nasty old CIA before the credits, or the last commercial, depending on the format.

'Really, honey. CIA has some good people in it, but basically it's just one more government agency.

'What about the FBI and Secret Service?' she asked.

'They're cops. Cops are different. My dad was a cop, remember?'

'Oh, yeah,' and then she went back to the 'Style' section of *The Washington Post*, which had both the

53

comics and the stories that interested her, mainly ones having to do with the sort of music that her father put quotation marks around.

Then there was a discreet knock at the door, and Andrea came in. At this time of day, she also acted as his private secretary, in this case delivering a dispatch from the State Department. Ryan took it, looked at it, and managed not to pound on the table, because his children were present.

'Thanks, Andrea,' he told her.

'Yes, Mr. President.' And Special Agent Price-O'Day went back out to the corridor.

Jack saw his wife looking at him. The kids couldn't read all his facial expressions, but his wife could. To Cathy, Ryan couldn't lie worth a damn, which was also why she didn't worry about his fidelity. Jack had the dissimulation ability of a two-year-old, despite all the help and training he got from Arnie. Jack caught the look and nodded. Yeah, it was China again. Ten minutes later, breakfast was fully consumed and the TV was turned off, and the Ryan family headed downstairs to work, to school, or to the day-care center at Johns Hopkins, depending on age, with the requisite contingent of Secret Service bodyguards. Jack kissed them all in their turn, except for little Jack—SHORTSTOP to the Secret Service—because John Patrick Ryan, Jr., didn't go in for that sissy stuff. *There was something to be said for having daughters*, Ryan thought, as he headed for the Oval Office. Ben Goodley was there, waiting with the President's Daily Brief.

'You have the one from SecState?' CARDSHARP asked.

'Yeah, Andrea delivered it.' Ryan fell into his

54

swivel chair and lifted the phone, punching the proper speed-dial button.

'Good morning, Jack,' SecState said in greeting, despite a short night's sleep gotten on the convertible sofa in his own office. Fortunately, his private bathroom also had a shower.

'Approved. Bring them all back,' SWORDSMAN told EAGLE.

'Who handles the announcement?' Secretary Adler asked.

'You do it. We'll try to low-key it,' the President said, with forlorn hope in his voice.

'Right,' Adler thought. 'Anything else?'

'That's it for now.'

'Okay, see ya, Scott.' Ryan replaced the phone. 'What about China?' he asked Goodley. 'Are they doing anything unusual?'

'No. Their military is active, but it's routine training activity only. Their most active sectors are up in their northeast and opposite Taiwan. Lesser activity in their southwest, north of India.'

'With all the good luck the Russians are having with oil and gold, are the Chinese looking north with envy?'

'It's not bad speculation, but we have no positive indications of that from any of our sources.' Everybody envied rich neighbors, after all. That's what had encouraged Saddam Hussein to invade Kuwait, despite having lots of oil under his own sand.

'*Any of our sources*' *includes* SORGE, the President reminded himself.

He pondered that for a second. 'Tell Ed I want a SNIE on Russia and China.'

'Quick?' Goodley asked. A Special National

55

Intelligence Estimate could take months to prepare.

'Three or four weeks. And I want to be able to hang my hat on it.'

'I'll tell the DCI,' Goodley promised.

'Anything else?' Ryan asked.

'That's it for now, sir.'

Jack nodded and checked his calendar. He had a fairly routine day, but the next one would largely be spent on Air Force One flying hither and yon across America, and he was overnighting in—he flipped the page on the printout—Seattle, before flying home to Washington and another full day. It was just as easy for him to use the VC-25A as a red-eye . . . oh, yeah, he had a breakfast speech in Seattle to the local Jaycees. He'd be talking about school reform. That generated a grunt. There just weren't enough nuns to go around. The School Sisters of Notre Dame had taught him at St. Matthew's Elementary School in northeast Baltimore back forty-plus years earlier—and taught him well, because the penalty for not learning or for misbehaving did not bear contemplation for a seven-year-old. But the truth of the matter was that he'd been a good, and fairly obedient—*dull*, Jack admitted to himself with a wry smile—child who'd gotten good marks because he'd had a good mom and a good dad, which was a lot more than too many contemporary American kids could say—*and how the hell was he supposed to fix* that? Jack asked himself. How could he bring back the ethos of his parents' generation, the importance of religion, and a world in which engaged people went to the altar as virgins? Now they were talking about telling kids that homosexual and lesbian sex was

56

okay. *What would Sister Frances Mary have said about* that? Jack wondered. A pity she wasn't around to crack some senators and representatives over the knuckles with her ruler. It had worked on him and his classmates at St. Matthew's . . .

The desk speaker buzzed. 'Senator Smithers just arrived at the West Entrance.' Ryan stood and went to his right, the door that came in from the secretaries' anteroom. For some reason, people preferred that one to the door off the corridor opposite the Roosevelt Room. Maybe it was more businesslike. But mainly they liked to see the President standing when the door opened, his hand extended and a smile on his face, as though he really was glad to see them. Sure, Wilbur.

Mary Smithers from Iowa, matronly, three kids and seven grandkids, he thought, *more talk about the Farm Bill.* What the hell was he supposed to know about farms? the President wondered. On those rare occasions that he purchased food, he did it at the supermarket—because that's where it all came from, wasn't it? One of the things on the briefing pages for his political appearances was always the local price for bread and milk in case some local reporter tested him. And chocolate milk came from brown cows.

*   *   *

'Accordingly, Ambassador Hitch and Assistant Secretary Rutledge will be flying back to Washington for consultations,' the spokesman told the audience.

'Does this signal a break in relations with China?' a reporter asked at once.

'Not at all. "Consultations" means just that. We will discuss the recent developments with our representatives so that our relations with China can more speedily be brought back to what they ought to be,' the spokesman replied smoothly.

The assembled reporters didn't know what to make of that and so three more questions of virtually identical content were immediately asked, and answers of virtually identical content repeated for them.

'He's good,' Ryan said, watching the TV, which was pirating the CNN (and other) coverage off the satellites. It wasn't going out live, oddly enough, despite the importance of the news being generated.

'Not good enough,' Arnie van Damm observed. 'You're going to get hit with this, too.'

'I figured. When?'

'The next time they catch you in front of a camera, Jack.'

And he had as much chance of ducking a camera as the leadoff hitter at opening day at Yankee Stadium, the President knew. Cameras at the White House were as numerous as shotguns during duck season, and there was no bag limit here.

*   *   *

'Christ, Oleg!' It took a lot to make Reilly gasp, but this one crossed the threshold. 'Are you serious?'

'So it would appear, Mishka,' Provalov answered.

'And why are you telling me?' the American asked. Information like this was a state secret equivalent to the inner thoughts of President

58

Grushavoy.

'There is no hiding it from you. I assume you tell everything we do together to Washington, and it was you who identified the Chinese diplomat, for which I and my country are in your debt.'

The amusing part of that was that Reilly had darted off to track Suvorov/Koniev without a thought, just as a cop thing, to help out a brother cop. Only afterward—about a nanosecond afterward, of course—had he thought of the political implications. And he'd thought this far ahead, but only as speculation, not quite believing that it could possibly have gone this far forward.

'Well, yes, I have to keep the Bureau informed of my operations here,' the legal attaché admitted, not that it was an earthshaking revelation.

'I know that, Mishka.'

'The Chinese wanted to kill Golovko,' Reilly whispered into his vodka. *'Fuck.'*

'My word exactly,' Provalov told his American friend. 'The question is—'

'Two questions, Oleg. First, why? Second, now what?'

'Third, who is Suvorov, and what is he up to?'

Which was obvious, Reilly thought. Was Suvorov merely a paid agent of a foreign country? Or was he part of the KGB wing of the Russian Mafia being paid by the Chinese to do something—but what, and to what purpose?

'You know, I've been hunting OC guys for a long time, but it never got anywhere near this big. This is right up there with all those bullshit stories about who "really" killed Kennedy.'

Provalov's eyes looked up. 'You're not saying . . .'

'No, Oleg. The Mafia isn't that crazy. You don't

go around looking to make enemies that big. You can't predict the consequences, and it isn't good for business. The Mafia is a business, Oleg. They try to make money for themselves. Even their political protection is aimed only at that, and that has limits, and they know what the limits are.'

'So, if Suvorov is Mafia, then he is only trying to make money?'

'Here it's a little different,' Reilly said slowly, trying to help his brain keep up with his mouth. 'Here your OC guys think more politically than they do in New York.' And the reason for that was that the KGB types had all grown up in an intensely political environment. Here politics really was power in a more direct sense than it had ever been in America, where politics and commerce had always been somewhat separate, the former protecting the latter (for a fee) but also controlled by it. Here it had always been, and still remained, the other way around. Business needed to rule politics because business was the source of prosperity, from which the citizens of a country derived their comforts. Russia had never prospered, because the cart kept trying to pull the horse. The recipient of the wealth had always tried to generate that wealth—and political figures are always pretty hopeless in that department. They are only good at squandering it. Politicians live by their political theories. Businessmen use reality and have to perform in a world defined by reality, not theory. That was why even in America they understood one another poorly, and never really trusted one another.

'What makes Golovko a target? What's the profit in killing him?' Reilly asked aloud.

'He is the chief adviser to President Grushavoy. He's never wanted to be an elected official, and therefore cannot be a minister per se, but he has the President's ear because he is both intelligent and honest—and he's a patriot in the true sense.'

Despite his background, Reilly didn't add. Golovko was KGB, formerly a deadly enemy to the West, and an enemy to President Ryan, but somewhere along the line they'd met each other and they'd come to respect each other—even *like* each other, so the stories in Washington went. Reilly finished off his second vodka and waved for another. He was turning into a Russian, the FBI agent thought. It was getting to the point that he couldn't hold an intelligent conversation without a drink or two.

'So, get him and thereby hurt your President, and thereby hurt your entire country. Still, it's one hell of a dangerous play, Oleg Gregoriyevich.'

'A *very* dangerous play, Mishka,' Provalov agreed. 'Who would do such a thing?'

Reilly let out a long and speculative breath. 'One very ambitious motherfucker.' He had to get back to the embassy and light up his STU-6 in one big fucking hurry. He'd tell Director Murray, and Murray would tell President Ryan in half a New York minute. Then what? It was way the hell over his head, Mike Reilly thought.

'Okay, you're covering this Suvorov guy.'

'We and the Federal Security Service now,' Provalov confirmed.

'They good?'

'Very,' the militia lieutenant admitted. 'Suvorov can't fart without us knowing what he had to eat.'

'And you have his communications penetrated.'

Oleg nodded. 'The written kind. He has a cell phone—maybe more than one, and covering them can be troublesome.'

'Especially if he has an encryption system on it. There's stuff commercially available now that our people have a problem with.'

'Oh?' Provalov's head came around. He was surprised for two reasons: first, that there was a reliable encryption system available for cell phones, and second, that the Americans had trouble cracking it.

Reilly nodded. 'Fortunately, the bad guys haven't found out yet.' Contrary to popular belief, the Mafia wasn't all that adept at using technology. Microwaving their food was about as far as they went. One Mafia don had thought his cell phone secure because of its frequency-hopping abilities, and then had entirely canceled that supposed advantage out by standing still while using it! The dunce-don had never figured that out, even after the intercept had been played aloud in Federal District Court.

'We haven't noticed any of that yet.'

'Keep it that way,' Reilly advised. 'Anyway, you have a national-security investigation.'

'It's still murder, and conspiracy to commit murder,' Provalov said, meaning it was still his case.

'Anything I can do?'

'Think it over. You have good instincts for Mafia cases, and that is probably what it is.'

Reilly tossed off his last drink. 'Okay. I'll see you tomorrow, right here?'

Oleg nodded. 'That is good.'

The FBI agent walked back outside and got into his car. Ten minutes later, he was at his desk. He

62

took the plastic key from his desk drawer and inserted it into the STU, then dialed Washington.

*   *   *

All manner of people with STU phones had access to Murray's private secure number, and so when the large system behind his desk started chirping, he just picked it up and listened to the hiss of static for thirty seconds until the robotic voice announced, 'Line is secure.'

'Murray,' he said.

'Reilly in Moscow,' the other voice said.

The FBI Director checked his desk clock. It was pretty damned late there. 'What's happening, Mike?' he asked, then got the word in three fast-spoken minutes.

*   *   *

'Yeah, Ellen?' Ryan said when the buzzer went off.

'The AG and the FBI Director want to come over, on something important, they said. You have an opening in forty minutes.'

'Fair enough.' Ryan didn't wonder what it was about. He'd find out quickly enough. When he realized what he'd just thought, he cursed the Presidency once more. He was becoming jaded. In *this* job?

*   *   *

'What the hell?' Ed Foley observed.

'Seems to be solid information too,' Murray told the DCI.

'What else do you know?'

'The fax just came in, only two pages, and nothing much more than what I just told you, but I'll send it over to you. I've told Reilly to offer total cooperation. Anything to offer from your side?' Dan asked.

'Nothing comes to mind. This is all news to us, Dan. My congrats to your man Reilly for turning it.' Foley was an information whore, after all. He'd take from anybody.

'Good kid. His father was a good agent, too.' Murray knew better than to be smug about it, and Foley didn't deserve the abuse. Things like this were not, actually, within CIA's purview, and not likely to be tumbled to by one of their operations.

For his part, Foley wondered if he'd have to tell Murray about SORGE. If this was for real, it had to be known at the very highest levels of the Chinese government. It wasn't a free-lance operation by their Moscow station. People got shot for fucking around at this level, and such an operation would not even occur to communist bureaucrats, who were not the most inventive people in the world.

'Anyway, I'm taking Pat Martin over with me. He knows espionage operations from the defensive side, and I figure I'll need the backup.'

'Okay, thanks. Let me go over the fax and I'll be back to you later today.'

He could hear the nod at the other end. 'Right, Ed. See ya.'

His secretary came in thirty seconds later with a fax in a folder. Ed Foley checked the cover sheet and called his wife in from her office.

CHAPTER THIRTY-FIVE

BREAKING NEWS

'Shit,' Ryan observed quietly when Murray handed him the fax from Moscow. 'Shit!' he added on further reflection. 'Is this for real?'

'We think so, Jack,' the FBI Director confirmed. He and Ryan went back more than ten years, and so he was able to use the first name. He filled in a few facts. 'Our boy Reilly, he's an OC expert, that's why we sent him over there, but he has FCI experience, too, also in the New York office. He's good, Jack,' Murray assured his President. 'He's going places. He's established a very good working relationship with the local cops—helped them out on some investigations, held their hands, like we do with local cops over here, y'know?'

'And?'

'And this looks gold-plated, Jack. Somebody tried to put a hit on Sergey Nikolay'ch, and it looks as though it was an agency of the Chinese government.'

'Jesus. Rogue operation?'

'If so, we'll find out when some Chinese minister dies of a sudden cerebral hemorrhage—induced by a bullet in the back of the head,' Murray told the President.

'Has Ed Foley seen this yet?'

'I called it in, and sent the fax over. So, yeah, he's seen it.'

'Pat?' Ryan turned to the Attorney General, the smartest lawyer Ryan had yet met, and that included all of his Supreme Court appointees.

'Mr. President, this is a stunning revelation, again, if we assume it's true, and not some sort of false-flag provocation, or a play by the Russians to make something happen—problem is, I can't see the rationale for such a thing. We appear to be faced with something that's too crazy to be true, and too crazy to be false as well. I've worked foreign counterintelligence operations for a long time. I've never seen nothing like this before. We've always had an understanding with the Russians that they wouldn't hit anybody in Washington, and we wouldn't hit anybody in Moscow, and to the best of my knowledge that agreement was never violated by either side. But this thing here. If it's real, it's tantamount to an act of war. That doesn't seem like a very prudent thing for the Chinese to do either, does it?'

POTUS looked up from the fax. 'It says here that your guy Reilly turned the connection with the Chinese . . . ?'

'Keep reading,' Murray told him. 'He was there during a surveillance and just kinda volunteered his services, and—bingo.'

'But can the Chinese really be this crazy . . .' Ryan's voice trailed off. 'This isn't the Russians messing with our heads?' he asked.

'What would be the rationale behind that?' Martin asked. 'If there is one, I don't see it.'

'Guys, nobody is *this* crazy!' POTUS nearly exploded. It was penetrating all the way into his mind now. The world wasn't rational yet.

'Again, sir, that's something you're better equipped to evaluate than we are,' Martin observed. It had the effect of calming Jack down a few notches.

'All the time I spent at Langley, I saw a lot of strange material, but this one really takes the prize.'

'What do we know about the Chinese?' Murray asked, expecting to hear a reply along the lines of *jack shit*, because the Bureau had not experienced conspicuous success in its efforts to penetrate Chinese intelligence operations in America, and figured that the Agency had the same problem and for much the same reason—Americans of Chinese ethnicity weren't thick in government service. But instead he saw that President Ryan instantly adopted a guarded look and said nothing. Murray had interviewed thousands of people during his career and along the way had picked up the ability to read minds a little bit. He read Ryan's right then and wondered about what he saw there.

'Not enough, Dan. Not enough,' Ryan replied tardily. His mind was still churning over this report. Pat Martin had put it right. It was too crazy to be true, and too crazy to be false. He needed the Foleys to go over this for him, and it was probably time to get Professor Weaver down from Brown University, assuming Ed and Mary Pat wouldn't throw a complete hissy-fit over letting him into both SORGE and this FBI bombshell. SWORDSMAN wasn't sure of much right now, but he was sure that he needed to figure this stuff out, and do it damned fast. American relations with China had just gone down the shitter, and now he had information to suggest they were making a direct attack on the Russian government. Ryan looked up at his guests. 'Thanks for this, guys. If you have anything else to tell me, let me know quick as you can. I have to ponder this one.'

'Yeah, I believe it, Jack. I've told Reilly to offer all the assistance he can and report back. They know he's doing that, of course. So, your pal Golovko wants you to know this one. How you handle that one's up to you, I suppose.'

'Yeah, I get all the simple calls.' Jack managed a smile. The worst part was the inability to talk things over with people in a timely way. Things like this weren't for the telephone. You wanted to see a guy's face and body language when you picked his brain—her brain, in MP's case—on a topic like this one. He hoped George Weaver was as smart as everyone said. Right now he needed a witch.

*   *   *

The new security pass was entirely different from his old SDI one, and he was heading for a different Pentagon office. This was the Navy section of the Pentagon. You could tell by all the blue suits and serious looks. Each of the uniformed services had a different corporate mentality. In the U.S. Army, everyone was from Georgia. In the Air Force, they were all from southern California. In the Navy, they all seemed to be swamp Yankees, and so it was here in the Aegis Program Office.

Gregory had spent most of the morning with a couple of serious commander-rank officers who seemed smart enough, though both were praying aloud to get the hell back on a ship and out to sea, just as Army officers always wanted to get back out in the field where there was mud to put on your boots and you had to dig a hole to piss in—but that's where the soldiers were, and any officer

68

worth his salt wanted to be where the soldiers were. For sailors, Gregory imagined, it was salt water and fish, and probably better food than the MREs inflicted on the guys in BDUs.

But from his conversations with the squids, he'd learned much of what he'd already known. The Aegis radar/missile system had been developed to deal with the Russian airplane and cruise-missile threat to the Navy's aircraft carriers. It entailed a superb phased-array radar called the SPY and a fair-to-middlin' surface-to-air missile originally called the Standard Missile, because, Gregory imagined, it was the only one the Navy had. The Standard had evolved from the SM-1 to the SM-2, actually called the SM-2-MR because it was a 'medium-range' missile instead of an ER, or extended-range, one, which had a booster stage to kick it out of the ships' launch cells a little faster and farther. There were about two hundred of the ER versions sitting in various storage sheds for the Atlantic and Pacific fleets, because full production had never been approved—because, somebody thought, the SM-2-ER might violate the 1972 Anti-Ballistic Missile Treaty, which had, however, been signed with a country called the Union of Soviet Socialist Republics, which country, of course, no longer existed. But after the 1991 war in the Persian Gulf, the Navy had looked at using the Standard Missile and Aegis system that shot it off against theater-missile threats like the Iraqi Scud. During that war, Aegis ships had actually been deployed into Saudi and other Gulf ports to protect them against the ballistic inbounds, but no missiles had actually been aimed that way, and so the system had never been combat-tested. Instead,

Aegis ships periodically sailed out to Kwajalein Atoll, where their theater-missile capabilities were tested against ballistic target drones, and where, most of the time, they worked. But that wasn't quite the same, Gregory saw. An ICBM reentry vehicle had a maximum speed of about seventeen thousand miles per hour, or twenty-five thousand feet per second, which was almost ten times the speed of a rifle bullet.

The problem here was, oddly enough, one of both hardware and software. The SM-2-ER-Block-IV missile had indeed been designed with a ballistic target in mind, to the point that its terminal guidance system was infrared. You could, theoretically, stealth an RV against radar, but anything plunging through the atmosphere at Mach 15-plus would heat up to the temperature of molten steel. He'd seen Minuteman warheads coming into Kwajalein from California's Vandenberg Air Force Base; they came in like man-made meteors, visible even in daylight, screaming in at an angle of thirty degrees or so, slowing down, but not visibly so, as they encountered thicker air. The trick was hitting them, or rather, hitting them hard enough to destroy them. In this, the new ones were actually easier to kill than the old ones. The original RVs had been metallic, some actually made of beryllium copper, which had been fairly sturdy. The new ones were lighter—therefore able to carry a heavier and more powerful nuclear warhead—and made from material like the tiles on the space shuttle. This was little different in feel from Styrofoam and not much stronger, since it was designed only to insulate against heat, and then only for a brief span of seconds. The space shuttles had suffered damage when their 747 ferry had flown through rainstorms, and some in the ICBM business referred to large raindrops as 'hydro meteors' for the damage they could do to a descending RV. On rare occasions when an RV had come down through a thunderstorm, relatively small hailstones had damaged them to the point that the nuclear warhead might not have functioned properly.

Such a target was almost as easy a kill as an aircraft—shooting airplanes down is easy if you hit them, not unlike dropping a pigeon with a shotgun. The trick remained hitting the damned things.

Even if you got close with your interceptor, close won you no cigars. The warhead on a SAM is little different from a shotgun shell. The explosive charge destroys the metal case, converting it into jagged fragments with an initial velocity of about five thousand feet per second. These are ordinarily quite sufficient to rip into the aluminum skin that constitutes the lift and control surfaces of the strength-members of an airplane's internal framing, turning an aircraft into a ballistic object with no more ability to fly than a bird stripped of its wings.

But hitting one necessitates exploding the warhead far enough from the target that the cone formed of the flying fragments intersects the space occupied by the target. For an aircraft, this is not difficult, but for a missile warhead traveling *faster* than the explosive-produced fragments, it is— which explained the controversy over the Patriot missiles and the Scuds in 1991.

The gadget telling the SAM warhead where and when to explode is generically called the 'fuse'. For

71

most modern missiles, the fusing system is a small, low-powered laser, which 'nutates', or turns in a circle to project its beam in a cone forward of its flight path, until the beam hits and reflects off the target. The reflected beam is received by a receptor in the laser assembly, and *that* generates the signal telling the warhead to explode. But quick as it is, it takes a finite amount of time, and the inbound RV is coming in very fast. So fast, in fact, that if the laser beam lacks the power for more than, say, a hundred meters of range, there isn't enough time for the beam to reflect off the RV in time to tell the warhead to explode soon enough to form the cone of destruction to engulf the RV target. Even if the RV is immediately next to the SAM warhead when the warhead explodes, the RV is going faster than the fragments, which cannot hurt it because they can't catch up.

And there's the problem, Gregory saw. The laser chip in the Standard Missile's nose wasn't very powerful, and the nutation speed was relatively slow, and that combination could allow the RV to slip right past the SAM, maybe as much as half the time, even if the SAM came within three meters of the target, and that was no good at all. They might actually have been better off with the old VT proximity fuse of World War II, which had used a non-directional RF emitter, instead of the new high-tech gallium-arsenide laser chip. But there was room for him to play. The nutation of the laser beam was controlled by computer software, as was the fusing signal. That was something he could fiddle with. To that end, he had to talk to the guys who made it, 'it' being the current limited-production test missile, the SM-2-ER-Block-IV,

72

and they were the Standard Missile Company, a joint venture of Raytheon and Hughes, right up the street in McLean, Virginia. To accomplish that, he'd have Tony Bretano call ahead. Why not let them know that their visitor was anointed by God, after all?

*   *   *

'My God, Jack,' Mary Pat said. The sun was under the yardarm. Cathy was on her way home from Hopkins, and Jack was in his private study off the Oval Office, sipping a glass of whiskey and ice with the DCI and his wife, the DDO. 'When I saw this, I had to go off to the bathroom.'

'I hear you, MP.' Jack handed her a glass of sherry—Mary Pat's favorite relaxing drink. Ed Foley picked a Samuel Adams beer in keeping with his working-class origins. 'Ed?'

'Jack, this is totally fucking crazy,' the Director of Central Intelligence blurted. 'Fucking' was not a word you usually used around the President, even this one. 'I mean, sure, it's from a good source and all that, but, Jesus, you just don't *do* shit like this.'

'Pat Martin was in here, right?' the Deputy Director (Operations) asked. She got a nod. 'Well, then he told you this is damned near an act of war.'

'Damned near,' Ryan agreed, with a small sip of his Irish whiskey. Then he pulled out his last cigarette of the day, stolen from Mrs. Sumter, and lit it. 'But it's a hard one to deny, and we have to fit this into government policy somehow or other.'

'We have to get George down,' Ed Foley said first of all.

'And show him SORGE, too?' Ryan asked. Mary

73

Pat winced immediately. 'I know we have to guard that one closely, MP, but, damn it, if we can't use it to figure out these people, we're no better off than we were before we had the source.'

She let out a long breath and nodded, knowing that Ryan was right, but not liking it very much. 'And our internal pshrink,' she said. 'We need a doc to check this out. It's crazy enough that we probably need a medical opinion.'

'Next, what do we say to Sergey?' Jack asked. 'He knows we know.'

'Well, start off with "keep your head down," I suppose,' Ed Foley announced. 'Uh, Jack?'

'Yeah?'

'You give this to your people yet, the Secret Service, I mean?'

'No . . . oh, yeah.'

'If you're willing to commit one act of war, why not another?' the DCI asked rhetorically. 'And they don't have much reason to like you at the moment.'

'But why Golovko?' MP asked the air. 'He's no enemy of China. He's a pro, a king-spook. He doesn't *have* a political agenda that I know about. Sergey's an *honest* man.' She took another sip of sherry.

'True, no political ambitions that I know of. But he is Grushavoy's tightest adviser on a lot of issues—foreign policy, domestic stuff, defense. Grushavoy likes him because he's smart and honest—'

'Yeah, that's rare enough in this town, too,' Jack acknowledged. That wasn't fair. He'd chosen his inner circle well, and almost exclusively of people with no political ambition, which made them an endangered species in the environs of Washington.

The same was true of Golovko, a man who preferred to serve rather than to rule, in which he was rather like the American President. 'Back to the issue at hand. Are the Chinese making some sort of play, and if so, what?'

'Nothing that I see, Jack,' Foley replied, speaking for his agency in what was now an official capacity. 'But remember that even with SORGE, we don't see that much of their inner thinking. They're so different from us that reading their minds is a son of a bitch, and they've just taken one in the teeth, though I don't think they really know that yet.'

'They're going to find out in less than a week.'

'Oh? How's that?' the DCI asked.

'George Winston tells me a bunch of their commercial contracts are coming up due in less than ten days. We'll see then what effect this has on their commercial accounts—and so will they.'

*　　　*　　　*

The day started earlier than usual in Beijing. Fang Gan stepped out of his official car and hurried up the steps into the building, Past the uniformed guard who always held the door open for him, and this time did not get a thank-you nod from the exalted servant of the people. Fang walked to his elevator, into it, then stepped off after arriving at his floor. His office door was only a few more steps. Fang was a healthy and vigorous man for his age. His personal staff leaped to their feet as he walked in—an hour early, they all realized.

'Ming!' he called on the way to his inner office.

'Yes, Comrade Minister,' she said, on going

75

through the still-open door.

'What items have you pulled off the foreign media?'

'One moment.' She disappeared and then reappeared with a sheaf of papers in her hand. '*London Times, London Daily Telegraph, Observer, New York Times, Washington Post, Miami Herald, Boston Globe.* The Western American papers are not yet available.' She hadn't included Italian or other European papers because she couldn't speak or read those languages well enough, and for some reason Fang only seemed interested in the opinions of English-speaking foreign devils. She handed over the translations. Again, he didn't thank her even peremptorily, which was unusual for him. Her minister was exercised about something.

'What time is it in Washington?' Fang asked next.

'Twenty-one hours, Comrade Minister,' she answered.

'So, they are watching television and preparing for bed?'

'Yes, Comrade Minister.'

'But their newspaper articles and editorials are already prepared.'

'That is the schedule they work, Minister. Most of their stories are done by the end of a normal working day. At the latest, news stories—aside from the truly unusual or unexpected ones—are completely done before the reporters go home for their dinner.'

Fang looked up at that analysis. Ming was a clever girl, giving him information on something he'd never really thought about. With that realization, he nodded for her to go back to her

76

desk.

*   *   *

For their part, the American trade delegation was just boarding their plane. They were seen off by a minor consular official who spoke plastic words from plastic lips, received by the Americans through plastic ears. Then they boarded their USAF aircraft, which started up at once and began rolling toward the runway.

'So, how do we evaluate this adventure, Cliff?' Mark Gant asked.

'Can you spell "disaster"?' Rutledge asked in return.

'That bad?'

The Assistant Secretary of State for Policy nodded soberly. Well, it wasn't his fault, was it? That stupid Italian clergyman gets in the way of a bullet, and then the widow of that other minister-person had to pray for him in public, *knowing* that the local government would object. And, of course, CNN had to be there for both events to stir the pot at home . . . How was a diplomat supposed to make peace happen if people kept making things worse instead of better?

'That bad, Mark. China may never get a decent trade agreement if this crap keeps going on.'

'All they have to do is change their own policies a little,' Gant offered.

'You sound like the President.'

'Cliffy, if you want to join a club, you have to abide by the club rules. Is that so hard to understand?'

'You don't treat great nations like the dentist

77

nobody likes who wants to join the country club.'

'Why is the principle different?'

'Do you really think the United States can govern its foreign policy by *principle*?' Rutledge asked in exasperation. So much so, in fact, that he'd let his mind slip a gear.

'The President does, Cliff, and so does your Secretary of State,' Gant pointed out.

'Well, if we want a trade agreement with China, we have to consider their point of view.'

'You know, Cliff, if you'd been in the State Department back in 1938, maybe Hitler could have killed all the Jews without all that much of a fuss,' Gant observed lightly.

It had the desired effect. Rutledge turned and started to object: 'Wait a minute—'

'It was just his internal policy, Cliff, wasn't it? So what, they go to a different church—gas 'em. Who cares?'

'Now look, Mark—'

'You look, Cliff. A country has to stand for certain things, because if you don't, who the fuck are you, okay? We're in the club—hell, we pretty much run the club. Why, Cliff? Because people know what we stand for. We're not perfect. You know it. I know it. They all know it. But they also know what we will and won't do, and so, we can be trusted by our friends, and by our enemies, too, and so the world makes a little sense, at least in our parts of it. And *that* is why we're respected, Cliff.'

'And all the weapons don't matter, and all the commercial power we have, what about them?' the diplomat demanded.

'How do you think we got them, Cliffy?' Gant demanded, using the diminutive of Rutledge's name again, just to bait him. 'We are what we are because people from all over the world came to America to work and live out their dreams. They worked hard. My grandfather came over from Russia because he didn't like getting fucked over by the czar, and he worked, and he got his kids educated, and they got *their* kids educated, and so now I'm pretty damned rich, but I haven't forgotten what Grandpa told me when I was little either. He told me this was the best place the world ever saw to be a Jew. Why, Cliff? Because the dead white European men who broke us away from England and wrote the Constitution had some good ideas and they lived up to them, for the most part. That's who we are, Cliff. And that means we have to *be* what we are, and *that* means we have to stand for certain things, and the world has to see us do it.'

'But we have so many flaws ourselves,' Rutledge protested.

'Of course we do! Cliff, we don't have to be perfect to be the best around, and we never stop trying to be better. My dad, when he was in college, he marched in Mississippi, and got his ass kicked a couple of times, but you know, it all worked out, and so now we have a black guy in the Vice Presidency. From what I hear, maybe he's good enough to take one more step up someday. Jesus, Cliff, how can you represent America to other nations if you don't get it?'

Diplomacy is business, Rutledge wanted to reply. *And I know how to do the business.* But why bother trying to explain things to this Chicago Jew? So, he rocked his seat back and tried to look dozy. Gant took the cue and stood for a seventy-foot walk. The

Air Force sergeants who pretended to be stewardesses aboard served breakfast, and the coffee was pretty decent. He found himself in the rear of the aircraft looking at all the reporters, and that felt a little bit like enemy territory, but not, on reflection, as much as it did sitting next to that diplo-jerk.

*   *   *

The morning sun that lit up Beijing had done the same to Siberia even earlier in the day.

'I see our engineers are as good as ever,' Bondarenko observed. As he watched, earthmoving machines were carving a path over a hundred meters wide through the primeval forests of pine and spruce. This road would serve both the gold strike and the oil fields. And this wasn't the only one. Two additional routes were being worked by a total of twelve crews. Over a third of the Russian Army's available engineers were on these projects, and that was a lot of troops, along with more than half of the heavy equipment in the olive-green paint the Russian army had used for seventy years.

'This is a "Hero Project," ' Colonel Aliyev said. And he was right. The 'Hero Project' idea had been created by the Soviet Union to indicate something of such great national importance that it would draw the youth of the nation in patriotic zeal—and besides, it was a good way to meet girls and see a little more of the world. This one was moving even faster than that, because Moscow had assigned the military to it, and the military was no longer worrying itself about an invasion from (or into) NATO. For all its faults, the Russian army still had access to a lot of human and material resources. Plus, there was real money in this project. Wages were very high for the civilians. Moscow wanted both of these resource areas brought on line—and quickly. And so the gold-field workers had been helicoptered in with light equipment, with which they'd built a larger landing area, which allowed still heavier equipment to be air-dropped, and with that a small, rough airstrip had been built. That had allowed Russian air force cargo aircraft to lift in truly heavy equipment, which was now roughing in a proper air-landing strip for when the crew extending the railroad got close enough to deliver the cement and rebar to create a real commercial-quality airport. Buildings were going up. Some of the first things that had been sent in were the components of a sawmill, and one thing you didn't have to import into this region was wood. Large swaths were being cleared, and the trees cut down to clear them were almost instantly transformed into lumber for building. First, the sawmill workers set up their own rough cabins. Now, administrative buildings were going up, and in four months, they expected to have dormitories for over a thousand of the miners who were already lining up for the highly paid job of digging this gold out of the ground. The Russian government had decided that the workers here would have the option of being paid in gold coin at world-price, and that was something few Russian citizens wanted to walk away from. And so expert miners were filling out their application forms in anticipation of the flights into the new strike. Bondarenko wished them luck. There were enough

81

mosquitoes there to carry off a small child and suck him dry of blood like mini-vampires. Even for gold coin, it was not a place he'd want to work.

The oil field was ultimately more important to his country, the general knew. Already, ships were fighting their way through the late-spring ice, shepherded by navy icebreakers like the *Yamal* and *Rossiya*, to deliver the drilling equipment needed to commence proper exploration for later production. But Bondarenko had been well briefed on this subject. This oil field was no pipe dream. It was the economic salvation of his country, a way to inject *huge* quantities of hard currency into Russia, money to buy the things it needed to smash its way into the twenty-first century, money to pay the workers who'd striven so hard and so long for the prosperity they and their country deserved.

And it was Bondarenko's job to guard it. Meanwhile, army engineers were furiously at work building harbor facilities so that the cargo ships would be able to land what cargo they had. The use of amphibious-warfare ships, so that the Russian Navy could land the cargo on the beaches as though it were battle gear, had been examined but discarded. In many cases, the cargo to be landed was larger than the main battle tanks of the Russian army, a fact which had both surprised and impressed the commanding general of the Far East Military District.

One consequence of all this was that most of Bondarenko's engineers had been stripped away for one project or another, leaving him with a few battalions organically attached to his fighting formations. And he had uses of his own for those engineers, the general grumbled. There were several places on the Chinese border where a couple of regiments could put together some very useful obstacles against invading mechanized forces. But they'd be visible, and too obviously intended to be used against Chinese forces, Moscow had told him, not caring, evidently, that the only way they could be used against the People's Liberation Army was if that army decided to come north and *liberate* Russia!

What was it about politicians? Bondarenko thought. Even the ones in America were the same, so he'd been told by American officers he'd met. Politicians didn't really care much about what something did, but they cared a great deal about what it *appeared* to do. *In that sense, all politicians of whatever political tilt all over the world were communists,* Bondarenko thought with an amused grunt, *more interested in show than reality.*

'When will they be finished?' the general-colonel asked.

'They've made amazing progress,' Colonel Aliyev replied. 'The routes will be fully roughed in—oh, another month or six weeks, depending on weather. The finishing work will take much longer.'

'You know what worries me?'

'What is that, Comrade General?' the operations officer asked.

'We've built an invasion route. For the first time, the Chinese could jump across the border and make good time to the north Siberian coast.' Before, the natural obstacles—mainly the wooded nature of the terrain—would have made that task difficult to the point of impossibility. But now there was a way to get there, and a reason to go there as well. Siberia now truly *was* something it had often

83

been thought to be, a treasure house of cosmic proportions. *Treasure house*, Bondarenko thought. *And I* am *the keeper of the keys.* He walked back to his helicopter to complete his tour of the route being carved out by army engineers.

CHAPTER THIRTY-SIX

SORGE REPORTS

President Ryan awoke just before six in the morning. The Secret Service preferred that he keep the shades closed, thus blocking the windows, but Ryan had never wanted to sleep in a coffin, even a large one, and so when he awoke momentarily at such times as 3:53 he preferred to see some sort of light outside the window, even if only the taillights of a patrolling police car or a lonely taxicab. Over the years, he'd become accustomed to waking early. That surprised him. As a boy, he'd always preferred to sleep late, especially on weekends. But Cathy had been the other way, like most doctors, and especially most surgeons: early to rise, and get to the hospital, so that when you worked on a patient you had all day to see how he or she tolerated the procedure.

So, maybe he'd picked it up from her, and in some sort of perverse one-upmanship he'd come to open his eyes even earlier. Or maybe it was a more recently acquired habit in this damned place, Jack thought, as he slid off the bed and padded off to the bathroom as another damned day started, this one like so many others, too damned early. What the hell was the matter? the President wondered. Why was it that he didn't need sleep as much anymore? Hell, sleep was one of the very few pure pleasures given to man on earth, and all he wanted was just a little more of it . . .

But he couldn't have it. It was just short of six in the morning, Jack told himself as he looked out the window. Milkmen were up, as were paperboys. Mailmen were in their sorting rooms, and in other places people who had worked through the night were ending their working days. That included a lot of people right here in the White House: protective troops in the Secret Service, domestic staff, some people Ryan knew by sight but not by name, which fact shamed him somewhat. They were *his* people, after all, and he was supposed to know about them, know their names well enough to speak them when he saw the owners thereof—but there were just too many of them for him to know. Then there were the uniformed people in the White House Military Office—called *Wham-o* by insiders—who supplemented the Office of Signals. There was, in fact, a small army of men and women who existed only to serve John Patrick Ryan—and through him the country as a whole, or that was the theory. What the hell, he thought, looking out the window. It was light enough to see. The streetlights were clicking off as their photoelectric sensors told them the sun was coming up. Jack pulled on his old Naval Academy robe, stepped into his slippers— he'd only gotten them recently; at home he just walked around barefoot, but a President couldn't do that in front of the troops, could he?—and moved quietly into the corridor.

There must have been some sort of bug or

85

motion sensor close to the bedroom door, Jack thought. He never managed to surprise anyone when he came out into the upstairs corridor unexpectedly. The heads always seemed to be looking in his direction and there was the instant morning race to see who could greet him first.

The first this time was one of the senior Secret Service troops, head of the night crew. Andrea Price-O'Day was still at her home in Maryland, probably dressed and ready to head out the door— what shitty hours these people worked on his behalf, Jack reminded himself—for the hourlong drive into D.C. And with luck she'd make it home—when? Tonight? That depended on his schedule for today, and he couldn't remember offhand what he had happening.

'Coffee, boss?' one of the younger agents asked.

'Sounds like a winner, Charlie.' Ryan followed him, yawning. He ended up in the Secret Service guard post for this floor, a walk-in closet, really, with a TV and a coffeepot—probably stocked by the kitchen staff—and some munchies to help the people get through the night.

'When did you come on duty?' POTUS asked.

'Eleven, sir,' Charlie Malone answered.

'Boring duty?'

'Could be worse. At least I'm not working the bad-check detail in Omaha anymore.'

'Oh, yeah,' agreed Joe Hilton, another one of the young agents on the deathwatch.

'I bet you played ball,' Jack observed.

Hilton nodded. 'Outside linebacker, sir. Florida State University. Not big enough for the pros, though.'

Only about two-twenty, and it's all lean meat, Jack

thought. Young Special Agent Hilton looked like a fundamental force of nature.

'Better off playing baseball. You make a good living, work fifteen years, maybe more, and you're healthy at the end of it.'

'Well, maybe I'll train my boy to be an outfielder,' Hilton said.

'How old?' Ryan asked, vaguely remembering that Hilton was a recent father. His wife was a lawyer at the Justice Department, wasn't she?

'Three months. Sleeping through the night now, Mr. President. Good of you to ask.'

I wish they'd just call me Jack. I'm not God, *am I?* But that was about as likely as his calling his commanding general Bobby-Ray back when he'd been Second Lieutenant John P. Ryan, USMC.

'Anything interesting happen during the night?'

'Sir, CNN covered the departure of our diplomats from Beijing, but that just showed the airplane taking off.'

'I think they just send the cameras down halfway hoping the airplane'll blow up so that they'll have tape of it—you know, like when the chopper comes to lift me out of here.' Ryan sipped his coffee. These junior Secret Service agents were probably a little uneasy to have 'The Boss,' as he was known within the Service, talking with them as if he and they were normal people. If so, Jack thought, tough shit. He wasn't going to turn into Louis XIV just to make *them* happy. Besides, he wasn't as good-looking as Leonardo DiCaprio, at least according to Sally, who thought that young actor was the cat's ass.

Just then, a messenger arrived with the day's copies of the morning's *Early Bird.* Jack took one

87

along with the coffee and headed back to read it over. A few editorials bemoaning the recall of the trade delegation—maybe it was the lingering liberalism in the media, the reason they were not, never had been, and probably never would be entirely comfortable with the amateur statesman in the White House. Privately, Ryan knew, they called him other things, some rather less polite, but the average Joe out there, Arnie van Damm told Jack once a week or so, still liked him a lot. Ryan's approval rating was still very high, and the reason for it, it seemed, was that Jack was perceived as a regular guy who'd gotten lucky—if they called *this* luck, POTUS thought with a stifled grunt.

He returned to reading the news articles, wandering back to the breakfast room, as he did so, where, he saw, people were hustling to get things set up—notified, doubtless, by the Secret Service that SWORDSMAN was up and needed to be fed. Yet more of the *His Majesty Effect*, Ryan groused. But he was hungry, and food was food, and so he wandered in, picked what he wanted off the buffet, and flipped the TV on to see what was happening in the world as he attacked his eggs Benedict. He'd have to devour them quickly, before Cathy appeared to yell at him about the cholesterol intake. All around him, to a radius of thirty miles or so, the government was coming to consciousness, or what passed for it, dressing, getting in their cars, and heading in, just as he was, but not as comfortably.

'Morning, Dad,' Sally said, coming in next and walking to the TV, which she switched to MTV without asking. It was a long way since that bright afternoon in London when he'd been shot, Jack thought. He'd been 'daddy' then.

*   *   *

In Beijing, the computer on Ming's desk had been in auto-sleep mode for just the right number of minutes. The hard drive started turning again, and the machine began its daily routine. Without lighting up the monitor, it examined the internal file of recent entries, compressed them, and then activated the internal modem to shoot them out over the 'Net. The entire process took about seventeen seconds, and then the computer went back to sleep. The data proceeded along the telephone lines in the city of Beijing until it found its destination server, which was, actually, in Wisconsin. There it waited for the signal that would call it up, after which it would be dumped out of the server's memory, and soon thereafter written over, eliminating any trace that it had ever existed.

In any case, as Washington woke up, Beijing was heading for sleep, with Moscow a few hours behind. The earth continued its turning, oblivious of what transpired in the endless cycle of night and day.

*   *   *

'Well?' General Diggs looked at his subordinate.
'Well, sir,' Colonel Giusti said, 'I think the cavalry squadron is in pretty good shape.' Like Diggs, Angelo Giusti was a career cavalryman. His job as commander of 1st Armored's cavalry squadron (actually a battalion, but the cav had its

89

own way of speaking) was to move out ahead of the division proper, locating the enemy and scouting out the land, being the eyes of Old Ironsides, but with enough combat power of its own to look after itself. A combat veteran of the Persian Gulf War, Giusti had smelled the smoke and seen the elephant. He knew what his job was, and he figured he had his troopers trained up about as well as circumstances in Germany allowed. He actually preferred the free-form play allowed by simulators to the crowded training fields of the Combat Maneuver Training Center, which was barely seventy-five square kilometers. It wasn't the same as being out there in your vehicles, but neither was it restricted by time and distance, and on the global SimNet system you could play against a complete enemy battalion, even a brigade if you wanted your people to get some sweat in their play. Except for the bumpy-float sensation of driving your Abrams around (some tankers got motion sickness from that), it conveyed the complexity better than any place except the NTC at Fort Irwin in the California desert, or the comparable facility the Army had established for the Israelis in the Negev.

Diggs couldn't quite read the younger officer's mind, but he'd just watched the Quarter Horse move around with no lack of skill. They'd played against some Germans, and the Germans, as always, were pretty good at the war business—but not, today, as good as First Tanks' cavalry troopers, who'd first outmaneuvered their European hosts, and then (to the surprise and distaste of the German brigadier who'd supervised the exercise) set an ambush that had cost them half a battalion of their Leos, as the Americans called the

Leopard-II main battle tanks. Diggs would be having dinner with the brigadier later today. Even the Germans didn't know night-fighting as well as the Americans did—which was odd, since their equipment was roughly comparable, and their soldiers pretty well trained . . . but the German army was still largely a conscript army, most of whose soldiers didn't have the time-in-service the Americans enjoyed.

In the wider exercise—the cavalry part had just been the 'real' segment of a wider command-post exercise, or CPX—Colonel Don Lisle's 2nd Brigade was handling the fuller, if theoretical, German attack quite capably. On the whole, the Bundeswehr was not having a good day. Well, it no longer had the mission of protecting its country against a Soviet invasion, and with that had gone the rather furious support of the citizenry that the West German army had enjoyed for so many years. Now the Bundeswehr was an anachronism with little obvious purpose, and the occupier of a lot of valuable real estate for which Germans could think up some practical uses. And so the former West German army had been downsized and mainly trained to do peacekeeping duty, which, when you got down to it, was heavily armed police work. The New World Order was a peaceful one, at least so far as Europeans were concerned. The Americans had engaged in combat operations to the rather distant interest of the Germans, who, while they'd always had a healthy interest in war-fighting, were now happy enough that their interest in it was entirely theoretical, rather like a particularly intricate Hollywood production. It also forced them to respect America a little more than they would have preferred. But some things couldn't be helped.

'Well, Angelo, I think your troopers have earned themselves a beer or two at the local Gasthauses. That envelopment you accomplished at zero-two-twenty was particularly adroit.'

Giusti grinned and nodded his appreciation. 'Thank you, General. I'll pass that one along to my S-3. He's the one who thought it up.'

'Later, Angelo.'

'Roger that one, sir.' Lieutenant Colonel Giusti saluted his divisional commander on his way.

'Well, Duke?'

Colonel Masterman pulled a cigar out of his BDU jacket and lit it up. One nice thing about Germany was that you could always get good Cuban ones here. 'I've known Angelo since Fort Knox. He knows his stuff, and he had his officers particularly well trained. Even had his own book on tactics and battle-drill printed up.'

'Oh?' Diggs turned. 'Is it any good?'

'Not bad at all,' the G-3 replied. 'I'm not sure that I agree with it all, but it doesn't hurt to have everyone singing out of the same hymnal. His officers all think pretty much the same way. So, Angelo's a good football coach. Sure enough he kicked the Krauts' asses last night.' Masterman closed his eyes and rubbed his face. 'These night exercises take it out of you.'

'How's Lisle doing?'

'Sir, last time I looked, he had the Germans well contained. Our friends didn't seem to know what he had around them. They were putzing around trying to gather information—short version, Giusti won the reconnaissance battle, and that decided things—again.'

'Again,' Diggs agreed. If there was any lesson out of the National Training Center, it was that one. Reconnaissance and counter-reconnaissance. Find the enemy. Don't let the enemy find you. If you pulled that off, it was pretty hard to lose. If you didn't, it was very hard to win.

'How's some sleep grab you, Duke?'

'It's good to have a CG who looks after his troopers, *mon Général.*' Masterman was sufficiently tired that he didn't even want a beer first.

And so with that decided, they headed for Diggs's command UH-60 Blackhawk helicopter for the hop back to the divisional kazerne. Diggs particularly liked the four-point safety belt. It made it a lot easier to sleep sitting up.

*   *   *

One of the things I have to do today, Ryan told himself, *is figure out what to do about the Chinese attempt on Sergey.* He checked his daily briefing sheet. Robby was out west again. That was too bad. Robby was both a good sounding board and a source of good ideas. So, he'd talk it over with Scott Adler, if he and Scott both had holes in their day, and the Foleys. *Who else?* Jack wondered. Damn, whom else could he trust with this? If this one leaked to the press, there'd be hell to pay. Okay, Adler had to be there. He'd actually met that Zhang guy, and if some Chinese minister-type had owned a piece of this, then he'd be the one, wouldn't he?

Probably. Not *certainly*, however. Ryan had been in the spook business too long to make that mistake. When you made *certainty* assumptions about things you weren't really sure about, you frequently walked right into a stone wall headfirst, and that could hurt. Ryan punched a button on his desk. 'Ellen?'

'Yes, Mr. President.'

'Later today, I need Scott Adler and the Foleys in here. It'll take about an hour. Find me a hole in the schedule, will you?'

'About two-thirty, but it means putting off the Secretary of Transportation's meeting about the air-traffic-control proposals.'

'Make it so, Ellen. This one's important,' he told her.

'Yes, Mr. President.'

It was by no means perfect. Ryan preferred to work on things as they popped into his mind, but as President you quickly learned that you served the schedule, not the other way around. Jack grimaced. So much for the illusion of power.

*　　　*　　　*

Mary Pat Foley strolled into her office, as she did nearly every morning, and as always turned on her computer—if there was one thing she'd learned from SORGE, it was to turn the damned thing all the way off when she wasn't using it. There was a further switch on her phone line that manually blocked it, much as if she'd pulled the plug out of the wall. She flipped that, too. It was an old story for an employee of an intelligence service. Sure, she was paranoid, but was she paranoid *enough*?

Sure enough, there was another e-mail from cgood@jadecastle.com. Chet Nomuri was still at work, and this download took a mere twenty-three seconds. With the download complete, she made sure she'd backed it up, then clobbered it out of her in-box so that no copies remained even in the ether world. Next, she printed it all up and called down for Joshua Sears to do the translations and some seat-of-the-pants analysis. SORGE had become routine in handling if not in importance, and by a quarter to nine she had the translation in hand.

'Oh, Lord. Jack's just going to love this one,' the DDO observed at her desk. Then she walked the document to Ed's larger office facing the woods. That's when she found out about the afternoon trip to the White House.

*   *   *

Mary Abbot was the official White House makeup artist. It was her job to make the President look good on TV, which meant making him look like a cheap whore in person, but that couldn't be helped. Ryan had learned not to fidget too much, which made her job easier, but she knew he was fighting the urge, which both amused and concerned her.

'How's your son doing at school?' Ryan asked.

'Just fine, thank you, and there's a nice girl he's interested in.'

Ryan didn't comment on that. He knew that there had to be some boy or boys at St. Mary's who found his Sally highly interesting (she was pretty, even to disinterested eyes), but he didn't want to think about that. It did make him grateful for the Secret Service, however. Whenever Sally went on a date, there would be at least a chase car full of

95

armed agents close by, and *that* would take the starch out of most teenaged boys. So, the USSS did have its uses, eh? *Girl children*, Jack thought, *were God's punishment on you for being a man.* His eyes were scanning his briefing sheets for the mini-press conference. The likely questions and the better sorts of answers to give to them. It seemed very dishonest to do it this way, but some foreign heads of government had the question prescreened so that the answers could be properly canned. Not a bad idea in the abstract, Jack thought, but the American media would spring for that about as quickly as a coyote would chase after a whale.

'There,' Mrs. Abbot said, as she finished touching up his hair. Ryan stood, looked in the mirror, and grimaced as usual.

'Thank you, Mary,' he managed to say.

'You're welcome, Mr. President.'

And Ryan walked out, crossing the hall from the Roosevelt Room to the Oval Office, where the TV equipment was set up. The reporters stood when he entered, as the kids at St. Matthew's had stood when the priest came into class. But in third grade, the kids asked easier questions. Jack sat down in a rocking swivel chair. Kennedy had done something similar to that, and Arnie thought it a good idea for Jack as well. The gentle rocking that a man did unconsciously in the chair gave him a homey look, the spin experts all thought—Jack didn't know that, and knowing it would have caused him to toss the chair out the window, but Arnie did and he'd eased the President into it merely by saying it looked good, and getting Cathy Ryan to agree. In any case, SWORDSMAN sat down, and relaxed in the comfortable chair, which was the other reason

Arnie had foisted it on him, and the real reason why Ryan had agreed. It was comfortable.

'We ready?' Jack asked. When the President asked that, it usually meant *Let's get this fucking show on the road!* But Ryan thought it was just a question.

Krystin Matthews was there to represent NBC. There were also reporters from ABC and Fox, plus a print reporter from the *Chicago Tribune.* Ryan had come to prefer these more intimate press conferences, and the media went along with it because the reporters were assigned by lot, which made it fair, and everyone had access to the questions and answers. The other good thing from Ryan's perspective was that a reporter was less likely to be confrontational in the Oval Office than in the raucous locker-room atmosphere of the pressroom, where the reporters tended to bunch together in a mob and adopt a mob mentality.

'Mr. President,' Krystin Matthews began. 'You've recalled both the trade delegation and our ambassador from Beijing. Why was that necessary?'

Ryan rocked a little in the chair. 'Krystin, we all saw the events in Beijing that so grabbed the conscience of the world, the murder of the cardinal and the minister, followed by the roughing-up—to use a charitable term for it—of the minister's widow and some members of the congregation.

He went on to repeat the points he'd made in his previous press conference, making particular note of the Chinese government's indifference to what had happened.

'One can only conclude that the Chinese government doesn't care. Well, we care. The American people care. And this administration cares. You cannot take the life of a human being as casually as though you are swatting an insect. The response we received was unsatisfactory, and so, I recalled our ambassador for consultations.'

'But the trade negotiations, Mr. President,' the *Chicago Tribune* broke in.

'It is difficult for a country like the United States of America to do business with a nation which does not recognize human rights. You've seen for yourself what our citizens think of all this. I believe you will find that they find those murders as repellent as I do, and, I would imagine, as you do yourself.'

'And so you will not recommend to Congress that we normalize trading relations with China?'

Ryan shook his head. 'No, I will not so recommend, and even if I did, Congress would rightly reject such a recommendation.'

'At what time might you change your position on this issue?'

'At such time as China enters the world of civilized nations and recognizes the rights of its common people, as all other great nations do.'

'So you are saying that China today is not a civilized country?'

Ryan felt as though he'd been slapped across the face with a cold, wet fish, but he smiled and went on. 'Killing diplomats is not a civilized act, is it?'

'What will the Chinese think of that?' Fox asked.

'I cannot read their minds. I do call upon them to make amends, or at least to consider the feelings and beliefs of the rest of the world, and then to reconsider their unfortunate action in that light.'

'And what about the trade issues?' This one came from ABC.

'If China wants normalized trade relations with the United States, then China will have to open its markets to us. As you know, we have a law on the books here called the Trade Reform Act. That law allows us to mirror-image other countries' trade laws and practices, so that whatever tactics are used against us, we can then use those very same tactics with respect to trade with them. Tomorrow, I will direct the Department of State and the Department of Commerce to set up a working group to implement TRA with respect to the People's Republic,' President Ryan announced, making the story for the day, and a bombshell it was.

* * *

'Christ, Jack,' the Secretary of the Treasury said in his office across the street. He was getting a live feed from the Oval Office. He lifted his desk phone and punched a button. 'I want a read of the PRC's current cash accounts, global,' he told one of his subordinates from New York. Then his phone rang.

'Secretary of State on Three,' his secretary told him over the intercom. SecTreas grunted and picked up the phone.

'Yeah, I saw it too, Scott.'

* * *

'So, Yuriy Andreyevich, how did it go?' Clark asked. It had taken over a week to set up, and mainly because General Kirillin had spent a few hours on the pistol range working on his technique. Now he'd just stormed into the officers' club bar

99

looking as though he'd taken one in the guts.

'Is he a Mafia assassin?'

Chavez had himself a good laugh at that. 'General, he came to us because the Italian police wanted to get him away from the Mafia. He got in the way of a mob assassination, and the local chieftain made noises about going after him and his family. What did he get you for?'

'Fifty euros,' Kirillin nearly spat.

'You were confident going in, eh?' Clark asked. 'Been there, done that.'

'Got the fuckin' T-shirt,' Ding finished the statement with a laugh. And fifty euros was a dent even in the salary of a Russian three-star.

'Three points, in a five-hundred-point match. I scored four ninety-three!'

'Ettore only got four ninety-six?' Clark asked. 'Jesus, the boy's slowing down.' He slid a glass in front of the Russian general officer.

'He's drinking more over here,' Chavez observed.

'That must be it.' Clark nodded. The Russian general officer was not, however, the least bit amused.

'Falcone is not human,' Kirillin said, gunning down his first shot of vodka.

'He could scare Wild Bill Hickok, and that's a fact. And you know the worst part about it?'

'What is that, Ivan Sergeyevich?'

'He's so goddamned humble about it, like it's fucking normal to shoot like that. Jesus, Sam Snead was never that good with a five-iron.'

'General,' Domingo said after his second vodka of the evening. The problem with being in Russia was that you tended to pick up the local customs, and one of those was drinking. 'Every man on my team is an expert shot, and by expert, I mean close to being on his country's Olympic team, okay? Big Bird's got us all beat, and none of us are used to losing any more'n you are. But I'll tell you, I'm goddamned glad he's on my team.' Just then, Falcone walked through the door. 'Hey, Ettore, come on over!'

He hadn't gotten any shorter. Ettore towered over the diminutive Chavez, and still looked like a figure from an El Greco painting. 'General,' he said in greeting to Kirillin. 'You shoot extremely well.'

'Not so good as you, Falcone,' the Russian responded.

The Italian cop shrugged. 'I had a lucky day.'

'Sure, guy,' Clark reacted, as he handed Falcone a shot glass.

'I've come to like this vodka,' Falcone said on gunning it down. 'But it affects my aim somewhat.'

'Yeah, Ettore.' Chavez chuckled. 'The general told us you blew four points in the match.'

'You mean you have done better than this?' Kirillin demanded.

'He has,' Clark answered. 'I watched him shoot a possible three weeks ago. That was five hundred points, too.'

'That was a good day,' Falcone agreed. 'I had a good night's sleep beforehand and no hangover at all.'

Clark had himself a good chuckle and turned to look around the room. Just then, another uniform entered the room and looked around. He spotted General Kirillin and walked over.

'Damn, who's this recruiting poster?' Ding

wondered aloud as he approached.

'Tovarisch General,' the man said by way of greeting.

'Anatoliy Ivan'ch,' Kirillin responded. 'How are things at the Center?'

Then the guy turned. 'You are John Clark?'

'That's me,' the American confirmed. 'Who are you?'

'This is Major Anatoliy Shelepin,' General Kirillin answered. 'He's chief of personal security for Sergey Golovko.'

'We know your boss.' Ding held out his hand. 'Howdy. I'm Domingo Chavez.'

Handshakes were exchanged all around.

'Could we speak in a quieter place?' Shelepin asked. The four men took over a corner booth in the club. Falcone remained at the bar.

'Sergey Nikolay'ch sent you over?' the Russian general asked.

'You haven't heard,' Major Shelepin answered. It was the way he said it that got everyone's attention. He spoke in Russian, which Clark and Chavez understood well enough. 'I want my people to train with you.'

'Haven't heard what?' Kirillin asked.

'We found out who tried to kill the Chairman,' Shelepin announced.

'Oh, he was the target? I thought they were after the pimp,' Kirillin objected.

'You guys want to tell us what you're talking about?' Clark asked.

'A few weeks ago, there was an assassination attempt in Dzerzhinskiy Square,' Shelepin responded, explaining what they'd thought at the time. 'But now it appears they hit the wrong target.'

'Somebody tried to waste Golovko?' Domingo asked. 'Damn.'

'Who was it?'

'The man who arranged it was a former KGB officer named Suvorov—so we believe, that is. He used two ex-Spetsnaz soldiers. They have both been murdered, probably to conceal their involvement, or at least to prevent them from discussing it with anyone.' Shelepin didn't add anything else. 'In any case, we have heard good things about your Rainbow troops, and we want you to help train my protective detail.'

'It's okay with me, so long as it's okay with Washington.' Clark stared hard into the bodyguard's eyes. He looked damned serious, but not very happy with the world at the moment.

'We will make the formal request tomorrow.'

'They are excellent, these Rainbow people,' Kirillin assured him. 'We're getting along well with them. Anatoliy used to work for me, back when I was a colonel.' The tone of voice told what he thought of the younger man.

There was more to this, Clark thought. A senior Russian official didn't just ask a former CIA officer for help with something related to his personal safety out of the clear blue. He caught Ding's eye and saw the same thought. Suddenly both were back in the spook business.

'Okay,' John said. 'I'll call home tonight if you want.' He'd do that from the American Embassy, probably on the STU-6 in the station chief's office.

CHAPTER THIRTY-SEVEN

FALLOUT

The VC-137 landed without fanfare at Andrews
Air Force Base. The base lacked a proper terminal
and the attendant jetways, and so the passengers
debarked on stairs grafted onto a flatbed truck.
Cars waited at the bottom to take them into
Washington. Mark Gant was met by two Secret
Service agents who drove him at once to the
Treasury Department building across the street
from the White House. He'd barely gotten used to
being on the ground when he found himself in the
Secretary's office.

'How'd it go?' George Winston asked.

'Interesting, to say the least,' Gant said, his mind
trying to get used to the fact that his body didn't
have a clue where it was at the moment. 'I thought
I'd be going home to sleep it off.'

'Ryan's invoking the Trade Recovery Act against
the Chinese.'

'Oh? Well, that's not all that much of a surprise,
is it?'

'Look at this,' SecTreas commanded, handing
over a recently produced printout. 'This' was a
report on the current cash holdings of the People's
Republic of China.

'How solid is this information?' TELESCOPE
asked TRADER.

The report was an intelligence estimate in all but
name. Employees within the Treasury Department
routinely kept track of international monetary

transactions as a means of determining the day-to-day strength of the dollar and other internationally traded currencies. That included the Chinese yuan, which had been having a slightly bad time of late.

'They're this thin?' Gant asked. 'I thought they were running short of cash, but I didn't know it was quite this bad . . .'

'It surprised me, too,' SecTreas admitted. 'It appears that they've been purchasing a lot of things on the international market lately, especially jet engines from France, and because they're late paying for the last round, the French company has decided to take a harder line—they're the only game in town. We won't let GE or Pratt and Whitney bid on the order, and the Brits have similarly forbidden Rolls-Royce. That makes the French the sole source, which isn't so bad for the French, is it? They've jacked up the price about fifteen percent, and they're asking for cash up front.'

'The yuan's going to take a hit,' Gant predicted. 'They've been trying to cover this up, eh?'

'Yeah, and fairly successfully.'

'That's why they were hitting us so hard on the trade deal. They saw this one coming, and they wanted a favorable announcement to bail them out. But they sure didn't play it very smart. Damn, you have this sort of a problem, you learn to crawl a little.'

'I thought so, too. Why, do you think?'

'They're proud, George. Very, very proud. Like a rich family that's lost its money but not its social position, and tries to make up for the one with the other. But it doesn't work. Sooner or later, people find out that you're not paying your bills, and then the whole world comes crashing in on you. You can put it off for a while, which makes sense if you have something coming in, but if the ship don't dock, you sink.' Gant flipped some pages, thinking: The other problem is that countries are run by politicians, people with no real understanding of money, who figure they can always maneuver their way out of whatever comes up. They're so used to having their own way that they never really think they can't have it that way all the time. One of the things Gant had learned working in D.C. was that politics was just as much about illusion as the motion-picture business was, which perhaps explained the affinity the two communities had for each other. But even in Hollywood you had to pay the bills, and you had to show a profit. Politicians always had the option of using T-bills to finance their accounts, and they also printed the money. Nobody expected the government to show a profit, and the board of directors was the voters, the people whom politicians conned as a way of life. It was all crazy, but that was the political game.

That's probably what the PRC leaders were thinking, Gant surmised. But sooner or later, reality raised its ugly head, and when it did all the time spent trying to avoid it was what really bit you on the ass. That was when the whole world said *gotcha*. And then you were well and truly got. In this case, the *gotcha* could be the collapse of the Chinese economy, and it would happen virtually overnight.

'George, I think State and CIA need to see this, and the President, too.

*   *   *

106

'Lord.' The President was sitting in the Oval Office, smoking one of Ellen Sumter's Virginia Slims and watching TV. This time it was C-SPAN. Members of the United States House of Representatives were speaking in the well about China. The content of the speeches was not complimentary, and the tone was decidedly inflammatory. All were speaking in favor of a resolution to condemn the People's Republic of China. C-SPAN2 was covering much the same verbiage in the Senate. Though the language was a touch milder, the import of the words was not. Labor unions were united with churches, liberals with conservatives, even free-traders with protectionists.

More to the point, CNN and the other networks showed demonstrations in the streets, and it appeared that Taiwan's 'We're the Good Guys' campaign had taken hold. Somebody (nobody was sure who yet) had even printed up stickers of the Red Chinese flag with the caption 'We Kill Babies and Ministers'. They were being attached to products imported from China, and the protesters were also busy identifying the American firms that did a lot of business on the Chinese mainland, with the aim of boycotting them.

Ryan's head turned. 'Talk to me, Arnie.'

'This looks serious, Jack,' van Damm said.

'Gee, Arnie, I can see that. How serious?'

'Enough that I'd sell stock in those companies. They're going to take a hit. And this movement may have legs . . .'

'What?'

'I mean it might not go away real soon. Next

you're going to see posters with stills from the TV coverage of those two clerics being murdered. That's an image that doesn't go away. If there's any product the Chinese sell here that we can get elsewhere, then a lot of Americans will start buying it elsewhere.'

The picture on CNN changed to live coverage of a demonstration outside the PRC Embassy in Washington. The signs said things like MURDERERS, KILLERS, and BARBARIANS!

'I wonder if Taiwan is helping to organize this . . .'

'Probably not—at least not yet,' van Damm thought. 'If I were they, I wouldn't exactly mind, but I wouldn't need to play with this. They'll probably increase their efforts to distinguish themselves from the mainland—and that amounts to the same thing. Look for the networks to do stories about the Republic of China, and how upset *they* are with all this crap in Beijing, how they don't want to be tarred with the same brush and all that,' the Chief of Staff said. 'You know, "Yes, we are Chinese, but *we* believe in human rights and freedom of religion." That sort of thing. It's the smart move. They have some good PR advisers here in D.C. Hell, I probably know some of them, and if I were on the payroll, that's what I would advise.'

That's when the phone rang. It was Ryan's private line, the one that usually bypassed the secretaries. Jack lifted it. 'Yeah?'

'Jack, it's George across the street. Got a minute? I want to show you something, buddy.'

'Sure. Come on over.' Jack hung up and turned to Arnie. 'SecTreas,' he explained. 'Says it's important.' The President paused. 'Arnie?'

'Yeah?'

'How much maneuvering room do I have with this?'

'The Chinese?' Arnie asked, getting a nod. 'Not a hell of a lot, Jack. Sometimes the people themselves decide what our policy is. And the people will be making policy now by voting with their pocketbooks. Next we'll see some companies announce that they're suspending their commercial contracts with the PRC. The Chinese already fucked Boeing over, and in the full light of day, which wasn't real smart. Now the people out there will want to fuck them back. You know, there are times when the average Joe Citizen stands up on his hind feet and gives the world the finger. When that happens, it's your job mainly to follow them, not to lead them,' the Chief of Staff concluded. His Secret Service code name was CARPENTER, and he'd just constructed a box for his President to stay inside.

Jack nodded and stubbed out the smoke. He might be the Most Powerful Man in the World, but his power came from the people, and as it was theirs to give, it was also sometimes theirs to exercise.

Few people could simply open the door to the Oval Office and walk in, but George Winston was one of them, mainly because the Secret Service belonged to him. Mark Gant was with him, looking as though he'd just run a marathon chased by a dozen armed and angry Marines in jeeps.

'Hey, Jack.'

'George. Mark, you look like hell,' Ryan said. 'Oh, you just flew in, didn't you?'

'Is this Washington or Shanghai?' Gant offered, as rather a wan joke.

'We took the tunnel. Jesus, have you seen the demonstrators outside? I think they want you to nuke Beijing,' SecTreas observed. The President just pointed at his bank of television sets by way of an answer.

'Hell, why are they demonstrating here? I'm on *their* side—at least I think I am. Anyway, what brings you over?'

'Check this out.' Winston nodded to Gant.

'Mr. President, these are the PRC's current currency accounts. We keep tabs on currency trading worldwide to make sure we know where the dollar is—which means we pretty much know where all the hard currency is in the world.'

'Okay.' Ryan knew about that—sort of. He didn't worry much about it, since the dollar was in pretty good shape, and the nonsqueaky wheel didn't need any grease. 'So?'

'So, the PRC's liquidity situation is in the shitter,' Gant reported. 'Maybe that's why they were so pushy in the trade talks. If so, they picked the wrong way to approach us. They demanded instead of asked.'

Ryan looked down the columns of numbers. 'Damn, where have they been dumping all their money?'

'Buying military hardware. France and Russia, mostly, but a lot went to Israel, too.' It was not widely known that the PRC had spent a considerable sum of money in Israel, mainly paid to IDI—Israel Defense Industries—to buy American-designed hardware manufactured under license in Israel. It was stuff the Chinese could not purchase

110

directly from America, including guns for their tanks and air-to-air missiles for their fighter aircraft. America had winked at the transactions for years. In conducting this business, Israel had turned its back on Taiwan, despite the fact that both countries had produced their nuclear weapons as a joint venture, back when they'd stuck together—along with South Africa—as international pariahs with no other friends in that particular area. In polite company, it was called *realpolitik*. In other areas of human activity, it was called *fuck your buddy*.

'And?' Ryan asked.

'And they've spent their entire trade surplus this way,' Gant reported. 'All of it, mainly on short-term purchase items, but some long-term as well, and for the long-term stuff they had to pay cash up front because of the nature of the transactions. The producers need the cash to run the production, and they don't want to get stuck holding the bag. Not too many people need five thousand tank guns,' Gant explained. 'The market is kinda exclusive.'

'So?'

'So, China is essentially out of cash. And they have real short-term cash needs. Like oil,' TELESCOPE went on. 'China's a net importer of oil. Production in their domestic fields falls well short, even though their needs are not really that great. Not too many Chinese citizens own cars. They have enough cash for three months' worth of oil, and then they come up short. The international oil market demands prompt payment. They can skate for a month, maybe six weeks, but after that, the tankers will turn around in mid-ocean and go somewhere else—they can do that, you know—and then the PRC runs out. It'll be like running into a wall, sir. *Smack.* No more oil, and then their country starts coming to a stop, including their military, which is their largest oil consumer. They've been running unusually high for some years because of increased activity in their maneuvers and training and stuff. They probably have strategic reserves, but we don't know exactly how much. And that can run out, too. We've been expecting them to make a move on the Spratly Islands. There's oil there, and they've been making noises about it off and on for about ten years, but the Philippines and other countries in the area have made claims, too, and they probably expect us to side with the Philippines for historical reasons. Not to mention, Seventh Fleet is still the biggest kid on the block in that part of the world.'

'Yeah.' Ryan nodded. 'If it came to a showdown, the Philippines appear to have the best claim on the islands, and we would back them up. We've shed blood together in the past, and that counts. Go on.'

'So, John Chinaman is short of oil, and he may not have the cash to pay for it, especially if our trade with them goes down the toilet. They need our dollars. The yuan isn't very strong anyway. International trading is also done in dollars, and as I just told you, sir, they've spent most of them.'

'What are you telling me?'

'Sir, the PRC is just about bankrupt. In a month or so, they're going to find that out, and it's going to be a bit of a shock for them.'

'When did *we* find this out?'

'That's my doing, Jack,' the Secretary of the Treasury said. 'I called up these documents earlier today, and then I had Mark go over them. He's our best man for economic modeling, even whacked out with jet lag.'

'So, we can squeeze them on this?'

'That's one option.'

'What if these demonstrations take hold?'

Gant and Winston shrugged simultaneously. 'That's where psychology enters into the equation,' said Winston. 'We can predict it to some extent on Wall Street—that's how I made most of my money—but psychoanalyzing a country is beyond my ken. That's your job, pal. I just run your accounting office across the street.'

'I need more than that, George.'

Another shrug. 'If the average citizen boycotts Chinese goods, and/or if American companies who do business over there start trimming their sails—'

'That's damned likely,' Gant interjected. 'This has got to have a lot of CEOs shitting their pants.'

'Well, if that happens, the Chinese get one in the guts, and it's going to hurt, big time,' TRADER concluded.

And how will they react to that? Ryan wondered. He punched his phone button. 'Ellen, I need one.' His secretary appeared in a flash and handed him a cigarette. Ryan lit it and thanked her with a smile and a nod.

'Have you talked this one over with State yet?'

A shake of the head. 'No, wanted to show it to you first.'

'Hmm. Mark, what did you make of the negotiations?'

'They're the most arrogant sons of bitches I've ever seen. I mean, I've met all sorts of big shots in my time, movers and shakers, but even the worst of them know when they need my money to do business, and when they know that, their manners get better. When you shoot a gun, you try to make sure you don't have it aimed at your own dick.'

That made Ryan laugh, while Arnie cringed. You weren't supposed to talk that way to the President of the United States, but some of these people knew that you could talk that way to John Patrick Ryan, the man.

'By the way, along those lines, I liked what you told that Chinese diplomat.'

'What's that, sir?'

'Their dicks aren't big enough to get in a pissing contest with us. Nice turn of phrase, if not exactly diplomatic.'

'How did you know that?' Gant asked, the surprise showing on his face. 'I never repeated that to anybody, not even to that jerk Rutledge.'

'Oh, we have ways,' Jack answered, suddenly realizing that he'd revealed something from a compartment named SORGE. *Oops.*

'Sounds like something you say at the New York Athletic Club,' SecTreas observed. 'But only if you're four feet or so away from the guy.

'But it appears it's true. At least in monetary terms. So, we have a gun we can point at their heads?'

'Yes, sir, we sure do,' Gant answered. 'It might take them a month to figure it out, but they won't be able to run away from it for very long.'

'Okay, make sure State and the Agency find this out. And, oh, tell CIA that they're supposed to get this stuff to me first. Intelligence estimates are their job.'

'They have an economics unit, but they're not all

114

that good,' Gant told the others. 'No surprise. The smart people in this area work The Street, or maybe academia. You can make more money at Harvard Business School than you can in government service.'

'And talent goes where the money is,' Jack agreed. Junior partners at medium-sized law firms made more than the President, which sometimes explained the sort of people who ended up here. Public service was supposed to be a sacrifice. It was for him—Ryan had proven his ability to make money in the trading business, but for him service to his country had been learned from his father, and at Quantico, long before he'd been seduced into the Central Intelligence Agency and then later tricked into the Oval Office. And once here, you couldn't run away from it. At least, not and keep your manhood. That was always the trap. Robert Edward Lee had called duty the most sublime of words. And he would have known, Ryan thought. Lee had felt himself trapped into fighting for what was at best a soiled cause because of his perceived duty to his place of birth, and therefore many would curse his name for all eternity, despite his qualities as a man and a soldier. *So, Jack,* he asked himself, *in* your *case, where do talent and duty and right and wrong and all that other stuf lie? What the hell are* you *supposed to do now?* He was supposed to know. All those people outside the White House's campuslike grounds expected him to know all the time where the right thing was, right for the country, right for the world, right for every working man, woman, and innocent little kid playing T-ball. *Yeah,* the President thought, *sure. You're anointed by the wisdom fairy when you walk in here every day, or kissed on the ear by the muse, or maybe Washington and Lincoln whisper to you in your dreams at night.* He sometimes had trouble picking his tie in the morning, especially if Cathy wasn't around to be his fashion adviser. But he was supposed to know what to do with taxes, defense, and Social Security— why? Because it was his job to know. Because he happened to live in government housing at One Thousand Six Hundred Pennsylvania Avenue and had the Secret goddamned Service protect him everywhere he went. At the Basic School at Quantico, the officers instructing newly commissioned Marine second lieutenants had told them about the loneliness of command. The difference between that and what he had here was like the difference between a fucking firecracker and a nuclear weapon. This kind of situation had started wars in the past. That wouldn't happen now, of course, but it had once. It was a sobering thought. Ryan took a last puff on his fifth smoke of the day and killed it in the brown glass ashtray he kept hidden in a desk drawer.

'Thanks for bringing me this. Talk it over with State and CIA,' he told them again. 'I want a SNIE on this, and I want it soon.'

'Right,' George Winston said, standing for the underground walk back to his building across the street.

'Mr. Gant,' Jack added. 'Get some sleep. You look like hell.'

'I'm allowed to sleep in this job?' TELESCOPE asked.

'Sure you are, just like I am,' POTUS told him with a lopsided smile. When they left, he looked at Arnie: 'Talk to me.'

116

'Speak to Adler, and have him talk to Hitch and Rutledge, which you ought to do, too,' Arnie advised.

Ryan nodded. 'Okay, tell Scott what I need, and that I need it fast.'

*   *   *

'Good news,' Professor North told her, as she came back into the room.

Andrea Price-O'Day was in Baltimore, at the Johns Hopkins Hospital, seeing Dr. Madge North, Professor of Obstetrics and Gynecology.

'Really?'

'Really,' Dr. North assured her with a smile. 'You're pregnant.'

Before anything else could happen, Inspector Patrick O'Day leapt to his feet and lifted his wife in his arms for a powerful kiss and a rib-cracking hug.

'Oh,' Andrea said almost to herself. 'I thought I was too old.'

'The record is well into the fifties, and you're well short of that,' Dr. North said, smiling. It was the first time in her professional career that she'd given this news to *two* people carrying guns.

'Any problems?' Pat asked.

'Well, Andrea, you are prime-ep. You're over forty and this is your first pregnancy, isn't it?'

'Yes.' She knew what was coming, but she didn't invite it by speaking the word.

'That means that there is an increased likelihood of Down's syndrome. We can establish that with an amniocentesis. I'd recommend we do that soon.'

'How soon?'

'I can do it today if you wish.'

117

'And if the test is . . . ?'

'Positive? Well, then you two have to decide if you want to bring a Down's child into the world. Some people do, but others don't. It's your decision to make, not mine,' Madge North told them. She'd done abortions in her career, but like most obstetricians, she much preferred to deliver babies.

'Down's—how and . . . I mean . . .' Andrea said, squeezing her husband's hand.

'Look, the odds are very much in your favor, like a hundred to one or so, and those are betting odds. Before you worry about it, the smart thing is to find out if there's anything to worry about at all, okay?'

'Right now?' Pat asked for his wife.

Dr. North stood. 'Yes, I have the time right now.'

'Why don't you take a little walk, Pat?' Special Agent Price-O'Day suggested to her husband. She managed to keep her dignity intact, which didn't surprise her husband.

'Okay, honey.' A kiss, and he watched her leave. It was not a good moment for the career FBI agent. His wife was pregnant, but now he had to wonder if the pregnancy was a good one or not. If not—then what? He was an Irish Catholic, and his church forbade abortion as murder, and murders were things he'd investigated—and even witnessed once. Ten minutes later, he'd killed the two terrorists responsible for it. That day still came back to him in perverse dreams, despite the heroism he'd displayed and the kudos he'd received for all of it.

But now, he was afraid. Andrea had been a fine stepmother for his little Megan, and both he and she wanted nothing in all the world more than this news—if it was, really, good news. It would

118

probably take an hour, and he knew he couldn't spend it sitting down in a doctor's outer office full of pregnant women reading old copies of *People* and *US Weekly*. But where to go? Whom to see?

Okay. He stood and walked out, and decided to head over to the Maumenee Building. It ought not be too hard to find. And it wasn't.

Roy Altman was the telltale. The big former paratrooper who headed the SURGEON detail didn't stand in one place like a potted plant, but rather circulated around, not unlike a lion in a medium-sized cage, always checking, looking with highly trained and experienced eyes for something that wasn't quite right. He spotted O'Day in the elevator lobby and waved.

'Hey, Pat! What's happening?' All the rivalry between the FBI and the USSS stopped well short of this point. O'Day had saved the life of SANDBOX and avenged the deaths of three of Altman's fellow agents, including Roy's old friend, Don Russell, who'd died like a man, gun in hand and three dead assassins in front of him. O'Day had finished Don's work.

'My wife's over being checked out,' the FBI inspector answered.

'Nothing serious?' Altman asked.

'Routine,' Pat responded, and Altman caught the scent of a lie, but not an important one.

'Is she around? While I'm here, I thought I'd stop over and say hi.'

'In her office.' Altman waved. 'Straight down, second on the right.'

'Thanks.'

'Bureau guy coming back to see SURGEON,' he said into his lapel mike.

119

'Roger,' another agent responded.

O'Day found the office door and knocked.

'Come in,' the female voice inside said. Then she looked up. 'Oh, Pat, how are you?'

'No complaints, just happened to be in the neighborhood, and—'

'Did Andrea see Madge?' Cathy Ryan asked. FLOTUS had helped make the appointment, of course.

'Yeah, and the little box doodad has a plus sign in it,' Pat reported.

'Great!' Then Professor Ryan paused. 'Oh, you're worried about something.' In addition to being an eye doctor, she knew trouble when she saw it.

'Dr. North is doing an amniocentesis. Any idea how long it takes?'

'When did it start?'

'Right about now, I think.'

Cathy knew the problem. 'Give it an hour. Madge is very good, and very careful in her procedures. They tap into the uterus and withdraw some of the amniotic fluid. That will give them some of the tissue from the embryo, and then they examine the chromosomes. She'll have the lab people standing by. Madge is senior staff, and when she talks, people listen.'

'She seems pretty competent.'

'She's a wonderful doc. She's *my* OB. You're worried about Down's, right?'

A nod. 'Yep.'

'Nothing you can do but wait.'

'Dr. Ryan, I'm—'

'My name's Cathy, Pat. We're friends, remember?' There was nothing like saving the life

120

of a woman's child to get on her permanent good side.

'Okay, Cathy. Yeah, I'm scared. It's not—I mean, Andrea's a cop, too, but—'

'But being good with a gun or just being tough doesn't help much right now, does it?'

'Not worth a damn,' Inspector O'Day confirmed quietly. He was about as used to being frightened as he was of flying the Space Shuttle, but potential danger to his wife and/or kid—*kids* now, maybe—the kind of danger in which he was utterly helpless—well, that was one of the buttons a capricious Fate could push while she laughed.

'The odds are way in your favor,' Cathy told him.

'Yeah, Dr. North said so ... but ...'

'Yeah. And Andrea's younger than I am.'

O'Day looked down at the floor, feeling like a total fucking wimp. More than once in his life, he'd faced down armed men—criminals with violent pasts—and intimidated them into surrender. Once in his life he'd had to use his Smith & Wesson 1076 automatic in anger, and both times he'd double-tapped the heads of the terrorists, sending them off to Allah—so they'd probably believed—to answer for the murder of the innocent woman. It hadn't been easy, exactly, but neither had it been all that hard. The endless hours of practice had made it nearly as routine as the working of his service automatic. But this wasn't danger to himself. He could deal with that. The worst danger, he was just learning, was to those you loved.

'Pat, it's okay to be scared. John Wayne was just an actor, remember?'

But that was it. The code of manhood to which most Americans subscribed was that of the Duke, and that code did not allow fear. In truth it was about as realistic as *Who Framed Roger Rabbit*, but foolish or not, there it was.

'I'm not used to it.'

Cathy Ryan understood. Most doctors did. When she'd been a straight ophthalmic surgeon, before specializing in lasers, she'd seen the patients and the patients' families, the former in pain, but trying to be brave, the latter just scared. You tried to repair the problems of one and assuage the fears of the other. Neither task was easy. The one was just skill and professionalism; the other involved showing them that, although this was a horrid emergency which they'd never experienced before, for Cathy Ryan, M.D., FACS, it was just another day at the office. She was the Pro from Dover. She could handle it. SURGEON was blessed with the demeanor that inspired confidence in all she met.

But even that didn't apply here. Though Madge North was a gifted physician, she was testing for a predetermined condition. Maybe someday it could be fixed—genetic therapy offered that hope, ten years or so down the line—but not today. Madge could merely determine what already was. Madge had great hands, and a good eye, but the rest of it was in God's hands, and God had already decided one way or the other. It was just a matter of finding out what His decision had been.

'This is when a smoke comes in handy,' the inspector observed, with a grimacing smirk.

'You smoke?'

He shook his head. 'Gave it up a long time ago.'

'You should tell Jack.'

The FBI agent looked up. 'I didn't know he smokes.'

'He bums them off his secretary every so often, the wimp,' Cathy told the FBI agent, with almost a laugh. 'I'm not supposed to know.'

'That's very tolerant for a doc.'

'His life's hard enough, and it's only a couple a day, and he doesn't do it around the kids, or Andrea'd have to shoot me for ripping his face off.'

'You know,' O'Day said, looking down again and speaking from the cowboy boots he liked to wear under his blue FBI suit, 'if it comes back that it's a Down's kid, what the hell do we do then?'

'That's not an easy choice.'

'Hell, under the law I don't get a choice. I don't even have a say in it, do I?'

'No, you don't.' Cathy didn't venture that this was an inequity. The law was firm on the point. The woman—in this case, the wife alone could choose to continue the pregnancy or terminate it. Cathy knew her husband's views on abortion. Her own views were not quite identical, but she did regard that choice as distasteful. 'Pat, why are you borrowing trouble?'

'It's not under my control.'

Like most men, Cathy saw, Pat O'Day was a control freak. She could understand that, because so was she. It came from using instruments to change the world to suit her wishes. But this was an extreme case. This tough guy was deeply frightened. He really ought not to be, but it was a question of the unknown for him. She knew the odds, and they were actually pretty good, but he was not a doctor, and all men, even the tough ones, she saw, feared the unknown. Well, it wasn't the first time she'd baby-sat an adult who needed his hand held—and this one had saved Katie's life.

'Want to walk over to the day-care center?'

'Sure.' O'Day stood.

It wasn't much of a walk, and her intention was to remind O'Day what this was all about—getting a new life into the world.

'SURGEON's on the way to the playpen,' Roy Altman told his detail. Kyle Daniel Ryan—SPRITE—was sitting up now, and playing very simply with very rudimentary toys under the watchful eyes of the lionesses, as Altman thought of them, four young female Secret Service agents who fawned over SPRITE like big sisters. But these sisters all carried guns, and they all remembered what had nearly happened to SANDBOX. A nuclear-weapons-storage site was hardly as well-guarded as this particular day-care center.

Outside the playroom was Trenton 'Chip' Kelley, the only male agent on the detail, a former Marine captain who would have frightened the average NFL lineman with a mere look.

'Hey, Chip.'

'Hi, Roy. What's happening?'

'Just strolling over to see the little guy.'

'Who's the muscle?' Kelley saw that O'Day was carrying heat, but decided he looked like a cop. But his left thumb was still on the button of his 'crash alarm,' and his right hand was within a third of a second of his service automatic.

'Bureau. He's cool,' Altman assured his subordinate.

' 'Kay.' Kelley opened the door.

'Who'd he play for?' O'Day asked Altman, once inside.

'The Bears drafted him, but he scared Ditka too much.' Altman laughed. 'Ex-Marine.'

124

'I believe it.' Then O'Day walked up behind Dr. Ryan. She'd already scooped Kyle up, and his arms were around her neck. The little boy was babbling, still months away from talking, but he knew how to smile when he saw his mommy.

'Want to hold him?' Cathy asked.

O'Day cradled the infant somewhat like a football. The youngest Ryan examined his face dubiously, especially the Zapata mustache, but Mommy's face was also in sight, and so he didn't scream.

'Hey, buddy,' O'Day said gently. Some things came automatically. When holding a baby, you don't stand still. You move a little bit, rhythmically, which the little ones seemed to like.

'It'll ruin Andrea's career,' Cathy said.

'Make for a lot better hours for her, and be nice to see her every night, but, yeah, Cathy, be kinda hard for her to run alongside the car with her belly sticking out two feet.' The image was good enough for a laugh. 'I suppose they'll put her on restricted duty.'

'Maybe. Makes for a great disguise, though, doesn't it?'

O'Day nodded. This wasn't so bad, holding a kid. He remembered the old Irish adage: *True strength lies in gentleness.* But what the hell, taking care of kids was also a man's duty. There was a lot more to being a man than just having a dick.

Cathy saw the display and had to smile. Pat O'Day had saved Katie's life, and done it like something out of a John Woo movie, except that Pat was a real tough guy, not the movie kind. His scenes weren't scripted; he'd had to do it for real, making it up as he'd gone along. He was a lot like

125

her husband, a servant of the law, a man who'd sworn an oath to Do the Right Thing every time, and like her husband, clearly a man who took his oaths seriously. One of those oaths concerned Pat's relationship with Andrea, and they all came down to the same thing: preserve, protect, defend. And now, this tiger with a tie was holding a baby and smiling and swaying back and forth, because that's what you did with a baby in your arms.

'How's your daughter?' Cathy asked.

'She and your Katie are good friends. And she's got a thing going with one of the boys at Giant Steps.'

'Oh?'

'Jason Hunt. I think it's serious. He gave Megan one of his Hot Wheels cars.' O'Day laughed. That's when his cell phone went off. 'Right side coat pocket,' he told the First Lady.

Cathy fished in his pocket and pulled it out. She flipped it open. 'Hello?'

'Who's this?' a familiar voice asked.

'Andrea? It's Cathy. Pat's right here.' Cathy took Kyle and handed off the phone, watching the FBI agent's face.

'Yeah, honey?' Pat said. Then he listened, and his eyes closed for two or three seconds, and that told the tale. His tense face relaxed. A long breath came out slowly, and the shoulders no longer looked like a man anticipating a heavy blow. 'Yeah, baby, I came over to see Dr. Ryan, and we're in the nursery. Oh, okay.' Pat looked over and handed over the phone. Cathy cradled it between her shoulder and ear.

'So, what did Madge say?' Cathy asked, already knowing most of it.

126

'Normal—and it's going to be a boy.'

'So, Madge was right, the odds were in your favor.' And they still were. Andrea was very fit. She wouldn't have any problems, Cathy was sure.

'Seven months from next Tuesday,' Andrea said, her voice already bubbling.

'Well, listen to what Madge says. I do,' Cathy assured her. She knew all the stuff Dr. North believed in. Don't smoke. Don't drink. Do your exercises. Take the classes on prepared delivery along with your husband. Come see me in five weeks for your next checkup. Read *What to Expect When You're Expecting.* Cathy handed the phone back. Inspector O'Day had taken a few steps and turned away. When he turned back to take the phone, his eyes were unusually moist.

'Yeah, honey, okay. I'll be right over.' He killed the phone and dumped it back in his pocket.

'Feel better?' she asked with a smile. One of the lionesses came over to take Kyle back. The little guy loved them all, and smiled up at her.

'Yes, ma'am. Sorry to bother you. I feel like a wuss.'

'Oh, bullcrap.' Rather a strong imprecation for Mrs. Dr. Ryan. 'Like I said, life isn't a movie, and this isn't the Alamo. I know you're a tough guy, Pat, and so does Jack. What about you, Roy?'

'Pat can work with me any day. Congratulations, buddy,' Altman added, turning back from the lead.

'Thanks, Pat,' O'Day told his colleague.

'Can I tell Jack, or does Andrea want to?' SURGEON asked.

'I guess you'll have to ask her about that one, ma'am.'

Pat O'Day was transformed, enough spring in his

127

step now to make him collide with the ceiling. He was surprised to see that Cathy was heading off to the OB-GYN building, but five minutes later it was obvious why. This was to be girl-girl bonding time. Even before he could embrace his wife, Cathy was there.

'Wonderful news, I'm so happy for you!'

'Yeah, well, I suppose the Bureau is good for something after all,' Andrea joked.

Then the bear with the Zapata mustache lifted her off the floor with a hug and a kiss. 'This calls for a small celebration,' the inspector observed.

'Join us for dinner tonight at the House?' SURGEON asked.

'We can't,' Andrea replied.

'Says who?' Cathy demanded. And Andrea had to bow to the situation.

'Well, maybe, if the President says it's okay.'

'*I* say it's okay, girl, and there are times when Jack doesn't count,' Dr. Ryan told them.

'Well, yes, then, I guess.'

'Seven-thirty,' SURGEON told them. 'Dress is casual.' It was a shame they were no longer regular people. This would have been a good chance for Jack to do steaks on the grill, something he remained very good at, and she hadn't made her spinach salad in months. Damn the Presidency anyway! 'And, Andrea, you *are* allowed two drinks tonight to celebrate. After that, one or two a week.'

Mrs. O'Day nodded. 'Dr. North told me.'

'Madge is a real stickler on the alcohol issue.' Cathy wasn't sure about the data on that, but then, she wasn't an OB-GYN, and she'd followed Dr. North's rules with Kyle and Katie. You just didn't fool around when you were pregnant. Life was too precious to risk.

CHAPTER THIRTY-EIGHT

DEVELOPMENTS

It's all handled electronically. Once a country's treasury was in its collection of gold bricks, which were kept in a secure, well-guarded place, or else traveled in a crate with the chief of state wherever he went. In the nineteenth century, paper currency had gained wide acceptance. At first, it had to be redeemable for gold or silver-something whose weight told you its worth—but gradually this, too, was discarded, because precious metals were just too damned heavy to lug around. But soon enough even paper currency became too bulky to drag about, as well. For ordinary citizens, the next step was plastic cards with magnetic strips on the back, which moved your *theoretical* currency from your account to someone else's when you made a purchase. For major corporations and nations, it meant something even more theoretical. It became an electronic expression. A nation determined the value of its currency by estimating what quantity of goods and services its citizens generated with their daily toil, and that became the volume of its monetary wealth, which was generally agreed upon by the other nations and citizens of the world. Thus it could be traded across national boundaries by fiber-optic or copper cables, or even by satellite transmissions, and so billions of dollars, pounds, yen, or the new euros moved from place to place via simple keystrokes. It was a lot easier and faster than shipping gold bricks, but, for all the convenience, the system that determined a person's or a nation's wealth was no less rigid, and at certain central banks of the world, a country's net collection of those monetary units was calculated down to a fraction of a percentage point. There was some leeway built into the system, to account for trades in process and so forth, but that leeway was also closely calculated electronically. What resulted was no different in its effect from the numbering of the bricks of King Croesus of Lydia. In fact, if anything, the new system that depended on the movement of electrons or photons from one computer to another was even more exact, and even less forgiving. Once upon a time, one could paint lead bricks yellow and so fool a casual inspector, but lying to a computerized accounting system required a lot more than that.

In China, the lying was handled by the Ministry of Finance, a bastard orphan child in a Marxist country peopled by bureaucrats who struggled on a daily basis to do all manner of impossible things. The first and easiest impossibility—because it had to be done—was for its senior members to cast aside everything they'd learned in their universities and Communist Party meetings. To operate in the world financial system, they had to understand and play by—and within—the world monetary rules, instead of the Holy Writ of Karl Marx.

The Ministry of Finance, therefore, was placed in the unenviable position of having to explain to the communist clergy that their god was a false one, that their perfect theoretical model just didn't play in the real world, and that therefore they had to bend to a reality which they had rejected. The bureaucrats in the ministry were for the most part observers, rather like children playing a computer game that they didn't believe in but enjoyed anyway. Some of the bureaucrats were actually quite clever, and played the game well, sometimes even making a profit on their trades and transactions. Those who did so won promotions and status within the ministry. Some even drove their own automobiles to work and were befriended by the new class of local industrialists who had shed their ideological straitjackets and operated as capitalists within a communist society. That brought wealth into their nation, and earned the tepid gratitude, if not the respect, of their political masters, rather as a good sheepdog might. This crop of industrialists worked closely with the Ministry of Finance, and along the way influenced the bureaucracy that managed the income that they brought into their country.

One result of all this activity was that the Ministry of Finance was surely and not so slowly drifting away from the True Faith of Marxism into the shadowy in-between world of socialist capitalism—a world with no real name or identity. In fact, every Minister of Finance had drifted away from Marxism to some greater or lesser extent, whatever his previous religious fervor, because one by one they had all seen that their country needed to play on this particular international playground, and to do that, had to play by the rules, and, oh, by the way, this game was bringing prosperity to the People's Republic in a way that fifty years of Marx and Mao had singularly failed to do.

As a direct result of this inexorable process, the

Minister of Finance was a candidate, not a full member of the Politburo. He had a voice at the table, but not a vote, and his words were judged by those who had never really troubled themselves to understand his words or the world in which he operated.

This minister was surnamed Qian, which, appropriately, meant coins or money, and he'd been in the job for six years. His background was in engineering. He'd built railroads in the northeastern part of his country for twenty years, and done so well enough to merit a change in posting. He'd actually handled his ministerial job quite well, the international community judged, but Qian Kun was often the one who had to explain to the Politburo that the Politburo couldn't do everything it wanted to do, which meant he was often about as welcome in the room as a plague rat. This would be one more such day, he feared, sitting in the back of his ministerial car on the way to the morning meeting.

*   *   *

Eleven hours away, on Park Avenue in New York, another meeting was under way. Butterfly was the name of a burgeoning chain of clothing stores which marketed to prosperous American women. It had combined new microfiber textiles with a brilliant young designer from Florence, Italy, into fully a six percent share of its market, and in America that was big money indeed.

Except for one thing. Its textiles were all made in the People's Republic, at a factory just outside the great port city of Shanghai, and then cut and sewn

132

into clothing at yet another plant in the nearby city of Yancheng.

The chairman of Butterfly was just thirty-two, and after ten years of hustling, he figured he was about to cash in on a dream he'd had from all the way back in Erasmus Hall High School in Brooklyn. He'd spent nearly every day since graduating Pratt Institute conceiving and building up his business, and now it was *his* time. It was time to buy that G so that he could fly off to Paris on a whim, get that house in the hills of Tuscany, and another in Aspen, and really live in the manner he'd earned.

Except for that one little thing. His flagship store at Park and 50th today had experienced something as unthinkable as the arrival of men from Mars. People had demonstrated there. People wearing Versace clothing had shown up with cardboard placards stapled to wooden sticks proclaiming their opposition to trade with BARBARIANS! and condemning Butterfly for doing business with such a country. Someone had even shown up with an image of the Chinese flag with a swastika on it, and if there was *anything* you didn't want associated with your business in New York, it was Hitler's odious logo.

'We've got to move fast on this,' the corporate counsel said. He was Jewish and smart, and had steered Butterfly through more than one minefield to bring it to the brink of ultimate success. 'This could kill us.'

He wasn't kidding, and the rest of the board knew it. Exactly four customers had gone past the protesters into the store today, and one of them had been returning something which, she said, she no longer wanted in her closet.

'What's our exposure?' the founder and CEO asked.

'In real terms?' the head of accounting asked. 'Oh, potentially four hundred.' By which he meant four hundred *million* dollars. 'It could wipe us out in, oh, twelve weeks.'

Wipe us out was not what the CEO wanted to hear. To bring a line of clothing this far was about as easy as swimming the Atlantic Ocean during the annual shark convention. This was his moment, but he found himself standing in yet another minefield, one for which he'd had no warning at all.

'Okay,' he responded as coolly as the acid in his stomach allowed. 'What can we do about it?'

'We can walk on our contracts,' the attorney advised.

'Is that legal?'

'Legal enough.' By which he meant that the downside exposure of shorting the Chinese manufacturers was less onerous than having a shop full of products that no person would buy.

'Alternatives?'

'The Thais,' Production said. 'There's a place outside Bangkok that would love to take up the slack. They called us today, in fact.'

'Cost?'

'Less than four percent difference. Three-point-six-three, to be exact, and they will be off schedule by, oh, maybe four weeks max. We have enough stock to keep the stores open through that, no problem,' Production told the rest of the board with confidence.

'How much of that stock is Chinese in origin?'

'A lot comes from Taiwan, remember? We can

have our people start putting the Good Guys stickers on them . . . and we can fudge that some, too.' Not all that many consumers knew the difference between one Chinese place name and another. A flag was much easier to differentiate.

'Also,' Marketing put in, 'we can start an ad campaign tomorrow. "Butterfly doesn't do business with dragons."' He held up an illustration that showed the corporate logo escaping a dragon's fiery breath. That it looked terminally tacky didn't matter for the moment. They had to take action, and they had to do it fast.

'Oh, got a call an hour ago from Frank Meng at Meng, Harrington, and Cicero,' Production announced. 'He says he can get some ROC textile houses on the team in a matter of days, and he says they have the flexibility to retool in less than a month—and if we green-light it, the ROC ambassador will officially put us on their good-guy list. In return, we just have to guarantee five years' worth of business, with the usual escape clauses.'

'I like it,' Legal said. The ROC ambassador would play fair, and so would his country. They knew when they had the tiger by the balls.

'We have a motion on the table,' the chairman and CEO announced. 'All in favor?'

With this vote, Butterfly was the first major American company to walk out on its contracts with the People's Republic. Like the first goose to leave Northern Canada in the fall, it announced that a new and chilly season was coming. The only potential problem was legal action from the PRC businesses, but a federal judge would probably understand that a signed contract wasn't quite the same thing as a suicide note, and perhaps even regard the overarching political question sufficient to make the contract itself void. After all, counsel would argue in chambers—and in front of a New York jury if necessary—when you find out you're doing business with Adolf Hitler, you *have* to take a step back. Opposing counsel would argue back, but he'd know his position was a losing one, and he'd tell his clients so before going in.

'I'll tell our bankers tomorrow. They're not scheduled to cut the money loose for another thirty-six hours.' This meant that one hundred forty million dollars would not be transferred to a Beijing account as scheduled. And now the CEO could contemplate going ahead with his order for the G. The corporate logo of a monarch butterfly leaving its cocoon, he thought, would look just great on the rudder.

*   *   *

'We don't know for sure yet,' Qian told his colleagues, 'but I am seriously concerned.'

'What's the particular problem today?' Xu Kun Piao asked.

'We have a number of commercial and other contracts coming due in the next three weeks. Ordinarily I would expect them to proceed normally, but our representatives in America have called to warn my office that there might be a problem.'

'Who are these representatives?' Shen Tang asked.

'Mainly lawyers whom we employ to manage our business dealings for us. Almost all are American citizens. They are not fools, and their advice is something a wise man attends carefully,' Qian said soberly.

'Lawyers are the curse of America,' Zhang Han San observed. 'And all civilized nations.' *At least here* we *decide the law*, he didn't have to explain.

'Perhaps so, Zhang, but if you do business with America you need such people, and they are very useful in explaining conditions there. Shooting the messenger may get you more pleasant news, but it won't necessarily be accurate.'

Fang nodded and smiled at that. He liked Qian. The man spoke the truth more faithfully than those who were supposed to listen for it. But Fang kept his peace on this. He, too, was concerned with the political developments caused by those two overzealous policemen, but it was too late to discipline them now. Even if Xu suggested it, Zhang and the others would talk him out of it.

*   *   *

Secretary Winston was at home watching a movie on his DVD player. It was easier than going to the movies, and he could do it without four Secret Service agents in attendance. His wife was knitting a ski sweater—she did her important Christmas presents herself, and it was something she could do while watching TV or talking, and it brought the same sort of relaxation to her that sailing his big offshore yacht did for her husband.

Winston had a multiline phone in the family room—and every other room in his Chevy Chase house—and the private line had a different ring so that he knew which one he had to answer himself.

'Yeah?'

137

'George, it's Mark.'

'Working late?'

'No, I'm home. Just got a call from New York. It may have just started.'

'What's that?' TRADER asked TELESCOPE.

'Butterfly—the ladies' clothing firm?'

'Oh, yeah, I know the name,' Winston assured his aide. Well he might: His wife and daughter loved the place.

'They're going to bail on their contracts with their PRC suppliers.'

'How big?'

'About a hundred forty.'

Winston whistled. 'That much?'

'That big,' Gant assured him. 'And they're a trend-setter. When this breaks tomorrow, it's going to make a lot of people think. Oh, one other thing.'

'Yeah?'

'The PRC just terminated its options with Caterpillar-equipment to finish up the Three Gorges project. That's about three-ten million, switching over to Kawa in Japan. That's going to be in the *Journal* tomorrow morning.

'That's real smart!' Winston grumbled.

'Trying to show us who's holding the whip, George.'

'Well, I hope they like how it feels going up their ass,' SecTreas observed, causing his wife to look over at him.

'Okay, when's the Butterfly story break?'

'It's too late for the *Journal* tomorrow, but it'll be on CNN-FN and CNBC for damned sure.'

'And what if other fashion houses do the same?'

'Over a billion, right away, and you know what they say, George, a billion here, a billion there, pretty soon you're talking real money.' It had been one of Everett McKinley Dirksen's better Washington observations.

'How much before their currency account goes in the tank?'

'Twenty, and it starts hurting. Forty, and they're in the shitter. Sixty, and they're fuckin' broke. Never seen a whole country sleeping over a steam vent, y'know? George, they also import food, wheat mainly, from Canada and Australia. That could *really* hurt.'

'Noted. Tomorrow.'

'Right.' The phone clicked off.

Winston picked up the controller to un-pause the DVD player, then had another thought. He picked up the mini-tape machine he used for notes and said, 'Find out how much of the PRC military purchases have been executed financially— especially Israel.' He clicked the STOP button, set it down, and picked the DVD controller back up to continue his movie, but soon found he couldn't concentrate on it very well. Something big was happening, and experienced as he was in the world of commerce, and now in the business of international transactions, he realized that he didn't have a handle on it. That didn't happen to George Winston very often, and it was enough to keep him from laughing at *Men in Black*.

*　　　*　　　*

Her minister didn't look very happy, Ming saw. The look on his face made her think that he might have lost a family member to cancer. She found out more when he called her in to dictate his notes. It took fully ninety minutes this time, and then two entire hours for her to transcribe them into her computer. She hadn't exactly forgotten what her computer probably did with them every night, but she hadn't thought about it in weeks. She wished she had the ability to discuss the notes' content with Minister Fang. Over the years of working for him, she'd acquired rather a sophisticated appreciation for the politics of her country, to the point that she could anticipate not only the thoughts of her master, but also those of some of his colleagues. She was in effect, if not in fact, a confidant of her minister, and while she could not counsel him on his job, if he'd had the wit to appreciate the effect of her education and her time inside his head, he might have used her far more efficiently than as a mere secretary. But she was a woman in a land ruled by men, and therefore voiceless. Orwell had been right. She'd read *Animal Farm* some years ago. Everyone *was* equal, but some *were* more equal than others. If Fang were smart, he'd use her more intelligently, but he wasn't, and he didn't. She'd talk to Nomuri-san about that tonight.

*　　　*　　　*

For his part, Chester was just finalizing an order for one thousand six hundred sixty-one high-end NEC desktops at the China Precision Machine Import and Export Corporation, which, among other things, made guided missiles for the People's Liberation Army. That would make Nippon Electric Company pretty happy. The sad part was that he couldn't rig these machine to talk as glibly as the two in the Council of Ministers, but that would have been too dangerous, if a good daydream over a beer and a smoke. Chester Nomuri, cyber-spy. Then his beeper started vibrating. He reached down and gave it a look. The number was 745-4426. Applied to the keys on a phone, and selecting the right letters, that translated in personal code to *shin gan*, 'heart and soul,' Ming's private endearment for her lover and an indication that she wanted to come over to his place tonight. That suited Nomuri just fine. So, he'd turned into James Bond after all. Good enough for a private smile, as he walked out to his car. He flipped open his shoephone, dialed up his email access, and sent his own message over the 'Net, 226-234: *bao bei*, 'beloved one'. She liked to hear him say that, and he didn't mind saying it. So, something other than TV for tonight. Good. He hoped he had enough of the Japanese scotch for the *aprés*-sex.

*   *   *

You knew you had a bad job when you welcomed a trip to the dentist. Jack had been going to the same one for nineteen years, but this time it involved a helicopter flight to a Maryland State Police barracks with its own helipad, followed by five minutes in a car to the dentist's office. He was thinking about China, but his principal bodyguard mistook his expression.

'Relax, boss,' Andrea told the President. 'If he makes you scream, I'll cap him.'

'You shouldn't be up so early,' Ryan responded crossly.

141

'Dr. North said I could work my regular routine until further notice, and I just started the vitamins she likes.'

'Well, Pat looks rather pleased with himself.' It had been a pleasant evening at the White House. It was always good to entertain guests who had no political agenda.

'What is it about you guys? You strut like roosters, but *we* have to do all the work!'

'Andrea, I would *gladly* switch jobs with you!' Ryan joked. He'd had this discussion with Cathy often enough, claiming that having a baby couldn't be all that hard—men had to do almost all of the tough work in life. But he couldn't joke with someone else's wife that way.

*　　　*　　　*

Nomuri heard his computer beep in the distance, meaning it had received and was now automatically encrypting and retransmitting the date e-mailed from Ming's desktop. It made an entertaining interruption to his current activity. It had been five days since their last tryst, and that was a long enough wait for him . . . and evidently for her as well, judging by the passion in her kisses. In due course, it was over, and they both rolled over for a smoke.

'How is the office?' Nomuri asked, with the answer to his question now residing in a server in Wisconsin.

'The Politburo is debating great finance. Qian, the minister in charge of our money, is trying to persuade the Politburo to change its ways, but they're not listening as Minister Fang thinks they ought.'

'Oh?'

'He's rather angry with his old comrades for their lack of flexibility.' Then Ming giggled. 'Chai said the minister was very flexible with her two nights ago.'

'Not a nice thing to say about a man, Ming,' Nomuri chided.

'I would never say it about you and your jade sausage, *shin gan*,' she said, turning for a kiss.

'Do they argue often there? In the Politburo, I mean?'

'There are frequent disagreements, but this is the first time in months that the matter has not been resolved to Fang's satisfaction. They are usually collegial, but this is a disagreement over ideology. Those can be violent—at least in intellectual terms.' Obviously, the Politburo members were too old to do much more than smack an enemy over the head with their canes.

'And this one?'

'Minister Qian says the country may soon be out of money. The other ministers say that is nonsense. Qian says we must accommodate the Western countries. Zhang and the others like him say we cannot show weakness after all they—especially the Americans—have done to us lately.'

'Don't they see that killing that Italian priest was a bad thing?'

'They see it as an unfortunate accident, and besides, he was breaking our laws.'

Jesus, Nomuri thought, *they really do think they're god-kings, don't they? 'Bao bei*, that is a mistake on their part.'

'You think so?'

143

'I have been to America, remember? I lived there for a time. Americans are very solicitous to their clergy, and they place a high value on religion. Spitting on it angers them greatly.'

'You think Qian is right, then?' she asked. 'You think America will deny us money for this foolish action?'

'I think it is possible, yes. Very possible, Ming.'

'Minister Fang thinks we should take a more moderate course, to accommodate the Americans somewhat, but he did not say so at the meeting.'

'Oh? Why?'

'He does not wish to depart too greatly from the path of the other ministers. You say that in Japan people fear not being elected. Here, well, the Politburo elects its own, and it can expel those who no longer fit in. Fang does not wish to lose his own status, obviously, and to make sure that doesn't happen, he takes a cautious line.'

'This is hard for me to understand, Ming. How do they select their members? How do the "princes" choose the new "prince"?'

'Oh, there are party members who have distinguished themselves ideologically, or sometimes from work in the field. Minister Qian, for example, used to be chief of railroad construction, and was promoted for that reason, but mainly they are picked for political reasons.'

'And Fang?'

'My minister is an old comrade. His father was one of Mao's faithful lieutenants, and Fang has always been politically reliable, but in recent years he has taken note of the new industries and seen how well they function, and he admires some of the people who operate them. He even has some into

144

his office from time to time for tea and talk.'

So, the old pervert is a progressive *here?* Nomuri wondered. Well, the bar for that was pretty low in China. You didn't have to jump real high, but that put him in advance of the ones who dug a trench under it, didn't it?

'Ah, so the people have no voice at all, do they?'

Ming laughed at that. 'Only at party meetings, and there you guard your voice.'

'Are you a member?'

'Oh, yes. I go to meetings once a month. I sit in the back. I nod when others nod, and applaud when they applaud, and I pretend to listen. Others probably listen better. It is not a small thing to be a party member, but my membership is because of my job at the ministry. I am here because they needed my language and computer skills—and besides, the ministers like to have young women under them,' she added.

'You're never on top of him, eh?'

'He prefers the ordinary position, but it is hard on his arms.' Ming giggled.

*   *   *

Ryan was glad to see that he was brushing enough. The dentist told him to floss as he always did, and RYan nodded, as he always did, and he'd never bought floss in his life and wasn't going to start now. But at least he'd undergone nothing more invasive than a couple of X-rays, for which, of course, he'd gotten the leather apron. On the whole, it had been ninety minutes torn off the front of his day. Back in the Oval Office, he had the latest SORGE, which was good enough for a

145

whispered 'damn'. He lifted the phone for Mary Pat at Langley.

'They're dense,' Ryan observed.

'Well, they sure as hell don't know high finance. Even I know better than this.'

'TRADER has to see this. Put him on the SORGE list,' POTUS ordered.

'With your day-to-day approval only,' the DDO hedged. 'Maybe he has a need-to-know on economics, but nothing else, okay?'

'Okay, for now,' Jack agreed. But George was coming along nicely on strategic matters, and might turn into a good policy adviser. He understood high-stress psychology better than most, and that was the name of the game. Jack broke the connection and had Ellen Sumter call the SecTreas over from across the street.

*   *   *

'So, what else do they worry about?' Chester asked.

'They're concerned that some of the workers and peasants are not as happy as they should be. You know about the riots they had in the coal region.'

'Oh?'

'Yes, the miners rioted last year. The PLA went in to settle things down. Several hundred people were shot, and three thousand arrested.' She shrugged while putting her bra back on. 'There is unrest, but that is nothing especially new. The army keeps control of things in the outlying regions. That's why they spend so much money, to keep the army reliable. The generals run the PLA's economic empire—all the factories and things—

146

and they're good at keeping a lid on things. The ordinary soldiers are just workers and peasants, but the officers are all party members, and they are reliable, or so the Politburo thinks. It's probably true,' Ming concluded. She hadn't seen her minister worry all that much about it. Power in the People's Republic decidedly grew from the barrel of a gun, and the Politburo owned all the guns. That made things simple, didn't it?

For his part, Nomuri had just learned things he'd never thought about before. He might want to make his own report on this stuff. Ming probably knew a lot of things that didn't go out as SONGBIRD material, and he'd be remiss not to send that to Langley, too.

*   *   *

'It's like a five-year-old in a gun store,' Secretary Winston observed. 'These people have no business making economic decisions for a city government, much less a major country. I mean, hell, as stupid as the Japanese were a few years ago, at least they know to listen to the coaches.'

'And?'

'And when they run into the brick wall, their eyes'll still be closed. That can smart some, Jack. They're going to get bit on the ass, and they don't see it coming.' Winston could mix metaphors with the best of 'em, Ryan saw.

'When?' SWORDSMAN asked.

'Depends on how many companies do what Butterfly did. We'll know more in a few days. The fashion business will be the lead indicator, of all things.'

'Really?'

'Surprised me, too, but this is the time for them to commit to the next season, and there's a *ton* of money in that business going on over there, man. Toss in all the toys for next Christmas. There's seventeen billion-plus just in that, Mark Gant tells me.'

'Damn.'

'Yeah, I didn't know Santa's reindeer had slanted eyes either, Jack. At least not to that extent.'

'What about Taiwan?' Ryan wondered.

'You're not kidding. They're jumping into the growing gap with both feet. Figure they pick up a quarter, maybe a third, of what the PRC is going to lose. Singapore's going to be next. And the Thais. This little bump in the road will go a long way to restore the damage done to their economy a few years back. In fact, the PRC's troubles might rebuild the whole South Asian economy. It could be a swing of fifty billion dollars out of China, and it has to go somewhere. We're starting to take bids, Jack. It won't be a bad deal for our consumers, and I'll bet those countries learn from Beijing's example, and kick their doors open a notch or so. So, our workers will profit from it, too—somewhat, anyway.

'Downside?'

'Boeing's squealing some. They wanted that triple-seven order, but you wait an' see. Somebody's going to take up that slack, too. One other thing.'

'Yeah?' Ryan asked.

'It's not just American companies bailing out on them. Two big Italian places, and Siemens in

Germany, they've announced termination of some business with their Chinese partners,' TRADER said.

'Will it turn into a general movement . . . ?'

'Too soon to say, but if I were these guys'— Winston shook the fax from CIA—'I'd be thinking about fence-mending real soon.'

'They won't do it, George.'

'Then they're going to learn a nasty lesson.'

CHAPTER THIRTY-NINE

THE OTHER QUESTION

'No action with our friend?' Reilly asked.

'Well, he continues his sexual adventures,' Provalov answered.

'Talk to any of the girls yet?'

'Earlier today, two of them. He pays them well, in euros or d-marks, and doesn't request any, uh, "exotic" services from them.'

'Nice to know he's normal in his tastes,' the FBI agent observed, with a grunt.

'We have numerous photos of him now. We've put an electronic tracker on his cars, and we've also planted a bug on his computer keyboard. That'll allow us to determine his encryption password, next time he makes use of it.'

'But he hasn't done anything incriminating yet,' Reilly said. He didn't even make it a question.

'Not under our observation,' Oleg confirmed.

'Damn, so, he was really trying to whack Sergey Golovko. Hard to believe, man.'

'That is so, but we cannot deny it. And on

Chinese orders.'

'That's like an act of war, buddy. It's a big fucking deal.' Reilly took a sip of his vodka.

'So it is, Mishka. Rather more complex than any case I've handled this year.' It was, Provalov thought, an artful understatement. He'd gladly go back to a normal homicide, a husband killing his wife for fucking a neighbor, or the other way around. Such things, nasty as they were, were far less nasty than this one was.

'How's he pick the girls up, Oleg?' Reilly asked.

'He doesn't call for them on the phone. He seems to go to a good restaurant with a good bar and wait until a likely prospect appears at his elbow.'

'Hmm, plant a girl on him?'

'What do you mean?'

'I mean get yourself a pretty girl who does this sort of thing for a living, brief her on what she ought to say, and set her in front of him like a nice fly on your fishhook. If he picks her up, maybe she can get him to talk.'

'Have you ever done such a thing?'

'We got a wiseguy that way in Jersey City three years ago. Liked to brag in front of women how tough he was, and the guys he whacked, that sort of thing. He's in Rahway State Prison now on a murder rap. Oleg, a lot more people have talked their way into prison than you'll ever catch on your own. Trust me. That's how it is for us, even.'

'I wonder if the Sparrow School has any graduates working . . . ?' Provalov mused.

*   *   *

150

It wasn't fair to do it at night, but nobody had ever said war was marked by fairness in its execution. Colonel Boyle was in his command post monitoring the operation of 1st Armored's Aviation Brigade. It was mainly his Apaches, though some Kiowa Warriors were up, too, as scouts for the heavy shooters. The target was a German heavy battalion, simulating a night's laagering after a day on the offense. In fact, they were pretending to be Russians—it was a NATO scenario that went back thirty years to the introduction of the first Huey Cobras, back in the 1970s, when the value of a helicopter gunship had first been noticed in Vietnam. And a revelation it had been. Armed for the first time in 1972 with TOW missiles, they'd proven to the tanks of the North Vietnamese just how fearsome a foe a missile-armed chopper could be, and that had been before night-vision systems had come fully on line. Now the Apache turned combat operations into sport shooting, and the Germans were still trying to figure a counter for it. Even their own night-vision gear didn't compensate for the huge advantage held by the airborne hunters. One idea that had almost worked was to lay a thermal-insulating blanket over the tanks so as to deny the helicopters the heat signature by which they hunted their motionless prey, but the problem there was the tank's main gun tube, which had proved impractical to conceal, and the blankets had never really worked properly, any more than a twin-bed coverlet could be stretched over a king-size bed. And so, now, the Apaches' laser-illumination systems were 'painting' the Leos for enough seconds to guarantee hits from the Hellfire missiles, and while the German tanks tried to shoot

151

back, they couldn't seem to make it work. And now the yellow 'I'm dead' lights were blinking, and yet another tank battalion had fallen victim to yet another administrative attack.

'They should have tried putting SAM teams outside their perimeter,' Colonel Boyle observed, watching the computer screen. Instead, the German colonel had tried IR lures, which the Apache gunners had learned to distinguish from the real thing. Under the rules of the scenario, proper tank decoys had not been allowed. They were a little harder to discriminate—the American-made ones almost exactly replicated the visual signature of an M1 tank, and had an internal heat source for fooling infrared gear at night-and-fired off a Hoffman pyrotechnic charge to simulate a return shot when they took a hit. But they were made so well for their mission that they could not be mistaken for anything other than what they were, either a real M1 main battle tank, and hence friendly, or a decoy, and thus not really useful in a training exercise, all in all a case of battlefield technology being too good for a training exercise.

'Pegasus Lead to Archangel, over,' the digital radio called. With the new radios, it was no longer a static-marred crackle.

'Archangel to Pegasus,' Colonel Boyle answered.

'Sir, we are Winchester and just about out of targets. No friendly casualties. Pegasus is RTB, over.'

'Roger, Pegasus. Looks good from here. Out.'

And with that, the Apache battalion of attack choppers and their Kiowa bird-dogs turned back for their airfield for the mission debrief and post-game beers.

Boyle looked over at General Diggs. 'Sir, I don't know how to do it much better than that.'

'Our hosts are going to be pissed.'

'The Bundeswehr isn't what it used to be. Their political leadership thinks peace has broken out all the way, and their troopers know it. They could have put some of their own choppers up to run interference, but my boys are pretty good at air-to-air—we train for it, and my pilots really like the idea of making ace on their own—but their chopper drivers aren't getting all the gas they need for operational training. Their best chopper drivers are down in the Balkans doing traffic observation.'

Diggs nodded thoughtfully. The problems of the Bundeswehr were not, strictly speaking, his problems. 'Colonel, that was well done. Please convey my pleasure to your people. What's next for you?'

'General, we have a maintenance stand-down tomorrow, and two days later we're going to run a major search-and-rescue exercise with my Blackhawks. You're welcome to come over and watch.'

'I just might, Colonel Boyle. You done good. Be seeing you.'

'Yes, sir.' The colonel saluted, and General Diggs walked out to his HMMWV, with Colonel Masterman in attendance.

'Well, Duke?'

'Like I told you, sir, Boyle's been feeding his boys and girls a steady diet of nails and human babies.'

'Well, his next fitness report's going to get him a star, I think.'

'His Apache commander's not bad either.'

'That's a fact,' the divisional G-3 agreed. 'Pegasus' was his call sign, and he'd kicked some serious ass this night.

'What's next?'

'Sir, in three days we have a big SimNet exercise against the Big Red One at Fort Riley. Our boys are pretty hot for it.'

'Divisional readiness?' Diggs asked.

'We're pushing ninety-five percent, General. Not much slack left to take up. I mean, sir, to go any farther, we gotta take the troops out to Fort Irwin or maybe the Negev Training Area. Are we as good as the Tenth Cav or the Eleventh? No, we don't get to play in the field as much as they do.' And, he didn't have to add, no division in any army in the world got the money to train that hard. 'But given the limitations we have to live with, there's not a whole lot more we can do. I figure we play hard on SimNet to keep the kids interested, but we're just about as far as we can go, sir.'

'I think you're right, Duke. You know, sometimes I kinda wish the Cold War could come back—for training purposes, anyway. The Germans won't let us play the way we used to back then, and that's what we need to take the next step.'

'Unless somebody springs for the tickets to fly a brigade out to California.' Masterman nodded.

'That ain't gonna happen, Duke,' Diggs told his operations officer. And more was the pity. First Tanks' troops were almost ready to give the Blackhorse a run for their money. Close enough, Diggs thought, that he'd pay to watch. 'How's a beer grab you, Colonel?'

'If the General is buying, I will gladly assist him in spending his money,' Duke Masterman said graciously, as their sergeant driver pulled up to the *kazerne*'s O-Club.

*   *

'Good morning, Comrade General,' Gogol said, pulling himself to attention.

Bondarenko had felt guilt at coming to see this old soldier so early in the morning, but he'd heard the day before that the ancient warrior was not one to waste daylight. And so he wasn't, the general saw.

'You kill wolves,' Gennady Iosifovich observed, seeing the gleaming pelts hanging on the wall of this rough cabin.

'And bear, but when you gild the pelts, they grow too heavy,' the old man agreed, fetching tea for his guests.

'These are amazing,' Colonel Aliyev said, touching one of the remaining wolf pelts. Most had been carried off.

'It's an amusement for an old hunter,' Gogol said, lighting a cigarette.

General Bondarenko looked at his rifles, the new Austrian-made one, and the old Russian M 1891 Mosin-Nagant sniper rifle.

'How many with this one?' Bondarenko asked.

'Wolves, bears?'

'Germans,' the general clarified, with coldness in his voice.

'I stopped counting at thirty, Comrade General. That was before Kiev. There were many more after that. I see we share a decoration,' Gogol observed, pointing to his visitor's gold star, for Hero of the Soviet Union, which he'd won in Afghanistan. Gogol had two, one from Ukraine and the other in

Germany.

'You have the look of a soldier, Pavel Petrovich, and a good one.' Bondarenko sipped his tea, served properly, a clear glass in a metal—was it silver?—holder.

'I served in my time. First at Stalingrad, then on the long walk to Berlin.'

I bet you did walk all the way, too, the general thought. He'd met his share of Great Patriotic War veterans, now mostly dead. This wizened old bastard had stared death in the face and spat at it, trained to do so, probably, by his life in these woods. He'd grown up with bears and wolves as enemies—as nasty as the German fascists had been, at least they didn't eat you—and so had been accustomed to wagering his life on his eye and his nerve. There was no real substitute for that, the kind of training you couldn't institute for an army. A gifted few learned how the hard way, and of those the lucky ones survived the war. Pavel Petrovich hadn't had an easy time. Soldiers might admire their own snipers, might value them for their skills, but you could never say 'comrade' to a man who hunted men as though they were animals—because on the other side of the line might be another such man who wanted to hunt *you*. Of all the enemies, that was the one you loathed and feared the most, because it became personal to see another man through a telescopic sight, to see his face, and take his life as a deliberate act against *one* man, even gazing at his face when the bullet struck. Gogol had been one of those, Gennady thought, a hunter of individual men. And he'd probably never lost a minute's sleep over it. Some men were just born to it, and Pavel

156

Petrovich Gogol was one of them. With a few hundred thousand such men, a general could conquer the entire world, but they were too rare for that . . .

. . . and maybe that was a good thing, Bondarenko mused.

'Might you come to my headquarters some night? I would like to feed you dinner and listen to your stories.'

'How far is it?'

'I will send you my personal helicopter, Sergeant Gogol.'

'And I will bring you a gilded wolf,' the hunter promised his guest.

'We will find an honored place for it at my headquarters,' Bondarenko promised in turn. 'Thank you for your tea. I must depart and see to my command, but I *will* have you to headquarters for dinner, Sergeant Gogol.' Handshakes were exchanged, and the general took his leave.

'I would not want him on the other side of a battlefield,' Colonel Aliyev observed, as they got into their helicopter.

'Do we have a sniper school in the command?'

'Yes, General, but it's mainly inactive.'

Gennady turned. 'Start it up again, Andrushka! We'll get Gogol to come and teach the children how it's done. He's a priceless asset. Men like that are the soul of a fighting army. It's our job to command our soldiers, to tell them where to go and what to do, but those are the men who do the fighting and the killing, and it's *our* job to make sure they're properly trained and supplied. And when they're too old, we use them to teach the new boys, to give them heroes they can touch and talk

to. How the *hell* did we ever forget that, Andrey?'
The general shook his head as the helicopter lifted
off.

*   *   *

Gregory was back in his hotel room, with three
hundred pages of technical information to digest as
he sipped his Diet Coke and finished off his french
fries. Something was wrong with the whole
equation, but he couldn't put his finger on it. The
Navy had tested its Standard 2-ER missile against
all manner of threats, mainly on computer, but also
against live targets at Kwajalein Atoll. It had done
pretty well, but there'd never been a full-up live
test against a for-real ICBM reentry vehicle. There
weren't enough of them to go around. Mainly they
used old Minuteman-II ICBMs, long since retired
from service and fired out of test silos at
Vandenberg Air Force Base in California, but those
were mostly gone. Russia and America had retired
all of their ballistic weapons, chiefly as a reaction to
the nuclear terrorist explosion at Denver and the
even more horrific aftermath that had barely been
averted. The negotiations to draw the numbers
down to zero—the last ones had been eliminated in
public just before the Japanese had launched their
sneak attack on the Pacific Fleet—had gone so
rapidly that a lot of the minor ancillary points had
scarcely been considered, and only later had it been
decided to take the 'spare' launchers whose
disposition had somehow been overlooked and
retain them for ABM testing (every month a
Russian officer checked the American ones at
Vandenberg, and an American officer counted the

158

Russian ones outside Plesetsk). The ABM tests were also monitored, but that entire area of effort was now largely theoretical. Both America and Russia retained a goodly number of nuclear warheads, and these could easily be affixed to cruise missiles, which, again, both sides had in relative abundance and no country could stop. It might take five hours instead of thirty-four minutes, but the targets would be just as dead.

Anti-missile work had been relegated to theater missiles, such as the ubiquitous Scuds, which the Russians doubtless regretted ever having built, much less sold to jerkwater countries that couldn't even field a single decent mechanized division, but who loved to parade those upgraded V-2-class ballistic stovepipes because they looked impressive as hell to the people on the sidewalks. But the new upgrades on Patriot and its Russian counterpart SAM largely negated that threat, and the Navy's Aegis system had been tested against them, with pretty good success. Like Patriot, though, Standard was really a point-defense weapon with damned little cross-range ability to cover an area instead of maybe twenty square miles of important sea-estate.

All in all, it was a pity that they'd never solved the power-throughput problem with his free-electron lasers. *Those* could have defended whole coastlines, if only . . . and if only his aunt had balls, Gregory thought, she'd be his uncle. There was talk of building a chemical laser aboard a converted 747 that could sure as hell clobber a ballistic launch during boost phase, but to do *that*, the 747 had to be fairly close to the launch point, and so *that* was just one more version of theater defense, and of little strategic use.

The Aegis system had real possibilities. The SPY radar system was first-rate, and though the computer that managed the information was the flower of 1975 technology—a current Apple Macintosh had it beat by a good three orders of magnitude in all categories of performance—intercepting a ballistic warhead wasn't a question of computing speed so much as kinetic energy—getting the kill vehicle to the right place at the right time. Even that wasn't so great a feat of engineering. The real work had been done as far back as 1959, with the Nike Zeus, which had turned into Spartan and shown great promise before being shitcanned by the 1972 treaty with the Soviet Union, which was, belatedly, just as dead as the Safeguard system, which had been aborted at half-built. Well, the fact of the matter was that MIRV technology had negated that entire defense concept. No, you had to kill the ICBM in boost phase to kill all the MIRVs at once, and do it over the enemy's territory so that if he had a primitive arming system he'd only fry his own turf. The method for doing that was the Brilliant Pebbles system developed at Lawrence-Livermore National Laboratory, and though it had never been given a full-up test, the technology was actually pretty straightforward. Being hit by a matchstick traveling at fifteen thousand miles per hour would ruin your entire day. But that would never happen. The drive to fund and deploy such a system had died with all the ballistic launchers. In a way, it was a pity, Gregory thought. Such a system would have been a really cool engineering accomplishment—but it had little practical application today. The PRC retained its land-based ballistic launchers, but there were only ten or so of them, and that was a long way from the fifteen hundred the Soviets had once pointed at America. The Chinese had a missile submarine, too, but Gregory figured that CINCPAC could make that go away if he had to. Even if it was just tied alongside the pier, one two-thousand-pound smart bomb could take it out of play, and the Navy had a lot of those.

So, he thought, *figure the PRC gets really pissed at Taiwan, and figure the Navy has an Aegis cruiser tied alongside so that its sailors can get drunk and laid in the city, and those folks in Beijing pick that moment to push the button on one of their ICBMs, how can the Navy keep its cruiser from turning into slag, and oh, by the way, keep the city of Taipei alive . . . ?*

The SM-2-ER had almost enough of the right ingredients to handle such a threat. If the missile was targeted on where the cruiser was, cross-range was not an issue. You just had to put the interceptor on the same line of bearing, because in essence the inbound rack wasn't moving at all, and you just had to put the SAM in the same place—Spot X—that the RV was going to be, at Time Y. The Aegis computer could figure where and when that was, and you weren't really hitting a bullet with a bullet. The RV would be about a meter across, and the kill-zone of the SAM's warhead would be about, what? Three meters across? Five? Maybe even eight or ten?

Call it eight, Al Gregory thought. Was the SM-2 *that* accurate? In absolute terms, probably yes. It had ample-sized control surfaces, and getting into the line of a jet aircraft—what the SM-2 had been designed to kill—had to take into account the maneuverability of the aircraft (pilots would do

161

their damnedest to avoid the things), and so the eight-meter globe of destruction could probably be made to intercept the inbound RV in terms of pure geometry.

The issue was speed. Gregory popped open another Diet Coke from the room's minibar and sat back on the bed to consider how troublesome that issue was. The inbound RV, at a hundred thousand feet, would be traveling at about sixteen thousand miles per hour, 23,466 feet per second, eight times the speed of a rifle bullet, 7,150 meters per second. That was pretty damned fast. It was about the same speed as a high-explosive detonation. You could have the RV sitting next to a ton of TNT at the moment the explosive went off, and the explosion couldn't catch up with the RV *That was FAST.*

So, the SAM's warhead has to go off well before it gets to where the RV is. Figuring out how much was a simple mathematical exercise. That meant that the proximity fuse on the SM-2 was the important variable in the equation, Gregory decided. He didn't know that he was wrong on this, didn't see what he was missing, and went on with his calculations. The software fix for the proximity laser fusing system looked less difficult than he'd imagined. Well, wasn't that good news?

*   *   *

It was another early day for Minister Fang Gan. He'd gotten a phone call at his home the previous night, and decided he had to arrive early for the appointment made then. This was a surprise for his staff, who were just setting up for the day when he

162

breezed in, not looking as cross as he felt for the disturbance of his adamantine routine. It wasn't their fault, after all, and they had the good sense not to trouble him, and thus generate artificial wrath.

Ming was just printing up her downloads from the Web. She had pieces that she thought would be of interest, especially one from *The Wall Street Journal*, and another from *Financial Times*. Both commented on what she thought might be the reason for the minister's early arrival. His 9:20 appointment was with Ren He-Ping, an industrialist friendly with her boss. Ren arrived early. The slender, elderly man looked unhappy— no, she thought, worried—about something. She lifted her phone to get permission, then stood and walked him into the inner office, racing back outside to fetch morning tea, which she hadn't had a chance to serve her boss yet.

Ming was back inside in less than five minutes, with the fine porcelain cups on a decorated serving tray. She presented the morning drinks to both men with an elegance that earned her a thank-you from her boss, and then she took her leave. Ren, she saw, wasn't any happier to be in with her minister.

'What is the problem, Ren?'

'In two weeks, I will have a thousand workers with nothing to do, Fang.'

'Oh? What is the reason for that, my friend?'

'I do much business with an American business. It is called Butterfly. They sell clothing to wealthy American women. My factory outside Shanghai makes the cloth, and my tailoring plant at Yancheng turns the fabric into clothing, which we

163

ship to America and Europe. We've been doing business with Butterfly for three years now, very satisfactorily for all concerned.'

'Yes? So, what, then, is the difficulty?'

'Fang, Butterfly just canceled an order worth one hundred forty million American dollars. They did it without any warning. Only last week they told us how happy they were with our products. We've invested a fortune into quality control to make sure they would stay with us—but they've left us like a dog in the street.'

'Why did this happen, Ren?' Minister Fang asked, fearing he knew the answer.

'Our representative in New York tells us that it's because of the deaths of the two clergymen. He tells us that Butterfly had no choice, that Americans demonstrated outside his establishment in New York and prevented people from going inside to buy his wares. He says that Butterfly cannot do business with me for fear of having their own business collapse.'

'Do you not have a contract with them? Are they not obligated to honor it?'

Ren nodded. 'Technically, yes, but business is a practical thing, Minister. If they cannot sell our goods, then they will not buy them from us. They cannot get the financing to do so from their bankers—bankers loan money in the expectation that it will be paid back, yes? There is an escape clause in the contract. We could dispute it in court, but it would take years, and we would probably not succeed, and it would also offend others in the industry, and thus prevent us from *ever* doing business in New York again. So, in practical terms there is no remedy.'

'Is this a temporary thing? Surely this difficulty will pass, will it not?'

'Fang, we also do business in Italy, with the House of d'Alberto, a major trend-setter in European fashion. They also canceled their relationship with us. It seems that the Italian man our police killed comes from a powerful and influential family. Our representative in Italy says that no Chinese firm will be able to do business there for some time. In other words, Minister, that "unfortunate incident" with the churchmen is going to have grave consequences.'

'But these people have to purchase their cloth somewhere,' Fang objected.

'Indeed they do. And they will do so in Thailand, Singapore, and Taiwan.'

'Is that possible?'

Ren nodded quickly and sadly. 'It is very possible. Sources have told me that they are busily contacting our former business partners to "take up the slack", as they put it. You see, the Taiwan government has launched an aggressive campaign to distinguish themselves from us, and it would appear that their campaign is, for the moment, highly successful.'

'Well, Ren, surely you can find other customers for your goods,' Fang suggested with confidence.

But the industrialist shook his head. He hadn't touched his tea and his eyes looked like wounds in a stone head. 'Minister, America is the world's largest such market, and it appears it will soon be closed to us. After that is Italy, and that door, also, has been slammed shut. Paris, London, even the avant-garde marketers in Denmark and Vienna will not even return our phone calls. I've had my

165

representatives contact all potential markets, and they all say the same thing: No one wants to do business with China. Only America could save us, but America will not.'

'What will this cost you?'

'As I told you, one hundred forty million dollars just from the Butterfly account alone, and another similar amount from our other American and European businesses.'

Fang didn't have to think long to calculate the take the PRC's government got from that.

'Your colleagues?'

'I have spoken with several. The news is the same. The timing could hardly be worse. *All* of our contracts are coming due at the same time. We are talking *billions* of dollars, Minister. *Billions,*' he repeated.

Fang lit a cigarette. 'I see,' he said. 'What would it take to fix this?'

'Something to make America happy, not just the government, but the citizens, too.'

'Is that truly important?' Fang asked, somewhat tiredly. He'd heard this rubbish so many times from so many voices.

'Fang, in America people can buy their clothing from any number of stores and manufacturers, any number of marketers. The people choose which succeeds and which fails. Women's clothing in particular is an industry as volatile as vapor. It does not take much to make such a company fail. As a result, those companies will not assume additional and unnecessary risks. To do business with the People's Republic, now, today, is something they see as an unnecessary risk.'

Fang took a drag and thought about that. It was,

actually, something he'd always known, intellectually, but never quite appreciated. America *was* a different place, and it *did* have different rules. And since China wanted American money, China had to abide by those rules. That wasn't politics. That was practicality.

'So, you want me to do what?'

'*Please*, tell your fellow ministers that this could mean financial ruin for us. Certainly for my industry, and we are a valuable asset for our country. We bring wealth into China. If you want that wealth to spend on other things, then you must pay attention to what we need in order to get you that wealth.' What Ren could not say was that he and his fellow industrialists were the ones who made the Politburo's economic (and therefore, also political) agenda possible, and that therefore the Politburo needed to listen to them once in a while. But Fang knew what the Politburo would say in reply. A horse may pull the cart, but you do not ask the horse where it wishes to go.

Such was political reality in the People's Republic of China. Fang knew that Ren had been around the world, that he had a sizable personal fortune which the PRC had graciously allowed him to accumulate, and that, probably more important, he had the intelligence and personal industry to thrive anywhere he chose to live. Fang knew also that Ren could fly to Taiwan and get financing to build a factory there, where he could employ others who looked and spoke Chinese, and he'd make money there *and* get some political influence in the bargain. Most of all, he knew that Ren knew this. Would he act upon it? Probably not. He was Chinese, a citizen of the mainland. This was *his* land, and he had no desire to leave it, else he would not be here now, pleading his case to the one minister—well, probably Qian Kun would listen also—whose ear might be receptive to his words. Ren was a patriot, but not a communist. What an odd duality that was . . .

Fang stood. This meeting had gone far enough. 'I will do this, my friend,' he told his visitor. 'And I will let you know what develops.'

'Thank you, Comrade Minister.' Ren bowed and took his leave, not looking better, but pleased that someone had actually listened to him. Listening was not what one expected of Politburo members.

Fang sat back down and lit another cigarette, then reached for his tea. He thought for a minute or so. 'Ming!' he called loudly. It took seven seconds by his watch.

'Yes, Minister?'

'What news articles do you have for me?' he asked. His secretary disappeared for another few seconds, then reappeared, holding a few pages.

'Here, Minister, just printed up. This one may be of particular interest.'

'This one' was a cover story from *The Wall Street Journal.* 'Major Shift in China Business?' it proclaimed. The question mark was entirely rhetorical, he saw in the first paragraph. Ren was right. He had to discuss this with the rest of the Politburo.

*   *   *

The second major item in Bondarenko's morning was observing tank gunnery. His men had the newest variant of the T-80UM main battle tank. It wasn't quite the newest T-99 that was just coming into production. This UM *did*, however, have a decent fire-control system, which was novel enough. The target range was about as simple as one could ask, large white cardboard panels with black tank silhouettes painted on them, and they were set at fixed, known ranges. Many of his gunners had never fired a live round since leaving gunnery school—such was the current level of training in the Russian Army, the general fumed.

Then he fumed some more. He watched one particular tank, firing at a target an even thousand meters away. It should have been mere spitting distance, but as he watched, first one, then two more, of the tracer rounds missed, all falling short, until the fourth shot hit high on the painted turret shape. With that feat accomplished, the tank shifted aim to a second target at twelve hundred meters and missed that one twice, before achieving a pinwheel in the geometric center of the target.

'Nothing wrong with that,' Aliyev said next to him.

'Except that the tank and the crew were all dead ninety seconds ago!' Bondarenko observed, followed by a particularly vile oath. 'Ever see what happens when a tank blows up? Nothing left of the crew but sausage! Expensive sausage.'

'It's their first time in a live-fire exercise,' Aliyev said, hoping to calm his boss down. 'We have limited practice ammunition, and it's not as accurate as warshots.'

'How many live rounds do we have?'

Aliyev smiled. 'Millions.' They had, in fact, warehouses full of the things, fabricated back in the 1970s.

'Then issue them,' the general ordered.

'Moscow won't like it,' the colonel warned. Warshots were, of course, far more expensive.

'I am not here to *please* them, Andrey Petrovich. I am here to *defend* them.' And someday he'd meet the fool who'd decided to replace the tank's loader crewman with a machine. It was slower than a soldier, and removed a crewman who could assist in repairing damage. Didn't engineers ever consider that tanks were actually supposed to go into *battle*? No, this tank had been designed by a committee, as all Soviet weapons had been, which explained, perhaps, why so many of them didn't work—or, just as badly, didn't protect their users. Like putting the gas tank inside the *doors* of the BTR armored personnel carrier. Who ever thought that a crewman might want to bail out of a damaged vehicle and perhaps even survive to fight afoot? The tank's vulnerability had been the very first thing the Afghans had learned about Soviet mobile equipment . . . and how many Russian boys had burned to death because of it? *Well,* Bondarenko thought, *I have a new country now, and Russia* does *have talented engineers, and in a few years perhaps we can start building weapons worthy of the soldiers who carry them.*

'Andrey, is there anything in our command which does work?'

'That's why we're training, Comrade General.' Bondarenko's service reputation was of an upbeat officer who looked for solutions rather than problems. His operations officer supposed that Gennady Iosifovich was overwhelmed by the scope of the difficulties, not yet telling himself that however huge a problem was, it had to be

170

composed of numerous small ones which *could* be addressed one at a time. Gunnery, for example. Today, it was execrable. But in a week it would be much better, especially if they gave the troops real rounds instead of the practice ones. Real 'bullets,' as soldiers invariably called them, made you feel like a man instead of a schoolboy with his workbook. There was much to be said for that, and like many of the things his new boss was doing, it made good sense. In two weeks, they'd be watching more tank gunnery, and seeing more hits than misses.

CHAPTER FORTY

FASHION STATEMENTS

'So, George?' Ryan asked.

'So, it's started. Turns out there are a ton of similar contracts coming due for the next season or something, plus Christmas toy contracts,' SecTreas told his President. 'And it's not just us. Italy, France, England, *everybody's* bugging out on them. The Chinese have made huge inroads into that industry, and they pissed off a lot of people in the process. Well, the chicken hasn't so much come home to roost as it's flown the coop, and that leaves our friends in Beijing holding the bag. It's a big bag, Jack. We're talking billions here.'

'How badly will that hurt them?' SecState asked.

'Scott, I grant you it seems a little odd that the fate of a nation could ride on Victoria's Secret brassieres, but money is money. They need it, and all of a sudden there's a big hole in their current account. How big? Billions. It's going to make a hell of a bellyache for them.'

'Any actual harm?' Ryan asked.

'Not my department, Jack,' Winston answered. 'That's Scott.'

'Okay.' Ryan turned his head to look at his other cabinet member.

'Before I can answer that, I need to know what net effect this will have on the Chinese economy.'

Winston shrugged. 'Theoretically, they could ride this out with minimal difficulties, but that depends on how they make up the shortfall. Their national industrial base is an incredibly muddled hodgepodge of private- and state-owned industries. The private ones are the efficient ones, of course, and the worst of the state-owned industries belong to their army. I've seen analyses of PLA operations that look like something out of *MAD magazine*, just impossible to credit on first reading. Soldiers don't generally know much about making things—they're better at breaking them—and tossing Marxism into the mix doesn't exactly help the situation. So, those "enterprises" piss away vast quantities of cash. If they shut those down, or just cut them back, they could kiss this little shortfall off and move on—but they won't.'

'That's right,' Adler agreed. 'The Chinese People's Liberation Army has a lot of political clout over there. The party controls it, but the tail wags the dog to a considerable extent. There's quite a bit of political and economic unrest over there. They need the army to keep things under control, and the PLA takes a big cut off the top of the national treasure because of that.'

'The Soviets weren't like that,' POTUS objected.

'Different country, different culture. Keep that in mind.'

'Klingons,' Ryan muttered, with a nod. 'Okay, go on.'

Winston took the lead. 'We can't predict the impact this will have on their society without knowing how they're going to react to the cash shortfall.'

'If they squeal when it starts to hurt, what do we do?' Ryan asked next.

'They're going to have to make nice, like reinstating the Boeing and Caterpillar orders, and doing it publicly.'

'They won't—they can't,' Adler objected. 'Too much loss of face. Asian mind-set. That won't happen. They might offer us concessions, but they'll have to be hidden ones.'

'Which is not politically acceptable to us. If I try to take *that* to Congress, first they'll laugh at me, then they'll crucify me.' Ryan took a sip of his drink.

'And they won't understand why you can't tell Congress what to do. They think you're a strong leader, and therefore you're supposed to make decisions on your own,' EAGLE informed his President.

'Don't they know *anything* about how our government works?' POTUS asked.

'Jack, I'm sure they have all sorts of experts who know more about the constitutional process than I do, but the Politburo members are not required to listen to them. They come from a very different political environment, and that's the one they understand. For us "the people" means popular opinion, polls, and ultimately elections. For them, it means the peasants and workers who are supposed to do what they're told.'

'We do business with these people?' Winston asked the ceiling.

'It's called realpolitik, George,' Ryan explained.

'But we can't pretend they don't exist. There's over a billion of them, and, oh, by the way, they also have nuclear weapons, on ballistic launchers, even.' Which added a decidedly unpleasant element to the overall equation.

'Twelve of them, according to CIA, and we can turn their country into a parking lot if we have to, just it'll take twenty-four hours instead of forty minutes,' Ryan told his guests, managing not to get a chill when he said it. The possibility was too remote to make him nervous. 'And they know that, and who wants to be the king of a parking lot? They *are* that rational, Scott, aren't they?'

'I think so. They rattle their saber at Taiwan, but not even much of that lately, not when we have Seventh Fleet there all the time.' Which, however, burned up a lot of fuel oil for the Navy.

'Anyway, this cash problem won't actually cripple their economy?' Jack asked.

'I don't think so, unless they're pretty damned dumb.'

'Scott, are they dumb?' Ryan asked State Department.

'Not that dumb—at least I don't think so,' State told the President.

'Good, then I can go upstairs and have another drink.' Ryan rose, and his guests did the same.

*　　　*　　　*

174

'This is lunacy!' Qian Kun growled at Fang half a world away, discussing what turned out to be the same set of issues.

'I will not disagree with you, Qian, but we must make our case to the rest of our colleagues.'

'Fang, this could mean ruin for us. With what shall we buy wheat and oil?'

'What are our reserves?'

The Finance Minister had to sit back and think about that one. He closed his eyes and tried to remember the numbers on which he got briefed the first Monday of every month. The eyes opened. 'The harvest from last year was better than average. We have food for about a year—assuming an average harvest this year, or even a slightly short one. The immediate problem is oil. We've been using a lot of that lately, with the PLA's constant exercises up north and on the coast. In oil, we have perhaps four months in reserve, and the money to purchase another two months. After that, we will have to cut back our uses. Now, we are self-sufficient in coal, and so we'll have all the electricity we need. The lights will burn. The trains will run, but the PLA will be crippled.' *Not that this is an entirely bad thing*, he didn't add. Both men acknowledged the value of the People's Liberation Army, but today it was really more of a domestic security service, like a large and well-armed police force, than a real guarantor of their national security, which had, really, no external threats to deal with.

'The army won't like that,' Fang warned.

'I am not overly concerned with their likes and dislikes, Fang,' the Finance Minister countered.

'We have a country to bring out of the nineteenth century. We have industries to grow, and people to feed and employ. The ideology of our youth has not been as successful in bringing this about as we were educated to expect.'

'Do you say that . . . ?'

Qian shifted in his chair. 'Remember what Deng said? It doesn't matter if the cat is black or white as long as it catches mice. And Mao exiled him soon thereafter, and so today we have two hundred million more mouths to feed, but the only additional funds with which we do it came to us from the black cat, not the white one. We live in a practical world, Fang. I, too, have my copy of *The Little Red Book*, but I've never tried to eat it.'

This former railroad engineer had been captured by his bureaucracy and his job, just like the last one had been—he'd died at the relatively young age of seventy-eight, before he could be expelled from his Politburo chair. Qian, a youthful sixty-six, would have to learn to watch his words, and his thoughts, more carefully. He was about to say so when Qian started speaking again.

'Fang, people like you and me, we must be able to speak freely to one another. We are not college students full of revolutionary zeal. We are men of years and knowledge, and we *must* have the ability to discuss issues frankly. We waste too much time in our meetings kneeling before Mao's cadaver. The man is *dead*, Fang. Yes, he was a great man, yes, he was a great leader for our people, but *no*, he *wasn't* the Lord Buddha, or Jesus, or whatever. He was only a man, and he had ideas, and most of them were right, but some of them were wrong, some of them don't work. The Great Leap

176

Forward accomplished nothing, and the Cultural Revolution, in addition to killing off undesirable intellectuals and troublemakers, also starved millions of our people to death, and that is not desirable, is it?'

'That is true, my young friend, but it is important how you present your ideas,' Fang warned his junior, non-voting member of the Politburo. *Present them stupidly, and you'll find yourself counting rice bags on a collective farm.* He was a little old to go barefoot into the paddies, even as punishment for ideological apostasy.

'Will you support me?' Qian asked.

'I will try,' was the halfhearted answer. He had to plead Ren HePing's case as well this day, and it wouldn't be easy.

*   *   *

They'd counted on the funds transfer at Qian's ministry. They had contracts to pay for. The tanker had long since been scheduled, because they were booked well in advance, and this carrier was just now coming alongside the loading pier off the coast of Iran. She'd load four hundred and fifty-six thousand tons of crude oil over a period of less than a day, then steam back out of the Persian Gulf, turn southeast for the passage around India, then transit the crowded Malacca Strait past Singapore and north to the huge and newly built oil terminal at Shanghai, where she'd spend thirty or forty hours offloading the cargo, then retrace her journey back to the Gulf for yet another load in an endless procession.

Except that the procession wasn't quite endless.

It would end when the money stopped, because the sailors had to be paid, the debt on the tanker serviced, and most of all, the oil had to be bought. And it wasn't just one tanker. There were quite a few of them on the China run. A satellite focused on just that one segment of the world's oil trade would have seen them from a distance, looking like cars on a highway going to and from the same two points continuously. And like cars, they didn't have to go merely between those two places. There were other ports at which to load oil, and others at which to offload it, and to the crews of the tankers, the places of origin and destination didn't really matter very much, because almost all of their time was spent at sea, and the sea was always the same. Nor did it matter to the owners of the tankers, or the agents who did the chartering. What mattered was that they got paid for their time.

For this charter, the money had been wire-transferred from one account to another, and so the crew stood at their posts watching the loading process—monitoring it mainly by watching various dials and gauges; you couldn't see the oil going through the pipes, after all. Various crew members were on the beach to see to the victualing of their ship, and to visit the chandlers to get books and magazines to read, videocassette movies, and drink to go with the food, plus whatever consumable supplies had been used up on the inbound trip. A few crewmen looked for women whose charms might be rented, but that was an iffy business in Iran. None of them knew or thought very much about who paid for their services. Their job was to operate the ship safely and efficiently. The ship's officers mainly had their wives along, for whom the

178

voyages were extended, if rather boring, pleasure cruises: Every modern tanker had a swimming pool and a deck for tanning, plus satellite TV for news and entertainment. And none of them particularly cared where the ship went, because for the women shopping was shopping, and any new port had its special charms.

This particular tanker, the *World Progress*, was chartered out of London, and had five more Shanghai runs scheduled until the charter ran out. The charter was paid, however, on a per-voyage basis, and the funds for this trip had been wired only seven days before. That was hardly a matter of concern for the owners or the ship's agent. After all, they were dealing with a nation-state, whose credit tended to be good. In due course, the loading was completed. A computerized system told the ship's first officer that the ship's trim was correct, and he so notified the master, who then told the chief engineer to wind up the ship's gas-turbine engines. This engine type made things easy, and in less than five minutes, the ship's power plant was fully ready for sea. Twenty minutes after that, powerful harbor tugs eased the ship away from the loading dock. This evolution is the most demanding for a tanker's crew, because only in confined waters is the risk of collision and serious damage quite so real. But within two hours, the tanker was under way under her own power, heading for the narrows at Bandar Abbas, and then the open sea.

*   *   *

'Yes, Qian,' Premier Xu said tiredly. 'Proceed.'

179

'Comrades, at our last meeting I warned you of a potential problem of no small proportions. That problem is with us now, and it is growing larger.'

'Are we running out of money, Qian?' Zhang Han San asked, with a barely concealed smirk. The answer amused him even more.

'Yes, Zhang, we are.'

'How can a nation run out of money?' the senior Politburo member demanded.

'The same way a factory worker can, by spending more than he has. Another way is to offend his boss and lose his job. We have done both,' Qian replied evenly.

'What "boss" do we have?' Zhang inquired, with a disarming and eerie gentleness.

'Comrades, that is what we call trade. We sell our goods to others in return for money, and we use that money to purchase goods from those others. Since we are not peasants from ancient times bartering a pig for a sheep, we must use money, which is the means of international exchange. Our trade with America has generated an annual surplus on the order of seventy billion American dollars.'

'Generous of the foreign devils,' Premier Xu observed to Zhang *sotto voce*.

'Which we have almost entirely spent for various items, largely for our colleagues in the People's Liberation Army of late. Most of these are long-term purchase items for which advance payment was necessary, as is normal in the international arms business. To this, we must add oil and wheat. There are other things which are important to our economy, but we will concentrate on these for the moment.' Qian looked around the table for

180

approval. He got it, though Marshal Luo Cong, Defense Minister, and commander-in-chief of the People's Liberation Army—*and* lord of the PLA's sizable industrial empire—was now looking on with a gimlet eye. The expenditures of his personal empire had been singled out, and that was not calculated to please him.

'Comrades,' Qian continued, 'we now face the loss of much, perhaps most, of that trade surplus with America, and other foreign countries as well. You see these?' He held up a fistful of telexes and e-mail printouts. 'These are cancellations of commercial business orders and funds transfers. Let me clarify. *These* are *billions* of lost dollars, money which in some cases we have already spent—but money we will never have because we have angered those with whom we do business.'

'Do you tell me that they have such power over us? Rubbish!' another member observed.

'Comrade, they have the power to buy our trade goods for cash, or *not* buy them for cash. If they choose *not* to buy them, we do *not* get the money we need to spend for Marshal Luo's expensive toys.' He used that word deliberately. It was time to explain the facts of life to these people, and a slap across the face was sure to get their attention. 'Now, let us consider wheat. We use wheat to make bread and noodles. If you have no wheat, you have no noodles.

'Our country does not grow enough wheat to feed our people. We know this. We have too many mouths to feed. In a few months, the great producing countries, America, Canada, Australia, Argentina, and so forth, they will all have wheat to sell—but with what shall we buy it? Marshal Luo, your army needs oil to refine into diesel fuel and jet fuel, does it not? We need the same things for our diesel trains, and our airlines. But we cannot produce all the oil we need for our domestic needs, and so we must buy it from the Persian Gulf and elsewhere—again, with what shall we buy it?'

'So, sell our trade goods to someone else?' a member asked, *with rather surprising innocence*, Qian thought.

'Who else might there be, comrade? There is only one America. We have also offended all of Europe. Whom does that leave? Australia? They are allied to Europe and America. Japan? They also sell to America, and *they* will move to replace our lost markets, not to buy from us. South America, perhaps? Those are all Christian countries, and we just killed a senior Christian churchman, didn't we? Moreover, in *their* ethical world, he died heroically. We have not just killed. We have created a holy martyr to their faith!

'Comrades, we have deliberately structured our industry base to sell to the American market. To sell elsewhere, we would first have to determine what they need that we can make, and then enter the market. You don't just show up with a boatload of products and exchange it for cash on the dock! It takes time and patience to become a force in such a market. Comrades, we have cast away the work of *decades*. The money we are losing will not come back for years, and until then, we must learn to live our national life differently.'

'What are you saying?' Zhang shot back.

'I am saying that the People's Republic faces economic ruin because two of our policemen killed those two meddling churchmen.'

'*That is not possible!*'

'It is not possible, Zhang? If you offend the man who gives you money, then he will give you no more. Can you understand that? We've gone far out of our way to offend America, and then we offended all of Europe as well. We have made ourselves outcasts—they call us barbarians because of that unhappy incident at the hospital. I do not defend them, but I must tell you what *they* say and think. And as long as they say those things and think those things, it is we who will pay for the error.'

'I refuse to believe this!' Zhang insisted.

'That is fine. You may come to my ministry and add up the numbers yourself.' Qian was feeling full of himself, Fang saw. Finally, he had them listening to him. Finally, he had them thinking about his thoughts and his expertise. 'Do you think I make this story up to tell in some country inn over rice wine?'

Then it was Premier Xu leaning forward and thinking aloud. 'You have our attention, Qian. What can we do to avert this difficulty?'

Having delivered his primary message quickly and efficiently, Qian Kun didn't know what to say now. There *wasn't* a way to avert it that these men would accept. But having given them a brief taste of the harsh truth, now he had to give them some more:

'We need to change the perception of American minds. We need to show them that we are not what they consider barbarians. We have to transform our image in their eyes. For starters, we must make amends for the deaths of those two priests.'

'Abase ourselves before the foreign devils?

183

Never!' Zhang snarled.

'Comrade Zhang,' Fang said, coming carefully to Qian's defense. 'Yes, we are the Middle Kingdom, and no, we are not the barbarians. They are. But sometimes one must do business with barbarians, and that might mean understanding their point of view, and adapting to it somewhat.'

'Humble ourselves before *them?'*

Yes, Zhang. We need what they have, and to get it, we must be acceptable to them.'

'And when they next demand that we make political changes, then what?' This was the premier, Xu, getting somewhat agitated, which was unusual for him.

'We face such decisions when and if they come,' Qian answered, pleasing Fang, who didn't want to risk saying *that* himself.

'We cannot risk that,' the Interior Minister, Tong Jie, responded, speaking for the first time. The police of the nation belonged to him, and he was responsible for civil order in the country—only if he failed would he call upon Marshal Luo, which would cause him both loss of face and loss of power at this table. In a real sense, the deaths of the two men had been laid at his place, for he had generated the formal orders on the suppression of religious activity in the PRC, increasing the harshness of law enforcement in order to increase the relative influence of his own ministry. 'If the foreigners insist upon internal political changes, it could bring us all down.'

And that was the core issue, Fang saw at once. The People's Republic rested absolutely upon the power of the party and its leaders, these men before him in this room. Like noblemen of old,

184

each was attended by a trusted servant, sitting in the chairs against the wall, around the table, waiting for the order to fetch tea or water. Each had his rationale for power, whether it was Defense, or Interior, or Heavy Industry, or in his particular case, friendship and general experience. Each had labored long and hard to reach this point, and none of them relished the thought of losing what he had, any more than a provincial governor under the Ching Dynasty would have willingly reverted to being a mere mandarin, because that meant at least ignominy, and just as likely, death. These men knew that if a foreign country demanded and got internal political concessions, then their grip on power would loosen, and that was the one thing they dared not risk. They ruled the workers and peasants, and because of that, they also feared them. The noblemen of old could fall back upon the teachings of Confucius, or Buddha; on a spiritual foundation for their temporal power. But Marx and Mao had swept all that away, leaving only force as their defense. And if to maintain their country's prosperity they had to diminish that force, what would then happen? They didn't know, and these men feared the unknown as a child feared the evil monsters under his bed at night, but with far more reason. It had happened, right here in Beijing, not all that many years before. Not one of these men had forgotten it. To the public, they'd always shown steadfast determination. But each of them, alone in his bathroom before the mirror, or lying in bed at night before sleep came, had shown fear. Because though they basked in the devotion of the peasants and workers, somehow each of them knew that the peasants and workers might fear them, but also hated them. Hated them for their arrogance, their corruption, for their privilege, their better food, their luxurious housing, their personal servants. Their servants, they all knew, loathed them as well, behind smiles and bows of obeisance, which could just as easily conceal a dagger, because that's how the peasants and workers had felt about the nobles of a hundred years before. The revolutionaries had made use of that hatred against the class enemies of that age, and new ones, they all knew, could make use of the same silent rage against themselves. And so they would cling to power with the same desperation as the nobles of old, except they would show even more ruthlessness, because unlike the nobles of old, they had no place to run to. Their ideology had trapped them in their golden cages more surely than any religion could.

Fang had never before considered all of these thoughts *in toto*. Like the others, he'd worried a lot when the college students had demonstrated, building up their 'goddess of liberty' out of plaster or papier-mâché—Fang didn't remember, though he did remember his sigh of relief when the PLA had destroyed it. It came as a surprise to him, the realization of how snared he was here in this place. The power he and his colleagues exercised was like something shown before a mirror that could be turned on them all instantly under the proper circumstances. They had immense power over every citizen in their country, but that power was all an illusion—

—and, no, they couldn't allow another country to dictate political practices to them, because their lives all depended on that illusion. It was like smoke on a calm day, seemingly a pillar to hold up the heavens, but the slightest wind could blow it all away, and then the heavens would fall. On them all.

But Fang also saw that there was no way out. If they didn't change to make America happy, then their country would run out of wheat and oil, and probably other things as well, and they would risk massive social change in a groundswell from below. But if to prevent that, they allowed some internal changes, they would just be inviting the same thing on themselves.

Which would kill them the more surely?

Did it matter? Fang asked himself. Either way, they'd be just as dead. He wondered idly how it would come, the fists of a mob, or bullets before a wall, or a rope. No, it would be bullets. That was how his country executed people. Probably preferable to the beheading sword of old. What if the swordsman missed his aim, after all? It must have been a horrid mess. He only had to look around the table to see that everyone here had similar thoughts, at least those with *enough* wit. All men feared the unknown, but now they had to choose which unknown to fear, and the choice was yet another thing to dread.

'So, Qian, you say we risk running out of things because we can no longer get the money we need to purchase them?' Premier Xu asked.

'That is correct,' the Finance Minister confirmed.

'In what other ways could we get money and oil?' Xu asked next.

'That is not within my purview, Chairman,' Qian answered.

'Oil is its own currency,' Zhang said. 'And there

is ample oil to our north. There is also gold, and many other things we need. Timber in vast quantities. And that which we need most of all—space, living space for our people.'

Marshal Luo nodded. 'We have discussed this before.'

'What do you mean?' Fang asked.

'The Northern Resource Area, our Japanese friends once called it,' Zhang reminded them all.

'*That* adventure ended in disaster,' Fang observed at once. 'We were fortunate not to have been damaged by it.'

'But we were not damaged at all,' Zhang replied lightly. 'We were not even implicated. We can be sure of that, can we not, Luo?'

'This is so. The Russians have never strengthened their southern defenses. They even ignore our exercises that have raised our forces to a high state of readiness.'

'Can we be sure of that?'

'Oh, yes,' the Defense Minister told them all. 'Tan?' he asked.

Tan Deshi was the chief of the Ministry of State Security, in charge of the PRC's foreign and domestic intelligence services. One of the younger men here at seventy, he was probably the healthiest of them all, a nonsmoker and a very light imbiber of alcohol. 'When we first began our increased exercises, they watched with concern, but after the first two years, they lost interest. We have over a million of our citizens living in eastern Siberia—it's illegal, but the Russians do not make much issue of it. A goodly number of them report to me. We have good intelligence of the Russian defenses.'

'And what is their state of readiness?' Tong Jie

asked.

'Generally, quite poor. They have one full-strength division, one at two-thirds, and the rest are hardly better than cadre-strength. Their new Far East commander, a General-Colonel Bondarenko, despairs of making things better, our sources tell us.'

'Wait,' Fang objected. 'Are we discussing the possibility of war with Russia here?'

'Yes,' Zhang Han San replied. 'We have done this before.'

'That is true, but on the first such occasion, we would have had Japan as an ally, and America neutralized. On the second, we assumed that Russia would have been broken up beforehand along religious lines. Who are our allies in this case? How has Russia been crippled?'

'We've been a little unlucky,' Tan answered. 'The chief minister—well, the chief adviser to their President Grushavoy is still alive.'

'What do you mean?' Fang asked.

'I mean that our attempt to kill him misfired.' Tan explained on for two minutes. The reaction around the table was one of mild shock.

'Tan had my approval,' Xu told them calmly.

Fang looked over at Zhang Han San. That's where the idea must have originated. His old friend might have hated capitalists, but that didn't stop him from acting like the worst pirate when it suited his goals. And he had Xu's ear, and Tan as his strong right arm. Fang thought he knew all of these men, but now he saw that his assumption had been in error. In each was something hidden, and sinister. They were far more ruthless than he, Fang saw.

'That is an act of war,' Fang objected.

'Our operational security was excellent. Our Russian agent, one Klementi Suvorov, is a former KGB officer we recruited ages ago when he was stationed here in Beijing. He's performed various functions for us for a long time and he has superb contacts within both their intelligence and military communities—that is, those segments of it that are now in the new Russian underworld. In fact he's a common criminal—a lot of the old KGB people have turned into that—but it works for us. He likes money, and for enough of it, he will do anything. Unfortunately in this case, a pure happenstance prevented the elimination of this Golovko person,' Tan concluded.

'And now?' Fang asked. Then he cautioned himself. He was asking too many questions, taking too much of a personal position here. Even in this room, even with these old comrades, it didn't pay to stand out too far.

'And now, that is for the Politburo to decide,' Tan replied blandly. It had to be affected, but was well acted in any case.

Fang nodded and leaned back, keeping his peace for the moment.

'Luo?' Xu asked. 'Is this feasible?'

The Marshal had to guard his words as well, not to appear too confident. You could get in trouble around this table by promising more than you could deliver, though Luo was in the unique position—somewhat shared by Interior Minister Tong—of having guns behind him and his position.

'Comrades, we have long examined the strategic issue here. When Russia was the Soviet Union, this operation was not possible. Their military was

190

much larger and better supported, and they had numerous intercontinental and theater ballistic missiles tipped with thermonuclear warheads. Now they have none, thanks to their bilateral agreement with America. Today, the Russian military is a shadow of what it was only ten or twelve years ago. Fully half of their draftees do not even report when called for service—if that happened here, we all know what would happen to the miscreants, do we not? They squandered much of their remaining combat power with their Chechen religious minority—and so, you might say that Russia is *already* splitting up along religious lines. In practical terms, the task is straightforward, if not entirely easy. The real difficulty facing us is distance and space, not actual military opposition. It's many kilometers from our border to their new oil field on the Arctic Ocean—much fewer to the new gold field. The best news of all is that the Russian army is itself building the roads we need to make the approach. It reduces our problems by two thirds right there. Their air force is a joke. We should be able to cope with it—they sell us their best aircraft, after all, and deny them to their own flyers. To make our task easier, we would do well to disrupt their command and control, their political stability and so forth. Tan, can you accomplish that?'

'That depends on what, exactly, is the task,' Tan Deshi replied.

'To eliminate Grushavoy, perhaps,' Zhang speculated. 'He is the only person of strength in Russia at the moment. Remove him, and their country would collapse politically.'

'Comrades,' Fang had to say, taking the risk,

'what we discuss here is bold and daring, but also fraught with danger. What if we fail?'

'Then, my friend, we are no worse off than we appear to be already,' Zhang replied. 'But if we succeed, as appears likely, we achieve the position for which we have striven since our youth. The People's Republic will become the foremost power in all the world.' As is our right, he didn't have to add. 'Chairman Mao never considered failing to destroy Chiang, did he?'

There was no arguing with that, and Fang didn't attempt it. The switchover from fear to adventurousness had been as abrupt as it was now becoming contagious. Where was the caution these men exercised so often? They were men on a floundering ship, and they saw a means of saving themselves, and having accepted the former proposition, they were catapulted into the latter. All he could do was lean back and watch the talk evolve, waiting—hoping—that reason would break out and prevail.

But from whom would it come?

CHAPTER FORTY-ONE

PLOTS OF STATE

'Yes, Minister?' Ming said, looking up from her almost—completed notes.

'You are careful with these notes, aren't you?'

'Certainly, Comrade Minister,' she replied at once. 'I never even print these documents up, as you well know. Is there a concern?'

Fang shrugged. The stresses of today's meeting were gradually bleeding off. He was a practical man of the world, and he was an elderly man. If there was a way to deal with the current problem, he would find it. If there wasn't, then he would endure. He always had. He was not the one taking the lead here, and his notes would show that he was one of the few cautious skeptics at the meeting. One of the others, of course, was Qian Kun, who'd walked out of the room shaking his head and muttering to his senior aide. Fang then wondered if Qian was keeping notes. It would have been a good move. If things went badly, those could be his only defense. At this level of risk, the hazard wasn't relegation to a menial job, but rather having one's ashes scattered in the river.

'Ming?'

'Yes, Minister?'

'What did you think of the students in the square all those years ago?'

'I was only in school then myself, Minister, as you know.'

'Yes, but what did you think?'

'I thought they were reckless. The tallest tree is always the first to be cut down.' It was an ancient Chinese adage, and therefore a safe thing to say. Theirs was a culture that discouraged taking such action—but perversely, their culture also lionized those who'd had the courage to do so. As with every human tribe, the criterion was simple. If you succeeded, then you were a hero, to be remembered and admired. If you failed, nobody would remember you anyway, except, perhaps, as a negative example. And so safety lay always in the middle course, and in safety was life.

The students had been too young to know all that. Too young to accept the idea of death. The bravest soldiers were always the young ones, those spirits of great passions and beliefs, those who had not lived long enough to reflect on what shape the world took when it turned against you, those too foolish to know fear. For children, the unknown was something you spent almost all your time exploring and finding out. Somewhere along the line, you discovered that you'd learned all that was safe to learn, and that's where most men stopped, except for the very few upon whom progress depended, the brave ones and the bold ones who walked with open eyes into the unknown, and humanity remembered those few who came back alive . . .

. . . and soon enough forgot those who did not.

But it was the substance of history to remember those who did, and the substance of Fang's society to remind them of those who didn't. Such a strange dichotomy. *What societies*, he wondered, *encourage people to seek out the unknown? How did they do? Did they thrive, or did they blunder about in the darkness and lose their substance in aimless, undirected wanderings?* In China, everyone followed the words and thoughts of Marx, as modified by Mao, because he had boldly walked into the darkness and returned with revolution, and changed the path of his nation. But there things had stopped, because no one was willing to proceed beyond the regions Mao had explored and illuminated—and proclaimed to be all that China and the world in general needed to know about. *Mao was like some sort of religious prophet, wasn't he?* Fang reflected.

. . . Hadn't China just killed a couple of those?

'Thank you, Ming,' he told her, waiting there for his next order. He didn't see her close the door as she went to her desk to transcribe the notes of this Politburo meeting.

*　　　*　　　*

'Dear God,' Dr. Sears whispered at his desk. As usual, the SORGE document had been printed up on the DDO's laser jet and handed over to him, and he'd walked back to his office to do the translation. Sometimes the documents were short enough to translate standing in front of her desk, but this one was pretty long. It was, in fact, going to take eight line-and-a-half-spaced pages off *his* laser printer. He took his time on this because of its content. He rechecked his translation. Suddenly he had doubts about his understanding of the Chinese language. He couldn't afford to mistranslate or misrepresent this sort of thing. It was just too hot. All in all, he took two and a half hours, more than double what Mrs. Foley probably expected, before he walked back.

'What took so long?' MP asked when he returned.

'Mrs. Foley, this is hot.'

'How hot?'

'Magma,' Sears said, as he handed the folder across.

'Oh?' She took the pages and leaned back in her comfortable chair to read it over. SORGE, source SONGBIRD. Her eyes cataloged the heading, yesterday's meeting of the Chinese Politburo. Then Sears saw it. Saw her eyes narrow as her hand reached for a butterscotch. Then her eyes shifted to him. 'You weren't kidding. Evaluation?'

'Ma'am, I can't evaluate the accuracy of the source, but if this is for real, well, then we're looking in on a process I've never seen before outside history books, and hearing words that nobody has ever heard in this building—not that I've ever heard about, anyway. I mean, every minister in their government is quoted there, and most of them are saying the same thing—'

'And it's not something we want them to say,' Mary Patricia Foley concluded his statement. 'Assuming this is all accurately reported, does it feel real?'

Sears nodded. 'Yes, ma'am. It sounds to me like real conversation by real people, and the content tracks with the personalities as I know them. Could it be fabricated? Yes, it could. If so, the source has been compromised in some way or other. However, I don't see that this could be faked without their wanting to produce a specific effect, and that would be an effect which would not be overly attractive to them.'

'Any recommendations?'

'It might be a good idea to get George Weaver down from Providence,' Sears replied. 'He's good at reading their minds. He's met a lot of them face-to-face, and he'll be a good backup for my evaluation.'

'Which is?' Mary Pat asked, not turning to the last page, where it would be printed up.

'They're considering war.'

The Deputy Director (Operations) of the Central Intelligence Agency stood and walked out her door, with Dr. Joshua Sears right behind her.

She took the short walk to her husband's office and went through the door without even looking at Ed's private secretary.

Ed Foley was having a meeting with the Deputy Director (Science and Technology) and two of his senior people when MP walked in. He looked up in surprise, then saw the blue folder in her hand. 'Yeah, honey?'

'Excuse me, but this can't wait even one minute.' Her tone of voice told as much as her words did.

'Frank, can we get together after lunch?'

'Sure, Ed.' DDS&T gathered his documents and his people and headed out.

When they were gone and the door closed, the DCI asked, 'SORGE?'

Mary Pat just nodded and handed the folder across, taking a seat on the couch. Sears remained standing. It was only then that he realized his hands were a little moist. That hadn't happened to him before. Sears, as head of the DI's Office of China Assessments, worked mainly on political evaluations: who was who in the PRC's political hierarchy, what economic policies were being pursued—the Society Page for the People's Republic, as he and his people thought of it, and joked about it over lunch in the cafeteria. He'd never seen anything like this, nothing hotter than handling internal dissent, and while their methods for handling such things tended to be a little on the rough side, as he often put it—mainly it meant summary execution, which was more than a *little* on the rough side for those affected—the distances involved helped him to take a more detached perspective. But not on this.

'Is this for real?' the DC asked.

'Dr. Sears thinks so. He also thinks we need to get Weaver down from Brown University.'

Ed Foley looked over at Sears. 'Call him. Right now.'

'Yes, sir.' Sears left the room to make the call.

'Jack has to see this. What's he doing now?'

'He's leaving for Warsaw in eight hours, remember? The NATO meeting, the photo opportunity at Auschwitz, stopping off at London on the way home for dinner at Buckingham Palace. Shopping on Bond Street,' Ed added. There were already a dozen Secret Service people in London working with the Metropolitan Police and MI-5, properly known as the Security Service. Twenty more were in Warsaw, where security concerns were not all that much of an issue. The Poles were very happy with America right now, and the leftover police agencies from the communist era still kept files on everyone who might be a problem. Each would have a personal baby-sitter for the entire time Ryan was in country. The NATO meeting was supposed to be almost entirely ceremonial, a basic feel-good exercise to make a lot of European politicians look pretty for their polyglot constituents.

'Jesus, they're talking about making a move on Grushavoy!' Ed Foley gasped, getting to page three. 'Are they totally off their fuckin' rockers?'

'Looks like they found themselves in a corner unexpectedly,' his wife observed. 'We may have overestimated their political stability.'

Foley nodded and looked up at his wife. 'Right now?'

'Right now,' she agreed.

Her husband lifted his phone and punched

speed-dial #1.

'Yeah, Ed, what is it?' Jack Ryan asked.

'Mary and I are coming over.'

'When?'

'Now.'

'That important?' the President asked.

'This is CRITIC stuff, Jack. You'll want Scott, Ben, and Arnie there, too. Maybe George Winston. The foundation of the issue is his area of expertise.

'China?'

'Yep.'

'Okay, come on over.' Ryan switched phones. 'Ellen, I need SecState, SecTreas, Ben, and Arnie in my office, thirty minutes from right now.

'Yes, Mr. President,' his secretary acknowledged. This sounded hot, but Robby Jackson was on his way out of town again, to give a speech in Seattle, at the Boeing plant of all places, where the workers and the management wanted to know about the 777 order to China. Robby didn't have much to say on that point, and so he'd talk about the importance of human rights and America's core beliefs and principles, and all that wave-the-flag stuff. The Boeing people would be polite about it, and it was hard to be impolite to a black man, especially one with Navy Wings of Gold on his lapel, and learning to handle this political bullshit was Robby's main task. Besides, it took pressure off Ryan, and that was Jackson's primary mission in life, and oddly enough, one which he accepted with relative equanimity. So, his VC-20B would be over Ohio right about now, Jack thought. Maybe Indiana. Just then Andrea came in.

'Company coming?' Special Agent Price-O'Day asked. She looked a little pale, Jack thought.

199

'The usual suspects. You feeling okay?' the President asked.

'Stomach is a little upset. Too much coffee with breakfast.'

Morning sickness? Ryan wondered. If so, too bad. Andrea tried so hard to be one of the boys. Admitting this female failing would scar her soul as though from a flamethrower. He couldn't say anything about it. Maybe Cathy could. It was a girl thing.

'Well, the DCI's coming over with something he says is important. Maybe they've changed the toilet paper in the Kremlin, as we used to say at Langley back when I worked there.'

'Yes, sir.' She smiled. Like most Secret Service agents, she'd seen the people and the secrets come and go, and if there were important things for her to know, she'd find out in due course.

*   *   *

General-Lieutenant Kirillin liked to drink as much as most Russians, and that was quite a lot by American standards. The difference between Russians and Brits, Chavez had learned, was that the Brits drank just as much, but they did it with beer, while the Russians made do with vodka. Ding was neither a Mormon nor a Baptist, but he was over his capacity here. After two nights of keeping up with the local Joneses, he'd nearly died on the morning run with his team, and only avoided falling out for fear of losing face before the Russian Spetsnaz people they were teaching to come up to Rainbow standards. Somehow he'd managed not to puke, though he had allowed Eddie Price to take

200

charge of the first two classes that day while he'd wandered off to drink a gallon of water to chase down three aspirins. Tonight, he'd decided, he'd cut off the vodkas at two . . . maybe three.

'How are our men doing?' the general asked.

'Just fine, sir,' Chavez answered. 'They like their new weapons, and they're picking up on the doctrine. They're smart. They know how to think before they act.'

'Does this surprise you?'

'Yes, General, it does. It was the same for me once, back when I was a squad sergeant in the Ninjas. Young soldiers tend to think with their dicks rather than their brains. I learned better, but I had to learn it the hard way in the field. It's sometimes a lot easier to get yourself into trouble than it is to think yourself out of it. Your Spetsnaz boys started off that way, but if you show them the right way, they listen pretty good. Today's exercise, for example. We set it up with a trap, but your captain stopped short on the way in and thought it through before he committed, and he passed the test. He's a good team leader, by the way. I'd say bump him to major.' Chavez hoped he hadn't just put the curse of hell on the kid, realizing that praise from a CIA officer wasn't calculated to be career-enhancing for a Russian officer.

'He's my nephew. His father married my sister. He's an academician, a professor at Moscow State University.'

'His English is superb. I'd take him for a native of Chicago.' And so Captain Leskov had probably been talent-scouted by KGB or its successor agency. Language skills of that magnitude didn't just happen.

'He was a parachutist before they sent him to Spetsnaz,' Kirillin went on, 'a good light-infantryman.'

'That's what Ding was, once upon a time,' Clark told the Russian.

'Seventh Light Infantry. They de-established the division after I left. Seems like a long time now.'

'How did you go from the American army into CIA?'

'His fault,' Chavez answered. 'John spotted me and foolishly thought I had potential.'

'We had to clean him up and send him to school, but he's worked out pretty well—even married my daughter.'

'He's still getting used to having a Latino in the family, but I made him a grandfather. Our wives are back in Wales.'

'So, how did you emerge from CIA into Rainbow?'

'My fault, again,' Clark admitted. 'I did a memo, and it perked to the top, and the President liked it, and he knows me, and so when they set the outfit up, they put me in charge of it. I wanted Domingo here to be part of it, too. He's got young legs, and he shoots okay.'

'Your operations in Europe were impressive, especially at the park in Spain.'

'Not our favorite. We lost a kid there.'

'Yeah,' Ding confirmed with a tiny sip of his drink. 'I was fifty yards away when that bastard killed Anna. Homer got him later on. Nice shot it was.'

'I saw him shoot two days ago. He's superb.'

'Homer's pretty good. Went home last fall on vacation and got himself a Dall sheep at eight hundred-plus yards up in Idaho. Hell of a trophy. He made it into the Boone and Crockett book in the top ten.

'He should go to Siberia and hunt tiger. I could arrange that,' Kirillin offered.

'Don't say that too loud.' Chavez chuckled. 'Homer will take you up on it.'

'He should meet Pavel Petrovich Gogol,' Kirillin went on.

'Where'd I hear that name?' Clark wondered at once.

'The gold mine,' Chavez handled the answer.

'He was a sniper in the Great Patriotic War. He has two gold stars for killing Germans, and he's killed hundreds of wolves. There aren't many like him left.'

'Sniper on a battlefield. The hunting must get real exciting.'

'Oh, it is, Domingo. It is. We had a guy in Third SOG who was good at it, but he damned near got his ass killed half a dozen times. You know—' John Clark had a satellite beeper, and it started vibrating in his belt. He picked it up and checked the number. 'Excuse me,' he said and looked for a good place. The Moscow officers' club had a courtyard, and he headed for it.

*   *   *

'What does this mean?' Arnie van Damm asked. The executive meeting had started with copies of the latest SORGE/SONGBIRD being passed out. Arnie was the fastest reader of the group, but not the best strategic observer.

'It doesn't mean anything good, pal,' Ryan

203

observed, turning to the third page.

'Ed,' Winston asked, looking up from page two. 'What can you tell me about the source? This looks like the insider-trading document from hell.'

'A member of the Chinese Politburo keeps notes on his conversations with the other ministers. We have access to those notes, never mind how.'

'So, this document and the source are both genuine?'

'We think so, yes.'

'How reliable?' TRADER persisted.

The DCI decided to take a long step out on a thin limb. 'About as reliable as one of your T-bills.'

'Okay, Ed, you say so.' And Winston's head went back down. In ten seconds, he muttered, 'Shit . . .'

'Oh, yeah, George,' POTUS agreed. ' "Shit" about covers it.'

'Concur, Jack,' SecState agreed.

Of those present, only Ben Goodley managed to get all the way through it without a comment. For his part, Goodley, for all the status and importance that came from his job as the President's National Security Adviser, felt particularly junior and weak at the moment. Mainly he knew that he was far the President's inferior in knowledge of national-security affairs, that he was in his post mainly as a high-level secretary. He was a carded National Intelligence Officer, one of whom, by law and custom, accompanied the President everywhere he went. His job was to convey information to the President. Former occupants of his corner office in the West Wing of the White House had often told their Presidents what to think and what to do. But he was just an information-conveyor, and at the moment, he felt weak even in that diminished capacity.

Finally, Jack Ryan looked up with blank eyes and a vacant face. 'Okay. Ed, Mary Pat, what do we have here?'

'It looks as if Secretary Winston's predictions on the financial consequences of the Beijing Incident might be coming true.'

'They're talking about precipitous consequences,' Scott Adler observed coolly. 'Where's Tony?'

'Secretary Bretano's down at Fort Hood, Texas, looking at the heavy troopers at Third Corps. He gets back late tonight. If we yank him back in a hurry, people will notice,' van Damm told the rest.

'Ed, will you object if we get this to him, secure?' No.

'Okay.' Ryan nodded and reached across his desk for his phone. 'Send Andrea in, please.' That took less than five seconds.

'Yes, Mr. President?'

'Could you walk this over to Signals, and have them TAPDANCE it to THUNDER?' He handed her the document. 'Then please bring it back here?'

'Yes, sir.'

'Thanks, Andrea,' Ryan told the disappearing form. Then he took a drink of water and turned to his guests. 'Okay, it looks pretty serious. How serious is it?'

'We're bringing Professor Weaver down from Brown to evaluate it for us. He's about the best guy in the country for reading their minds.'

'Why the hell doesn't he work for me?' Jack asked.

'He likes it at Brown. He comes from Rhode Island. We've offered him a job across the river half

205

a dozen times that I know of,' DCI Foley told Ryan, 'but he always says the same thing.'

'Same at State, Jack. I've known George for fifteen years or more. He doesn't want to work for the government.'

'Your kind of man, Jack,' Arnie added for a little levity.

'Besides, he can make more money as a contractor, can't he? Ed, when he comes down, make sure he comes in to see me.'

'When? You're flying out in a few hours,' Ed pointed out.

'Shit.' Ryan remembered it now. Callie Weston was just finishing up the last of his official speeches in her office across the street. She was even coming across on Air Force One with the official party. Why was it that you couldn't deal with things one at a time? Because at this level, they just didn't arrive that way.

'All right,' Jack said next. 'We need to evaluate how serious this is, and then figure a way to forestall it. That means—what?'

'One of several things. We can approach them quietly,' SecState Adler said. 'You know, tell them that this has gone too far, and we want to work with them on the sly to ameliorate the situation.'

'Except Ambassador Hitch is over here now, consulting, remember? Where's he doing it today, Congressional or Burning Tree?' POTUS asked. Hitch enjoyed golf, a hobby he could hardly pursue in Beijing. Ryan could sympathize. He was lucky to get in one round a week, and what swing he'd once had was gone with the wind.

'The DCM in Beijing is too junior for something like this. No matter what we said through him, they

206

wouldn't take it seriously enough.'

'And what, exactly, could we give them?' Winston asked. 'There's nothing big enough to make them happy that we could keep quiet. They'd have to give us something so that we could justify giving them anything, and from what I see here, they don't want to give us anything but a bellyache. We're limited in our action by what the country will tolerate.'

'You think they'd tolerate a shooting war?' Adler snapped.

'Be cool, Scott. There are practical considerations. Anything juicy enough to make these Chinese bastards happy has to be approved by Congress, right? To get such a concession through Congress would mean giving them the justification for it.' Winston waved the secret document in his hand. 'But we can't do that because Ed here would have a fit, and even if we did, somebody on the Hill would leak it to the papers in a New York minute, and half of them would call it danegeld, and say fuck the Chinks, millions for defense but not one penny for tribute. Am I right?'

'Yes,' Arnie answered. 'The other half would call it responsible statesmanship, but the average Joe out there wouldn't much like it. The average citizen would expect you to call Premier Xu on the phone and say, "Better not do this, buddy," and expect it to stick.'

'Which would, by the way, kill SONGBIRD,' Mary Pat added as a warning, lest they take that option seriously. 'That would end a human life, and deny us further information that we need to have. And from my reading of this report, Xu would deny

207

everything and just keep going forward. They really think they're in a corner, but they can't see a way to smart themselves out of it.'

'The danger is . . . ?' TRADER asked.

'Internal political collapse,' Ryan explained. 'They're afraid that if anything upsets the political or economic conditions inside the country, the whole house of cards comes tumbling down. With serious consequences for the current royal family of the PRC.'

'Called the chop.' Ben Goodley had to say something, and that was an easy one. 'Actually a rifle bullet today.' It didn't help him feel much better. He was out of his depth and he knew it.

That's when the President's STU rang. It was SecDef Tony Bretano, THUNDER. 'Yeah,' Ryan said. 'Putting you on speaker, Tony. Scott, George, Arnie, Ed, Mary Pat, and Ben are here, and we just read what you got.'

'I presume this is real?'

'Real as hell,' Ed Foley told the newest member of the SORGE/ SONGBIRD chorus.

'This is worrisome.'

'On that we are agreed, Tony. Where are you now?'

'Standing on top of a Bradley in the parking lot. Never seen so many tanks and guns in my life. Feels like real power here.'

'Yeah, well, what you just read shows you the limits of our power.'

'So I gather. If you want to know what I think we should do about it—well, make it clear to them somehow that this would be a really bad play for them.'

'How do we do that, Tony?' Adler asked.

'Some animals—the puffer fish, for example. When threatened, it swallows a gallon of water and expands its size—makes it look too big to eat.'

Ryan was surprised to hear that. He'd no idea that Bretano knew anything about animals. He was a physics and science guy. Well, maybe he watched the Discovery Channel like everyone else.

'Scare them, you mean?'

'Impress them, better way of putting it.'

'Jack, we're going to Warsaw—we can let Grushavoy know about this . . . how about we invite him into NATO? The Poles are there already. It would commit all of Europe to come to Russia's defense in the event of an invasion. I mean, that's what alliances and mutual-defense treaties are all about. "You're not just messing with me, Charlie. You're messing with all my friends, too." It's worked for a long time.'

Ryan considered that one, and looked around the room. 'Thoughts?'

'It's something,' Winston thought.

'But what about the other NATO counties? Will they buy into this? The whole purpose of NATO,' Goodley reminded them, 'was to protect them from the Russians.'

'The Soviets,' Adler corrected. 'Not the same thing anymore, remember.'

'The same people, the same language, sir,' Goodley persisted. He felt pretty secure on this one. 'What you propose is an elegant possible solution to the present problem, but to make it happen we'd have to share SORGE with other countries, wouldn't we?' The suggestion made the Foleys both wince. There were few things on the planet as talkative as a chief of government.

'What the hell, we've been watching their military with overheads for a long time. We can say that we're catching stuff there that makes us nervous. Good enough for the unwashed,' the DCI offered.

'Next, how do we persuade the Russians?' Jack wondered aloud. 'This could be seen in Moscow as a huge loss of face.'

'We have to explain the problem to them. The danger is to their country, after all,' Adler pronounced.

'But they're not unwashed. They'll want to know chapter and verse, and it is *their* national security we're talking about here,' Goodley added.

'You know who's in Moscow now?' Foley asked POTUS.

'John?'

'RAINBOW SIX. John and Ding both know Golovko, and he's Grushavoy's number-one boy. It's a nice, convenient back channel. Note that this also confirms that the Moscow rocket was aimed at him. Might not make Sergey Nikolay'ch feel better, but he'd rather know than guess.

'Why can't those stupid fucking people just say they're sorry they shot those two people?' Ryan wondered crossly.

'Why do you think pride is one of the Seven Deadly Sins?' the DCI asked in reply.

*   *   *

Clark's portable phone was a satellite type with a built-in encryption system, really just a quarter-inch-thick plastic pad that actually made the phone easier to cradle against his shoulder. Like most such phones, it took time to synchronize with its companion on the other end, the task made harder by the delay inherent in the use of satellites.

'Line is secure,' the synthetic female voice said finally.

'Who's this?'

'Ed Foley, John. How's Moscow?'

'Pleasant. What gives, Ed?' John asked. The DCI didn't call from D.C. on a secure line to exchange pleasantries.

'Get over to the embassy. We have a message we want you to deliver.'

'What sort?'

'Get to the embassy. It'll be waiting. Okay?'

'Roger. Out.' John killed the phone and walked back inside.

'Anything important?' Chavez asked.

'We have to go to the embassy to see somebody,' Clark replied, simulating anger at the interruption of his quiet time of the day.

'See you tomorrow then, Ivan and Domingo,' Kirillin saluted them with his glass.

'What gives?' Chavez asked from thirty feet away.

'Not sure, but it was Ed Foley who paged me.'

'Something important?'

'I guess we'll just have to wait and see.'

'Who drives?'

'Me.' John knew Moscow fairly well, having learned it first on missions in the 1970s that he was just as happy to forget about, when his daughters had been the age of his new grandson.

The drive took twenty minutes, and the hard part turned out to be persuading the Marine guard that they really were entitled to come inside after normal business hours. To this end, the man waiting for them, Tom Barlow, proved useful. The Marines knew him, and he knew them, and that made everything okay, sort of.

'What's the big deal?' Jack asked, when they got to Barlow's office.

'This.' He handed the fax across, a copy to each. 'Might want to take a seat, guys.'

'*Madre de Dios*,' Chavez gasped thirty seconds later.

'Roger that, Domingo,' his boss agreed. They were reading a hastily laundered copy of the latest SORGE dispatch.

'We got us a source in Beijing, 'mano.'

'Hang a big roger on that one, Domingo. And we're supposed to share the take with Sergey Nikolay'ch. Somebody back home is feeling real ecumenical.'

'Fuck!' Chavez observed. Then he read on a little. 'Oh, yeah, I see. This does make some sense.'

'Barlow, we have a phone number for our friend?'

'Right here.' The CIA officer handed over a Post-it note and pointed to a phone. 'He'll be out at his dacha, out in the Lenin Hills. They haven't changed the name yet. Since he found out he was the target, he's gotten a little more security-conscious.'

'Yeah, we've met his baby-sitter, Shelepin,' Chavez told Barlow. 'Looks pretty serious.'

'He'd better be. If I read this right, he might be called up to bat again, or maybe Grushavoy's detail.'

'Is this for real?' Chavez had to wonder. 'I mean, this is *causas belli* stuff.'

'Well, Ding, you keep saying that international relations is two countries fucking each other.' Then he dialed the phone. 'Tovarisch Golovko,' he told the voice that answered it, adding in Russian, 'It's Klerk, Ivan Sergeyevich. That'll get his attention,' John told the other two.

'Greetings, Vanya,' a familiar voice said in English. 'I will not ask how you got this number. What can I do for you?'

'Sergey, we need to see you at once on an important matter.'

'What sort of matter?'

'I am the mailman, Sergey. I have a message to deliver to you. It is worthy of your attention. Can Domingo and I see you this evening?'

'Do you know how to get here?'

Clark figured he'd find his way out to the woods. 'Just tell the people at the gate to expect two capitalist friends of Russia. Say about an hour from now?'

'I will be waiting.'

'Thank you, Sergey' Clark replaced the phone. 'Where's the pissparlor, Barlow?'

'Down the hall on the right.'

The senior field intelligence officer folded the fax and tucked it into his coat pocket. Before having a talk about something like this, he needed a bathroom.

CHAPTER FORTY-TWO

BIRCH TREES

They drove into the sunset, west from the Russian capital. Traffic had picked up in Moscow since his last real adventure here, and you could use the center lane in the wide avenues. Ding handled navigation with a map, and soon they were beyond the ring roads around the Russian capital and entering the hills that surrounded the city. They passed a memorial which neither had ever seen before, three huge—

'What the hell is that?' Ding asked.

'This is as close as the Germans got in 1941,' John explained. 'This is where they stopped 'em.'

'What do you call those things?' 'Those things' were immense steel I-beams, three of them welded at ninety-degree angles to look like enormous jacks.

'Hedgehogs, but in the SEALs we called 'em horned scullies. Hard to drive a tank over one,' Clark told his younger partner.

'They take their history serious here, don't they?'

'You would, too, if you stopped somebody who wanted to erase your country right off the map, sonny. The Germans were pretty serious back then, too. It was a very nasty war, that one.'

'Guess so. Take the next right, Mr. C.'

Ten minutes later, they were in a forest of birch trees, as much a part of the Russian soul as vodka and borscht. Soon thereafter they came to a guard

214

shack. The uniformed guard held an AK-74 and looked surprisingly grim. *Probably briefed on the threat to Golovko and others*, John imagined. But he'd also been briefed on who was authorized to pass, and they only had to show their passports to get cleared, the guard also giving them directions about which country lane to take.

'The houses don't look too bad,' Chavez observed.

'Built by German POWs,' John told him. 'Ivan doesn't exactly like the Germans very much, but he does respect their workmanship. These were built for the Politburo members, mainly after the war, probably. There's our place.'

It was a wood-frame house, painted brown and looking like a cross between a German country house and something from an Indiana farm, Clark thought. There were guards here, too, armed and walking around. *They'd been called from the first shack*, John figured. One of them waved. The other two stood back, ready to cover the first one if something untoward happened.

'You are Klerk, Ivan Sergeyevich?'

'*Da,*' John answered. 'This is Chavez, Domingo Stepanovich.'

'Pass, you are expected,' the guard told them.

It was a pleasant evening. The sun was down now, and the stars were making their appearance in the sky. There was also a gentle westerly breeze, but Clark thought he could hear the ghosts of war here. Hans von Kluge's panzer grenadiers, men wearing the *feldgrau* of the Wehrmacht. World War II on this front had been a strange conflict, like modern TV wrestling. No choice between good and bad, but only between bad and worse, and on that score it had been six-five and pick 'em. But their host probably wouldn't see history that way, and Clark had no intention of bringing up the subject.

Golovko was there, standing on the sheltered porch by the furniture, dressed casually. Decent shirt, but no tie. He wasn't a tall man, about halfway between Chavez and himself in height, but the eyes always showed intelligence, and now they also showed interest. He was curious about the purpose of this meeting, as well he might be.

'Ivan Sergeyevich,' Golovko said in greeting. Handshakes were exchanged, and the guests conducted inside. Mrs. Golovko, a physician, was nowhere in evidence. Golovko first of all served vodka, and directed them to seats.

'You said you had a message for me.' The language for this meeting was to be English, John saw.

'Here it is.' Clark handed the pages across.

'*Spasiba.*' Sergey Nikolay'ch sat back in his chair and started to read.

He would have been a fine poker player, John thought. His face changed not at all through the first two pages. Then he looked up.

'Who decided that I needed to see this?' he asked.

'The President,' Clark answered.

'Your Ryan is a good comrade, Vanya, and an honorable man.' Golovko paused. 'I see you have improved your human-intelligence capabilities at Langley.'

'That's probably a good supposition, but I know nothing of the source here, Chairman Golovko,' Clark answered.

'This is, as you say, hot.'

216

'It is all of that,' John agreed, watching him turn another page.

'Son of a bitch!' Golovko observed, finally showing some emotion.

'Yeah, that's about what I said,' Chavez entered the conversation.

'They are well-informed. This does not surprise me. I am sure they have ample espionage assets in Russia,' Golovko observed, with anger creeping into his voice. 'But this is—this is naked aggression they discuss.'

Clark nodded. 'Yep, that's what it appears to be.'

'This is genuine information?' Golovko asked.

'I'm just the mailman, Chairman,' Clark replied. 'I vouch for nothing here.'

'Ryan is too good a comrade to play agent provocateur. This is madness.' And Golovko was telling his guests that he had no good intelligence assets in the Chinese Politburo, which actually surprised John. It wasn't often that CIA caught the Russians short at anything. Golovko looked up. 'We once had a source for such information, but no longer.'

'I've never worked in that part of the world, Chairman, except long ago when I was in the Navy.' And the Chinese part of that, he didn't explain, was mainly getting drunk and laid in Taipei.

'I've traveled to Beijing several times in a diplomatic capacity, not recently. I cannot say that I've ever really understood those people.' Golovko finished reading the document and set it down. 'I can keep this?'

'Yes, sir,' Clark replied.

'Why does Ryan give us this?'

'I'm just the delivery boy, Sergey Nikolay'ch, but

I should think the motive is in the message. America does not wish to see Russia hurt.'

'Decent of you. What concessions will you require?'

'None that I am aware of.'

'You know,' Chavez observed, 'sometimes you just want to be a good neighbor.'

'At this level of statecraft?' Golovko asked skeptically.

'Why not? It does not serve American interests to see Russia crippled and robbed. How big are these mineral finds, anyway?' John asked.

'Immense,' Golovko replied. 'I'm not surprised you've learned of them. Our efforts at secrecy were not serious. The oil field is one to rival the Saudi reserves, and the gold mine is very rich indeed. Potentially, these finds could save our economy, could make us a truly wealthy nation and a fit partner for America.'

'Then you know why Jack sent this over. It's a better world for both of us if Russia prospers.'

'Truly?' Golovko was a bright man, but he'd grown up in a world in which both America and Russia had often wished each other dead. Such thoughts died hard, even in so agile a mind as his.

'Truly,' John confirmed. 'Russia is a great nation, and you are great people. You are fit partners for us.' He didn't add that, this way, America wouldn't have to worry about bailing them out. Now they'd have the wherewithal to see to their own enrichment, and America needed only offer expertise and advice about how to enter the capitalist world with both feet, and open eyes.

'This from the man who helped arrange the defection of the KGB chairman?' Golovko asked.

'Sergey, as we say at home, that was business, not personal. I don't have a hard-on for Russians, and you wouldn't kill an American just for entertainment purposes, would you?'

Indignation: 'Of course not. That would be *nekulturniy*.'

'It is the same with us, Chairman.'

'Hey, man,' Chavez added. 'From when I was a teenager, I was trained to kill your people, back when I was an Eleven-Bravo carrying a rifle, but, guess what, we're not enemies anymore, are we? And if we're not enemies, then we can be friends. You helped us out with Japan and Iran, didn't you?'

'Yes, but we saw that we were the ultimate target of both conflicts, and it was in our national interest.'

'And perhaps the Chinese have us as *their* ultimate target. Then this is in our interest. They probably don't like us any more than they like you.'

Golovko nodded. 'Yes, one thing I do know about them is their sense of racial superiority.'

'Dangerous way for people to think, man. Racism means your enemies are just insects to be swatted,' Chavez concluded, impressing Clark with the mixture of East LA accent and master's-degree analysis of the situation at hand. 'Even Karl Marx didn't say that he was better than anybody else 'cuz of his skin color, did he?'

'But Mao did,' Golovko added.

'Doesn't surprise me,' Ding went on. 'I read his *Little Red Book* in graduate school. He didn't want to be just a political leader. Hell, he wanted to be God. Let his ego get in the way of his brain—not an uncommon affliction for people who take countries over, is it?'

'Lenin was not such a man, but Stalin was,' Golovko observed. 'So, then Ivan Emmetovich is a friend of Russia. What shall I do with this?'

'That's up to you, pal,' Clark told him.

'I must speak to my President. Yours comes to Poland tomorrow, doesn't he?'

'I think so.'

'I must make some phone calls. Thank you for coming, my friends. Perhaps another time I will be able to entertain you properly.'

'Fair enough.' Clark stood and tossed off the end of his drink. More handshakes, and they left the way they'd come.

'Christ, John, what happens now?' Ding asked, as they drove back out.

'I suppose everybody tries to beat some sense into the Chinese.'

'Will it work?'

A shrug and arched eyebrows: 'News at eleven, Domingo.'

*   *   *

Packing for a trip isn't easy, even with a staff to do it all for you. This was particularly true for SURGEON, who was not only concerned about what she wore in public while abroad, but was also the Supreme Authority on her husband's clothes, a status which her husband tolerated rather than entirely approved. Jack Ryan was still in the Oval Office trying to do business that couldn't wait—actually it mostly could, but there were fictions in government that had to be honored—and also waiting for the phone to ring.

'Arnie?'

'Yeah, Jack?'

'Tell the Air Force to have another G go over to Warsaw in case Scott has to fly to Moscow on the sly.'

'Not a bad idea. They'll probably park it at some air force base or something.' Van Damm went off to make the phone call.

'Anything else, Ellen?' Ryan asked his secretary.

'Need one?'

'Yeah, before Cathy and I wing off into the sunset.' Actually, they were heading east, but Mrs. Sumter understood. She handed Ryan his last cigarette of the day.

'Damn,' Ryan breathed with his first puff. He'd be getting a call from Moscow sure as hell— wouldn't he? That depended on how quickly they digested the information, or maybe Sergey would wait for the morning to show it to President Grushavoy. Would he? In Washington, something that hot would be graded CRITIC and shoved under the President's nose inside twenty minutes, but different countries had different rules, and he didn't know what the Russians did. For damned sure he'd be hearing from one of them before he stepped off the plane at Warsaw. But for now . . . He stubbed the smoke out, reached inside his desk for the breath spray, and zapped his mouth with the acidic stuff before leaving the office and heading outside—the West Wing and the White House proper are not connected by an indoor corridor, due to some architectural oversight. In any case, inside six minutes he was on the residential level, watching the ushers organize his bags. Cathy was there, trying to supervise, under

221

the eyes of the Secret Service as well, who acted as though they worried about having a bomb slipped in. But paranoia was their job. Ryan walked over to his wife. 'You need to talk to Andrea.'

'What for?'

'Stomach trouble, she says.'

'Uh-oh.' Cathy had suffered from queasiness with Sally, but that was ages ago, and it hadn't been severe. 'Not really much you can do about it, you know.'

'So much for medical progress,' Jack commented. 'She probably could use some girl–girl support anyway.'

Cathy smiled. 'Oh, sure, womanly solidarity. So, you're going to bond with Pat?'

Jack grinned back at her. 'Yeah, maybe he'll teach me to shoot a pistol better.'

'Super,' SURGEON observed dryly.

'Which dress for the big dinner?' POTUS asked FLOTUS.

'The light-blue one.'

'Slinky,' Jack said, touching her arm.

The kids showed up then, shepherded up to the bedroom level by their various detail leaders, except for Kyle, who was carried by one of his lionesses. Leaving the kids was never particularly easy, though all concerned were somewhat accustomed to it. The usual kisses and hugs took place, and then Jack took his wife's hand and led her to the elevator.

It let them off at the ground level, with a straight walk out to the helicopter pad. The VH-3 was there, with Colonel Malloy at the controls. The Marines saluted, as they always did. The President and First Lady climbed inside and buckled into the comfortable seats, under the watchful eyes of a Marine sergeant, who then went forward to report to the pilot in the right-front seat.

Cathy enjoyed helicopter flight more than her husband did, since she flew in one twice a day. Jack was no longer afraid of it, but he did prefer driving a car, which he hadn't been allowed to do in months. The Sikorsky lifted up gently, pivoted in the air, and headed off to Andrews. The flight took about ten minutes. The helicopter alighted close to the VC-25A, the Air Force's version of the Boeing 747; it was just a few seconds to the stairs, with the usual TV cameras to mark the event.

'Turn and wave, honey,' Jack told Cathy at the top of the steps. 'We might make the evening news.'

'Again?' Cathy grumped. Then she waved and smiled, not at people, but at cameras. With this task completed, they went inside the aircraft and forward to the Presidential compartment. There they buckled in, and were observed to do so by an Air Force NCO, who then told the pilot it was okay to spool up the engines and taxi to the end of Runway Zero-one-right. Everything after that was ordinary, including the speech from the pilot, followed by the usual, stately takeoff roll of the big Boeing, and the climb out to thirty-eight thousand feet. Aft, Ryan was sure, everyone was comfortable, because the worst seat on this aircraft was as good as the best first-class seat on any airline in the world. On the whole this seemed a serious waste of the taxpayers' money, but to the best of his knowledge no taxpayer had ever complained very loudly.

The expected happened off the coast of Maine.

223

'Mr. President?' a female voice asked.

'Yeah, Sarge?'

'Call for you, sir, on the STU. Where do you want to take it?'

Ryan stood. 'Topside.'

The sergeant nodded and waved. 'This way, sir.'

'Who is it?'

'The DCI.'

Ryan figured that made sense. 'Let's get Secretary Adler in on this, too.'

'Yes, sir,' she said as he started up the spiral stairs.

Upstairs, Ryan settled into a working-type seat vacated for him by an Air Force NCO who handed him the proper phone. 'Ed?'

'Yeah, Jack. Sergey called.'

'Saying what?'

'He thinks it's a good idea you coming to Poland. He requests a high-level meeting, on the sly if possible.'

Adler took the chair next to Ryan and caught the comment.

'Scott, feel like a hop to Moscow?'

'Can we do it quietly?' SecState asked.

'Probably.'

'Then, Yes. Ed, did you field the NATO suggestion?'

'Not my turf to try that, Scott,' the Director of Central Intelligence replied.

'Fair enough. Think they'll spring for it?'

'Three-to-one, yes.'

'I'll agree with that,' Ryan concurred. 'Golovko will like it, too.'

'Yeah, he will, once he gets over the shock,' Adler observed, with irony in his voice.

'Okay, Ed, tell Sergey that we are amenable to a covert meeting. SecState flying into Moscow for consultations. Let us know what develops.'

'Will do.'

'Okay, out.' Ryan set the handset down and turned to Adler. 'Well?'

'Well, if they spring for it, China will have something to think about.' This statement was delivered with a dollop of hope.

The problem, Ryan thought once again as he stood, *is that Klingons don't think quite the same way we do.*

*   *   *

The bugs had them all smirking. Suvorov/Koniev had picked up another expensive hooker that night, and her acting abilities had played out in the proper noises at the proper moments. *Or maybe he was really that good in bed*, Provalov wondered aloud, to the general skepticism of the others in the surveillance van. *No*, the others thought, *this girl was too much of a professional to allow herself to get into it that much.* They all thought that was rather sad, lovely as she was to look at. But they knew something their subject didn't know. This girl had been a 'dangle', pre-briefed to meet Suvorov/Koniev.

Finally the noise subsided, and they heard the distinctive *snap* of an American Zippo lighter, and the usual post-sex silence of a sated man and a (simulatedly) satisfied woman.

'So, what sort of work do you do, Vanya?' the female voice asked, showing the expected professional interest of an expensive hooker in a

225

wealthy man she might wish to entertain again.

'Business' was the answer.

'What sort?' Again, just the right amount of interest. The good news, Provalov thought, was that she didn't need coaching. The Sparrow School must have been fairly easy to operate, he realized. Women did this sort of thing from instinct.

'I take care of special needs for special people,' the enemy spy answered. His revelation was followed by a feminine laugh.

'I do that, too, Vanya.'

'There are foreigners who need special services which I was trained to handle under the old regime.'

'You were KGB? Really?' Excitement in her voice. This girl was good.

'Yes, one of many. Nothing special about it.'

'To you, perhaps, but not to me. Was there really a school for women like me? Did KGB train women to . . . to take care of the needs of men.'

A man's laugh this time: 'Oh, yes, my dear. There was such a school. You would have done well there.'

Now the laugh was coquettish. 'As well as I do now?'

'No, not at what you charge.'

'But am I worth it?' she asked.

'Easily,' was the satisfied answer.

'Would you like to see me again, Vanya?' Real hope, or beautifully simulated hope, in the question.

'*Da*, I would like that very much, Maria.'

'So, you take care of people with special needs. What needs are those?' She could get away with this because men so enjoyed to be found

226

fascinating by beautiful women. It was part of their act of worship at this particular altar, and men *always* went for it.

'Not unlike what I was trained to do, Maria, but the details need not concern you.

Disappointment: 'Men always say that,' she grumped. 'Why do the most interesting men have to be so mysterious?'

'In that is our fascination, woman,' he explained. 'Would you prefer that I drove a truck?'

'Truck drivers don't have your . . . your manly abilities,' she replied, as if she'd learned the difference.

'A man could get hard just listening to this bitch,' one of the FSS officers observed.

'That's the idea,' Provalov agreed. 'Why do you think she can charge so much?'

'A real man need not pay for it.'

'Was I that good?' Suvorov/Koniev asked in their headphones.

'Any better and I would have to pay you, Vanya,' she replied, with joy in her voice. Probably a kiss went along with the proclamation.

'No more questions, Maria. Let it lie for now,' Oleg Gregoriyevich urged to the air. She must have heard him.

'You know how to make a man feel like a man,' the spy/assassin told her. 'Where did you learn this skill?'

'It just comes naturally to a woman,' she cooed.

'To some women, perhaps.' Then the talking stopped, and in ten minutes, the snoring began.

'Well, that's more interesting than our normal cases,' the FSS officer told the others.

'You have people checking out the bench?'

227

'Hourly.' There was no telling how many people delivered messages to the dead-drop, and they probably weren't all Chinese nationals. No, there'd be a rat-line in this chain, probably not a long one, but enough to offer some insulation to Suvorov's handler. That would be good fieldcraft, and they had to expect it. So, the bench and its dead-drop would be checked out regularly, and in that surveillance van would be a key custom-made to fit the lock on the drop-box, and a photocopier to make a duplicate of the message inside. The FSS had also stepped up surveillance of the Chinese Embassy. Nearly every employee who carne outside had a shadow now. To do this properly meant curtailing other counterespionage operations in Moscow, but this case had assumed priority over everything else. It would soon become even more important, but they didn't know that yet.

*   *   *

'How many engineers do we have available?' Bondarenko asked Allyev in the east Siberian dawn.

'Two regiments not involved with the road-building,' the operations officer answered.

'Good. Get them all down here immediately to work on the camouflage on these bunkers, and to set up false ones on the other side of these hills. Immediately, Andrey.'

'Yes, General, I'll get them right on it.'

'I love the dawn, the most peaceful time of day.'

'Except when the other fellow uses it for his attack.' Dawn was the universal time for a major offensive, so that one had all the light of the day to pursue it.

'If they come, it will be right up this valley.'

'Yes, it will.'

'They will shoot up the first line of defenses—what they think they are, that is,' Bondarenko predicted, pointing. The first line was composed of seemingly real bunkers, made of rebarred concrete, but the gun tubes sticking out of them were fake. Whatever engineer had laid out these fortifications had been born with an eye for terrain worthy of Alexander of Macedon. They *appeared* to be beautifully sited, but a little too much so. Their positioning was a little too predictable, and they were visible, if barely so, to the other side, and something *barely* visible would be the first target hit. There were even pyrotechnic charges in the false bunkers, so that after a few direct hits they'd explode, and really make the enemy feel fine for having hit them. Whoever had come up with *that* idea had been a genius of a military engineer.

But the real defenses on the front of the hills were tiny observation posts whose buried phone lines led back to the real bunkers, and beyond them to artillery positions ten or more kilometers back. Some of these were old, also pre-sited, but the rockets they launched were just as deadly today as they'd been in the 1940s, design progeny of the Katushka artillery rockets the Germans had learned to hate. Then came the direct-fire weapons. The first rank of these were the turrets of old German tanks. The sights and the ammunition still worked, and the crewmen knew how to use them, and they had escape tunnels leading to vehicles that would probably allow them to survive

229

a determined attack. The engineers who had laid this line out were probably all dead now, and General Bondarenko hoped they'd been buried honorably, as soldiers deserved. This line wouldn't stop a determined attack—no fixed line of defenses could accomplish that—but it would be enough to make an enemy wish he'd gone somewhere else.

But the camouflage needed work, and that work would be done at night. A high-flying aircraft tracing over the border with a side-looking camera could see far into his country and take thousands of useful, pretty pictures, and the Chinese probably had a goodly collection of such pictures, plus whatever they could get from their own satellites, or from the commercial birds that anyone could employ now for money—

'Andrey, tell intelligence to see if we can determine if the Chinese have accessed commercial photo satellites.'

'Why bother? Don't they have their own—'

'We don't know how good their reconsats are, but we do know that the new French ones are as good as anything the Americans had up until 1975 or so, and that's good enough for most purposes.'

'Yes, General.' Aliyev paused. 'You think something is going to happen here?'

Bondarenko paused, frowning as he stared south over the river. He could see into China from this hilltop. The ground looked no different, but for political reasons it was alien land, and though the inhabitants of that land were no different ethnically from the people native to *his* land, the political differences were enough to make the sight of them a thing of concern, even fear, for him. He shook his head.

'Andrey Petrovich, you've heard the same intelligence briefings I've heard. What concerns me is that their army has been far more active than ours. They have the ability to attack us, and we do not have the ability to defeat them. We have less than three full-strength divisions, and the level of their training is inadequate. We have much to do before I will begin to feel comfortable. Firming up this line is the easiest thing to do, and the easiest part of firming it up is hiding the bunkers. Next, we'll start rotating the soldiers back to the training range and have them work on their gunnery. That will be easy for them to do, but it hasn't been done in ten months! So much to do, Andrushka, so much to do.'

'That is so, Comrade General, but we've made a good beginning.'

Bondarenko waved his hand and growled, 'Ahh, a good beginning will be a year from now. We've taken the first morning piss in what will be a long day, Colonel. Now, let's fly east and see the next sector.'

*　　　*　　　*

General Peng Xi-Wang, commander of the Red Banner 34th Shock Army, only sixteen kilometers away, looked through powerful spotting glasses at the Russian frontier. Thirty-fourth Shock was a Type A Group Army, and comprised about eighty thousand men. He had an armored division, two mechanized ones, a motorized infantry division, and other attachments, such as an independent artillery brigade under his direct command. Fifty years of age, and a party member since his twenties, Peng was a long-term professional soldier who'd enjoyed the last ten years of his life. Since commanding his tank regiment as a senior colonel, he'd been able to train his troops incessantly on what had become his home country.

The Shenyang Military District comprised the northeastern most part of the People's Republic. It was composed of hilly, wooded land, and had warm summers and bitter winters. There was a touch of early ice on the Amur River below Peng now, but from a military point of view, the trees were the real obstacle. Tanks could knock individual trees down, but not every ten meters. No, you had to drive between and around them, and while there was room for that, it was hard on the drivers, and it ate up fuel almost as efficiently as tipping the fuel drum over on its side and just pouring it out. There were some roads and railroad rights-of-way, and if he ever went north, he'd be using them, though that made for good ambush opportunities, if the Russians had a good collection of antitank weapons. But the Russian doctrine, going back half a century, was that the best antitank weapon was a better tank. In their war with the fascists, the Soviet army had enjoyed possession of a superb tank in the T-34. They'd built a lot of the Rapier antitank guns, and duly copied NATO guided antitank weapons, but you dealt with those by blanketing an area with artillery fire, and Peng had lots of guns and mountains of shells to deal with the unprotected infantrymen who had to steer the missiles into their targets. He wished he had the Russian-designed Arena anti-missile system, which had been designed to protect their tanks from the swarm of NATO's deadly insects, but he didn't, and he heard it didn't work all that well anyway.

The spotting glasses were Chinese copies of a German Zeiss model adopted for use by the Soviet Army of old. They zoomed from twenty- to fifty-power, allowing him an intimate view of the other side of the river. Peng came up here once a month or so, which allowed him to inspect his own border troops, who stood what was really a defensive watch, and a light one at that. He had little concern about a Russian attack into his country. The People's Liberation Army taught the same doctrine as every army back to the Assyrians of old: The best defense is a good offense. If a war began here, better to begin it yourself. And so Peng had cabinets full of plans to attack into Siberia, prepared by his operations and intelligence people, because that was what operations people did.

'Their defenses look ill-maintained,' Peng observed.

'That is so, Comrade,' the colonel commanding the border-defense regiment agreed. 'We see little regular activity there.'

'They are too busy selling their weapons to civilians for vodka,' the army political officer observed. 'Their morale is poor, and they do not train anything like we do.'

'They have a new theater commander,' the army's intelligence chief countered. 'A General-Colonel Bondarenko. He is well regarded in Moscow as an intellect and as a courageous battlefield commander from Afghanistan.'

'That means he survived contact once,' Political observed. 'Probably with a Kabul whore.'

'It is dangerous to underestimate an adversary,' Intelligence warned.

'And foolish to overestimate one.'

Peng just looked through the glasses. He'd heard his intelligence and political officer spar before. Intelligence tended to be an old woman, but many intelligence officers were like that, and Political, like so many of his colleagues, was sufficiently aggressive to make Genghis Khan seem womanly. As in the theater, officers played the roles assigned to them. His role, of course, was to be the wise and confident commander of one of his country's premier striking arms, and Peng played that role well enough that he was in the running for promotion to General First Class, and if he played his cards very carefully, in another eight years or so, maybe Marshal. With that rank came real political power and personal riches beyond counting, with whole factories working for his own enrichment. Some of those factories were managed by mere colonels, people with the best of political credentials who knew how to kowtow to their seniors, but Peng had never gone that route. He enjoyed soldering far more than he enjoyed pushing paper and screaming at worker-peasants. As a new second lieutenant, he'd fought the Russians, not very far from this very spot. It had been a mixed experience. His regiment had enjoyed initial success, then had been hammered by a storm of artillery. That had been back when the Red Army, the real Soviet Army of old, had fielded whole artillery *divisions* whose concentrated fire could shake the very earth and sky, and that border clash had incurred the wrath of the nation the Russians had once been. But no longer. Intelligence told him that the Russian troops on the far side of this cold river were not even a

234

proper shadow of what had once been there. Four divisions, perhaps, and not all of them at full strength. So, however clever this Bondarenko fellow was, if a clash came, he'd have his hands very full indeed.

But that was a political question, wasn't it? Of course. All the really important things were.

'How are the bridging engineers?' Peng asked, surveying the watery obstacle below.

'Their last exercise went very well, Comrade General,' Operations replied. Like every other army in the world, the PLA had copied the Russian 'ribbon' bridge, designed by Soviet engineers in the 1960s to force crossings of all the streams of Western Germany in a NATO/Warsaw Pact war so long expected, but never realized. Except in fiction, mainly Western fiction that had had the NATO side win in every case. Of course. Would capitalists spend money on books that ended their culture? Peng chuckled to himself Such people enjoyed their illusions . . .

. . . almost as much as his own country's Politburo members. That's the way it was all over the world, Peng figured. The rulers of every land held images in their heads, and tried to make the world conform to them. Some succeeded, and those were the ones who wrote the history books.

'So, what do we expect here?'

'From the Russians?' Intelligence asked. 'Nothing that I have heard about. Their army is training a little more, but nothing to be concerned about. If they wanted to come south across that river, I hope they can swim in the cold.'

'The Russians like their comforts too much for that. They've grown soft with their new political

235

regime,' Political proclaimed.

'And if we are ordered north?' Peng asked.

'If we give them one hard kick, the whole rotten mess will fall down,' Political answered. He didn't know that he was exactly quoting another enemy of the Russians.

CHAPTER FORTY-THREE

DECISIONS

The colonel flying Air Force One executed an even better landing than usual. Jack and Cathy Ryan were already awake and showered to alertness, helped by a light breakfast heavy on fine coffee. The President looked out the window to his left and saw troops formed up in precise lines, as the aircraft taxied to its assigned place.

'Welcome to Poland, babe. What do you have planned?'

'I'm going to spend a few hours at their big teaching hospital. Their chief eye-cutter wants me to look at his operation.' It was always the same for FLOTUS, and she didn't mind. It came from being an academic physician, treating patients, but also teaching young docs, and observing how her counterparts around the world did their version of her job. Every so often, you saw something new that was worth learning from, or even copying, because smart people happened everywhere, not just at the Johns Hopkins University School of Medicine. It was the one part of the First Lady folderol that she actually enjoyed, because she

236

could learn from it, instead of just being a somewhat flat-chested Barbie doll for the world to gawk at. To this end she was dressed in a beige business suit, whose jacket she would soon exchange for a doc's proper white lab coat, which was always her favorite item of apparel. Jack was wearing one of his dark-blue white-pinstriped President-of-the-United States suits, with a maroon striped tie because Cathy liked the color combination, and she really did decide what Jack wore, except for the shirt. SWORDSMAN wore only white cotton shirts with button-down collars, and despite Cathy's lobbying for something different, on that issue he stood firm. This had caused Cathy to observe more than once that he'd wear the damned things with his tuxedos if convention didn't demand otherwise.

The aircraft came to a halt, and the stagecraft began. The Air Force sergeant—this one always a man—opened the door on the left side of the aircraft to see that the truck-mounted stairs were already in place. Two more non-coms scurried down so that they could salute Ryan when he walked down. Andrea Price-O'Day was talking over her digital radio circuit to the chief of the Secret Service advance team to make sure it was safe for the President to appear in the open. She'd already heard that the Poles had been as cooperative as any American police force, and had enough security deployed here to defend against an attack by space aliens or Hitler's Wehrmacht. She nodded to the President and Mrs. Ryan.

'Showtime, babe,' Jack told Cathy, with a dry smile.

'Knock 'em dead, Movie Star,' she said in reply.

237

It was one of their inside jokes.

John Patrick Ryan, President of the United States of America, stood in the door to look out over Poland, or at least as much of it as he could see from this vantage. The first cheers erupted then, for although he'd never even been close to Poland before, he was a popular figure here, for what reason Jack Ryan had no idea. He walked down, carefully, telling himself not to trip and spill down the steps. It looked bad to do so, as one of his antecedents had learned the hard way. At the bottom, the two USAF sergeants snapped off their salutes, which Ryan unconsciously returned, and then he was saluted again by a Polish officer. They did it differently, Jack saw, with ring and little finger tucked in, like American Cub Scouts. Jack nodded and smiled to this officer, then followed him to the receiving line. There was the U.S. ambassador to introduce him to the Polish President. Together they walked down a red carpet to a small lectern, where the Polish President welcomed Ryan, and Ryan make remarks to demonstrate his joy at visiting this ancient and important new American ally. Ryan had a discordant memory of the 'Polack' jokes so popular when he'd been in high school, but managed not to relate any to the assembled throng. This was followed by a review past the honor guard of soldiers, about three companies of infantrymen, all spiffed up for this moment; Jack walked past them, looking in each face for a split second and figuring they just wanted to go back to barracks to change into their more comfortable fatigues, where they'd say that this Ryan guy looked okay for a damned American chief of state, and wasn't it good that this

238

pain-in-the-ass duty was over. Then Jack and Cathy (carrying flowers given to her by two cute Polish kids, a boy and a girl, age six or so, because that was the best age to greet an important foreign woman) got into the official car, an American limo from the U.S. Embassy, for the drive into town. Once there, Jack looked over to the ambassador.

'What about Moscow?'

Ambassadors had once been Very Important People, which explained why each still had to be approved by vote of the United States Senate. When the Constitution had been drafted, world travel had been done by sailing ship, and an ambassador in a foreign land was the United States of America, and had to be able to speak for his country entirely without guidance from Washington. Modern communications had transformed ambassadors into glorified mailmen, but they still, occasionally, had to handle important matters with discretion, and this was such a case.

'They want the Secretary to come over as soon as possible. The backup aircraft is at a fighter base about fifteen miles from here. We can get Scott there within the hour,' Stanislas Lewendowski reported.

'Thanks, Stan. Make it happen.'

'Yes, Mr. President,' the ambassador, a native of Chicago, agreed with a curt nod.

'Anything we need to know?'

'Aside from that, sir, no, everything's pretty much under control.'

'I hate it when they say that,' Cathy observed quietly. 'That's when I look up for the falling sandbag.'

'Not here, ma'am,' Lewendowski promised.

'Here things *are* under control.'

That's nice to hear, President Ryan thought, *but what about the rest of the fucking world?*

*   *   *

'Eduard Petrovich, this is not a happy development,' Golovko told his President.

'I can see that,' Grushavoy agreed tersely. 'Why did we have to learn this from the Americans?'

'We had a very good source in Beijing, but he retired not long ago. He's sixty-nine years old and in ill health, and it was time to leave his post in their Party Secretariat. Sadly, we had no replacement for him,' Golovko admitted. 'The American source appears to be a man of similar placement. We are fortunate to have this information, regardless of its source.'

'Better to have it than not to have it,' Eduard Petrovich admitted. 'So, now what?'

'Secretary of State Adler will be joining us in about three hours, at the Americans' request. He wishes to consult with us directly on a 'matter of mutual interest.' That means the Americans are as concerned with this development as we are.'

'What will they say?'

'They will doubtless offer us assistance of some sort. Exactly what kind, I cannot say.'

'Is there anything I don't already know about Adler and Ryan?'

'I don't think so. Scott Adler is a career diplomat, well regarded everywhere as an experienced and expert diplomatic technician. He and Ryan are friends, dating back to when Ivan Emmetovich was Deputy Director of CIA. They

240

get along well and do not have any known disagreements in terms of policy. Ryan I have known for over ten years. He is bright, decisive, and a man of unusually fine personal honor. A man of his word. He was the enemy of the Soviet Union, and a skilled enemy, but since our change of systems he has been a friend. He evidently wishes us to succeed and prosper economically, though his efforts to assist us have been somewhat disjointed and confused. As you know, we have assisted the Americans in two black operations, one against China and one against Iran. This is important, because Ryan will see that he owes us a debt. He is, as I said, an honorable man, and he will wish to repay that debt, as long as it does not conflict with his own security interests.'

'Will an attack on China be seen that way?' President Grushavoy asked.

Golovko nodded decisively. 'Yes, I believe so. We know that Ryan has said privately that he both likes and admires Russian culture, and that he would prefer that America and Russia should become strategic partners. So, I think Secretary Adler will offer us substantive assistance against China.'

'What form will it take?'

'Eduard Petrovich, I am an intelligence officer, not a gypsy fortune-teller . . .' Golovko paused. 'We will know more soon, but if you wish me to make a guess . . .'

'Do so,' the Russian President commanded. The SVR Chairman took a deep breath and made his prediction:

'He will offer us a seat on the North Atlantic Council.' That startled Grushavoy:

'Join NATO?' he asked, with an open mouth.

'It would be the most elegant solution to the problem. It allies us with the rest of Europe, and would face China with a panoply of enemies if they attack us.'

'And if they make this offer to us . . . ?'

'You should accept it at once, Comrade President,' the chief of the RSV replied. 'We would be fools not to.'

'What will they demand in return?'

'Whatever it is, it will be far less costly than a war against China.'

Grushavoy nodded thoughtfully. 'I will consider this. Is it really possible that America can recognize Russia as an ally?'

'Ryan will have thought this idea through. It conforms to his strategic outlook, and, as I said, I believe he honestly admires and respects Russia.'

'After all his time in CIA?'

'Of course. That is why he does. He knows us. He ought to respect us.'

Grushavoy thought about that one. Like Golovko, he was a Russian patriot who loved the very smell of Russian soil, the birch forests, the vodka and the borscht, the music and literature of his land. But he was not blind to the errors and ill fortune his country had endured over the centuries. Like Golovko, Grushavoy had come to manhood in a nation called the Union of Soviet Socialist Republics, and had been educated to be a believer in Marxism-Leninism, but he'd gradually come to see that, although the path to political power had required worshiping at that godless altar, the god there had been a false one. Like many, he'd seen that the previous system simply didn't work. But unlike all but a small and courageous few, he'd spoken out about the system's shortcomings. A lawyer, even under the Soviet system when law had been subordinated to political whim, he'd crusaded for a rational system of laws which would allow people to predict the reaction of the state to their actions with something akin to confidence. He'd been there when the old system had fallen, and had embraced the new system as a teenager embraced his first love. Now he was struggling to bring order—lawful order, which was harder still—to a nation which had known only dictatorial rule for centuries. If he succeeded, he knew he'd be remembered as one of the giants of human political history. If he failed, he'd just be remembered as one more starry-eyed visionary unable to turn his dream into reality. The latter, he thought in quiet moments, was the more likely outcome.

But despite that concern, he was playing to win. Now he had the gold and oil discoveries in Siberia, which had appeared as if gifts from the merciful God his education had taught him to deny. Russian history predicted—nay, demanded—that such gifts be taken from his country, for such had always been their hateful ill luck. Did God hate Russia? Anyone familiar with the past in his ancient country would think so. But today hope appeared as a golden dream, and Grushavoy was determined not to let this dream evaporate as all the others had. The land of Tolstoy and Rimsky-Korsakov had given much to the world, and now it deserved something back. Perhaps this Ryan fellow would indeed be a friend of his country and his people. His country needed friends. His country had the resources to exist alone, but to make use of those resources, he needed assistance, enough to allow Russia to enter the world as a complete and self-sufficient nation, ready to be a friend to all, ready to give and to take in honor and amity. The wherewithal was within his reach, if not quite within his hand. To take it would make him an Immortal, would make Eduard Petrovich Grushavoy the man who raised up his entire country. To do that he'd need help, however, and while that abraded his sense of *amour propre*, his patriotism, his duty to his country required that he set self aside.

'We shall see, Sergey Nikolay'ch. We shall see.'

*　　　*　　　*

'The time is ripe,' Zhang Han San told his colleagues in the room of polished oak. 'The men and weapons are in place. The prize lies right before our eyes. That prize offers us economic salvation, economic security such as we have dreamed of for decades, the ability,' he went on, 'to make China the world's preeminent power. That is a legacy to leave our people such as no leader has ever granted his descendants. We need only take it. It lies almost in our hands, like a peach upon a tree.'

'It is feasible?' Interior Minister Tong Jie asked cautiously.

'Marshal?' Zhang handed the inquiry off to the Defense Minister.

Luo Cong leaned forward. He and Zhang had spent much of the previous evening together with maps, diagrams, and intelligence estimates. 'From a military point of view, yes, it is possible. We have four Type A Group armies in the Shenyang Military District, fully trained and poised to strike north. Behind them are six Type B Group armies with sufficient infantry to support our mechanized forces, and four more type C Group armies to garrison the land we take. From a strictly military point of view, the only issues are moving our forces into place and then supplying them. That is mainly a question of railroads, which will move supplies and men. Minister Qian?' Luo asked. He and Zhang had considered this bit of stage-managing carefully, hoping to co-opt a likely opponent of their proposed national policy early on.

The Finance Minister was startled by the question, but pride in his former job and his innate honesty compelled him to respond truthfully: 'There is sufficient rolling stock for your purposes, Marshal Luo,' he replied tersely. 'The concern will be repairing damage done by enemy air strikes on our rights-of-way and bridges. That is something the Railroad Ministry has examined for decades, but there is no precise answer to it, because we cannot predict the degree of damage the Russians might inflict.'

'I am not overly worried about that, Qian,' Marshal Luo responded. 'The Russian air force is in miserable shape due to all their activity against their Muslim minorities. They used up a goodly fraction of their best weapons and spare parts. We estimate that our air-defense groups should preserve our transportation assets with acceptable losses. Will we be able to send railroad-construction personnel into Siberia to extend our railheads?'

Again Qian felt himself trapped. 'The Russians

245

have surveyed and graded multiple rights-of-way over the years in their hopes for extending the Trans-Siberian Railroad and settling people into the region. Those efforts date back to Stalin. Can we lay track rapidly? Yes. Rapidly enough for your purposes? Probably not, Comrade Marshal,' Qian replied studiously. If he didn't answer honestly, his seat at this table would evaporate, and he knew it.

'I am not sanguine on this prospect, comrades,' Shen Tang spoke for the Foreign Ministry.

'Why is that, Shen?' Zhang asked.

'What will other nations do?' he asked rhetorically. 'We do not know, but I would not be optimistic, especially with the Americans. They become increasingly friendly with the Russians. President Ryan is well known to be friendly with Golovko, chief advisor to President Grushavoy.'

'A pity that Golovko still lives, but we were unlucky,' Tan Deshi had to concede.

'Depending on luck is dangerous at this level,' Fang Gan told his colleagues. 'Fate is no man's friend.'

'Perhaps the next time,' Tan responded.

'Next time,' Zhang thought aloud, 'better to eliminate Grushavoy and so throw their country into total chaos. A country without a President is like a snake without a head. It may thrash about, but it harms no one.'

'Even a severed head can bite,' Fang observed. 'And who is to say that Fate will smile upon this enterprise?'

'A man can wait for fate to decide for him, or he can seize the foul woman by the throat and take her by force—as we have all done in our time,' Zhang added with a cruel smile.

Much more easily done with a docile secretary than with Destiny herself, Zhang, Fang didn't say aloud. He could go only so far in this forum, and he knew it. 'Comrades, I counsel caution. The dogs of war have sharp teeth, but any dog may turn and bite his master. We have all seen *that* happen, have we not? Some things, once begun, are less easily halted. War is such a thing, and it is not to be undertaken so lightly.'

'What would you have us do, Fang?' Zhang asked. 'Should we wait until we run out of oil and wheat? Should we wait until we need troops to quell discord among our own people? Should we wait for Fate to decide for us, or should we choose our own destiny?'

The only reply to that came from Chinese culture itself, the ancient beliefs that came to all of the Politburo members almost as genetic knowledge, unaffected by political conditioning: 'Comrades, Destiny awaits us all. It chooses us, not we it. What you propose here, my old friend, could merely accelerate what comes for us in any case, and who among us can say if it will please or displease us?' Minister Fang shook his head. 'Perhaps what you propose is necessary, even beneficial,' he allowed, 'but only after the alternatives have been examined fully and discarded.'

'If we are to decide,' Luo told them, 'then we must decide soon. We have good campaigning weather before us. That season will only last so long. If we strike soon—in the next two weeks—we can seize our objectives, and then time works *for* us. Then winter will set in and make offensive campaigning virtually impossible against a determined defense. Then we can depend upon Shen's ministry to safeguard and consolidate what we have seized, perhaps to share our winnings with the Russians . . . for a time,' he added cynically. China would never share such a windfall, they all knew. It was merely a ploy fit to fool children and mushy-headed diplomats, which the world had in abundance, they all knew.

Through all this, Premier Xu had sat quietly, observing how the sentiments went, before making his decision and calling for a vote whose outcome would, of course, be predetermined. There was one more thing that needed asking. Not surprisingly, the question came from Tan Deshi, chief of the Ministry of State Security:

'Luo, my friend, how soon would the decision have to be made to ensure success? How easily could the decision be called back if circumstances warrant?'

'Ideally, the "go" decision would be made today, so that we can start moving our forces to their preset jumping-off places. To stop them—well, of course, you can stop the offensive up to the very moment the artillery is to open fire. It is much harder to advance than it is to stay in place. Any man can stand still, no matter where he is.' The preplanned answer to the preplanned question was as clever as it was misleading. Sure, you could always stop an army poised to jump off, about as easily as you could stop a Yangtze River flood.

'I see,' Tan said. 'In that case, I propose that we vote on *conditional* approval of a "go" order, subject to change at any time by majority vote of the Politburo.'

Now it was Xu's turn to take charge of the

meeting: 'Comrades, thank you all for your views on the issue before us. Now we must decide what is best for our country and our people. We shall vote on Tan's proposal, a conditional authorization for an attack to seize and exploit the oil and gold fields in Siberia.'

As Fang had feared, the vote was already decided, and in the interests of solidarity, he voted with the rest. Only Qian Kun wavered, but like all the others, he sided with the majority, because it was dangerous to stand alone in any group in the People's Republic, most of all this one. And besides, Qian was only a candidate member, and didn't have a vote at this most democratic of tables.

The vote turned out to be unanimous.

Long Chun, it would be called: Operation SPRING DRAGON.

*   *   *

Scott Adler knew Moscow as well as many Russian citizens did, he'd been here so many times, including one tour in the American Embassy as a wet-behind-the-ears new foreign-service officer, all those years before, during the Carter Administration. The Air Force flight crew delivered him on time, and they were accustomed to taking people on covert missions to odd places. This mission was less unusual than most. His aircraft rolled to a stop at the Russian fighter base, and the official car rolled up even before the mechanical steps unfolded. Adler hustled out, unaccompanied even by an aide. A Russian official shook hands with him and got him into the car for the drive into Moscow. Adler was at ease. He knew that he was offering Russia a gift fit for the world's largest Christmas tree, and he didn't think they were stupid enough to reject it. No, the Russians were among the world's most skillful diplomats and geopolitical thinkers, a trait that went back sixty years or more. It had struck him as sad, back in 1978, that their adroit people had been chained to a doomed political system—even back then, Adler had seen the demise of the Soviet Union coming. Jimmy Carter's 'human rights' proclamation had been that President's best and least appreciated foreign-policy play, for it had injected the virus of rot into their political empire, begun the process of eating away their power in Eastern Europe, and also of letting their own people start to ask questions. It was a pot that Ronald Reagan had sweetened—upping the ante with his defense buildup that had stretched the Soviet economy to the breaking point and beyond, allowing George Bush to be there when they'd tossed in their cards and cast off from the political system that stretched back to Vladimir ll'ych Ulyanov, Lenin himself, the founding father, even the god of Marxism-Leninism. It was usually sad when a god died . . .

. . . but not in this case, Adler thought as the buildings flashed by.

Then he realized that there was one more large but false god out there, Mao Zedong, awaiting final interment in history's rubbish heap. When would that come? Did this mission have a role to play in that funeral? Nixon's opening to China had played a role in the destruction of the Soviet Union, which historians still had not fully grasped. Would its final echo be found in the fall of the People's Republic itself? That remained to be seen.

The car pulled into the Kremlin through the Spaskiy Gate, then proceeded to the old Council of Ministers Building. There Adler alighted and hurried inside, into an elevator to a third-floor meeting room.

'Mr. Secretary.' The greeting came from Golovko. Adler should have found him an *eminence gris*, he thought. But Sergey Nikolay'ch was actually a man of genuine intellect and the openness that resulted directly from it. He was not even a pragmatist, but a man who sought what was best for his country, and would search for it everywhere his mind could see. *A seeker of truth*, SecState thought. That sort of man he and America could live with.

'Chairman. Thank you for receiving us so quickly.'

'Please come with me, Mr. Adler.' Golovko led him through a set of high double doors into what almost appeared to be a throne room. EAGLE couldn't remember if this building went back to the czars. President Eduard Petrovich Grushavoy was waiting for him, already standing politely, looking serious but friendly.

'Mr. Adler,' the Russian President said, with a smile and an extended hand.

'Mr. President, a pleasure to be back in Moscow.'

'Please.' Grushavoy led him to a comfortable set of chairs with a low table. Tea things were already out, and Golovko handled the serving like a trusted earl seeing to the needs of his king and guest.

'Thank you. I've always loved the way you serve your tea in Russia.' Adler stirred his and took a sip.

'So, what do you have to say to us?' Grushavoy

251

asked in passable English.

'We have shown you what has become for us a cause for great concern.

'The Chinese,' the Russian President observed. Everyone knew all of this, but the beginning of the conversation would follow the conventions of high-level talk, like lawyers discussing a major case in chambers.

'Yes, the Chinese. They seem to be contemplating a threat to the peace of the world. America has no wish to see that peace threatened. We've all worked very hard—your country and mine—to put an end to conflict. We note with gratitude Russia's assistance in our most recent conflicts. Just as we were allies sixty years ago, so Russia has acted again lately. America is a country that remembers her friends.'

Golovko let out a breath slowly. Yes, his prediction was about to come true. Ivan Emmetovich was a man of honor, and a friend of his country. What came back to him was the time he'd held a pistol to Ryan's head, the time Ryan had engineered the defection of KGB chairman Gerasimov all those years before. Sergey Nikolay'ch had been enraged back then, as furious as he had ever been in a long and stressful professional life, but he'd held back from firing the pistol because it would have been a foolish act to shoot a man with diplomatic status. Now he blessed his moderation, for now Ivan Emmetovich Ryan offered to Russia what he had always craved from America: predictability. Ryan's honor, his sense of fair play, the personal honesty that was the most crippling aspect of his newly acquired political persona, all combined to make him a person upon whom Russia could depend. And at this moment, Golovko could do that which he'd spent his life trying to do: He could see the future that lay only a few short minutes away.

'This Chinese threat, it is real, you think?' Grushavoy asked.

'We fear it is,' the American Secretary of State answered. 'We hope to forestall it.'

'But how will we accomplish that? China knows of our military weakness. We have de-emphasized our defense capabilities of late, trying to shift the funds into areas of greater value to our economy. Now it seems we might pay a bitter price for that,' the Russian President worried aloud.

'Mr. President, we hope to help Russia in that respect.'

'How?'

'Mr. President, even as we speak, President Ryan is also speaking with the NATO chiefs of state and government. He is proposing to them that we invite Russia to sign the North Atlantic Treaty. That will ally the Russian Federation with all of Europe. It ought to make China take a step back to consider the wisdom of a conflict with your country.'

'Ahh,' Grushavoy breathed. 'So, America offers Russia a full alliance of state?'

Adler nodded. 'Yes, Mr. President. As we were allies against Hitler, so today we can again be allies against all potential enemies.'

'There are many complications in this, talks between your military and ours, for example—even talks with the NATO command in Belgium. It could take months to coordinate our country with NATO.'

'Those are technical matters to be handled by

diplomatic and military technicians. At this level, however, we offer the Russian Federation our friendship in peace and in war. We place the word and the honor of our countries at your disposal.'

'What of the European Union, their Common Market of economic alliances?'

'That, sir, is something left to the EEC, but America will encourage our European friends to welcome you completely into the European community, and offer all influence we can muster to that end.'

'What do you ask in return?' Grushavoy asked. Golovko hadn't offered that prediction. This could be the answer to many Russian prayers, though his mind made the leap to see that Russian oil would be a major boon to Europe, and hence a matter of mutual, not unilateral, profit.

'We ask for nothing special in return. It is in the American interest to help make a stable and peaceful world. We welcome Russia into that world. Friendship between your people and ours is desirable to everyone, is it not?'

'And in our friendship is profit also for America,' Golovko pointed out.

Adler sat back and smiled agreement. 'Of course. Russia will sell things to America, and America will sell things to Russia. We will become neighbors in the global village, friendly neighbors. We will compete economically, giving and taking from each other, as we do with many other countries.'

'The offer you make is this simple?' Grushavoy asked.

'Should it be more complicated?' the SecState asked. 'I am a diplomat, not a lawyer. I prefer simple things to complex ones.'

Grushavoy considered all this for half a minute or so. Usually, diplomatic negotiations lasted weeks or months to do even the simplest of things, but Adler was right: Simple was better than complex, and the fundamental issue here was simple, though the downstream consequences might be breathtaking. America offered salvation to Russia, not just a military alliance, but the opening of all doors to economic development. America and Europe would partner with the Russian Federation, creating what could become both an open and integrated community to span the northern hemisphere. It stood to make Eduard Petrovich Grushavoy the Russian who brought his country a full century into the present/future of the world, and for all the statues of Lenin and Stalin that had been toppled, well, maybe some of his own likeness would be erected. It was a thought to appeal to a Russian politician. And after a few minutes, he extended his hand across the low table of tea things.

'The Russian Federation gladly accepts the offer of the United States of America. Together we once defeated the greatest threat to human culture. Perhaps we can do so again—better yet, together we may forestall it.'

'In that case, sir, I will report your agreement to my President.'

Adler checked his watch. It had taken twenty minutes. Damn, you could make history in a hurry when you had your act together, couldn't you? He stood. 'I must be off then to make my report.'

'Please convey my respects to President Ryan. We will do our best to be worthy allies to your country.'

'He and I have no doubts of that, Mr. President.' Adler shook hands with Golovko and walked to the door. Three minutes after that, he was back in his car and heading back to the airport. Once there, the aircraft had barely begun to taxi when he got on the secure satellite phone.

*   *   *

'Mr. President?' Andrea said, coming up to Ryan just as the plenary session of the NATO chiefs was about to begin. She handed over the secure portable phone. 'It's Secretary Adler.'

Ryan took the phone at once. 'Scott? Jack here. What gives?'

'It's a done deal, Jack.'

'Okay, now I have to sell it to these guys. Good job, Scott. Hurry back.'

'We're rolling now, sir.' The line went dead. Ryan tossed the phone to Special Agent Price-O'Day.

'Good news?' she asked.

'Yep.' Ryan nodded and walked into the conference room.

'Mr. President.' Sir Basil Charleston came up to him. The chief of the British Secret Intelligence Service, he'd known Ryan longer than anyone else in the room had. One odd result of Ryan's path to the Presidency was that the people who knew him best were all spooks, mainly NATO ones, and these found themselves advising their chiefs of government on how to deal with America. Sir Basil had served no less than five Prime Ministers of Her Majesty's Government, but now he was in rather a higher position than before.

'Bas, how are you?'

'Doing quite well, thank you. May I ask a question?'

'Sure.' *But I don't have to answer it*, Jack's smile added in reply.

'Adler is in Moscow now. Can we know why?'

'How will your PM react to inviting Russia into NATO?'

That made Basil blink, Ryan saw. It wasn't often that you could catch this guy unawares. Instantly, his mind went into overdrive to analyze the new situation. 'China?' he asked after about six seconds.

Jack nodded. 'Yeah. We may have some problems there.'

'Not going north, are they?'

'They're thinking about it,' Ryan replied.

'How good is your information on that question?'

'You know about the Russian gold strike, right?'

'Oh, yes, Mr. President. Ivan's been bloody lucky on both scores.'

'Our intel strike in Beijing is even better.'

'Indeed?' Charleston observed, letting Jack know that the SIS had also been pretty much shut out there.

'Indeed, Bas. It's class-A information, and it has us worried. We're hoping that pulling Russia into NATO can scare them off. Grushavoy just agreed on it. How do you suppose the rest of these folks will react to it?'

'They'll react cautiously, but favorably, after they've had a chance to consider it.'

'Will Britain back us on this play?' Ryan asked.

'I must speak with the PM. I'll let you know.'

With that, Sir Basil walked over to where the British Prime Minister was chatting with the German Foreign Minister. Charleston dragged him off and spoke quietly into his ear. Instantly, the Prime Minister's eyes, flaring a little wide, shot over to Ryan. The British PM was somewhat trapped, somewhat unpleasantly because of the surprise factor, but the substance of the trap was that Britain and America *always* supported each other. The 'special relationship' was as alive and well today as it had been under the governments of Franklin Roosevelt and Winston Churchill. It was one of the few constants in the diplomatic world for both countries, and it belied Kissinger's dictum that great nations didn't have friendships, but rather interests. Perhaps it was the exception proving the rule, but if so, exception it was. Both Britain and America would hurl themselves in front of a train for the other. The fact that in England, President Ryan was Sir John Ryan, KCVO, made the alliance even more firm. In acknowledgment of that, the Prime Minister of the United Kingdom walked over to the American chief of state.

'Jack, will you let us in on this development?'

'Insofar as I can. I may give Basil a little more on the side, but, yeah, Tony, this is for real, and we're damned worried about it.'

'The gold and the oil?' the PM asked.

'They seem to think they're in an economic box. They're just about out of hard currency, and they're hurting for oil and wheat.'

'You can't make an arrangement for that?'

'After what they did? Congress would hang me from the nearest lamppost.'

'Quite,' the Brit had to agree. BBC had run its

258

own news mini-series on human rights in the PRC, and the Chinese hadn't come off very well. Indeed, despising China was the new European sport, which hadn't helped their foreign-currency holdings at all. As China had trapped themselves, so the Western nations had been perversely co-opted into building the wall. The citizens of these democracies wouldn't stand for economic or trade concessions any more than the Chinese Politburo could see its way to making the political sort. 'Rather like Greek tragedy, isn't it, Jack?'

'Yeah, Tony, and our tragic flaw is adherence to human rights. Hell of a situation, isn't it?'

'And you're hoping that bringing Russia into NATO will give them pause?'

'If there's a better card to play, I haven't seen it in my deck, man.'

'How set are they on the path?'

'Unknown. Our intelligence on this is very good, but we have to be careful making use of it. It could get people killed, and deny us the information we need.'

'Like our chap Penkovskiy in the 1960s.' One thing about Sir Basil, he knew how to educate his bosses on how the business of intelligence worked.

Ryan nodded, then proceeded with a little of his own disinformation. It was business, and Basil would understand: 'Exactly. I can't have that man's life on my conscience, Tony, and so I have to treat this information very carefully.'

'Quite so, Jack. I understand fully.'

'Will you support us on this?'

The PM nodded at once. 'Yes, old boy, we must, mustn't we?'

'Thanks, pal.' Ryan patted him on the shoulder.

CHAPTER FORTY-FOUR

THE SHAPE OF A NEW WORLD ORDER

It took all day, lengthening what was supposed to have been a pro forma meeting of the NATO chiefs into a minor marathon. It took all of Scott Adler's powers of persuasion to smooth things over with the various foreign ministers, but with the assistance of Britain, whose diplomacy had always been of the Rolls-Royce class, after four hours there was a head-nod-and-handshake agreement, and the diplomatic technicians were sent off to prepare the documents. All this was accomplished behind closed doors, with no opportunity for a press leak, and so when the various government leaders made it outside, the media learned of it like a thunderbolt from a clear sky. What they did not learn was the real reason for the action. They were told it had to do with the new economic promise in the Russian Federation, which seemed reasonable enough, and when you came down to it, was the root cause in any case.

In fact most of the NATO partners didn't know the whole story, either. The new American intelligence was directly shared only with Britain, though France and Germany were given some indications of America's cause for concern. For the rest, the simple logic of the situation was enough to offer appeal. It would look good in the press, and for most politicians all over the world, that was sufficient to make them doff their clothes and run about a public square naked. Secretary Adler cautioned his President about the dangers of drawing sovereign nations into treaty obligations without telling them all the reasons behind them, but even he agreed that there was little other choice in the matter. Besides, there *was* a built-in escape clause that the media wouldn't see at first, and hopefully, neither would the Chinese.

The media got the story out in time for the evening news broadcasts in America and the late-night ones in Europe, and the TV cameras showed the arrival of the various VIPs at the official dinner in Warsaw.

'I owe you one, Tony,' Ryan told the British Prime Minister with a salute of his wineglass. The white wine was French, from the Loire Valley, and excellent. The hard liquor of the night had been an equally fine Polish vodka.

'Well, one can hope that it gives our Chinese friends pause. When will Grushavoy arrive?'

'Tomorrow afternoon, followed by more drinking. Vodka again, I suppose.' The documents were being printed up at this very moment, and then would be bound in fine leather, as such important documents invariably were, after which they'd be tucked away in various dusty basement archives, rarely to be seen by the eyes of men again.

'Basil tells me that your intelligence information is unusually good, and rather frightening,' the PM observed, with a sip of his own.

'It is all of that, my friend. You know, we're supposed to think that this war business is a thing of the past.'

'So they thought a hundred years ago, Jack. It didn't quite work out that way, did it?'

'True, but that was then, and this is now. And

the world really has changed in the past hundred years.'

'I hope that is a matter of some comfort to Franz Ferdinand, and the ten million or so chaps who died as an indirect result of his demise, not to mention Act Two of the Great European Civil War,' the Prime Minister observed.

'Yeah, day after tomorrow, I'm going down to Auschwitz. That ought to be fun.' Ryan didn't really want to go, but he figured it was something of an obligation under the circumstances, and besides, Arnie thought it would look good on TV, which was why he did a lot of the things he did.

'Do watch out for the ghosts, old boy. I should think there are a number of them there.'

'I'll let you know,' Ryan promised. Would it be like Dickens's *A Christmas Carol?* he wondered. The ghost of horrors past, accompanied by the ghost of horrors present, and finally the ghost of horrors yet to be? But he was in the business of preventing such things. That's what the people of his country paid him for. Maybe $250,000 a year wasn't much for a guy who'd twice made a good living in the trading business, but it was a damned sight more than most of the taxpayers made, and they gave it to him in return for his work. That made the obligation as sacred as a vow sworn to God's own face. Auschwitz had happened because other men hadn't recognized their obligation to the people whom *they* had been supposed to serve. Or something like that. Ryan had never quite made the leap of imagination necessary to understand the thought processes of dictators. Maybe Caligula had really figured that the lives of the Roman people were his possessions to use and discard like

262

peanut shells. Maybe Hitler had thought that the German people existed only to serve his ambition to enter the history books—and if so, sure enough it had happened, just not quite the way he'd hoped it would. Jack Ryan knew objectively that he'd be in various history books, but he tried to avoid thinking about what future generations would make of him. Just surviving in his job from day to day was difficult enough. The problem with history was that you couldn't transport yourself into the future so that you could look back with detachment and see what the hell you were supposed to do. No, making history was a damned sight harder than studying it, and so he'd decided to avoid thinking about it altogether. He wouldn't be around to know what the future thought anyway, so there was no sense in worrying about it, was there? He had his own conscience to keep him awake at night, and that was hard enough.

Looking around the room, he could see the chiefs of government of more than fifteen countries, from little Iceland to the Netherlands to Turkey. He was President of the United States of America, by far the largest and most powerful country of the NATO alliance—until tomorrow, anyway, he corrected himself—and he wanted to take them all aside and ask each one how the hell he (they were all men at the moment) reconciled his self and his duties. How did you do the job honorably? How did you look after the needs of every citizen? Ryan knew that he couldn't reasonably expect to be universally loved. Arnie had told him that—that he only needed to be liked, not loved, by half-plus-one of the voters in America—but there had to be more to the job than that, didn't there? He knew all of his fellow chief executives by name and sight, and he'd been briefed in on each man's character. That one there, he had a mistress only nineteen years old. That one drank like a fish. That one had a little confusion about his sexual preference. And that one was a crook who'd enriched himself hugely on the government payroll. But they were all allies of his country, and therefore they were officially his friends. And so Jack had to ignore what he knew of them and treat them like what they appeared to be rather than what they really were, and the really funny part of that was that they felt themselves to be his superiors because they were better politicians than he was. And the funniest part of all was that they were right. They *were* better politicians than he was, Ryan thought, sipping his wine. The British Prime Minister walked off to see his Norwegian counterpart, as Cathy Ryan rejoined her husband.

'Well, honey, how did it go?'

'The usual. Politics. Don't any of these women have a real job?' she asked the air.

'Some do,' Jack remembered from his briefings. 'Some even have kids.'

'Mainly grandkids. I'm not old enough for that yet, thank God.'

'Sorry, babe. But there are advantages to being young and beautiful,' POTUS told FLOTUS.

'And you're the best-looking guy here,' Cathy replied with a smile.

'But I'm too tired. Long day at the bargaining table.'

'Why are you bringing Russia into NATO?'

'To stop a war with China,' Jack replied

honestly. It was time she knew. The answer to her question got her attention.

'What?'

'I'll fill you in later, babe, but that's the short version.'

'A war?'

'Yeah. It's a long story, and we hope that what we agreed to do today will prevent it.'

'You say so,' Cathy Ryan observed dubiously.

'Meet anybody you like?'

'The French President is very charming.'

'Oh, yeah? He was a son of a bitch in the negotiating session today. Maybe he's just trying to get in your knickers,' Jack told his wife. He'd been briefed in on the French President, and he was reputed to be a man of 'commendable vigor,' as the State Department report delicately put it. Well, the French had a reputation as great lovers, didn't they?

'I'm spoke for, Sir John,' she reminded him.

'And so am I, my lady.' He could have Roy Altman shoot the Frenchman for making a move on his wife, Ryan thought with amusement, but that would cause a diplomatic incident, and Scott Adler always got upset about those ... Jack checked his watch. It was about time to call this one a day. Soon some diplomat would make a discreet announcement that would end the evening. Jack hadn't danced with his wife. The sad truth was that Jack couldn't dance a lick, which was a source of minor contention with his wife, and a shortcoming he planned to correct someday ... maybe.

The party broke up on time. The embassy had comfortable quarters, and Ryan found his way to the king-sized bed brought in for his and Cathy's use.

*   *   *

Bondarenko's official residence at Chabarsovil was a very comfortable one, befitting a four-star resident and his family. But his wife didn't like it. Eastern Siberia lacked the social life of Moscow, and besides, one of their daughters was nine months pregnant, and his wife was in St. Petersburg to be there when the baby arrived. The front of the house overlooked a large parade ground. The back, where his bedroom was, looked into the pine forests that made up most of this province. He had a large personal staff to look after his needs. That included a particularly skilled cook, and communications people. It was one of the latter who knocked on his bedroom door at three in the local morning.

'Yes, what is it?'

'An urgent communication for you, Comrade General,' the voice answered.

'Very well, wait a minute.' Gennady Iosifovich rose and donned a cloth robe, punching on a light as he went to open the door. He grumbled as any man would at the loss of sleep, but generals had to expect this sort of thing. He opened the door without a snarl at the NCO who handed over the telex.

'Urgent, from Moscow,' the sergeant emphasized.

'Da, spasiba,' the general replied, taking it and walking back toward his bed. He sat in the comfortable chair that he usually dumped his tunic on and picked up the reading glasses that he didn't actually need, but which made reading easier in the semidarkness. It was something urgent—well, urgent enough to wake him up in the middle of the fucking—

'My God,' CINC–FAR EAST breathed to himself, halfway down the cover sheet. Then he flipped it over to read the substance of the report.

In America it would be called a Special National Intelligence Estimate. Bondarenko had seen them before, even helped draft some, but never one like this.

It is believed that there is an imminent danger of war between Russia and the People's Republic of China. The Chinese objective in offensive operations will be to seize the newly-discovered gold and oil deposits in eastern Siberia by rapid mechanized assault north from their border west of Khabarovsk. The leading elements will include the 34th Shock Army, a Type A Group Army . . .

This intelligence estimate is based upon national intelligence assets with access to the political leaders of the PRC and the quality of the intelligence is graded '1A,' the report went on, meaning that the SVR regarded it as Holy Writ. Bondarenko hadn't seen that happen very much.

Far East Command is directed to make all preparations to meet and repel such an attack . . .

'With what?' the general asked the papers in his hand. 'With what, comrades?' With that he lifted the bedside phone. 'I want my staff together in forty minutes,' he told the sergeant who answered. He would not take the theatrical step of calling a full alert just yet. That would follow his staff meeting. Already his mind was examining the

267

problem. It would continue to do so as he urinated, then shaved, his mind running in small circles, a fact which he recognized but couldn't change, and the fact that he couldn't change it didn't slow the process one small bit. The problem he faced as he scraped the whiskers from his face was not an easy one, perhaps an impossible one, but his four-star rank made it *his* problem, and he didn't want to be remembered by future Russian military students as the general who'd not been up to the task of defending his country against a foreign invasion. He was here, Bondarenko told himself, because he was the best operational thinker his country had. He'd faced battle before, and comported himself well enough not only to live but to wear his nation's highest decorations for bravery. He'd studied military history his whole life. He'd even spent time with the Americans at their battle laboratory in California, something he lusted to copy and re-create in Russia as the best possible way to prepare soldiers for battle, but which his country couldn't begin to afford for years. He had the knowledge. He had the nerve. What he lacked were the assets. But history was not made by soldiers who had what they needed, but by those who did not. When the soldiers had enough, the political leaders went into the books. Gennady Iosifovich was a soldier, and a *Russian* soldier. His country was *always* taken by surprise, because for whatever reason her political leaders didn't ever see war coming, and because of that soldiers had to pay the price. A distant voice told him that at least he wouldn't be shot for failure. Stalin was long dead, and with him the ethos of punishing those whom he had failed to warn or prepare. But Bondarenko didn't listen to that voice. Failure was too bitter an alternative for him to consider while he lived.

*   *   *

The Special National Intelligence Estimate made its way to American forces in Europe and the Pacific even more quickly than to Chabarsovil. For Admiral Bartolomeo Vito Mancuso, it came before a scheduled dinner with the governor of Hawaii. His Public Affairs Officer had to knock that one back a few hours while CINCPAC called his staff together.

'Talk to me, Mike,' Mancuso commanded his J-2, BG Michael Lahr.

'Well, it hasn't come totally out of left field, sir,' the theater intelligence coordinator replied. 'I don't know anything about the source of the intelligence, but it looks like high-level human intelligence, probably with a political point of origin. CIA says it's highly reliable, and Director Foley is pretty good. So, we have to take this one very seriously.' Lahr paused for a sip of water.

'Okay, what we know is that the PRC is looking with envious eyes at the Russian mineral discoveries in the central and northern parts of eastern Siberia. That plays into the economic problems they got faced with after the killings in Beijing caused the break in trade talks, and it also appears that their other trading partners are backing away from them as well. So, the Chinese now find themselves in a really tight economic corner, and that's been a *causas belli* as far back as we have written history.'

'What can we do to scare them off?' asked the

269

general commanding Pacific Fleet Marine Force.

'What we're doing tomorrow is to make the Russian federation part of NATO. Russian President Grushavoy will be flying to Warsaw in a few hours to sign the North Atlantic Treaty. *That* makes Russia an ally of the United States of America, and of *all* the NATO members. So, the thinking is that if China moves, they're not just taking on Russia, but all the rest of the North Atlantic Council as well, and *that* ought to give them pause.'

'And if it doesn't?' Mancuso asked. As a theater commander-in-chief, he was paid to consider diplomatic failure rather than success.

'Then, sir, if the Chinese strike north, we have a shooting war on the Asian mainland between the People's Republic of China and an American ally. That means we're going to war.'

'Do we have any guidance from Washington along those lines?' CINCPAC asked.

Lahr shook his head. 'Not yet, Admiral. It's developing a little fast for that, and Secretary Bretano is looking to us for ideas.'

Mancuso nodded. 'Okay. What can we do? What kind of shape are we in?'

The four-star commanding Seventh Fleet leaned forward: 'I'm in pretty decent shape. My carriers are all available or nearly so, but my aviators could use some more training time. Surface assets—well, Ed?'

Vice Admiral Goldsmith looked over to his boss. 'We're good, Bart.'

COMSUBPAC nodded. 'It'll take a little time to surge more of my boats west, but they're trained up, and we can give their navy a major bellyache if

270

we have to.'

Then eyes turned to the Marine. 'I hope you're not going to tell me to invade the Chinese mainland with one division,' he observed. Besides, all of Pacific Fleet didn't have enough amphibious-warfare ships to land more than a brigade landing force, and they knew that. Good as the Marines were, they couldn't take on the entire People's Liberation Army.

'What sort of shape are the Russians in?' Seventh Fleet asked General Lahr.

'Not good, sir. Their new Commander Far East is well regarded, but he's hurting for assets. The PLA has him outnumbered a good eight to one, probably more. So, the Russians don't have much in the way of deep-strike capabilities, and just defending themselves against air attack is going to be a stretch.'

'That's a fact,' agreed the general commanding the Air Force assets in the Pacific Theater. 'Ivan's pissed away a lot of his available assets dealing with the Chechens. Most of their aircraft are grounded with maintenance problems. That means his drivers aren't getting the stick time they need to be proficient airmen. The Chinese, on the other hand, have been training pretty well for several years. I'd say their air force component is in pretty good shape.'

'What can we move west with?'

'A lot,' the USAF four-star answered. 'But will it be enough? Depends on a lot of variables. It'll be nice to have your carriers around to back us up.' Which was unusually gracious of the United States Air Force.

'Okay,' Mancuso said next. 'I want to see some

271

options. Mike, let's firm up our intelligence estimates on what the Chinese are capable of, first of all, and second, what they're thinking.'

'The Agency is altering the tasking of its satellites. We ought to be getting a lot of overheads soon, plus our friends on Taiwan—they keep a pretty good eye on things for us.'

'Are they in on this SNIE?' Seventh Fleet asked.

Lahr shook his head. 'No, not yet. This stuff is being held pretty close.'

'Might want to tell Washington that they have a better feel for Beijing's internal politics than we do,' the senior Marine observed. 'They ought to. They speak the same language. Same thought processes and stuff. Taiwan ought to be a prime asset to us.'

'Maybe, maybe not,' Lahr countered. 'If a shooting war starts, they won't jump in for the fun of it. Sure, they're our friends, but they don't really have a dog in this fight yet, and the smart play for them is to play it cautious. They'll go to a high alert status, but they will not commence offensive operations on their own hook.'

'Will we really back the Russians if it comes to that? More to the point, will the Chinese regard that as a credible option on our part?' COMAIRPAC asked. He administratively 'owned' the carriers and naval air wings. Getting them trained was his job.

'Reading their minds is CIA's job, not ours,' Lahr answered. 'As far as I know, DIA has no high-quality sources in Beijing, except what we get from intercepts out of Fort Meade. If you're asking me for a personal opinion, well, we have to remember that their political assessments are made by Maoist politicians who tend to see things their own way rather than with what we would term an objective outlook. Short version, I don't know, and I don't know anyone who does, but the asset that got us this information tells us that they're serious about this possible move. Serious enough to bring Russia into NATO. You could call that rather a desperate move towards deterring the PRC, Admiral.'

'So, we regard war as a highly possible eventuality?' Mancuso summarized.

'Yes, sir,' Lahr agreed.

'Okay, gentlemen. Then we treat it that way. I want plans and options for giving our Chinese brethren a bellyache. Rough outlines after lunch tomorrow, and firm options in forty-eight hours. Questions?' There were none. 'Okay, let's get to work on this.'

*　　　*　　　*

Al Gregory was working late. A computer-software expert,. he was accustomed to working odd hours, and this was no exception. At the moment he was aboard USS *Gettysburg*, an Aegis-class cruiser. The ship was not in the water, but rather in dry dock, sitting on a collection of wooden blocks while undergoing propeller replacement. *Gettysburg* had tangled with a buoy that had parted its mooring chain and drifted into the fairway, rather to the detriment of the cruiser's port screw. The yard was taking its time to do the replacement because the ship's engines were about due for programmed maintenance anyway. This was good for the crew. Portsmouth Naval Shipyard, part of the Norfolk Naval Base complex, wasn't exactly a garden spot, but it was where most of the crew's families lived, and that made it attractive enough.

Gregory was in the ship's CIC, or Combat Information Center, the compartment from which the captain 'fought' the ship. All the weapons systems were controlled from this large space. The SPY radar display was found on three side-by-side displays about the size of a good big-screen TV The problem was the computers that drove the systems.

'You know,' Gregory observed to the senior chief who maintained the systems, 'an old iMac has a ton more power than this.'

'Doc, this system is the flower of 1975 technology,' the senior chief protested. 'And it ain't all that hard to track a missile, is it?'

'Besides, Dr. Gregory,' another chief put it, 'that radar of mine is still the best fucking system ever put to sea.'

'That's a fact,' Gregory had to agree. The solid-state components could combine to blast six *megawatts* of RF power down a one-degree line of bearing, enough to make a helicopter pilot, for example, produce what cruel physicians called FLKs: funny-looking kids. And more than enough to track a ballistic reentry vehicle at a thousand miles or more. The limitation there also was computer software, which was the new gold standard in just about every weapons system in the world.

'So, when you want to track an RV, what do you do?'

'We call it "inserting the chip",' the senior chief answered.

'What? It's hardware?' Al asked. He had trouble believing that. This wasn't a computer that you slid

274

a board into.

'No, sir, it's software. We upload a different control program.'

'Why do you need a second program for that? Can't your regular one track airplanes and missiles?' the TRW vice president demanded.

'Sir, I just maintain and operate the bitch. I don't design the things. RCA and IBM do that.'

'Shit,' Gregory observed.

'You could talk to Lieutenant Olson,' the other chief thought aloud. 'He's a Dartmouth boy. Pretty smart for a j.g.'

'Yeah,' the first chief agreed. 'He writes software as sort of a hobby.'

'Dennis the Menace. Weps and the XO get annoyed with him sometimes.

'Why?' Gregory asked.

'Because he talks like you, sir,' Senior Chief Leek answered. 'But he ain't in your pay grade.'

'He's a good kid, though,' Senior Chief Matson observed. 'Takes good care of his troops, and he knows his stuff, doesn't he, Tim?'

'Yeah, George, good kid, going places if he stays in.'

'He won't. Computer companies are already trying to recruit him. Shit, Compaq offered him three hundred big ones last week.'

'That's a living wage,' Chief Leek commented. 'What did Dennis say.

'He said no. I told him to hold out for half a mil.' Matson laughed as he reached for some coffee.

'What d'ya think, Dr. Gregory? The kid worth that kinda money in the 'puter business?'

'If he can do really good code, maybe,' Al replied, making a mental note to check out this

275

Lieutenant Olson himself. TRW always had room for talent. Dartmouth was known for its computer science department. Add field experience to that, and you had a real candidate for the ongoing SAM project. 'Okay, if you insert the chip, what happens?'

'Then you change the range of the radar. You know how it works, the RF energy goes out forever on its own, but we only accept signals that bounce back within a specific time gate. This'—Senior Chief Leek held up a floppy disk with a hand-printed label on it—'changes the gate. It extends the effective rage of the SPY out to, oh, two thousand kilometers. Damned sight farther than the missiles'll go. I was on *Port Royal* out at Kwajalein five years ago doing a theater-missile test, and we were tracking the inbound from the time it popped over the horizon all the way in.'

'You hit it?' Gregory asked with immediate interest.

Leek shook his head. 'Guidance-fin failure on the bird, it was an early Block-IV We got within fifty meters, but that was a cunt hair outside the warhead's kill perimeter, and they only allowed us one shot, for some reason or other nobody ever told me about. *Shiloh* got a kill the next year. Splattered it with a skin-skin kill. The video of that one is a son of a bitch,' the senior chief assured his guest.

Gregory believed it. When an object going one way at fourteen thousand miles per hour got hit by something going the other way at two thousand miles per hour, the result could be quite impressive. 'First-round hit?' he asked.

'You bet. The sucker was coming straight at us,

and this baby doesn't miss much.'

'We always clean up with Vandal tests off Wallops Island,' Chief Matson confirmed.

'What are those exactly?'

'Old Talos SAMs,' Matson explained. 'Big stovepipes, ramjet engines, they can come in on a ballistic track at about twenty-two hundred miles per hour. Pretty hot on the deck, too. That's what we worry about. The Russians came out with a sea-skimmer we call Sunburn—'

'Aegis-killer, some folks call it,' Chief Leek added. 'Low and fast.'

'But we ain't missed one yet,' Matson announced. 'The Aegis system's pretty good. So, Dr. Gregory, what exactly are you checking out?'

'I want to see if your system can be used to stop a ballistic inbound.'

'How fast?' Matson asked.

'A for-real ICBM. When you detect it on radar, it'll be doing about seventeen thousand miles per hour, call it seventy-six hundred meters per second.'

'That's real fast,' Leek observed. 'Seven, eight times the speed of a rifle bullet.'

'Faster'n a theater ballistic weapon like a Scud. Not sure we can do it,' Matson worried.

'This radar system'll track it just fine. It's very similar to the Cobra Dane system in the Aleutians. Question is, can your SAMs react fast enough to get a hit?'

'How hard's the target?' Matson asked.

'Softer than an aircraft. The RV's designed to withstand heat, not an impact. Like the space shuttle. When you fly it through a rainstorm, it plays hell with the tiles.'

277

'Oh, yeah?'

'Yep.' Gregory nodded. 'Like Styrofoam coffee cups.'

'Okay, so then the problem's getting the SM2 close enough to have the warhead pop off when the target's in the fragmentation cone.'

'Correct.' They might be enlisted men, Gregory thought, but that didn't make them dumb.

'Software fix in the seeker head, right?'

'Also correct. I've rewritten the code. Pretty easy job, really. I reprogrammed the way the laser mutates. Ought to work okay if the infrared homing system works as advertised. At least it did in the computer simulations up in Washington.'

'It worked just fine on *Shiloh*, Doc. We got the videotape aboard somewhere,' Leek assured him. 'Wanna see it?'

'You bet,' Dr. Gregory said with enthusiasm.

'Okay.' Senior Chief Leek checked his watch. 'I'm free now. Let me head aft for a smoke, and then we'll *roll the videotape*,' he said, sounding like Warner Wolf on WCBS New York.

'You can't smoke in here?'

Leek grunted annoyance. 'It's the New Navy, Doc. The cap'n's a health Nazi. You gotta go aft to light up. Not even in chief's quarters,' Leek groused.

'I quit,' Matson said. 'Not a pussy like Tim here.'

'My ass,' Leek responded. 'There's a few real men left aboard.'

'How come you sit sideways here?' Gregory asked, rising to his feet to follow them aft. 'The important displays go to the right side of the ship instead of fore and aft. How come?'

' 'Cuz it helps you puke if you're in a seaway.'

278

Matson laughed. 'Whoever designed these ships didn't like sailors much, but at least the air-conditioning works.' It rarely got above sixty degrees in the CIC, causing most of the men who worked there to wear sweaters. Aegis cruisers were decidedly not known for their comforts.

*   *   *

'This is serious?' Colonel Allyev asked. It was a stupid question, and he knew it. But it just had to come out anyway, and his commander knew that.

'We have orders to treat it that way, Colonel,' Bondarenko replied crossly. 'What do we have to stop them?'

'The 265th Motor-Rifle Division is at roughly fifty percent combat efficiency,' the theater operations officer replied. 'Beyond that, two tank regiments at forty percent or so. Our reserve formations are mostly theoretical,' Aliyev concluded. 'Our air assets—one regiment of fighter-interceptors ready for operations, another three who don't have even half their aircraft fit to fly.'

Bondarenko nodded at the news. It was better than it had been upon his arrival in theater, and he'd done well to bring things that far, but that wouldn't impress the Chinese very much.

'Opposition?' he asked next. Far East's intelligence officer was another colonel, Vladimir Konstantinovich Tolkunov.

'Our Chinese neighbors are in good military shape, Comrade General. The nearest enemy formation is Thirty-fourth Shock Army, a Type A Group Army commanded by General Peng Xi-

279

Wang,' he began, showing off what he knew. 'That one formation has triple or more our mechanized assets, and is well trained. Chinese aircraft—well, their tactical aircraft number over two thousand, and we must assume they will commit everything to this operation. Comrades, we do not have anything like the assets we need to stop them.'

'So, we will use space to our advantage,' the general proposed. 'Of that we have much. We will fight a holding action and await reinforcements from the west. I'll be talking with Stavka later today. Let's draw up what we'll need to stop these barbarians.'

'All down one line of railroad,' Aliyev observed. 'And our fucking engineers have been busily clearing a route for the Chinks to take to the oil fields. General, first of all, we need to get our engineers working on minefields. We have millions of mines, and the route the Chinese will take is easily predicted.'

The overall problem was that the Chinese had strategic, if not tactical, surprise. The former was a political exercise, and like Hitler in 1941, the Chinese had pulled it off. At least Bondarenko would have tactical warning, which was more than Stalin had allowed his Red Army. He also expected to have freedom of maneuver, because also unlike Stalin, his President Grushavoy would be thinking with his brain instead of his balls. With freedom of maneuver Bondarenko would have the room to play a mobile war with his enemy, denying the Chinese a chance at decisive engagement, allowing hard contact only when it served his advantage. Then he'd be able to wait for reinforcements to give him a chance to fight a set-piece battle on his own terms, at a place and time of his choosing.

'How good are the Chinese, really, Pavel?'

'The People's Liberation Army has not engaged in large-scale combat operations for over fifty years, since the Korean War with the Americans, unless you cite the border clashes we had with them in the late '60s and early '70s. In that case, the Red Army dealt with them well, but to do that we had massive firepower, and the Chinese were only fighting for limited objectives. They are trained largely on our old model. Their soldiers will not have the ability to think for themselves. Their discipline is worse than draconian. The smallest infraction can result in summary execution, and that makes for obedience. At the operational level, their general officers are well-trained in theoretical terms. Qualitatively, their weapons are roughly the equal of ours. With their greater funding, their training levels mean that their soldiers are intimately familiar with their weapons and rudimentary tactics,' Zhdanov told the assembled staff. 'But they are probably not our equal in operational-maneuver thinking. Unfortunately, they do have numbers going for them, and quantity has a quality all its own, as the NATO armies used to say of us. What they will want to do, and what I fear they will, is try to roll over us quickly—just crush us and move on to their political and economic objectives as quickly as possible.'

Bondarenko nodded as he sipped his tea. This was mad, and the maddest part of all was that he was playing the role of a NATO commander from 1975—maybe a German one, which was truly insane—faced with adverse numbers, but blessed, as the Germans had not been, with space to play

281

with, and Russians had always used space to their advantage. He leaned forward:

'Very well. Comrades, we will *deny* them the opportunity for decisive engagement. If they cross the border, we will fight a maneuver war. We will sting and move. We will hurt them and withdraw before they can counterattack. We will give them land, but we will *not* give them blood. The life of every single one of our soldiers is precious to us. The Chinese have a long way to go to their objectives. We will let them go a lot of that way, and we will bide our time and husband our men and equipment. We will make them pay for what they take, but we will not—we must not—give them the chance to catch our forces in decisive battle. Are we understood on that?' he asked his staff. 'When in doubt, we will run away and deny the enemy what he wants. When we have what we need to strike back, we will make him wish he never heard of Russia, but until then, let him chase his butterflies.'

'What of the border guards?' Aliyev asked.

'They will hurt the Chinese, and then they will pull out. Comrades, I cannot emphasize this enough: the life of every single private soldier is important to us. Our men will fight harder if they know we care about them, and more than that, they *deserve* our care and solicitude. If we ask them to risk their lives for their country, their country *must* be loyal to them in return. If we achieve that, they will fight like tigers. The Russian soldier knows how to fight. We must all be worthy of him. You are all skilled professionals. This will be the most important test of our lives. We must all be equal to our task. Our nation depends on us. Andrey

Petrovich, draw up some plans for me. We are authorized to call up reserves. Let us start doing that. We have hectares of equipment for them to use. Unlock the gates and let them start drawing gear, and God permit the officers assigned to those cadres are worthy of their men. Dismissed.' Bondarenko stood and walked out, hoping his declamation had been enough for the task.

But wars were not won by speeches.

CHAPTER FORTY-FIVE

GHOSTS OF HORRORS PAST

President Grushavoy arrived in Warsaw with the usual pomp and circumstance. A good actor, Ryan saw, watching the arrival on TV. You never would have guessed from his face that his country was looking at a major war. Grushavoy passed the same receiving line, doubtless composed of the same troops Ryan had eyeballed on his arrival, made a brief but flowery arrival speech citing the long and friendly history shared by Poland and Russia (conveniently leaving out the equally long and less-than-friendly parts), then got into a car for the city, accompanied, Ryan was glad to see, by Sergey Nikolay'ch Golovko.

In the President's hand was a fax from Washington outlining what the Chinese had in the way of war assets to turn loose on their northern neighbors, along with an estimate from the Defense Intelligence Agency on what they called the 'correlation of forces,' which, Jack remembered, was a term of art used by the Soviet army of old. Its estimate of the situation was not especially favorable. Almost as bad, America didn't have much with which to help the Russians. The world's foremost navy was of little direct use in a land war. The United States Army had a division and a half of heavy troops in Europe, but that was thousands of miles from the expected scene of action. The Air Force had all the mobility it needed to project force anywhere on the globe, and that could give anyone a serious headache, but airplanes could not by themselves defeat an army. No, this would be largely a Russian show, and the Russian army, the fax said, was in terrible shape. The DIA had some good things to say about the senior Russian commander in theater, but a smart guy with a .22 against a dumb one with a machine gun was still at a disadvantage. So, he hoped the Chinese would be taken aback by this day's news, but CIA and State's estimate of that possibility was decidedly iffy.

'Scott?' Ryan asked his Secretary of State.

'Jack, I can't say. This ought to discourage them, but we can't be sure how tight a corner they think they are in. If they think they're trapped, they might still lash out.'

'God damn it, Scott, is this the way nations do business?' Jack demanded. 'Misperceptions? Fears? Outright stupidity?'

Adler shrugged. 'It's a mistake to think a chief of government is any smarter than the rest of us, Jack. People make decisions the same way, regardless of how big and smart they are. It comes down to how they perceive the question, and how best they can serve their own needs, preserve their own personal

284

well-being. Remember that we're not dealing with clergymen here. They don't have much in the way of consciences. Our notion of right and wrong doesn't play in that sort of mind. They translate what's good for their country into what's good for themselves, just like a king in the twelfth century, but in this case there isn't any bishop around to remind them that there may be a God looking down at them with a notebook.' They'd gone out of their way, Adler didn't have to say, to eliminate a cardinal-archbishop just to get themselves into this mess.

'Sociopaths?' the President asked.

Secretary Adler shrugged. 'I'm not a physician, just a diplomat. When you negotiate with people like this, you dangle what's good for their country—them—in front of their eyes and hope they reach for it. You play the game without entirely understanding them. These people do things neither one of us would ever do. And they run a major country, complete with nuclear weapons.'

'Great,' Ryan breathed. He stood and got his coat. 'Well, let's go watch our new ally sign up, shall we?'

Ten minutes later, they were in the reception room of the Lazienski Palace. There was the usual off-camera time for the various chiefs of government to socialize over Perrier-and-a-twist before some nameless protocol official opened the double doors to the table, chairs, documents, and TV cameras.

The speech from President Grushavoy was predictable in every detail. The NATO alliance had been established to protect Western Europe

285

against what his country had once been, and his former country had established its own mirror-image alliance called the Warsaw Pact right here in this very city. But the world had turned, and now Russia was pleased to join the rest of Europe in an alliance of friends whose only wish was peace and prosperity for all. Grushavoy was pleased indeed to be the first Russian in a very long time to be a real part of the European community, and promised to be a worthy friend and partner of his newly close neighbors. (The military ramifications of the North Atlantic Treaty were not mentioned at all.) And everyone present applauded. And Grushavoy pulled out an ancient fountain pen borrowed from the collection at The Hermitage in St. Petersburg to sign in the name of his country, and so bring membership in NATO up by one. And everyone applauded again as the various chiefs of state and government walked over to shake their new ally's hand. And the shape of the world changed yet again.

'Ivan Emmetovich,' Golovko said, as he approached the American President.

'Sergey Nikolay'ch,' Ryan said in quiet reply.

'What will Beijing think of this?' the chief of the Russian intelligence service asked.

'With luck, we'll know in twenty-four hours,' Ryan answered, knowing that this ceremony had gone out on CNN's live global feed, and positive that it was being watched in China.

'I expect the language will be profane.'

'They've said nasty things about me lately,' Jack assured him.

'That you should have carnal relations with your mother, no doubt.'

286

'Actually, that I should have oral sex with her,' the President confirmed distastefully. 'I suppose everybody says things like that in private.'

'In person, it can get a man shot.'

Ryan grunted grim semi-amusement. 'Bet your ass, Sergey.'

'Will this work?' Golovko asked.

'I was going to ask you that. You're closer to them than we are.'

'I do not know,' the Russian said, with a tiny sip of his vodka glass. 'And if it does not . . .'

'In that case, you have some new allies.'

'And what of the precise wording of Articles Five and Six of the treaty?'

'Sergey, you may tell your President that the United States will regard an attack on any part of the territory of the Russian Federation as operative under the North Atlantic Treaty. On that, Sergey Nikolay'ch, you have the word and the commitment of the United States of America,' SWORDSMAN told his Russian acquaintance.

'Jack, if I may address you in this way, I have told my President more than once that you are a man of honor, and a man of your word.' The relief on his face was obvious.

'Sergey, from you those words are flattering. It's simple, really. It's your land, and a nation like ours cannot just stand by and watch a robbery of this scale taking place. It corrupts the foundations of international peace. It's our job to remake the world into a peaceful place. There's been enough war.'

'I fear there will be another,' Golovko said, with characteristic honesty.

'Then together your country and mine will make

it the very last.'

'Plato said, "Only the dead have seen the end of war."'

'So, are we to be bound by the words of a Greek who lived twenty-five centuries ago? I prefer the words of a Jew who lived five centuries later. It's time, Sergey. It's fucking time,' Ryan said forcefully.

'I hope you are right. You Americans, always so madly optimistic . . .'

'There's a reason for that.'

'Oh? What would that be?' the Russian asked.

Jack fixed his eyes on his Russian colleague. 'In my country, all things *are* possible. They will be in your country, too, if you just allow it. Embrace democracy, Sergey. Embrace freedom. Americans are not genetically different from the rest of the world. We're mongrels. We have the blood of every country on earth in our veins. The only thing different between us and the rest of the world is our Constitution. Just a set of rules. That's all, Sergey, but it has served us well. You've been studying us for how long?'

'Since I joined KGB? Over thirty-five years.'

'And what have you learned of America and how it works?' Ryan asked.

'Obviously not enough,' Golovko answered honestly. 'The spirit of your country has always puzzled me.'

'Because it's too simple. You were looking for complexity. We allow people to pursue their dreams, and when the dreams succeed, we reward them. Others see that happen and chase after their own dreams.'

'But the class issues?'

'What class issues? Sergey, not everybody goes to Harvard. I didn't, remember? My father was a cop. I was the first guy in my family to finish college. Look how I turned out. Sergey, we do not have class distinctions in America. You can be what you choose to be, if you are willing to work at it. You can succeed or you can fail. Luck helps,' Ryan admitted, 'but it comes down to work.'

'All Americans have stars in their eyes,' the Chairman of the SVR observed tersely.

'The better to see the heavens,' Ryan responded.

'Perhaps. Just so they don't come crashing down on us.'

*　　　*　　　*

'So, what does this mean for us?' Xu Kun Piao asked, in an entirely neutral voice.

Zhang Han San and his premiere had been watching the CNN feed in the latter's private office, complete with simultaneous translation through headphones now discarded. The senior Minister Without Portfolio made a dismissive wave of the hand.

'I've read the North Atlantic Treaty,' he said. 'It does not apply to us at all. Articles Five and Six limit its military application to events in Europe and North America only—all right, it includes Turkey, and, as originally written, Algeria, which was part of France in 1949. For incidents at sea, it applies only to the Atlantic Ocean and the Mediterranean Sea, and then only north of the Tropic of Cancer. Otherwise, the NATO countries would have been compelled to join in the Korean War and Vietnam on the American side. Those

289

things did not happen because the treaty did not apply outside its defined area. Nor does it apply to us. Treaty documents have discrete language and discrete application,' he reminded his party chief. 'They are not open-ended.'

'I am concerned even so,' Xu responded.

'Hostilities are not activities to be undertaken lightly,' Zhang admitted. 'But the real danger to us is economic collapse and the resulting social chaos. *That*, comrade, could bring down our entire social order, and *that* is something we cannot risk. But, when we succeed in seizing the oil and gold, we need not worry about such things. With our own abundant oil supply, we will not face an energy crisis, and with gold we can buy anything we require from the rest of the world. My friend, you must understand the West. They worship money, and they base their economies on oil. With those two things they must do business with us. Why did America intervene in the Kuwait affair? Oil. Why did Britain, France, and all the other nations join in? Oil. He who has oil is their friend. We shall have oil. It is that simple,' Zhang concluded.

'You are very confident.'

The minister nodded. 'Yes, Xu, I am, because I have studied the West for many years. The way they think is actually very predictable. The purpose of this treaty might be to frighten us, I suppose, but it is at most a paper tiger. Even if they wished to provide military assistance to Russia, they do not have the ability to do so. And I do not believe that they have that wish. They cannot know our plans, because if they did, they would have pressed their advantage over us in terms of currency reserves at the trade talks, but they did not, did they?' Zhang

asked.

'Is there no way they could know?'

'It is most unlikely. Comrade Tan has no hint of foreign espionage in our country at anything approaching a high level, and his sources in Washington and elsewhere have not caught a sniff of such information being available to them.'

'Then why did they just broaden NATO?' Xu demanded.

'Is it not obvious? Russia is becoming rich with oil and gold, and the capitalist states wish to partake in the Russians' good fortune. That is what they said in the press, isn't it? It is fully in keeping with the capitalist ethos: mutual greed. Who can say, perhaps in five years they will invite us into NATO for the same reason,' Zhang observed with an ironic leer.

'You are confident that our plans have not been compromised?'

'As we come to a higher alert level and begin moving troops, we may expect some reaction from the Russians. But the rest of them? Bah! Tan and Marshal Luo are confident as well.'

'Very well,' Xu said, not entirely persuaded, but agreeing even so.

*   *   *

It was morning in Washington. Vice President Jackson was de facto boss of the crisis-management team, a place assured by his previous job, Director of Operations—J-3—for the Joint Chiefs of Staff. One nice thing about the White House was the good security, made better still by bringing people in via helicopter and car, and by the fact that the

Joint Chiefs could teleconference in from their meeting room—'the Tank'—over a secure fiber-optic link.

'Well?' Jackson asked, looking at the large television on the wall of the Situation Room.

'Mancuso has his people at work in Hawaii. The Navy can give the Chinese a bad time, and the Air Force can move a lot of assets to Russia if need be,' said Army General Mickey Moore, Chairman of the Joint Chiefs. 'It's the land side of the equation that has me worried. We could theoretically move one heavy division—First Armored—from Germany east, along with some attachments, and maybe NATO will join in with some additional stuff, but the Russian army is in miserable shape at the moment, especially in the Far East, and there's also the additional problem that China has twelve CSS-4 intercontinental ballistic missiles. We figure eight or more of them are aimed at us.'

'Tell me more,' TOMCAT ordered.

'They're Titan-II clones. Hell,' Moore went on, 'I just found out the background earlier today. They were designed by a CalTech-educated Air Force colonel of Chinese ethnicity who defected over there in the 1950s. Some bonehead trumped up some security charges against him—turned out they were all bullshit, would you believe—and he bugged out with a few suitcases' worth of technical information right out of JPL, where he was working at the time. So, the ChiComms built what were virtually copies of the old Martin-Marietta missile, and, like I said, we figure eight of them are aimed back at us.'

'Warheads?'

'Five-megaton is our best guess. City-busters.

292

The birds are bitches to maintain, just like ours were. We figure they're kept defueled most of the time, and they probably need two to four hours to bring them up to launch readiness. That's the good news. The bad news is that they upgraded the protection on the silos over the last decade, probably as a result of what we did in the Iraq bombing campaign and also the B-2 strikes into Japan on their SS-19 clones. The current estimate is that the covers are fifteen feet of rebarred concrete plus three feet of armor-class steel. We don't have a conventional bomb that'll penetrate that.'

'Why not?' Jackson demanded in considerable surprise.

'Because the GBU-29 we cobbled together to take out that deep bunker in Baghdad was designed to hang on the F-111. It's the wrong dimensions for the B-2's bomb bay, and the 111s are all at the boneyard in Arizona. So, we have the bombs, okay, but nothing to deliver them with. Best option to take those silos out would be air-launched cruise missiles with W-80 warheads, assuming the President will authorize a nuclear strike on them.'

'What warning will we have that the Chinese have prepared the missiles for launch?'

'Not much,' Moore admitted. 'The new silo configuration pretty well prevents that. The silo covers are massive beasts. We figure they plan to blow them off with explosives, like we used to do.'

'Do we have nuke-tipped cruise missiles?'

'No, the President has to authorize that. The birds and the warheads are co-located at Whiteman Air Force Base along with the B-2s. It would take a day or so to mate them up. I'd recommend that the President authorize that if this Chinese situation goes any farther,' Moore concluded.

And the best way to deliver nuclear-tipped cruise missiles—off Navy submarines or carrier-based strike aircraft—was impossible because the Navy had been completely stripped of its nuclear weapons inventory, and fixing that would not be especially easy, Jackson knew. The fallout of the nuclear explosion in Denver, which had brought the world to the brink of a full-scale nuclear exchange, had caused Russia and America to take a deep breath and then to eliminate all of their ballistic launchers. Both sides still had nuclear weapons, of course. For America they were mostly B-61 and -83 gravity bombs and W-80 thermonuclear warheads that could be affixed to cruise missiles. Both systems could be delivered with a high degree of confidence and accuracy, and stealth. The B-2A bomber was invisible to radar (and hard enough to spot visually unless you were right next to it) and the cruise missiles smoked in so low that they merged not merely with ground clutter but with highway traffic as well. But they lacked the speed of ballistic weapons. That was the trouble with the fearsome weapons, but that was also their advantage. Twenty-five minutes from turning the 'enable-launch' key to impact—even less for the sea-launched sort, which usually flew shorter distances. But those were all gone, except for the ones kept for ABM tests, and those had been modified to make them difficult to fit with warheads.

'Well, we just try to keep this one conventional. How many nuclear weapons could we deliver if we had to?'

'First strike, with the B-2s?' Moore asked. 'Oh, eighty or so. If you figure two per target, enough to turn every major city in the PRC into a parking lot. It would kill upwards of a hundred million people,' the Chairman added. He didn't have to say that he had no particular desire to do that. Even the most bloodthirsty soldiers were repelled by the idea of killing civilians in such numbers, and those who made four-star rank got there by being thoughtful, not psychotic.

'Well, if we let them know that, they ought to think hard about pissing us off that big,' Jackson decided.

'They ought to be *that* rational, I suppose,' Mickey Moore agreed. 'Who wants to be the ruler of a parking lot?' But the problem with that, he didn't add, was that people who started wars of aggression were never completely rational.

*   *   *

How do we go about calling up reserves?' Bondarenko asked.

Theoretically, almost every Russian male citizen was liable to such a call-up, because most of them had served in their country's military at one time or another. It was a tradition that dated back to the czars, when the Russian army had been likened to a steamroller because of its enormous mass.

The practical problem today, however, was that the state didn't know where they all lived. The state required that the veterans of uniformed service tell the army when they moved from one residence to another, but the men in question, since until recently they'd needed the state's permission to move anywhere, assumed that the state knew where they were and rarely bothered, and the country's vast and cumbersome bureaucracy was too elephantine to follow up on such things. As a result, neither Russia, nor the Soviet Union before it, had done much to test its ability to call up trained soldiers who'd left their uniforms behind. There were whole reserve divisions that had the most modern of equipment, but it had never been moved after being rolled into their warehouses, and was attended only by cadres of active-duty mechanics who actually spent the time to maintain it, turning over the engines in accordance with written schedules which they followed as mindlessly as the orders that had been drafted and printed. And so, the general commanding the Far East Military Theater had access to thousands of tanks and guns for which he had no soldiers, along with mountains of shells and virtual lakes of diesel fuel.

The word 'camouflage', meaning a trick to be played or a ruse, is French in origin. It really ought to be Russian, however, because Russians were the world's experts at this military art. The storage sites for the real tanks that formed the backbone of Bondarenko's theoretical army were so skillfully hidden that only his own staff knew where they were. A good fraction of the sites had even evaded American spy satellites that had searched for years for the locations. Even the roads leading to the storage sites were painted with deceptive colors, or planted with false conifer trees. This was all one more lesson of World War II, when the Soviet Army had totally befuddled the Germans so often that one wondered why the Wehrmacht even bothered employing intelligence officers, they had been snookered so frequently.

'We're getting orders out now,' Colonel Aliyev replied. 'With luck, half of them ought to find people who've worn the uniform. We could do better if we made a public announcement.'

'No,' Bondarenko replied. 'We can't let them know we're getting ready. What about the officer corps?'

'For the reserve formations? Well, we have an ample supply of lieutenants and captains, just no privates or NCOs for them to command. I suppose if we need to we can field a complete regiment or so of junior officers driving tanks,' Aliyev observed dryly.

'Well, such a regiment ought to be fairly proficient,' the general observed with what passed for light humor. 'How fast to make the callup happen?'

'The letters are already addressed and stamped. They should all be delivered in three days.'

'Mail them at once. See to it yourself, Andrey' Bondarenko ordered.

'By your command, Comrade General.' Then he paused. 'What do you make of this NATO business?'

'If it brings us help, then I am for it. I'd love to have American aircraft at my command. I remember what they did to Iraq. There are a lot of bridges I'd like to see dropped into the rivers they span.'

'And their land forces?'

'Do not underestimate them. I've seen how they train, and I've driven some of their equipment. It's excellent, and their men know how to make use of it. One company of American tanks, competently led and supported, can hold off a whole regiment. Remember what they did to the army of the United Islamic Republic. Two active-duty regiments and a brigade of territorials crushed two heavy corps as if it were a sand-table exercise. That's why I want to upgrade our training. Our men are as good as theirs, Andrey Petrovich, but their training is the best I have ever seen. Couple that to their equipment, and there you have their advantage.'

'And their commanders?'

'Good, but no better than ours. Shit, they copy our doctrine time and again. I've challenged them on this face-to-face, and they freely admit that they admire our operational thinking. But they make better use of our doctrine than we do—because they train their men better.'

'And they train better because they have more money to spend.'

'There you have it. They don't have tank commanders painting rocks around the motor pool, as we do,' Bondarenko noted sourly. He'd just begun to change that, but just-begun was a long way from mission-accomplished. 'Get the call-up letters out, and remember, we must keep this quiet. Go. I have to talk to Moscow.'

'Yes, Comrade General.' The G-3 made his departure.

*   *   *

'Well, ain't that something?' Major General Diggs commented after watching the TV show.

'Makes you wonder what NATO is for,' Colonel Masterman agreed.

'Duke, I grew up expecting to see T-72 tanks rolling through the Fulda Gap like cockroaches on a Bronx apartment floor. Hell, now they're our friends?' He had to shake his head in disbelief. 'I've met a few of their senior people, like that Bondarenko guy running the Far East Theater. He's pretty smart, serious professional. Visited me at Fort Irwin. Caught on real fast, really hit it off with Al Hamm and the Blackhorse. Our kind of soldier.'

'Well, sir, I guess he really is now, eh?'

That's when the phone rang. Diggs lifted it. 'General Diggs. Okay, put him through . . . Morning, sir . . . Just fine, thanks, and—yes? What's that? . . . This is serious, I presume . . . Yes, sir. Yes, sir, we're ready as hell. Very well, sir. Bye.' He set the phone back down. 'Duke, good thing you're sitting down.'

'What gives?'

'That was SACEUR. We got alert orders to be ready to entrain and move east.'

'East where?' the divisional operations officer asked, surprised. An unscheduled exercise in Eastern Germany, maybe?

'Maybe as far as Russia, the eastern part. Siberia, maybe,' Diggs added in a voice that didn't entirely believe what it said.

'What the hell?'

'NCA is concerned about a possible dust-up between the Russians and the Chinese. If it happens, we may have to go east to support Ivan.'

'What the hell?' Masterman observed yet again.

'He's sending his J-2 down to brief us in on what he's got from Washington. Ought to be here in half an hour.'

'Who else? Is this a NATO tasking?'

'He didn't say. Guess we'll have to wait and see. For the moment just you and the staff, the ADC, and the brigade sixes are in on the brief.'

'Yes, sir,' Masterman said, there being little else he could say.

*　　　*　　　*

The Air Force sends a number of aircraft when the President travels. Among these were C-5B Galaxies. Known to the Navy as 'the aluminum cloud' for its huge bulk, the transport is capable of carrying whole tanks in its cavernous interior. In this case, however, they carried VH-60 helicopters, larger than a tank in dimensions, but far lighter in weight.

The VH-60 is a version of the Sikorsky Blackhawk troop-carrier, somewhat cleaned up and appointed for VIP passengers. The pilot was Colonel Dan Malloy, a Marine with over five thousand hours of stick time in rotary-ring aircraft, whose radio call-sign was 'Bear'. Cathy Ryan knew him well. He usually flew her to Johns Hopkins in the morning in a twin to this aircraft. There was a co-pilot, a lieutenant who looked impossibly young to be a professional aviator, and a crew chief, a Marine staff sergeant E-6 who saw to it that everyone was properly strapped in, something that Cathy did better than Jack, who was not used to the different restraints in this aircraft.

Aside from that the Blackhawk flew superbly, not at all like the earthquake-while-sitting-on-a-chandelier sensation usually associated with such contrivances. The flight took almost an hour, with the President listening in on the headset/ear protectors. Overhead, all aerial traffic was closed down, even commercial flights in and out of every commercial airport to which they came close. The Polish government was concerned with his safety.

'There it is,' Malloy said over the intercom. 'Eleven o'clock.'

The aircraft banked left to give everyone a good look out the polycarbonate windows. Ryan felt a sudden sense of enforced sobriety come over him. There was a rudimentary railroad station building with two tracks, and another spur that ran off through the arch in yet another building. There were a few other structures, but mainly just concrete pads to show where there had been a large number of others, and Ryan's mind could see them from the black-and-white movies shot from aircraft, probably Russian ones, in World War II. They'd been oddly warehouse-like buildings, he remembered. But the wares stored in them had been human beings, though the people who'd built this place hadn't seen it that way; they had regarded them as vermin, insects or rats, something to be eliminated as efficiently and coldly as possible.

That's when the chill hit. It was not a warm morning, the temperature in the upper fifties or so, Jack thought, but his skin felt colder than that number indicated. The chopper landed softly, and the sergeant got the door open and the President stepped out onto the landing pad that had recently been laid for just this purpose. An official of the Polish government came up and shook his hand, introducing himself, but Ryan missed it all, suddenly a tourist in Hell itself, or so it felt. The official who would be serving as guide led them to a car for the short drive closer to the facility. Jack slid in beside his wife.

'Jack . . .' she whispered.

'Yeah,' he acknowledged. 'Yeah, babe, I know.' And he spoke not another word, not even hearing the well-prepared commentary the Pole was giving him.

'Arbeit Macht Frei' the wrought-iron arch read. *Work makes free* was the literal meaning, perhaps the most callously cynical motto ever crafted by the twisted minds of men calling themselves civilized. Finally, the car stopped, and they got out into the air again, and again the guide led them from place to place, telling them things they didn't hear but rather felt, because the very air seemed heavy with evil. The grass was wonderfully green, almost like a golf course from the spring rain . . . from the nutrients in the soil? Jack wondered. Lots of those. More than two million people had met death in this place. Two million. Maybe three. After a while, counting lost its meaning, and it became just a number, a figure on a ledger, written in by some accountant or other who'd long since stopped considering what the digits represented.

He could see it in his mind, the human shapes, the bodies, the heads, but thankfully not the faces of the dead. He presently found himself walking along what the German guards had called *Himmel Straße*, the Road to Heaven. But why had they called it that? Was it pure cynicism, or did they really believe there was a God looking down on what they did, and if so, what had they thought He thought of this place and their activity? What kind of men could they have been? Women and children had been slaughtered immediately upon arrival here because they had little value as workers in the industrial facilities that I. G. Farben had built, so as to take the last measure of utility from the people sent here to die—to make a little profit from their last months. Not just Jews, of course; the Polish aristocracy and the Polish priesthood had been killed here. Gypsies. Homosexuals. Jehovah's Witnesses. Others deemed undesirable by Hitler's government. Just insects to be eliminated with Zyklon-B gas, a derivative of pesticide research by the German chemical industries.

Ryan had not expected this to be a pleasant side-trip. What he'd anticipated was an educational experience, like visiting the battlefield at Antietam, for example.

But this hadn't been a battlefield, and it didn't feel like at all like one.

What must it have been like for the men who'd liberated this place in 1944? Jack wondered. Even hardened soldiers, men who'd faced death every day for years, must have been taken aback by what they'd found here. For all its horrors, the battlefield remained a place of honor, where men tested men in the most fundamental way—it was cruel and final, of course, but there was the purity of fighting men contesting with other fighting men, using weapons, but—but that was rubbish, Jack thought. There was little nobility to be found in war . . . and far less in this place. On a battlefield, for whatever purpose and with whatever means, men fought against *men*, not women and kids. There was some honor to be had in the former, but not . . . this. This was crime on a vast scale, and as evil as war was, at the human level it stopped short of what men called crime, the deliberate infliction of harm upon the innocent. How could men do such a thing? Germany was today, as it had been then, a Christian country, the same nation that had brought forth Martin Luther, Beethoven, and Thomas Mann. Did it all come down to their leader? Adolf Hitler, a nebbish of a man, born to a middle-grade civil servant, a failure at everything he'd tried . . . except demagoguery. He'd been a fucking genius at that . . .

. . . But why had Hitler hated anyone so much as to harness the industrial might of his nation not for conquest, which was bad enough, but for the base purpose of cold-blooded extermination? That, Jack knew, was one of history's most troublesome mysteries. Some said Hitler had hated the Jews because he'd seen one on the streets of Vienna and simply disliked him. Another expert in the field, a Jew himself, had posed the proposition that a Jewish prostitute had given the failed Austrian painter gonorrhea, but there was no documentary evidence upon which to base that. Yet another school of thought was more cynical still, saying that Hitler hadn't really cared about the Jews one way or another, but needed an enemy for people to hate so that he could become leader of Germany, and had merely seized upon the Jews as a target of opportunity, just something against which to mobilize his nation. Ryan found this alternative unlikely, but the most offensive of all. For whatever reason, he'd taken the power his country had given him and turned it to this purpose. In doing so, Hitler had cursed his name for all time to come, but that was no consolation to the people whose remains fertilized the grass. Ryan's wife's boss at

Johns Hopkins was a Jewish doc named Bernie Katz, a friend of many years. How many such men had died here? How many potential Jonas Salks? Maybe an Einstein or two? Or poets, or actors, or just ordinary workers who would have raised ordinary kids . . .

. . . and when Jack had sworn the oath of office mandated by the United States Constitution, he'd really sworn to protect such people as those, and maybe such people as these, too. As a man, as an American, and as President of the United States, did he not have a duty to prevent such things from ever happening again? He actually believed that the use of armed force could only be justified to protect American lives and vital American security interests. But was that all America was? What about the principles upon which his nation was founded? Did America only apply them to specific, limited places and goals? What about the rest of the world? Were these not the graves of real people?

John Patrick Ryan stood and looked around, his face as empty right now as his soul, trying to understand what had taken place here, and what he could—what he *had* to learn from this. He had immense power at his fingertips every day he lived in the White House. How to use it? How to apply it? What to fight against? More important, what to fight *for*?

'Jack,' Cathy said quietly, touching his hand.

'Yeah, I've seen enough, too. Let's get the hell away from this place.' He turned to the Polish guide and thanked him for words he'd scarcely heard and started walking back to where the car was. Once more they passed under the wrought-iron arch of a lie, doing what two or three million people had never done.

If there were such a thing as ghosts, they'd spoken to him without words, but done it in one voice: *Never again.* And silently, Ryan agreed. Not while he lived. Not while America lived.

CHAPTER FORTY-SIX

JOURNEY HOME

They waited for SORGE, and rarely had anyone waited more expectantly even for the arrival of a firstborn child. There was a little drama to it, too, because SORGE didn't deliver every day, and they could not always see a pattern in when it appeared and when it didn't. Ed and Mary Pat Foley both awoke early that morning, and lay in bed for over an hour with nothing to do, then finally arose to drink their breakfast coffee and read the papers in the kitchen of their middle-class home in suburban Virginia. The kids went off to school, and then the parents finished dressing and walked out to their 'company' car, complete with driver and escort vehicle. The odd part was that their car was guarded but their house was not, and so a terrorist only had to be smart enough to attack the house, which was not all that hard. The *Early Bird* was waiting for them in the car, but it had little attraction for either of them this morning. The comic strips in the *Post* had been more interesting, especially 'Non Sequitur,' their favorite morning chuckle, and the sports pages.

306

'What do you think?' Mary Pat asked Ed. That managed to surprise him, since his wife didn't often ask his opinion of a field-operations question.

He shrugged as they passed a Dunkin' Donuts box. 'Coin toss, Mary.'

'I suppose. I sure hope it comes up heads this time.'

'Jack's going to ask us in . . . an hour and a half, I suppose.'

'Something like that,' the DDO agreed in a breathy voice.

'The NATO thing ought to work, ought to make them think things over,' the DCI thought aloud.

'Don't bet the ranch on it, honey bunny,' Mary Pat warned.

'I know.' Pause. 'When does Jack get on the airplane to come home?'

She checked her watch. 'About two hours.'

'We should know by then.'

'Yeah,' she agreed.

Ten minutes later, informed of the shape of the world en route by National Public Radio's *Morning Edition*, they arrived at Langley, again parking in the underground garage, and again taking the elevator up to the seventh floor, where, again, they split up, going to their separate offices. In this, Ed surprised his wife. She'd expected him to hover over her shoulder as she flipped on her office computer, looking for another brownie recipe, as she called it. This happened at seven-fifty-four.

'You've got mail,' the electronic voice announced as she accessed her special Internet account. Her hand wasn't quite shaking when she moved the mouse to click on the proper icon, but nearly so. The letter came up, went through the

307

descrambling process, and came up as cleartext she couldn't read. As always, MP saved the document to her hard drive, confirmed that it was saved, then printed up a hard copy, and finally deleted the letter from her electronic in-box, completely erasing it off the Internet. Then she lifted her phone.

'Please have Dr. Sears come up right away,' she told her secretary.

Joshua Sears had also come in early this morning, and was sitting at his desk reading the *New York Times* financial page when the call came. He was in the elevator in under a minute, and then in the office of the Deputy Director (Operations).

'Here,' Mary Pat said, handing over the six pages of ideographs. 'Take a seat.'

Sears sat in a comfortable chair and started his translation. He could see that the DDO was a little exercised about this, and his initial diagnosis came as he turned to page two.

'This isn't good news,' he said, without looking up. 'Looks like Zhang is guiding Premier Xu in the direction he wants. Fang is uneasy about it, but he's going along, too. Marshal Luo is fully on the team. I guess that's to be expected. Luo's always been a hardball guy,' Sears commented. 'Talk here's about operational security, concern that we might know what they're up to—but they think they're secure,' Sears assured the DDO.

As many times as she'd heard that sort of thing, it never failed to give her a severe case of the chills, hearing the enemy (to Mary Pat nearly everyone was an enemy) discuss the very possibility that she'd devoted her entire professional life to realizing. And almost always you heard their voices saying that, no, there wasn't anyone like her out there hearing them. She'd never really left her post in Moscow, when she'd been control officer for Agent CARDINAL. He'd been old enough to have been her grandfather, but she'd thought of him as her own newborn, as she gave him taskings, and collected his take, forwarding it back to Langley, always worried for his safety. She was out of that game now, but it came down to the same thing. Somewhere out there was a foreign national sending America information of vital interest. She knew the person's name, but not her face, not her motivation, just that she liked to share her bed with one of her officers, and she kept the official diary for this Minister Fang, and her computer sent it out on the Web, on a path that ended at her seventh-floor desk.

'Summary?' she asked Dr. Sears.

'They're still on the warpath,' the analyst replied. 'Maybe they'll turn off it at some later date, but there is no such indication here.'

'If we warn them off . . . ?'

Sears shrugged. 'No telling. Their real concern is internal political dissension and possible collapse. This economic crisis has them worried about political ruin for them all, and that's all they're worried about.'

'Wars are begun by frightened men,' the DDO observed.

'That's what history tells us,' Sears agreed. 'And it's happening again, right before our eyes.'

'Shit,' Mrs. Foley observed. 'Okay, print it up and get it back to me, fast as you can.'

'Yes, ma'am. Half hour. You want me to show this to George Weaver, right?'

'Yeah.' She nodded. The academic had been going over the Sorge data for several days, taking his time to formulate his part of the SNIE slowly and carefully, which was the way he worked. 'You mind working with him?'

'Not really. He knows their heads pretty well, maybe a little better than I do—he has a master's in psychology from Yale. Just he's a little slow formulating his conclusions.'

'Tell him I want something I can use by the end of the day.'

'Will do,' Sears promised, rising for the door. Mary Pat followed him out, but took a different turn.

'Yeah?' Ed Foley said, when she came into his office.

'You'll have the write-up in half an hour or so. Short version: They are not impressed by the NATO play.'

'Oh, shit,' the DCI observed at once.

'Yeah,' his wife agreed. 'Better find out how quick we can get the information to Jack.'

'Okay.' The DCI lifted his secure phone and punched the speed-dial button for the White House.

*   *   *

There was one last semi-official meeting at the American Embassy before departure, and again it was Golovko speaking for his President, who was away schmoozing with the British Prime Minister.

'What did you make of Auschwitz?' the Russian asked.

'It ain't Disney World,' Jack replied, taking a sip

of coffee. 'Have you been there?'

'My uncle Sasha was part of the force that liberated the camp,' Sergey replied. 'He was a tank commander—a colonel—in the Great Motherland War.'

'Did you talk to him about it?'

'When I was a boy. Sasha—my mother's brother, he was—was a true soldier, a hard man with hard rules for life, and a committed communist. That must have shaken him, though,' Golovko went on. 'He didn't really talk about what effect it had on him. Just that it was ugly, and proof to him of the correctness of his cause. He said he had an especially good war after that—he got to kill more Germans.'

'And what about the things—'

'Stalin did? We never spoke of that in my family. My father was NKVD, as you know. He thought that whatever the state did was correct. Not unlike what the *fascisti* thought at Auschwitz, I admit, but he would not have seen it that way. Those were different times, Ivan Emmetovich. Harder times. Your father served in the war as well, as I recall.'

'Paratrooper, One-Oh-First. He never talked much about it, just the funny things that happened. He said the night drop into Normandy was pretty scary, but that's all—he never said what it was like running around in the dark with people shooting at him.'

'It cannot be very enjoyable, to be a soldier in combat.'

'I don't suppose it is. Sending people out to do it isn't fun, either. God damn it, Sergey! I'm supposed to protect people, not risk their lives.'

'So, you are not like Hitler. And not like Stalin,'

the Russian added graciously. 'And neither is Eduard Petrovich. It is a gentler world we live in, gentler than that of our fathers and our uncles. But not gentle enough yet. When will you know how our Chinese friends reacted to yesterday's events?'

'Soon, I hope, but we're not exactly sure. You know how that works.'

'*Da.*' You depended on the reports of your agents, but you were never sure when they would come in, and in the expectation came frustration. Sometimes you wanted to wring their necks, but that was both foolish and morally wrong, as they both knew.

'Any public reaction?' Ryan asked. The Russians would have seen it sooner than his own people.

'A nonreaction, Mr. President. No public comment at all. Not unexpected, but somewhat disappointing.'

'If they move, can you stop them?'

'President Grushavoy has asked that very question of Stavka, his military chiefs, but they have not yet answered substantively. We are concerned with operational security. We do not wish the PRC to know that we know anything.'

'That can work against you,' Ryan warned.

'I said that very thing this morning, but soldiers have their own ways, don't they? We are calling up some reserves, and warning orders have gone out to some mechanized troops. The cupboard, however, as you Americans say, is somewhat bare at the moment.'

'What have you done about the people who tried to kill you?' Ryan asked, changing the subject.

'The main one is under constant observation at the moment. If he tries something else, we will then

312

speak to him,' Golovko promised. 'The connection, again, is Chinese, as you know.'

'I've heard.'

'Your FBI agent in Moscow, that Reilly fellow, is very talented. We could have used him in Second Directorate.'

'Yeah, Dan Murray thinks a lot of him.'

'If this Chinese matter goes further, we need to set up a liaison group between your military and ours.'

'Work through SACEUR,' Ryan told him. He'd already thought that one through. 'He has instructions to cooperate with your people.'

'Thank you, Mr. President. I will pass that along. So, your family, it is well?' You couldn't have this sort of meeting without irrelevant pleasantries.

'My oldest, Sally, is dating. That's hard on Daddy,' Ryan admitted.

'Yes.' Golovko allowed himself a smile. 'You live in fear that she will come upon such a boy as you were, yes?'

'Well, the Secret Service helps keep the little bastards under control.'

'There is much to be said for men with guns, yes,' the Russian agreed with some amusement, to lighten the moment.

'Yeah, but I think daughters are God's punishment on us for being men.' That observation earned Ryan a laugh.

'Just so, Ivan Emmetovich, just so.' And Sergey paused again. Back to business: 'It is a hard time for both of us, is it not?'

'Yeah, it is that.'

'Perhaps the Chinese will see us standing together and reconsider their greed. Together our

313

fathers' generation killed Hitler, after all. Who can stand against the two of us?'

'Sergey, wars are not rational acts. They are not begun by rational men. They're begun by people who don't care a rat-fuck about the people they rule, who're willing to get their fellow men killed for their own narrow purposes. This morning I saw such a place. It was Satan's amusement park, I suppose, but not a place for a man like me. I came away angry. I wouldn't mind having a chance to see Hitler, long as I have a gun in my hand when I do.' It was a foolish thing to say, but Golovko understood.

'With luck, together we will prevent this Chinese adventure.'

'And if not?'

'Then together we will defeat them, my friend. And perhaps that will be the last war of all.'

'I wouldn't bet on it,' the President replied. 'I've had that thought before myself, but I suppose it's a worthy goal.'

'When you find out what the Chinese say . . . ?'

'We'll get the word to you.'

Golovko rose. 'Thank you. I will convey that to my President.'

Ryan walked the Russian to the door, then headed off to the ambassador's office.

'This just came in.' Ambassador Lewendowski handed over the fax. 'Is this as bad as it looks?' The fax was headed EYES-ONLY PRESIDENT, but it had come into *his* embassy.

Ryan took the pages and started reading. 'Probably. If the Russians need help via NATO, will the Poles throw in?'

'I don't know. I can ask.'

314

The President shook his head. 'Too soon for that.'

'Did we bring the Russians into NATO with the knowledge of this?' The question showed concern that stopped short of outrage at the violation of diplomatic etiquette.

Ryan looked up. 'What do you think?' He paused. 'I need your secure phone.'

Forty minutes later, Jack and Cathy Ryan walked up the steps into their airplane for the ride home. SURGEON was not surprised to see her husband disappear into the aircraft's upper communications level, along with the Secretary of State. She suspected that her husband might have stolen a smoke or two up there, but she was asleep by the time he came back down.

For his part, Ryan wished he had, but couldn't find a smoker up there. The two who indulged had left their smokes in their luggage to avoid the temptation to violate USAF regulations. The President had a single drink and got into his seat, rocking it back for a nap, during which he found himself dreaming of Auschwitz, mixing it up with scenes remembered from *Schindler's List*. He awoke over Iceland, sweating, to see his wife's angelic sleeping face, and to remind himself that, bad as the world was, it wasn't quite that bad anymore. And his job was to keep it that way.

*   *   *

'Okay, is there any way to make them back off?' Robby Jackson asked the people assembled in the White House Situation Room.

Professor Weaver struck him as just one more

academic, long of wind and short of conclusion. Jackson listened anyway. This guy knew more about the way the Chinese thought. He must. His explanation was about as incomprehensible as the thought processes he was attempting to make clear.

'Professor,' Jackson said finally, 'that's all well and good, but what the hell does something that happened nine centuries ago tell us about today? These are Maoists, not royalists.'

'Ideology is usually just an excuse for behavior, Mr. Vice President, not a reason for it. Their motivations are the same today as they would have been under the Chin Dynasty, and they fear exactly the same thing: the revolt of the peasantry if the economy goes completely bad,' Weaver explained to this pilot, a technician, he thought, and decidedly not an intellectual. At least the President had some credentials as a historian, though they weren't impressive to the tenured Ivy League department chairman.

'Back to the real question here: What can we do to make them back off, short of war?'

'Telling them that we know of their plans might give them pause, but they will make their decision on the overall correlation of forces, which they evidently believe to be fully in their favor, judging from what I've been reading from this SORGE fellow.'

'So, they won't back off?' the VP asked.

'I cannot guarantee that,' Weaver answered.

'And blowing our source gets somebody killed,' Mary Pat Foley reminded the assembly.

'Which is just one life against many,' Weaver pointed out.

Remarkably, the DDO didn't leap across the

table to rip his academic face off. She respected Weaver as an area specialist/consultant. But fundamentally he was one more ivory-tower theoretician who didn't consider the human lives that rode on decisions like that one. Real people had their lives end, and that was a big deal to those real people, even if it wasn't to this professor in his comfortable office in Providence, Rhode Island.

'It also cancels out a vital source of information in the event that they go forward anyway—which could adversely affect our ability to deal with the real-world military threat, by the way.'

'There is that, I suppose,' Weaver conceded diffidently.

'Can the Russians stop them?' Jackson asked. General Moore took the question.

'It's six-five and pick 'em,' the Chairman of the Joint Chiefs answered. 'The Chinese have a lot of combat power to unleash. The Russians have a lot of room to absorb it, but not the combat power to repel it per se. If I had to bet, I'd put my money on the PRC—unless we come in. Our airpower could alter the equation somewhat, and if NATO comes in with ground forces, the odds change. It depends on what reinforcements we and the Russians can get into the theater.'

'Logistics?'

'A real problem,' Mickey Moore conceded. 'It all comes down one railway line. It's double-tracked and electrified, but that's the only good news about it.'

'Does anybody know how to run an operation like that down a railroad? Hell, we haven't done it since the Civil War,' Jackson thought aloud.

'Just have to wait and see, sir, if it comes to that.

317

The Russians have doubtless thought it over many times. We'll depend on them for that.'

'Great,' the Vice President muttered. A lifelong USN sailor, he didn't like depending on anything except people who spoke American and wore Navy Blue.

'If the variables were fully in our favor, the Chinese wouldn't be thinking about this operation as seriously as they evidently are.' Which was about as obvious as the value of a double play with the bases loaded and one out in the bottom of the ninth.

'The problem,' George Winston told them, 'is that the prize is just too damned inviting. It's like the bank doors have been left open over a three-day weekend, and the local cops are on strike.'

'Jack keeps saying that a war of aggression is just an armed robbery writ large,' Jackson told them.

'That's not far off,' SecTreas agreed. Professor Weaver thought the comparison overly simplistic, but what else could you expect of people like these?

'We can warn them off when we start seeing preparations on our overheads,' Ed Foley proposed. 'Mickey, when will we start seeing that?'

'Conceivably, two days. Figure a week for them to get ramped up. Their forces are pretty well in theater already, and it's just a matter of getting them postured—putting them all near their jump-off points. Then doing the final approach march will happen, oh, thirty-six hours before they start pulling the strings on their field guns.'

'And Ivan can't stop them?'

'At the border? Not a chance,' the general answered, with an emphatic shake of the head.

'They'll have to play for time, trading land for time. The Chinese have a hell of a long trip to get the oil. That's their weakness, a huge flank to protect and a god-awful vulnerable logistics train. I'd look out for an airborne assault on either the gold or the oil fields. They don't have much in the way of airborne troops or airlift capacity, but you have to figure they'll try it anyway. They're both soft targets.

'What can we send in?'

'First thing, a lot of air assets, fighters, fighter-bombers, and every aerial tanker we can scrape up. We may not be able to establish air superiority, but we can quickly deny it to them, make it a fifty-fifty proposition almost at once, and then start rolling their air force back. Again it's a question of numbers, Robby, and a question of how well their flyers are trained. Probably better than the Russians, just because they have more hours on the stick, but technically the Russians actually have generally better aircraft, and probably better doctrine—except they haven't had the chance to practice it.'

Robby Jackson wanted to grumble that the situation had too many unknowns, but if there hadn't been, as Mickey Moore had just told him, the Chinese wouldn't be leaning on their northern border. Muggers went after little old ladies with their Social Security money, not cops who had just cashed their paychecks on the way home from work. There was much to be said for carrying a gun on the street, and as irrational as street crime or war-starting might be, those who did it were *somewhat* reflective in their choices.

*   *   *

319

Scott Adler hadn't slept at all on the flight, as he'd played over and over in his mind the question of how to stop a war from starting. That was the primary mission of a diplomat, wasn't it? Mainly he considered his shortcomings. As the prime foreign-affairs officer of his country, he was supposed to know—he was *paid* to know—what to say to people to deflect them from irrational actions. At base that could mean telling them, *Do this and the full power and fury of America will descend on you and ruin your whole day.* Better to cajole them into being reasonable, because in reasonableness was their best salvation as a nation in the global village. But the truth was that the Chinese thought in ways that he could not replicate within his own mind, and so he wasn't sure what to say to make them see the light. The worst part of all was that he'd met this Zhang guy in addition to Foreign Minister Shen, and all he knew for sure was that they did not look upon reality as he did. They saw blue where he saw green, and he couldn't understand their strange version of green well enough to explain it into blue. A small voice chided him for possible racism, but this situation was too far gone for political correctness. He had a war to stop, and he didn't know how. He ended up staring at the bulkhead in front of his comfortable glove-leather seat and wishing it was a movie screen. He felt like seeing a movie now, something to get his mind off the hamster wheel that just kept turning and turning. Then he felt a tap on his shoulder, and turned to see his President, who motioned him to the circular staircase to the upper level. Again they chased two Air Force communicators off their seats.

'Thinking over the newest SORGE?'

'Yep.' EAGLE nodded.

'Any ideas?'

The head moved in a different plane now. 'No. Sorry, Jack, but it just isn't there. Maybe you need a new SecState.'

Ryan grunted. 'No, just different enemies. The only thing I see is to tell them we know what they're up to, and that they'd better stop.'

'And when they tell us to shove it up our collective ass, then what?'

'You know what we need right now?' SWORDSMAN asked.

'Oh, yeah, a couple hundred Minuteman or Trident missiles would work just fine to show them the light. Unfortunately . . .'

'Unfortunately, we did away with them to make the world a safer place. Oops,' Ryan concluded.

'Well, we have the bombs and the aircraft to deliver them, and—'

'No!' Ryan hissed. 'No, God damn it, I will not initiate a nuclear war in order to stop a conventional one. How many people do you want me to kill?'

'Easy, Jack. It's my job to present options, remember? Not to advocate them—not that one anyway.' He paused. 'What did you think of Auschwitz?'

'It's the stuff of nightmares—wait a minute, your parents, right?'

'My father—Belzec in his case, and he lucked out and survived.'

'Does he talk about it?'

'Never. Not a single word, even to his rabbi. Maybe a pshrink. He went to one for a few years, but I never knew what for.'

'I can't let anything like that happen again. To stop that—yeah, to stop that,' Ryan speculated aloud, 'yeah, I might drop a B-83.'

'You know the lingo?'

'A little. I got briefed in a long time ago, the names for the hardware stuck in my mind. Funny thing, I've never had nightmares about *that*. Well, I've never read into the SIOP—Single Integrated Operation Plan, the cookbook for ending the world. I think I'd eat a gun before I did that.'

'A whole lot of Presidents had to think those things over,' Adler pointed out.

'Before my time, Scott, and they never expected them to happen anyway. They all figured they'd smart their way through it. 'Til Bob Fowler came along and damned near stumbled into calling in the codes. That was some wild Sunday night,' Ryan said, remembering.

'Yeah, I know the story. You kept your head screwed on straight. Not many others did.'

'Yeah. And look where it got me,' POTUS observed with a grim chuckle. He looked out a window. They were over land now, probably Labrador, lots of green and lakes, and few straight lines to show the hand of man on the land. 'What do we do, Scott?'

'We try to warn them off. They'll do things we can see with satellites, and then we can call them on it. Our last play will be to tell them that Russia is an American ally now, and messing with Ivan means messing with Uncle Sam. If that doesn't stop them, nothing else will.'

'Offer some danegeld to buy them off?' the President wondered.

'A waste of time. I don't think it would work, but I'd be for-damned sure they'd see it as a sign of weakness and be encouraged by it. No, they respect strength, and we have to show them that. Then they'll react one way or another.'

'They're going to go,' Jack thought.

'Coin toss. Hope it comes up tails, buddy.'

'Yeah.' Ryan checked his watch. 'Early morning in Beijing.'

'They'll be waking up and heading in for work,' Adler agreed. 'What exactly can you tell me about this SORGE source?'

'Mary Pat hasn't told me much, probably best that way. One of the things I learned at Langley. You can know too much sometimes. Better not to know their faces, and especially their names.'

'In case something bad happens?'

'When it does, it's pretty bad. Don't want to think what these people would do. Their version of the Miranda warning is, "You can scream all you want. We don't mind."'

'Funny,' SecState thought.

'Actually it's not all that effective as an interrogation technique. They end up telling you exactly what you want to hear, and you end up dictating it to them instead of getting what they really know.'

'What about the appeals process?' Scott asked, with a yawn. Finally, belatedly, he was getting sleepy.

'In China? That's when the shooter asks if you prefer the left ear or the right ear.' Ryan stopped himself. Why was he making bad jokes on *this* subject?

*　　　*　　　*

The busy place in the Washington, D.C., area was the National Reconnaissance Office. A joint venture of CIA and the Pentagon, NRO ran the reconsats, the big camera birds circling the earth at low–medium altitude, looking down with their hugely expensive cameras that rivaled the precision and expense of the Hubble space telescope. There were three photo-birds up, circling the earth every two hours or so, and passing over the same spot twice a day each. There was also a radar-reconnaissance satellite that had much poorer resolution than the Lockheed- and TRW-made KH-11s, but which could see through clouds. This was important at the moment, because a cold front was tracing across the Chinese–Siberian border, and the clouds at its forward edge blanked out all visual light, much to the frustration of the NRO technicians and scientists whose multibillion-dollar satellites were useful only for weather forecasting at the moment. Cloudy with scattered showers, and chilly, temperature in the middle forties, dropping to just below freezing at night.

The intelligence analysts, therefore, closely examined the 'take' from the Lacrosse radar-intelligence bird because that was the only game in town at the moment.

'The clouds go all the way down to six thousand feet or so. Even a Blackbird wouldn't be much use at the moment,' one of the photo-interpreters observed. 'Okay, what do we have here . . .? Looks like a higher level of railroad activity, looks like flatcars mostly. Something on them, but too much clutter to pick out the shapes.'

'What do they move on flatcars?' a naval officer asked.

'Tracked vehicles,' an Army major answered, 'and heavy guns.'

'Can we confirm that supposition from this data?' the Navy guy asked.

'No,' the civilian answered. 'But . . . there, that's the yard. We see six long trains sitting still in the yard. Okay, where's the . . .' He accessed his desktop computer and called up some visual imagery. 'Here we go. See these ramps? They're designed to offload rolling equipment from the trains.' He turned back to the Lacrosse 'take.' 'Yeah, these here look like tank shapes coming off the ramps, and forming up right here in the assembly areas, and that's the shape of an armored regiment. That's three hundred twenty-two main battle tanks, and about a buck and a quarter of APCs, and so . . . yeah, I'd estimate that this is a full armored division detraining. Here's the truck park . . . and this grouping here, I'm not sure. Looks bulky . . . square or rectangular shapes. Hmm,' the analyst concluded. He turned back to his own desktop and queried some file images. 'You know what this looks like?'

'You going to tell us?'

'Looks like a five-ton truck with a section of ribbon bridge on it. The Chinese copied the Russian bridge design—hell, everybody did. It's a beautiful little design Ivan cobbled together. Anyway, on radar, it looks like this and'—he turned back to the recent satellite take—'that's pretty much what these look like, isn't it? I'll call that eighty percent likelihood. So, this group here I'll call two engineer regiments accompanying this tank division.'

'Is that a lot of engineers to back up a single division?' the naval officer asked.

'Sure as hell,' the Army major confirmed.

'I'd say so,' the photo-interpreter agreed. 'The normal TO and E is one battalion per division. So, this is a corps or army vanguard forming up, and I'd have to say they plan to cross some rivers, guys.'

'Go on,' the senior civilian told him.

'They're postured to head north.'

'Okay,' the Army officer said. 'Have you ever seen this before?'

'Two years ago, they were running an exercise, but that was one engineer regiment, not two, and they left this yard and headed. southeast. That one was a pretty big deal. We got a lot of visual overheads. They were simulating an invasion or at least a major assault. That one used a full Group A army, with an armored division and two mechanized divisions as the assault force, and the other mech division simulating a dispersed defense force. The attacking team won that one.'

'How different from the way the Russians are deployed on their border?' This was the Navy intelligence officer.

'Thicker—I mean, for the exercise the Chinese defenders were thicker on the ground than the Russians are today.'

'And the attacking force won?'

'Correct.'

'How realistic was the exercise?' the major asked.

'It wasn't Fort Irwin, but it was as honest as they can run one, and probably accurate. The attackers had the usual advantages in numbers and initiative.

They punched through and started maneuvering in the defender's trains area, had themselves a good old time.'

The naval officer looked at his colleague in green. 'Just what they'd be thinking if they wanted to head north.'

'Concur.'

'Better call this one in, Norm.'

'Yep.' And both uniformed officers headed to the phones.

'When's the weather clear?' the lingering civilian asked the tech.

'Call it thirty-six hours. It'll start to clear tomorrow night, and we have the taskings already programmed in.' He didn't have to say that the nighttime capabilities on the KH11 satellites weren't all that different from in the daylight—you just didn't get much in the way of color.

CHAPTER FORTY-SEVEN

OUTLOOKS AND ALL-NIGHTERS

Westbound jet lag, or travel-shock, as President Ryan preferred to call it, is always easier than eastbound's, and he'd gotten sleep on the airplane. Jack and Cathy walked off Air Force One and to the waiting helicopter, which got them to the landing pad on the South Lawn in the usual ten minutes. This time FLOTUS walked directly into the White House while POTUS walked left toward the West Wing, but to the Situation Room rather than the Oval Office. Vice President Jackson was waiting for him there, along with the usual suspects.

'Hey, Robby.'

'How was the flight, Jack?'

'Long.' Ryan stretched to get his muscles back under control. 'Okay, what's happening?'

'Ain't good, buddy. We have Chinese mechanized troops heading for the Russian border. Here's what we got in from NRO.' Jackson personally spread out the printouts from the photo-intelligence troops. 'We got mechanized forces here, here, and here, and these are engineers with bridging equipment.'

'How long before they're ready?' Ryan asked.

'Potentially as little as three days,' Mickey Moore answered. 'More likely five to seven.'

'What are we doing?'

'We have a lot of warning orders out, but nobody's moving yet.'

'Do they know we're onto this?' the President asked next.

'Probably not, but they must know we're keeping an eye on things, and they must know our reconnaissance capabilities. It's been in the open media for twenty-some years,' Moore answered.

'Nothing from them to us over diplomatic channels?'

'*Bupkis,*' Ed Foley said.

'Don't tell me they don't care. They have to care.'

'Maybe they care, Jack,' the DCI responded. 'But they're not losing as much sleep over it as they are over internal political problems.'

'Anything new from SORGE?'

Foley shook his head. 'Not since this morning.'

'Okay, who's our senior diplomat in Beijing?'

'The DCM at the embassy, but he's actually fairly junior, new in the post,' the DCI said.

'Okay, well, the note we're going to send won't be,' Ryan said. 'What time is it over there?'

'Eight-twelve in the morning,' Jackson said, pointing to a wall clock set on Chinese time.

'So, SORGE didn't report anything from their working day yesterday?'

'No. That happens two or three days per week. It's not unusual,' Mary Pat pointed out. 'Sometimes that means the next one will be extra meaty.'

Everyone looked up when Secretary Adler came in; he had driven instead of helicoptered in from Andrews. He quickly came up to speed.

'That bad?'

'They look serious, man,' Jackson told SecState.

'Sounds like we have to send them that note.'

'They're too far gone down this road to stop,' another person said. 'It's not likely that any note will work.'

'Who are you?' Ryan asked.

'George Weaver, sir, from Brown. I consult to the Agency on China.'

'Oh, okay. I've read some of your work. Pretty good stuff, Dr. Weaver. So, you say they won't turn back. Tell us why,' the President commanded.

'It's not because they fear revelation of what they're up to. Their people don't know, and won't find out until Beijing tells them. The problem, as you know, is that they fear a potential economic collapse. If their economy goes south, sir, then you get a revolt of the masses, and that's the one thing they really fear. They don't see a way to avoid that other than getting rich, and the way for them to get rich is to seize the newly discovered Russian assets.'

'Kuwait writ large?' Ryan asked.

'Larger and more complex, but, yes, Mr. President, the situation is fundamentally similar. They regard oil both as a commodity and as an entry card into international legitimacy. They figure that if they have it, the rest of the world will have to do business with them. The gold angle is even more obvious. It's the quintessential trading commodity. If you have it, you can sell it for anything you care to purchase. With those assets and the cash they can buy with them, they figure to bootstrap their national economy to the next level, and they just assume that the rest of the world will play along with them because they're going to be rich, and capitalists are only interested in money.'

'They're really that cynical, that shallow?' Adler asked, somewhat shocked at the thought, even after all he'd already been through.

'Their reading of history justifies that outlook, Mr. Secretary. Their analysis of our past actions, and those of the rest of the world, lead them to this conclusion. I grant you that they fail to appreciate what we call our reasons for the actions we took, but in strictly and narrowly factual terms, that's how the world looks to them.'

'Only if they're idiots,' Ryan observed tiredly. 'We're dealing with idiots.'

'Mr. President, you're dealing with highly sophisticated political animals. Their outlook on the world is different from ours, and, true, they do not understand us very well, but that does not make them fools,' Weaver told the assembly.

Fine, Ryan thought for what seemed the hundredth time, *but then they're Klingons.* There was no sense saying that to Weaver. He'd simply launch into a long-winded rebuttal that wouldn't take the discussion anywhere. And Weaver would be right. Fools or geniuses, you only had to understand *what* they were doing, not *why*. The *what* might not make sense, but if you knew it, you also knew what had to be stopped.

'Well, let's see if they understand this,' Ryan said. 'Scott, tell the PRC that if they attack into Russia, America will come to Russia's aid, as required by the North Atlantic Treaty, and—'

'The NATO Treaty doesn't actually say that,' Adler warned.

'I say it does, Scott, and more to the point, I told the Russians it does. If the Chinese realize we're not kidding, will it make a difference?'

'That opens up a huge can of worms, Jack,' Adler warned. 'We have thousands of Americans in China, thousands. Businessmen, tourists, a lot of people.'

'Dr. Weaver, how will the Chinese treat foreign nationals in time of war?'

'I would not want to be there to find out. The Chinese can be fine hosts, but in time of war, if, for example, they think you're a spy or something, it could get very difficult. The way they treat their own citizens—well, we've seen that on TV, haven't we?'

'Scott, we also tell them that we hold their government leaders *personally* responsible for the safety and well-being of American citizens in their country. I mean that, Scott. If I have to, I'll sign the orders to track them down and bury their asses. Remind them of Tehran and our old friend Daryaei. That Zhang guy met him once, according

331

to the former Indian Prime Minister, and I had him taken all the way out,' Ryan announced coldly. 'Zhang would do well to consider that.'

'They will not respond well to such threats,' Weaver warned. 'It's just as easy to say we have a lot of their citizens here, and—'

'We can't do that, and they know it,' Ryan shot back.

'Mr. President, I just told you, our concept of laws is alien to them. That sort of threat is one they *will* understand, and they will take it seriously. The question then is how valuable they regard the lives of their own citizens.

'And that is?'

'Less than we do,' Weaver answered.

Ryan considered that. 'Scott, make sure they know what the Ryan Doctrine means,' he ordered. 'If necessary, I *will* put a smart bomb through their bedroom windows, even if it takes us ten years to find them.'

'The DCM will make that clear. We can also alert our citizens to get the next bird out.'

'Yeah, I'd want to get the hell out of Dodge City,' Robby Jackson observed. 'And you can get that warning out over CNN.'

'Depending on how they respond to our note. It's eight-thirty in the morning over there. Scott, that note has to be in their hands before lunch.'

SecState nodded. 'Right.'

'General Moore, we have warning orders cut to the forces we can deploy?'

'Yes, sir. We can have Air Force units in Siberia in less than twenty-four hours. Twelve hours after that, they'll be ready to launch missions.'

'What about bases, Mickey?' Jackson asked.

'Tons of 'em, from when they worried about splashing B-52s. Their northern coast is lousy with airstrips. We have our Air Attaché in Moscow sitting down with their people right now,' General Moore said. The colonel in question was pulling a serious all-nighter. 'The Russians, he says, are being very cooperative.'

'How secure will the bases be?' the Vice President asked next.

'Their main protection will be distance. The Chinese will have to reach the best part of a thousand miles to hit them. We've tagged ten E-3B AWACS out of Tinker Air Force Base to go over and establish continuous radar coverage, plus a lot of fighters to do BARCAP Once that's done, we'll think about what missions we'll want to fly. Mainly defensive at first, until we get firmly established.'

Moore didn't have to explain to Jackson that there was more to moving an Air Force than just the aircraft. With each fighter squadron went mechanics, ordnancemen, and even air-traffic controllers. A fighter plane might have only one pilot, but it needed an additional twenty or more personnel to make it a functioning weapon. For more complex aircraft, the numbers just went higher.

'What about CINCPAC?' Jackson asked.

'We can give their navy a serious headache. Mancuso's moving his submarines and other ships.'

'These images aren't all that great,' Ryan observed, looking down at the radar overheads.

'We'll have visuals late tomorrow,' Ed Foley told him.

'Okay, when we do, we'll have to show them to NATO, see what they'll do to help us out.'

'First Armored has orders to stand by to entrain. The German railroads are in better shape today than they were in 1990 for DESERT SHIELD,' the Chairman of the Joint Chiefs informed them. 'We can change trains just east of Berlin. The Russian railroads have a different gauge. It's wider. That actually helps us, wider cars for our tracks to ride on. We figure we can move First Armored to the far side of the Urals in about seven days.'

'Who else?' Ryan asked.

'Not sure,' Moore answered.

'The Brits'll go with us. Them we can depend on,' Adler told them all. 'And Grushavoy was talking to their Prime Minister. We need to talk to Downing Street to see what developed from that.'

'Okay, Scott, please look into that. But first let's get that note drafted for Beijing.'

'Right,' SecState agreed, and headed for the door.

'Jesus, I hope we can get them to see sense,' Ryan said to the maps and imagery before his eyes.

'Me, too, Jack,' the Vice President agreed. 'But don't bet the farm on it.'

What Adler had said to him on the flight from Warsaw came back to him. If only America still had ballistic missiles, deterrence would have been far easier. But Ryan had played a role in eliminating the damned things, and it seemed a very strange thing for him to regret now.

*   *   *

The note was generated and sent to the embassy in Beijing in less than two hours. The Deputy Chief of Mission or DCM in the embassy was a career

334

foreign-service officer named William Kilmer. The formal note arrived as e-mail, and he had a secretary print it up in proper form and on expensive paper, which was folded into an envelope of creamy texture for hand delivery. He called the Chinese Foreign Ministry, requesting an urgent meeting with Foreign Minister Sheri Tang. This was granted with surprising alacrity, and Kilmer walked to his own automobile, a Lincoln Town Car, and drove himself to the Ministry.

Kilmer was in his middle thirties, a graduate of the College of William and Mary in Virginia and Georgetown University in Washington. A man on his way up, his current position was rather ahead of his years, and the only reason he'd gotten it was that Ambassador Carl Hitch had been expected to be a particularly good mentor for bringing him along from AAA ball into the bigs. This mission, delivering *this* note, made him think about just how junior he was. But he couldn't very well run from the job, and career-wise he was taking a big step. Assuming he didn't get shot. Unlikely, but . . .

The walk to Shen's office was a lonely one. The corridor seemed to stretch into infinity as he stepped down it in his best suit and shiny black shoes. The building and its appointments were supposed to be imposing, to show representatives of foreign countries just how impressive the People's Republic of China was. Every country did it this way, some better than others. In this case the architect had earned his money, Kilmer thought. Finally—but sooner than he'd expected when he'd begun—he found the door and turned right to enter the secretaries' anteroom. Shen's male executive assistant led the American into a more

335

comfortable waiting room and fetched water for him. Kilmer waited for the expected five minutes, because you didn't just barge in to see a senior government minister of a major power, but then the high doors—they were always double doors at this level of diplomacy—opened and he was beckoned in.

Shen was wearing a Mao jacket today instead of the usual Western-style business suit, a dark blue in color. He approached his guest and extended his hand.

'Mr. Kilmer, a pleasure to see you again.'

'Thank you for allowing this impromptu audience, Minister.'

'Please have a seat.' Shen waved to some chairs surrounding the usual low table. When both of them were seated, Shen asked, 'What can I do for you this day?'

'Minister, I have a note from my government to place into your hand.' With that, Kilmer pulled the envelope from his coat pocket and handed it across.

The envelope was not sealed. Shen withdrew the two-page diplomatic message and leaned back to read it. His face didn't alter a dot before he looked up.

'This is a most unusual communication, Mr. Kilmer.'

'Minister, my government is seriously concerned with recent deployments of your military.'

'The last note delivered from your embassy was an insulting interference with our internal affairs. Now you threaten us with war?'

'Sir, America makes no threats. We remind you that since the Russian Federation is now a signatory of the North Atlantic Treaty, any hostilities directed at Russia will compel America to honor her treaty commitments.

'And you threaten the senior members of our government if something untoward should happen to Americans in our country? What do you take us for, Mr. Kilmer?' Shen asked in an even, unexcited voice.

'Minister, we merely point out that, as America extends to all of our visitors the protection of our laws, we hope that the People's Republic will do the same.'

'Why should we treat American citizens any differently from the way we treat our own?'

'Minister, we merely request your assurance that this will be the case.'

'Why should it not be the case? Do you accuse us of plotting a war of aggression against our neighbor?'

'We take note of recent military actions by the People's Republic and request clarification.'

'I see.' Shen folded the papers back up and set them on the table. 'When do you request a reply?'

'As soon as you find it convenient to do so, Minister,' Kilmer answered.

'Very well. I will discuss this matter with my colleagues on the Politburo and reply to you as quickly as we can.'

'I will convey that good news to Washington, Minister. I will not take more time from your day, sir. Thank you very much indeed for your time.' Kilmer stood and shook hands one more time. Kilmer walked through the anteroom without a glance left or right, turned left in the corridor, and headed toward the elevators. The corridor seemed just as long for this little walk, he thought, and the clicking of his heels on the tile floor seemed unusually loud. Kilmer had been an FSO long enough to know that Shen should have reacted more irately to the note. Instead he had received it like an invitation to an informal dinner at the embassy. That meant something, but Kilmer wasn't sure what. Once in his car, he started composing his dispatch to Foggy Bottom, then quickly realized that this was something he'd better report by voice first over the STU.

*   *   *

'How good is he, Carl?' Adler asked the ambassador.

'He's an okay kid, Scott. Photographic memory, talent I wish I had. Maybe he was promoted a little fast, but he's got the brains he needs, just a little short on field experience. I figure in another three years or so, he'll be ready to run his own embassy and start his way up the ladder.'

In a place like Lesotho, SecState thought, which was a place to make 'backwater' seem a compliment. Well, you had to start somewhere. 'How will Shen react?'

'Depends. If they're just maneuvering troops on routine training, they might be a little angry. If it's for real and we've caught them with their hands in the cookie jar, they'll act hurt and surprised.' Hitch paused for a yawn. 'Excuse me. The real question is whether it'll make them think things over.'

'Will it? You know most of 'em.'

'I don't know,' Hitch admitted uncomfortably. 'Scott, I've been there a while, sure, but I can't say that I fully understand them. They make decisions on political considerations that Americans have a hard time comprehending.'

'The President calls them Klingons,' Adler told the ambassador.

Hitch smiled. 'I wouldn't go that far, but there is logic in the observation.' Then Adler's intercom buzzed.

'Call from William Kilmer in Beijing on the STU, Mr. Secretary,' the secretary's voice said.

'This is Scott Adler,' SecState said when he lifted the phone. 'Ambassador Hitch is here with me. You're on speaker.'

'Sir, I made the delivery. Minister Shen hardly blinked. He said he'd get back to us soon, but not exactly when, after he talked it over with his Politburo colleagues. Aside from that, not much of a reaction at all. I can fax you the transcript in about half an hour. The meeting didn't last ten minutes.'

Adler looked over at Hitch, who shook his head and didn't look happy at the news.

'Bill, how was his body language?' Hitch asked.

'Like he was on Prozac, Carl. No physical reaction at all.'

'Shen tends to be a little hyperactive,' Hitch explained. 'Sometimes he has trouble sitting still. Conclusions, Bill?'

'I'm worried,' Kilmer replied at once. 'I think we have a problem here.'

'Thank you, Mr. Kilmer. Send the fax quick as you can.' Adler punched the phone button and looked at his guest. 'Oh, shit.'

'Yeah. How soon will we know how they're going to react to this?'

'Tomorrow morning, I hope, we—'

'We have a source inside their government?' Hitch asked. The blank look he got in reply was answer enough.

*   *   *

'Thanks, Scott,' Ryan said, hanging up the phone. He was back in the Oval Office now, sitting in his personally-fitted swivel chair, which was about as comfortable as any artifact could make him. It didn't help much at the moment, but he supposed it was one less thing to worry about.

'So.'

'So, we wait to see if SORGE tells us anything.'

'SORGE?' Professor Weaver asked.

'Dr. Weaver, we have a sensitive source of information that sometimes gives us information on what their Politburo is thinking,' Ed Foley told the academic. 'And that information does not leave this room.'

'Understood.' Academic or not, Weaver played by the rules. 'That's the name for the special stuff you've been showing me?'

'Correct.'

'It's a hell of a source, whoever it is. It reads like a tape of their meetings, captures their personalities, especially Zhang. He's the real bad actor here. He's got Premier Xu pretty well wrapped around his little finger.'

'Adler's met him, during the shuttle talks after the Airbus shoot-down at Taipei,' Ryan said.

'And?' Weaver asked. He knew the name and the words, but not the man.

'And he's powerful and not a terribly nice chap,'

the President answered. 'He had a role in our conflict with Japan, and also the fracas with the UIR last year.'

'Machiavelli?'

'That's pretty close, more a theoretician than a lead actor, the man-behind-the-throne sort of guy. Not an ideologue per se, but a guy who likes to play in the real world—patriot, Ed?' Ryan asked the DCI.

'We've had our pshrink profile him.' Foley shrugged. 'Part sociopath, part political operator. A guy who enjoys the exercise of power. No known personal weaknesses. Sexually active, but a lot of their Politburo members are. Maybe it's a cultural thing, eh, Weaver?'

'Mao was like that, as we all know. The emperors used to have rather large stables of concubines.'

'That's what people did before TV, I suppose,' Arnie van Damm observed.

'Actually that's not far from the truth,' Weaver agreed. 'The carryover to today is cultural, and it's a fundamental form of personal power that some people like to exercise. Women's lib hasn't made it into the PRC yet.'

'I must be too Catholic,' the President thought aloud. 'The idea of Mao popping little girls makes my skin crawl.'

'They didn't mind, Mr. President,' Weaver told him. 'Some would bring their little sisters over after they got in bed with the Great Leader. It's a different culture, and it has different rules from ours.'

'Yeah, just a little different,' observed the father of two daughters, one just starting to date. What would the fathers of those barely nubile little girls have thought? Honored to have their daughters deflowered by the great Mao Zedong? Ryan had a minor chill from the thought, and dismissed it. 'Do they care about human life at all? What about their soldiers?'

'Mr. President, the Judeo-Christian Bible wasn't drafted in China, and efforts by missionaries to get Christianity going over there were not terribly successful—and when Mao came along, he suppressed it fairly effectively, as we saw again recently. Their view of man's place in nature is different from ours, and, no, they do not value a single human life as we do. We're talking here about communists who view everything through a political lens, and that is over and above a culture in which a human life had little import. So, you could say it's a very infelicitous confluence of belief systems from our point of view.'

Infelicitous, Ryan thought, *there's a delicate turn of phrase. Were talking about a government that killed off twenty million plus of its own people along the way, just in a few months, in pursuit of political perfection.* 'Dr. Weaver, best guess: What's their Politburo going to say?'

'They will continue on the path they're on,' Weaver answered quickly. He was surprised at the reaction.

'God damn it, doesn't anybody think common sense is going to break out?' Ryan snarled. He looked around the room, to see people suddenly looking down at the royal-blue rug.

'Mr. President, they fear war less than they fear the alternatives to war,' Weaver answered, rather courageously, Arnie van Damm thought. 'To repeat, if they don't enrich their country in oil and gold, they fear an economic collapse that will destroy their entire political order, and that, to them, is more frightening than the prospect of losing a hundred thousand soldiers in a war of conquest.'

'And I can stop it only by dropping a nuclear bomb on their capital—which will, by the way, kill a couple of million ordinary people. God damn it!' Ryan swore again.

'More like five million, maybe as many as ten,' General Moore pointed out, earning him a withering look from his Commander-in-Chief. 'Yes, sir, that would work, but I agree the price of doing it's a little high.'

'Robby?' Jack turned to his Vice President in hope of hearing something encouraging.

'What do you want me to say, Jack? We can hope they realize that this is going to cost them more than they expect, but it would appear the odds are against it.'

'One other thing we need to do is prepare the people for this,' Arnie said. 'Tomorrow we should alert the press, and then you'll have to go on TV and tell everybody what's happening and why.'

'You know, I really don't like this job very much—excuse me. That's rather a puerile thing to say, isn't it?' SWORDSMAN apologized.

'Ain't supposed to be fun, Jack,' van Damm observed. 'You've played the game okay to this point, but you can't always control the other people at the card table.'

The President's phone rang. Jack answered it. 'Yes? Okay.' He looked up. 'Ed, it's for you.'

Foley stood and walked to take the phone.

'Foley . . . Okay, good, thanks.' He replaced the phone. 'Weather's clearing over Northeast China. We'll have some visual imagery in half an hour.'

'Mickey, how fast can we get aerial recon assets in place?' Jackson asked.

'We have to fly them in. We have things we can stage out of California, but it's a lot more efficient to fly them over in a C-17 and lift them off from a Siberian airfield. We can do that in, oh . . . thirty-six hours from your order.'

'The order is given,' Ryan said. 'What sort of aircraft are they?'

'They're UAVs, sir. Unmanned Aerial Vehicles, used to call them drones. They're stealthy and they stay up a long time. We can download real-time video from them. They're fabulous for battlefield reconnaissance, the best new toys the Air Force has fielded, so far as the Army is concerned. I can get them going right now.'

'Do it,' Ryan told him.

'Assuming we have a place to land them. But we could stage them out of Elmendorf in Alaska if we have to.' Moore lifted the phone and made his call to the National Military Command Center, the NMCC, in the Pentagon.

*   *   *

For General Peng, things were getting busy. The operation order was topped with the ideographs Long Chun, SPRING DRAGON. The 'dragon' part sounded auspicious, since for thousands of years the dragon had been the symbol of imperial rule and also good fortune. There was still plenty of daylight. That suited Peng, and he hoped it would suit his soldiers. Daylight made for good hunting, and made it harder for large bodies of men to hide or move unseen, and that suited his mission.

He was not without misgivings. He was a general officer with orders to fight a war, and nothing makes such a man reflective like instructions to perform the things he'd claimed the ability to do. He would have preferred more artillery and air support, but he had a good deal of the former, and probably enough of the latter. At the moment, he was going over intelligence estimates and maps. He'd studied the Russian defenses on the far side of the border for years, to the point of occasionally putting reconnaissance specialists across the river to scout out the bunkers that had faced south for fifty years. The Russians were good military engineers, and those fixed defenses would take some dealing with.

But his attack plan was a simple one. Behind a massive artillery barrage, he'd put infantry across the Amur River in assault boats to deal with the Russian bunkers, simultaneously bringing up engineers to span the river with ribbon bridges in order to rush his mechanized forces across, up the hills on the far side, then farther north. He had helicopters, though not enough of the attack kind to suit his needs. He'd complained about this, but so had every other senior officer in the People's Liberation Army. The only thing about the Russian Army that worried him were their Mi-24 attack helicopters. They were clumsy machines but dangerous in their capabilities, if wisely used.

His best intelligence came from reams of Humint from Chinese citizens living illegally but comfortably in Russia—shopkeepers and workers, a fair number of whom were officers or stringers for the Ministry for State Security. He would have preferred more photographs, but his country had only a single orbiting reconnaissance satellite, and the truth was that the imagery purchased from the French SPOT commercial satellite company was better, at one-meter resolution, than his own country could manage. It was also easier to acquire over the Internet, and for that his intelligence coordinator had a blank check. They showed the nearest Russian mechanized formation over a hundred kilometers away. That confirmed the human intelligence that had said only things within artillery range were garrison units assigned to the border defenses. It was interesting that the Russian high command had not surged forces forward, but they didn't have many to surge, and defending a border, with its numerous crenellations and meanders, used up manpower as a sponge used up water—and they didn't have that many troops to squander. He also possessed information that this General-Colonel Bondarenko was training his troops harder than his predecessor had, but that was not much cause for concern. The Chinese had been training hard for years, and Ivan would take time to catch up.

No, his only concern was distance. His army and its neighbors had a long way to go. Keeping them supplied would be a problem, because as Napoleon said that an army marched on its stomach, so tanks and tracked vehicles floated on a sea of diesel oil. His intelligence sources gave locations for large Russian stocks, but he couldn't count on seizing them intact, desirable though that might be, and even though he had plans for helicopter assaults on every one he had charted.

Peng put out his sixtieth cigarette of the day and looked up at his operations officer. 'Yes?'

'The final order has arrived. Jump off at 0330 in three days.'

'Will you have everything in place by then?' Peng asked.

'Yes, Comrade General, with twenty-four hours to spare.'

'Good. Let's make sure that all our men are well fed. It may be a long time between meals for the next few weeks.'

'That order has already been given, Comrade General,' the colonel told him.

'And total radio silence.'

'Of course, Comrade General.'

*   *   *

'Not a whisper,' the sergeant said. 'Not even carrier waves.'

The RC-135 Rivet Joint aircraft was the first USAF bird to deploy, flying out of Anderson Air Force base on the island of Guam. It had refueled over the Sea of Okhotsk and entered Russian airspace over the port city of Ayan, and now, two hours later, was just east of Skovorodino on the Russian side of the border. The Rivet Joint was an extensively modified windowless version of the old Boeing 707, crammed with radio-receiving equipment and crewed with experienced ferret personnel, one of only two USAF crews who spoke passable Chinese.

'Sergeant, what's it mean when you have a lot of soldiers in the field and no radios?' the colonel in command of the mission asked. It was a rhetorical question, of course.

'Same thing it means when your two-year-old isn't making any noise, sir. He's crayoning the wall, or doing something else to get his bottom smacked.' The sergeant leaned back in the pilot-type seat, looking at the numerous visual scans tuned to known PLA frequencies. The screen was blank except for mild static. Maybe there'd been some chatter as the PLA had moved units into place, but now there was nothing but some commercial FM traffic, mainly music that was as alien to the American flight crew as Grand Ol' Opry would have been in Beijing. Two crewmen listening to the civilian stations noted that the lyrics of the Chinese love ballads were as mindless as those of their Nashville counterparts, though the stations were leaning more heavily to patriotic songs at the moment.

*   *   *

The same was noted at Fort Meade, Maryland. The National Security Agency had a lot of ferret satellites up and circling the globe, including two monster Rhyolite-types in geosynchronous orbit over the equator, and all were tuned to Chinese military and government channels. The FM-radio chatter associated with military formations had trended down to zero in the last twelve hours, and to the uniformed and civilian analysts alike that meant just one thing: A quiet army is an army planning to do something.

*   *   *

348

The people at the National Reconnaissance Office had the main tasking in finishing up a Special National Intelligence Estimate, because people tended to believe photographs more than mere words. The imagery had been computer-matched with the radar-imaging satellites' 'take', but surprisingly to no one, the assembly areas were mostly empty now. The tanks and other tracked vehicles had lingered only long enough to get reorganized after the train trip, and had moved out north, judging by the ruts they'd left in the mainly dirt roads of the region. They'd taken the time to spread their camouflage nets over the re-deployed tanks, but that, too, had been a pro forma waste of time, because they could as little hide the track marks of hundreds of such vehicles as they could hide a mountain range. And scarcely any such effort had been taken with the hundreds of supply trucks, which, they saw, were still moving in tight little convoys, at about thirty kilometers per hour, heading for assembly areas just a few klicks south of where the shooters were. The imagery was printed up on six of the big laser printers custom-made for the NRO, and driven to the White House, where people were mainly sitting around in the Oval Office pulling a Presidential all-nighter, which was rather more special than those done by the deliveryman, an Army sergeant E-5 in this case. The civilian analyst who'd come with him stayed inside while the NCO walked back out to the government Ford sedan, having left behind a Newport hundred-millimeter cigarette for the President.

'Jack, you're bad,' Jackson observed. 'Bumming

a smoke off that innocent young boy.'

'Stick it, Robby,' POTUS replied with a grin. The smoke made him cough, but it helped him stay awake as much as the premium coffee did. 'You handle the stress your way, I'll handle it my way. Okay, what do we have here?' the President asked the senior analyst.

'Sir, this is as many armored vehicles in one area as I have ever seen in China, plus all their equipment. They're going north, and soon, in less than three days, I'd say.'

'What about air?' Jackson asked.

'Right here, sir.' The analyst's finger traced over one of the photos. 'Dedicated fighter base at Jinxi is a good example. Here's a squadron of Russian-made Su-27s, plus a whole regiment of J-7s. The Sukhoi's a pretty good fighter plane, similar in mission and capabilities to an early F-15. The -7's a day-fighter knockoff of the old MiG-21, modified for ground attack as well as mixing up in the furball. You can count sixty-eight aircraft. Probably at least four were in the air when the satellite went overhead. Note the fueling trucks right on the ramp, and this aircraft has ground crew tinkering with it. We estimate that this base was stood-down for five days—'

'—getting everything ready?' Jackson asked. That's how people did it.

'Yes, sir. You will also note missile noses peeking out under the wings of all these aircraft. They appear to be loaded for combat.'

'White ones on the rails,' Robby observed. 'They're planning to go do some work.'

'Unless our note gets them to calm down,' Ryan said, with a minor degree of hope in his voice. A

350

very minor note, the others in the room thought. The President got one last puff off the purloined Newport and stubbed it out. 'Might it help for me to make a direct personal call to Premier Xu?'

'Honest answer?' It was Professor Weaver, rather the worse for wear at four in the Washington morning.

'The other sort isn't much use to me at the moment,' Ryan replied, not quite testily.

'It will look good in the papers and maybe the history books, but it is unlikely to affect their decision-making process.'

'It's worth a try,' Ed Foley said in disagreement. 'What do we have to lose?'

'Wait until eight, Jack,' van Damm thought. 'We don't want him to think we've been up all night. It'll inflate his sense of self-worth.'

Ryan turned to look at the windows on his south wall. The drapes hadn't been closed, and anyone passing by could have noted that the lights had been on all night. But, strangely, he didn't know if the Secret Service ever turned them off at night.

'When do we start moving forces?' Jack asked next.

'The Air Attaché will call from Moscow when his talks have been concluded. Ought to be any time.'

The President grunted. 'Longer night than ours.'

'He's younger than we are,' Mickey Moore observed. 'Just a colonel.'

'If this goes, what are our plans like?' van Damm asked.

'Hyperwar,' Moore answered. 'The world doesn't know the new weapons we've been developing. It'll make DESERT STORM look like slow motion.'

CHAPTER FORTY-EIGHT

OPENING GUNS

While others were pulling all-nighters, Gennady Iosifovich Bondarenko was forgetting what sleep was supposed to have been. His teleprinter was running hot with dispatches from Moscow, reading that occupied his time, and not always to his profit. Russia had still not learned to leave people alone when they were doing their jobs, and as a result, his senior communications officer cringed when he came in with new 'FLASH' traffic.

'Look,' the general said to his intelligence officer. 'What I need is information on what equipment they have, where they are, and how they are postured to move north on us. Their politics and objectives are not as important to me as where they are right now!'

'I expect to have hard information from Moscow momentarily. It will be American satellite coverage, and—'

'God damn it! I remember when we had our own fucking satellites. What about aerial reconnaissance?'

'The proper aircraft are on their way to us now. We'll have them flying by tomorrow noon, but do we dare send them over Chinese territory?' Colonel Tolkunov asked.

'Do we dare not to?' CINC–FAR EAST demanded in reply.

'General,' the G-2 said, 'the concern is that we would be giving the Chinese a political excuse for

352

the attack.'

'Who said that?'

'Stavka.'

Bondarenko's head dropped over the map table. He took a breath and closed his eyes for three blissful seconds, but all that achieved was to make him wish for an hour—no, just thirty minutes of sleep. That's all, he thought, just thirty minutes.

'A political excuse,' the general observed. 'You know, Vladimir Konstantinovich, once upon a time, the Germans were sending highflying reconnaissance aircraft deep into Western Russia, scouting us out prior to their invasion. There was a special squadron of fighters able to reach their altitude, and their regimental commander asked for permission to intercept them. He was relieved of his command on the spot. I suppose he was lucky that he wasn't shot. He ended up a major ace and a Hero of the Soviet Union before some German fighter got him. You see, Stalin was afraid of provoking Hitler, too!'

'Comrade Colonel?' Heads turned. It was a young sergeant with an armful of large-format photographs.

'Here, quickly!'

The sergeant laid them on the table, obscuring the topographical maps that had occupied the previous four hours. The quality wasn't good. The imagery had been transmitted over a fax machine instead of a proper photographic printer, but it was good enough for their purposes. There were even inserts, small white boxes with legends typed in, in English, to tell the ignorant what was in the pretty little pictures. The intelligence officer was the first to make sense of it all.

'Here they come,' the colonel breathed. He checked the coordinates and the time indicated in the lower-right corner of the top photo. 'That's a complete tank division, and it's right'—he turned back to the printed map—'right here, just as we expected. Their marshaling point is Harbin. Well, it had to be. All their rail lines converge there. Their first objective will be Belogorsk.'

'And right up the valley from there,' Bondarenko agreed. 'Through this pass, then northwest.' One didn't need to be a Nobel laureate to predict a line of advance. The terrain was the prime objective condition to which all ambitions and plans had to bend. Bondarenko could read the mind of the enemy commander well enough, because any trained soldier would see the contour lines on the map and analyze them the same way. Flat was better than sloped. Clear was better than wooded. Dry was better than wet. There was a lot of sloped terrain on the border, but it smoothed out, and there were too many valleys inviting speedy advance. With enough troops, he could have made every one of those valleys a deathtrap, but if he'd had enough troops, the Chinese wouldn't be lined up on his border. They'd be sitting in their own prepared defenses, fearing him. But that was not the shape of the current world for Commander-in-Chief Far East.

The 265th Motor Rifle was a hundred kilometers back from the border. The troops were undergoing frantic gunnery training now, because that would generate the most rapid return for investment. The battalion and regimental officers were in their command posts running map-table exercises, because Bondarenko needed them thinking, not shooting. He had sergeants for that. The good news for Bondarenko was that his soldiers enjoyed shooting live rounds, and their skill levels were improving rapidly. The bad news was that for every trained tank crew he had, the Chinese had over twenty.

'What an ambush we could lay, if we only had the men,' Tolkunov breathed.

'When I was in America, watching them train, I heard a good if-only joke. If only your aunt had balls, then she'd be your uncle, Vladimir Konstantinovich.'

'Quite so, Comrade General.' They both turned back to the maps and the photos.

*　　　*　　　*

'So, they know what we're doing,' Qian Kun observed. 'This is not a good development.'

'You can know what a robber will do, but if he has a pistol and you don't, what difference does it make?' Zhang Han San asked in return. 'Comrade Marshal?'

'One cannot hide so large a movement of troops,' Marshal Luo said blandly. 'Tactical surprise is always hard to achieve. But we do have strategic surprise.'

'That is true,' Tan Deshi told the Politburo. 'The Russians have alerted some of their divisions for movement, but they are all in the west, and days away, and all wiil approach down this rail line, and our air force can close it, can't you, Luo?'

'Easily,' the Defense Minister agreed.

'And what of the Americans?' Fang Gan asked. 'In that note we just got, they have told us that they

355

regard the Russians as allies. How many times have people underestimated the Americans, Zhang? Including yourself,' he added.

'There are objective conditions which apply even to the Americans, for all their magic,' Luo assured the assembly.

'And in three years we will be selling them oil and gold,' Zhang assured them all in turn. 'The Americans have no political memory. They always adapt to the changing shape of the world. In 1949, they drafted the NATO Treaty, which included their bitter enemies in Germany. Look at what they did with Japan, after dropping atomic bombs on them. The only thing we should consider: though few Americans will be deployed, and they will have to take their chances along with everyone else, perhaps we should avoid inflicting too many casualties. We would also do well to treat prisoners and captured civilians gently—the world does have sensibilities we must regard somewhat, I suppose.'

'Comrades,' Fang said, summoning up his courage for one last display of his inner feelings. 'We still have the chance to stop this from happening, as Marshal Luo told us some days ago. We are not fully committed until shots are fired. Until then, we can say we were running a defense exercise, and the world will go along with that explanation, for the reasons my friend Zhang has just told us. But once hostilities are begun, the tiger is out of the cage. Men defend what is theirs with tenacity. You will recall that Hitler underestimated the Russians, to his ultimate sorrow. Iran underestimated the Americans just last year, causing disaster for them and the death of their leader. Are we *sure* that we can prevail in this adventure?' he asked. 'Sure? We gamble with the life of our country here. We ought not to forget that.'

'Fang, my old comrade, you are wise and thoughtful as ever,' Zhang responded graciously. 'And I know you speak on behalf of our nation and our people, but as we must not underestimate our enemies, so we ought not to underestimate ourselves. We fought the Americans once before, and we gave them the worst military defeat in their history, did we not?'

'Yes, we did surprise them, but in the end we lost a *million* men, including Mao's own son. And why? Because we *over*estimated our own abilities.'

'Not this time, Fang,' Luo assured them all. 'Not this time. We will do to the Russians the same thing we did to the Americans at the Yalu River. We will strike with power and surprise. Where they are weak, we will rush through. Where they are strong, we will encircle and surround. In 1950, we were a peasant army with only light weapons. Today,' Luo went on, 'we are a fully modern army. We can do things today such as even the Americas could not dream of back then. We *will* prevail,' the Defense Minister concluded with firm conviction.

'Comrades, do we wish to stop now?' Zhang asked, to focus the debate. 'Do we wish to doom our country's economic and political future? For that is the issue at hand. If we stand still, we risk national death. Who among us wishes to stand still then?'

Predictably no one, not even Qian, moved to pick up that gauntlet. The vote was entirely pro forma, and unanimous. As always, the Politburo achieved collegiality for its own sake. The ministers

357

returned to their various offices. Zhang buttonholed Tan Deshi for several minutes before heading back to his. An hour after that, he dropped in on his friend, Fang Gan.

'You are not cross with me?' Fang asked.

'The voice of caution is something that does not offend me, my old friend,' Zhang said, graciously taking his seat opposite the other's desk. He could afford to be gracious. He had won.

'I am afraid of this move, Zhang. We *did* underestimate the Americans in 1950, and it cost us many men.'

'We have the men to spare,' the senior Minister Without Portfolio pointed out. 'And it will make Luo feel valuable.'

'As if he needs that.' Fang gestured his displeasure with that strutting martinet.

'Even a dog has his uses,' his visitor pointed out.

'Zhang, what if the Russians are more formidable than you think?'

'I've taken care of that. We will create instability in their country in two days, the very day our attack begins.'

'How?'

'You'll recall we had that failed attempt against Grushavoy's senior advisor, that Golovko fellow.'

'Yes, and I counseled against that, too,' Fang reminded his visitor.

'And there, perhaps, you were right,' Zhang acknowledged, to smooth his host's feathers. 'But Tan has developed the capability, and what better way to destabilize Russia than to eliminate their President? This we can do, and Tan has his orders.'

'You assassinate a government chief in a foreign land?' Fang asked, surprised at this level of

358

boldness. 'What if you fail?'

'We commit an act of war against Russia anyway. What have we to lose by this? Nothing—but there is much to gain.'

'But the political implications . . .' Fang breathed.

'What of them?'

'What if they turn the tables on us?'

'You mean attempt to attack Xu personally?' The look on his face provided the real answer to the question: *China would be better of without the nonentity.* But even Zhang would not say that aloud, even in the privacy of this room. 'Tan assures me that our physical security is perfect. Perfect, Fang. There are no foreign intelligence operations of consequence in our country.'

'I suppose every nation says such a thing—right before the roof caves in on them. We've done well with our spying in America, for example, and for that our good Comrade Tan is to be congratulated, but arrogance falls before the blow, and such blows are never anticipated. We would do well to remember that.'

Zhang dismissed the thought: 'One cannot fear everything.'

'That is true, but to fear nothing is also imprudent.' Fang paused to mend fences. 'Zhang, you must think me an old woman.'

That made the other minister smile. 'Old woman? No, Fang, you are a comrade of many years' standing, and one of our most thoughtful thinkers. Why, do you suppose, I brought you onto the Politburo?'

To get my votes, of course, Fang didn't answer. He had the utmost respect for his senior colleague, but he wasn't blind to his faults. 'For that I am grateful.'

'For that the *people* ought to be grateful, you are so solicitous to their needs.'

'Well, one must remember the peasants and workers out there. We serve them, after all.' The ideological cant was just perfect for the moment. 'This is not an easy job we share.'

'You need to relax a little. Get that girl Ming out there, take her to your bed. You've done it before.' It was a weakness both men shared. The tension of the moment abated, as Zhang wished it to.

'Chai sucks better,' Fang replied, with a sly look.

'Then take her to your flat. Buy her some silk drawers. Get her drunk. They all like that.'

'Not a bad idea,' Fang agreed. 'It certainly helps me sleep.'

'Then do it by all means! We'll need our sleep. The next few weeks will be strenuous for us—but more so for our enemies.'

'One thing, Zhang. As you said, we must treat the captives well. One thing the Americans do not forgive rapidly is cruelty to the helpless, as we have seen here in Beijing.'

'Now, *they* are old women. They do not understand the proper use of strength.'

'Perhaps so, but if we wish to do business with them, as you say, why offend them unnecessarily?'

Zhang sighed and conceded the point, because he knew it to be the smart play. 'Very well. I will tell Luo.' He checked his watch. 'I must be off. I've having dinner with Xu tonight.'

'Give him my best wishes.'

'Of course.' Zhang rose, bowed to his friend, and took his leave. Fang took a minute or so before rising and walking to the door. 'Ming,' he called, on opening it. 'Come here.' He lingered at the door as the secretary came in, allowing his eyes to linger on Chai. Their eyes met and she winked, adding a tiny feminine smile. Yes, he needed his sleep tonight, and she would help.

'The Politburo meeting ran late this day,' Fang said, settling into his chair and doing his dictation. It took twenty-five minutes, and he dismissed Ming to do her daily transcription. Then he had Chai come in, gave her an order, and dismissed her. In another hour, the working day ended. Fang walked down to his official car, with Chai in trail. Together they rode to his comfortable apartment, and there they got down to business.

* * *

Ming met her lover at a new restaurant called the Jade Horse, where the food was better than average.

'You look troubled,' Nomuri observed.

'Busy time at the office,' she explained. 'There is big trouble to come.'

'Oh? What sort of trouble?'

'I cannot say,' she demurred. 'It will probably not affect your company.'

And Nomuri saw that he'd taken his agent to the next—actually the last—step. She no longer thought about the software on her office computer. He never brought the subject up. Better that it should happen below the visible horizon. Better that she should forget what she was doing. Your conscience doesn't worry about things you've forgotten. After dinner, they walked back to

Nomuri's place, and the CIA officer tried his best to relax her. He was only partially successful, but she was properly appreciative and left him at quarter to eleven. Nomuri had himself a nightcap, a double, and checked to make sure his computer had relayed her almost-daily report. Next week he hoped to have software he could cross-load to hers over the 'Net, so that she'd be transmitting the reports directly out to the recipe network. If Bad Things were happening in Beijing, NEC might call him back to Japan, and he didn't want SONGBIRD's reports to stop going to Langley.

*   *   *

As it happened, this one was already there, and it had generated all manner of excitement.

It was enough to make Ed Foley wish he'd lent a STU to Sergey Golovko, but America didn't give away its communications secrets that readily, and so the report had been redrafted and sent by secure fax to the U.S. Embassy in Moscow, then hand-carried to SVR headquarters by a consular officer not associated with the CIA. Of course, now they'd assume that he was a spook, which would cause the Russians to shadow him everywhere he went, and use up trained personnel of the FSS. Business was still business, even in this New World Order.

Golovko, predictably, bounced hard off his high office ceiling.

*   *   *

John Clark got the news over his secure satellite phone.

362

'What the hell?' RAINBOW SIX asked sitting still in his personal car not far from Red Square.

'You heard me,' Ed Foley explained.

'Okay, now what?'

'You're tight with their special-operations people, right?'

'Somewhat,' Clark allowed. 'We're training them.'

'Well, they might come to you for advice of some sort. You have to know what's happening.'

'Can I tell Ding?'

'Yes,' the DCI agreed.

'Good. You know, this proves the Chavez Premise.'

'What's that?' Foley asked.

'He likes to say that international relations is largely composed of one nation fucking another.'

It was enough to make Foley laugh, five thousand miles and eight time zones away. 'Well, our Chinese friends are sure playing rough.'

'How good is the information?'

'It's Holy Writ, John. Take it to the bank,' Ed assured his distant field officer.

We have some *source in Beijing*, Clark didn't observe aloud. 'Okay, Ed. If they come to me, I'll let you know. We cooperate, I presume.'

'Fully,' the DCI assured him. 'We're allies now. Didn't you see CNN?'

'I thought it was the Sci-Fi Channel.'

'You ain't the only one. Have a good one, John.'

'You, too, Ed. Bye.' Clark thumbed the END button and went on just to himself. 'Holy jumpin' Jesus.' Then he restarted the car and headed off to his rendezvous with Domingo Chavez.

Ding was at the bar that RAINBOW had adopted

during its stay in the Moscow area. The boys congregated in a large corner booth, where they complained about the local beer, but appreciated the clear alcohol preferred by the natives.

'Hey, Mr. C,' Chavez said in greeting.

'Just got a call from Ed on my portable.'

'And?'

'And John Chinaman is planning to start a little war with our hosts, and that's the good news,' Clark added.

'What the fuck is the bad news?' Chavez asked, with no small incredulity in his voice.

'Their Ministry of State Security just put a contract out on Eduard Petrovich,' John went on.

'Are they fuckin' crazy?' the other CIA officer asked the booth.

'Well, starting a war in Siberia isn't exactly a rational act. Ed let us in because he thinks the locals might want our help soon. Supposedly they know the local contact for the ChiComms. You have to figure a hot takedown's going to evolve from this, and we've been training their troopies. I figure we might be invited in to watch, but they probably wont want us to assist.'

'Agreed.'

That's when General Kirillin came in, with a sergeant at his side. The sergeant stood by the door with his overcoat unbuttoned and his right hand close to the opening. The senior officer spotted Clark and came directly over.

'I don't have your cell-phone number.'

'What do you want us for today, General?' Clark asked.

'I need for you to come with me. We have to see Chairman Golovko.'

'Do you mind if Domingo comes along?'

'That is fine,' Kirillin replied.

'I've talked to Washington recently. How much do you know?' Clark asked his Russian friend.

'Much, but not all. That's why we need to see Golovko.' Kirillin waved them to the door, where his sergeant was doing his best Doberman imitation.

'Something happening?' Eddie Price asked. No one was guarding his expression, and Price knew how to read faces.

'Tell you when we get back,' Chavez told him. The staff car waiting outside had a chase car with four men in it, and the sergeant/bodyguard accompanying the general was one of the few enlisted men who'd been let into the cross-training that RAINBOW had been running. The Russians, they knew, were coming along very well. It didn't hurt to draw people hand-selected from an already elite unit.

The cars moved through Moscow traffic with less than the usual regard for traffic and safety laws, then pulled into the main gate at #2 Dzerzhinskiy Square. The elevator was held for them, and they made the top floor in a hurry.

'Thank you for coming so quickly. I assume you've spoken with Langley,' Golovko observed.

Clark held up his cell phone.

'The encryption unit is so small?'

'Progress, Chairman,' Clark observed. 'I'm told this intelligence information is to be taken seriously.'

'Foleyeva has a fine source in Beijing. I've seen some of the "take" from him. It would appear, first, that a deliberate attempt was made on my life, and now another is planned for President Grushavoy. I've already notified him. His security people are fully alerted. The Chinese lead agent in Moscow has been identified and is under surveillance. When he receives his instructions, we will arrest him. But we do not know who his contacts are. We assume they are former Spetsnaz people loyal to him, criminals, of course, doing special work for the underworld we've grown up here.'

That made sense, John thought. 'Some people will do anything for money, Sergey Nikolay'ch. How can we help you?'

'Foley has instructed you to assist? Good of him. Given the nature of how the intelligence came to us, an American observer seems appropriate. For the takedown, we will use police, with cover from General Kirillin's people. As RAINBOW commander, this will be your task.'

Clark nodded. It wasn't all that demanding. 'Fair enough.'

'We'll keep you safe,' the general assured him.

'And you expect the Chinese to launch a war on Russia?'

'Within the week,' Golovko nodded.

'The oil and the gold?' Chavez asked.

'So it would seem.'

'Well, that's life in the big city,' Ding observed.

'We will make them regret this barbaric act,' Kirillin told everyone present.

'That remains to be seen,' Golovko cautioned. He knew what Bondarenko was saying to Stavka.

'And with you guys in NATO, we're coming to help out?' Clark asked.

'Your President Ryan is a true comrade,' the Russian agreed.

'That means RAINBOW, too, then,' John thought aloud. 'We're all NATO troopers.'

'Ain't never fought in a real war before,' Chavez thought aloud. But now he was a simulated major, and he might just get drafted into this one. His life insurance, he remembered, was fully paid up.

'It's not exactly fun, Domingo,' Clark assured him. *And I'm getting little old for this shit.*

*　　*　　*

The Chinese Embassy was under continuous and expert surveillance by a large team of officers from the Russian Federal Security Service. Almost all of them were formerly of the KGB's Second Chief Directorate. Reconstituted under a new agency's aegis, they performed the same function as the FBI's Intelligence Division, and they gave away little to their American counterparts. No fewer than twenty of them were assigned to this task. They comprised all physical types, male and female, prosperous- and impoverished-looking, middle-aged and old—but no really young ones, because this case was too important for inexperienced officers. The vehicles assigned to the task included everything from dump trucks to motorbikes, and every mobile group had at least one radio, of types so advanced that the Russian Army didn't have them yet.

Kong Deshi emerged from the PRC embassy at seven-forty. He walked to the nearest Metro station and took the escalator down. This was entirely routine. At the same time, another minor consular officer left and headed in a different direction, but the FSS officers didn't know to watch him. He walked three blocks to the second lamppost on a busy street and, passing it, he pulled a strip of white paper tape from his coat pocket and stuck it vertically on the metal post. Then he walked on to a restaurant and had dinner alone, having fulfilled a mission whose purpose he didn't know. He was the flagman for the MSS in the embassy, but was not a trained intelligence officer.

Third Secretary Kong rode the train for the proper number of stops and got off, with four FSS officers in trail, another one waiting in the station, and two more at the top of the long escalator to the surface. Along the way, he purchased a newspaper from one of the kiosks on the street. Twice he stopped, once to light a cigarette and the other time to look around as if lost and trying to get his bearings. Both efforts, of course, were to spot a tail, but the FSS people were too numerous, some too near, and the close ones studiously, but not too studiously, looking elsewhere. The truth of the matter, as known to the FBI and the British Security Service as well, is that once a contact is identified, he is as naked and helpless as a newborn in the jungle, as long as those shadowing him are not total fools. These KGB-trained professionals were anything but fools. The only thing they didn't know was the identity of the flagman, but that, as usual, was something you might never get. The problem there was that you never knew how quickly to get the dead-drop that was about to be made.

The other problem for the control agent, Kong Deshi, was that once the location of the dead-drop was identified, it was as easily watched as the single cloud in an otherwise clear sky. The size of the surveillance troop was just to make sure there wasn't another drop. And there wasn't. Kong sat down on the expected bench. Here he violated fieldcraft by acting as though he could read a newspaper in the diminishing light, but as there was a streetlamp close by, it wouldn't tip off the casual onlooker.

'There,' one of the FSS men observed. Kong's right hand made the emplacement. Three minutes later, he folded his paper and strolled off, in the same direction he'd been heading. The FSS detail let him go a long way before they moved in.

Again it was done from a van, and again the locksmith was inside and waiting with the custom-made key. Also in the van was a high-end American laptop computer with the onetime cipher pad preprogrammed in, an exact copy of Suvorov/Koniev's desktop machine in his upscale flat on the ring road. And so, the senior FSS officer on the case thought, their quarry was like a tiger prowling through the jungle with ten unknown rifles aimed at it, powerful, and dangerous, perhaps, but utterly doomed.

The transfer case was delivered. The locksmith popped it open. The contents were unfolded and photocopied, then replaced, and the case was resealed and returned to its spot on the metal plate under the bench. Already a typist was keying in the random letters of the message, and inside of four minutes, the clear-text came up.

'*Yob tvoyu mat!*' the senior officer observed. 'They want him to kill President Grushavoy!'

'What is that?' a junior officer asked. The case-leader just handed over the laptop computer and let him read the screen.

369

'This is an act of war,' the major breathed. The colonel nodded.

'It is that, Gregoriy.' And the van pulled away. He had to report this, and do it immediately.

*   *   *

Lieutenant Provalov was home when the call came. He grumbled the usual amount as he re-dressed and headed to FSS headquarters. He hadn't grown to love the Federal Security Service, but he had come to respect it. With such resources, he thought, he could end crime in Moscow entirely, but they didn't share resources, and they retained the above-the-law arrogance their antecedent agency had once displayed. Perhaps it was necessary. The things they investigated were no less serious than murder, except in scale. Traitors killed not individuals, but entire regions. Treason was a crime that had been taken seriously in his country for centuries, and one that his nation's long-standing institutional paranoia had always feared as much as it had hated.

They were burning more than the usual amount of midnight oil here, Provalov saw. Yefremov was standing in his office, reading a piece of paper with the sort of blank look on his face that frequently denoted something monstrous.

'Good evening, Pavel Georgiyevich.'

'Lieutenant Provalov. Here.' Yefremov handed over the paper. 'Our subject grows ambitious. Or at least his controllers do.'

The militia lieutenant took the page and read it quickly, then returned to the top to give it a slower redigestion.

'When did this happen?'

'Less than an hour ago. What observations do you make?'

'We should arrest him at once!' the cop said predictably.

'I thought you'd say that. But instead we will wait and see whom he contacts. Then we will snatch him up. But first, I want to see the people he notifies.'

'What if he does it from a cell phone or a pay phone?'

'Then we will have the telephone company identify them for us. But I want to see if he has a contact within an important government office. Suvorov had many colleagues where he was in KGB. I want to know which of them have turned mercenary, so that we can root all of them out. The attack on Sergey Nikolay'ch displayed a frightening capability. I want to put an end to it, to scoop that all up, and send them all to a labor camp of strict regime.' The Russian penal system had three levels of camps. Those of 'mild' regime were unpleasant. The 'medium' ones were places to avoid. But those of 'strict' regime were hell on earth. They were particularly useful for getting the recalcitrant to speak of things they preferred to keep quiet about in ordinary circumstances. Yefremov had the ability to control which scale of punishment a man earned. Suvorov already merited death, in Russia, usually delivered by a bullet . . . but there were worse things than death.

'The President's security detail has been warned?'

The FSS officer nodded. 'Yes, though that was a tender one. How can we be sure that one of them is not compromised? That nearly happened to the American President last year, you may have heard, and it is a possibility we have to consider. They are all being watched. But Suvorov had few contacts with the Eighth Directorate when he was KGB, and none of the people he knew ever switched over to there.'

'You are sure of that?'

'We finished the cross-check three days ago. We've been busy checking records. We even have a list of people Suvorov might call. Sixteen of them, in fact. All of their phones have been tapped, and all are being watched.' But even the FSS didn't have the manpower to put full surveillance details on those potential suspects. This had become the biggest case in the history of the FSS, and few of the KGB's investigations had used up this much manpower, even back to Oleg Penkovskiy.

'What about the names Amalrik and Zimyanin?'

'Zimyanin came up in our check, but not the other. Suvorov didn't know him, but Zimyanin did—they were comrades in Afghanistan—and presumably recruited the other himself. Of the sixteen others, seven are prime suspects, all Spetsnaz, three officers and four non-coms, all of them people who've put their talent and training on the open market. Two are in St. Petersburg, and might have been implicated in the elimination of Amalrik and Zimyanin. It would appear that their comradeship was lacking,' Yefremov observed dryly. 'So, Provalov, do you have anything to add?'

'No, it would seem that you have covered all likely investigative avenues.'

'Thank you. Since it remains a murder case, you will accompany us when we make the arrest.'

'The American who assisted us . . . ?'

'He may come along,' Yefremov said generously. 'We'll show him how we do things here in Russia.'

*   *   *

Reilly was back in the U.S. Embassy on the STU, talking to Washington.

'Holy shit,' the agent observed.

'That about covers it,' Director Murray agreed. 'How good's their Presidential-protective detail?'

'Pretty good. As good as the Secret Service? I don't know what their investigative support is like, but on the physical side, I'd have to say they're okay.'

'Well, they've certainly been warned by now. Whatever they have is going to be perked up a notch or two. When will they do the takedown on this Suvorov guy?'

'Smart move is to sit on it until he makes a move. Figure the Chinese will get the word to him soon—like now, I suppose—and then he'll make some phone calls. That's when I'd put the arm on him, and not before.'

'Agreed,' Murray observed. 'We want to be kept informed on all this. So, stroke your cop friend, will ya?'

'Yes, sir.' Reilly paused. 'This war scare is for real?'

'It looks that way,' Murray confirmed. 'We're ramping up to help them out, but I'm not sure how it's going to play out. The President's hoping that the NATO gig will scare them off, but we're not sure of that either. The Agency's running in circles trying to figure the PRC out. Aside from that, I don't know much.'

That surprised Reilly. He'd thought Murray was tight with the President, but supposed now that this information was too compartmentalized.

*   *   *

'I'll take that,' Colonel Aliyev said to the communications officer.

'It's for the immediate attention of—'

'He needs sleep. To get to him, you must go through me,' the operations officer announced, reading through the dispatches. 'This one can wait . . . this one I can take care of. Anything else?'

'This one's from the President!'

'President Grushavoy needs a lucid general more than he needs an answer to this, Pasha.' Aliyev could use some sleep, too, but there was a sofa in the room, and its cushions were calling out to him.

'What's Tolkunov doing?'

'Updating his estimate.'

'Is it getting better in any way?' Comms asked.

'What do you think?' Ops replied.

'Shit.'

'That's about right, comrade. Know where we can purchase chopsticks for us to eat with?'

'Not while I have my service pistol,' the colonel replied. At nearly two meters in height, he was much too tall to be a tanker or an infantryman. 'Make sure he sees these when he wakes. I'll fix it with Stavka.'

'Good. I'm going to get a few hours, but wake me, not him,' Aliyev told his brother officer.

'*Da.*'

They were small men in the main. They started arriving at Never, a small railroad town just east of Skovorodino, on day-coaches tacked onto the regular rail service on the Trans-Siberian Railroad. Getting off, they found officers in uniform directing them to buses. These headed down a road paralleling the railroad right-of-way southeast toward a tunnel drilled ages before in the hills over the diminutive Urkan River. Beside the tunnel was an opening which appeared to the casual viewer to be a siding for service equipment for the railroad. And so it was, but this service tunnel went far into the hillside, and branching off it were many more, all constructed in the 1930s by political prisoners, part of Iosef Stalin's gulag labor empire. In these man-made caverns were three hundred T-55 tanks, built in the mid-1960s and never used, but rather stored here to defend against an invasion from China, along with a further two hundred BTR-60 wheeled infantry carriers, plus all the other rolling stock for a Soviet-pattern tank division. The post was garrisoned by a force of four hundred conscripts who, like generations before them, served their time servicing the tanks and carriers, mainly moving from one to another, turning over the diesel engines and cleaning the metal surfaces, which was necessary because of water seepage through the stone roof. The 'Never Depot,' it was called on classified maps, one of several such places close to the main rail line that went from Moscow to Vladivostok. Cunningly hidden, partially in plain sight, it was one of the aces that General-Colonel Bondarenko had hidden up his sleeve.

As were the men. They were mostly in their thirties, confused, and more than a little angry at having been called away from their homes. However, like good Russians, or indeed good citizens in any land, they got their notices, figured that their country had a need, and it *was* their country, and so about three-fourths of them went as summoned. Some saw familiar faces from their time in the conscript army of the Soviet Union—these men were mainly from that time—and greeted old friends, or ignored those less happily remembered. Each was given a preprinted card telling him where to go, and so the tank crews and infantry squads formed up, the latter finding their uniforms and light weapons, plus ammunition, waiting in the assigned motor-carrier. The tank crewmen were all small men, about 167 centimeters in height—about five feet six inches to an American—because the interiors of the old Russian tanks did not permit tall men to fit inside.

The tankers returning to the steeds of their youth knew the good and bad points of the T-55s. The engines were made of roughly machined parts and would grind off a full kilogram of metal shavings into the oil sumps during the first few hours of running, but, they all figured, that would have been taken care of by the routine turning-over of the engines in the depot. The tanks were, in fact, in surprisingly good shape, better than the ones they'd used on active duty. This seemed both strange and unsurprising to the returning soldiers, because the Red Army had made little logical sense when they'd been in it, but that, for a Soviet citizen of the 1970s and '80s, was not unexpected either.

Most remembered their service with some fondness, and for the usual reasons, the chance to travel and see new, different things, and the comradeship of men their own age—a time of life in which young men seek out the new and the exciting. The poor food, miserable pay, and strenuous duty were largely forgotten, though exposure to the rolling equipment brought back some of it with the instant memory that accompanied smells and feels from the past. The tanks all had full internal fuel tanks, plus the oil drums affixed to the rear that had made all of the men cringe when thinking about a battlefield—one live round could turn every tank into a pillar of fire, and so that was the fuel you burned off first, just so you could pull the handle to dump the damned things off when the first bullet flew.

Most agreeably of all, those who pressed the start buttons felt and heard the familiar rumble after only a few seconds of cranking. The benign environment of this cavern had been kind to these old, but essentially unused, tanks. They might have been brand new, fresh from the assembly lines of the massive factory at Nizhnyi Tagil, for decades the armory of the Red Army. The one thing that had changed, they all saw, was that the red star was gone from the glacis plate, replaced with an all-too-visible representation of their new white-blue-red flag, which, they all thought, was far too good an aiming point. Finally they were all called away from their vehicles by the young reserve officers, who, they saw, looked a little worried. Then the speeches began, and the reservists found out why.

*　　　*　　　*

'Damn, isn't she a lovely one,' the FSS officer said, getting into the car. They'd followed their subject to yet another expensive restaurant, where he'd dined alone, then walked into the bar, and within five minutes fixed upon a woman who'd also arrived alone, pretty in her black, red-striped dress that looked to have been copied from some Italian designer. Suvorov/Koniev was driving back toward his flat, with a total of six cars in trail, three of them with light-change switches on their dashboards to alter their visual appearance at night. The cop riding in the number-two car thought that was an especially clever feature.

He was taking his time, not racing his car to show his courage, but instead dazzling the girl with his man-of-the-world demeanor, the investigators thought. The car slowed as it passed one corner, a street with old iron lampposts, then changed direction, if not abruptly, then unexpectedly.

'Shit, he's going to the park,' the senior FSS guy said, picking up his radio microphone to say this over the air. 'He must have spotted a flag somewhere.'

And so he did, but first he dropped off what appeared to be a very disappointed woman, holding some cash in her hand to ease the pain. One of the FSS cars paused to pick her up for questioning, while the others continued their distant pursuit, and five minutes later, it happened. Suvorov/Koniev parked his car on one side of the park and walked across the darkened grass to the other, looking about as he did so, not noticing the fact that five cars were circling.

'That's it. He picked it up.' He'd done it

skillfully, but that didn't matter if you knew what to look for. Then he walked back to his car. Two of the cars headed directly over to his flat, and the three in trail just kept going when he pulled in.

*   *   *

'He said he felt suddenly ill. I gave him my card,' she told the interrogators. 'He gave me fifty euros for my trouble.' Which was fair payment, she thought, for wasting half an hour of her valuable time.

'Anything else? Did he look ill?'

'He said that the food suddenly disagreed with him. I wondered if he'd gotten cold feet as some men do, but not this one. He is a man of some sophistication. You can always tell.'

'Very well. Thank you, Yelena. If he calls you, please let us know.'

'Certainly.' It had been a totally painless interview, which came as rather a surprise for her, and for that reason she'd cooperated fully, wondering what the hell she'd stumbled into. A criminal of some sort? Drug trafficker, perhaps? If he called her, she'd call these people and to hell with him. Life for a woman of her trade was difficult enough.

*   *   *

'He's on the computer,' an electronics specialist said at FSS headquarters. He read the keystrokes off the keyboard bug they'd planted, and they not only showed up on his screen, but also ran live on a duplicate of the subject desktop system. 'There,

379

there's the clear-text. He's got the message.'

There was a minute or so of thoughtful pause, and then he began typing again. He logged onto his e-mail service and started typing up messages. They all said some variant of 'contact me as soon as you can,' and that told them what he was up to. A total of four letters had gone out, though one suggested forwarding to one or more others. Then he logged off and shut his computer down.

'Now, let's see if we can identify his correspondents, shall we?' the senior investigator told his staff. That took all of twenty minutes. What had been routine drudgery was now as exciting as watching the World Cup football final.

*   *   *

The Myasishchev M-5 reconnaissance aircraft lifted off from Taza just before dawn. An odd-looking design with its twin booms, it was a forty-years-too-late Russian version of the venerable Lockheed U-2, able to cruise at seventy thousand feet at a sedate five hundred or so knots and take photographs in large numbers with high resolution. The pilot was an experienced Russian air force major with orders not to stray within ten kilometers of the Chinese border. This was to avoid provoking his country's potential enemies, and that order was not as easy to execute as it had been to write down in Moscow, because the borders between countries are rarely straight lines. So, the major programmed his autopilot carefully and sat back to monitor his instruments while the camera systems did all the real work. The main instrument he monitored was his threat-receiver, essentially a radio scanner programmed to note the energy of radar transmitters. There were many such transmitters on the border, most of the low- to mid-frequency search types, but then a new one came up. This was on the X-band, and it came from the south, and that meant that a Chinese surface-to-air missile battery was illuminating him with a tracking-and-targeting radar. *That* got his attention, because although seventy thousand was higher than any commercial aircraft could fly, and higher than many fighters could reach, it was well within the flight envelope of a SAM, as an American named Francis Gary Powers had once discovered over Central Russia. A fighter could outmaneuver most SAMs, but the M-5 was not a fighter and had trouble outmaneuvering clouds on a windless day. And so he kept his eye on the threat—receiver's dials while his ears registered the shrill *beep-beep* of the aural alert. The visual display showed that the pulse-repetition rate was in the tracking rather than the lock-up mode. So, a missile was probably not in the air, and the sky was clear enough that he'd probably see the smoke trail that such missiles always left, and today—no, no smoke coming up from the ground. For defensive systems, he had only a primitive chaff dispenser and prayer. Not even a white-noise jammer, the major groused. But there was no sense in worrying. He *was* ten kilometers inside his own country's airspace, and whatever SAM systems the Chinese possessed were probably well inside their own borders. It would be a stretch for them to reach him, and he could always turn north and run while punching loose a few kilos of shredded aluminum foil to give the inbound missile something else to chase. As it played out, the mission involved four complete sweeps of the border region, and that required ninety otherwise boring minutes before he reprogrammed the M-5 back to the old fighter base outside Taza.

The ground crew supporting the mission had also been deployed from the Moscow area. As soon as the M-5 rolled to a stop, the film cassettes were unloaded and driven to the portable film lab for development, then forwarded, still wet, to the interpreters. They saw few tanks, but lots of tracks in the ground, and that was all they needed to see.

CHAPTER FORTY-NINE

DISARMING

'I know, Oleg. I understand that we developed the intelligence in Washington and forwarded it to your people immediately,' Reilly said to his friend.

'You must be proud of that,' Provalov observed.

'Wasn't the Bureau that did it,' Reilly responded. The Russians would be touchy about having Americans provide them with such sensitive information. Maybe Americans would have reacted the same way. 'Anyway, what are you going to do about it?'

'We're trying to locate his electronic correspondents. We have their addresses, and they are all on Russian-owned ISPs. FSS probably has them all identified by now.'

'Arrest them when?'

'When they meet Suvorov. We have enough to

make the arrests now.'

Reilly wasn't sure about that. The people Suvorov wanted to meet could always say that they came to see him by invitation without having a clue as to the purpose of the meeting, and a day-old member of the bar could easily enough sell the 'reasonable doubt' associated with that to a jury. Better to wait until they all did something incriminating, and then squeeze one of them real hard to turn state's evidence on the rest. But the rules and the juries were different here.

*   *   *

'Anatoliy, what are you thinking about?' Golovko asked.

'Comrade Chairman, I am thinking that Moscow has suddenly become dangerous,' Major Shelepin replied. 'The idea of former Spetsnaz men conspiring to commit treason on this scale sickens me. Not just the threat, but also the infamy of it. These men were my comrades in the army, trained as I was to be guardians of the State.' The handsome young officer shook his head.

'Well, when this place was the KGB, it happened to us more than once. It is unpleasant, yes, but it is reality. People are corruptible. It is human nature,' Golovko said soothingly. *Besides, the threat isn't against me now*, he didn't add. An unworthy thought, perhaps, but that also was human nature. 'What is President Grushavoy's detail doing now?'

'Sweating, I should imagine. Who can say that this is the only threat? What if this Kong bastard has more than one such agent in Moscow? We should pick him up, too.'

383

'So we shall, when the time comes. He's been observed to do only one dead-drop over the past week, and we control that one—yes, yes, I know,' Sergey added, when he saw the beginnings of Anatoliy's objections. 'He isn't the only MSS operative in Moscow, but he's probably the only one on this case. Security considerations are universal. They must worry that one of their officers might be in *our* employ, after all. There are many wheels in such an operation, and they don't all turn in the same direction, my young friend. You know what I miss?'

'I should imagine it is having the second chief directorate under the same roof. That way the operation would be run cooperatively.'

Golovko smiled. 'Correct, Anatoliy Ivan'ch. For now, we can only do our job and wait for others to do theirs. And, yes, waiting is never an entertaining way to spend one's time.' With that observation, both men resumed staring at the desk phones, waiting for them to ring.

*   *   *

The only reason that surveillance hadn't been tightened any more was that there wasn't enough room for the additional personnel, and Suvorov might take note of the thirty people who followed him everywhere. That day he awoke at his normal hour, washed up, had coffee and kasha for breakfast, left the apartment building at 9:15, and drove his car into the city, with a good deal of elusive company. He parked his car two blocks from Gor'kiy Park and walked the rest of the way there.

384

So did four others, also under surveillance. They met at a magazine kiosk at precisely 9:45 and walked together toward a coffee shop that was disagreeably crowded, too much so for any of the watchers to get close enough to listen in, though the faces were observed. Suvorov/Koniev did most of the talking, and the other four listened intently, and nods started.

Yefremov of the Federal Security Service kept his distance. He was senior enough that he could no longer guarantee that his face was unknown, and had to trust the more junior men to get in close, their earpieces removed and radio transmitters turned off, wishing they could read lips like the people in spy movies.

For Pavel Georgiyevich Yefremov, the question was, what to do now? Arrest them all and risk blowing the case—or merely continue to shadow, and risk having them go forward . . . and perhaps accomplish the mission?

The question would be answered by one of the four contacts. He was the oldest of them, about forty, a Spetsnaz veteran of Afghanistan with the Order of the Red Banner to his name. His name was Igor Maximov. He held up his hand, rubbing forefinger and thumb, and, getting the answer to his question, he shook his head and politely took his leave. His departure was a cordial one, and his personal two-man shadow team followed him to the nearest Metro station while the others continued talking.

On learning this, Yefremov ordered him picked up. That was done when he got off the Metro train five kilometers away at the station near his flat, where he lived with his wife and son. The man did not resist and was unarmed. Docile as a lamb, he accompanied the two FSS officers to their headquarters.

'Your name is Maximov, Igor Il'ych,' Yefremov told him. 'You met with your friend Suvorov, Klementi Ivan'ch, to discuss participation in a crime. We want to hear your version of what was discussed.'

'Comrade Yefremov, I met some old friends for coffee this morning and then I left. Nothing in particular was discussed. I do not know what you are talking about.'

'Yes, of course,' the FSS man replied. 'Tell me, do you know two former Spetsnaz men like yourself, Amalrik and Zimyanin?'

'I've heard the names, but I don't know the faces.'

'Here are the faces.' Yefremov handed over the photos from the Leningrad Militia. 'They are not pleasant to look upon.'

Maximov didn't blanch, but he didn't look at the photos with affection either. 'What happened to them?'

'They did a job for your comrade, Suvorov, but he was evidently displeased with how they went about it, and so, they went swimming in the River Neva. Maximov, we know that you were Spetsnaz. We know that you earn your living today doing illegal things, but that is not a matter of concern to us at the moment. We want to know exactly what was said at the coffee shop. You will tell us this, the easy way or the hard way. The choice is yours.' When he wanted to, Yefremov could come on very hard to his official guests. In this case, it wasn't difficult. Maximov was not a stranger to violence, at least on the giving side. The receiving side was something he had no wish to learn about.

'What do you offer me?'

'I offer you your freedom in return for your cooperation. You left the meeting before any conclusions were reached. That is why you are here. So, do you wish to speak now, or shall we wait a few hours for you to change your mind?'

Maximov was not a coward—Spetsnaz didn't have many of those, in Yefremov's experience—but he was a realist, and realism told him that he had nothing to gain by noncooperation.

'He asked me and the others to participate in a murder. I presume it will be a difficult operation, otherwise why would he need so many men? He offers for this twenty thousand euros each. I decided that my time is more valuable than that.'

'Do you know the name of the target?'

Maximov shook his head. 'No. He did not say. I did not ask.'

'That is good. You see, the target is President Grushavoy.' That got a reaction, as Maximov's eyes flared.

'That is state treason,' the former Spetsnaz sergeant breathed, hoping to convey the idea that he'd never do such a thing. He learned fast.

'Yes. Tell me, is twenty thousand euros a good price for a murder?'

'I would not know. If you want me to tell you that I have killed for money, no, Comrade Yefremov, I will not say that.'

But you have, and you'd probably participate in this one if the price went high enough. In Russia, E20,000 was a considerable sum. But Yefremov had much bigger fish to fry. 'The others at the meeting, what do you know of them?'

'All are Spetsnaz veterans. Ilya Suslov and I served together east of Qandahar. He's a sniper, a very good one. The others, I know them casually, but I never served with them.'

Sniper. Well, those were useful, and President Grushavoy appeared in public a lot. He was scheduled to have an outdoor rally the very next day, in fact. It was time to wrap this up.

'So, Suvorov spoke of a murder for hire?'

'Yes, he did.'

'Good. We will take your statement. You were wise to cooperate, Igor Il'ych.' Yefremov had a junior officer lead him away. Then he lifted his phone. 'Arrest them all,' he told the field commander.

'The meeting broke up. We have all of them under surveillance. Suvorov is en route back to his flat with one of the three.'

'Well, assemble the team and arrest them both.'

*　　　*　　　*

'Feeling better?' Colonel Aliyev asked.

'What time is it?'

'Fifteen-forty, Comrade General,' Colonel Aliyev replied. 'You slept for thirteen hours. Here are some dispatches from Moscow.'

'You let me sleep that long?' the general demanded, instantly angry.

'The war has not begun. Our preparations, such as they are, are progressing, and there seemed no sense in waking you. Oh, we have our first set of reconnaissance photos. Not much better than the American ones we had faxed to us. Intelligence has firmed up its estimate. It's not getting any better. We have support now from an American ELINT aircraft, but they tell us that the Chinese aren't using their radios, which is not a surprise.

'God damn it, Andrey!' the general responded, rubbing his unshaven face with both hands.

'So, court-martial me after you've had your coffee. I got some sleep, too. You have a staff. I have a staff, and I decided to let them do their jobs while we slept,' the operations officer said defiantly.

'What of the Never Depot?'

'We have a total of one hundred eighty tanks operating with full crews. Shorter on the infantry component and artillery, but the reservists seem to be functioning with some degree of enthusiasm, and the 265th Motor Rifle is starting to act like a real division for the first time.' Aliyev walked over a mug of coffee with milk and sugar, the way Bondarenko preferred it. 'Drink, Gennady Iosifovich.' Then he pointed to a table piled with buttered bread and bacon.

'If we live, I will see you promoted, Colonel.'

'I've always wanted to be a general officer. But I want to see my children enter university, too. So, let's try to stay alive.'

'What of the border troops?'

'I have transport assigned to each post—where possible, two sets of transport. I've sent some of the reservists in BTRs to make sure they have a little protection against the artillery fire when they pull out. We have a lot of guns in the photos from the M-5, Comrade General. And fucking mountains of shells. But the border troops have ample protection, and the orders have gone out so that they will not need permission to leave their posts when the situation becomes untenable—at the company-officer level, that is,' Aliyev added. Commissioned officers were less likely to bug out than enlisted men.

'No word on when?'

The G-3 shook his head. 'Nothing helpful from Intelligence. The Chinese are still moving trucks and such around, from what we can tell. I'd say another day, maybe as many as three.'

*   *   *

'So?' Ryan asked.

'So, the overheads show they're still moving the chess pieces on the board,' Foley answered. 'But most of them are in place.'

'What about Moscow?'

'They're going to arrest their suspects soon. Probably going to pick up the control officer in Moscow, too. They'll sweat him some, but he does have diplomatic immunity, and you can't squeeze him much.' Ed Foley remembered when KGB had arrested his wife in Moscow. It hadn't been pleasant for her—and less so for him—but they hadn't roughed her up, either. Messing with people who traveled on diplomatic passports didn't happen often, despite what they'd seen on TV a few weeks before. And the Chinese probably regretted that one a lot, pronouncements on the SORGE feeds to the contrary notwithstanding.

'Nothing from inside to encourage us?'

'Nope.' The DCI shook his head.

'We ought to start moving the Air Force,' Vice President Jackson urged.

390

'But then it could be seen as a provocation,' Secretary Adler pointed out. 'We can't give them any excuse.'

'We can move First Armored into Russia, say it's a joint training exercise with our new NATO allies,' TOMCAT said. 'That could buy us a few days.'

Ryan weighed that and looked over at the Chairman of the Joint Chiefs. 'Well, General?'

'It can't hurt all that much. They're already working with Deutsche Rail to get the move organized.'

'Then do it,' the President ordered.

'Yes, sir.' General Moore moved to make the call.

Ryan checked his watch. 'I have a reporter to talk to.'

'Have fun,' Robby told his friend.

*   *   *

Zhigansk, on the west side of the Lena River, had once been a major regional air-defense center for the old Soviet PVO Strany, the Russian air-defense command. It had a larger-than-average airfield with barracks and hangars, and had been largely abandoned by the new Russian military, with just a caretaker staff to maintain the facility in case it might be needed someday. This turned out to be a piece of lucky foresight, because the United States Air Force started moving in that day, mainly transport aircraft from the central part of America that had staged through Alaska and flown over the North Pole to get there. The first of thirty C-5 Galaxy transports landed at ten in the morning local time, taxiing to the capacious but vacant ramps to offload their cargo under the direction of ground crewmen who'd ridden in the large passenger area aft of the wing box in the huge transports. The first things wheeled off were the Dark Star UAVs. They looked like loaves of French bread copulating atop slender wings, and were long-endurance, stealthy reconnaissance drones that took six hours to assemble for flight. The crews got immediately to work, using mobile equipment shipped on the same aircraft.

Fighter and attack aircraft came into Suntar, far closer to the Chinese border, with tankers and other support aircraft—including the American E-3 Sentry AWACS birds—just west of there at Mirnyy. At these two air bases, the arriving Americans found their Russian counterparts, and immediately the various staffs started working together. American tankers could not refuel Russian aircraft, but to everyone's relief the nozzles for ground fueling were identical, and so the American aircraft could make use of the take fuel from the Russian JP storage tanks, which, they found, were huge, and mainly underground to be protected against nuclear airbursts. The most important element of cooperation was the assignment of Russian controllers to the American AWACS, so that Russian fighters could be controlled from the American radar aircraft. Almost at once, some E-3s lifted off to test this capability, using arriving American fighters as practice targets for controlled intercepts. They found immediately that the Russian fighter pilots reacted well to the directions, to the pleased surprise of the American controllers.

They also found almost immediately that the American attack aircraft couldn't use Russian bombs and other ordnance. Even if the shackle points had been the same (they weren't), the Russian bombs had different aerodynamics from their American counterparts, and so the computer software on the American aircraft could not hit targets with them—it would have been like trying to jam the wrong cartridge into a rifle: even if you could fire the round, the sights would send it to the wrong point of impact. So, the Americans would have to fly in the bombs to be dropped, and shipping bombs by air was about as efficient as flying in gravel to build roads. Bombs came to fighter bases by ship, train, truck, and forklift, not by air. For this reason, the B-1s and other heavy-strike aircraft were sent to Andersen Air Force Base on Guam, where there *were* some bomb stores to be used, even though they were a long way from the supposed targets.

The air forces of the two sides established an immediate and friendly rapport, and in hours—as soon as the American pilots had gotten a little mandated crew rest—they were planning and flying missions together with relative ease.

*　　　*　　　*

The Quarter Horse went first. Under the watchful eyes of Lieutenant Colonel Angelo Giusti, the M1A2 main battle tanks and M3 Bradley cavalry scout vehicles rolled onto the flatcars of Deutsche Rail, accompanied by the fuel and other support trucks. Troops went into coaches at the head end of the train 'consists' and were soon heading east to Berlin, where they'd change over to the Russian-gauge cars for the further trip east. Oddly, there were no TV cameramen around at the moment, Giusti saw. That couldn't last, but it was one less distraction for the unit that was the eyes of First Tanks. The division's helicopter brigade was sitting at its own base, awaiting the availability of Air Force transports to ferry them east. Some genius had decided against having the aircraft fly themselves, which, Giusti thought, they were perfectly able to do, but General Diggs had told him not to worry about it. Giusti would worry about it, but not out loud. He settled into a comfortable seat in the lead passenger coach, along with his staff, and went over maps just printed up by the division's cartography unit, part of the intelligence shop. The maps showed the terrain they might be fighting for. Mostly they predicted where the Chinese would be going, and that wasn't overly demanding.

*   *   *

'So, what are we going to do?' Bob Holtzman asked.

'We're beginning to deploy forces to support our allies,' Ryan answered. 'We hope that the PRC will see this and reconsider the activities that now appear to be under way.'

'Have we been in contact with Beijing?'

'Yes.' Ryan nodded soberly. 'The DCM of our embassy in Beijing, William Kilmer, delivered a note from us to the Chinese government, and we are now awaiting a formal reply.'

'Are you telling us that you think there will be a shooting war between Russia and China?'

'Bob, our government is working very hard to

forestall that possibility, and we call on the Chinese government to think very hard about its position and its actions. War is no longer a policy option in this world. I suppose it once was, but no longer. War only brings death and ruin to people. The world has turned a corner on this thing. The lives of people—including the lives of soldiers—are too precious to be thrown away. Bob, the reason we have governments is to serve the needs and the interests of *people*, not the ambitions of rulers. I hope the leadership of the PRC will see that.' Ryan paused. 'A couple of days ago, I was at Auschwitz. Bob, that was the sort of experience to get you thinking. You could *feel* the horror there. You could hear the screams, smell the death smell, you could *see* the lines of people being led off under guns to where they were murdered. Bob, all of a sudden it wasn't just black-and-white TV anymore.

'It came to me then that there is no excuse at all for the government of a country, any country, to engage in killing for profit. Ordinary criminals rob liquor stores to get money. Countries rob countries to get oil or gold or territory. Hitler invaded Poland for *Lebensraum*, for room for Germany to expand—but, damn it, there were already people living there, and what he tried to do was to steal. That's all. Not statecraft, not vision. Hitler was a *thief* before he was a murderer. Well, the United States of America will not stand by and watch that happen again.' Ryan paused and took a sip of water.

'One of the things you learn in life is that there's only one thing really worth having, and that's love. Well, by the same token there's only one thing worth fighting for, and that is justice. Bob, that's what America fights for, and if China launches a war of aggression—a war of robbery—America will stand by her ally and stop it from happening.'

'Many say that your policy toward China has helped to bring this situation about, that your diplomatic recognition of Taiwan—' Ryan cut him off angrily.

'Bob, I will not have any of that! The Republic of China's government is a freely elected one. America *supports* democratic governments. Why? Because we stand *for* freedom and self-determination. Neither I nor America had anything to do with the cold-blooded murders we saw on TV, the death of the Papal Nuncio, Cardinal DiMilo, and the killing of the Chinese minister Yu Fa An. We had nothing to do with that. The revulsion of the entire civilized world came about because of the PRC's actions. Even then, China could have straightened it out by investigating and punishing the killers, but they chose not to, and the world reacted—to what they did all by themselves.'

'But what is this all about? Why are they massing troops on the Russian border?'

'It appears that they want what the Russians have, the new oil and gold discoveries. Just as Iraq once invaded Kuwait. It was for oil, for money, really. It was an armed robbery, just like a street thug does, mugging an old lady for her Social Security check, but somehow, for some reason, we sanctify it when it happens at the nation-state level. Well, no more, Bob. The world will no longer tolerate such things. And America will not stand by and watch this happen to our ally. Cicero once said that Rome grew great not through conquest, but rather through defending her allies. A nation

396

acquires respect from acting for things, not *against* things. You measure people not by what they are against, but by what they are *for*. America stands *for* democracy, *for* the self-determination of people. We stand *for* freedom. We stand *for* justice. We've told the People's Republic of China that if they launch a war of aggression, then America will stand with Russia and against the aggressor. We believe in a peaceful world order in which nations compete on the economic battlefield, not with tanks and guns. There's been enough killing. It's time for that to stop, and America will be there to make it stop.

'The world's policeman?' Holtzman asked. Immediately, the President shook his head.

'Not that, but we will defend our allies, and the Russian Federation is an ally. We stood with the Russian people to stop Hitler. We stand with them again,' Ryan said.

'And again we send our young people off to war?'

'There need be no war, Bob. There is no war today. Neither America nor Russia will start one. That question is in the hands of others. It isn't hard, it isn't demanding, for a nation-state to stand its military down. It's a rare professional soldier who relishes conflict. Certainly no one who's seen a battlefield will voluntarily rush to see another. But I'll tell you this: If the PRC launches a war of aggression, and if because of them American lives are placed at risk, then those who make the decision to set loose those dogs are putting their own lives at risk.'

'The Ryan Doctrine?' Holtzman asked.

'Call it anything you want. If it's acceptable to kill some infantry private for doing what his government tells him, then it's also acceptable to kill the people who tell the government what to do, the ones who send that poor, dumb private out in harm's way.'

Oh, shit, Arnie van Damm thought, hovering in the doorway of the Oval Office. *Jack, did you have to say* that?

'Thank you for your time, Mr. President,' Holtzman said. 'When will you address the nation?'

'Tomorrow. God willing, it'll be to say that the PRC has backed off. I'll be calling Premier Xu soon to make a personal appeal to him.'

'Good luck.'

*   *   *

'We are ready,' Marshal Luo told the others. 'The operation commences early tomorrow morning.'

'What have the Americans done?'

'They've sent some aircraft forward, but aircraft do not concern me,' the Defense Minister replied. 'They can sting, as a mosquito does, but they cannot do real harm to a man. We will make twenty kilometers the first day, and then fifty per day thereafter—maybe more, depending on how the Russians fight. The Russian Air Force is not even a paper tiger. We can destroy it, or at least push it back out of our way. The Russians are starting to move mechanized troops east on their railroad, but we will pound on their marshaling facility at Chita with our air assets. We can dam them up and stop them to protect our left flank until we move troops in to wall that off completely.'

'You are confident, Marshal?' Zhang asked—rhetorically, of course.

'We'll have their new gold mine in eight days, and then it's ten more to the oil,' the marshal predicted, as though describing how long it would take to build a house.

'Then you are ready?'

'Fully,' Luo insisted.

'Expect a call from President Ryan later today,' Foreign Minister Shen warned the premier.

'What will he say?' Xu asked.

'He will give you a personal plea to stop the war from beginning.'

'If he does, what ought I to say?'

'Have your secretary say you are out meeting the people,' Zhang advised. 'Don't talk to the fool.'

Minister Shen wasn't fully behind his country's policy, but nodded anyway. It seemed the best way to avoid a personal confrontation, which Xu would not handle well. His ministry was still trying to get a feel for how to handle the American President. He was so unlike other governmental chiefs that they still had difficulty understanding how to speak with him.

'What of our answer to their note?' Fang asked.

'We have not given them a formal answer,' Shen told him.

'It concerns me that they should not be able to call us liars,' Fang said. 'That would be unfortunate, I think.'

'You worry too much, Fang,' Zhang commented, with a cruel smile.

'No, in that he is correct,' Shen said, rising to his colleague's defense. 'Nations must be able to trust the words of one another, else no intercourse at all is possible. Comrades, we must remember that there will be an 'after the war,' in which we must be able to reestablish normal relations with the nations of the world. If they regard us as outlaw, that will be difficult.'

'That makes sense,' Xu observed, speaking his own opinion for once. 'No, I will not accept the call from Washington, and no, Fang, I will not allow America to call us liars.'

'One other development,' Luo said. 'The Russians have begun high-altitude reconnaissance flights on their side of the border. I propose to shoot down the next one and say that their aircraft intruded on our airspace. Along with other plans, we will use that as a provocation on their part.'

'Excellent,' Zhang observed.

*   *   *

'So?' John asked.

'So, he is in this building,' General Kirillin clarified. 'The takedown team is ready to go up and make the arrest. Care to observe?'

'Sure,' Clark agreed with a nod. He and Chavez were both dressed in their RAINBOW ninja suits, black everything, plus body armor, which struck them both as theatrical, but the Russians were being overly solicitous to their hosts, and that included official concern for their safety. 'How is it set up?'

'We have four men in the apartment next door. We anticipate no difficulties,' Kirillin told his guests. 'So, if you will follow me.'

'Waste of time, John,' Chavez observed in Spanish.

'Yeah, but they want to do a show-and-tell.' The two of them followed Kirillin and a junior officer to

400

the elevator, which whisked them up to the proper floor. A quick, furtive look showed that the corridor was clear, and they moved like cats to the occupied apartment.

'We are ready, Comrade General,' the senior Spetsnaz officer, a major, told his commander. 'Our friend is sitting in his kitchen discussing matters with his guest. They're looking at how to kill President Grushavoy tomorrow on his way to parliament. Sniper rifle,' he concluded, 'from eight hundred meters.'

'You guys make good ones here,' Clark observed. Eight hundred was close enough for a good rifleman, especially on a slow-moving target like a walking man.

'Proceed, Major,' Kirillin ordered.

With that, the four-man team walked back out into the corridor. They were dressed in their own RAINBOW suits, black Nomex, and carrying the equipment Clark and his people had brought over, German MP-10 submachine guns, and .45 Beretta sidearms, plus the portable radios from E-Systems. Clark and Chavez were wearing identical gear, but not carrying weapons. Probably the real reason Kirillin had brought them over, John thought, was to show them how much his people had learned, and that was fair enough. The Russian troopers looked ready. Alert and pumped up, but not nervous, just the right amount of tenseness.

The officer in command moved down the corridor to the door. His explosives man ran a thin line of det-cord explosive along the door's edges and stepped aside, looking at his team leader for the word.

'Shoot,' the major told him—

—and before Clark's brain could register the single-word command, the corridor was sundered with the crash of the explosion that sent the solid-core door into the apartment at about three hundred feet per second. Then the Russian major and a lieutenant tossed in flashbangs sure to disorient anyone who might have been there with a gun of his own. It was hard enough for Clark and Chavez, and they'd known what was coming and had their hands over their ears. The Russians darted into the apartment in pairs, just as they'd been trained to do, and there was no other sound, except for a scream down the hall from a resident who hadn't been warned about the day's activities. That left John Clark and Domingo Chavez just standing there, until an arm appeared and waved them inside.

The inside was a predictable mess. The entry door was now fit only for kindling and toothpicks, and the pictures that decorated the wall did so without any glass in the frames. The blue sofa had a ruinous scorch mark on the right side, and the carpet was cratered by the other flash-bang.

Suvorov and Suslov had been sitting in the kitchen, always the heart of any Russian home. That had placed them far enough away from the explosion to be unhurt, though both looked stunned by the experience, and well they might be. There were no weapons in evidence, which was surprising to the Russians but not to Clark, and the two supposed miscreants were now facedown on the tile floor, their hands manacled behind them and guns not far behind their heads.

'Greetings, Klementi Ivan'ch,' General Kirillin said. 'We need to talk.'

402

The older of the two men on the floor didn't react much. First, he was not really able to, and second, he knew that talking would not improve his situation. Of all the spectators, Clark felt the most sympathy for him. To run a covert operation was tense enough. To have one blown—it had never happened to John, but he'd thought about the possibility often enough—was not a reality that one wished to contemplate. Especially in this place, though since it was no longer the Soviet Union, Suvorov could take comfort in the fact that things might have been a little worse. But not that much worse, John was sure. It was time for him to say something.

'Well executed, Major. A little heavy on the explosives, but we all do that. I say that to my own people almost every time.'

'Thank you, General Clark.' The senior officer of the strike team beamed, but not too much, trying to look cool for his subordinates. They'd just done their first real-life mission, and pleased as they all were, the attitude they had to adopt was *of course we did it right*. It was a matter of professional pride.

'So, Yuriy Andreyevich, what will happen with them now?' John asked in his best Leningrad Russian.

'They will be interrogated for murder and conspiracy to commit murder, plus state treason. We picked up Kong half an hour ago, and he's talking,' Kirillin added, lying. Suvorov might not believe it, but the statement would get his mind wandering in an uncomfortable direction. 'Take them out!' the general ordered. No sooner had that happened than an FSS officer came in to light up the desktop computer to begin a detailed check of its contents. The protection program Suvorov had installed was bypassed because they knew the key to it, from the keyboard bug they'd installed earlier. Computers, they all agreed, must have been designed with espionage in mind—but they worked both ways.

'Who are you?' a stranger in civilian clothes asked.

'John Clark' was the surprising answer in Russian. 'And you?'

'Provalov. I am a lieutenant-investigator with the militia.'

'Oh, the RPG case?'

'Correct.'

'I guess that's your man.'

'Yes, a murderer.'

'Worse than that,' Chavez said, joining the conversation.

'There is nothing worse than murder,' Provalov responded, always the cop.

Chavez was more practical in his outlook. 'Maybe, depends on if you need an accountant to keep track of all the bodies.'

'So, Clark, what do you think of the operation?' Kirillin asked, hungry for the American's approval.

'It was perfect. It was a simple operation, but flawlessly done. They're good kids, Yuriy. They learn fast and they work hard. They're ready to be trainers for your special-operations people.'

'Yeah, I'd take any of them out on a job,' Ding agreed. Kirillin beamed at the news, unsurprising as it was.

CHAPTER FIFTY

THUNDER AND LIGHTNING

'They got him,' Murray told Ryan. 'Our friend Clark was there to watch. Damned ecumenical of the Russkies.'

'Just want to be an ally back to us, I suppose, and RAINBOW is a NATO asset. You suppose he'll sing?'

'Like a canary, probably,' the FBI Director predicted. 'The Miranda Rule never made it to Russia, Jack, and their interrogation techniques are a little more—uh, enthusiastic than ours are. Anyway, it's something to put on TV, something to get their public seriously riled up. So, boss, this war going to stop or go?'

'We're trying to stop it, Dan, but—'

'Yeah, I understand,' Murray said. 'Sometimes big shots act just like street hoods. Just with bigger guns.'

This bunch has H-bombs, Jack didn't say. It wasn't something you wanted to talk about right after breakfast. Murray hung up and Ryan checked his watch. It was time. He punched the intercom button on his phone.

'Ellen, could you come in, please?'

It took the usual five seconds. 'Yes, Mr. President.'

'I need one, and it's time to call Beijing.'

'Yes, sir.' She handed Ryan a Virginia Slim and went back to the anteroom.

Ryan saw one of the phone lights go on and waited, lighting his smoke. He had his speech to

405

Premier Xu pretty well canned, knowing that the Chinese leader would have a good interpreter nearby. He also knew that Xu would still be in the office. He'd been working pretty late over the past few days—it wasn't hard to figure out why. Starting a potential world war had to be a time-consuming business. So, it would be less than thirty seconds to make the guy's phone ring, then Ellen Sumter would talk to the operator on the far end—the Chinese had full-time switchboard operators rather than secretary-receptionists as in the White House—and the call would be put through. So, figure another thirty seconds, and then Jack would get to make his case to Xu: *Let's reconsider this one, buddy, or something bad will happen. Bad for our country. Bad for yours. Probably worse for yours.* Mickey Moore had promised something called Hyperwar, and that would be seriously bad news for someone unprepared for it. The phone light stayed on, but Ellen wasn't beeping him to get on the line . . . why? Xu was still in his office. The embassy in Beijing was supposed to be keeping an eye on the guy. Ryan didn't know how, but he was pretty sure they knew their job. It might have been as easy as having an embassy employee—probably an Agency guy—stand on the street with a cell phone and watch a lit-up office window, then report to the embassy, which would have an open line to Foggy Bottom, which had many open lines to the White House. But then the light on the phone blinked out, and the intercom started:

'Mr. President, they say he's out of the office,' Mrs. Sumter said.

'Oh?' Ryan took a long puff. 'Tell State to confirm his location.'

406

'Yes, Mr. President.' Then forty seconds of silence. 'Mr. President, the embassy says he's in his office, as far as they can tell.'

'And his people said . . . ?'

'They said he's out, sir.'

'When will he be back?'

'I asked. They said they didn't know.'

'Shit,' Ryan breathed. 'Please get me Secretary Adler.'

'Yeah, Jack,' SecState said a few seconds later.

'He's dodging my call, Scott.'

'Xu?'

'Yeah.'

'Not surprising. They—the Chinese Politburo—don't trust him to talk on his own without a script.'

Like Arnie and me, Ryan thought with a mixture of anger and humor. 'Okay, what's it mean, Scott?'

'Nothing good, Jack,' Adler replied. 'Nothing good.'

'So, what do we do now?'

'Diplomatically, there's not much we can do. We've sent them a stiff note, and they haven't answered. Your position vis-à-vis them and the Russian situation is as clear as we can make it. They know what we're thinking. If they don't want to talk to us, it means they don't care anymore.

'Shit.'

'That's right,' the Secretary of State agreed.

'You're telling me we can't stop it?'

'Correct.' Adler's tone was matter-of-fact.

'Okay, what else?'

'We tell our civilians to get the hell out of China. We're set up to do that here.'

'Okay, do it,' Ryan ordered, with a sudden flip of his stomach.

'Right.'

'I'll get back to you.' Ryan switched lines and punched the button for the Secretary of Defense.

'Yeah,' Tony Bretano answered.

'It looks like it's going to happen,' Ryan told him.

'Okay, I'll alert all the CINCs.'

In a matter of minutes, FLASH traffic was dispatched to each of the commanders-in-chief of independent commands. There were many of them, but at the moment the most important was CINCPAC, Admiral Bart Mancuso in Pearl Harbor. It was just after three in the morning when the STU next to his bed started chirping.

'This is Admiral Mancuso,' he said, more than half asleep.

'Sir, this is the watch officer. We have a war warning from Washington. China. "Expect the commencement of hostilities between the PRC and the Russian Federation to commence within the next twenty-four hours. You are directed to take all measures consistent with the safety of your command." Signed Bretano, SecDef, sir,' the lieutenant commander told him.

Mancuso already had both feet on the floor of the bedroom. 'Okay, get my staff together. I'll be in the office in ten minutes.'

'Aye, aye, sir.'

The chief petty officer assigned to drive him was already outside the front door, and Mancuso noted the presence of four armed Marines in plain sight. The senior of them saluted while the others studiously looked outward at a threat that probably wasn't there . . . but might be. Minutes later, he walked into his hilltop headquarters overlooking the naval base. Brigadier General Lahr was there, waiting for him.

'How'd you get in so fast?' CINCPAC asked him.

'Just happened to be in the neighborhood, Admiral,' the J-2 told him. He followed Mancuso into the inner office.

'What's happening?'

'The President tried to phone Premier Xu, but he didn't take the call. Not a good sign from our Chinese brethren,' the theater intelligence officer observed.

'Okay, what's John Chinaman doing?' Mancuso asked, as a steward's mate brought in coffee.

'Not much in our area of direct interest, but he's got a hell of a lot of combat power deployed in the Shenyang Military District, most of it right up on the Amur River.' Lahr set up a map stand and started moving his hand on the acetate overlay, which had a lot of red markings on it. For the first time in his memory, Mancuso saw Russian units drawn in blue, which was the 'friendly' color. It was too surprising to comment on.

'What are we doing?'

'We're moving a lot of air assets into Siberia. The shooters are here at Suntar. Reconnaissance assets back here at Zhigansk. The Dark Stars ought to be up and flying soon. It'll be the first time we've deployed 'em in a real shooting war, and the Air Force has high hopes for them. We have some satellite overheads that show where the Chinese are. They've camouflaged their heavy gear, but the Lacrosse imagery sees right through the nets.'

'And?'

'And it's over half a million men, five Group-A mechanized armies. That's one armored division,

409

two mechanized infantry, and one motorized infantry each, plus attachments that belong directly to the army commander. The forces deployed are heavy in tanks and APCs, fair in artillery, but light in helicopters. The air assets belong to somebody else. Their command structure for coordinating air and ground isn't as streamlined as it ought to be, and their air forces aren't very good by our standards, but their numbers are better than the Russians'. Manpower-wise, the Chinese have a huge advantage on the ground. The Russians have space to play with, but if it comes down to a slugging match, bet your money on the People's Liberation Army.'

'And at sea?'

'Their navy doesn't have much out of port at the moment, but overheads show they're lighting up their boilers alongside. I would expect them to surge some ships out. Expect them to stay close in, defensive posture, deployment just to keep their coast clear.'

Mancuso didn't have to ask what he had out. Seventh Fleet was pretty much out to sea after the warnings from previous weeks. His carriers were heading west. He had a total of six submarines camped out on the Chinese coast, and his surface forces were spun up. If the People's Liberation Army Navy wanted to play, they'd regret it.

'Orders?'

'Self-defense only at this point,' Lahr said.

'Okay, we'll close to within two hundred fifty miles of their coast minimum for surface ships. Keep the carriers an additional hundred back for now. The submarines can close in and shadow any PLAN forces at will, but no shooting unless attacked, and I don't want anyone counter-detected. The Chinese have that one reconsat up. I don't want it to see anything painted gray.' Dodging a single reconnaissance satellite wasn't all that difficult, since it was entirely predictable in course and speed. You could even keep out of the way of two. When the number got to three, things became difficult.

*   *   *

In the Navy, the day never starts because the day never ends, but that wasn't true for a ship sitting in wooden blocks. Then things changed, if not to an eight-hour day, then at least to a semi-civilian job where most of the crew lived at home and drove in every morning (for the most part) to do their jobs. That was principally preventive maintenance, which is one of the U.S. Navy's religions. It was the same for Al Gregory; in his case, he drove his rented car in from the Norfolk motel and blew a kiss at the rent-a-cop at the guard shack, who waved everyone in. Once there had been armed Marines at the gates, but they'd gone away when the Navy had been stripped of its tactical nuclear weapons. There were still some nukes at the Yorktown ordnance station, because the Trident warheads hadn't yet all been disassembled out at Pantex in Texas, and some still occupied their mainly empty bunkers up on the York River, awaiting shipment west for final disposal. But not at Norfolk, and the ships that had guards mainly depended on sailors carrying Beretta M9 pistols which they might, or might not, know how to use properly. That was the case on USS *Gettysburg*,

411

whose sailors recognized Gregory by sight and waved him aboard with a smile and a greeting.

'Hey, Doc,' Senior Chief Leek said, when the civilian came into CIC. He pointed to the coffee urn. The Navy's real fuel was coffee, not distillate fuel, at least as far as the chiefs were concerned.

'So, anything good happening?'

'Well, they're going to put a new wheel on today.'

'Wheel?'

'Propeller,' Leek explained. 'Controllable pitch, reversible screw, made of high-grade manganese-bronze. They're made up in Philadelphia, I think. It's interesting to watch how they do it, long as they don't drop the son of a bitch.'

'What about your toy shop?'

'Fully functional, Doc. The last replacement board went in twenty minutes ago, didn't it, Mr. Olson?' The senior chief addressed his assistant CIC officer, who came wandering out of the darkness and into view. 'Mr. Olson, this here's Dr. Gregory from TRW.'

'Hello,' the young officer said, stretching his hand out. Gregory took it.

'Dartmouth, right?'

'Yep, physics and mathematics. You?'

'West Point and Stony Brook, math,' Gregory said.

'Hudson High?' Chief Leek asked. 'You never told me that.'

'Hell, I even did Ranger School between second- and first-class years,' he told the surprised sailors. People looked at him and often thought 'pussy.' He enjoyed surprising them. 'Jump School, too. Did nineteen jumps, back when I was young and

412

foolish.'

'Then you went into SDI, I gather,' Olson observed, getting himself some CIC coffee. The black-gang coffee, from the ship's engineers, was traditionally the best on any ship, but this wasn't bad.

'Yeah, spent a lot of years in that, but it all kinda fizzled out, and TRW hired me away before I made bird. When you were at Dartmouth, Bob Jastrow ran the department?'

'Yeah, he was involved in SDI, too, wasn't he?'

Gregory nodded. 'Yeah, Bob's pretty smart.' In his lexicon, *pretty smart* meant doing the calculus in your head.

'What do you do at TRW?'

'I'm heading up the SAM project at the moment, from my SDI work, but they lend me out a lot to other stuff. I mainly do software and the theoretical engineering.'

'And you're playing with our SM-2s now?'

'Yeah, I've got a software fix for one of the problems. Works on the 'puter, anyway, and the next job's reprogramming the seeker heads on the Block IVs.'

'How you going to do that?'

'Come on over and I'll show you,' Gregory said. He and Olson wandered to a desk, with the chief in tow. 'The trick is fixing the way the laser nutates. Here's how the software works . . .' This started an hour's worth of discussion, and Senior Chief Leek got to watch a professional software geek explaining his craft to a gifted amateur. Next they'd have to sell all this to the Combat Systems Officer—'Weps'—before they could run the first computer simulations, but it looked to Leek as

413

though Olson was pretty well sold already. Then they'd have to get the ship back in the water to see if all this bullshit actually worked.

* * *

The sleep had worked, Bondarenko told himself. Thirteen hours, and he hadn't even awakened to relieve his bladder—so, he must have really needed it. Then and there he decided that Colonel Aliyev would screen successfully for general's stars.

He walked into his evening staff meeting feeling pretty good, until he saw the looks on their faces.

'Well?' he asked, taking his seat.

'Nothing new to report,' Colonel Tolkunov reported for the intelligence staff. 'Our aerial photos show little, but we know they're there, and they're still not using their radios at all. Presumably they have a lot of phone lines laid. There are scattered reports of people with binoculars on the southern hilltops. That's all. But they're ready, and it could start at any time—oh, yes, just got this from Moscow,' the G-2 said. 'The Federal Security Service arrested one K. I. Suvorov on suspicion of conspiring to assassinate President Grushavoy.'

'What?' Aliyev asked.

'Just a one-line dispatch with no elaboration. It could mean many things, none of them good,' the intelligence officer told them. 'But nothing definite either.'

'An attempt to unsettle our political leadership? That's an act of war,' Bondarenko said. He decided he had to call Sergey Golovko himself about that one!

'Operations?' he asked next.

414

'The 265th Motor Rifle is standing-to. Our air-defense radars are all up and operating. We have interceptor aircraft flying combat air patrol within twenty kilometers of the border. The border defenses are on full alert, and the reserve formation—'

'Have a name for it yet?' the commanding general asked.

'Boyar,' Colonel Aliyev answered. 'We have three companies of motorized infantry deployed to evacuate the border troops if necessary, the rest are out of their depot and working up north of Never. They've done gunnery all day.'

'And?'

'And for reservists they did acceptably,' Aliyev answered. Bondarenko didn't ask what that meant, partly because he was afraid to.

'Anything else we can do? I want ideas, comrades,' General Bondarenko said. But all he saw were headshakes. 'Very well. I'm going to get some dinner. If anything happens, I want to know about it. Anything at all, comrades.' This generated nods, and he walked back to his quarters. There he got on the phone.

'Greetings, General,' Golovko said. It was still afternoon in Moscow. 'How are things at your end?'

'Tense, Comrade Chairman. What can you tell me of this attempt on the President?'

'We arrested a chap named Suvorov earlier today. We're interrogating him and one other right now. We believe that he was an agent of the Chinese Ministry of State Security, and we believe also that he was conspiring to kill Eduard Petrovich.'

'So, in addition to preparing an invasion, they also wish to cripple our political leadership?'

'So it would seem,' Golovko agreed gravely.

'Why weren't we given fuller information?' Far East demanded.

'You weren't?' The chairman sounded surprised.

'No!' Bondarenko nearly shouted.

'That was an error. I am sorry, Gennady Iosifovich. Now, you tell me: Are you ready?'

'All of our forces are at maximum alert, but the correlation of forces is adverse in the extreme.'

'Can you stop them?'

'If you give me more forces, probably yes. If you do not, probably no. What help can I expect?'

'We have three motor-rifle divisions on trains at this moment crossing the Urals. We have additional air power heading to you, and the Americans are beginning to arrive. What is your plan?'

'I will not try to stop them at the border. That would merely cost me all of my troops to little gain. I will let the Chinese in and let them march north. I will harass them as much as possible, and then when they are well within our borders, I will kill the body of the snake and watch the head die. *If*, that is, you give me the support I need.'

'We are working on it. The Americans are being very helpful. One of their tank divisions is now approaching Poland on trains. We'll send them right through to where you are.'

'What units?'

'Their First Tank division, commanded by a Negro chap named Diggs.'

'Marion Diggs? I know him.'

'Oh?'

'Yes, he commanded their National Training

416

Center and also commanded the force they deployed to the Saudi kingdom last year. He's excellent. When will he arrive?'

'Five days, I should imagine. You'll have three Russian divisions well before then. Will that be enough, Gennady?'

'I do not know,' Bondarenko replied. 'We have not yet taken the measure of the Chinese. Their air power worries me most of all. If they attack our railhead at Chita, deploying our reinforcements could be very difficult.' Bondarenko paused. 'We are well set up to move forces laterally, west to east, but to stop them we need to move them northeast from their drop-off points. It will be largely a race to see who can go north faster. The Chinese will also be using infantry to wall off the western flank of their advance. I've been training my men hard. They're getting better, but I need more time and more men. Is there any way to slow them down politically?'

'All political approaches have been ignored. They pretend nothing untoward is happening. The Americans have approached them as well, in hope of discouraging them, but to no avail.'

'So, it comes to a test of arms?'

'Probably,' Golovko agreed. 'You're our best man, Gennady Iosifovich. We believe in you, and you will have all the support we can muster.'

'Very well,' the general replied, wondering if it would be enough. 'I will let you know of any developments here.'

General Bondarenko knew that a proper general—the sort they had in movies, that is— would now eat the combat rations his men were having, but no, he'd eat the best food available

417

because he needed his strength, and false modesty would not impress his men at all. He did refrain from alcohol, which was probably more than his sergeants and privates were doing. The Russian soldier loves his vodka, and the reservists had probably all brought their own bottles to ease the chill of the nights—such would be the spoken excuse. He could have issued an order forbidding it, but there was little sense in drafting an order that his men would ignore. It only undermined discipline, and discipline was something he needed. That would have to come from within his men. The great unknown, as Bondarenko thought of it. When Hitler had struck Russia in 1941—well, it was part of Russian mythology, how the ordinary men of the land had risen up with ferocious determination. From the first day of the war, the courage of the Russian soldier had given the Germans pause. Their battlefield skills might have been lacking, but never their courage. For Bondarenko, both were needed; a skillful man need not be all that brave, because skill would defeat what bravery would only defy. Training. It was always training. He yearned to train the Russian soldier as the Americans trained their men. Above all, to train them to think—to encourage them to think. A thinking *German* soldier had nearly destroyed the Soviet Union—how close it had been was something the movies never admitted, and it was hard enough to learn about it at the General Staff academies, but three times it had been devilishly close, and for some reason the gods of war had sided with Mother Russia on all three occasions.

What would those gods do now? That was the question. Would his men be up to the task? Would *he* be up to the task? It was his name that would be remembered, for good or ill, not those of the private soldiers carrying the AK-74 rifles and driving the tanks and infantry carriers. Gennady Iosifovich Bondarenko, general-colonel of the Russian Army, commander-in-chief Far East, hero or fool? Which would it be? Would future military students study his actions and cluck their tongues at his stupidity or shake their heads in admiration of his brilliant maneuvers?

It would have been better to be a colonel again, close to the men of his regiment, even carrying a rifle of his own as he'd done at Dushanbe all those years before, to take a personal part in the battle, and take direct fire at enemies he could see with his own eyes. That was what came back to him now, the battle against the Afghans, defending that mis-sited apartment block in the snow and the darkness. He'd earned his medals that day, but medals were always things of the past. People respected him for them, even his fellow soldiers, the pretty ribbons and metal stars and medallions that hung from them, but what did they mean, really? Would he find the courage he needed to be a commander? He was sure here and now that that sort of courage was harder to find than the sort that came from mere survival instinct, the kind that was generated in the face of armed men who wished to steal your life away.

It was so easy to look into the indeterminate future with confidence, to know what had to be done, to suggest and insist in a peaceful conference room. But today he was in his quarters, in command of a largely paper army that happened to be facing a real army composed of men and steel, and if he failed to deal with it, his name would be cursed for all time. Historians would examine his character and his record and say, well, yes, he was a brave colonel, and even an adequate theoretician, but when it came to a real fight, he was unequal to the task. And if he failed, men would die, and the nation he'd sworn to defend thirty years before would suffer, if not by his hand, then by his responsibility.

And so General Bondarenko looked at his plate of food and didn't eat, just pushed the food about with his fork, and wished for the tumbler of vodka that his character denied him.

*   *   *

General Peng Xi-Wang was finishing up what he expected to be his last proper meal for some weeks. He'd miss the long-grain rice that was not part of combat rations—he didn't know why that was so: The general who ran the industrial empire that prepared rations for the frontline soldiers had never explained it to him, though Peng was sure that he never ate those horrid packaged foods himself. He had a staff to taste-test, after all. Peng lit an after-dinner smoke and enjoyed a small sip of rice wine. It would be the last of those for a while, too. His last pre-combat meal completed, Peng rose and donned his tunic. The gilt shoulderboards showed his rank as three stars and a wreath.

Outside his command trailer, his subordinates waited. When he came out, they snapped to attention and saluted as one man, and Peng saluted back. Foremost was Colonel Wa Cheng-Gong, his operations officer. Wa was aptly named. Cheng-

Gong, his given name, meant 'success'.

'So, Wa, are we ready?'

'Entirely ready, Comrade General.'

'Then let us go and see.' Peng led them off to his personal Type 90 command-post vehicle. Cramped inside, even for people of small size, it was further crowded by banks of FM radios, which fed the ten-meter-tall radio masts at the vehicle's four corners. There was scarcely room for the folding map table, but his battle staff of six could work in there, even when on the move. The driver and gunner were both junior officers, not enlisted men.

The turbocharged diesel caught at once, and the vehicle lurched toward the front. Inside, the map table was already down, and the operations officer showed their position and their course to men who already knew it. The large roof hatch was opened to vent the smoke. Every man aboard was smoking a cigarette now.

*   *   *

'Hear that?' Senior Lieutenant Valeriy Mikhailovich Komanov had his head outside the top hatch of the tank turret that composed the business end of his bunker. It was the turret of an old—ancient—JS-3 tank. Once the most fearsome part of the world's heaviest main-battle tank, this turret had never gone anywhere except to turn around, its already thick armor upgraded by an additional twenty centimeters of appliqué steel. As part of a bunker, it was only marginally slower than the original tank, which had been underpowered at best, but the monster 122-mm gun still worked, and worked even better here, because underneath it was not the cramped confines of a tank hull, but rather a spacious concrete structure which gave the crewmen room to move and turn around. That arrangement cut the reloading speed of the gun by more than half, and didn't hurt accuracy either, because this turret had better optics. Lieutenant Komanov was, notionally, a tanker, and his platoon here was twelve tanks instead of the normal three, because these didn't move. Ordinarily, it was not demanding duty, commanding twelve six-man crews, who didn't go anywhere except to the privy, and they even got to practice their gunnery at a duplicate of this emplacement at a range located twenty kilometers away. They'd been doing that lately, in fact, at the orders of their new commanding general, and neither Komanov nor his men minded, because for every soldier in the world, shooting is fun, and the bigger the gun, the greater the enjoyment. Their 122-mms had a relatively slow muzzle velocity, but the shell was large enough to compensate for it. Lately, they'd gotten to shoot at worn-out old T-55s and blown the turret off each one with a single hit, though getting the single hit had taken the crews, on the average, 2.7 shots fired.

They were on alert now, a fact which their eager young lieutenant was taking seriously. He'd even had his men out running every morning for the last two weeks, not the most pleasant of activities for soldiers detailed to sit inside concrete emplacements for their two years of conscripted service. It wasn't easy to keep their edge. One naturally felt secure in underground concrete structures capped with thick steel and surrounded with bushes which made their bunker invisible from fifty meters away. Theirs was the rearmost of the platoons, sitting on the south slope of Hill 432—its summit was 432 meters high—facing the north side of the first rank of hills over the Amur Valley. Those hills were a lot lower than the one they were on, and also had bunkers on them, but those bunkers were fakes—not that you could tell without going inside, because they'd also been made of old tank turrets—in their case from truly ancient KV-2s that had fought the Germans before rusting in retirement—set in concrete boxes. The additional height of their hill meant that they could see into China, whose territory started less than four kilometers away. And that was close enough to hear things on a calm night.

Especially if the thing they heard was a few hundred diesel engines starting up at once.

'Engines,' agreed Komanov's sergeant. 'A fucking lot of them.'

The lieutenant hopped down from his perch inside the turret and walked the three steps to the phone switchboard. He lifted the receiver and punched the button to the regimental command post, ten kilometers north.

'This is Post Five Six Alfa. We can hear engines to our south. It sounds like tank engines, a lot of them.'

'Can you see anything?' the regimental commander asked.

'No, Comrade Colonel. But the sound is unmistakable.'

'Very well. Keep me informed.'

'Yes, comrade. Out.' Komanov set the phone back in its place. His most-forward bunker was Post Five Nine, on the south slope of the first rank of hills. He punched that button.

'This is Lieutenant Komanov. Can you see or hear anything?'

'We see nothing,' the corporal there answered. 'But we hear tank engines.'

'You see nothing?'

'Nothing, Comrade Lieutenant,' Corporal Vladimirov responded positively.

'Are you ready?'

'We are fully ready,' Vladimirov assured him. 'We are watching the south.'

'Keep me informed,' Komanov ordered, unnecessarily. His men were alert and standing-to. He looked around. He had a total of two hundred rounds for his main gun, all in racks within easy reach of the turret. His loader and gunner were at their posts, the former scanning the terrain with optical sights better than his own officer's binoculars. His reserve crewmen were just sitting in their chairs, waiting for someone to die. The door to the escape tunnel was open. A hundred meters through that was a BTR-60 eight-wheeled armored personnel carrier ready to get them the hell away, though his men didn't expect to make use of it. Their post was impregnable, wasn't it? They had the best part of a meter of steel on the gun turret, and three meters of reinforced concrete, with a meter of dirt atop it—and besides, they were hidden in a bush. You couldn't hit what you couldn't see, could you? And the Chinks had slitty little eyes and couldn't see very well, could they? Like all the men in this crew, Komanov was a European Russian, though there were Asians under his command. This part of his country was a mishmash of nationalities and languages, though all had learned Russian, if not at home, then in school.

'Movement,' the gunner said. 'Movement on Rice Ridge.' That was what they called the first ridge line in Chinese territory. 'Infantrymen.'

'You're sure they're soldiers?' Komanov asked.

'I suppose they might be shepherds, but I don't see any sheep, Comrade Lieutenant.' The gunner had a wry sense of humor.

'Move,' the lieutenant told the crewman who'd taken his place in the command hatch. He reclaimed the tank commander's seat. 'Get me the headset,' he ordered next. Now he'd be connected to the phone system with a simple push-button microphone. With that, he could talk to his other eleven crews or to regiment. But Komanov didn't don the earphones just yet. He wanted his ears clear. The night was still, the winds calm, just a few gentle breezes. They were a good distance from any real settlement, and so there were no sounds of traffic to interfere. Then he leveled his binoculars on the far ridge. Yes, there was the ghostly suggestion of movement there, almost like seeing someone's hair blowing in the wind. But it wasn't hair. It could only be people. And as his gunner had observed, they would not be shepherds.

For ten years, the officers in the border bunkers had cried out for low-light goggles like those issued to the Spetsnaz and other elite formations, but, no, they were too expensive for low-priority posts, and so such things were only seen here when some special inspection force came through, just long enough for the regular troops to drool over them. No, they were supposed to let their eyes adapt to the darkness . . . *as though they think we're cats,*

425

Komanov thought. But all the interior battle lights in the bunkers were red, and that helped. He'd forbidden the use of white lights inside the post for the past week.

Brothers of this tank turret had first been produced in late 1944—the JS-3 had stayed in production for many years, *as though no one had summoned the courage to stop producing something with the name Iosif Stalin on it*, he thought. Some of them had rolled into Germany, invulnerable to anything the Fritzes had deployed. And the same tanks had given serious headaches to the Israelis, with their American- and English-built tanks, as well.

'This is Post Fifty. We have a lot of movement, looks like infantry, on the north slope of Rice Ridge. Estimate regimental strength,' his earphones crackled.

'How many high-explosive shells do we have?' Komanov asked.

'Thirty-five,' the loader answered.

And that was a goodly amount. And there were fifteen heavy guns within range of Rice Ridge, all of them old ML-20 152-mm howitzers, all sitting on concrete pads next to massive ammo bunkers. Komanov checked his watch. Almost three-thirty. Ninety minutes to first light. The sky was cloudless. He could look up and see stars such as they didn't have in Moscow, with all its atmospheric pollution. No, the Siberian sky was clear and clean, and above his head was an ocean of light made brighter still by a full moon still high in the western sky. He focused his eyes through his binoculars again. Yes, there *was* movement on Rice Ridge.

426

'So?' Peng asked.

'At your command,' Wa replied.

Peng and his staff were forward of their guns, the better to see the effect of their fire.

*   *   *

But seventy thousand feet over General Peng's head was Marilyn Monroe. Each of the Dark Star drones had a name attached to it, and given the official name of the platform, the crews had chosen the names of movie stars, all of them, of course, of the female persuasion. This one even had a copy of the movie star's Playboy centerfold from 1953 skillfully painted on the nose, but the eyes looking down from the stealthy UAV were electronic and multi-spectrum rather than china blue. Inside the fiberglass nosecone, a directional antenna cross-linked the 'take' to a satellite, which then distributed it to many places. The nearest was Zhigansk. The farthest was Fort Belvoir, Virginia, within spitting distance of Washington, D.C., and that one sent its feed via fiberoptic cable to any number of classified locations. Unlike most spy systems, this one showed real-time movie-type imagery.

'Looks like they're getting ready, sir,' an Army staff sergeant observed to his immediate boss, a captain. And sure enough, you could see soldiers ramming shells into the breeches of their field pieces, followed by the smaller cloth bags that contained the propellant. Then the breeches were slammed shut, and the guns elevated. The 30-30-

class blank cartridges were inserted into the firing ports of the breechblocks, and the guns were fully ready. The last step was called 'pulling the string,' and was fairly accurate. You just jerked the lanyard rope to fire the blank cartridge and that ignited the powder bags, and then the shell went north at high speed.

'How many guns total, Sergeant?' the captain asked.

'A whole goddamned pisspot full, sir.'

'I can see that. What about a number?' the officer asked.

'North of six hundred, and that's just in this here sector, Cap'n. Plus four hundred mobile rocket launchers.'

'We spotted air assets yet?'

'No, sir. The Chinese aren't nighttime flyers yet, least not for bombing.'

*   *   *

Eagle Seven to Zebra, over,' the AWACS senior controller radioed back to Zhigansk.

'Zebra to Seven, reading you five-by-five,' the major running the ground base replied.

'We got bogies, call it thirty-two coming north out of Siping, estimate they're Sierra-Uniform Two-Sevens.'

'Makes sense,' the major on the ground told his wing commander. 'Siping's their 667th Regiment. That's their best in terms of aircraft, and stick-time. That's their varsity, Colonel.'

'Who do we have to meet them?'

'Our Russian friends out of Nelkan. Nearest American birds are well north and—'

428

'—and we haven't got orders to engage anybody yet,' the colonel agreed. 'Okay, let's get the Russians alerted.'

'Eagle Seven to Black Falcon Ten, we have Chinese fighters three hundred kilometers bearing one-nine-six your position, angels thirty, speed five hundred knots. They're still over Chinese territory, but not for much longer.'

'Understood,' the Russian captain responded. 'Give me a vector.'

'Recommend intercept vector two-zero-zero,' the American controller said. His spoken Russian was pretty good. 'Maintain current speed and altitude.'

'Roger.'

On the E-3B's radar displays, the Russian Su-27s turned to head for the Chinese Su-27s. The Russians would have radar contact in about nine minutes.

*   *   *

'Sir, this don't look real nice,' another major in Zhigansk said to his general.

'Then it's time to get a warning out,' the USAF two-star agreed. He lifted a phone that went to the Russian regional command post. There hadn't as yet been time to get a proper downlink to them.

*   *   *

'General, a call from the American technical mission at Zhigansk,' Tolkunov said.

'This is General Bondarenko.'

'Hello, this is Major General Gus Wallace. I just

set up the reconnaissance shop here. We just put up a stealthy recon-drone over the Russian Chinese border at . . .' He read off the coordinates. 'We show people getting ready to fire some artillery at you, General.'

'How much?' Bondarenko asked.

'Most I've ever seen, upwards of a thousand guns total. I hope your people are hunkered down, buddy. The whole damned world's about to land on 'em.'

'What can you do to help us?' Bondarenko asked.

'My orders are not to take action until they start shooting,' the American replied. 'When that happens, I can start putting fighters up, but not much in the way of bombs. We hardly have any to drop,' Wallace reported. 'I have an AWACS up now, supporting your fighters in the Chulman area, but that's all for now. We have a C-130 ferrying you a downlink tomorrow so that we can get you some intelligence directly. Anyway, be warned, General, it looks here as though the Chinese are going to launch their attack momentarily.'

'Thank you, General Wallace.' Bondarenko hung up and looked at his staff. 'He says it's going to start at any moment.'

*   *   *

And so it did. Lieutenant Komanov saw it first. The line of hills his men called Rice Ridge was suddenly backlit by yellow flame that could only be the muzzle flashes of numerous field guns. Then came the upward-flying meteor shapes of artillery rockets.

'Here it comes,' he told his men. Unsurprisingly, he kept his head up so that he could see. His head, he reasoned, was a small target. Before the shells landed, he felt the impact of their firing; the rumble came through the ground like a distant earthquake, causing his loader to mutter, 'Oh, shit,' probably the universal observation of men in their situation.

'Get me regiment,' Komanov ordered.

'Yes, Lieutenant,' the voice answered.

'We are under attack, Comrade Colonel, massive artillery fire to the south. Guns and rockets are coming our—'

Then the first impacts came, mainly near the river, well to his south. The exploding shells were not bright, but like little sparks of light that fountained dirt upward, followed by the noise. That *did* sound like an earthquake. Komanov had heard artillery fire before, and seen what the shells do at the far end, but this was as different from that as an exploding oil tank was from a cigarette lighter.

'Comrade Colonel, our country is at war,' Post Five Six Alfa reported to command. 'I can't see enemy troop movement yet, but they're coming.

'Do you have any targets?' regiment asked.

'No, none at this time.' He looked down into the bunker. His various positions could just give a direction to a target, and when another confirmed it and called in its own vector, they'd have a pre-plotted artillery target for the batteries in the rear—

—but those were being hit already. The Chinese rockets were targeted well behind him, and that's what their targets had to be. He turned his head to

431

see the flashes and hear the booms from ten kilometers back. A moment later, there was a fountaining explosion skyward. One of the first flight of Chinese rockets had gotten lucky and hit one of the artillery positions in the rear. *Bad news for that gun crew*, Komanov thought. The first casualties in this war. There would be many more . . . perhaps including himself. Surprisingly, that thought was a distant one. Someone was attacking *his* country. It wasn't a supposition or a possibility anymore. He could see it, and feel it. This was *his* country they were attacking. He'd grown up in this land. His parents lived here. His grandfather had fought the Germans here. His grandfather's two brothers had, too, and both had died for their country, one west of Kiev and the other at Stalingrad. And now these Chink bastards were attacking his country, too? More than that, they were attacking *him*, Senior Lieutenant Valeriy Mikhailovich Komanov. These *foreigners* were trying to kill him, his men, *and* trying to steal part of his country.

Well, fuck that! he thought.

'Load HE!' he told his loader.

'Loaded!' the private announced. They all heard the breech clang shut.

'No target, Comrade Lieutenant,' the gunner observed.

'There will be, soon enough.'

'Post Five Nine, this is Five Six Alfa. What can you see?'

'We just spotted a boat, a rubber boat, coming out of the trees on the south bank . . . more, more, more, many of them, maybe a hundred, maybe more.'

'Regiment, this is Fifty-six Alfa, fire mission!' Komanov called over the phone.

*   *   *

The gunners ten kilometers back were at their guns, despite the falling Chinese shells and rockets that had already claimed three of the fifteen gun crews. The fire mission was called in, and the preset concentration dialed in from range books so old they might as well have been engraved in marble. In each case, the high-explosive projectile was rammed into the breech, followed by the propellant charge, and the gun cranked up and trained to the proper elevation and azimuth, and the lanyards pulled, and the first Russian counterstrokes in the war just begun were fired.

Unknown to them, fifteen kilometers away a fire-finder radar was trained on their positions. The millimeter-wave radar tracked the shells in flight and a computer plotted their launch points. The Chinese knew that the Russians had guns covering the border, and knew roughly where they would be—the performance of the guns told that tale—but not exactly where, because of the skillful Russian efforts at camouflage. In this case, those efforts didn't matter too greatly. The calculated position of six Russian howitzers was instantly radioed to rocket launchers that were dedicated counter-battery weapons. One Type-83 launcher was detailed to each target, and each of them held four monster 273-mm rockets, each with a payload of 150 kilograms of submunitions, in this case eighty hand grenade-sized bomblets. The first rocket launched three minutes after the first

Russian counter-fire salvo, and required less than two minutes of flight time from its firing point ten kilometers inside Chinese territory. Of the first six fired, five destroyed their targets, and then others, and the Russian gunfire died in less than five minutes.

*   *   *

'Why did it stop?' Komanov asked. He'd seen a few rounds hit among the Chinese infantry just getting out of their boats on the Russian side of the river. But the shriek of shells overhead passing south had just stopped after a few minutes. 'Regiment, this is Five Six Alfa, why has our fire stopped?'

'Our guns were taking counter-battery fire from the Chinese. They're trying to get set back up now,' was the encouraging reply. 'What is your situation?'

'Position Five-Zero has taken a little fire, but not much. Mainly they're hitting the reverse slope of the southern ridge.' That was where the fake bunkers were, and the concrete lures were fulfilling their passive mission. This line of defenses had been set up contrary to published Russian doctrine, because whoever had set them up had known that all manner of people can read books. Komanov's own position covered a small saddle-pass through two hills, fit for advancing tanks. If the Chinese came north in force, if this was not just some sort of probe aimed at expanding their borders—they'd done that back in the late 1960s—this was a prime invasion route. The maps and the terrain decided that.

'That is good, Lieutenant. Now listen: Do not expose your positions unnecessarily. Let them in close before you open up. Very close.' That, Komanov knew, meant a hundred meters or so. He had two heavy machine guns for that eventuality. But he wanted to kill tanks. That was what his main gun had been designed to do.

'Can we expect more artillery support?' he asked his commander.

'I'll let you know. Keep giving us target information.'

'Yes, Comrade Colonel.'

*   *   *

For the fighter planes, the war began when the first PLAAF crossed over the Amur. There were four Russian fighter-interceptors up, and these, just like the invaders, were Sukhoi-27. Those on both sides had been made in the same factories, but the Chinese pilots had triple the recent flight time of the defending Russians, who were outnumbered eight to one.

Countering that, however was the fact that the Russian aircraft had support from the USAF E-3B Sentry AWACS aircraft, which was guiding them to the intercept. Both sets of fighters were flying with their target-acquisition radars in standby mode. The Chinese didn't know what was out there. The Russians did. That was a difference.

'Black Falcon Ten, this is Eagle Seven. Recommend you come right to new course two-seven-zero. I'm going to try an' bring you up on the Chinese from their seven o'clock.' It would also keep them out of Chinese radar coverage.

'Understood, Eagle. Coming right to two-seven-zero.' The Russian flight leader spread his formation out and settled down as much as he could, with his eyes tending to look off to his left.

'Okay, Black Falcon Ten, that's good. Your targets are now at your nine o'clock, distance thirty kilometers. Come left now to one-eight-zero.

'Coming left,' the Russian major acknowledged. 'We will try to start the attack Fox-Two,' he advised. He knew American terminology. That meant launching infrared seekers, which did not require the use of radar, and so did not warn anyone that he was in harm's way. The Marquis of Queensberry had never been a fighter pilot.

'Roger that, Falcon. This boy's smart,' the controller commented to his supervisor.

'That's how you stay alive in this business,' the lieutenant colonel told the young lieutenant at the Nintendo screen.

'Okay, Falcon Ten, recommend you come left again. Targets are now fifteen kilometers . . . make that seventeen kilometers to your north. You should have tone shortly.'

'*Da.* I have tone,' the Russian pilot reported, when he heard the warble in his headset. 'Flight, prepare to fire . . . Fox-Two!' Three of the four aircraft loosed a single missile each. The fourth pilot was having trouble with his IR scanner. In all cases, the blazing rocket motors wrecked their night vision, but none of the pilots looked away as they'd been trained to do, and instead watched their missiles streak after fellow airmen who did not yet know they were under attack. It took twenty seconds, and as it turned out, two missiles were targeted on the same Chinese aircraft. That one took two hits and exploded. The second died from its single impact, and then things really got confusing. The Chinese fighters scattered on command from their commander, doing so in a preplanned and well-rehearsed maneuver, first into two groups, then into four, each of which had a piece of sky to defend. Everyone's radar came on, and in another twenty seconds, a total of forty missiles were flying, and with this began a deadly game of chicken. The radar-homing missiles needed a radar signal to guide them, and that meant that the firing fighter could not switch off or turn away, only hope that his bird would kill its target and switch off his radar before his missile got close.

'Damn,' the lieutenant observed, in his comfortable controller's seat in the E-3B. Two more Chinese fighters blinked into larger bogies on his screen and then started to fade, then another, but there were just too many of the Chinese air-to-air missiles, and not all of the Chinese illumination radars went down. One Russian fighter took three impacts and disintegrated. Another one limped away with severe damage, and as quickly as it had begun, this air encounter ended. Statistically, it was a Russian win, four kills for one loss, but the Chinese would claim more.

'Any chutes?' the senior controller asked over the intercom. The E-3 radar could track those, too.

'Three, maybe four ejected. Not sure who, though, not till we play the tape back. Damn, that was a quick one.'

The Russians didn't have enough planes up to do a proper battle. Maybe next time, the colonel thought. The full capabilities of a fighter/AWACS team had never been properly demonstrated in combat, but this war held the promise to change that, and when it happened, some eyes would be opened.

437

CHAPTER FIFTY-ONE

FALLING BACK

Senior Lieutenant Valeriy Mikhailovich Komanov learned something he'd never suspected. The worst part of battle—at least to a man in a fixed emplacement—was knowing that the enemy was out there, but being unable to shoot at him. The reverse slopes of the ridge to his immediate south had to be swarming with Chinese infantry, and his supporting artillery had been taken out in the first minutes of the battle. Whoever had set up the artillery positions had made the mistake of assuming that the guns were too far back and too shielded by terrain for the enemy to strike at them. Fire-finder radar/computer systems had changed that, and the absence of overhead cover had doomed the guncrews to rapid death, unless some of them had found shelter in the concrete-lined trenches built into their positions. He had a powerful gun at his fingertips, but it was one that could not reach over the hills to his south because of its flat trajectory. As envisioned, this defense line would have included leg infantry who'd depend on and also support the bunker strongpoints—and be armed with mortars which could reach over the close-in hills and punish those who were there but unseen behind the terrain feature. Komanov could only engage those he could see, and they—

'There, Comrade Lieutenant,' the gunner said. 'A little right of twelve o'clock, some infantry just crested the ridge. Range one thousand five

438

hundred meters.'

'I see them.' There was just a hint of light on the eastern horizon now. Soon there would be enough light to see by. That would make shooting easier, but for both sides. In an hour, his bunker would be targeted, and they'd get to see just how thick their armor protection really was.

'Five Six Alfa, this is Five Zero. We have infantry eleven hundred meters to our south. Company strength and moving north toward us.'

'Very well. Do not engage until they are within two hundred meters.' Komanov automatically doubled the shooting range at which he'd been trained to open fire. What the hell, he thought, his crews would do that in their own minds anyway. A man thinks differently when real bullets are flying.

As if to emphasize that, shells started landing on the crest immediately behind his position, close enough to make him duck down.

'So they see us?' his loader asked.

'No, they're just barraging the next set of hills to support their infantrymen.'

'Look, look there, they're on top of false bunker One Six,' the gunner said. Komanov shifted his glasses—

Yes, they were there, examining the old KV 2 gun turret with its vertical sides and old 15 5-mm gun. As he watched, a soldier hung a satchel charge on the side and backed away. Then the charge went off, destroying something that had never worked anyway. *That would make some Chinese lieutenant feel good*, Komanov thought. Well, Five Six Alfa would change his outlook somewhat, in another twenty or thirty minutes.

The bad part was that now he had perfect

targets for his supporting artillery, and those old six-inch guns would have cut through them like a harvester's scythe. Except the Chinese were *still* hitting those positions, even though the Russian fire had stopped. He called Regiment again to relay his information.

'Lieutenant,' his colonel answered, 'the supporting battery has been badly hit. You are on your own. Keep me posted.'

'Yes, Comrade Colonel. Out.' He looked down at his crew. 'Don't expect supporting fire.' The weapons of World War III had just destroyed those of World War I.

'Shit,' the loader observed.

'We'll be in the war soon, men. Be at ease. The enemy is now closer . . .'

'Five hundred meters,' the gunner agreed.

*   *   *

'Well?' General Peng asked at his post atop Rice Ridge.

'We've found some bunkers but they are all unoccupied,' Colonel Wa reported. 'So far, the only fire we've taken has been indirect artillery, and we've counterbatteried that to death. The attack is going completely to plan, Comrade General.' They could see the truth of that. The bridging engineers were rolling up to the south bank of the Amur now, with folded sections of ribbon bridge atop their trucks. Over a hundred Type 90 main-battle tanks were close to the river, their turrets searching vainly for targets so that they could support the attacking infantry, but there was nothing for them to shoot at, and so the tankers, like the generals,

440

had nothing to do but watch the engineers at work. The first bridge section went into the water, flipping open to form the first eight meters of highway across the river. Peng checked his watch. Yes, things were going about five minutes ahead of schedule, and that was good.

*   *   *

Post Five Zero opened up first with its 12.7-mm machine gun. The sound of it rattled across the hillside. Five Zero was thirty-five hundred meters to his east, commanded by a bright young sergeant named Ivanov. *He opened up too early*, Komanov thought, reaching for targets a good four hundred meters away, but there was nothing to complain about, and the heavy machine gun could easily reach that far . . . yes, he could see bodies crumpling from the heavy slugs—

—then a crashing *BOOM* as the main gun let loose a single round, and it reached into the saddle they defended, exploding there amidst a squad or so.

'Comrade Lieutenant, can we?' his gunner asked.

'No, not yet. Patience, Sergeant,' Komanov replied, watching to the east to see how the Chinese reacted to the fire. Yes, their tactics were predictable, but sound. The lieutenant commanding them first got his men down. Then they set up a base of fire to engage the Russian position, and then they started maneuvering left and right. Aha, a section was setting up something . . . something on a tripod. An anti-tank recoilless rifle, probably. He could have turned his gun to

441

take it out, but Komanov didn't want to give away his position yet.

'Five Zero, this is Five Six Alfa, there's a Chinese recoilless setting up at your two o'clock, range eight hundred,' he warned.

'Yes, I see it!' the sergeant replied. And he had the good sense to engage it with his machine gun. In two seconds, the green tracers reached out and ripped through the gun section once, twice, three times, just to be sure. Through his binoculars, he could see some twitching, but that was all.

'Well done, Sergeant Ivanov! Look out, they're moving to your left under terrain cover.'

But there wasn't much of that around here. Every bunker's field of fire had been bulldozed, leveling out almost all of the dead ground within eight hundred meters of every position.

'We shall see about that, Comrade Lieutenant.' And the machine gun spoke again. Return fire was coming in now. Komanov could see tracers bouncing off the turret's thick armor into the sky.

'Regiment, Five Six Alfa here. Post Five Zero is under deliberate attack now from infantry, and—'

Then more artillery shells started landing, called in directly on Five Zero. He hoped Ivanov was now under his hatch. The turret had a coaxial machine gun, an old but powerful PK with the long 7.62-mm cartridge. Komanov let his gunner survey the threat to his bunker while he watched how the Chinese attacked Sergeant Ivanov's. Their infantry moved with some skill, using what ground they had, keeping fire on the exposed gun turret—enough artillery fell close enough to strip away the bushes that had hidden it at first. Even if your bullets bounced off, they were still a distraction to those inside. It was the big shells that concerned the lieutenant. A direct hit might penetrate the thinner top armor, mightn't it? An hour before, he would have said no, but he could see now what the shells did to the ground, and his confidence had eroded quickly.

'Comrade Lieutenant,' his gunner said. 'The people headed for us are turning away to attack Ivanov. Look.'

Komanov turned around to see. He didn't need his binoculars. The sky was improving the light he had, and now he could see more than shadows. They were man shapes, and they were carrying weapons. One section was rushing to his left, three of them carrying something heavy. On reaching a shallow intermediate ridgeline, they stopped and started putting something together, some sort of tube . . .

. . . it was an HJ-8 anti-tank missile, his mind told him, fishing up the information from his months of intelligence briefings. They were about a thousand meters to his left front, within range of Ivanov . . .

. . . and within range of his big DshKM machine gun. Komanov stood on his firing stand and yanked back hard on the charging handle, leveling the gun and sighting carefully. His big tank gun could do this, but so could he . . .

So, you want to kill Sergeant Ivanov? his mind asked. Then he thumbed the trigger lever, and the big gun shook in his hands. His first burst was about thirty meters short, but his second was right on, and three men fell. He kept firing to make sure he'd destroyed their rocket launcher. He realized a moment later that the brilliant green tracers had just announced his location for all to see—tracers work in both directions. That became clear in two minutes, when the first artillery shells began landing around Position Five Six Alfa. He only needed one close explosion to drop down and slam his hatch. The hatch was the weakest part of his position's protection, with only a fifth of the protective thickness of the rest—else he'd be unable to open it, of course—and if a shell hit *that*, he and his crew would all be dead. The enemy knew their location now, and there was no sense in hiding.

'Sergeant,' he told his gunner. 'Fire at will.'

'Yes, Comrade Lieutenant!' And with that, the sergeant loosed his first high-explosive round at a machine-gun crew eight hundred meters away. The shell hit the gun itself and vaporized the infantrymen operating it. 'There's three good Chinks!' he exulted. 'Load me another!' The turret started turning, and the gunner started hunting.

*   *   *

'Getting some resistance now,' Wa told Peng. 'There are Russian positions on the southern slope of the second ridge. We're hitting them now with artillery.'

'Losses?'

'Light,' the operations officer reported, listening in on the tactical radio.

'Good,' said General Peng. His attention was almost entirely on the river. The first bridge was about a third complete now.

*   *   *

'Those bridging engineers are pretty good,' General Wallace thought, watching the 'take' from Marilyn Monroe.

'Yes, sir, but it might as well be a peacetime exercise. They're not taking any fire,' the junior officer observed, watching another section being tied off. 'And it's a very efficient bridge design.'

'Russian?'

The major nodded. 'Yes, sir. We copied it, too.'

'How long?'

'The rate they're going? About an hour, maybe an hour ten.'

'Back to the gunfight,' Wallace ordered.

'Sergeant, let's go back to the ridge,' the officer told the NCO who was piloting the UAC. Thirty seconds later, the screen showed what looked like a tank sunk in the mud surrounded by a bunch of infantrymen.

'Jesus, that looks like real fun,' Wallace thought. A fighter pilot by profession, the idea of fighting in the dirt appealed to him about as much as anal sex.

'They're not going to last much longer,' the major said. 'Look here. The gomers are behind some of the bunkers now.'

'And look at all that artillery.'

*   *   *

A total of a hundred heavy field guns were now pounding Komanov's immobile platoon. That amounted to a full battery fixed on each of them, and heavy as his buried concrete box was, it was shaking now, and the air inside filled with cement dust, as Komanov and his crew struggled to keep up with all the targets.

'This is getting exciting, Comrade Lieutenant,' the gunner observed, as he loosed his fifteenth main-gun shot.

Komanov was in his commander's cupola, looking around and seeing, rather to his surprise, that his bunker and all the others under his command could not deal with the attackers. It was a case of intellectual knowledge finally catching up with what his brain had long proclaimed as evident common sense. He actually was *not* invincible here. Despite his big tank gun and his two heavy machine guns, he could not deal with all these *insects* buzzing about him. It was like swatting flies with an icepick. He reckoned that he and his crew had personally killed or wounded a hundred or so attackers—but no tanks. Where were the tanks he yearned to kill? He could do that job well. But to deal with infantry, he needed supporting artillery fire, plus foot soldiers of his own. Without them, he was like a big rock on the sea coast, indestructible, but the waves could just wash around him. And they were doing that now, and then Komanov remembered that all the rocks by the sea *were* worn down by the waves, and eventually toppled by them. His war had lasted three hours, not even that much, and he was fully surrounded, and if he wanted to survive, it would soon be time to leave.

The thought enraged him. Desert his post? *Run away?* But then he remembered that he had orders allowing him to do so, if and when his post became untenable. He'd received the orders with a confident chuckle. Run away from an impregnable mini-fortress? What nonsense. But now he was alone. Each of his posts was alone. And—

—the turret rang like an off-tone bell with a direct impact of a heavy shell, and then—

—'*Shit!*' the gunner screamed. 'Shit! My gun's damaged!'

Komanov looked out of one of his vision slits, and yes, he could see it. The gun tube was scorched and . . . and actually bent. Was that possible? A gun barrel was the sturdiest structure men could make—but it was slightly bent. And so it was no longer a gun barrel at all, but just an unwieldy steel club. It had fired thirty-four rounds, but it would fire no more. With that gone, he'd never kill a Chinese tank. Komanov took a deep breath to collect himself and his thoughts. Yes, it was time.

'Prepare the post for destruction!' he ordered.

'Now?' the gunner asked incredulously.

'Now!' the lieutenant ordered. 'Set it up!'

There was a drill for this, and they'd practiced it. The loader took a demolition charge and set it among the racked shells. The electrical cable was in a spool, which he played out. The gunner ignored this, cranking the turret right to fire his coaxial machine gun at some approaching soldiers, then turning rapidly the other way to strike at those who'd used his reaction to the others' movement for cover to move themselves. Komanov stepped down from the cupola seat and looked around. There was his bed, and the table at which they'd all eaten their food, and the toilet room and the shower. This bunker had become home, a place of both comfort and work, but now they had to surrender it to the Chinese. It was almost inconceivable, but it could not be denied. In the movies, they'd fight to the death here, but fighting to the death was a lot more comfortable for actors who could start a new film the next week.

'Come on, Sergeant,' he ordered his gunner, who took one last long burst before stepping down and heading toward the escape tunnel.

Komanov counted off the men as they went, then headed out. He realized he hadn't phoned his intentions back to Regiment, and he hesitated, but, no, there wasn't time for that now. He'd radio his action from the moving BTR.

The tunnel was low enough that they had to run bent over, but it was also lit, and there was the outer door. When the reserve gunner opened it, they were greeted by the much louder sound of falling shells.

'You fucking took long enough,' a thirtyish sergeant snarled at them. 'Come on!' he urged, waving them to his BTR-60.

'Wait.' Komanov took the twist-detonator and attached the wire ends to the terminals. He sheltered behind the concrete abutment that contained the steel door and twisted the handle once.

The demolition charge was ten kilograms of TNT. It and the stored shells created an explosion that roared out of the escape tunnel with a sound like the end of the world, and on the far side of the hill the heavy turret of the never-finished JS-3 tank rocketed skyward, to the amazed pleasure of the Chinese infantrymen. And with that, Komanov's job was done. He turned and followed his men to board the eight-wheeled armored personnel carrier. It was ensconced on a concrete pad under a grass-covered concrete roof that had prevented anyone from seeing it, and now it raced down the hill to the north and safety.

448

　　　　*　　　　*　　　　*

'Bugging out,' the sergeant told the major, tapping the TV screen taking the feed from Marilyn Monroe. 'This bunch just blew up their gun turret. That's the third one to call it a day.'

'Surprised they lasted this long,' General Wallace said. Sitting still in a combat zone was an idea entirely foreign to him. He'd never done fighting while moving slower than four hundred knots, and he considered that speed to be practically standing still.

'I bet the Russians will be disappointed,' the major said.

'When do we get the downlink to Chabarsovil?'

'Before lunch, sir. We're sending a team down to show them how to use it.'

　　　　*　　　　*　　　　*

The BTR was in many ways the world's ultimate SUV, with eight driving wheels, the lead four of which turned with the steering wheel. The reservist behind that wheel was a truck driver in civilian life, and knew how to drive only with his right foot pressed to the floor, Komanov decided. He and his men bounced inside like dice in a cup, saved from head injury only by their steel helmets. But they didn't complain. Looking out of the rifle-firing ports, they could see the impact of Chinese artillery, and the quicker they got away from that, the better they'd all feel.

'How was it for you?' the lieutenant asked the sergeant commanding the vehicle.

449

'Mainly we were praying for you to be a coward. What with all those shells falling around us. Thank God for whoever built that garage we were hidden in. At least one shell fell directly on it. I nearly shit myself,' the reservist reported with refreshing candor. They were communicating in face-to-face shouts.

'How long to regimental headquarters?'

'About ten minutes. How many did you get?'

'Maybe two hundred,' Komanov thought, rather generously. 'Never saw a tank.'

'They're probably building their ribbon bridges right now. It takes a while. I saw a lot of that when I was in Eighth Guards Army in Germany. Practically all we practiced was crossing rivers. How good are they?'

'They're not cowards. They advance under fire even when you kill some of them. What happened to our artillery?'

'Wiped out, artillery rockets, came down like a blanket of hail, Comrade Lieutenant, *crump*,' he replied with a two-handed gesture.

'Where is our support?'

'Who the fuck do you think we are?' the sergeant asked in reply. They were all surprised when the BRT skidded to an unwarned stop. 'What's happening?' he shouted at the driver.

'Look!' the man said in reply, pointing.

Then the rear hatches jerked open and ten men scrambled in, making the interior of the BTR as tight as a can of fish.

'Comrade Lieutenant!' It was Ivanov from Five Zero.

'What happened?'

'We took a shell on the hatch,' he replied, and

the bandages on his face told the truth of the tale. He was in some pain, but happy to be moving again. 'Our BTR took a direct hit on the nose, killed the driver and wrecked it.'

'I've never seen shelling like this, not even in exercises in Germany and the Ukraine,' the BTR sergeant said. 'Like the war movies, but different when you're really in it.'

'*Da*,' Komanov agreed. It was no fun at all, even in his bunker, but especially out here. The sergeant lit up a cigarette, a Japanese one, and held on to the overhead grip to keep from rattling around too much. Fortunately, the driver knew the way, and the Chinese artillery abated, evidently firing at random target sets beyond visual range of their spotters.

*   *   *

'It's started, Jack,' Secretary of Defense Bretano said. 'I want to release our people to start shooting.'

'Who, exactly?'

'Air Force, fighter planes we have in theater, to start. We have AWACS up and working with the Russians already. There's been one air battle, a little one, already. And we're getting feed from reconnaissance assets. I can cross-link them to you if you want.'

'Okay, do that,' Ryan told the phone. 'And on the other issue, okay, turn 'em loose,' Jack said. He looked over at Robby.

'Jack, it's what we pay 'em for, and believe me, they don't mind. Fighter pilots live for this sort of thing—until they see what happens, though they

451

mainly never do. They just see the broke airplane, not the poor shot-up bleeding bastard inside, trying to eject while he's still conscious,' Vice President Jackson explained. 'Later on, a pilot may think about that a little. I did. But not everyone. Mainly you get to paint a kill on the side of your aircraft, and we all want to do that.'

*   *   *

'Okay, people, we are now in this fight,' Colonel Bronco Winters told his assembled pilots. He'd gotten four kills over Saudi the previous year, downing those poor dumb ragheaded gomers who flew for the country that had brought biological warfare to his own nation. One more, and he'd be a no-shit fighter ace, something he dreamed about all the way back to his doolie year at Colorado Springs. He'd been flying the F-15 Eagle fighter for his entire career, though he hoped to upgrade to the new F-22A Raptor in two or three more years. He had 4,231 hours in the Eagle, knew all its tricks, and couldn't imagine a better aircraft to go up in. So, now he'd kill Chinese. He didn't understand the politics of the moment, and didn't especially care. He was on a Russian air base, something he'd never expected to see except through a gunsight, but that was okay, too. He thought for a moment that he rather liked Chinese food, especially the things they did to vegetables in a wok, but those were American Chinese, not the commie kind, and that, he figured, was that. He'd been in Russia for just over a day, long enough to turn down about twenty offers to snort down some vodka. Their fighter pilots seemed smart enough, maybe a little

452

too eager for their own good, but friendly and respectful when they saw the four kills painted on the side panel of his F-15-Charlie, the lead fighter of the 390th Fighter Squadron. He hopped off the Russian jeep—they called it something else that he hadn't caught—at the foot of his fighter. His chief mechanic was there.

'Got her all ready for me, Chief?' Winters asked, as he took the first step on the ladder.

'You bet,' replied Chief Master Sergeant Neil Nolan. 'Everything is toplined. She's as ready as I can make her. Go kill us some, Bronco.' It was a squadron rule that when a pilot had his hands on his aircraft, he went only by his call-sign.

'I'll bring you the scalps, Nolan.' Colonel Winters continued his climb up the ladder, patting the decorated panel as he went. Chief Master Sergeant Nolan scurried up to help him strap in, then dropped off, detached the ladder, and got clear.

Winters began his start-up procedures, first of all entering his ground coordinates, something they still did on the Eagle despite the new GPS locator systems, because the F-15C had inertial navigation in case it broke (it never did, but procedure was procedure). The instruments came on-line, telling Winters that his Eagle's conformal fuel tanks were topped off, and he had a full load of four AIM-120 AMRAAM radar-guided missiles, plus four more of the brand-new AIM-9X Sidewinders, the super-snake version of a missile whose design went back to before his mom and dad had married in a church up on Lenox Avenue in Harlem.

'Tower, this is Bronco with three, ready to taxi, over.'

'Tower, Bronco, you are cleared to taxi. Wind is three-zero-five at ten. Good luck, Colonel.'

'Thank you, Tower. Boars, this is lead, let's get goin'.' With that, he tripped his brakes and the fighter started moving, driven by its powerful Pratt & Whitney engines. A bunch of Russians, mainly groundcrewmen, but judging by the outfits, some drivers as well, were out on the ramp watching him and his flight. *Okay*, he thought, *we'll show 'em how we do things downtown.* The four taxied in pairs to the end of the runway and then roared down the concrete slabs, and pulled back into the air, wingman tucked in tight. Seconds later, the other two pulled up and they turned south, already talking to the nearest AWACS, Eagle Two.

'Eagle Two, this is Boar Leader in the air with four.'

'Boar Leader, this is Eagle Two. We have you. Come south, vector one-seven-zero, climb and maintain flight level three-three. Looks like there's going to be some work for ya today, over.'

'Suits me. Out.' Colonel Winters—he'd just been deep-dip selected for his bird as a full bull colonel—wiggled a little in his seat to get things just right, and finished his climb to 33,000 feet. His radar system was off, and he wouldn't speak unnecessarily because someone out there might be listening, and why spoil the surprise? In a few minutes, he'd be entering the coverage of Chinese border radar stations. Somebody would have to do something about that. Later today, he hoped, the Little Weasel F-16s would go and see about those. But his job was Chinese fighter aircraft, and any bombers that might offer themselves. His orders were to remain over Russian airspace for the entire

454

mission, and so if Joe Chink didn't want to come out and play, it would be a dull day. But Joe had Su-27s, and he thought those were pretty good. And Joe Chink Fighter Pilot probably thought he was pretty good, too.

So, they'd just have to see.

Otherwise, it was a good day for flying, two-tenths clouds and nice clean country air to fly in. His falcon's eyes could see well over a hundred miles from up here, and he had Eagle Two to tell him where the gomers were. Behind him, a second and third flight of four Eagles were each taking off. The Wild Boars would be fully represented today.

*   *   *

The train ride was fairly jerky. Lieutenant Colonel Giusti squirmed in his upright coach seat, trying to get a little bit comfortable, but the Russian-made coach in which he and his staff were riding hadn't been designed with creature comforts in mind, and there was no sense grumbling about it. It was dark outside, the early morning that children sensibly take to be nighttime, and there wasn't much in the way of lights out there. They were in Eastern Poland now, farm country, probably, as Poland was evolving into the Iowa of Europe, lots of pig farms to make the ham for which this part of the world was famous. Vodka, too, probably, and Colonel Giusti wouldn't have minded a snort of that at the moment. He stood and walked down the aisle of the car. Nearly everyone aboard was asleep or trying to be. Two sensible NCOs were stretched out on the floor instead of curled up on the seats. The dirty floor wouldn't do their uniforms much good,

455

but they were heading to combat operations, where neatness didn't really count all that much. Personal weapons were invariably stowed in the overhead racks, in the open for easy access, because they were all soldiers, and they didn't feel very comfortable without a usable weapon close by. He continued aft. The next coach had more troopers from Headquarters Company. His squadron sergeant major was in the back of that one, reading a paperback.

'Hey, Colonel,' the sergeant major said in greeting. 'Long ride, ain't it?'

'At least three more days to go, maybe four.'

'Super,' the senior non-com observed. 'This is worse'n flying.'

'Yeah, well, at least we got our tracks with us.'

'Yes, sir.'

'How's the food situation?'

'Well, sir, we all got our MREs, and I got me a big box of Snickers bars stashed. Any word what's happening in the world?'

'Just that it's started in Siberia. The Chinese are across the border and Ivan's trying to stop 'em. No details. We ought to get an update when we go through Moscow, after lunchtime, I expect.'

'Fair 'nuff.'

'How are the troopers taking things?'

'No problems, bored with the train ride, want to get back in their tracks, the usual.'

'How's their attitude?'

'They're ready, Colonel,' the sergeant-major assured him.

'Good.' With that, Giusti turned and headed back to his seat, hoping he'd get a few hours anyway, and there wasn't much of Poland to see

456

anyway. The annoying part was being so cut off. He had satellite radios in his vehicles, somewhere on the flatcars aft of this coach, but he couldn't get to them, and without them he didn't know what was happening up forward. A war was on. He knew that. But it wasn't the same as knowing the details, knowing where the train would stop, where and when he'd get to offload his equipment, get the Quarter Horse organized, and get back on the road, where they belonged.

The train part was working well. The Russian train service seemingly had a million flatcars designed expressly to transport tracked vehicles, undoubtedly intended to take their battle tanks west, into Germany for a war against NATO. Little had the builders ever suspected that the cars would be used to bring American tanks east to help defend Russia against an invader. Well, nobody could predict the future more than a few weeks. At the moment, he would have settled for five days or so.

The rest of First Armored was stretched back hundreds of miles on the east-west rail line. Colonel Don Lisle's Second Brigade was just finishing up boarding in Berlin, and would be tail-end Charlie for the division. They'd cross Poland in daylight, for what that was worth.

The Quarter Horse was in the lead, where it belonged. Wherever the drop-off point was, they'd set up perimeter security, and then lead the march farther east, in a maneuver called Advance to Contact, which was where the 'fun' started. And he needed to be well-rested for that, Colonel Giusti reminded himself. So he settled back in his seat and closed his eyes, surrendering his body to the jerks and sways of the train car.

*   *   *

Dawn patrol was what fighter pilots all thought about. The title for the duty went back to a 1930s Errol Flynn movie and the term had probably originated with a real mission name, meaning to be the first up on a new day, to see the sun rise, and to seek out the enemy right after breakfast.

Bronco Winters didn't look much like Errol Flynn, but that was okay. You couldn't tell a warrior by the look *on* his face, though you could by the look on his face. He was a fighter pilot. As a youngster in New York, he'd ride the subway to La Guardia Airport, just to stand at the fence and watch the airplanes take off and land, knowing even then that he wanted to fly. He'd also known that fighters would be more fun than airliners, and known finally that to fly fighters he had to enter a service academy, and to do that he'd have to study. And so he'd worked hard all through school, especially in math and science, because airplanes were mechanical things, and that meant that science determined how they worked. So, he was something of a math whiz—that had been his college major at Colorado Springs—but his interest in it had ended the day he'd walked into Columbus Air Force Base in Mississippi, because once he got his hands on the controls of an aircraft, the 'study' part of his mission was accomplished, and the 'learning' part really began. He'd been the number-one student in his class at Columbus, quickly and easily mastering the Cessna Tweety Bird trainer, and then moving on to fighters, and since he'd been

458

number one in his class, he'd gotten his choice—and that choice, of course, had been the F-15 Eagle fighter, the strong and handsome grandson of the F-4 Phantom. An easy plane to fly, it was a harder one to fight, since the controls for the combat systems are located on the stick and the throttles, all in buttons of different shapes so that you could manage all the systems by feel, and keep your eyes up and out of the aircraft instead of having to look down at instruments. It was something like playing two pianos at the same time, and it had taken Winters a disappointing six months to master. But now those controls came as naturally as twirling the wax into his Bismarck mustache, his one non-standard affectation, which he'd modeled on Robin Olds, a legend in the American fighter community, an instinctive pilot and a thinking—and therefore a very dangerous—tactician. An ace in World War II, an ace in Korea, and also an ace over North Vietnam, Olds was one of the best who'd ever strapped a fighter plane to his back, and one whose mustache had made Otto von Bismarck himself look like a pussy.

Colonel Winters wasn't thinking about that now. The thoughts were there even so, as much a part of his character as his situational awareness, the part of his brain that kept constant track of the three-dimensional reality around him at all times. Flying came as naturally to him as it did to the gyrfalcon mascot at the Air Force Academy. And so did hunting, and now he was hunting. His aircraft had instrumentation that downloaded the take from the AWACS aircraft a hundred fifty miles to his rear, and he divided his eye time equally between the sky around him and the display three feet from his 20-

10 brown eyes . . .

. . . there . . . two hundred miles, bearing one-seven-two, four bandits heading north. Then four more, and another flight of four. Joe Chink was coming up to play, and the pigs were hungry.

'Boar Lead, this is Eagle Two.' They were using encrypted burst-transmission radios that were very difficult to detect, and impossible to listen in on.

'Boar Lead.' But he kept his transmission short anyway. Why spoil the surprise?

'Boar Lead, we have sixteen bandits, one-seven-zero your position at angels thirty, coming due north at five hundred knots.'

'Got 'em.'

'They're still south of the border, but not for long,' the young controller on the E-3B advised. 'Boar, you are weapons-free at this time.'

'Copy weapons-free,' Colonel Winters acknowledged, and his left hand flipped a button to activate his systems. A quick look down to his weapons-status display showed that everything was ready to fire. He didn't have his tracking/ targeting radar on, though it was in standby mode. The F-15 had essentially been designed as an appendage to the monstrous radar in its nose—a design consideration that had defined the size of the fighter from the first sketch on paper—but over the years the pilots had gradually stopped using it, because it could warn an enemy with the right sort of threat receiver, telling him that there was an Eagle in the neighborhood with open eyes and sharp claws. Instead he could now cross-load the radar information from the AWACS, whose radar signals were unwelcome, but nothing an enemy could do anything about, and not directly threatening. The Chinese would be directed and controlled by ground radar, and the Boars were just at the fuzzy edge of that, maybe spotted, maybe not. Somewhere to his rear, a Rivet Joint EC-135 was monitoring both the radar and the radios used by the Chinese ground controllers, and would cross-load any warnings to the AWACS. But so far none of that. So, Joe Chink was coming north.

'Eagle, Boar, say bandit type, over.'

'Boar, we're not sure, but probably Sierra-Uniform Two-Sevens by point of origin and flight profile, over.'

'Roger.' Okay, good, Winters thought. They thought the Su-27 was a pretty hot aircraft, and for a Russian-designed bird it was respectable. They put their best drivers into the Flanker, and they'd be the proud ones, the ones who thought they were as good as he was. *Okay, Joe, let's see how good you are.* 'Boar, Lead, come left to one-three-five.'

'Two.' 'Three.' 'Four,' the flight acknowledged, and they all banked to the left. Winters took a look around to make sure he wasn't leaving any contrails to give away his position. Then he checked his threat receiver. It was getting some chirps from Chinese search radar, but still below the theoretical detection threshold. That would change in twenty miles or so. But then they'd just be unknowns on the Chinese screens, and fuzzy ones at that. Maybe the ground controllers would radio a warning, but maybe they'd just peer at their screens and try to decide if they were real contacts or not. The robin's-egg blue of the Eagles wasn't all that easy to spot visually, especially when you had the sun behind you, which was the oldest trick in

461

the fighter-pilot bible, and one for which there was still no solution . . .

The Chinese passed to his right, thirty miles away, heading north and looking for Russian fighters to engage, because the Chinese would want to control the sky over the battlefield they'd just opened up. That meant that they'd be turning on their own search radars, and when that happened, they'd spend most of their time looking down at the scope instead of out at the sky, and that was dangerous. When he was south of them, Winters brought his flight right, west, and down to twenty thousand feet, well below Joe Chink's cruising altitude, because fighter pilots might look back and up, but rarely back and down, because they'd been taught that height, like speed, was life. And so it was . . . most of the time. In another three minutes, they were due south of the enemy, and Winters increased power to maximum dry thrust so as to catch up. His flight of four split on command into two pairs. He went left, and then his eyes spotted them, dark flecks on the brightening blue sky. They were painted the same light gray the Russians liked—and that would be a real problem if Russian Flankers entered the area, because you didn't often get close enough to see if the wings had red stars or white-blue-red flags painted on them.

The audio tone came next. His Sidewinders could see the heat bloom from the Lyul'ka turbofan engines, and that meant he was just about close enough. His wingman, a clever young lieutenant, was now about five hundred yards to his right, doing his job, which was covering his leader. *Okay*, Bronco Winters thought. He had a good hundred knots of overtake speed now.

'Boar, Eagle, be advised these guys are heading directly for us at the moment.

'Not for long, Eagle,' Colonel Winters responded. They weren't flecks anymore. Now they were twin-rudder fighter aircraft. Cruising north, tucked in nice and pretty. His left forefinger selected Sidewinder to start, and the tone in his earphones was nice and loud. He'd start with two shots, one at the left-most Flanker, and the other at the rightmost . . . right about . . .

'Fox-Two, Fox-Two with two birds away,' Bronco reported. The smoke trails diverged, just as he wanted them to, streaking in on their targets. His gunsight camera was operating, and the picture was being recorded on videotape, just as it had been over Saudi the previous year. He needed one kill to make ace—

—he got the first six seconds later, and the next half a second after that. Both Flankers tumbled right. The one on the left nearly collided with his wingman, but missed, and tumbled violently as pieces started coming off the airframe. The other one was rolling and then exploded into a nice white puffball. The first pilot ejected cleanly, but the second didn't.

Tough luck, Joe, Winters thought. The remaining two Chinese fighters hesitated, but both then split and started maneuvering in diverging directions. Winters switched on his radar and followed the one to the left. He had radar lock and it was well within the launch parameters for his AMRAAM. His right forefinger squeezed the pickle switch.

'Fox-One, Fox-One, Slammer on guy to the west.' He watched the Slammer, as it was called, race in. Technically a fire-and-forget weapon like

463

the Sidewinder, it accelerated almost instantly to mach-two-plus and rapidly ate up the three miles between them. It only took about ten seconds to close and explode a mere few feet over the fuselage of its target, and that Flanker disintegrated with no chute coming away from it.

Okay, three. This morning was really shaping up, but now the situation went back to World War I. He had to search for targets visually, and searching for jet fighters in a clear sky wasn't . . .

. . . there . . .

'You with me, Skippy?' he called on the radio.

'Got you covered, Bronco,' his wingman replied. 'Bandit at your one o'clock, going left to right.'

'On him,' Winters replied, putting his nose on the distant spot in the sky. His radar spotted it, locked onto it, and the IFF transponder didn't say friendly. He triggered off his second Slammer: 'Fox-One on the south guy! Eagle, Boar Lead, how we doing?'

'We show five kills to this point. Bandits are heading east and diving. Razorback is coming in from your west with four, angels three-five at six hundred, now at your ten o'clock. Check your IFF, Boar Lead.' The controller was being careful, but that was okay.

'Boar, Lead, check IFF now!'

'Two.' 'Three.' 'Four,' they all chimed in. Before the last of them confirmed his IFF transponder was in the transmit setting, his second Slammer found its target, running his morning's score to four. *Well, damn*, Winters thought, *this morning is* really *shaping up nice.*

'Bronco, Skippy is on one!' his wingman reported, and Winters took position behind, low, and left of his wingman. 'Skippy' was First Lieutenant Marto Acosta, a red-haired infant from Wichita who was coming along nicely for a child with only two hundred hours in type.

'Fox-Two with one,' Skippy called. His target had turned south, and was heading almost straight into the streaking missile. Winters saw the Sidewinder go right into his right-side intake, and the resulting explosion was pretty impressive.

'Eagle, Boar Lead, give me a vector, over.'

'Boar Lead, come right at zero-nine-zero. I have a bandit at ten miles and low, angels ten, heading south at six-hundred-plus.'

Winters executed the turn and checked his radar display. 'Got him!' And this one also was well within the Slammer envelope. 'Fox-One with Slammer.' His fifth missile of the day leaped off the rail and rocketed east, angling down, and again Winters kept his nose on the target, ensuring that he'd get it on tape . . . yes! 'That's a splash. Bronco has a splash, I think that's five.'

'Confirm five kills to Bronco,' Eagle Two confirmed. 'Nice going, buddy.'

'What else is around?'

'Boar Lead, the bandits are running south on burner, just went through Mach One. We show a total of nine kills plus one damage, with six bandits running back to the barn, over.'

'Roger, copy that, Eagle. Anything else happening at the moment?'

'Ah, that's a negative, Boar Lead.'

'Where's the closest tanker?'

'You can tank from Oliver-Six, vector zero-zero-five, distance two hundred, over.'

'Roger that. Flight, this is Bronco. Let's

assemble and head off to tank. Form up on me.'

'Two. Three. Four.'

'How we doing?'

'Sloppy has one,' his wingman reported.

'Ducky has two,' the second element leader chimed in.

'Ghost Man has two and a scratch.'

It didn't add up, Winters thought. Hell, maybe the AWACS guys got confused. That's why they had videotape. All in all, not a bad morning. Best of all, they'd put a real dent in the ChiComm Flanker inventory, and probably punched a pinhole in the confidence of their Su-27 drivers. Shaking up a fighter jock's confidence was almost as good as a kill, especially if they'd bagged the squadron commander. It would make the survivors mad, but it would make them question themselves, their doctrine, and their aircraft. And that was good.

*   *   *

'So?'

'The border defenses did about as well as one could reasonably expect,' Colonel Aliyev replied. 'The good news is that most of our men escaped with their lives. Total dead is under twenty, with fifteen wounded.'

'What do they have across the river now?'

'Best guess, elements of three mechanized divisions. The Americans say that they now have six bridges completed and operating. So, we can expect that number to increase rapidly. Chinese reconnaissance elements are pushing forward. We've ambushed some of them, but no prisoners yet. Their direction of advance is exactly what we anticipated, as is their speed of advance to this point.'

'Is there any good news?' Bondarenko asked.

'Yes, General. Our air force and our American friends have given their air force a very bloody nose. We've killed over thirty of their aircraft with only four losses to this point, and two of the pilots have been rescued. We've captured six Chinese pilots. They're being taken west for interrogation. It's unlikely that they'll give us any really useful information, though I am sure the air force will want to grill them for technical things. Their plans and objectives are entirely straightforward, and they are probably right on, or even slightly in advance of their plans.'

None of this was a surprise to General Bondarenko, but it was unpleasant even so. His intelligence staff was doing a fine job of telling him what they knew and what they expected, but it was like getting a weather report in winter: Yes, it was cold, and yes, it was snowing, and no, the cold and the snow will probably not stop, and isn't it a shame you don't have a warm coat to wear? He had nearly perfect information, but no ability to do anything to change the news. It was all very good that his airmen were killing Chinese airmen, but it was the Chinese tanks and infantry carriers that he had to stop.

'When will we be able to bring air power to bear on their spearheads?'

'We will start air-to-ground operations this afternoon with Su-31 ground-attack aircraft,' Aliyev replied. 'But . . .'

'But what?' Bondarenko demanded.

'But isn't it better to let them come in with

467

minimal interference for a few days?' It was a courageous thing for his operations officer to say. It was also the right thing, Gennady Iosifovich realized on reflection. If his only strategic option was to lay a deep trap, then why waste what assets he had before the trap was fully set? This was not the Western Front in June of 1941, and he didn't have Stalin sitting in Moscow with a figurative pistol to his head.

No, in Moscow now, the government would be raising all manner of political hell, probably calling for an emergency meeting of the United Nations Security Council, but that was just advertising. It was his job to defeat these yellow barbarians, and doing that was a matter of using what power he had in the most efficient manner possible, and that meant drawing them out. It meant making their commander as confident as a schoolyard bully looking down at a child five years his junior. It meant giving them what the Japanese had once called the Victory Disease. Make them feel invincible, and *then* leap at them like a tiger dropping from a tree.

'Andrey, only a few aircraft, and tell them not to risk themselves by pressing their attacks too hard. We can hurt their air force, but their ground forces—we let them keep their advantage for a while. Let them get fat on this fine table set before them for a while.'

'I agree, Comrade General. It's a hard pill to swallow, but in the end, harder for them to eat— assuming our political leadership allows us to do the right thing.'

'Yes, that is the real issue at hand, isn't it?'

CHAPTER FIFTY-TWO

DEEP BATTLE

General Peng crossed over into Russia in his command vehicle, well behind the first regiment of heavy tanks. He thought of using a helicopter, but his operations staff warned him that the air battle was not going as well as the featherheads in the PLAAF had told him to expect. He felt uneasy, crossing the river in an armored vehicle on a floating bridge—like a brick tied to a balloon—but he did so, listening as his operations officer briefed him on the progress to this point.

'The Americans have surged a number of fighter aircraft forward, and along with them their E-3 airborne radar fighter-control aircraft. These are formidable, and difficult to counter, though our air force colleagues say that they have tactics to deal with them. I will believe that when I see it,' Colonel Wa observed. 'But that is the only bad news so far. We are several hours ahead of schedule. Russian resistance is lighter than I expected. The prisoners we've taken are very disheartened at their lack of support.'

'Is that a fact?' Peng asked, as they left the ribbon bridge and thumped down on Russian soil.

'Yes, we have ten men captured from their defensive positions—we'll see them in a few minutes. They had escape tunnels and personnel carriers set to evacuate the men. They didn't expect to hold for long,' Colonel Wa went on. 'They *planned* to run away, rather than defend to the last as we expected. I think they lack the heart for combat, Comrade General.'

That information got Peng's attention. It was important to know the fighting spirit of one's enemy: 'Did any of them stand and fight to the end?'

'Only one of their bunker positions. It cost us thirty men, but we took them out. Perhaps their escape vehicle was destroyed and they had no choice,' the colonel speculated.

'I want to see one of these positions at once,' Peng ordered.

'Of course, Comrade General.' Wa ducked inside and shouted an order to the track driver. The Type 90 armored personnel carrier lurched to the right, surprising the MP who was trying to do traffic control, but he didn't object. The four tall radio whips told him what sort of track this was. The command carrier moved off the beaten track directly toward an intact Russian bunker.

General Peng got out, ducking his head as he did so, and walked toward the mainly intact old gun turret. The 'inverted frying pan' shape told him that this was off an old Stalin-3 tank—a very formidable vehicle, once upon a time, but now an obvious relic. A team of intelligence specialists was there. They snapped to attention when they saw the general approach.

'What did we kill it with?' Peng asked.

'We didn't, Comrade General. They abandoned it after firing fifteen cannon shots and about three hundred machine gun rounds. They didn't even destroy it before we captured it,' the intelligence captain reported, waving the general down the tank hatch. 'It's safe. We checked for booby traps.'

Peng climbed down. He saw what appeared to be a comfortable small barracks, shell storage for their big tank gun, ample rounds for their two machine guns. There were empty rounds for both types of guns on the floor, along with wrappers for field rations. It appeared to be a comfortable position, with bunks, shower, toilet, and plenty of food storage. Something worth fighting for, the general thought. 'How did they leave?' Peng asked.

'This way,' the young captain said, leading him north into the tunnel. 'You see, the Russians planned for everything.' The tunnel led under the crest of the hill to a covered parking pad for— probably for a BTR, it looked like, confirmed by the wheel tracks on the ground immediately off the concrete pad.

'How long did they hold?'

'We took the place just less than three hours after our initial bombardment. So, we had infantry surrounding the main gun emplacement, and soon thereafter, they ran away,' the captain told his army commander.

'I see. Good work by our assault infantry.' Then Peng saw that Colonel Wa had brought his command track over the hill to the end of the escape tunnel, allowing him to hop right aboard.

'Now what?' Wa asked.

'I want to see what we did to their artillery support positions.'

Wa nodded and relayed the orders to the track commander. That took fifteen minutes of bouncing and jostling. The fifteen heavy guns were still there, though the two Peng passed had been knocked over and destroyed by counter-battery fire. The position they visited was mainly intact, though a number of rockets had fallen close aboard, near enough that three bodies were still lying there untended next to their guns, the bodies surrounded by sticky pools of mainly dried blood. More men had survived, probably. Close to each gun was a two-meter-deep narrow trench lined with concrete that the bombardment hadn't done more than chip. Close by also was a large ammo-storage bunker with rails on which to move the shells and propellant charges to the guns. The door was open.

'How many rounds did they get off?' he asked.

'No more than ten,' another intelligence officer, this one a major, replied. 'Our counter-battery fire was superb here. The Russian battery was fifteen guns, total. One of them got off twenty shots, but that was all. We had them out of action in less than ten minutes. The artillery-tracker radars worked brilliantly, Comrade General.'

Peng nodded agreement. 'So it would appear. This emplacement would have been fine twenty or thirty years ago—good protection for the gunners and a fine supply of shells, but they did not anticipate an enemy with the ability to pinpoint their guns so rapidly. If it stands still, Wa, you can kill it.' Peng looked around. 'Still, the engineers who sited this position and the other one, they were good. It's just that this sort of thing is out of date. What were our total casualties?'

'Killed, three hundred fifty, thereabouts. Wounded, six hundred twenty,' operations replied. 'It was not exactly cheap, but less than we expected. If the Russians had stood and fought, it could have been far worse.'

'Why did they run so soon?' Peng asked. 'Do we know?'

'We found a written order in one of the bunkers, authorizing them to leave when they thought things were untenable. That surprised me,' Colonel Wa observed. 'Historically, the Russians fight very hard on the defense, as the Germans found. But that was under Stalin. The Russians had discipline then. And courage. Not today, it would seem.'

'Their evacuation was conducted with some skill,' Peng thought out loud. 'We ought to have taken more prisoners.'

'They ran too fast, Comrade General,' operations explained.

'He who fights and runs away,' General Peng quoted, 'lives to fight another day. Bear that in mind, Colonel.'

'Yes, Comrade General, but he who runs away is not an immediate threat.'

'Let's go,' the general said, heading off to his command track. He wanted to see the front, such as it was.

* * *

'So?' Bondarenko asked the lieutenant. The youngster had been through a bad day, and being required to stand and make a report to his theater commander made it no better. 'Stand easy, boy. You're alive. It could have been worse.'

'General, we could have held if we'd been given a little support,' Komanov said, allowing his frustration to appear.

'There was none to give you. Go on.' The general pointed at the map on the wall.

'They crossed here, and came through this saddle, and over this ridge to attack us. Leg infantry, no vehicles that we ever saw. They had man-portable anti-tank weapons, nothing special or unexpected, but they had massive artillery support. There must have been an entire battery concentrated just on my one position. Heavy guns, fifteen-centimeter or more. And artillery rockets that wiped out our artillery support almost immediately.'

'That's the one surprise they threw at us,' Aliyev confirmed. 'They must have a lot more of those fire-finder systems than we expected, and they're using their Type 83 rockets as dedicated counter-battery weapons, like the Americans did in Saudi. It's an effective tactic. We'll have to go after their counter-battery systems first of all, or use self-propelled guns to fire and move after only two or three shots. There's no way to spoof them that I know of, and jamming radars of that type is extremely difficult.'

'So, we have to work on a way to kill them early on,' Bondarenko said. 'We have electronic-intelligence units. Let them seek out those Chink radars and eliminate them with rockets of our own.' He turned. 'Go, on. Lieutenant. Tell me about the Chinese infantry.'

'They are not cowards, Comrade General. They take fire and act properly under it. They are well-drilled. My position and the one next to us took down at least two hundred, and they kept coming. Their battle drill is quite good, like a soccer team. If you do *this*, they do *that*, almost instantly. For certain, they call in artillery fire with great skill.'

'They had the batteries already lined up, Lieutenant, lined up and waiting,' Aliyev told the junior officer. 'It helps if you are following a prepared script. Anything else?'

'We never saw a tank. They had us taken out before they finished their bridges. Their infantry looked well-prepared, well-trained, even eager to move forward. I did not see evidence of flexible thinking, but I did not see much of anything, and as you say, their part of the operation was preplanned, and thoroughly rehearsed.'

'Typically, the Chinese tell their men a good deal about their planned operations beforehand. They don't believe in secrecy the way we do,' Aliyev said. 'Perhaps it makes for comradely solidarity on the battlefield.'

'But things are going their way, Andrey. The measure of an army is how it reacts when things go badly. We haven't seen that yet, however.' *And would they ever?* Bondarenko wondered. He shook his head. He had to banish that sort of thinking from his mind. If he had no confidence, how could his men have it? 'What about your men, Valeriy Mikhailovich? How did they fight?'

'We *fought*, Comrade General,' Komanov assured the senior officer. 'We killed two hundred, and we would have killed many more with a little artillery support.'

'Will your men fight some more?' Aliyev asked.

'Fuck, yes!' Komanov snarled back. 'Those little bastards are invading *our* country. Give us the right weapons, and we'll fucking kill them all!'

'Did you graduate tank school?'

Komanov bobbed his head like a cadet. 'Yes, Comrade General, eighth in my class.'

'Give him a company with BOYAR,' the general told his ops officer. 'They're short of officers.'

Major General Marion Diggs was in the third train out of Berlin; it wasn't his choosing, just the way things worked out. He was thirty minutes behind Angelo Giusti's cavalry squadron. The Russians were running their trains as closely together as safety allowed, and probably even shading that somewhat. What *was* working was that the Russian national train system was fully electrified, which meant that the engines accelerated well out of stations and out of the slow orders caused by track problems, which were numerous.

Diggs had grown up in Chicago. His father had been a Pullman porter with the Atcheson, Topeka and Santa Fe Railroad, working the Super Chief between Chicago and Los Angeles until the passenger service had died in the early 1970s; then, remarkably enough, he'd changed unions to become an engineer. Marion remembered riding with him as a boy, and loving the feel of such a massive piece of equipment under his hands—and so, when he'd gone to West Point, he'd decided to be a tanker, and better yet, a cavalryman. Now he owned a lot of heavy equipment.

It was his first time in Russia, a place he certainly hadn't expected to see when he'd been in the first half of his uniformed career, when the Russians he'd worried about seeing had been mainly from First Guards Tank and Third Shock armies, those massive formations that had once sat in East Germany, always poised to take a nice little drive to Paris, or so NATO had feared.

But no more, now that Russia was part of NATO, an idea that was like something from a bad

476

science-fiction movie. There was no denying it, however. Looking out the windows of the train car, he could see the onion-topped spires of Russian Orthodox churches, ones that Stalin had evidently failed to tear down. The railyards were pretty familiar. Never the most artistic examples of architecture or city planning, they looked the same as the dreary yards leading into Chicago or any other American city. No, only the train yards that you built under your Christmas tree every year were pretty. But they didn't have any Christmas trees in evidence here. The train rolled to a stop, probably waiting for a signal to proceed—

—but no, this looked to be some sort of military terminal. Russian tanks were in evidence off to the right, and a lot of sloped concrete ramps—the Russians had probably built this place to ship their own tracked vehicles west, he judged.

'General?' a voice called.

'Yo!'

'Somebody here to see you, sir,' the same voice announced.

Diggs stood and walked back to the sound. It was one of his junior staff officers, a new one fresh from Leavenworth, and behind him was a Russian general officer.

'You are Diggs?' the Russian asked in fair English.

'That's right.'

'Come with me please.' The Russian walked out onto the platform. The air was fresh, but they were under low, gray clouds this morning.

'You going to tell me how things are going out east?' Diggs asked.

'We wish to fly you and some of your staff to

Chabarsovil so that you can see for yourself.'

That made good sense, Diggs thought. 'How many?'

'Six, plus you.'

'Okay.' The general nodded and reached for the captain who'd summoned him from his seat. 'I want Colonels Masterman, Douglas, Welch, Turner, Major Hurst, and Lieutenant Colonel Garvey.'

'Yes, sir.' The boy disappeared.

'How soon?'

'The transport is waiting for you now.'

One of theirs, Diggs thought. He'd never flown on a Russian aircraft before. How safe would it be? How safe would it be to fly into a war zone? Well, the Army didn't pay him to stay in safe places.

'Who are you?'

'Nosenko, Valentin Nosenko, general major, Stavka.'

'How bad is it?'

'It is not good, General Diggs. Our main problem will be getting reinforcements to the theater of action. But they have rivers to cross. The difficulties, as you Americans say, should even out.'

Diggs's main worry was supply. His tanks and Bradleys all had basic ammo loads already aboard, and two and a half additional such loads for each vehicle were on supply trucks sitting on other trains like this one. After that, things got a little worrisome, especially for artillery. But the biggest worry of all was diesel fuel. He had enough to move his division maybe three or four hundred miles. That was a good long way in a straight line, but wars never allowed troops to travel in straight lines. That translated to maybe two hundred miles of actual travel at best, and that was not an

478

impressive number at all. Then there was the question of jet fuel for his organic aircraft. So, his head logistician, Colonel Ted Douglas, was the first guy he needed, after Masterman, his operations brain. The officers started showing up.

'What gives, sir?' Masterman asked.

'We're flying east to see what's going on.'

'Okay, let me make sure we have some communications gear.' Masterman disappeared again. He left the train car, along with two enlisted men humping satellite radio equipment.

'Good call, Duke,' LTC Garvey observed. He was communications and electronic intelligence for First Tanks.

'Gentlemen, this is General Nosenko from Stavka. He's taking us east, I gather?'

'Correct, I am an intelligence officer for Stavka. This way, please.' He led them off, to where four cars were waiting. The drive to a military airport took twenty minutes.

'How are your people taking this?' Diggs asked.

'The civilians, you mean? Too soon to tell. Much disbelief, but some anger. Anger is good,' Nosenko said. 'Anger gives courage and determination.'

If the Russians were talking about anger and determination, the situation must be pretty bad, Diggs thought, looking out at the streets of the Moscow suburbs.

'What are you moving east ahead of us?'

'So far, four motor-rifle divisions,' Nosenko answered. 'Those are our best-prepared formations. We are assembling other forces.'

'I've been out of touch. What else is NATO sending? Anything?' Diggs asked next.

'A British brigade is forming up now, the men

479

based at Hohne. We hope to have them on the way here in two days.'

'No way we'd go into action without at least the Brits to back us up,' Diggs said. 'Good, they're equipped about the same way we are.' And better yet, they trained according to the same doctrine. *Hohne*, he thought, their 22nd Brigade from Haig Barracks, Brigadier Sam Turner. Drank whiskey like it was Perrier, but a good thinker and a superior tactician. And his brigade was all trained up from some fun and games down at Grafenwöhr. 'What about Germans?'

'That's a political question,' Nosenko admitted.

'Tell your politicians that Hitler's dead, Valentin. The Germans are pretty good to have on your side. Trust me, buddy. We play with them all the time. They're down a little from ten years ago, but the German soldier ain't no dummy, and neither are his officers. Their reconnaissance units are particularly good.'

'Yes, but that is a political question,' Nosenko repeated. And that, Diggs knew, was that, at least for now.

The aircraft waiting was an Il-86, known to NATO as the Camber, manifestly the Russian copy of Lockheed's C-141 Starlifter. This one had Aeroflot commercial markings, but retained the gun position in the tail that the Russians liked to keep on all their tactical aircraft. Diggs didn't object to it at the moment. They'd scarcely had the chance to sit down and strap in when the aircraft started rolling.

'In a hurry, Valentin?'

'Why wait, General Diggs? There's a war on,' he reminded his guest.

'Okay, what do we know?'

Nosenko opened the map case he'd been carrying and laid out a large sheet on the floor as the aircraft lifted off. It was of the Chinese–Russian border on the Amur River, with markings already penciled on. The American officers all leaned over to look.

'They came in here, and drove across the river . . .'

* * *

'How fast are they moving?' Bondarenko asked.

'I have a reconnaissance company ahead of them. They report in every fifteen minutes,' Colonel Tolkunov replied. 'They are moving in a deliberate manner. Their reconnaissance screen is composed of WZ-501 tracked APCs, heavy on radios, light on weapons. They are on the whole not very enterprising, however. As I said, deliberate. They move by leapfrogging half a kilometer at a bound, depending on terrain. We're monitoring their radios. They're not encrypted, though their spoken language is deceptive in terminology. We're working on that.'

'Speed of advance?'

'Five kilometers in an hour is the fastest we've seen, usually slower than that. Their main body is still getting organized, and they haven't set up a logistics train yet. I'd expect them to attempt no more than thirty kilometers in a day on flat open ground, based on what I've seen so far.'

'Interesting.' Bondarenko looked back at his maps. They'd start going north-northwest because that's what the terrain compelled them to do. At this speed, they'd be at the gold strike in six or seven days.

Theoretically, he could move 265th Motor Rifle to a blocking position . . . here . . . in two days and make a stand, but by then they'd have at least three, maybe eight, mechanized divisions to attack his one full-strength unit, and he couldn't gamble on that so soon. The good news was that the Chinese were bypassing his command post—*contemptuously?* he wondered, *or just because there was nothing there to threaten them, and so nothing to squander force on?* No, they'd run as fast and hard as they could, bringing up foot infantry to wall off their line of advance. That was classic tactics, and the reason was because it worked. Everyone did it that way, from Hannibal to Hitler.

So, their lead elements moved deliberately, and they were still forming up their army over the Amur bridgehead.

'What units have we identified?'

'The lead enemy formation is their 34th Red Banner Shock Army, Commanded by Peng Xi-Wang. He is politically reliable and well-regarded in Beijing, an experienced soldier. Expect him to be the operational army group commander. The 34th Army is mainly across the river now. Three more Group A mechanized armies are lined up to cross as well, the 31st, 29th, and 43rd. That's a total of sixteen mechanized divisions, plus a lot of other attachments. We think the 65th Group B Army will be next across. Four infantry divisions plus a tank brigade. Their job will be to hold the western flank, I would imagine.' That made sense. There was no Russian force east of the breakthrough worthy of the name. A classic operation would also wheel east to Vladivostok on the Pacific Coast, but that would only distract forces from the main objection. So, the turn east would wait for at least a week, probably two or three, with just light screening forces heading that way for the moment.

'What about our civilians?' Bondarenko asked.

'They're leaving the towns in the Chinese path as best they can, mainly cars and buses. We have MP units trying to keep them organized. So far nothing has happened to interfere with the evacuation,' Tolkunov said. 'See, from this it looks as if they're actually bypassing Belogorsk, just passing east of it with their reconnaissance elements.'

'That's the smart move, isn't it?' Bondarenko observed. 'Their real objective is far to the north. Why slow down for anything? They don't want land. They don't want people. They want oil and gold. Capturing civilians will not make those objectives any easier to accomplish. If I were this Peng fellow, I would be worried about the extent of my drive north. Even unopposed, the natural obstacles are formidable, and defending his line of advance will be a beast of a problem.' Gennady paused. Why have any sympathy for this barbarian? His mission was to kill him and all his men, after all. But how? If even marching that far north was a problem—and it was—then how much harder would it be to strike through the same terrain with less-prepared troops? The tactical problems on both sides were the kind men in his profession did not welcome.

'General Bondarenko?' a foreign voice asked.

'Yes?' He turned to see a man dressed in an American flight suit.

'Sir, my name is Major Dan Tucker. I just flew in with a downlink for our Dark Star UAVs. Where do you want us to set up, sir?'

'Colonel Tolkunov? Major, this is my chief of intelligence.'

The American saluted sloppily, as air force people tended to do. 'Howdy, Colonel.'

'How long to set up?'

The American was pleased that this Tolkunov's English was better than his own Russian. 'Less than an hour, sir.'

'This way.' The G-2 led him outside. 'How good are your cameras?'

'Colonel, when a guy's out taking a piss, you can see how big his dick is.'

Tolkunov figured that was typical American braggadocio, but it set him wondering.

*   *   *

Captain Feodor Il'ych Aleksandrov commanded the 265th Motor Rifle's divisional reconnaissance element—the division was supposed to have a full battalion for this task, but he was all they had—and for that task he had eight of the new BRM reconnaissance tracks. These were evolutionary developments of the standard BMP infantry combat vehicle, upgraded with better automotive gear—more reliable engine and transmission systems—plus the best radios his country made. He reported directly to his divisional commander, and also, it seemed, to the theater intelligence coordinator, some colonel named Tolkunov. That chap, he'd discovered, was very concerned with his personal safety, always urging him to stay close—

but not too close—not to be spotted, and to avoid combat of any type. His job, Tolkunov had told him at least once every two hours for the last day and a half, was to stay alive and to keep his eye on the advancing Chinese. He wasn't supposed to so much as injure one little hair on their cute little Chink heads, just stay close enough that if they mumbled in their sleep, to copy down the names of the girlfriends they fucked in their dreams.

Aleksandrov was a young captain, only twenty-eight, and rakishly handsome, an athlete who ran for personal pleasure—and running, he told his men, was the best form of exercise for a soldier, especially a reconnaissance specialist. He had a driver, gunner, and radio operator for each of his tracks, plus three infantrymen whom he'd personally trained to be invisible.

The drill was for them to spend about half their time out of their vehicles, usually a good kilometer or so ahead of their Chinese counterparts, either behind trees or on their bellies, reporting back with monosyllabic comments on their portable radios, which were of Japanese manufacture. The men moved light, carrying only their rifles and two spare magazines, because they weren't supposed to be seen or heard, and the truth was that Aleksandrov would have preferred to send them out unarmed, lest they be tempted to shoot someone out of patriotic anger. However, no soldier would ever stand for being sent out on a battlefield weaponless, and so he'd had to settle for ordering them out with bolts closed on empty chambers. The captain was usually out with his men, their BRM carriers hidden three hundred or so meters away in the trees.

485

In the past twenty-four hours, they'd become intimately familiar with their Chinese opponents. These were also trained and dedicated reconnaissance specialists, and they were pretty good at their jobs, or certainly appeared to be. They were also moving in tracked vehicles, and also spent a lot of their time on foot, ahead of their tracks, hiding behind trees and peering to the north, looking for Russian forces. The Russians had even started giving them names.

'It's the gardener,' Sergeant Buikov said. That one liked touching trees and bushes, as though studying them for a college paper or something. The gardener was short and skinny, and looked like a twelve-year-old to the Russians. He seemed competent enough, carrying his rifle slung on his back, and using his binoculars often. He was a Chinese lieutenant, judging by his shoulderboards, probably commander of this platoon. He ordered his people around a lot, but didn't mind taking the lead. So, he was probably conscientious. *He is, therefore, the one we should kill first*, Aleksandrov thought. Their BRM reconnaissance track had a fine 30-mm cannon that could reach out and turn the gardener into fertilizer from a thousand meters or so, but Captain Aleksandrov had forbidden it, worse luck, Buikov thought. He was from this area, a woodsman of sorts who'd hunted in the forests many times with his father, a lumberjack. 'We really ought to kill him.'

'Boris Yevgeniyevich, do you wish to alert the enemy to our presence?' Aleksandrov asked his sergeant.

'I suppose not, my captain, but the hunting season is—'

'—closed, Sergeant. The season is closed, and no, he is not a wolf that you can shoot for your own pleasure, and—down,' Aleksandrov ordered. The gardener was looking their way with his field glasses. Their faces were painted, and they had branches tucked into their field clothing to break up their outlines, but he was taking no chances. 'They'll be moving soon. Back to the track.'

The hardest part of their drill was to avoid leaving tracks for the Chinese to spot. Aleksandrov had 'discussed' this with his drivers, threatening to shoot anyone who left a trail. (He knew he couldn't do that, of course, but his men weren't quite sure.) Their vehicles even had upgraded mufflers to reduce their sound signature. Every so often, the men who designed and built Russian military equipment got things right, and this was such a case. Besides, they didn't crank their engines until they saw the Chinese doing the same. Aleksandrov looked up. Okay, the gardener was waving to those behind him, the wave that meant to bring their vehicles up. They were doing another leapfrog jump, with one section standing fast and providing over-watch cover for the next move, should something happen. He had no intention of making anything happen, but of course they couldn't know that. Aleksandrov was surprised that they were maintaining their careful drill into the second day. They weren't getting sloppy yet. He'd expected that, but it seemed that the Chinese were better drilled even than his expectations, and were assiduously following their written doctrine. Well, so was he.

'Move now, Captain?' Buikov asked.

'No, let's sit still and watch. They ought to stop

at that little ridge with the logging road. I want to see how predictable they are, Boris Yevgeniyevich.' But he did trigger his portable radio. 'Stand by, they're jumping again.'

The other radio just clicked on and off, creating a whisper of static, rather than a spoken reply. Good, his men were adhering to their radio discipline. The second echelon of Chinese tracks moved forward carefully, at about ten-kilometer speed, following this opening in the forest. Interesting, he thought, that they weren't venturing too far into the adjoining woods. No more than two or three hundred meters. Then he cringed. A helicopter chattered overhead. It was a Gazelle, a Chinese copy of the French military helicopter. But his track was back in the woods, and every time it stopped, the men ran outside to stretch the camo-net around it. His men, also, were well-drilled. And *that*, he told his men, was why they didn't dare leave a visible trail if they wanted to live. It wasn't much of a helicopter, but it did carry rockets—and their BRM was an armored personnel carrier, but it wasn't *that* armored.

'What's he doing?' Buikov asked.

'If he's looking, he's not being very careful about it.'

The Chinese were driving up a pathway built ages ago for an unbuilt spur off the Trans-Siberian Railroad. It was wide, in some places five hundred meters, and fairly well-graded. Someone in years past had thought about building this spur to exploit the unsurveyed riches of Siberia—enough to cut down a lot of trees, and they'd barely grown back in the harsh winters. Just saplings in this pathway now, easily ground into splinters by tracked

488

vehicles. Farther north, the work was being continued by army engineers, making a path to the new gold find, and beyond that to the oil discoveries on the Arctic Coast. When they got that far, the Chinese would find a good road, ready-made for a mechanized force to exploit. But it was a narrow one, and the Chinese would have to learn about flank security if they kept this path up.

Aleksandrov remembered a Roman adventure into Germany, a soldier named Quintilius Varus, commanding three legions, who'd ignored his flanks, and lost his army in the process to a German named Armenius. Might the Chinese make a similar mistake? No, everyone knew of the Teutonenberg Forest disaster. It was a textbook lesson in every military academy in the known world. Quintilius Varus had been a political commander, given that command because he'd been beloved of his emperor, Caesar Augustus, obviously not because of his operational skill. It was a lesson probably better remembered by soldiers than by politicians. And the Chinese army was commanded by soldiers, wasn't it?

'That's the fox,' Buikov said. This was the other officer in the Chinese unit, probably the subordinate of the gardener. Similar in size, but he had less interest in plants than he had in darting about. As they watched, he disappeared into the tree line to the east, and if he went by the form card, he'd be invisible for five to eight minutes.

'I could use a smoke,' Sergeant Buikov observed.

'That will have to wait, Sergeant.'

'Yes, Comrade Captain. May I have a sip of water, then?' he asked petulantly. It wasn't water he wanted, of course.

'Yes, I'd like a shot of vodka, too, but I neglected to bring any with me, as, I am sure, you did as well.'

'Regrettably, yes, Comrade Captain. A good slug of vodka helps keep the chill away in these damp woods.'

'And it also dulls the senses, and we need our senses, Boris Yevgeniyevich, unless you enjoy eating rice. Assuming the Chinks take prisoners, which I rather doubt. They do not like us, Sergeant, and they are not a civilized people. Remember that.'

So, they don't go to the ballet. Neither do I, Sergeant Buikov didn't say aloud. His captain was a Muscovite, and spoke often of cultural matters. But like his captain, Buikov had no love for the Chinese, and even less now that he was looking at Chinese soldiers on the soil of his country. He only regretted not killing some, but killing was not his job. His job was watching them piss on his country, which somehow only made him angrier.

'Captain, will we ever get to shoot them?' the sergeant asked.

'In due course, yes, it will be our job to eliminate their reconnaissance elements, and yes, Boris, I look forward to that as well.' *And, yes, I could use a smoke as well. And I'd love a glass of vodka right now.* But he'd settle for some black bread and butter, which he did have in his track, three hundred meters to the north.

Six and a half minutes this time. The fox had at least looked into the woods to the east, probably listened for the sound of diesel engines, but heard nothing but the chirping of birds. Still, this Chink lieutenant was the more conscientious of the two, in Buikov's opinion. *They should kill him first, when*

490

the time came, the sergeant thought. Aleksandrov tapped the sergeant on the shoulder. 'Our turn to leapfrog, Boris Yevgeniyevich.'

'By your command, Comrade Captain.' And both men moved out, crouching for the first hundred meters, and taking care not to make too much noise, until they heard the Chinese tracks start their engines. In five more minutes, they were back in their BRM and heading north, slowly picking their way through the trees, Aleksandrov buttered some bread and ate it, sipping water as he did so. When they'd traveled a thousand meters, their vehicle stopped, and the captain got on his big radio.

*   *   *

'Who is Ingrid?' Tolkunov asked.

'Ingrid Bergman,' Major Tucker replied. 'Actress, good-lookin' babe in her day. All the Dark Stars are named for movie stars, Colonel. The troops did it.' There was a plastic strip on the monitor top to show which Dark Star was up and transmitting. Marilyn Monroe was back at Zhigansk for service, and Grace Kelly was the next one up, scheduled to go in fifteen hours. 'Anyway'—he flipped a switch and then played a little with his mouse control—'there's the Chinese lead elements.'

'Son of a bitch,' Tolkunov said, demonstrating his knowledge of American slang.

Tucker grinned. 'Pretty good, ain't it? Once I sent one over a nudist colony in California—that's like a private park where people walk around naked all the time. You can tell the difference

491

between the flatchested ones and the ones with nice tits. Tell the natural blondes from the peroxide ones, too. Anyway, you use this mouse to control the camera—well, somebody else is doing it now up at Zhigansk. Anything in particular that you're interested in?'

'The bridges on the Amur,' Tolkunov said at once. Tucker picked up a radio microphone.

'This is Major Tucker. We have a tasking request. Slew Camera Three onto the big crossing point.'

'Roger,' the speaker next to the monitor said.

The picture changed immediately, seeming to race across the screen like a ribbon from ten o'clock down to four o'clock. Then it stabilized. The field of view must have been four kilometers across. It showed a total of what appeared to be eight bridges, each of them approached by what looked like a parade of insects.

'Give me control of Camera Three,' Tucker said next.

'You got it, sir,' the speaker acknowledged.

'Okay.' Tucker played with the mouse more than the keyboard, and the picture zoomed in— 'isolated'—on the third bridge from the west. There were three tanks on it at once, moving at about ten kilometers per hour south to north. The display showed a compass rose in case you got disoriented, and it was even in color. Tolkunov asked why.

'No more expensive than black-and-white cameras, and we put it on the system because it sometimes shows you things you don't get from gray. First time for overheads, even the satellites don't do color yet,' Tucker explained. Then he frowned. 'The angle's wrong, can't get the divisional markings on the tanks without moving the platform. Wait.' He picked up the microphone again. 'Sergeant, who's crossing the bridges now?'

'Appears to be their Three-Oh-Second armored division, sir, part of the Twenty-Ninth Group A Army. The Thirty-Fourth Army is fully across now. We estimate one full regiment of the Three-Oh-Second is across and moving north at this time,' the intel weenie reported, as though relating the baseball scores from yesterday.

'Thanks, Sarge.'

'Roger that, Maj.'

'And they can't see this drone?' Tolkunov asked.

'Well, on radar it's pretty stealthy, and there's another little trick we have on it. Goes back to World War II, called Project Yehudi back then, you put lights on the thing.'

'What?' Tolkunov asked.

'Yeah, you spot airplanes because they're darker'n the sky, but if you put lightbulbs on 'em, they turn invisible. So, there are lights on the airframe, and a photo sensor dials the brightness automatically. They're damned near impossible to spot—they cruise at sixty thousand feet, way the hell above contrail level, and they got no infrared signature at all, hardly—even if you know where to look, and they tell me you can't hardly *make* an air-to-air missile lock onto one. Pretty cool toy, eh?'

'How long have you had this?'

'I've been working on it, oh, about four years now.'

'I've heard of Dark Star, but this capability is amazing.'

Tucker nodded. 'Yeah, it's pretty slick. Nice to

know what the other guy's doing. First time we deployed it was over Yugoslavia, and once we learned how to use it, and how to coordinate it with the shooters, well, we learned to make their lives pretty miserable. Tough shit, Joe.'

'Joe?'

'Joe Chink.' Tucker pointed at the screen. 'That's what we mainly call him.' The friendly nickname for Koreans had once been Luke the Gook. 'Now, Ingrid doesn't have it yet, but Grace Kelly does, a laser designator, so you can use these things to clobber targets. The fighter just lofts the bomb in from, oh, maybe twenty miles away, and we guide it into the target. I've only done that at Red Flag, and we can't do it from here with this terminal, but they can up at Zhigansk.'

'Guide bombs from six hundred kilometers away?'

'Yeah. Hell, you can do it from Washington if you want. It all goes over the satellite, y'know?'

Yob tvoyu maht!'

'Soon we're going to make the fighter jocks obsolete, Colonel. Another year or so and we'll be doing terminal guidance on missiles launched from a coupla hundred miles away. Won't need fighter pilots then. Guess I'll have to buy me a scarf. So, Colonel, what else do you want to see?'

*   *   *

The Il-86 landed at a rustic fighter base with only a few helicopters on it, Colonel Mitch Turner noted. As divisional intelligence officer, he was taking in a lot of what he saw in Russia, and what he saw wasn't all that encouraging. Like General Diggs, he'd entered the Army when the USSR had been the main enemy and principal worry for the United States Army, and now he was wondering how many of the intelligence estimates he'd help draft as a young spook officer had been pure fantasy. Either that or the mighty had fallen farther and faster than any nation in history. The Russian army wasn't even a shadow of what the Red Army had been. The 'Rompin', Stompin' Russian Red Ass' so feared by NATO was as dead as the stegosaurus toys his son liked to play with, and right now that was not such a good thing. The Russian Federation looked like a rich family of old with no sons to defend it, and the girl kids were getting raped. Not a good thing. The Russians, like America, still had nuclear weapons—bombs, deliverable by bombers and tactical fighters. However, the Chinese had missiles to deliver theirs, and they were targeted at cities, and the Big Question was whether the Russians had the stones to trade a few cities and, say, forty million people for a gold mine and some oil fields. Probably not, Turner figured. Not something a smart man would do. Similarly, they could not afford a war of attrition against a country with nine times as many people *and* a healthier economy, even over this ground. No, if they were to defeat the Chinese, it had to be with maneuver and agility, but their military was in the shitter, and neither trained nor equipped to play maneuver warfare.

This, Turner thought on reflection, *was going to be an interesting war*. It was not the sort he wanted to fight. Better to clobber a dumb little enemy than mix it up with a smart powerful one. It might not be glorious, but it was a hell of a lot safer.

'Mitch,' General Diggs said, as they stood to walk off the airplane. 'Thoughts?'

'Well, sir, we might have picked a better place to fly to. Way things look, this is going to be a little exciting.'

'Go on,' the general ordered.

'The other side has better cards. More troops, better-trained troops, more equipment. Their task, crossing a lot of nasty country, is not enviable, but neither is the Russian task, defending against it. To win they have to play maneuver warfare. But I don't see that they have the horsepower to pull it off.'

'Their boss out here, Bondarenko. He's pretty good.'

'So was Erwin Rommel, sir, but Montgomery whupped his ass.'

There were staff cars lined up to drive them into the Russian command post. The weather was clearer here, and they were close enough to the Chinese that a clear sky wasn't something to enjoy any more.

CHAPTER FIFTY-THREE

DEEP CONCERNS

'So, what's happening there?' Ryan asked.

'The Chinese are seventy miles inside Russia. They have a total of eight divisions over the river, and they're pushing north,' General Moore replied, moving a pencil across the map spread on the conference table. 'They blew through the Russian border defenses pretty fast—it was essentially the Maginot Line from 1940. I wouldn't have expected it to hold very long, but our overheads showed them punching through fairly professionally with their leading infantry formations, supported by a lot of artillery. Now they have their tanks across—about eight hundred to this point, with another thousand or so to go.'

Ryan whistled. 'That many?'

'When you invade a major country, sir, you don't do it on the cheap. The only good news at this point is that we've really given their air force a bloody nose.'

'AWACS and -15s?' Jackson asked.

'Right.' The Chairman of the Joint Chiefs nodded. 'One of our kids made ace in a single engagement. A Colonel Winters.'

'Bronco Winters,' Jackson said. 'I've heard the name. Fighter jock. Okay, what else?'

'Our biggest problem on the air side is going to be getting bombs to our airmen. Flying bombs in is not real efficient. I mean, you can use up a whole C-5 just to deliver half the bombs for one squadron of F-15Es, and we've got a lot of other things for the C-5s to do. We're thinking about sending the bombs into Russia by train to Chita, say, and then flying them up to Suntar from there, but the Russian railroad is moving just tanks and vehicles for now, and that isn't going to change soon. We're trying to fight a war at the end of one railroad line. Sure, it's double-tracked, but it's still just one damned line. Our logistical people are already taking a lot of Maalox over this one.'

'Russian airlift capacity?' Ryan asked.

'FedEx has more,' General Moore replied. 'In

fact, FedEx has a lot more. We're going to ask you to authorize call-up of the civilian reserve air fleet, Mr. President.'

'Approved,' Ryan said at once.

'And a few other little things,' Moore said. He closed his eyes. It was pushing midnight, and nobody had gotten much sleep lately. 'VMH-1 is standing-to. We're in a shooting war with a country that has nuclear weapons on ballistic launchers. So, we have to think about the possibility—remote maybe, but still a possibility—that they could launch at us. So, VMH-1 and the Air Force's First Heli at Andrews are standing-to. We can get a chopper here to lift you and your family out in seven minutes. That concerns you, Mrs. O'Day,' Moore said to Andrea.

The President's Principal Agent nodded. 'We're dialed in. It's all in The Book,' she said. That nobody had opened that particular book since 1962 was beside the point. It was written down. Mrs. Price-O'Day looked a little peaked.

'You okay?' Ryan asked.

'Stomach,' she explained.

'Try some ginger?' Jack went on.

'Nothing much works for this, Dr. North tells me. Please excuse me, Mr. President.' She was embarrassed that he'd noticed her discomfort. She always wanted to be one of the boys. But the boys didn't get pregnant, did they?

'Why don't you drive home?'

'Sir, I—'

'*Go*,' Ryan said. 'That's an order. You're a woman, and you're pregnant. You can't be a cop all the time, okay? Get some relief here and go. Right now.'

Special Agent Price-O'Day hesitated, but she did have an order, so she walked out the door. Another agent came in immediately.

'Machismo from a woman. What's the goddamned world coming to?' Ryan asked the assembly.

'You're not real liberated, Jack,' Jackson observed with a grin.

'It's called objective circumstances, I think. She's still a girl, even if she does carry a pistol. Cathy says she's doing fine. This nausea stuff doesn't last forever. Probably feels like it to her, though. Okay, General, what else?'

'Kneecap and Air Force One are on hot-pad alert 'round the clock. So, if we get a launch warning, in seven minutes or less, you and the Vice President are on choppers, five more minutes to Andrews, and three more after that you're doing the takeoff roll. The drill is, your family goes to Air Force One and you go to Kneecap,' he concluded. Kneecap was actually the National Emergency Airborne Command Post (NEACP), but the official acronym was too hard to pronounce. Like the VC-25A that served as Air Force One, Kneecap was a converted 747 that was really just a wrapper for a bunch of radios flying in very close formation.

'Gee, that's nice to know. What about my family?' POTUS asked.

'In these circumstances, we keep a chopper close to where your wife and kids are at all times, and then they'll fly in whatever direction seems the safest at the moment. If that's not Andrews, then they'll get picked up later by a fixed-wing aircraft and taken to whatever place seems best. It's all theoretical,' Moore explained, 'but something you might as well know about.'

'Can the Russians stop the Chinese?' Ryan asked, turning his attention back to the map.

'Sir, that remains to be seen. They *do* have the nuclear option, but it's not a card I would expect them to play. The Chinese *do* have twelve CSS-4 ICBMs. It's essentially a duplicate of our old Titan-II liquid fuels, with a warhead estimated to be between three and five megatons.'

'City-buster?' Ryan asked.

'Correct. No counterforce capability, and there's nothing we have left to use against it in that role anyway. The CEP on the warhead is estimated to be plus or minus a thousand meters or so. So, it'd do a city pretty well, but that's about all.'

'Any idea where they're targeted?' Jackson asked. Moore nodded at once.

'Yes. The missile is pretty primitive, and the silos are oriented on their targets because the missile doesn't have much in the way of cross-range maneuverability. Two are targeted on Washington. Others on LA, San Francisco, and Chicago. Plus Moscow, Kiev, St. Petersburg. They're all leftovers from the Bad Old Days, and they haven't been modified in any way.'

'Any way to take them out?' Jackson asked.

'I suppose we could stage a mission with fighter or bomber aircraft and go after the silos with PGMs,' Moore allowed. 'But we'd have to fly the bombs to Suntar first, and even then it'll be rather a lengthy mission for the F-117s.'

'What about B-2s out of Guam?' Jackson asked.

'I'm not sure they can carry the right weapons. I'll have to check that.'

'Jack, this is something we need to think about, okay?'

'I hear you, Robby. General, have somebody look into this, okay?'

'Yes, sir.'

* * *

'Gennady Iosifovich!' General Diggs called on entering the map room.

'Marion Ivanovich!' The Russian came over to take his hand, followed by a hug. He even kissed his guest, in the Russian fashion, and Diggs flinched from this, in the American fashion. 'In!'

And Diggs waited for ten seconds: 'Out!' Both men shared the laugh of an insider's joke.

'The turtle bordello is still there?'

'It was the last time I looked, Gennady.' Then Diggs had to explain to the others. 'Out at Fort Irwin—we collected all the desert tortoises and put them in a safe place so the tanks wouldn't squish 'em and piss off the tree-huggers. I suppose they're still in there making little turtles, but the damned things screw so slow they must fall asleep doing it.'

'I have told that story many times, Marion.' Then the Russian turned serious. 'I am glad to see you. I will be more glad to see your division.'

'How bad is it?'

'It is not good. Come.' They walked over to the big wall map. 'These are their positions as of thirty minutes ago.'

'How are you keeping track of them?'

'We now have your Dark Star invisible drones, and I have a smart young captain on the ground watching them as well.'

501

'That far . . .' Diggs said. Colonel Masterman was right beside him now. 'Duke?' Then he looked at his Russian host. 'This is Colonel Masterman, my G-3. His last job was as a squadron commander in the Tenth Cav.'

'Buffalo Soldier, yes?'

'Yes, sir,' Masterman confirmed with a nod, but his eyes didn't leave the map. 'Ambitious bastards, aren't they?'

'Their first objective will be here,' Colonel Aliyev said, using a pointer. 'This is the Gogol Gold Strike.'

'Well, hell, if you're gonna steal something, might as well be a gold mine, right?' Duke asked rhetorically. 'What do you have to stop them with?'

'Two-Six-Five Motor Rifle is here.' Aliyev pointed.

'Full strength?'

'Not quite, but we've been training them up. We have four more motor-rifle divisions en route. The first arrives at Chita tomorrow noon.' Aliyev's voice was a little too optimistic for the situation. He didn't want to show weakness to Americans.

'That's still a long way to move,' Masterman observed. He looked over at his boss.

'What are you planning, Gennady?'

'I want to take the four Russian divisions north to link up with the 265th, and stop them about here. Then, perhaps, we will use your forces to cross east through here and cut them off.'

Now it wasn't the Chinese who were being ambitious, both Diggs and Masterman thought. Moving First Infantry Division (Mechanized) from Fort Riley, Kansas, to Fort Carson, Colorado, would have been about the same distance, but it would have been on flat ground and against no opposition. Here that task would involve a lot of hills and serious resistance. *Those factors* did *make a difference*, the American officers thought.

'No serious contact yet?'

Bondarenko shook his head. 'No, I'm keeping my mechanized forces well away from them. The Chinese are advancing against no opposition.'

'You want 'em to fall asleep, get sloppy?' Masterman asked.

'*Da,* better that they should get overconfident.'

The American colonel nodded. That made good sense, and as always, war was as much a psychological game as a physical one. 'If we jump off the trains at Chita, it's still a long-approach march to where you want us, General.'

'What about fuel?' Colonel Douglas asked.

'That is the one thing we have plenty of,' answered Colonel Aliyev. 'The blue spots on the map, fuel storage—it is the same as your Number Two Diesel.'

'How much?' Douglas asked.

'At each fuel depot, one billion two hundred fifty million liters.'

'Shit!' Douglas observed. '*That* much?'

Aliyev explained, 'The fuel depots were established to support a large mobile force in a border conflict. They were built in the time of Nikita Sergeyevich Khrushchev. Huge concrete-and-steel storage tanks, all underground, well hidden.'

'They must be,' Mitch Turner observed. 'I've never been briefed on them.'

'So, we evaded even your satellite photos, yes?' That pleased the Russian. 'Each depot is manned by a force of twenty engineers, with ample electric pumps.'

'I like the locations,' Masterman said. 'What's this unit here?'

'That is BOYAR, a reserve mechanized force. The men have just been called up. Their weapons are from a hidden equipment-storage bunker. It's a short division, old equipment—T-55s and such— but serviceable. We're keeping that force hidden,' Aliyev said.

The American G-3 arched his eyebrows. Maybe they were out-manned, but they weren't dumb. That BOYAR force was in a particularly interesting place . . . if Ivan could make proper use of it. Their overall operational concept looked good— theoretically. A lot of soldiers could come up with good ideas. The problem was executing them. Did the Russians have the ability to do that? Russia's military theorists were as good as any the world had ever seen—good enough that the United States Army regularly stole their ideas. The problem was that the U.S. Army could apply those theories to a real battlefield, and the Russians could not.

'How are your people handling this?' Masterman asked.

'Our soldiers, you mean?' Aliyev asked. 'The Russian soldier knows how to fight,' he assured his American counterpart.

'Hey, Colonel, I am not questioning their guts,' Duke assured his host. 'How's their spirit, for one thing?'

Bondarenko handled that one: 'Yesterday I had to face one of my young officers, Komanov, from the border defenses. He was furious that we were unable to give him the support he needed to defeat the Chinese. And I was ashamed,' the general admitted to his guests. 'My men have the spirit. Their training is lacking—I just got here a few months ago, and my changes have barely begun to take effect. But, you will see, the Russian soldier has *always* risen to the occasion, and he will today—if we here are worthy of him.'

Masterman didn't share a look with his boss. Diggs had spoken well of this Russian general, and Diggs was both a good operational soldier and a good judge of men. But the Russian had just admitted that his men weren't trained up as well as they ought to be. The good news was that on the battlefield, men learned the soldier's trade rapidly. The bad news was that the battlefield was the most brutal Darwinian environment on the face of the planet. Some men would learn, but others would die in the process, and the Russians didn't have all that many they could afford to lose. This wasn't 1941, and they weren't fighting with half their population base this time around.

'You're going to want us to move out fast when the trains drop us off at Chita?' Tony Welch asked. He was the divisional chief of staff.

'Yes,' Aliyev confirmed.

'Okay, well, then I need to get down there and look over the facilities. What about fuel for our choppers?'

'Our air force bases have fuel storage similar to the diesel depots,' Aliyev told him. 'Your word is infrastructure, yes? That is the one thing we have much of. When will they arrive?'

'The Air Force is still working that out. They're going to fly our aviation brigade in. Apaches first.

Dick Boyle's chomping at the bit.'

'We will be very pleased to see your attack helicopters. We have all too few of our own, and our air force is also slow delivering them.'

'Duke,' Diggs said, 'get on the horn to the Air Force. We need some choppers right the hell now, just so we can get around and see what we need to see.'

'Roger,' Masterman replied.

'Let me get a satellite radio set up,' Lieutenant Colonel Garvey said, heading for the door.

*   *   *

Ingrid Bergman was heading south now. General Wallace wanted a better idea for the Chinese logistical tail, and now he was getting it. The People's Republic of China was in many ways like America had been at the turn of the previous century. Things moved mainly by rail. There were no major highways as Americans understood them, but a lot of railroads. Those were efficient for moving large quantities of anything over medium-to-long distances, but they were also inflexible, and hard to repair—especially the bridges—and most of all the tunnels, and so that was what he and his targeting people were looking at. The problem was that they had few bombs to drop. None of his attack assets—mainly F-15E Strike Eagles at the moment—had flown over with bombs on their wings, and he had barely enough air-to-mud munitions for an eight-ship strike mission. It was like going to a dance and finding no girls there. The music was fine, and so was the fruit punch, but there really wasn't anything to do. Perversely, his

506

-15E crews didn't mind. They got to play fighter plane, and all such people prefer shooting other airplanes down to dropping bombs on mud soldiers. It just came with the territory. The one thing he had going now was that his scarf-and-goggles troops were playing hell with the PRC air force, with over seventy confirmed kills already for not a single air-to-air loss. The advantage of having E-3B AWACS aircraft was so decisive that the enemy might as well have been flying World War I Fokkers, and the Russians were learning rapidly how to make use of E-3B support. Their fighters were good aerodynamic platforms, just lacking in legs. The Russians had never built a fighter with fuel capacity for more than about one hour's flight time. Nor had they ever learned how to do midair refueling, as the Americans had. And so the Russian MiG and Sukhoi fighters could go up, take their instructions from the AWACS, and participate in one engagement, but then they had to return to base for gas. Half of the kills his Eagle drivers had collected so far were of Chinese fighters that had broken off their fights to RTB for gas as well. It wasn't fair, but Wallace, like all Air Force fighter types, could hardly have cared less about being fair in combat.

But Wallace was fighting a defensive war to this point. He was successfully defending Russian airspace. He was not taking out Chinese targets, not even attacking the Chinese troops on the ground in Siberia. So, though his fighters were having a fine, successful war, they just weren't accomplishing anything important. To that end, he lifted his satellite link to America.

'We ain't got no bombs, General,' he told

507

Mickey Moore.

'Well, your fellow Air Scouts are maxed out on taskings, and Mary Diggs is screaming to get some trash haulers to get him his chopper brigade moved to where he needs it.'

'Sir, this is real simple. If you want us to kill some Chinese targets, we have to have bombs. I hope I'm not going too fast for you,' Wallace added.

'Go easy, Gus,' Moore warned.

'Well, sir, maybe it just looks a little different in Washington, but where I'm sitting right now, I have missions, but not the tools to carry those missions out. So, you D.C. people can either send me the tools or rescind the missions. Your call, sir.'

'We're working on it,' the Chairman of the Joint Chiefs assured him.

*　　　*　　　*

'Do I have any orders?' Mancuso asked the Secretary of Defense.

'Not at this time,' Bretano told CINCPAC.

'Sir, may I ask why? The TV says we're in a shooting war with China. Am I supposed to play or not?'

'We are considering the political ramifications,' THUNDER explained.

'Excuse me, sir?'

'You heard me.'

'Mr. Secretary, all I know about politics is voting every couple of years, but I have a lot of gray ships under my command, and they're technically known as *war*ships, and my country is at war.' The frustration in Mancuso's voice was plain.

508

'Admiral, when the President decides what to do, you will find out. Until then, ready your command for action. It's going to happen. I'm just not sure when.'

'Aye, aye, sir.' Mancuso hung up and looked at his subordinates. 'Political ramifications,' he said. 'I didn't think Ryan was like that.'

'Sir,' Mike Lahr soothed. 'Forget "political" and think "psychological," okay? Maybe Secretary Bretano just used the wrong word. Maybe the idea is to hit them when it'll do the most good—because we're messing with their heads, sir, remember?'

'You think so?'

'Remember who the Vice President is? He's one of us, Admiral. And President Ryan isn't a pussy, is he?'

'Well . . . no, not that I recall,' CINCPAC said, remembering the first time he'd met the guy, and the shoot-out he'd had aboard *Red October*. No, Jack Ryan wasn't a pussy. 'So, what do you suppose he's thinking?'

'The Chinese have a land war going on—air and land, anyway. Nothing's happening at sea. They may not expect anything to happen at sea. But they are surging some ships out, just to establish a defense line for the mainland. If we get orders to hit those ships, the purpose will be to make a psychological impact. So, let's plan along those lines, shall we? Meanwhile, we keep getting more assets in place.'

'Right.' Mancuso nodded and turned to face the wall. Pacific Fleet was nearly all west of the dateline now, and the Chinese had probably no clue where his ships were, but he knew about them. USS *Tucson* was camped out on *406*, the single

PRC ballistic-missile submarine. It was known to the west as a 'Xia' class SSBN, and his intelligence people disagreed on the sub's actual name, but '406' was the number painted on its sail, and that was how he thought of it. None of that mattered to Mancuso. The first shoot order he planned to issue would go to *Tucson*—to put that missile-armed sub at the bottom of the Pacific Ocean. He remembered that the PRC had nuclear-tipped missiles, and those in his area of responsibility would disappear as soon as he had authorization to deal with them. USS *Tucson* was armed with Mark 48 ADCAP fish, and they'd do the job on that target, assuming that he was right and President Ryan wasn't a pussy after all.

*　　　*　　　*

'And so, Marshal Luo?' Zhang Han San asked.

'Things go well,' he replied at once. 'We crossed the Amur River with trivial losses, captured the Russian positions in a few hours, and are now driving north.'

'Enemy opposition?'

'Light. Very light, in fact. We're starting to wonder if the Russians have any forces deployed in sector at all. Our intelligence suggests the presence of two mechanized divisions, but if they're there, they haven't advanced to establish contact with us. Our forces are racing forward, making better than thirty kilometers per day. I expect to see the gold mine in seven days.'

'Is anything going badly?' Qian asked.

'Only in the air. The Americans have deployed fighters to Siberia, and as we all know, the

Americans are very clever with their machines, especially the ones that fly. They have inflicted some losses on our fighter aircraft,' the Defense Minister admitted.

'How large are the losses?'

'Total, over one hundred. We've gotten twenty-five or so of theirs in return, but the Americans are masters of aerial combat. Fortunately, their aircraft can do little to hinder the advance of our tanks, and, as you have doubtless noted, they have not attacked into our territory at all.'

'Why is that, Marshal?' Fang asked.

'We are not certain,' Luo answered, turning to the MSS chief. 'Tan?'

'Our sources are not certain, either. The most likely explanation is that the Americans have made a political decision not to attack us directly, but merely to defend their Russian "ally" in a pro forma way. I suppose there is also the consideration that they do not wish to take losses from our air defenses, but the main reason for their restraint is undoubtedly political.'

Heads nodded around the table. It was indeed the most likely explanation for the American lack of action, and all of these men understood political considerations.

'Does this mean that they are measuring their action against us in such a way as to cause us minimal injury?' Tong Jie asked. It was so much the better for him, of course, since the Interior Ministry would have to deal with the internal dislocations that systematic attacks might cause.

'Remember what I said before,' Zhang pointed out. 'They *will* do business with us once we've secured our new territory. So, they already anticipate this. It seems plain that they will support their Russian friends, but only so much. What else are the Americans but mercenaries? This President Ryan, what was he?'

'He was a CIA spy, and by all accounts an effective one,' Tan Deshi reminded them.

'No,' Zhang disagreed. 'He was a trader in stocks before he joined CIA, and then he was a stock trader again after he left—and whom does he bring into his cabinet? Winston, another hugely rich capitalist, a trader in stocks and securities, a typical American rich man. I tell you, money is the key to understanding these people. They do business. They have no political ideology, except to fatten their purses. To do that, you try not to make blood enemies, and now, here, with us, they do not try to anger us too greatly. I tell you, I understand these people.'

'Perhaps,' Qian said. 'But what if there are objective circumstances which prevent more aggressive action?'

'Then why is their navy not taking action? Their navy is most formidable, but it does nothing, correct, Luo?'

'Not to this point, but we are wary of them,' the marshal warned. He was a soldier, not a sailor, even though the PLAN did come under his command. 'We have patrol aircraft looking for them, but so far we have not spotted anything. We know they are not in harbor, but that is all.'

'They do nothing with their navy. They do nothing with their land forces. They sting us slightly with their air forces, but what is that? The buzzing of insects.' Zhang dismissed the issue.

'How many have underestimated America, and

this Ryan fellow, and done so to their misfortune?' Qian demanded. 'Comrades, I tell you, this is a dangerous situation we are in. Perhaps we can succeed, all well and good if that comes to pass, but overconfidence can be any man's undoing.'

'And overestimating one's enemy ensures that you will never do anything,' Zhang Han San countered. 'Did we get to where we are, did our country get to where we are, by timidity? The Long March was not made by cowards.' He looked around the table, and no one summoned the character to argue with him.

'So, things go well in Russia?' Xu asked the Defense Minister.

'Better than the plan,' Luo assured them all.

'Then we proceed,' the Premier decided for them all, once others had made the real decisions. The meeting soon adjourned, and the ministers went their separate ways.

'Fang?'

The junior Minister-Without-Portfolio turned to see Qian Kun coming after him in the corridor. 'Yes, my friend?'

'The reason the Americans have not taken firmer action is that they act at the end of a single railroad to move them and their supplies. This takes time. They have not dropped bombs on us, probably, because they don't have any. And where does Zhang get this rubbish about American ideology?'

'He is wise in the ways of international affairs,' Fang replied.

'Is he? Is he really? Is he not the one who tricked the Japanese into commencing a war with America? And why—so that we and they could seize Siberia. And then did he not quietly support Iran and their attempt to seize the Saudi kingdom? And why? So that we could then use the Muslims as a hammer to beat Russia into submission—so that we could seize Siberia. Fang, all he thinks about is Siberia. He wishes to see it under our flag before he dies. Perhaps he wishes to have his ashes buried in a golden urn, like the emperors,' Qian hissed. 'He's an adventurer, and those men come to bad ends.'

'Except those who succeed,' Fang suggested.

'How many of them succeed, and how many die before a stone wall?' Qian shot back. 'I say the Americans will strike us, and strike us hard once their forces are assembled. Zhang follows his own political vision, not facts, not reality. He may lead our country to its doom.'

'Are the Americans so formidable as that?'

'If they are not, Fang, why does Tan spend so much of his time trying to steal their inventions? Don't you remember what America did to Japan and Iran? They are like the wizards of legend. Luo tells us that they've savaged our air force. How often has he told us how formidable our fighters are? All the money we spent on those wonderful aircraft, and the Americans slaughter them like hogs fattened for market! Luo claims we've gotten twenty-five of theirs. He *claims* only twenty-five. More likely we've gotten one or two! Against over a hundred losses, but Zhang tells us the Americans don't want to challenge us. Oh, really? What held them back from smashing Japan's military, and then annihilating Iran's?' Qian paused for breath. 'I fear this, Fang. I fear what Zhang and Luo have gotten us into.'

'Even if you are right, what can we do to stop it?' the minister asked.

'Nothing,' Qian admitted. 'But *someone* must speak the truth. *Someone* must warn of the danger that lies before us, if we are to have a country left at the end of this misbegotten adventurism.'

'Perhaps so. Qian, you are as ever a voice of reason and prudence. We will speak more,' Fang promised, wondering how much of the man's words was alarmism, and how much was good sense. He'd been a brilliant administrator of the state railroads, and therefore was a man with a firm grasp on reality.

Fang had known Zhang for most of his adult life. He was a highly skilled player on the political stage, and a brilliantly gifted manipulator of people. But Qian was asking if those talents translated into a correct perception of reality, and did he *really* understand America and Americans—and most of all, this Ryan fellow? Or was he just forcing oddly-shaped pegs into the slots he'd engraved in his own mind? Fang admitted that he didn't know, and more to the point, didn't know the answers to the implicit questions. He did not know himself whether Zhang was right or not. And he really should. But who might? Tan of the Ministry of State Security? Shen of the Foreign Ministry? Who else? Certainly not Premier Xu. All he did was to confirm the consensus achieved by others, or to repeat the words spoken into his ear by Zhang.

Fang walked to his office thinking about all these things, trying to organize his thoughts. Fortunately, he had a system for achieving that.

*　　　*　　　*

515

It started in Memphis, the headquarters of Federal Express. Faxes and telexes arrived simultaneously, telling the company that its wide-body cargo jets were being taken into federal service under the terms of a Phase I call-up of the Civilian Reserve Air Fleet. That meant that all freight-capable aircraft that the federal government had helped to finance (that was nearly all of them, because no commercial bank could compete with Washington when it came to financing things) were now being taken, along with their crews, under the control of the Air Mobility Command. The notice wasn't welcome, but neither was it much of a surprise. Ten minutes later came follow-up messages telling the aircraft where to go, and soon thereafter they started rolling. The flight crews, the majority of them military-trained, wondered where their ultimate destinations were, sure that they'd be surprising ones. The pilots would not be disappointed in this.

FedEx would have to make do with its older narrow-body aircraft, like the venerable Boeing 727s with which the company had gotten started two decades earlier. That, the dispatchers knew, would be a stretch, but they had assistance agreements with the airlines, which they would now activate in order to try to keep up with the continuing shipment of legal documents and live lobsters all over America.

*   *   *

'Just how inefficient is it?' Ryan asked.

'Well we can deliver one day's worth of bombs in

516

three days' worth of flying—maybe two if we stretch things a little, but that's as good as it's going to get,' Moore told him. 'Bombs are heavy things, and getting them around uses up a lot of jet fuel. General Wallace has a nice list of targets to service, but to do that he needs bombs.'

'Where are the bombs going to come from?'

'Andersen Air Force Base on Guam has a nice pile,' Moore said. 'Ditto Elmendorf in Alaska, and Mountain Home in Idaho. Various other places. It's not so much a question of time and distance as of weight. Hell, the Russian base he's using at Suntar is plenty big for his purposes. We just have to get the bombs to him, and I've just shunted a lot of Air Force lifters to Germany to start loading First Armored's aviation assets to where Diggs is. That's going to take four days of nonstop flying.'

'What about crew rest?' Jackson asked.

'What?' Ryan looked up.

'It's a Navy thing, Jack. The Air Force has union rules on how much they can fly. Never had those rules out on the boats,' Robby explained. 'The C-5 has a bunk area for people to sleep. I was just being facetious.' He didn't apologize. It was late— actually 'early' was the correct adjective—and nobody in the White House was getting much sleep.

For his part, Ryan wanted a cigarette to help him deal with the stress, but Ellen Sumter was home and in bed, and no one on night duty in the White House smoked, to the best of his knowledge. But that was the wimp part of his character speaking, and he knew it. The President rubbed his face with his hands and looked over at the clock. He had to get some sleep.

'It's late, Honey Bunny,' Mary Pat said to her husband.

'I never would have guessed. Is that why my eyes keep wanting to close?'

There was, really, no reason for them to be here. CIA had little in the way of assets in the PRC. SORGE was the only one of value. The rest of the intelligence community, DIA and NBA, each of them larger than the Central Intelligence Agency in terms of manpower, didn't have any directly valuable human sources either, though NSA was doing its utmost to tap in on Chinese communications. They were even listening in on cell phones through their constellation of geosynchronous ferret satellites, downloading all of the 'take' through the Echelon system and then forwarding the 'hits' to human linguists for full translation and evaluation. They were getting some material, but not all that much. SORGE was the gemstone of the collection, and both Edward and Mary Patricia Foley were really staying up late to await the newest installment in Minister Fang's personal diary. The Chinese Politburo was meeting every day, and Fang was a dedicated diarist, not to mention a man who enjoyed the physical attractions of his female staff. They were even reading significance into the less regular writings of WARBLER, who mainly committed to her computer his sexual skills, occasionally enough to make Mary Pat blush. Being an intelligence officer was often little different from being a paid voyeur, and the staff psychiatrist translated all of the prurient stuff

518

into what was probably a very accurate personality profile, but to them it just meant that Fang was a dirty old man who happened to exercise a lot of political power.

'It's going to be another three hours at best,' the DCI said.

'Yeah,' his wife agreed.

'Tell you what . . .' Ed Foley rose off the couch, tossed away the cushions, and reached in to pull out the foldaway bed. It was marginally big enough for two.

'When the staff sees this, they'll wonder if we got laid tonight.'

'Baby, I have a headache,' the DCI reported.

CHAPTER FIFTY-FOUR

PROBES AND PUSHES

Much of life in the military is mere adherence to Parkinson's Law, the supposition that work invariably expands to fill the time allocated for it. In this case, Colonel Dick Boyle arrived on the very first C-5B Galaxy, which, immediately upon rolling to a stop, lifted its nose 'visor' door to disgorge the first of three UH-60A Blackhawk helicopters, whose crewmen just as immediately rolled it to a vacant piece of ramp to unfold the rotor blades, assure they were locked in place, and ready the aircraft for flight after the usual safety checks. By that time, the C-5B had refueled and rolled off into the sky to make room for the next Galaxy, this one delivering AH-64 Apache attack helicopters—in this case complete with weapons and other accoutrements for flying real missions against a real armed enemy.

Colonel Boyle busied himself with watching everything, even though he knew that his troops were doing their jobs as well as they could be done, and would do those jobs whether he watched and fussed over them or not. Perversely, what Boyle wanted to do was to fly to where Diggs and his staff were located, but he resisted the temptation because he felt he should be supervising people whom he'd trained to do their jobs entirely without supervision. That lasted three hours until he finally saw the logic of the situation and decided to be a commander rather than a shop supervisor, and lifted off for Chabarsovil. The flying was easy enough, and he preferred the medium-low clouds, because there had to be fighters about, and not all of them would be friendly. The GPS navigation system guided him to the right location, and the right location, it turned out, was a concrete helipad with soldiers standing around it. They were wearing the 'wrong' uniform, a state of mind that Boyle knew he'd have to work on. One of them escorted Boyle into a building that looked like the Russian idea of a headquarters, and sure enough, it was.

'Dick, come on over,' General Diggs called. The helicopter commander saluted as he approached.

'Welcome to Siberia, Dick,' Marion Diggs said in greeting.

'Thank you, sir. What's the situation?'

'Interesting,' the general replied. 'This is General Bondarenko. He's the theater commander.' Boyle saluted again. 'Gennady, this is

Colonel Boyle, who commands my aviation brigade. He's pretty good.'

'What's the air situation, sir?' Boyle asked Diggs.

'The Air Force is doing a good job on their fighters so far.'

'What about Chinese helicopters?'

'They do not have many,' another Russian officer said. 'I am Colonel Aliyev, Andrey Petrovich, theater operations. The Chinese do not have many helicopters. We've only seen a few, mainly scouts.'

'No troop carriers? No staff transport?'

'No,' Aliyev answered. 'Their senior officers prefer to move around in tracked vehicles. They are not married to helicopters as you Americans are.'

'What do you want me to do, sir?' Boyle asked Diggs.

'Take Tony Turner to Chita. That's the railhead we're going to be using. We need to get set up there.'

'Drive the tracks in from there, eh?' Boyle looked at the map.

'That's the plan. There are closer points, but Chita has the best facilities to off-load our vehicles, so our friends tell us.'

'What about gas?'

'The place you landed is supposed to have sizable underground fuel tanks.'

'More than you will need,' Aliyev confirmed. Boyle thought that was quite a promise.

'And ordnance?' Boyle asked. 'We've got maybe two days' worth on the C-5s so far. Six complete loads for my Apaches, figuring three missions per day.'

'Which version of the Apache?' Aliyev asked.

'Delta, Colonel. We've got the Longbow radar.'

'Everything works?' the Russian asked.

'Colonel, not much sense bringing them if they don't,' Boyle replied, with a raised eyebrow. 'What about secure quarters for my people?'

'At the base where you landed, there will be secure sleeping quarters for your aviators—bombproof shelters. Your maintenance people will be housed in barracks.'

Boyle nodded. It was the same everywhere. The weenies who built things acted as if pilots were more valuable than the people who maintained the aircraft. And so they were, until the aircraft needed repairs, at which point the pilot was as useful as a cavalryman without a horse.

'Okay, General. I'll take Tony to this Chita place and then I'm going back to see to my people's needs. I could sure use one of Chuck Garvey's radios.'

'He's outside. Grab one on your way.'

'Okay, sir. Tony, let's get moving,' he said to the chief of staff.

'Sir, as soon as we get some infantry in, I want to put security on those fueling points,' Masterman said. 'Those places need protecting.'

'I can give you what you need,' Aliyev offered.

'Fine by me,' Masterman responded. 'How many of those secure radios did Garvey bring?'

'Eight, I think. Two are gone already,' General Diggs warned. 'Well, there'll be more on the train. Go tell Boyle to send two choppers here for our needs.'

'Right.' Masterman ran for the door.

The ministers all had offices and, as in every other such office in the world, the cleanup crews came in, in this case about ten every night. They picked up all sorts of trash, from candy wrappers to empty cigarette packs to papers, and the latter went into special burn-bags. The janitorial staff was not particularly smart, but they had had to pass background checks and go through security briefings that were heavy on intimidation. They were not allowed to discuss their jobs with anyone, not even a spouse, and not *ever* to reveal what they saw in the wastebaskets. In fact, they never thought much about it—they were less interested in the thoughts or ideas of the Politburo members than they were in the weather forecasts. They'd rarely even seen the ministers whose offices they cleaned, and none of the crew had ever so much as spoken a single word to any of them; they just tried to be invisible on those rare occasions when they saw one of the godlike men who ruled their nation. Maybe a submissive bow, which was not even acknowledged by so much as a look, because they were mere furniture, menials who did peasants' work because, as peasants, that was all they were suited for. The peasants knew what computers were, but such machines were not for the use of such men as they were, and the janitorial staff knew it.

And so when one of the computers made a noise while a cleaner was in the office, he took no note of it. Well, it seemed odd that it should whir when the screen was dark, but why it did what it did was a mystery to him, and he'd never even been so bold as to touch the thing. He didn't even dust the keyboard as he cleaned the desktop—no, he always avoided the keys.

And so, he heard the whir begin, continue for a few seconds, then stop, and he paid no mind to it.

* * *

Mary Pat Foley opened her eyes when the sun started casting shadows on her husband's office wall and rubbed her eyes reluctantly. She checked her watch. Seven-twenty. She was usually up long before this—but she usually didn't go to bed after four in the morning. Three hours of sleep would probably have to do. She stood and headed into Ed's private washroom. It had a shower, like hers. She'd make use of her own shortly, and for the moment settled for some water splashed on her face and a reluctant look in the mirror that resulted in a grimace at what the look revealed.

The Deputy Director (Operations) of the Central Intelligence Agency shook her head, and then her entire body to get the blood moving, and then put her blouse on. Finally, she shook her husband's shoulder.

'Out of the hutch, Honey Bunny, before the foxes get you.'

'We still at war?' the DCI asked from behind closed eyes.

'Probably. I haven't checked yet.' She paused for a stretch and slipped her feet into her shoes. 'I'm going to check my e-mail.'

'Okay, I'll call downstairs for breakfast,' Ed told her.

'Oatmeal. No eggs. Your cholesterol is too high,' Mary Pat observed.

'Yeah, baby,' he grumbled in submissive reply.

'That's a good Honey Bunny.' She kissed him and headed out.

Ed Foley made his bathroom call, then sat at his desk and lifted the phone to call the executive cooking staff. 'Coffee. Toast. Three-egg omelet, ham, and hash browns.' Cholesterol or not, he had to get his body working.

*　　　*　　　*

'You've got mail,' the mechanical voice said.

'Great.' The DDO breathed. She downloaded it, going through the usual procedures to save and print, but rather more slowly this morning because she was groggy and therefore mistake-prone. That sort of thing made her slow down and be extra careful, something she'd learned to do as the mother of a newborn. And so in four minutes instead of the usual two, she had a printed hard copy of the latest SORGE feed from Agent SONGBIRD. Six pages of relatively small ideographs. Then she lifted the phone and punched the speed-dial button for Dr. Sears.

'Yes?'

'This is Mrs. Foley. We got one.'

'On the way, Director.' She had some coffee before he arrived, and the taste, if not the effect of the caffeine, helped her face the day.

'In early?' she asked.

'Actually I slept in last night. We need to improve the selection on the cable TV,' he told her, hoping to lighten the day a little. One look at her eyes told him how likely that was.

'Here.' She handed the sheets across. 'Coffee?'

525

'Yes, thank you.' His eyes didn't leave the page as his hand reached out for the Styrofoam cup. 'This is good stuff today.'

'Oh?'

'Yeah, it's Fang's account of a Politburo discussion of how the war's going . . . they're trying to analyze our actions . . . yeah, that's about what I'd expect . . .'

'Talk to me, Dr. Sears,' Mary Pat ordered.

'You're going to want to get George Weaver in on this, too, but what he's going to say is that they're projecting their own political outlook onto us generally, and onto President Ryan in particular . . . yeah, they're saying that we are not hitting them hard for political reasons, that they think we don't want to piss them off too much . . .' Sears took a long sip of coffee. 'This is really good stuff. It tells us what their political leadership is thinking, and what they're thinking isn't very accurate.' Sears looked up. 'They misunderstand us worse than we misunderstand them, Director, even at this level. They see President Ryan's motivation as a strictly political calculation. Zhang says that he's laying back so that we can do business with them, after they consolidate their control over the Russian oil and gold fields.'

'What about their advance?'

'They say—that is, Marshal Luo says—that things are going according to plan, that they're surprised at the lack of Russian opposition, and also surprised that we haven't struck any targets within their borders.'

'That's because we don't have any bombs over there yet. Just found that out myself. We're having to fly the bombs in so that we can drop them.'

'Really? Well, they don't know that yet. They think it's deliberate inaction on our part.'

'Okay, get me a translation. When will Weaver get in?'

'Usually about eight-thirty.'

'Go over this with him as soon as he arrives.'

'You bet.' Sears took his leave.

*　　　*　　　*

'Bedding down for the night?' Aleksandrov asked.

'So it would seem, Comrade Captain,' Buikov answered. He had his binoculars on the Chinese. The two command-reconnaissance vehicles were together, which only seemed to happen when they secured for the night. It struck both men as odd that they confined their activities to daylight, but that wasn't a bad thing for the Russian watchers, and even soldiers needed their sleep. More than most, in fact, both of the Russians would have said. The stress and strain of keeping track of the enemies of their country—and doing so *within* their own borders—were telling on both of them.

The Chinese drill was thorough, but predictable. The two command tracks were together. The others were spread out, mainly in front of them, but one three hundred meters behind to secure their rear. The crews of each track stayed together as a unit. Each broke out a small petrol stove for cooking their rice—*probably rice*, the Russians all thought. And they settled down to get four or five hours of sleep before waking, cooking breakfast, and moving out before dawn. Had they not been enemies, their adherence to so demanding a drill might have excited admiration. Instead, Buikov

527

found himself wondering if he could get two or three of their BRMs to race up on the invaders and immolate them with the 30-mm rapid-fire cannons on their tracked carriers. But Aleksandrov would never allow it. You could always depend on officers to deny the sergeants what they wanted to do.

The captain and his sergeant walked back north to their track, leaving three other scouts to keep watch on their 'guests,' as Aleksandrov had taken to calling them.

'So, Sergeant, how are you feeling?' the officer asked in a quiet voice.

'Some sleep will be good.' Buikov looked back. There was now a ridgeline in addition to the trees between him and the Chinks. He lit a cigarette and let out a long, relaxed breath. 'This is harder duty than I expected it to be.'

'Oh?'

'Yes, Comrade Captain. I always thought we could kill our enemies. Baby-sitting them is very stressful.'

'That is so, Boris Yevgeniyevich, but remember that if we do our job properly, then Division will be able to kill more than just one or two. We are their eyes, not their teeth.'

'As you say, Comrade Captain, but it is like making a movie of the wolf instead of shooting him.'

'The people who make good wildlife movies win awards, Sergeant.'

The odd thing about the captain, Buikov thought, *was that he was always trying to reason with you.* It was actually rather endearing, as if he was trying to be a teacher rather than an officer.

'What's for dinner?'

'Beef and black bread, Comrade Captain. Even some butter. But no vodka,' the sergeant added sourly.

'When this is over, I will allow you to get good and drunk, Boris Yevgeniyevich,' Aleksandrov promised.

'If we live that long, I will toast your health.' The track was where they'd left it, and the crew had spread out the camouflage netting. *One thing about this officer*, Buikov thought, *he got the men to do their duty without much in the way* of *complaint. The same sort of good comradely solidarity my grandfather spoke about as he told his endless tales* of *killing Germans on the way to Vienna, just like in all the movies*, the sergeant thought.

The black bread was canned, but tasty, and the beef, cooked on their own small petrol heater, wasn't so bad as to choke a dog. About the time they finished, Sergeant Grechko appeared. He was the commander of the unit's #3 BRM, and he was carrying . . .

'Is that what I think it is?' Buikov asked. 'Yuriy Andreyevich, you are a comrade!'

It was a half-liter bottle of vodka, the cheapest 'BOΔKA' brand, with a foil top that tore off and couldn't be resealed.

'Whose idea is this?' the captain demanded.

'Comrade Captain, it is a cold night, and we are Russian soldiers, and we need something to help us relax,' Grechko said. 'It's the only bottle in the company, and one slug each will not harm us, I think,' the sergeant added reasonably.

'Oh, all right.' Aleksandrov extended his metal cup, and received perhaps sixty grams. He waited for the rest of his crew to get theirs, and saw that the bottle was empty. They all drank together, and sure enough, it tasted just fine to be Russian soldiers out in the woods, doing their duty for their Motherland.

'We'll have to refuel tomorrow,' Grechko said.

'There will be a fuel truck waiting for us, forty kilometers north at the burned-down sawmill. We'll go up there one at a time, and hope our Chinese guests do not get overly ambitious in their advance.'

*   *   *

'That must be your Captain Aleksandrov,' Major Tucker said. 'Fourteen hundred meters from the nearest Chinese. That's pretty close,' the American observed.

'He's a good boy,' Aliyev said, 'Just reported in. The Chinese follow their drill with remarkable exactitude. And the main body?'

'Twenty-five miles back—forty kilometers or so. They're laagering in for the night, too, but they're actually building campfires, like they want us to know where they are.' Tucker worked the mouse to show the encampments. The display was green-on-green now. The Chinese armored vehicles showed as bright spots, especially from the engines, which glowed from residual heat.

'This is amazing,' Aliyev said in frank admiration.

'We decided back around the end of the 1970s that we could play at night when everybody else can't. It took a while to develop the technology, but it by-God works, Colonel. All we need now is some Smart Pigs.'

'What?'

'You'll see, Colonel. You'll see,' Tucker promised. Best of all, this 'take' came from Grace Kelly, and she *did* have a laser designator plugged in to the fuselage, tooling along now at 62,000 feet and looking down with her thermal-imaging cameras. Under Tucker's guidance, the UAV kept heading south, to continue the catalog of the Chinese units advancing into Siberia. There were sixteen ribbon bridges on the Amur River now, and a few north of there, but the really vulnerable points were around Harbin, well to the south, inside Chinese territory. Lots of railroad bridges between there and Bei'an, the terminus of the railroad lifeline to the People's Liberation Army. Grace Kelly saw a lot of trains, mainly diesel engines, but even some old coal-burning steam engines that had come out of storage in order to keep the weapons and supplies coming north. Most interesting of all was the recently built traffic circle, where tank cars were unloading something, probably diesel fuel, into what appeared to be a pipeline that PLAA engineers were working very hard to extend north. That was something they'd copied from America. The U.S. and British armies had done the same thing from Normandy east to the front in late 1944, and *that*, Tucker knew, was a target worthy of note. Diesel fuel wasn't just the food of a field army. It was the very air it breathed.

There were huge numbers of idle men about. Laborers, probably, there to repair damaged tracking, and the major bridging points had SAM and FLAK batteries in close attendance. So, Joe Chink knew that the bridges were important, and he was doing his best to guard them.

For what good that would do, Tucker thought. He got on the satellite radio to talk things over with the crew up at Zhigansk, where General Wallace's target book was being put together. The crunchies on the ground were evidently worried about taking on the advancing People's Liberation Army, but to Major Tucker, it all looked like a collection of targets. For point targets, he wanted J-DAMs, and for area targets, some smart pigs, the J-SOWS, and then Joe Chink was going to take one on the chin, and probably, like all field armies, this one had a glass jaw. If you could just hit it hard enough.

*   *   *

The Russians on the ground had no idea what FedEx was, and were more than a little surprised that any private, nongovernment corporation could actually own something as monstrous as a Boeing 747F freighter aircraft.

For their part, the flight crews, mainly trained by the Navy or Air Force, had never expected to see Siberia except maybe through the windows of a B-52H strategic bomber. The runways were unusually bumpy, worse than most American airports, but there was an army of people on the ground, and when the swinging door on the nose came up, the ground crews waved the forklifts in to start collecting the palletized cargo. The flight crews didn't leave the aircraft. Fueling trucks came up and connected the four-inch hoses to the proper nozzle points and started refilling the capacious tanks so that the aircraft could leave as soon as possible, to clear the ramp space. Every -747F had a bunking area for the spare pilots who'd come along for the ride. They didn't even get a drink, those who'd sleep for the return flight, and they had to eat the boxed lunches they'd been issued at Elmendorf on the outbound flight. In all, it took fifty-seven minutes to unload the hundred tons of bombs, which was scarcely enough for ten of the F-15Es parked at the far end of the ramp, but that was where the forklifts headed.

*   *   *

'Is that a fact?' Ryan observed.

'Yes Mr. President,' Dr. Weaver replied. 'For all their sophistication, these people can be very insular in their thinking, and as a practical matter, we are all guilty of projecting our own ways of thinking into other people.'

'But I have people like you to advise me. Who advises them?' Jack asked.

'They have some good ones. Problem is, their Politburo doesn't always listen.'

'Yeah, well, I've seen that problem here, too. Is this good news or bad news, people?'

'Potentially it could be both, but let's remember that we understand them now a lot better than they understand us,' Ed Foley told those present. 'That gives us a major advantage, if we play our cards intelligently.'

Ryan leaned back and rubbed his eyes. Robby Jackson wasn't in much better shape, though he'd slept about four hours in the Lincoln Bedroom (unlike President Lincoln—it was called that simply because a picture of the sixteenth President hung on the wall). The good Jamaican coffee helped everyone at least simulate consciousness.

'I'm surprised that their Defense Minister is so narrow,' Robby thought aloud, his eyes tracing over the SORGE dispatch. 'You pay the senior operators to be big-picture thinkers. When operations go as well as the one they're running, you get suspicious. I did, anyway.'

'Okay, Robby, you used to be God of Operations across the river. What do you recommend?' Jack asked.

'The idea in a major operation is always to play with the other guy's head. To lead him down the path you want him to go, or to get inside his decision cycle, just prevent him from analyzing the data and making a decision. I think we can do that here.'

'How?' Arnie van Damm asked.

'The common factor of every successful military plan in history is this: You show the guy what he expects and hopes to see, and then when he thinks he's got the world by the ass, you cut his legs off in one swipe.' Robby leaned back, holding court for once. 'The smart move is to let them keep going for a few more days, make it just seem easier and easier for them while we build up our capabilities, and then when we hit them, we land on them like the San Francisco earthquake—no warning at all, just the end of the fuckin' world hits 'em. Mickey, what's their most vulnerable point?'

General Moore had that answer: 'It's always logistics. They're burning maybe nine hundred tons of diesel fuel a day to keep those tanks and tracks moving north. They have a full five thousand engineers working like beavers running a pipeline to keep up with their lead elements. We cut that, and they can make up some of the shortfall with fuel trucks, but not all of it—'

'And we use the Smart Pig to take care of those,' Vice President Jackson finished.

'That's one way to handle it,' General Moore agreed.

'Smart Pig?' Ryan asked.

Robby explained, concluding: 'We've been developing this and a few other tricks for the last eight years. I spent a month out at China Lake a few years ago with the prototype. It works, if we have enough of them.'

'Gus Wallace has that at the top of his Christmas list.'

'The other trick is the political side,' Jackson concluded.

'Funny, I have an idea for that. How is the PRC presenting this war to its people?'

It was Professor Weaver's turn: 'They're saying that the Russians provoked a border incident— same thing Hitler did with Poland in 1939. The Big Lie technique. They've used it before. Every dictatorship has. It works if you control what your people see.'

'What's the best weapon for fighting a lie?' Ryan asked.

'The truth, of course,' Arnie van Damm answered for the rest. 'But they control their news distribution. How do we get the truth to their population?'

'Ed, how is the SORGE data coming out?'

'Over the 'Net, Jack. So?'

'How many Chinese citizens own computers?'

'Millions of them—the number's really jumped in the past couple of years. That's why they're ripping that patent off Dell Computer that we

535

made a stink about in the trade talks and—oh, yeah
. . .' Foley looked up with a smile. 'I like it.'

'That could be dangerous,' Weaver warned.

'Dr. Weaver, there's no safe way to fight a war,'
Ryan said in reply. 'This isn't a negotiation
between friends. General Moore?'

'Yes, sir.'

'Get the orders out.'

'Yes, sir.'

'The only question is, will it work?'

'Jack,' Robby Jackson said, 'It's like with
baseball. You play the games to find out who the
best is.'

*   *   *

The first reinforcing division to arrive at Chita was
the 201st. The trains pulled into the built-for-the-
purpose offloading sidings. The flatcars had been
designed (and built in large numbers) to transport
tracked military vehicles. To that end, flip-down
bridging ramps were located at each end of every
single car, and when those were tossed down in
place, the tanks could drive straight off onto the
concrete ramps to where every train had backed
up. It was a little demanding—the width of the cars
was at best marginal for the tank tracks—but the
drivers of each vehicle kept their path straight,
breathing a small sigh of relief when they got to the
concrete. Once on the ground, military police
troops, acting as traffic cops, directed the armored
vehicles to assembly areas. The 201st Motor Rifle
Division's commander and his staff were there
already, of course, and the regimental officers got
their marching orders, telling them what roads to

take northeast to join Bondarenko's Fifth Army, and by joining it, to make it a real field army rather than a theoretical expression on paper.

The 201st, like the follow-on divisions, the 80th, 34th, and 94th, were equipped with the newest Russian hardware, and were at their full TO&E. Their immediate mission was to race north and east to get in front of the advancing Chinese. It would be quite a race. There weren't many roads in this part of Russia, and what roads there were here were unpaved gravel, which suited the tracked vehicles. The problem would be diesel fuel, because there were few gas stations for the trucks which ran the roads in peacetime pursuits, and so the 201st had requisitioned every tanker truck its officers could locate, and even that might not be enough, the logisticians all worried, not that they had much choice in the matter. If they could get their tanks there, then they'd fight them as pillboxes if it came to that.

About the only thing they had going for them was the network of telephone lines, which enabled them to communicate without using radios. The entire area was under the strictest possible orders for radio silence, to deny all conceivable knowledge to the enemy; and the air forces in the area, American and Russian, were tasked to eliminate all tactical reconnaissance aircraft that the Chinese would be sending about. So far, they'd been successful. A total of seventeen J-6 and -7 aircraft, thought to be the reconnaissance variants of their classes, had been 'splashed' short of Chita.

*　　　*　　　*

537

The Chinese problem with reconnaissance was confirmed in Paris, of all places. SPOT, the French corporation which operated commercial photosatellites, had received numerous requests for photos of Siberia, and while many of them came from seemingly legitimate western businesses, mainly news agencies, all had been summarily denied. Though not as good as American reconnaissance satellites, the SPOT birds were good enough to identify all the trains assembled at Chita.

And since the People's Republic of China still had a functioning embassy in Moscow, the other concern was that their Ministry of State Security had Russian nationals acting as paid spies, feeding data to Russia's new enemy. Those individuals about whom the Russian Federal Security Service had suspicions were picked up and questioned, and those in custody were interrogated vigorously.

This number included Mementi Ivanovich Suvorov.

'You were in the service of an enemy country,' Pavel Yefremov observed. 'You killed for a foreign power, and you conspired to kill our country's President. We know all this. We've had you under surveillance for some time now. We have this.' He held up a photocopy of the onetime pad recovered from the dead-drop on the park bench. 'You may talk now, or you may be shot. It is your life at risk, not mine.'

In the movies, this was the part where the suspect was supposed to say defiantly, 'You're going to kill me anyway,' except that Suvorov had no more wish to die than anyone else. He loved life as much as any man, and he'd never expected to be caught any more than the most foolish of street criminals did. If anything, he'd expected arrest even less than one of those criminals, because he knew how intelligent and clever he was, though this feeling had understandably deflated over the last few days.

The outlook of Klementi Ivan'ch Suvorov was rather bleak at the moment. He *was* KGB-trained, and he knew what to expect—a bullet in the head—unless he could give his interrogators something sufficiently valuable for them to spare his life, and at the moment even life in a labor camp of strict regime was preferable to the alternative.

'Have you truly arrested Kong?'

'We told you that before, but, no, we have not. Why tip them off that we've penetrated their operation?' Yefremov said honestly.

'Then you can use me against them.'

'How might we do that?' the FSS officer asked.

'I can tell them that the operation they propose is going forward, but that the situation in Siberia wrecked my chance to execute it in a timely fashion.'

'And if Kong cannot leave their embassy—we have it guarded and isolated now, of course—how would you get that information to him?'

'By electronic mail. Yes, you can monitor their landlines, but to monitor their cellular phones is more difficult. There's a backup method for me to communicate with him electronically.'

'And the fact that you haven't made use of it so far will not alert them?'

'The explanation is simple. My Spetsnaz contact was frightened off by the outbreak of hostilities, and so was I.'

'But we've already checked your electronic accounts.'

'Do you think they are all written down?' He tapped the side of his head. 'Do you think I am totally foolish?'

'Go on, make your proposal.'

'I will propose that I can go forward with the mission. I require them to authorize it by a signal— the way they set the shades in their windows, for example.'

'And for this?'

'And for this I will not be executed,' the traitor suggested.

'I see,' Yefremov said quietly. He would have been perfectly content to shoot the traitor right here and now, but it might be politically useful to go forward with his proposal. He'd kick that one upstairs.

*　　　*　　　*

The bad part about watching them was that you had to anticipate everything they did, and that meant that they got to have more sleep, about an hour's worth, Aleksandrov figured, and no more than that only because they were predictable. He'd had his morning tea. Sergeant Buikov had enjoyed two morning cigarettes with his, and now they lay prone on wet dew-dampened ground, with their binoculars to their eyes. The Chinese had also had soldiers out of their tracks all night, set about a hundred meters away from them, so it seemed. *They weren't very adventurous*, the captain thought. He would have spread his sentries much farther out, at least half a kilometer, in pairs with radios to go with their weapons. For that matter, he would have set up a mortar in the event that they spotted something dangerous. But the fox and the gardener seemed to be both conservative and confident, which was an odd combination of characteristics.

But their morning drill was precise. The petrol heaters came out for tea—*probably tea*, they all figured—and whatever it was that they had for breakfast. Then the camouflage nets came down. The outlying sentries came in and reported in person to their officers, and everyone mounted up. The first hop on their tracks was a short one, not even half a kilometer, and again the foot-scouts dismounted and moved forward, then quickly reported back for the second, much longer morning frog leap forward.

'Let's move, Sergeant,' Aleksandrov ordered, and together they ran to their BRM for their first trek into the woods for their own third installment of frog leap backwards.

*   *   *

'There they go again,' Major Tucker said, after getting three whole hours of sleep on a thin mattress four feet from the Dark Star terminal. It was Ingrid Bergman up again, positioned so that she could see both the reconnaissance element and main body of the Chinese army. 'You know, they really stick to the book, don't they?'

'So it would seem,' Colonel Tolkunov agreed.

'So, going by that, tonight they'll go to about here.' Tucker made a green mark on the acetate-covered map. 'That puts them at the gold mine day after tomorrow. Where do you plan to make your stand?' the major asked.

'That depends on how quickly the Two Zero One can get forward.'

'Gas?' Tucker asked.

'Diesel fuel, but, yes, that is the main problem with moving so large a force.'

'Yeah, with us it's bombs.'

'When will you begin to attack Chinese targets?' Tolkunov asked.

'Not my department, Colonel, but when it happens, you'll see it here, live and in color.'

*   *   *

Ryan had gotten two hours of nap in the afternoon, while Arnie van Damm covered his appointments (the Chief of Staff needed his sleep, too, but like most people in the White House, he put the President's needs before his own), and now he was watching TV, the feed from Ingrid Bergman.

'This is amazing,' he observed. 'You could almost get on the phone and tell a guy where to go with his tank.'

'We try to avoid that, sir,' Mickey Moore said at once. In Vietnam it had been called the 'squad leader in the sky' when battalion commanders had directed sergeants on their patrols, not always to the enlisted men's benefit. The miracle of modern communications could also be a curse, with the expected effect that the people in harm's way would ignore their radios or just turn the damned things off until they had something to say themselves.

Ryan nodded. He'd been a second lieutenant of

Marines once, and though it hadn't been for long, he remembered it as demanding work for a kid just out of college.

'Do the Chinese know we're doing this?'

'Not as far as we can tell. If they did, they'd sure as hell try to take the Dark Star down, and we'd notice if they tried. That's not easy, though. They're damned near invisible on radar, and tough to spot visually, so the Air Force tells me.'

'Not too many fighters can reach sixty thousand feet, much less cruise up there,' Robby agreed. 'It's a stretch even for a Tomcat.' His eyes, too, were locked on the screen. No officer in the history of military operations had ever had a capability akin to this, not even two percent of it, Jackson was sure. Most of war-fighting involved finding the enemy so that you knew where to kill him. These new things made it like watching a Hollywood movie—and if the Chinese knew they were there, they'd freak. Considerable efforts had been designed into Dark Star to prevent that from happening. Their transmitters were directional, and locked onto satellites, instead of radiating outward in the manner of a normal radio. So, they might as well have been black holes up there, orbiting twelve miles over the battlefield.

'What's the important thing here?' Jack asked General Moore.

'Logistics, sir, always logistics. Told you this morning, sir, they're burning up a lot of diesel fuel, and replenishing that is a mother of a task. The Russians have the same problem. They're trying to race a fresh division north of the Chinese spearhead, to made a stand around Aldan, close to where the gold strike is. It's only even money they

543

can make it, even over roads and without opposition. They have to move a lot of fuel, too, and the other problem for them is that it'll wear out the tracks on their vehicles. They don't have lowboy trailers like ours, and so their tanks have to do it all on their own. Tanks are a lot more delicate to operate than they look. Figure they'll lose a quarter to a third of their strength just from the approach march.'

'Can they fight?' Jackson asked.

'They're using the T-80U. It would have given the M60A3 a good fight, but no, not as good as our first-flight M1, much less the M1A2, but against the Chinese M-90, call it an even match, qualitatively. It's just that the Chinese have a lot more of them. It comes down to training. The Russian divisions that they're sending into the fight are their best-trained and -equipped. Question is, are they good enough? We'll just have to see.'

'And our guys?'

'They start arriving at Chita tomorrow morning. The Russians want them to assemble and move east-southeast. The operational concept is for them to stop the Chinese cold, and then we chop them off from their supplies right near the Amur River. It makes sense theoretically,' Mickey Moore said neutrally, 'and the Russians say they have all the fuel we'll need in underground bunkers that have been there for damned near fifty years. We'll see.'

CHAPTER FIFTY-FIVE

LOOKS AND HURTS

General Peng was all the way forward now, with
the leading elements of his lead armored division,
the 302nd. Things were going well for him—
sufficiently well, in fact, that he was becoming
nervous about it. *No opposition at all?* he asked
himself. Not so much as a single rifle round, much
less a barrage of artillery. Were the Russians totally
asleep, totally devoid of troops in this sector? They
had a full army group command section at
Chabarsovil, commanded by that Bondarenko
fellow, who was reported to be a competent, even a
courageous, officer. But where the hell were his
troops? Intelligence said that a complete Russian
motor-rifle division was here, the 265th, and a
Russian motor-rifle division was a superbly
designed mechanized formation, with enough tanks
to punch a hole in most things, and manned with
enough infantry to hold any position for a long
time. Theoretically. But where the hell was it? And
where were the reinforcements the Russians had to
be sending? Peng had asked for information, and
the air force had supposedly sent photo-
reconnaissance aircraft to look for his enemies, but
with no result. He had expected to be mainly on his
own for this campaign, but not *entirely* on his own.
Fifty kilometers in advance of the 302nd Armored
was a reconnaissance screen that had reported
nothing but some tracks in the ground that might
or might not have been fresh. The few helicopter

545

flights that had gone out had reported nothing. They should have spotted *something*, but no, only some civilians, who for the most part got the hell out of the way and stayed there.

Meanwhile, his troops had crewed up this ancient railroad right-of-way, but it wasn't much worse than traveling along a wide gravel road. His only potential operational concern was fuel, but two hundred 10,000-liter fuel trucks were delivering an adequate amount from the pipeline the engineers were extending at a rate of forty kilometers per day from the end of the railhead on the far bank of the Amur. In fact, that was the most impressive feat of the war so far. Well behind him, engineer regiments were laying the pipe, then covering it under a meter of earth for proper concealment. The only things they couldn't conceal were the pumping stations, but they had the spare parts to build plenty more should they be destroyed.

No, Peng's only real concern was the location of the Russian Army. The dilemma was that either his intelligence was faulty, and there *were* no Russian formations in his area of interest, or it was accurate and the Russians were just running away and denying him the chance to engage and destroy them. But since when did Russians *not* fight for their land? Chinese soldiers surely would. And it just didn't fit with Bondarenko's reputation. None of this situation made sense. Peng sighed. *But battlefields were often that way*, he told himself. For the moment, he was on—actually slightly ahead of—schedule, and his first strategic objective, the gold mine, was three days away from his leading reconnaissance element. He'd never seen a gold mine before.

*   *   *

'I'll be damned!' Pavel Petrovich said. 'This is *my* land. No Chink's going to chase me off of it!'

'They are only three or four days away, Pasha.'

'So? I have lived here for over fifty years. I'm not going to leave now.' The old man was well to the left of defiant. The chief of the mining company had come personally to drive him out, and expected him to come willingly. But he'd misread the old man's character.

'Pasha, we can't leave you here in their way. This is their objective, the thing they invaded us to steal—'

'Then I shall *fight* for it!' he retorted. 'I killed Germans, I've killed bears, I've killed wolves. Now, I will kill Chinese. I'm an old man, not an old *woman*, comrade!'

'Will you fight against enemy soldiers?'

'And why not?' Gogol asked. 'This is *my* land. I know all its places. I know where to hide, and I know how to shoot. I've killed soldiers before.' He pointed to his wall. The old service rifle was there, and the mining chief could easily see the notches he'd cut on the stock with a knife, one for every German. 'I can hunt wolves and bear. I can hunt men, too.

'You're too old to be a soldier. That's a young man's job.'

'I need not be an athlete to squeeze a trigger, comrade, and I know these woods.' To emphasize his words, Gogol stood and took down his old sniper rifle from the Great Patriotic War, leaving the new Austrian rifle. The meaning was clear. He'd fought with this arm before, and he was quite willing to do so again. Hanging on his wall still were a number of the gilded wolf skins, most of which had single holes in the head. He touched one, then looked back at his visitors. 'I am a Russian. I will fight for my land.'

The mining chief figured he'd buck this information up to the military. Maybe they could take him out. For himself, he had no particular desire to entertain the Chinese army, and so he took his leave. Behind him, Pavel Petrovich Gogol opened a bottle of vodka and enjoyed a snort. Then he cleaned his rifle and thought of old times.

*   *   *

The train terminal was well-designed for their purposes, Colonel Welch thought. Russian engineers might have designed things clunky, but they'd also designed them to work, and the layout here was a lot more efficient than it looked on first inspection. The trains reversed direction on what American railroaders called a wye—Europeans called it a turning triangle—which allowed trains to back up to any one of ten offloading ramps, and the Russians were doing it with skill and aplomb. The big VL80T electric locomotive eased backwards, with the conductors on the last car holding the air-release valve to activate the brakes when they reached the ramp. When the trains stopped, the soldiers jumped from their passenger coaches and ran back to their individual vehicles to start them up and drive them off. It didn't take longer than thirty minutes to empty a train. That impressed Colonel Welch, who'd used the Auto Train to take his family to Disney World, and the offloading procedure in Sanford, Florida, usually took an hour and a half or so. Then there was no further waiting. The big VL (Vladimir Lenin) engines immediately moved out for the return trip west to load up another ten thousand tons of train cars and cargo. It certainly appeared as though the Russians could make things happen when they had to.

'Colonel?' Welch turned to see a Russian major, who saluted crisply.

'Yes?'

'The first train with your personnel is due in four hours twenty minutes. We'll take them to the southern assembly area. There is fuel there if they need it, and then we have guides to direct them east.'

'Very good.'

'Until then, if you wish to eat, there is a canteen inside the station building.'

'Thank you. We're okay at the moment.' Welch walked over to where his satellite radio was set up, to get that information to General Diggs.

*　　　*　　　*

Colonel Bronco Winters now had seven red stars painted on the side panel of his F-15C, plus four of the now-defunct UIR flags. He could have painted on some marijuana or coca leaves as well, but that part of his life was long past, and those kills had been blacker than his uncle Ernie, who still lived in Harlem. So, he was a double-ace, and the Air Force hadn't had many of those on active duty in a

549

very long time. He took his flight to what they had taken to calling Bear Station, on the western edge of the Chinese advance.

It was an Eagle station. There were now over a hundred F-16 fighters in Siberia, but they were mainly air-to-mud rather than air-to-air, and so the fighting part of the fighter mission was his department, while the -16 jocks grumbled about being second-class citizens. Which they were, as far as Colonel Winters thought. Damned little single-engine pukes.

Except for the F-16CGs. They were useful because they were dedicated to taking out enemy radars and SAM sites. The Siberian Air Force (so they now deemed themselves) hadn't done *any* air-to-mud yet. They had orders not to, which offended the guys whose idea of fun was killing crunchies on the ground instead of more manly pursuits. They didn't have enough bombs for a proper bombing campaign yet, and so they were coming up just to ride guard on the E-3Bs in case Joe Chink decided to go after them—it was a hard mission, but marginally doable, and Bronco was surprised that they hadn't made the attempt yet. It was a sure way to lose a lot of fighter planes, but they'd lost a bunch anyway, and why not lose them to a purpose . . . ?

'Boar Lead, this is Eagle Two, over.'

'Boar Leader.'

'We show something happening, numerous bandits one-four-five your position, angels three-three, range two hundred fifty miles, coming north at six hundred knots—make that count thirty-plus bandits, looks like they're coming right for us, Boar Lead,' the controller on the AWACS reported.

'Roger, copy that. Boar, Lead,' he told his flight of four. 'Let's get our ears perked up.'

'Two.' 'Three.' 'Four,' the rest of his flight chimed in.

'Boar Leader, this is Eagle Two. The bandits just went supersonic, and they are heading right for us. Looks like they're not kidding. Vector right to course one-three-five and prepare to engage.'

'Roger, Eagle. Boar Lead, come right to one-three-five.'

'Two.' 'Three.' 'Four.'

Winters checked his fuel first of all. He had plenty. Then he looked at his radar display for the picture transmitted from the AWACS, and sure enough, there was a passel of bandits inbound, like a complete ChiComm regiment of fighters. The bastards had read his mind.

'Damn, Bronco, this looks like a knife fight coming.'

'Be cool, Ducky, we got better knives.'

'You say so, Bronco,' the other element leader answered.

'Let's loosen it up, people,' Colonel Winters ordered. The flight of four F-15Cs separated into two pairs, and the pairs slipped apart as well so that each could cover the other, but a single missile could not engage both.

The display between his legs showed that the Chinese fighters were just over a hundred miles off now, and the velocity vectors indicated speeds of over eight hundred knots. Then the picture dirtied up some.

'Boar Lead, looks like they just dropped off tanks.'

'Roger that.' So, they'd burned off fuel to get

altitude, and now they were committed to the battle with full internal fuel. That would give them better legs than usual, and they had closed to less than two hundred miles between them and the E-3B Sentry they clearly wanted to kill. There were thirty people on that converted 707, and Winters knew a lot of them. They'd worked together for years, mainly in exercises, and each controller on the Sentry had a specialty. Some were good at getting you to a tanker. Some were good at sending you out to hunt. Some were best at defending themselves against enemies. This third group would now take over. The Sentry crewmen would think this wasn't cricket, that it wasn't exactly fair to chase deliberately after a converted obsolete airliner . . . just because it acted as bird-dog for those who were killing off their fighter-pilot comrades. *Well, that's life*, Winters thought. But he wasn't going to give any of these bandits a free shot at another USAF aircraft.

Eighty miles now. 'Sloppy, follow me up,' the colonel ordered.

'Roger, Lead.' The two clawed up to forty thousand feet, so that the cold ground behind the targets would give a better contrast for their infrared seekers. He checked the radar display again. There had to be a good thirty of them, and that was a lot. If the Chinese were smart, they'd have two teams, one to engage and distract the American fighters, and the other to blow through after their primary target. He'd try to concentrate on the latter, but if the former group's pilots were competent, that might not be easy.

The warbling tone started in his headphones. The range was now sixty miles. *Why not now?* he asked himself. They were beyond visual range, but not beyond range of his AMA missiles. Time to shoot 'em in the lips.

'Going Slammer,' he called on the radio.

'Roger, Slammer,' Skippy replied from half a mile to his right.

'Fox-One!' Winters called, as the first one leapt off the rails. The first Slammer angled left, seeking its designated target, one of the enemy's leading fighters. The closure speed between missile and target would be well over two thousand miles per hour. His eyes dropped to the radar display. His first missile appeared to hit—yes, the target blip expanded and started dropping. Number Eight. Time for another: 'Fox-One!'

'Fox-One,' his wingman called. Seconds later: 'Kill!' Lieutenant Acosta called.

Winters's second missile somehow missed, but there wasn't time for wondering why. He had six more AMRAAMs, and he pickled four of them off in the next minute. By that time, he could see the inbound fighters. They were Shenyang J-8IIs, and they had radars and missiles, too. Winters flipped on his jammer pod, wondering if it would work or not, and wondering if their infrared missiles had all-aspect targeting like his Sidewinders. He'd probably find out soon, but first he fired off two 'winders. 'Breaking right, Skippy.'

'I'm with you, Bronco,' Acosta replied.

Damn, Winters thought, *there are still at least twenty of the fuckers.* He headed down, speeding up as he went and calling for a vector.

'Boar Lead, Eagle, there's twenty-three of them left and they're still coming. Dividing into two elements. You have bandits at your seven o'clock and closing.'

Winters reversed his turn and racked his head against the g-forces to spot it. Yeah, a J-8 all right, the Chinese two-engine remake of the MiG-21, trying to get position to launch on him—no, two of the bastards. He reefed the turn in tight, pulling seven gees, and after ten endless seconds, getting his nose on the targets. His left hand selected Sidewinder and he triggered two off.

The bandits saw the smoke trails of the missiles and broke apart, in opposite directions. One would escape, but both the heat-seekers locked on the guy to the right, and both erased his aircraft from the sky. But where had the other one gone? Winters' eyes swept a sky that was both crowded and empty at the same time. His threat receiver made its unwelcome screeching sound, and now he'd find out if the jammer pod worked or not. Somebody was trying to lock him up with a radar-guided missile. His eyes swept around looking for who that might be, but he couldn't see anyone—

—Smoke trail! A missile, heading in his general direction, but then it veered and exploded with its target—friend or foe, Winters couldn't tell.

'Boar Flight, Lead, check in!' he ordered.

'Two.' 'Three.' A pause before: 'Four!'

'Skippy, where are you?'

'Low and right, one mile, Leader. Heads up, there's a bandit at your three and closing.'

'Oh, yeah?' Winters yanked his fighter to the right and was rewarded with an immediate warbling tone—but was it friend or foe? His wingman said the latter, but he couldn't tell, until—

Whoever it was, it had launched at him, and so

he triggered a Sidewinder in reply, then dove hard for the deck while punching off flares and chaff to distract it. It worked. The missile, a radar seeker, exploded harmlessly half a mile behind him, but his Sidewinder didn't miss. He'd just gotten another kill, but he didn't know how many today, and there wasn't time to think things over.

'Skippy, form up on me, we're going north.'

'Roger, Bronco.'

Winters had his radar on, and he saw at least eight enemy blips to the north. He went to afterburner to chase, checking his fuel state. Still okay. The Eagle accelerated rapidly, but just to be safe, he popped off a string of chaff and flares in case some unknown Chinese was shooting at him. The threat receiver was screeching continuously now, though not in the distinctive chirping tone that suggested lock-up. He checked his weapons board. Three AIM-9X Sidewinders left. Where the hell had this day gone to?

'Ducky is hit, Ducky is hit!' a voice called. 'Aw, shit!'

'Ghost Man here, got the fucker for you, Ducky. Come right, let me give you a damage check.'

'One engine gone, other one's running hot,' the second element leader reported, in a voice more angry than afraid. He didn't have time for fear yet. Another thirty seconds or so and that would start to take hold, Winters was sure.

'Ducky, you're trailing vapor of some sort, recommend you find a place to set it down.'

'Eagle Two, Bronco, what's happening?'

'Bronco, we have six still inbound, putting Rodeo on it now. You have a bandit at your one o'clock at twenty miles, angels three-one, speed

555

seven-five-zero.'

'Roger that, Eagle. I'm on him.' Winters came a little right and got another acquisition tone. 'Fox-Two!' he called. The smoke trail ran straight for several miles, then corkscrewed to the left as it approached the little dot of gray-blue and . . . yes!

'Rodeo Lead,' a new voice called. 'Fox-One, Fox-One with two!'

'Conan, Fox-One!'

Now things were really getting nervous. Winters knew that he might be in the line of fire for those Slammers. He looked down to see that the light on his IFF was a friendly, constant green. The Identification Friend or Foe was supposed to tell American radars and missiles that he was on their side, but Winters didn't entirely trust computer chips with his life, and so he squinted his eyes to look for smoke trails that weren't going sideways. His radar could see the AWACS now, and it was moving west, taking the first part of evasive action, but its radar was still transmitting, even with Chinese fighters within . . . twenty miles? Shit! But then two more blips disappeared, and the remaining ones all had friendly IFF markers.

Winters checked his weapons display. No missiles left. How had all that happened? He was the United States Air Force champ for situational awareness, but he'd just lost track of a combat action. He couldn't remember firing all his missiles.

'Eagle Two, this is Boar Lead. I'm Winchester. Do you need any help?' 'Winchester' meant out of weapons. That wasn't entirely true. He still had a full magazine of 20-mm cannon shells, but suddenly all the gees and all the excitement were pulling on him. His arms felt leaden as he eased his

Eagle back to level flight.

'Boar Lead, Eagle. Looks like we're okay now, but that was kinda exciting, fella.'

'Roger that, Eagle. Same here. Anything left?'

'Negative, Boar. Rodeo Lead got the last two. I think we owe that major a couple of beers.'

'I'll hold you to that, Eagle,' Rodeo Lead observed.

'Ducky, where are you?' Winters called next.

'Kinda busy, Bronco,' a strained voice replied. 'I got a hole in my arm, too.

'Bronco, Ghost Man. Ducky's got some holes in the airframe. I'm going to shepherd him back to Suntar. Thirty minutes, about.'

'Sloppy, where you be?'

'Right behind you, Leader. I think I got four, maybe five, in that furball.'

'Any weapons left?'

'Stammer and 'winder, one each. I'll look after you, Colonel,' Lieutenant Acosta promised. 'How'd you make out?'

'Two, maybe more, not sure,' the squadron commander answered. The final tally would come from the AWACS, plus a check of his own videotape. Mainly he wanted to get out of the aircraft and take a good stretch, and he now had time to worry about Major Don Boyd—Ducky— and his aircraft.

*   *   *

'So, we want to mess with their heads, Mickey?' Admiral Dave Seaton asked.

'That's the idea,' the Chairman of the Joint Chiefs told the chief of naval operations.

557

'Makes sense. Where are their heads at?'

'According to what CIA says, they think we're limiting the scope of operations for political reasons—to protect their sensibilities, like.'

'No foolin'?' Seaton asked with no small degree of incredulity.

Moore nodded. 'Yep.'

'Well, then it's like a guy holding aces and eights, isn't it?' the CNO thought aloud, referring to the last poker hand held by James Butler—'Wild Bill'—Hickok in Deadwood, South Dakota. 'We just pick the mission that's sure to flip them out.'

'What are you thinking?' Moore asked.

'We can slam their navy pretty hard. Bart Mancuso's a pretty good operator. What are they most afraid of . . . ?' Seaton leaned back in his swivel chair. 'First thing Bart wants to do is take out their missile submarine. It's at sea now with *Tucson* in trail, about twenty thousand yards back.'

'That far?'

'It's plenty close enough. It's got an SSN in close proximity to protect it. So, *Tucson* takes 'em both out—zap.' Moore didn't get the terminology, but Seaton was referring to the Chinese ships as 'it,' meaning an enemy, a target worthy only of destruction. 'Beijing might not know it's happened right away, unless they've got an 'I'm Dead' buoy on the sail. Their surface navy's a lot easier. That'll be mainly aircraft targets, some missiles to keep the surface community happy.'

'Submarine-launched missiles?'

'Mickey, you don't sink ships by making holes that let air in. You sink ships by making holes that let water in,' Seaton explained. 'Okay, if this is supposed to be for psychological effect, we hit

558

everything simultaneously. That'll mean staging a lot of assets, and it runs the risk of being overly complicated, having the other guy catch a sniff of what's happening before we do anything. It's a risk. Do we really want to run it?'

'Ryan's thinking "big picture". Robby's helping him.'

'Robby's a fighter pilot,' Seaton agreed. 'He likes to think in terms of movie stuff. Hell, Tom Cruise is taller than he is,' Seaton joked.

'Good operational thinker. He was a pretty good J-3,' Moore reminded the senior sailor.

'Yeah, I know, it's just that he likes to make dramatic plays. Okay, we can do it, only it complicates things.' Seaton looked out the window for a second. 'You know what might really flip them out?'

'What's that?' Moore asked. Seaton told him. 'But it's not possible for us to do, is it?'

'Maybe not, but we're not dealing with professional military people, are we? They're politicians, Mickey. They're used to dealing with images instead of reality. So, we give them an image.'

'Do you have the pieces in place to do that?'

'Let me find out.'

'This is crazy, Dave.'

'And deploying First Armored to Russia isn't?' the CNO demanded.

*   *   *

Lieutenant Colonel Angelo Giusti was now certain that he'd be fully content never to ride on another train as long as he lived. He didn't know that all of

559

the Russian State Railroad's sleeper cars were being used to transport Russian army forces—they'd never sent any of the cars as far west as Berlin, not to slight the Americans, but because it had simply never occurred to anyone to do so. He took note of the fact that the train veered off to the north, off the main track, thumping over various switches and interlockings as it did so, and then the train came to a halt and started going backwards slowly. They seemed to be in the yard alone. They'd passed numerous westbound trains in the past two hours, all with engines dragging empty flatcars, and the conductor who appeared and disappeared regularly had told them that this was the approximate arrival time scheduled, but he hadn't really believed it, on the premise that a railroad with such uncomfortable seats probably didn't adhere to decent schedules either. But here they were, and the offloading ramps were obvious for what they were.

'People, I think we're here,' the commander of the Quarter Horse told his staff.

'Praise Jesus,' one of them observed. A few seconds later, the train jolted to a stop, and they were able to walk out onto the concrete platform, which, they saw, stretched a good thousand meters to the east. Inside of five minutes, the soldiers of Headquarters Troop were out and walking to their vehicles, stretching and grousing along the way.

'Hey, Angie,' called a familiar voice.

Giusti looked to see Colonel Welch and walked up to him with a salute.

'What's happening?' Giusti asked.

'It's a mess out east of here, but there is good news.'

'What might that be?'

'There's plenty of fuel stashed for us. I've been flying security detachments out, and Ivan says he's got fuel depots that're the size of fuckin' supertankers. So, we're not going to run out of gas.'

'That's good to know. What about my choppers?' Welch just pointed. There was an OH-58D Kiowa Warrior sitting not three hundred yards away. 'Thank God for that. What's the bad news?'

'The PLA has four complete Group-A armies in Siberia and heading north. There hasn't been any heavy contact yet because Ivan's refusing combat at the moment, until they can get something big enough to meet them with. They have one motor-rifle division in theater and four more heading up there. The last of 'em just cleared this railyard an hour and a half ago.'

'That's, what? Sixteen heavy divisions in the invasion force?'

Welch nodded. 'Thereabouts.'

'What's my mission?'

'Assemble your squadron and head southeast. The idea is First Armored will cut off the bottom of the break-in and interrupt their supply line. Russian blocking force will then try to stop them about two hundred miles northeast of here.'

'Can they do it?' Four Russian divisions against sixteen Chinese didn't seem especially favorable odds.

'Not sure,' Welch admitted. 'Your job is to get out and establish lead security for the division. Advance to and secure the first big fuel depot. We'll play it from there.'

'Support?'

'At the moment, the Air Force is mainly doing

fighter work. No deep strikes yet because they don't have enough bombs to sustain any kind of campaign.'

'What about resupply?'

'We have two basic loads for all the tracks. That'll have to do for a while. At least we have four units of fire for the artillery.' That meant four days' worth of shells—based on what the Army computed that a day of combat required. The supply weenies who did those calculations weren't stingy on shells to shoot at the other guy. And in the entire Persian Gulf war, not a single tank had completely shot out its first basic load of shells, they both knew. But that was a different war. No two were ever the same, and they only got worse.

Giusti turned when he heard the first engine start up. It was an M3A2 Bradley Scout track, and the sergeant in the commander's hatch looked happy to be moving. A Russian officer took over as traffic cop, waving the Brad forward, then right toward the assembly area. The next train backed up to the next ramp over. That would be 'A' or Avenger Troop, with the first of Quarter Horse's really heavy equipment, nine of the M1A2 main battle tanks.

'How long before everything's here?' Giusti asked.

'Ninety minutes, they told me,' Welch answered. 'We'll see.'

*   *   *

'What's this?' a captain asked the screen in front of him. The E-3B entry designated Eagle Two was back on the ground at Zhigansk. Its crew was more than a little shaken. Being approached by real fighters with real blood in their eyes was qualitatively different from exercises and postmission analysis back stateside. The tapes of the engagement had been handed off to the wing intelligence staff, who viewed the battle with some detachment, but they could see that the PLAAF had thrown a full regiment of first-line fighters at the AWACS, and more than that, done it on a one-way mission. They'd come in on burner, and that would have denied them a trip back to their base. So, they'd been willing to trade over thirty fighters for a single E-3B. But there was more to the mission than that, the captain saw.

'Look here,' he told his colonel. 'Three, no, four reconnaissance birds went northwest.' He ran the tape forward and backward. 'We didn't touch any of them. Hell, they didn't even see them.'

'Well, I'm not going to fault the Sentry crew for that, Captain.'

'Not saying that, sir. But John Chinaman just got some pictures of Chita, and also of these Russian units moving north. The cat's out of the bag, Colonel.'

'We've got to start thinking about some counter-air missions on these airfields.'

'We have bombs to do it?'

'Not sure, but I'm taking this to General Wallace. What's the score on the air fight?'

'Colonel Winters got four for sure and two probables. Damn, that guy's really cleaning up. But it was the -16 guys saved the AWACS. These two J-8s got pretty damned close before Rodeo splashed them.'

'We'll put some more coverage on the E-3s from

now on,' the colonel observed.

'Not a bad idea, sir.'

*   *   *

'Yes?' General Peng said, when his intelligence officer came up to him.

'Aerial reconnaissance reports large mechanized formations one hundred fifty kilometers west of us, moving north and northeast.'

'Strength?' the general asked.

'Not sure. Analysis of the photos is not complete, but certainly regimental strength, maybe more.'

'Where, exactly?'

'Here, Comrade General.' The intelligence officer unfolded a map and pointed. 'They were spotted here, here, and from here to here. The pilot said large numbers of tanks and tracked vehicles.'

'Did they shoot at him?'

'No, he said there was no fire at all.'

'So, they are rushing to where they are going . . . racing to get to our flank, or to get ahead of us . . .?' Peng considered this, looking down at the map. 'Yes, that's what I would expect. Any reports from our front?'

'Comrade General, our reconnaissance screen reports that they have seen the tracks of vehicles, but no visual sightings of the enemy at all. They have taken no fire, and seen nothing but civilians.'

*   *   *

'Quickly,' Aleksandrov urged.

How the driver and his assistant had gotten the ZIL-157 to this place was a mystery whose solution didn't interest the captain. That it had gotten here was enough. His lead BRM at that moment had been Sergeant Grechko's, and he'd filled up his tanks, and then radioed to the rest of the company, which for the first time broke visual contact with the advancing Chinese and raced north to top off as well. It was dangerous and against doctrine to leave the Chinese unseen, but Aleksandrov couldn't guarantee that they'd all have a chance to refuel otherwise. Then Sergeant Buikov had a question.

'When do *they* refuel, Comrade Captain? We haven't seen them do it, have we?'

That made his captain stop and think. 'Why, no, we haven't. Their tanks must be as empty as ours.'

'They had extra fuel drums the first day, remember? They dropped them off sometime yesterday.'

'Yes, so maybe they have one more day of fuel, maybe only half a day, but then someone must refill them—but who will that be, and how . . .?' the officer wondered. He turned to look. The fuel came out of the portable pump at about forty liters or ten gallons per minute. Grechko had taken his BRM south to reestablish contact with the Chinese. They were still sitting still, between frog-leap bounds, probably half an hour away if they stuck with their drill, from which they hadn't once deviated. And people had once said that the Red Army was inflexible . . .

'There, that's it,' Aleksandrov's driver said. He handed the hose back and capped the tank.

'You,' the captain told the driver of the fuel

truck. 'Go east.'

'To where?' the man asked. 'There's nothing there.'

That stopped his thinking for a few seconds. There had been a sawmill here once, and you could see the wide swaths of saplings left over from when whoever had worked here had cut trees for lumber. It was the closest thing to open ground they'd seen in over a day.

'I came from the west. I can get back there now, with the truck lighter, and it's only six kilometers to the old logging road.'

'Very well, but do it quickly, corporal. If they see you, they'll blast you.

'Farewell then, Comrade Captain.' The corporal got back into the truck, started up, and turned to the north to loop around.

'I hope someone gives him a drink tonight. He's earned it,' Buikov said. There was much more to any army than the shooters.

'Grechko, where are you?' Aleksandrov called over his radio.

'Four kilometers south of you. They're still dismounted, Captain. Their officer seems to be talking on the radio.'

'Very well. You know what to do when they remount.' The captain set the radio microphone down and leaned against his track. This business was getting very old. Buikov lit a smoke and stretched.

'Why can't we just kill a *few* of them, Comrade Captain? Would it not be worth it to get *some* sleep?'

'How many times must I tell you what our fucking mission is, Sergeant!' Aleksandrov nearly screamed at his sergeant.

'Yes, Captain,' Buikov responded meekly.

CHAPTER FIFTY-SIX

MARCH TO DANGER

Lieutenant Colonel Giusti started off in his personal HMMWV, the new incarnation of the venerable Jeep. *Using a Bradley would have been more comfortable, even more sensible, but overly dramatic*, he thought, *and there wouldn't be any contact anytime soon.* Besides, the right front seat in this vehicle was better for his back after the endless train ride. In any case, he was following a Russian UAZ-469, which looked like a Russian interpretation of an American SUV, and whose driver knew the way. The Kiowa Warrior helicopter he'd seen at the railyard was up and flying, scouting ahead and reporting back that there was nothing there but mostly empty road, except for some civilian traffic being kept out of the way by Russian MPs. Right behind Giusti's command vehicle was a Bradley flying the red-and-white guidon of the First of the Fourth Cavalry. The regiment had, for American arms, a long and distinguished history— its combat action had begun on July 30, 1857, against the Cheyenne Indians at Solomon River— and this campaign would add yet another battle streamer to the regimental standard . . . and Giusti hoped he'd live long enough to attach it himself. The land here reminded him of Montana, rolling foothills with pine trees in abundance. The views were decently long, just what a mechanized trooper liked, because it meant you could engage an enemy at long range. American soldiers especially preferred that, because they had weapons that could reach farther than those of most other armies.

'DARKHORSE SIX to SABRE SIX, over,' the radio crackled.

'SABRE SIX,' LTC Giusti responded.

'SABRE , I'm now at checkpoint Denver. The way continues to be clear. Negative traffic, negative enemy indications, over. Proceeding east to checkpoint Wichita.'

'Roger that, thank you, out.' Giusti checked the map to be sure he knew exactly where the chopper was.

So, twenty miles ahead there was still nothing to be concerned about, at least according to the captain flying his lead helicopter. *Where would it start?* Giusti wondered. On the whole, he would have preferred to stand still and sit in on the divisional commander's conference, just to find out what the hell was happening, but as cavalry-screen commander, it was his job to go out forward and find the enemy, then report back to IRON SIX, the divisional commander. He really didn't have much of a mission yet, aside from driving up to the Russian fuel depot, refueling his vehicles there, and setting up security, then pulling out and continuing his advance as the leading elements of the First Armored's heavy forces got there. It was his job, in short, to be the ham in the sandwich, as one of his troop commanders liked to joke. But this ham could bite back. Under his command were three troops of armored cavalry, each with nine M1A2

568

Abrams main-battle tanks and thirteen M3A2 Bradley cavalry scout vehicles, plus a FISTV track for forward observers to call in artillery support— somewhere behind him, the First Armored's artillery would be off-loading soon from its train, he hoped. His most valuable assets were D and E troops, each with eight OH-58D Kiowa Warrior helicopters, able both to scout ahead and to shoot with Hellfire and Stinger missiles. In short, his squadron could look after itself, within reasonable limits.

As they got closer, his troopers would become more cautious and circumspect, because good as they were, they were neither invincible nor immortal. America had fought against China only once, in Korea nearly sixty years earlier, and the experience had been satisfactory to neither side. For America, the initial Chinese attack had been unexpected and massive, forcing an ignominious retreat from the Yalu River. But for China, once America had gotten its act together, the experience had cost a million lives, because firepower was always the answer to raw numbers, and America's lasting lesson from its own Civil War was that it was better to expend *things* than to expend *people*. The American way of war was not shared by everyone, and in truth it was tailored to American material prosperity as much as to American reverence for human life, but it was the American way, and that was the way its warriors were schooled.

*　　　*　　　*

'I think it's about time to roll them back a little,' General Wallace observed over the satellite link to

Washington.

'What do you propose?' Mickey Moore asked.

'For starters, I want to send my F-16CGs after their radar sites. I'm tired of having them use radar to direct their fighters against my aircraft. Next, I want to start going after their logistical choke points. In twelve hours, the way things are going, I'll have enough ordnance to start doing some offensive warfare here. And it's about time for us to start, General,' Wallace said.

'Gus, I have to clear that with the President,' the Chairman told the Air Force commander in Siberia.

'Okay, fine, but tell him we damned near lost an AWACS yesterday—with a crew of thirty or so—and I'm not in a mood to write that many letters. We've been lucky so far, and an AWACS is a hard kill. Hell, it cost them a full regiment of fighters to fail in that mission. But enough's enough. I want to go after their radar sites, and I want to do some offensive counter-air.'

'Gus, the thinking here is that we want to commence offensive operations in a systematic way for maximum psychological effect. That means more than just knocking some antennas down.'

'General, I don't know what it looks like over there, but right here it's getting a little exciting. Their army is advancing rapidly. Pretty soon our Russian friends are going to have to make their stand. It'll be a whole lot easier if the enemy is short on gas and bullets.'

'We know that. We're trying to figure a way to shake up their political leadership.'

'It isn't politicians coming north trying to kill us, General. It's soldiers and airmen. We have to start

570

crippling them before they ruin our whole damned day.'

'I understand that, Gus. I will present your position to the President,' the Chairman promised.

'Do that, will ya?' Wallace killed the transmission, wondering what the hell the lotus-eaters in Washington were thinking about, assuming they were thinking at all. He had a plan, and he thought it was a pretty good systematic one. His Dark Star drones had given him all the tactical intelligence he needed. He knew what targets to hit, and he had enough ordnance to do the hitting, or at least to start doing it.

If they let me, Wallace thought.

*   *   *

'Well, it wasn't a complete waste,' Marshal Luo said. 'We got some pictures of what the Russians are doing.'

'And what's that?' Zhang asked.

'They're moving one or two—probably two—divisions northeast from their rail assembly point at Chita. We have good aerial pictures of them.'

'And still nothing in front of our forces?'

Luo shook his head. 'Our reconnaissance people haven't seen anything more than tracks in the ground. I have to assume there are Russians in those woods somewhere, doing reconnaissance of their own, but if so, they're light forces who're working very hard to keep out of the way. We know they've called up some reserves, but they haven't shown up either. Maybe their reservists didn't report. Morale in Russia is supposed to be very low, Tan tells us, and that's all we've really seen.

The men we captured are very disheartened because of their lack of support, and they didn't fight all that well. Except for the American airplanes, this war is going extremely well.'

'And they haven't attacked our territory yet?' Zhang wanted to be clear on that.

Another shake of the head. 'No, and I can't claim that they're afraid to do it. Their fighter aircraft are excellent, but to the best of our knowledge they haven't even attempted a photo-reconnaissance mission. Maybe they just depend on satellites now. Certainly those are supposed to be excellent sources of information for them.'

'And the gold mine?'

'We'll be there in thirty-six hours. And at that point we can make use of the roads their own engineers have been building to exploit the mineral finds. From the gold mine to the oil fields—five to seven days, depending on how well we can run supplies up.'

'This is amazing, Luo,' Zhang observed. 'Better than my fondest hopes.'

'I almost wish the Russians would stand and fight somewhere, so that we could have a battle and be done with it. As it is, my forces are stringing out somewhat, but only because the lead elements are racing forward so well. I've thought about slowing them down to maintain unit integrity, but—'

'But speed works for us, doesn't it?' Zhang observed.

'Yes, it would seem to,' the Defense Minister agreed. 'But one prefers to keep units tightly grouped in case there is some contact. However, if the enemy is running, one doesn't want to give him pause to regroup. So, I'm giving General Peng and his divisions free rein.'

'What forces are you facing?'

'We're not sure. Perhaps a regiment or so could be ahead of us, but we see no evidence of it, and two more regiments are trying to race ahead of us, or attack our flank, but we have flank security out to the west, and they've seen nothing.'

*   *   *

Bondarenko hoped that someday he'd meet the team that had developed this American Dark Star drone. Never in history had a commander possessed such knowledge as this, and without it he would have been forced to commit his slender forces to battle just to ascertain what stood against him. Not now. He probably had a better feel for the location of the advancing Chinese than their own commander did.

Better yet, the leading regiment of the 201st Motor Rifle Division was only a few kilometers away, and the leading formation was the division's steel fist, its independent tank regiment of ninety-five T-80U main-battle tanks.

The 265th was ready for the reinforcement, and its commander, Yuriy Sinyavskiy, proclaimed that he was tired of running away. A career professional soldier and mechanized infantryman, Sinyavskiy was a profane, cigar-chomping man of forty-six years, now leaning over a map table in Bondarenko's headquarters.

'This, this is my ground, Gennady Iosifovich,' he said, stabbing at the point with his finger. It was just five kilometers north of the Gogol Gold Field, a line of ridges twenty kilometers across, facing open ground the Chinese would have to cross. 'And put the Two-Oh-First's tanks just here on my right. When we stop their advance guard, they can blow in from the west and roll them up.'

'Reconnaissance shows their leading division is strung out somewhat,' Bondarenko told him.

It was a mistake made by every army in the world. The sharpest teeth of any field force are its artillery, but even self-propelled artillery, mounted on tracks for cross-country mobility, can't seem to keep up with the mechanized forces it is supposed to support. It was a lesson that had even surprised the Americans in the Persian Gulf, when they'd found their artillery could keep up with the leading tank echelons only with strenuous effort, and across flat ground. The People's Liberation Army had tracked artillery, but a lot of it was still the towed variety, and was being pulled behind trucks that could not travel cross-country as well as the tracked kind.

General Diggs observed the discussion, which his rudimentary Russian could not quite keep up with, and Sinyavskiy spoke no English, which really slowed things down.

'You still have a lot of combat power to stop, Yuriy Andreyevich,' Diggs pointed out, waiting for the translation to get across.

'If we cannot stop them completely, at least we can give them a bloody nose' was the belated reply.

'Stay mobile,' Diggs advised. 'If I were this General Peng, I'd maneuver east—the ground is better suited for it—and try to wrap you up from your left.'

'We will see how maneuver-minded they are,' Bondarenko said for his subordinate. 'So far all they have done is drive straight forward, and I think they are becoming complacent. See how they are stretched out, Marion. Their units are too far separated to provide mutual support. They are in a pursuit phase of warfare, and that makes them disorganized, *and* they have little air support to warn them of what lies ahead. I think Yuriy is right: This is a good place for a stand.'

'I agree it's good ground, Gennady, just don't marry the place, okay?' Diggs warned.

Bondarenko translated that for his subordinate, who answered back in machine-gun Russian around his cigar.

'Yuriy says it is a place for a fucking, not a wedding. When will you join your command, Marion?'

'My chopper's on the way in now, buddy. My cavalry screen is at the first fuel depot, with First Brigade right behind. We should be in contact in a day and a half or so.'

They'd already discussed Diggs's plan of attack. First Armored would assemble northwest of Belogorsk, fueling at the last big Russian depot, then leap out in the darkness for the Chinese bridgehead. Intelligence said that the PLA's 65th Type-B Group Army was there now, digging in to protect the left shoulder of their break-in. Not a mechanized force, it was still a lot for a single division to chew on. If the Chinese plan of attack had a weakness, it was that they'd bet all their mechanized forces on the drive forward. The forces left behind to secure the breakthrough were at best motorized—carried by wheeled vehicles instead of tracked ones—and at worst leg infantry, who had to walk where they went. That made them slow and vulnerable to men who sat down behind steel as they went to battle in their tracked vehicles.

But there were a hell of a lot of them, Diggs reminded himself.

Before he could leave, General Sinyavskiy reached into his hip pocket and pulled out a flask. 'A drink for luck,' he said in his only words of broken English.

'Hell, why not?' Diggs tossed it off. It was good stuff, actually. 'When this is all over, we will drink again,' he promised.

'*Da,*' the general replied. 'Good luck, Diggs.'

'Marion,' Bondarenko said. 'Be careful, comrade.'

'You, too, Gennady. You got enough medals, buddy. No sense getting your ass shot off trying to win another.'

'Generals are supposed to die in bed,' Bondarenko agreed on the way to the door.

Diggs trotted out to the UH-60. Colonel Boyle was flying this one. Diggs donned the crash helmet, wishing they'd come up with another name for the damned thing, and settled in the jump seat behind the pilots.

'How we doing, sir?' Boyle asked, letting the lieutenant take the chopper back off.

'Well, we have a plan, Dick. Question is, will it work?'

'Do I get let in on it?'

'Your Apaches are going to be busy.'

'There's a surprise,' Boyle observed.

'How are your people?'

'Ready' was the one-word reply. 'What are we calling this?'

'CHOPSTICKS.' Diggs then heard a laugh over the

intercom wire.

'I love it.'

*   *   *

'Okay, Mickey,' Robby Jackson said. 'I understand Gus's position. But we have a big picture here to think about.'

They were in the Situation Room looking at the Chairman on TV from the Pentagon room known as The Tank. It was hard to hear what he was muttering that way, but the way he looked down was a sufficient indication of his feelings about Robby's remark.

'General,' Ryan said, 'the idea here is to rattle the cage of their political leadership. Best way to do that is to go after them in more places than one, overload 'em.'

'Sir, I agree with that idea, but General Wallace has his point, too. Taking down their radar fence will degrade their ability to use their fighters against us, and they still have a formidable fighter force, even though we've handled them pretty rough so far.'

'Mickey, if you handle a girl this way down in Mississippi, it's called rape,' the Vice President observed. 'Their fighter pilots look at their aircraft now and they see caskets, for Christ's sake. Their confidence has got to be gone, and that's all a fighter jock has to hold onto. Trust me on this one, will ya?'

'But Gus—'

'But Gus is too worried about his force. Okay, fine, let him send some Charlie-Golfs against their picket fence, but mainly we want those birds armed

577

with Smart Pigs to go after their ground forces. The fighter force can look after itself.'

For the first time, General Mickey Moore regretted Ryan's choice of Vice President. Robby was thinking like a politician rather than an operational commander—and that came as something of a surprise. He was seemingly less worried about the safety of his forces than of . . .

. . . *than of what the overall objective was*, Moore corrected himself. And *that* was not a completely bad way to think, was it? Jackson had been a pretty good J-3 not so long before, hadn't he?

American commanders no longer thought of their men as expendable assets. That was not a bad thing at all, but sometimes you had to put forces in harm's way, and when you did that, some of them did not come home. And that was what they were paid for, whether you liked it or not. Robby Jackson had been a Navy fighter pilot, and he hadn't forgotten the warrior ethos, despite his new job and pay grade.

'Sir,' Moore said, 'what orders do I give General Wallace?'

*   *   *

'Cecil B. goddamned DeMille,' Mancuso observed crossly.

'Ever wanted to part the Red Sea?' General Lahr asked.

'I ain't God, Mike,' CINCPAC said next.

'Well, it *is* elegant, and we *do* have most of the pieces in place,' his J-2 pointed out.

'This is a political operation. What the hell are we, a goddamned focus group?'

'Sir, you going to continue to rant, or are we going to get to work on this?'

Mancuso wished for a *lupara* to blast a hole in the wall, or Mike Lahr's chest, but he *was* a uniformed officer, and he *did* now have orders from his Commander-in-Chief.

'All right. I just don't like to have other people design my operations.'

'And you know the guy.'

'Mike, once upon a time, back when I had three stripes and driving a submarine was all I had to worry about, Ryan and I helped steal a whole Russian submarine, yeah—and if you repeat that to anyone, I'll have one of my Marines shoot your ass. Sink some of their ships, yeah, splash a few of their airplanes, sure, but "trailing our coat" in sight of land? Jesus.'

'It'll shake them up some.'

'If they don't sink some of my ships in the attempt.'

*　　　*　　　*

'Hey, Tony,' the voice on the phone said. It took Bretano a second to recognize it.

'Where are you now, Al?' the Secretary of Defense asked.

'Norfolk. Didn't you know? I'm on USS *Gettysburg* upgrading their SAMs. It was your idea, wasn't it?'

'Well, yeah, I suppose it was,' Tony Bretano agreed, thinking back.

'You must have seen this Chinese thing coming a long way off, man.'

'As a matter of fact, we—' The SecDef paused

for a second. 'What do you mean?'

'I mean, if the ChiComms loft an ICBM at us, this Aegis system does give us something to fall back on, if the computer simulations are right. They ought to be. I wrote most of the software,' Gregory went on.

Secretary Bretano didn't want to admit that he hadn't really thought about that eventuality. Thinking things through was one of the things he was paid for, after all. 'How ready are you?'

'The electronics stuff is okay, but we don't have any SAMs aboard. They're stashed at some depot or something, up on the York River, I think they said. When they load them aboard, I can upgrade the software on the seeker heads. The only missiles aboard, the ones I've been playing with, they're blue ones, exercise missiles, not shooters, I just found out. You know, the Navy's a little weird. The ship's in a floating dry dock. They're going to lower us back in the water in a few hours.' He couldn't see his former boss's face at the moment. If he could, he would have recognized the *oh, shit* expression on his Italian face.

'So, you're confident in your systems?'

'A full-up test would be nice, but if we can loft three or four SAMs at the inbound, yeah, I think it oughta work.'

'Okay, thanks, Al.'

'So, how's this war going? All I see on TV is how the Air Force is kicking some ass.'

'They are, the TV's got that right, but the rest— can't talk about it over the phone. Al, let me get back to you, okay?'

'Yes, sir.'

In his office, Bretano switched buttons. 'Ask

Admiral Seaton to come in to see me.' That didn't take very long.

'You rang, Mr. Secretary,' the CNO said when he came in.

'Admiral, there's a former employee of mine from TRW in Norfolk right now. I set him up to look at upgrading the Aegis missile system to engage ballistic targets.'

'I heard a little about that. How's his project going?' Dave Seaton asked.

'He says he's ready for a full-up test. But, Admiral, what if the Chinese launch one of their CSS-4s at us?'

'It wouldn't be good,' Seaton replied.

'Then how about we take our Aegis ships and put them close to the likely targets?'

'Well, sir, the system's not certified for ballistic targets yet, and we haven't really run a test, and—'

'Is it better than nothing?' the SecDef asked, cutting him off.

'A little, I suppose.'

'Then let's make that happen, and make it happen right now.'

Seaton straightened up. 'Aye aye, sir.'

'*Gettysburg* first. Have her load up what missiles she needs, and bring her right here,' Bretano ordered.

'I'll call SACLANT right now.'

*   *   *

It was the strangest damned thing, Gregory thought. This ship—not an especially big ship, smaller than the one he and Candi had taken a cruise on the previous winter, but still an oceangoing *ship*—was in an elevator. That's what a floating dry dock was. They were flooding it now, to make it go down, back into the water to see if the new propeller worked. Sailors who worked on the dry dock were watching from their perches on—whatever the hell you called the walls of the damned thing.

'Weird, ain't it, sir?'

Gregory smelled the smoke. It had to be Senior Chief Leek. He turned. It was.

'Never seen this sort of thing before.'

'Nobody does real often, 'cept'n those guys over there who operate this thing. Did you take the chance to walk under the ship?'

'Walk *under* ten thousand tons of metal?' Gregory responded. 'I don't think so.'

'You was a soldier, wasn't you?'

'Told you, didn't I? West Point, jump school, ranger school, back when I was young and foolish.'

'Well, Doc, it's no big deal. Kinda interesting to see how she's put together, 'specially the sonar dome up forward. If I wasn't a radar guy, I probably woulda been a sonar guy, 'cept there's nothing for them to do anymore.

Gregory looked down. Water was creeping across the gray metal floor—*deck?* he wondered—of the dry dock.

'Attention on deck!' a voice called. Sailors turned and saluted, including Chief Leek.

It was Captain Bob Blandy *Gettysburg*'s CO. Gregory had met him only once, and then just to say hello.

'Dr. Gregory.'

'Captain.' They shook hands.

'How's your project been going?'

'Well, the simulations look good. I'd like to try it

against a live target.'

'You got sent to us by the SecDef?'

'Not exactly, but he called me in from California to look at the technical aspects of the problem. I worked for him when he was head of TRW.'

'You're an SDI guy, right?'

'That and SAMs, yes, sir. Other things. I'm one of the world's experts on adaptive optics, from my SDI days.'

'What's that?' Captain Blandy asked.

'The rubber mirror, we called it. You use computer-controlled actuators to warp the mirror to compensate for atmospheric distortions. The idea was to use that to focus the energy beam from a free-electron laser. But it didn't work out. The rubber mirror worked just fine, but for some reason we never figured out, the damned lasers didn't scale up the way we hoped they would. Didn't come up to the power requirements to smoke a missile body.' Gregory looked down in the dry dock again. It certainly took its time, but they probably didn't want to drop anything this valuable. 'I wasn't directly involved in that, but I kibitzed some. It turned out to be a monster of a technical problem. We just kept bashing our heads against the wall until we got tired of the squishy sound.'

'I know mechanical engineering, some electrical, but not the high-energy stuff. So, what do you think of our Aegis system?'

'I love the radar. Just like the Cobra Dane the Air Force has up at Shemya in the Aleutians. A little more advanced, even. You could probably bounce a signal off the moon if you wanted to.'

'That's a little out of our range gate,' Blandy observed. 'Chief Leek here been taking good care of you?'

'When he leaves the Navy, we might have a place for him at TRW. We're part of the ongoing SAM project.'

'And Lieutenant Olson, too?' the skipper asked.

'He's a very bright young officer, Captain. I can think of a lot of companies who might want him.' If Gregory had a fault, it was being too truthful.

'I ought to say something to discourage you from that, but—'

'Cap'n!' A sailor came up. 'Flash-traffic from SACLANT, sir.' He handed over a clipboard. Captain Blandy signed the acknowledgment sheet and took the message. His eyes focused very closely.

'Do you know if the SecDef knows what you're up to?'

'Yes, Captain, he does. I just spoke to Tony a few minutes ago.'

'What the hell did you tell him?'

Gregory shrugged. 'Not much, just that the project was coming along nicely.'

'Uh-huh. Chief Leek, how's your hardware?'

'Everything's a hundred percent on line, Cap'n. We got a job, sir?' the senior chief asked.

'Looks like it. Dr. Gregory, if you will excuse me, I have to see my officers. Chief, we're going to be getting under way soon. If any of your troops are on the beach, call 'em back. Spread the word.'

'Aye aye, sir.' He saluted as Captain Blandy hustled back forward. 'What's that all about?'

'Beats me, Chief.'

'What do I do? Getting under way?' Gregory asked.

'Got your toothbrush? If not, you can buy one in

the ship's store. Excuse me, Doc, I have to do a quick muster.' Leek tossed his cigarette over the side and went the same way that the captain had.

And there was precisely nothing for Gregory to do. There was no way for him to leave the ship, except to jump down into the flooding floating dry dock, and that didn't look like a viable option. So, he headed back into the superstructure and found the ship's store open. There he bought a toothbrush.

* * *

Bondarenko spent the next three hours with Major General Sinyavskiy, going over approach routes and fire plans.

'They have fire-finder radar, Yuriy, and their counter-battery rockets have a long reach.'

'Can we expect any help from the Americans?'

'I'm working on that. We have superb reconnaissance information from their movie-star drones.'

'I need the location of their artillery. If we can take that away from them, it makes my job much easier.'

'Tolkunov!' the theater commander yelled. It was loud enough that his intelligence coordinator came running.

'Yes, Comrade General!'

'Vladimir Konstantinovich, we'll be making our stand here,' Bondarenko said, pointing to a red line on the map. 'I want minute-to-minute information of the approaching Chinese formations—especially their artillery.'

'I can do that. Give me ten minutes.' And the

585

G-2 disappeared back out to where the Dark Star terminal was. Then his boss thought about it.

'Come on, Yuriy, you have to see this.'

'General,' Major Tucker said by way of greeting. Then he saw a second one. 'General,' he said again.

'This is General Sinyavskiy. He commands Two-Six-Five. Would you please show him the advancing Chinese?' It wasn't a question or a request, just phrased politely because Tucker was a foreigner.

'Okay, it's right here, sir, we've got it all on videotape. Their leading reconnaissance elements are . . . here, and their leading main-force units are right here.'

'Fuck,' Sinyavskiy observed in Russian. 'Is this magic?'

'No, this is—' Bondarenko switched languages. 'Which unit is this, Major?'

'Grace Kelly again, sir. *To Catch a Thief* with Cary Grant, Hitchcock movie that one was. The sun'll be down in another hour or so and we'll be getting it all on the thermal-imaging systems. Anyway, here's their leading battalion, all look like their Type-90 tanks. They're keeping good formation discipline, and they just refueled about an hour ago, so, figure they're good for another two hundred or so kilometers before they stop again.'

'Their artillery?'

'Lagging behind, sir, except for this tracked unit here.' Tucker played with the mouse some and brought up another picture.

'Gennady Iosifovich, how can we fail with such information?' the division commander asked.

'Yuriy remember when we thought about attacking the Americans?'

586

'Madness. The Chinks can't see this drone?' Sinyavskiy asked, somewhat incredulously.

'It's stealthy, as they call it, invisible on radar.'

'*Nichevo.*'

'Sir, I have a direct line to our headquarters at Zhigansk. If you guys are going to make a stand, what do you want from us?' Tucker asked. 'I can forward your request to General Wallace.'

'I have thirty Su-25 attack bombers and also fifty Su-24 fighter bombers standing by, plus two hundred Mi-24 helicopters.' Getting the last in theater had been agonizingly slow, but finally they were here, and they were the Ace of Diamonds Bondarenko had facedown on the card table. He hadn't let so much as one approach the area of operations yet, but they were two hundred kilometers away, fueled and armed, their flight crews flying to practice their airmanship and shooting live weapons as rehearsal—for some, the first live weapons they'd ever shot.

'That's going to be a surprise for good old Joe,' Tucker observed with a whistle. 'Where'd you hide them, sir? Hell, General, I didn't know they were around.'

'There are a few secure places. We want to give our guests a proper greeting when the time is right,' Gennady Iosifovich told the young American officer.

'So, what do you want us to do, sir?'

'Take down their logistics. Show me this Smart Pig you've been talking to Colonel Tolkunov about.'

'That we can probably do, sir,' Tucker said. 'Let me get on the phone to General Wallace.'

'So, they're turning me loose?' Wallace asked.

'As soon as contact is imminent between Russian and Chinese ground forces.' Mickey Moore then gave him his targets. 'It's most of the things you wanted to hit, Gus.'

'I suppose,' the Air Force commander allowed, somewhat grudgingly. 'And if the Russians ask for help?'

'Give it to them, within reason.'

'Right.'

*   *   *

LTC Giusti, SABRE SIX, got off the helicopter at the Number Two fueling point and walked toward General Diggs.

'They weren't kidding,' Colonel Masterman was saying. 'This *is* a fuckin' lake.' One and a quarter *billion* liters translated to more than three hundred million gallons, or nearly a million tons of fuel, about the carrying capacity of four supertankers, all of Number Two Diesel, or close enough that the fuel injectors on his tanks and Bradleys wouldn't notice the difference. The manager of the site, a civilian, had said that the fuel had been there for nearly forty years, since Khrushchev had had a falling-out with Chairman Mao, and the possibility of war with the *other* communist country had turned from an impossibility into a perceived likelihood. Either it was remarkable prescience or paranoid wish fulfillment, but in either case it worked to the benefit of First Armored Division.

The off-loading facilities could have been better,

but the Soviets evidently hadn't had much experience with building gas stations. It was more efficient to pump the fuel into the division's fuel bowsers, which then motored off to fill the tanks and tracks four or six at a time.

'Okay, Mitch, what do we have on the enemy?' General Diggs asked his intelligence officer.

'Sir, we've got a Dark Star tasked directly to us now, and she'll be up for another nine hours. We're up against a leg-infantry division. They're forty kilometers that way, mainly sitting along this line of hills. There's a regiment of ChiComm tanks supporting them.'

'Artillery?'

'Some light and medium, all of it towed, setting up now, with fire-finder radars we need to worry about,' Colonel Turner warned. 'I've asked General Wallace to task some F-16s with HARMs to us. They can tune the seekers on those to the millimeter-band the fire-finders use.'

'Make that happen,' Diggs ordered.

'Yes, sir.'

'Duke, how long to contact?' the general asked his operations officer.

'If we move on schedule, we'll be in their neighborhood about zero-two-hundred.'

'Okay, let's get the brigade commanders briefed in. We party just after midnight,' Diggs told his staff, not even regretting his choice of words. He was a soldier about to go into combat, and with that came a different and not entirely pleasant way of thinking.

CHAPTER FIFTY-SEVEN

HYPERWAR

It had been rather a tedious couple of days for USS *Tucson*. She'd been camped out on *406* for sixteen days, and was holding station seventeen thousand yards—eight and a half nautical miles—astern of the Chinese boomer, with a nuclear-powered fast-attack camped out just to the south of it at the moment. The SSN, at least, supposedly had a name, *Hai Long*, the intelligence weenies said it was. But to *Tucson*'s sonarman, *406* was Sierra-Eleven, and *Hai Long* was Sierra-Twelve, and so they were known to the fire-control tracking party.

Tracking both targets was not demanding. Though both had nuclear power plants, the reactor systems were noisy, especially the feed pumps that ran cooling water through the nuclear pile. That, plus the sixty-hertz generators, made for two pairs of bright lines on the waterfall sonar display, and tracking both was about as difficult as watching two blind men in an empty shopping mall parking lot at high noon on a cloudless day. But it was more interesting than tracking whales in the North Pacific, which some of PACFLT's boats had been tasked to do of late, to keep the tree-huggers happy.

Things had gotten a little more interesting lately. *Tucson* ran to periscope/antenna depth twice a day, and the crew had learned, much to everyone's surprise, that Chinese and American armed forces were trading shots in Siberia, and *that* meant, the crew figured, that *406* might have to be made to disappear, and *that* was a mission, and while it might not exactly be fun, it was what they were paid to do, which made it a worthwhile activity.

406 had submarine-launched ballistic missiles aboard, twelve Ju Lang-1 CSS-N-3s, each with a single megaton-range warhead. The name meant 'Great Wave,' so the intelligence book said. It also said they had a range of less than three thousand kilometers, which was less than half the range needed to strike California, though it could hit Guam, which was American territory. That didn't really matter. What did matter was that *406* and *Hai Long* were ships of war belonging to a nation with which the United States was now trading shots.

The VLS radio fed off an antenna trailed off the after corner of *Tucson*'s sail, and it received transmissions from a monstrous, mainly underground transmitter located in Michigan's Upper Peninsula. The tree-huggers complained that the energy emanating from this radio confused migrating geese in the fall, but no hunters had yet complained about smaller bags of waterfowl, and so the radio remained in service. Built to send messages to American missile submarines, it still transmitted to the fast-attacks that remained in active service. When a transmission was received, a bell went off in the submarine's communications room, located aft of the attack center, on the starboard side.

The bell *ding*ed. The sailor on watch called his officer, a lieutenant, j.g., who in turn called the captain, who took the submarine back up to antenna depth. Once there, he elevated the

591

communications laser to track in on the Navy's own communications satellite, known as SSIX, the Submarine Satellite Information Exchange, telling it that he was ready for a transmission. The reply action message came over a directional S-band radio for the higher bandwidth. The signal was cross-loaded into the submarine's crypto machines, decoded, and printed up.

TO: USS TUCSON (SSN-770)
FROM: CINCPAC

1. UPON RECEIVING 'XQT SPEC OP' SIGNAL FROM VLS YOU WILL ENGAGE AND DESTROY PRC SSBN AND ANY PRC SHIPS IN CONTACT.
2. REPORT RESULTS OF ATTACK VIA SSIX.
3. SUBSEQUENT TO THIS OPERATION, CONDUCT UNRESTRICTED OPERATIONS AGAINST PRC NAVAL UNITS.
4.YOU WILL NOT RPT NOT ENGAGE COMMERCIAL TRAFFIC OF ANY KIND.
CINCPAC SENDS

END MESSAGE

'Well, it's about goddamned time,' the CO observed to his executive officer.

'Doesn't say when to expect it,' the XO observed.

'Call it two hours,' the captain said. 'Let's close to ten thousand yards. Get the troops perked up. Spin up the weapons.'

'Aye.'

'Anything else close?'

'There's a Chinese frigate off to the north, about thirty miles.'

'Okay, after we do the subs, we'll Harpoon that one, then we'll close to finish it off, if necessary.'

'Right.' The XO went forward to the attack center. He checked his watch. It was dark topside. It didn't really matter to anyone aboard the submarine, but darkness made everybody feel a little more secure for some reason or other, even the XO.

*　　　*　　　*

It was tenser now. Giusti's reconnaissance troopers were now within twenty miles of the expected Chinese positions. That put them inside artillery range, and that made the job serious.

The mission was to advance to contact, and to find a hole in the Chinese positions for the division to exploit. The secondary objective was to shoot through the gap and break into the Chinese logistical area, just over the river from where they'd made their breakthrough. There they would rape and pillage, as LTC Giusti thought of it, probably turning north to roll up the Chinese rear with one or two brigades, and probably leaving the third to remain in place astride the Chinese line of communications as a blocking force.

His troopers had all put on their 'makeup,' as some called it, their camouflage paint, darkening the natural light spots of the face and lightening the dark ones. It had the overall effect of making them look like green and black space aliens. The advance would be mounted, for the most part, with the cavalry scouts mostly staying in their Bradleys and depending on the thermal-imaging viewers used by the driver and gunner to spot enemies. They'd be jumping out occasionally, though, and so everyone checked his PVS-11 personal night-vision system. Every trooper had three sets of fresh AA batteries that were as important as the magazines for their M16A2 rifles. Most of the men gobbled down an MRE ration and chased it with water, and often some aspirin or Tylenol to ward off minor aches and pains that might come from bumps or sprains. They all traded looks and jokes to lighten the stress of the night, plus the usual brave words meant as much for themselves as for others. Sergeants and junior officers reminded the men of their training, and told them to be confident in their abilities.

Then, on radioed command, the Bradleys started off, leading the heavier main-battle tanks off to the enemy, moving initially at about ten miles per hour.

The squadron's helicopters were up, all sixteen of them, moving very cautiously because armor on a helicopter is about as valuable as a sheet of newspaper, and because someone on the ground only needed a thermal-imaging viewer to see them, and a heat-seeking missile would snuff them out of the sky. The enemy had light flak, too, and that was just as deadly.

The OH-58D Kiowa Warriors had good night-vision systems, and in training the flight crews had learned to be confident of them, but people didn't often die in training. Knowing that there were people out there with live weapons and the orders to make use of them made everyone discount some of the lessons they'd learned. Getting shot down in one of those exercises meant being told over the radio to land, and maybe getting a tongue-lashing from the company commander for screwing up, which usually ended with a reminder that in real combat operations, he'd be dead, his wife a widow, and his children orphans. But they weren't, really, and so those words were never taken as seriously as they were now. Now it could be real, and all of the flight crews had wives or sweethearts, and most of them had children as well.

And so they moved forward, using their own night-vision equipment to sweep the ground ahead, their hands a little more tingly than usual on the controls.

*   *   *

Division Headquarters had its own Dark Star terminal set up, with an Air Force captain running it. Diggs didn't much like being so far in the rear with his men going out in harm's way, but command wasn't the same thing as leadership. He'd been told that years before at Fort Leavenworth's Command and General Staff School, and he'd experienced it in Saudi Arabia only the previous year, but even so, he felt the need to be out forward, close to his men, so that he could share the danger with them. But the best way for him to mitigate the danger to them was to stay back here and establish effective control over operations, along with Colonel Masterman.

'Cookstoves?' Masterman asked.

'Yep,' the USAF captain—his name was Frank

Williams—agreed. 'And these bright ones are campfires. Cool night. Ground temperature's about forty-three degrees, air temperature is forty-one. Good contrast for the thermal viewing systems. They seem to use the kind of stoves we had in the Boy Scouts. Damn, there's a bunch of 'em. Like hundreds.'

'Got a hole in their lines?'

'Looks thin right here, 'tween these two hills. They have a company on this hilltop, and another company here—I bet they're in different battalions,' Williams said. 'Always seems to work that way. The gap between them looks like a little more 'n a kilometer, but there's a little stream at the bottom.'

'Bradleys don't mind getting a little wet,' Diggs told the junior officer. 'Duke?'

'Best bet for a blow-through I've seen so far. Aim Angelo for it?'

Diggs thought about that. It meant committing his cavalry screen, and that also meant committing at least one of his brigades, but such decisions were what generals were for. 'What else is around?'

'I'd say their regimental headquarters is right about here, judging by the tents and trucks. You're going to want to hit it with artillery, I expect.

'Right about the time QUARTER HORSE gets there. No sense alerting them too soon,' Masterman suggested. General Diggs thought it over one more time and made his first important decision of the night:

'Agreed. Duke, tell Giusti to head for that gap.'

'Yes, sir.' Colonel Masterman moved off toward the radios. They were doing this on the fly, which wasn't exactly the way they preferred, but that was often the world of real-time combat operations.

'Roger,' Diggs called.

Colonel Roger Ardan was his divisional artillery commander—GUNFIGHTER SIX on the divisional radio net—a tall thin man, rather like a not-tall-enough basketball player.

'Yes, sir.'

'Here's your first fire mission. We're going to shoot Angelo Giusti through this gap. Company of infantry here and here, and what appears to be a regimental command post here.'

'Enemy artillery?'

'Some one-twenty-twos here, and what looks like two-oh-threes, eight inch, right here.'

'No rocket-launchers?'

'None I've seen yet. That's a little odd, but they're not around that I can see,' Captain Williams told the gunner.

'What about radars?' Colonel Ardan asked.

'Maybe one here, but hard to tell. It's under some camo nets.' Williams selected the image with his mouse and expanded it.

'We'll take that one on general principles. Put a pin in it,' Ardan said.

'Yes, sir. Print up a target list?'

'You bet, son.'

'Here you go,' Williams said. A command generated two sheets of paper out of the adjacent printer, with latitude-longitude positions down to the second of angle. The captain handed it across.

'How the hell did we ever survive without GPS and overheads?' Ardan wondered aloud. 'Okay, General, this we can do. When?'

'Call it thirty minutes.'

'We'll be ready,' GUNFIGHTER promised. 'I'll

597

TOT the regimental command post.'

'Sounds good to me,' Diggs observed.

*   *   *

First Armored had a beefed-up artillery brigade. The second and the third battalions of the First Field Artillery Regiment had the new Paladin self-propelled 155-mm howitzer, and the 2nd Battalion, 6th Field Artillery, had self-propelled eight-inch, plus the division's Multiple Launch Rocket System tracks, which ordinarily were under the direct order of the divisional commander, as his personal shotgun. These units were six miles behind the leading cavalry troops, and on order left the roads they were on and pulled off to firing positions north and south of the gravel track. Each of them had a Global Positioning Satellite, or GPS, receiver, and these told them where they were located down to an accuracy of less than three meters. A transmission over the joint Tactical Information Distribution System, or J-TIDS, told them the locations of their targets, and onboard computers computed azimuth and range to them. Then they learned the shell selection, either 'common' high-explosive or VT (for variable-time). These were loaded and the guns trained onto the distant targets, and the gunners just waited for the word to pull the strings. Their readiness was radioed back to the divisional HQ.

*   *   *

'All set, sir,' Colonel Ardan reported.

'Okay, we'll wait to see how Angelo's doing.'

598

'Your screen is right here,' Captain Williams told the senior officers. For him it was like being in a skybox at a football game, except that one team didn't know he was there, and didn't know the other team was on the field as well. 'They're within three kicks of the enemy's first line of outposts.'

'Duke, tell Angelo. Get it out on the IVIS.'

'Done,' Masterman replied. The only thing they couldn't do was cross-deck the 'take' from the Dark Star drone.

*   *   *

SABRE SIX was now in his Bradley instead of the safer Abrams main-battle tank. He could see better out of this one, Giusti judged.

'IVIS is up,' the track commander called. Colonel Giusti ducked down and twisted around the gun-turret structure to see where the sergeant was sitting. Whoever had designed the Bradley hadn't considered that a senior officer might use it—and his squadron didn't have one of the new 'God' tracks yet, with the IVIS display in the back.

'First enemy post is right over there, sir, at eleven o'clock, behind this little rise,' the sergeant said, tapping the screen.

'Well, let's go say hi.'

'Roger that, Colonel. Kick it, Charlie,' he told the driver. For the rest of the crew: 'Perk it up, people. Heads up. We're in Indian Country.'

*   *   *

'How are things up north?' Diggs asked Captain Williams.

599

'Let's see.' The captain deselected Marilyn Monroe and switched over to the 'take' from Grace Kelly. 'Here we go, the leading Chinese elements are within fifteen klicks of the Russians. Looks like they're settled in for the night, though. Looks like we'll be in contact first.'

'Oh, well.' Diggs shrugged. 'Back to Miss Monroe.'

'Yes, sir.' More computer maneuvers. 'Here we are. Here's your leading cavalry element, two klicks from John Chinaman's first hole in the ground.'

Diggs had grown up watching boxing on TV. His father had been a real fan of Muhammad Ali, but even when Ali had lost to Leon Spinks, he'd known the other guy was in the ring with him. Not now. The camera zoomed in to isolate the hole. There were two men there. One was hunched down smoking a cigarette, and that must have ruined the night vision of one of them, maybe both, which explained why they hadn't seen anything yet, though they ought to have heard something . . . the Brad wasn't all that quiet . . .

'There, he just woke up a little,' Williams said. On the TV screen, the head turned abruptly. Then the other head came up, and the bright point of the cigarette went flying off to their right front. Giusti's track was coming in from their left, and now both heads were oriented in that general direction.

'How close can you get?' Diggs asked.

'Let's see . . .' In five seconds, the two nameless Chinese infantrymen in their hand-dug foxhole took up half the screen. Then Williams did a split screen, like the picture-in-picture feature of some television sets. The big part showed the two doomed soldiers, and the little one was locked on

600

the leading Bradley Scout, whose gun turret was now turning a little to the left . . . about eleven hundred meters now . . .

They had a field phone in the hole, Diggs could see now, sitting on the dirt between the two grunts. Their hole was the first in the enemy combat outpost line, and their job would have been to report back when something evil this way came. They heard something, but they weren't sure what it was, were probably waiting until they saw it. *The PLA didn't have night-vision goggles, at least not at this level*, Diggs thought. That was important information. 'Okay, back it off.'

'Right, sir.' Williams dumped the close-up of the two grunts, returning to the picture that showed both them and the approaching Brad. Diggs was sure that Giusti's gunner could see them now. It was just a question of when he chose to take the first shot, and that was a call for the guy in the field to make, wasn't it?

'There!' The muzzle of the 25-mm chain gun flashed three times, causing the TV screen to flare, and there was a line of the tracers, streaking to the hole—

—and the two grunts were dead, killed by three rounds of high-explosive incendiary-tracer ammunition. Diggs turned.

'GUNFIGHTER, commence firing!'

'Fire!' Colonel Ardan said into his microphone. Moments later, the ground shook under their feet, and a few seconds after that came the distant sound of thunder, and more than ninety shells started arcing into the air.

*　　　*　　　*

601

Colonel Ardan had ordered a TOT, or time-on-target barrage, on the regimental command post behind the small pass that the Quarter Horse was driving for. An American invention from World War II, TOT was designed so that every round fired from the various guns targeted on the single spot on the map would arrive at the same instant, and so deny the people there the chance to dive for cover at the first warning. In the old days, that had meant laboriously computing the flight time of every single shell, but computers did that now in less time than it took to frame the thought. This particular mission had fallen to 2nd/6th and its eight-inchers, universally regarded as the most accurate heavy guns in the United States Army. Two of the shells were common impact-fused high-explosive, and the other ten were VT. That stood for 'variable time,' but really meant that in the nose of each shell was a tiny radar transponder set to explode the shell when it was about fifty feet off the ground. In this way, the fragments lancing away from the exploding shell were not wasted into the ground, but instead made an inverted cone of death about two hundred feet across at its base. The common shells would have the effect of making craters, immolating those who might be in individual shelter holes.

Captain Williams switched Marilyn's focus to the enemy command post. From a high perspective the thermal cameras even caught the bright dots of the shells racing through the night. Then the camera zoomed back in on the target. By Diggs's estimation, all of the shells landed in less than two seconds. The effects were horrific. The six tents there evaporated, and the glowing green stick figures of human beings fell flat and stopped moving. Some pieces separated from one another, an effect Diggs had never seen.

'Whoa!' Williams observed. 'Stir-fry.'

What was *it about the Air Force*? General Diggs wondered. *Or maybe it was just the kid's youth.*

On the screen, some people were still moving, having miraculously survived the first barrage, but instead of moving around (or of running away, because artillery barrages didn't arrive in groups of only one) they remained at their posts, some looking to the needs of the wounded. It was courageous, but it doomed most of them to death. The only one or two people in the regimental command post who were going to live were the ones who'd pick winning lottery tickets later in life. If there were going to be as many as two, that is. The second barrage landed twenty-eight seconds after the first, and then a third thirty-one seconds after that, according to the time display in the upper right corner of the screen.

'Lord have mercy,' Colonel Ardan observed in a whisper. He'd never in his career seen the effect of fire in this way. It had always been a distant, detached thing to the cannon-cocker, but now he saw what his guns actually did.

'Target, cease fire,' Diggs said, using tanker-talk for *It's dead, you killed it, find another one.* A year before in the sands of Saudi Arabia, he'd watched combat on a computer screen and felt the coldness of war, but this was infinitely worse. This was like watching a Hollywood special-effects movie, but it wasn't computer-generated animation. He'd just watched the command section of an infantry

603

regiment, perhaps forty people, erased from the face of the earth in less than ninety seconds, and they had, after all, been human beings, something this young Air Force captain didn't seem to grasp. To him it was doubtless some sort of Nintendo game. Diggs decided that it was probably better to think of it that way.

The two infantry companies on the hilltops north and south of the little pass were clobbered by a full battery each. The next question was what that would generate. With the regimental CP down, things might get a little confusing for the divisional commander. Somebody would hear the noise, and if someone from regiment had been on the phone, the disconnect first of all would make people think, *huh*, because that was the normal human reaction, even for soldiers in a combat zone; bad phone connections were probably the rule rather than the exception, and they'd probably use phones rather than radios because they were more secure and more reliable—except when shellfire killed the phone and/or cut the lines. So, the enemy division commander was probably just waking up with a tug on his shoulder, then he'd be a little confused by what he was told.

'Captain, do we know where the enemy's divisional CP is yet?'

'Probably right here, sir. Not completely sure, but there's a bunch of trucks.'

'Show me on a map.'

'Here, sir.' The computer screen again. Diggs had a sudden thought: This young Air Force officer might eat his meals off it. More to the point, the CP was just in range of his MLRS batteries. And it had a lot of radio masts. Yeah, that was where the

ChiComm general was.

'GUNFIGHTER, I want this hit right now.'

'Yes, sir.' And the command went out over JTIDS to the 2nd/6th Field Artillery. The MLRS tracks were already set up awaiting orders, and the target assigned was well within the stewing angle for their launchers. The range, forty-three kilometers, was just within their capability. Here also the work was done by computer. The crewmen trained the weapons on the correct azimuth, locked their suspension systems to stabilize the vehicles, and closed the shutters on their windows to protect against blast and the ingress of the rocket exhaust smoke, which was lethal when breathed. Then it was just a matter of pushing the red firing button, which happened on command of the battery commander, and all nine vehicles unleashed their twelve rockets each, about a second apart, every one of which contained 644 grenade-sized submunitions, all targeted on an area the size of three football fields.

The effect of this, Diggs saw three minutes after giving the order, was nearly seventy *thousand* individual explosions in the target area, and as bad as it had been for the regimental CP, that had been trick or treat compared to this. Whatever division he'd been facing was now as thoroughly decapitated as though by Robespierre himself.

*   *   *

After the initial fire, Lieutenant Colonel Giusti found that he had no targets. He sent one troop through the gap while holding the north side of it himself, taking no fire at all. The falling 155s on the hills to his front and rear explained much of that, for surely it was a storm of steel and explosives. Someone somewhere fired off a parachute flare, but nothing developed from it. Twenty minutes after the initial barrage, the leading elements of First Brigade came into view. He waited until they were within a hundred meters before pulling off to the east to rejoin his squadron in the shallow valley. He was now technically inside enemy lines, but as with the first good hit in a football game, the initial tension was now gone, and there was a job to be done.

*   *   *

Dick Boyle, like most aviators, was qualified in more than one sort of aircraft and he could have chosen to fly-lead the mission in an Apache, which was one of the really enjoyable experiences for a rotary-wing pilot, but instead he remained in his UH-60 Blackhawk, the better to observe the action. His target was the independent tank brigade which was the organizational fist of the 65th Type B Group Army, and to service that target he had twenty-eight of his forty-two AH-64D Apache attack helicopters, supported by twelve Kiowa Warriors and one other Blackhawk.

The Chinese tank force was twenty miles northwest of their initial crossing point, agreeably sitting in open ground in circular formation so as to have guns pointing in all directions, none of which were a matter of concern to Dick Boyle and his men. It had probably made sense to laager them that way forty years ago, but not today, not in the night with Apaches nearby. With his OH-58Ds playing the scout role, the attack formation swept in from the north, down the valley. Whatever colonel was in command of this force had selected a place from which he could move to support any of the divisions in the 65th Army, but that merely concentrated his vehicles in a single spot, about five hundred meters across. Boyle's only worry was SAMs and maybe flak, but he had Dark Star photos to tell him where that all was, and he had a team of four Apaches delegated to handle the threat first of all.

It was in the form of two missile batteries. One was composed of four DK-9 launchers very similar to the American Chaparral, with four Sidewinder-class heat-seekers mounted on a tracked chassis. Their range would be about seven miles, just a touch longer than the effective range of his Hellfire missiles. The other was their HQ-61A, which Boyle thought of as the Chinese version of the Russian SA-6. There were fewer of these, but they had ten miles of range and supposedly a very capable radar system, and also had a hard floor of about a hundred meters, below which they couldn't track a target, which was a good thing to know, if true. His tactic would be to detect them and take them out as quickly as possible, depending on his EH-60 electronic-intelligence helicopter to sniff them out. The code for one of these was HOLIDAY. The heat-seekers were called DUCKS.

The Chinese soldiers on the ground would also have simple man-portable heat-seekers that were about as capable as the old American Redeye missile, but his Apaches had suppressed exhausts that were expected to defeat the heat-seekers—and those who had voiced the expectations weren't flying tonight. They never did.

*   *   *

There were more air missions tonight, and not all of them were over Russian territory. Twenty F-117A Stealth fighters had deployed to Zhigansk, and they'd mainly sat on the ground since their first arrival, waiting for bombs to be flown over, along with the guidance package attachments that changed them from simple ballistic weapons to smart bombs that went deliberately for a special piece of real estate. The special weapons for the Black Jets were the GBU-27 laser-guided hard-target penetrators. These were designed not merely to hit objects and explode, but to lance inside them before detonating, and they had special targets. There were twenty-two such targets tonight, all located in or near the cities of Harbin and Bei'an, and every one was a railroad bridge abutment.

The People's Republic depended more on its rail transportation than most countries, because it lacked the number of motor vehicles to necessitate the construction of highways, and also because the inherent efficiency of railroads appealed to the economic model in the heads of its political leaders. They did not ignore the fact that such a dependence on a single transportation modality could make them vulnerable to attack, and so at every potential chokepoint, like river crossings, they'd used the ample labor force of their country to build multiple bridges, all of heavily-built rebarred concrete abutments. *Surely*, they'd thought, *six separate crossing points at a single river couldn't* all *be damaged beyond timely repair.*

The Black Jets refueled from the usual KC-135 tanker aircraft and continued south, unseen by the radar fence erected by the PRC government along its northeastern border, and kept going. The heavily automated aircraft continued to their destinations on autopilot. They even made their bombing runs on autopilot, because it was too much to expect a pilot, however skilled, both to fly the aircraft and guide the infrared laser whose invisible grounded dot the bomb's seeker-head sought out. The attacks were made almost simultaneously, just a minute apart from east to west at the six parallel bridges over the Songhua Jiang River at Harbin. Each bridge had major pier abutments on the north and south bank. Both were attacked in each case. The bomb drops were easier than contractor tests, given the clear air and the total lack of defensive interference. In every case, the first set of six bombs fell true, striking the targets at Mach-1 speed and penetrating in for a distance of twenty-five to thirty feet before exploding. The weapons each had 535 pounds of Tritonal explosive. Not a particularly large quantity, in tight confinement it nevertheless generated hellish power, rupturing the hundred of tons of concrete around it like so much porcelain, albeit without the noise one would expect from such an event.

Not content with this destruction, the second team of F-117s struck at the northern abutments, and smashed them as well. The only lives directly lost were those of the engineer and fireman of a northbound diesel locomotive pulling a trainload of ammunition for the army group across the Amur

River, who were unable to stop their train before running over the edge.

The same performance was repeated in Bei'an, where five more bridges were dropped into the Wuyur He River, and in this dual stroke, which had lasted a mere twenty-one minutes, the supply line to the Chinese invasion force was sundered for all time to come. The eight aircraft left over—they'd been a reserve force in case some of the bombs should fail to destroy their targets—headed for the loop siding near the Amur used by tank cars. This was, oddly enough, not nearly as badly hit as the bridges, since the deep-penetrating bombs went too far into the ground to create much of surface craters, though some train cars were upset, and one of them caught fire. All in all, it had been a routine mission for the F-117s. Attempts to engage them with the SAM batteries in the two cities failed because the aircraft never appeared on the search-radar screens, and a missile launch was not even attempted.

*   *   *

The bell went off again, and the ELF message printed up as EQT SPEC OP or 'execute special operation' in proper English. *Tucson* was now nine thousand yards behind Sierra-Eleven, and fifteen from Sierra-Twelve.

'We're going to do one fish each. Firing order Two, One. Do we have a solution light?' the captain asked.

'Valid solutions for both fish,' the weapons officer replied.

'Ready Tube Two.'

'Tube Two is ready in all respects, tube flooded, outer door is open, sir.'

'Very well. Match generated bearings and . . . shoot!'

The handle was turned on the proper console. 'Tube Two fired electrically, sir.' *Tucson* shuddered through her length with the sudden explosion of compressed air that ejected the weapon into the seawater.

'Unit is running hot, straight, and normal, sir,' Sonar reported.

'Very well, ready Tube One,' the captain said next.

'Tube One is ready in all respects, tube is flooded, outer door is open,' Weps announced again.

'Very well. match generated bearings and shoot!' This command came as something of an exclamation. The captain figured he owed it to the crew, which was at battle stations, of course.

'Tube One fired electrically, sir,' the petty officer announced after turning the handle again, with exactly the same physical effect on the ship.

'Unit Two running hot, straight, and normal, sir,' Sonar said again. And with that, the captain took the five steps to the Sonar Room.

'Here we go, Cap'n,' the leading sonarman said, pointing to the glass screen with a yellow grease pencil.

The nine thousand yards' distance to *406* translated to four and a half nautical miles. The target was traveling at a depth of less than a hundred feet, maybe transmitting to its base on the radio or something, and steaming along at a bare five knots, judging by the blade count. That worked out to a running time of just under five minutes for the first target, and then another hundred sixty seconds or so to the second one. The second shot would probably get a little more complicated than the first. Even if they failed to hear the Mark 48 ADCAP torpedo coming, a deaf man could not miss the sound of 800 pounds of Torpex going off underwater three miles away, and he'd try to maneuver, or do something more than break out the worry beads and say a few Hail Maos, or whatever prayer these people said. The captain leaned back into the attack center.

'Reload ADCAP into Tube Two, and a Harpoon into Tube One.'

'Aye, Cap'n,' the Weapons Officer acknowledged.

'Where's that frigate?' he asked the lead sonarman.

'Here, sir, Luda-class, an old clunker, steam-powered, bearing two-one-six, tooling along at about fourteen knots, by blade count.'

'Time on Unit Two,' the skipper called.

'Minute twenty seconds to impact, sir.' The captain looked at the display. If Sierra-Eleven had sonarmen on duty, they weren't paying much attention to the world around them. That would change shortly.

'Okay, go active in thirty seconds.'

'Aye, aye.'

On the sonar display, the torpedo was dead on the tone line from *406*. It seemed a shame to kill a submarine when you didn't even know its name . . .

'Going active on Unit Two,' Weps called.

'There it is, sir,' the sonarman said, pointing to a different part of the screen. The ultrasonic sonar lit up a new line, and fifteen seconds later—

'—Sierra-Eleven just kicked the gas, sir, look here, cavitation and blade count is going up, starting a turn to starboard . . . ain't gonna matter, sir,' the sonarman knew from the display. You couldn't outmaneuver a -48.

'What about—Twelve?'

'He's heard it, too, Cap'n. Increasing speed and—' The sonarman flipped his headphones off. 'Yeow! That hurt.' He shook his head hard. 'Unit impact on Sierra-Eleven, sir.'

The captain picked up a spare set of headphones and plugged them in. The sea was still rumbling. The target's engine sounds had stopped almost at once—the visual display confirmed that, though the sixty-hertz line showed her generators were still—no, they stopped, too. He heard and saw the sound of blowing air. Whoever he was, he was trying to blow ballast and head for the roof, but without engine power . . . no, not much of a chance of that, was there? Then he shifted his eyes to the visual track of Sierra-Twelve. The fast-attack had been a little more awake, and was turning radically to port, and really kicking on the power. His plant noise was way up, as was his blade count . . . and he was blowing ballast tanks, too . . . why?

'Time on Unit One?' the captain called.

'Thirty seconds for original plot, probably a little longer now.'

Not much longer, the skipper thought. The ADCAP was motoring along on the sunny side of sixty knots this close to the surface . . . Weps went active on it, and the fish was immediately in acquisition. A well-trained crew would have fired off a torpedo of their own, just to scare their attacker off, and maybe escape if the first fish missed—not much of a play, but it cost you nothing to do it, and maybe got you the satisfaction of having company arrive in hell right after you knocked on the door . . . but they didn't even get a decoy off. They must have all been asleep . . . certainly not very awake . . . not very alert . . . didn't they know there was a war going on . . . ? Twenty-five seconds later, they found out the hard way, when another splotch appeared on the sonar display.

Well, he thought, *two for two. That was pretty easy.* He stepped back into the attack center and lifted a microphone. 'Now hear this. This is the captain speaking. We just launched two fish on a pair of ChiComm submarines. We won't be seeing either one of them anymore. Well done to everybody. That is all.' Then he looked over at his communications officer: 'Prepare a dispatch to CINCLANT. "Four Zero Six destroyed at . . . Twenty-Two-Fifty-Six Zulu along with escorting SSN. Now engaging Frigate." Send that off when we get to antenna depth.'

'Yes, sir.'

'Tracking party, we have a frigate bearing two-one-six. Let's get a track on him so we can Harpoon his ass.'

'Aye, sir,' said the lieutenant manning the tracking plot.

*   *   *

It was approaching six in the evening in Washington, where everybody who was somebody

614

was watching TV, but not the commercial kind. The Dark Star feeds were going up on encrypted satellite links, and being distributed around Washington over dedicated military fiber-optic lines. One of those, of course, led to the White House Situation Room.

'Holy God,' Ryan said. 'It's like some kind of fucking video game. How long have we had this capability?'

'It's pretty new, Jack, and yeah,' the Vice President agreed, 'it is kind of obscene—but, well, it's just what the operators see. I mean, the times I splashed airplanes, I got to see it, just I was in a G-suit with a Tomcat strapped to my back. Somehow this feels dirtier, man. Like watching a guy and a gal go at it, and not in training films—'

'What?'

'That's what you call porno flicks on the boats, Jack, "training films". But this is like peeking in a window on a guy's wedding night, and he doesn't know about it . . . feels kinda dirty.'

'The people will like it,' Arnie van Damm predicted. 'The average guy out there, especially kids, to them it'll be like a movie.'

'Maybe so, Arnie, but it's a snuff film. Real lives being snuffed out, and in large numbers. That division CP Diggs got with his MLRS rockets—I mean, Jesus Christ. It was like an act of an angry pagan god, like the meteor that got the dinosaurs, like a murderer wasting a kid in a schoolyard,' Robby said, searching for just how dirty it felt to him. But it was business, not personal, for what little consolation that might be to the families of the departed.

615

*   *   *

'Getting some radio traffic,' Tolkunov told General Bondarenko. The intelligence officer had half a dozen electronic-intelligence groups out, listening in on the frequencies used by the PLA. They usually spoke in coded phrases which were difficult to figure out, especially since the words changed on a day-to-day basis, along with identifying names for the units and personalities involved.

But the security measures tended to fall by the wayside when an emergency happened, and senior officers wanted hard information in a hurry. In this case, Bondarenko had watched the take from Grace Kelly and felt little pity for the victims, wishing only that he'd been the one inflicting the casualties, because it was *his* country the Chinks had invaded.

'The American artillery doctrine is impressive, isn't it?' Colonel Tolkunov observed.

'They've always had good artillery. But so do we, as this Peng fellow will discover in a few hours,' CINC–FAR EAST replied. 'What do you think he'll do?'

'It depends on what he finds out,' the G-2 replied. 'The information that gets to him will probably be fairly confusing, and it will concern him, but less than his own mission.'

And that made sense, Gennady Iosifovich had to agree. Generals tended to think in terms of the missions assigned to them, leaving the missions of others to those others, trusting them to do the jobs assigned to *them.* It was the only way an army could function, really. Otherwise you'd be so worried about what was happening around you that you'd

616

never get your own work done, and the entire thing would quickly grind to a halt. It was called tunnel vision when it didn't work, and good teamwork when it did.

'What about the American deep strikes?'

'Those Stealth aircraft are amazing. The Chinese rail system is complete disrupted. Our guests will soon be running short of fuel.'

'Pity,' Bondarenko observed. The Americans were efficient warriors, and their doctrine of deep-strike, which the Russian military had scarcely considered, could be damned effective if you brought it off, and if your enemy couldn't adapt to it. Whether the Chinese could adapt was something they'd have to see about. 'But they still have sixteen mechanized divisions for us to deal with.'

'That is so, Comrade General,' Tolkunov agreed.

*　　　*　　　*

'FALCON THREE to FALCON LEADER, I see me a SAM track. It's a Holiday,' the pilot reported. 'Hilltop two miles west of the CLOVERLEAF—wait, there's a Duck there, too.'

'Anything else?' FALCON LEAD asked. This captain commanded the Apaches tasked to SAM suppression.

'Some light flak, mainly two-five mike-mike set up around the SAMs. Request permission to fire, over.'

'Stand by,' FALCON LEAD replied. 'EAGLE LEAD, this is FALCON LEAD, over.'

'EAGLE LEAD copies, FALCON,' Boyle replied from his Blackhawk.

'We have SAM tracks in view. Permission to engage, over.'

Boyle thought fast. His Apaches now had the tank laager in sight and surrounded on three sides. Okay, Falcon was approaching the hill overlooking the laager, code-named CLOVERLEAF. Well, it was about time.

'Permission granted. Engage the SAMs. Out.'

'Roger, engaging. FALCON THREE, this is LEAD. Take 'em out.'

'Take your shot, Billy,' the pilot told his gunner.

'Hellfire, now!' The gunner in the front seat triggered off his first missile. The seven-inch-wide missile leaped off its launch-rail with a flare of yellow light, and immediately tracked on the laser dot. Through his thermal viewer, he saw a dismounted crewman looking that way, and he immediately pointed toward the helicopter. He was yelling to get someone's attention, and the race was between the inbound missile and human reaction time. The missile had to win. He got the attention of someone, maybe his sergeant or lieutenant, who then looked in the direction he was pointing. You could tell by the way he cocked his head that he didn't see anything at first, while the first one was jerking his arm like a fishing pole, and the second one saw it, but by that time there was nothing for him to do but throw himself to the ground, and even that was a waste of energy. The Hellfire hit the base of the launcher assembly and exploded, killing everything within a ten-meter circle.

'Tough luck, Joe.' Then the gunner switched over to the other one, the Holiday launcher. This crew had been alerted by the sound, and he could see them scurrying to light up their weapon. They'd just about gotten to their places when the Duck launcher blew up.

Next came the flak. There were six gun mounts, equally divided between 25- and 35-mm twin gun sets, and those could be nasty. The Apache closed in. The gunner selected his own 20-mm cannon and walked it across every site. The impacts looked like flashbulbs, and the guns were knocked over, some with exploding ammo boxes.

'EAGLE LEAD, FALCON THREE, this hilltop is cleaned off. We're circling to make sure. No coverage over the CLOVERLEAF now. It's wide open.

'Roger that.' And Boyle ordered his Apaches in.

It was about as fair as putting a professional boxer into the ring against a six-year-old. The Apaches circled the laagered tanks just like Indians in the movies around a circled wagon train, except in this one, the settlers couldn't fire back. The Chinese tank crewmen were mainly sleeping outside, next to their mounts. Some crews were in their vehicles, standing guard after a fashion, and some dismounted crewmen were walking around on guard, holding Type 68 rifles. They'd been alerted somewhat by the explosions on the hilltop overlooking the laager. Some of the junior officers were shouting to get their men up and into their tanks, not knowing the threat, but thinking naturally enough that the safe place to be was behind armor, from which place they could shoot back to defend themselves. They could scarcely have been more wrong.

The Apaches danced around the laager, sideslipping as the gunners triggered off their missiles. Three of the PLA tanks used their thermal viewers and actually saw helicopters and shot at them, but the range of the tank guns was only half that of the Hellfires, and all of the rounds fell well short, as did the six handheld HN-5 Sams that were fired into the night. The Hellfires, however, did not, and in every case—only two of them missed—the huge warheads had the same effect on the steel tanks that a cherry bomb might have on a plastic model. Turrets flew into the air atop pillars of flame, then crashed back down, usually upside-down on the vehicles to which they'd been attached. There'd been eighty-six tanks here, and that amounted to three missiles per helicopter, with a few lucky gunners getting a fourth shot. All in all, the destruction of this brigade took less than three minutes, leaving the colonel who'd been in command to stand at his command post with openmouthed horror at the loss of the three hundred soldiers he'd been training for over a year for this very moment. He even survived a strafing of his command section by a departing Apache, seeing the helicopter streak overhead so quickly that he didn't even have time to draw his service pistol.

'EAGLE LEAD, FALCON LEAD. The CLOVERLEAF is toast, and we are RTB, over.'

Boyle could do little more than shake his head. 'Roger, FALCON. Well done, Captain.'

'Roger, thank you, sir. Out.' The Apaches formed up and headed northwest to their base to refuel and rearm for the next mission. Below, he could see the First Brigade, blown through the gap in Chinese lines, heading southeast into the Chinese logistics area.

$$* \qquad * \qquad *$$

Task Force 77 had been holding station east of the Formosa Strait until receiving orders to race west. The various Air Bosses had word that one of their submarines had eliminated a Chinese boomer and fast-attack submarine, which was fine with them, and probably just peachy for the task force commander. Now it was their job to go after the People's Liberation Army Navy, which, they all agreed, was a hell of a name for a maritime armed force. The first aircraft to go off, behind the F-14Ds flying barrier combat air patrol, or BARCAP, for the Task Force, were the E-2C Hawkeye radar aircraft, the Navy's two-engine prop-driven mini-AWACS. These were tasked to finding targets for the shooters, mainly F/A-18 Hornets.

This was to be a complex operation. The Task Force had three SSNs assigned to 'sanitize' the area of ChiComm submarines. The Task Force commander seemed especially concerned with the possibility of a Chinese diesel-powered SSK punching a hole in one of his ships, but that was not an immediate concern for the airmen, unless they could find one tied alongside the pier.

The only real problem was target identification. There was ample commercial shipping in the area, and they had orders to leave that entirely alone, even ships flying the PRC flag. Anything with a SAM radar would be engaged beyond visual range. Otherwise, a pilot had to have eyeballs on the target before loosing a weapon. Of weapons they had plenty, and ships were fragile targets as far as missiles and thousand-pound bombs were concerned. The overall target was the PLAN South Sea Fleet, based at Guangszhou (better known to Westerners as Canton). The naval base there was well-sited for attack, though it was defended by surface-to-air missile batteries and some flak.

The F-14s on the lead were guided to aerial targets by the Hawkeyes. Again since there was commercial air traffic in the sky, the fighter pilots had to close to visual range for a positive ID of their targets. This could be dangerous, but there was no avoiding it.

What the Navy pilots didn't know was that the Chinese knew the electronic signature of the APD-138 radar on the E-2Cs, and therefore they also knew that something was coming. Fully a hundred Chinese fighters scrambled into the air and set up their own combat air patrol over their East Coast. The Hawkeyes spotted that and radioed a warning to the advancing fighters, setting the stage for a massive air engagement in the predawn darkness.

There was no elegant way to go about it. Two squadrons of Tomcats, twenty-four in all, led the strike force. Each carried four AIM-54C Phoenix missiles, plus four AIM-9X Sidewinders, The Phoenixes were old—nearly fifteen years old for some of them, and in some cases the solid-fuel motor bodies were developing cracks that would soon become apparent. They had a theoretical range of over a hundred miles, however, and that made them useful things to hang on one's airframe.

The Hawkeye crews had orders to make careful determination of what was a duck and what was a goose, but it was agreed quickly that two or more aircraft flying in close formation were not Airbuses full of civilian passengers, and the Tomcats were authorized to shoot a full hundred miles off the Chinese mainland. The first salvo was composed of forty-eight. Of these, six self-destructed within five hundred yards of their launching aircraft, to the displeased surprise of the pilots involved. The remaining forty-two streaked upward in a ballistic path to a height of over a hundred thousand feet before tipping over at Mach-5 speed and switching on their millimeter-band Doppler homing radars. By the end of their flight, their motors were burned out, and they did not leave the smoke trail that pilots look for. Thus, though the Chinese pilots knew that they'd been illuminated, they couldn't see the danger coming, and therefore could not see anything to evade. The forty-two Phoenixes started going off in their formations, and the only survivors were those who broke into radical turns when they saw the first warheads go off. All in all, the forty-eight launches resulted in thirty-two kills. The surviving Chinese pilots were shaken but also enraged. As one man, they turned east and lit up their search radars, looking for targets for their own air-to-air missiles. These they found, but beyond range of their weapons. The senior officer surviving the initial attack ordered them to go to afterburner and streak east, and at a range of sixty miles, they fired off their PL-10 radar-guided air-to-air missiles. These were a copy of the Italian Aspide, in turn a copy of the old American AIM-7E Sparrow. To track a target, they required that the launching aircraft keep itself and its radar pointed at the target. In this case, the Americans were heading in as well, with their own radars emitting, and what happened was a great game of chicken, with the fighter pilots on either side unwilling to turn and run—and besides, they all figured that to do so merely guaranteed one's death. And so the race was between airplanes and missiles, but the PL-10 had a speed of Mach 4 against the Phoenix's Mach 5.

Back on the Hawkeyes, the crewmen kept track of the engagement. Both the aircraft and the streaking missiles were visible on the scopes, and there was a collective holding of breath for this one.

The Phoenixes hit first, killing thirty-one more PLAAF fighters, and also turning off their radars rather abruptly. That made some of their missiles 'go dumb,' but not all, and the six Chinese fighters that survived the second Phoenix barrage found themselves illuminating targets for a total of thirty-nine PL-10s, which angled for only four Tomcats.

The American pilots affected by this saw them coming, and the feeling wasn't particularly pleasant. Each went to afterburner and dove for the deck, losing every bit of chaff and flares he had in his protection pods, plus turning the jamming pods up to max power. One got clean away. Another lost most of them in the chaff, where the Chinese missiles exploded like fireworks in his wake, but one of the F-14s had nineteen missiles chasing him alone, and there was no avoiding them all. The third missile got close enough to trigger its warhead, and then nine more, and the Tomcat was reduced to chaff itself, along with its two-man crew. That left one Navy fighter whose radar-intercept officer ejected safely, though the pilot did not.

The remaining Tomcats continued to bore in. They were out of Phoenix missiles now, and closed to continue the engagement with Sidewinders.

624

Losing comrades did nothing more than anger them for the moment, and this time it was the Chinese who turned back and headed for their coast, chased by a cloud of heat-seeking missiles.

This bar fight had the effect of clearing the way for the strike force. The PLAN base had twelve piers with ships alongside, and the United States Navy went after its Chinese counterpart—as usually happened, on the principle that in war people invariably kill those most like themselves before going after the different ones.

The first to draw the wrath of the Hornets were the submarines. They were mainly old Romeo-class diesel boats, long past whatever prime they'd once had. They were mainly rafted in pairs, and the Hornet drivers struck at them with Skippers and SLAMs. The former was a thousand-pound bomb with a rudimentary guidance package attached, plus a rocket motor taken off obsolete missiles, and they proved adequate to the task. The pilots tried to guide them between the rafted submarines, so as to kill two with a single weapon, and that worked in three out of five attempts. SLAM was a land-attack version of the Harpoon anti-ship missile, and these were directed at the port and maintenance facilities without which a naval base is just a cluttered beach. The damage done looked impressive on the videotapes. Other aircraft tasked to a mission called IRON HAND sought out Chinese missile and flak batteries, and engaged those at safe distance with HARM anti-radiation missiles which sought out and destroyed acquisition and illumination radars with high reliability.

All in all, the first U.S. Navy attack on the mainland of East Asia since Vietnam went off well, eliminating twelve PRC warships and laying waste to one of its principal naval bases.

Other bases were attacked with Tomahawk cruise missiles launched mainly from surface ships. Every PLAN base over a swath of five hundred miles of coast took one form of fire or another, and the ship count was jacked up to sixteen, all in a period of a little over an hour. The American tactical aircraft returned to their carriers, having spilled the blood of their enemies, though also having lost some of their own.

CHAPTER FIFTY-EIGHT

POLITICAL FALLOUT

It was a difficult night for Marshal Luo Cong, the Defense Minister for the People's Republic of China. He'd gone to bed about eleven the previous night, concerned with the ongoing operations of his military forces, but pleased that they seemed to be going well. And then, just after he'd closed his eyes, the phone rang.

His official car came at once to convey him to his office, but he didn't enter it. Instead he went to the Defense Ministry's communications center, where he found a number of senior- and mid-level officers going over fragmentary information and trying to make sense of it. Minister Luo's presence didn't help them, but just added stress to the existing chaos.

Nothing seemed clear, except that they could identify holes in their information. The 65th Army had seemingly dropped off the face of the earth. Its commanding general had been visiting one of his divisions, along with his staff, and hadn't been heard from since 0200 or so. Nor had the division's commanding general. In fact, nothing at all was known about what was happening up there. To fix that, Marshal Luo ordered a helicopter to fly up from the depot at Sunwu. Then came reports from Harbin and Bei'an of air raids that had damaged the railroads. A colonel of engineers was dispatched to look into that.

But just when he thought he'd gotten a handle on the difficulties in Siberia, then came reports of an air attack on the fleet base at Guangszhou, and then the lesser naval bases at Haikuo, Shantou, and Xiachuandao. In each case, the headquarters facilities seemed hard-hit, since there was no response from the local commanders. Most disturbing of all was the report of huge losses to the fighter regiments in the area—reports of American naval aircraft making the attacks. Then finally, worst of all, a pair of automatic signals, the distress buoys from his country's only nuclear-powered missile submarine and the hunter submarine detailed to protect her, the *Hai Long*, were both radiating their automated messages. It struck the marshal as unlikely to the point of impossibility that so many things could have happened at once. And yet there was more. Border radar emplacements were off the air and could not be raised on radio or telephone. Then came another phone call from Siberia. One of the divisions on the left shoulder of the breakthrough—the one the commanding general of 65th Type B Group Army had been visiting a few hours before—reported . . .

that is, a junior communications officer said a subunit of the division reported, that unknown armored forces had lanced through its western defenses, going east, and . . . disappeared?

'How the hell does an enemy attack successfully *and disappear*?' the marshal had demanded, in a voice to make the young captain wilt. 'Who reported this?'

'He identified himself as a major in the Third Battalion, 745th Guards Infantry Regiment, Comrade Marshal,' was the trembling reply. 'The radio connection was scratchy, or so it was reported to us.'

'And who made the report?'

'A Colonel Zhao, senior communications officer in the intelligence staff of 71st Type C Group Army north of Bei'an. They are detailed to border security in the breakthrough sector,' the captain explained.

'I know that!' Luo bellowed, taking out his rage on the nearest target of opportunity.

'Comrade Marshal,' said a new voice. It was Major General Wei Dao-Ming, one of Luo's senior aides, just called in from his home after one more of a long string of long days, and showing the strain, but trying to smooth the troubled waters even so. 'You should let me and my staff assemble this information in such a way that we can present it to you in an orderly manner.'

'Yes, Wei, I suppose so.' Luo knew that this was good advice, and Wei was a career intelligence officer, accustomed to organizing information for his superiors. 'Quick as you can.'

'Of course, Comrade Minister,' Wei said, to remind Luo that he was a political figure now

628

rather than the military officer he'd grown up as.

Luo went to the VIP sitting room, where green tea was waiting. He reached into the pocket of his uniform tunic and pulled out some cigarettes, strong unfiltered ones to help him wake up. They made him cough, but that was all right. By the third cup of tea, Wei returned with a pad of paper scribbled with notes.

'So, what is happening?'

'The picture is confused, but I will tell you what I know, and what I think,' Wei began.

'We know that General Qi of Sixty-fifth Army is missing, along with his staff. They were visiting 191st Infantry Division, just north and west of our initial breakthrough. The 191st is completely off the air as well. So is the 615th Independent Tank Brigade, part of Sixty-fifth Army. Confused reports talk of an air attack on the tank brigade, but nothing precise is known. The 735th Guards Infantry Regiment of the 191st division is also off the air, cause unknown. You ordered a helicopter out of Sunwu to take a look and report back. The helicopter will get off at dawn. Well and good.

'Next, there are additional reports from that sector, none of which make sense or help form any picture of what is happening. So, I have ordered the intelligence staff of the Seventy-first Army to send a reconnaissance team across the river and ascertain what's happening there and report back. That will take about three hours.

'The good news is that General Peng Xi-Wang remains in command of 34th Shock Army, and will be at the gold mine before midday. Our armored spearhead is deep within enemy territory. I expect the men are waking up right now and will be

629

moving within the hour to continue their attack.

'Now, this news from the navy people is confusing, but it's not really a matter of consequence. I've directed the commander of South Sea Fleet to take personal charge of the situation and report back. So say about three hours for that.

'So, Comrade Minister, we will have decent information shortly, and then we can start addressing the situation. Until then, General Peng will soon resume his offensive, and by evening, our country will be much richer,' Wei concluded. He knew how to keep his minister happy. His reward for this was a grunt and a nod. 'Now,' General Wei went on, 'why don't you get a few hours of sleep while we maintain the watch?'

'Good idea, Wei.' Luo took two steps to the couch and lay down across it. Wei opened the door, turned off the lights, then he closed the door behind himself. The communications center was only a few more steps.

'Now,' he said, stealing a smoke from a major, 'what the hell is happening out there?'

'If you want an opinion,' a colonel of intelligence said, 'I think the Americans just flexed their muscles, and the Russians will do so in a few hours.'

'What? Why do you say that? And why the Russians?'

'Where has their air force been? Where have their attack helicopters been? We don't know, do we? Why don't we know? Because the Americans have swatted our airplanes out of the sky like flies, that's why.'

'We've deluded ourselves that the Russians don't

want to fight, haven't we? A man named Hitler once thought the same thing. He died a few years later, the history books say. We similarly deluded ourselves into thinking the Americans would not strike us hard for political reasons. Wei, some of our political leaders have been off chasing the dragon!' The aphorism referred to opium-smoking, a popular if illegal pastime in the southern part of China a few centuries before. 'There were no political considerations. They were merely building up their forces, which takes time. And the Russians didn't fight us because they wanted us to get to the end of the logistical string, and then the fucking Americans cut that string off at Harbin and Bei'an! General Peng's tanks are nearly *three* hundred kilometers inside Russia now, with only *two* hundred kilometers of fuel in their tanks, and there'll be no more fuel coming up to them. We've taken over two *thousand* tanks and turned their crews into badly trained light infantry! That is what's happening, Comrade Wei,' the colonel concluded.

'You can say that sort of thing to me, Colonel. Say it before Minister Luo, and your wife will pay the state for the bullet day after tomorrow,' Wei warned.

'Well, I know it,' Colonel Geng He-ping replied. 'What will happen to you later today, Comrade General Wei, when you organize the information and find out that I am correct?'

'The remainder of today will have to take care of itself' was the fatalistic reply. 'One thing at a time, Geng.' Then he assembled a team of officers and gave them each a task to perform, found himself a chair to sit in, and wondered if Geng might have a good feel for the situation—

'Colonel Geng?'

'Yes, Comrade General?'

'What do you know of the Americans?'

'I was in our embassy in Washington until eighteen months ago. While there, I studied their military quite closely.'

'And—are they capable of what you just said?'

'Comrade General, for the answer to that question, I suggest you consult the Iranians and the Iraqis. I'm wondering what they might try next, but thinking exactly like an American is a skill I have never mastered.'

*   *   *

'They're moving,' Major Tucker reported with a stretch and a yawn. 'Their reconnaissance element just started rolling. Your people have pulled way back. How come?'

'I ordered them to collect Comrade Gogol before the Chinese kill him,' Colonel Tolkunov told the American. 'You look tired.'

'Hell, what's thirty-six hours in the same chair?' *A helluva sore back, that's what it is,* Tucker didn't say. Despite the hours, he was having the time of his life. For an Air Force officer who'd flunked out of pilot training, making him forever an 'unrated weenie' in Air Force parlance, a fourth-class citizen in the Air Force pecking order—below even helicopter pilots—he was earning his keep more and better than he'd ever done. He'd probably been more valuable to his side in this war than even that Colonel Winters, with all his air-to-air snuffs. But if anyone ever said such a thing to him, he'd have to *aw-shucks* it and look humbly down at his shoes. *Humble, my ass*, Tucker thought. He was proving the value of a new and untested asset, and doing so like the Red Baron in his red Fokker Trimotor. The Air Force was not a service whose members cultivated humility, but his lack of pilot's wings had compelled him to do just that for all ten of his years of uniformed service. The next generation of UAVs would have weapons attached, and maybe even be able to go air-to-air, and then, maybe, he'd show those strutting fighter jock-itches who had the real balls in this man's Air Force. Until then, he'd just have to be content gathering information that helped the Russians kill Joe Chink and all his brothers, and if this was Nintendo War, then little Danny Tucker was the by-God cock of the by-God walk in *this* virtual world.

'You have been most valuable to us, Major Tucker.'

'Thank you, sir. Glad to help,' Tucker replied with his best little-boy smile. *Maybe I'll grow me a good mustache.* He set the thought aside with a smile, and sipped some instant coffee from a MRE pack—the extra caffeine was about the only thing keeping him up at the moment. But the computer was doing most of the work, and it showed the Chinese reconnaissance tracks moving north.

*   *   *

'Son of a bitch,' Captain Aleksandrov breathed. He'd heard about Gogol's wolf pelts on state radio, but he hadn't seen the TV coverage, and the sight took his breath away. Touching one, he halfway expected it to be cold and stiff like wire, but, no, it was like the perfect hair of a perfect blonde . . .

'And who might you be?' The old man was holding a rifle and had a decidedly gimlet eye.

'I am Captain Fedor Il'ych Aleksandrov, and I imagine you are Pavel Petrovich Gogol.'

A nod and a smile. 'You like my furs, Comrade Captain?'

'They are unlike anything I have ever seen. We have to take these with us.'

'Take? Take where? I'm not going anywhere,' Pasha said.

'Comrade Gogol, I have my orders—to get you away from here. Those orders come from Headquarters Far East Command, and those orders will be obeyed, Pavel Petrovich.'

'No Chink is going to chase me off my land!' His old voice thundered.

'No, Comrade Gogol, but soldiers of the Russian Army will not leave you here to die. So, that is the rifle you killed Germans with?'

'Yes, many, many Germans,' Gogol confirmed.

'Then come with us, and maybe you can kill some yellow invaders.'

'Who exactly are you?'

'Reconnaissance company commander, Two-Six-Five Motor Rifle Division. We've been playing hide-and-seek with the Chinks for four long days, and now we're ready to do some real fighting. Join us, Pavel Petrovich. You can probably teach us a few things we need to know.' The young handsome captain spoke in his most reasonable and respectful tones, for this old warrior truly deserved it. The tone turned the trick.

'You promise me I will get to take one shot?'

'My word as a Russian officer, Comrade,'

Aleksandrov pledged, with a bob of his head.

'Then I come.' Gogol was already dressed for it—the heat in his cabin was turned off. He shouldered his old rifle and an ammunition pack containing forty rounds—he'd never gone into the field with more than that—and walked to the door. 'Help me with my wolves, boy, will you.'

'Gladly, Grandfather.' Then Aleksandrov found out how heavy they were. But he and Buikov managed to toss them inside their BRM, and the driver headed off.

'Where are they?'

'About ten kilometers back. We've been in visual contact with them for days, but they've pulled us back. Away from them.'

'Why?'

'To save you, you old fool,' Buikov observed with a laugh. 'And to save these pelts. These are too good to drape over the body of some Chinese strumpet!'

'I think, Pasha—I am not sure,' the captain said, 'but I think it's time for our Chinese guests to get a proper Russian welcome.'

'Captain, look!' the driver called.

Aleksandrov lifted his head out the big top hatch and looked forward. A senior officer was waving to him to come forward more quickly. Three minutes later, they halted alongside him.

'You are Aleksandrov?'

'Yes, Comrade General!' the young man confirmed to the senior officer.

'I am General Sinyavskiy. You've done well, boy. Come out here and talk to me,' he ordered in a gruff voice that was not, however, unkind.

Aleksandrov had only once seen his senior

635

commander, and then only at a distance. He was not a large man, but you didn't want him as a physical enemy in a small room. He was chewing on a cigar that had gone out seemingly hours before, and his blue eyes blazed.

'Who is this?' Sinyavskiy demanded. Then his face changed. 'Are you the famous Pasha?' he asked more respectfully.

'Senior Sergeant Gogol of the Iron and Steel Division,' the old man said with great dignity, and a salute which Sinyavskiy returned crisply.

'I understand you killed some Germans in your day. How many, Sergeant?'

'Count for yourself, Comrade General,' Gogol said, handing his rifle over.

'Damn,' the general observed, looking at the notches, like those on the pistol of some American cowboy. 'I believe you really did it. But combat is a young man's game, Pavel Petrovich. Let me get you to a place of safety.'

Gogol shook his head. 'This captain promised me one shot, or I would not have left my home.'

'Is that a fact?' The commanding general of 265th Motor Rifle looked around. 'Captain Aleksandrov, very well, we'll give our old comrade his one shot.' He pointed to a place on the map before him. 'This should be a good spot for you. And when you can, get him the hell away from there,' Sinyavskiy told the young man. 'Head back this way to our lines. They'll be expecting you. Boy, you've done a fine job shadowing them all the way up. Your reward will be to see how we greet the bastards.'

'Behind the reconnaissance element is a large force.'

'I know. I've been watching them on TV for a day and a half, but our American friends have cut off their supplies. And we will stop them, and we will stop them right here.'

Aleksandrov checked the map reference. It looked like a good spot with a good field of fire, and best of all, an excellent route to run away on. 'How long?' he asked.

'Two hours, I should think. Their main body is catching up with the screen. Your first job is to make their screen vehicles disappear.'

'Yes, Comrade General, that we can do for you!' the captain responded with enthusiasm.

*   *   *

Sunrise found Marion Diggs in a strangely bizarre environment. Physically, the surroundings reminded him of Fort Carson, Colorado, with its rolling hills and patchy pine woods, but it was unlike America in its lack of paved roads or civilization, and that explained why the Chinese had invaded here. With little civilian population out here, there was no infrastructure or population base to provide for the area's defense, and that had made things a lot easier for John Chinaman. Diggs didn't mind it, either. It was like his experience in the Persian Gulf—no noncombatants to get in the way—and that was good.

But there were a lot of Chinese to get in the way. Mike Francisco's First Brigade had debouched into the main logistics area for the Chinese advance. The ground was carpeted with trucks and soldiers, but while most of them were armed, few were organized into cohesive tactical units, and that

637

made all the difference. Colonel Miguel Francisco's brigade of four battalions had been organized for combat with the infantry and tank battalions integrated into unified battalion task groups of mixed tanks and Bradleys, and these were sweeping across the ground like a harvesting machine in Kansas in August. If it was painted green, it was shot.

The monstrous Abrams main-battle tanks moved over the rolling ground like creatures from Jurassic Park—alien, evil, and unstoppable, their gun turrets traversing left and right—but without firing their main guns. The real work was being done by the tank commanders and their M2 .50 machine guns, which could turn any truck into an immobile collection of steel and canvas. Just a short burst into the engine made sure that the pistons would never move again, and the cargo in the back would remain where it was, for inspection by intelligence officers, or destruction by explosives-carrying engineer troops who came behind the tanks in their HMMWVs. Some resistance was offered by the Chinese soldiers, but only by the dumb ones, and never for long. Even those with man-portable anti-tank weapons rarely got close enough to use them, and those few who popped up from Wolfholes only scratched the paint on the tanks, and usually paid for their foolishness with their lives. At one point, a battalion of infantry did launch a deliberate attack, supported by mortars that forced the tank and Bradley crews to button up and reply with organized fire. Five minutes of 155-mm fire and a remorseless advance by the Bradleys, spitting fire from their chain guns and through the firing ports for the mounted infantry inside, made them look like fire-breathing dragons, and these dragons were not a sign of good luck for the Chinese soldiers. That battalion evaporated in twenty minutes, along with its dedicated but doomed commander.

Intact enemy armored vehicles were rarely seen by the advancing First Brigade. Where it went, Apache attack helicopters had gone before, looking for targets for their Hellfire missiles, and killing them before the ground troops could get close. All in all, it was a perfect military operation, totally unfair in the balance of forces. It wasn't the least bit sporting, but a battlefield is not an Olympic stadium, and there were no uniformed officials to guard the supposed rules of fair play.

The only exciting thing was the appearance of a Chinese army helicopter, and two Apaches blazed after it and destroyed it with air-to-air missiles, dropping it in the Amur River close to the floating bridges, which were now empty of traffic but not yet destroyed.

*   *   *

'What have you learned, Wei?' Marshal Luo asked, when he emerged from the conference room he'd used for his nap.

'The picture is still unclear in some respects, Comrade Minister,' the general answered.

'Then tell me what is clear,' Luo ordered.

'Very well. At sea, we have lost a number of ships. This evidently includes our ballistic missile submarine and its escorting hunter submarine, cause unknown, but their emergency beacons deployed and transmitted their programmed messages starting at about zero-two-hundred hours. Also lost are seven surface warships of various types from our South Sea Fleet. Also, seven fleet bases were attacked by American aircraft, believed to be naval carrier aircraft, along with a number of surface-to-air missile and radar sites on the southeastern coast. We've succeeded in shooting down a number of American aircraft, but in a large fighter battle, we took serious losses to our fighter regiments in that region.'

'Is the American Navy attacking us?' Luo asked.

'It appears that they are, yes,' General Wei answered, choosing his words with care. 'We estimate four of their aircraft carriers, judging by the number of aircraft involved. As I said, reports are that we handled them roughly, but our losses were severe as well.'

'What are their intentions?' the minister asked.

'Unclear. They've done serious damage to a number of bases, and I doubt we have a single surface ship surviving at sea. Our navy personnel have not had a good day,' Wei concluded. 'But that is not really a matter of importance.'

'The attack on the missile submarine is,' Luo replied. 'That is an attack on a strategic asset. That is something we must consider.' He paused. 'Go on, what else?'

'General Qi of Sixty-fifth Army is missing and presumed dead, along with all of his senior staff. We've made repeated attempts to raise him by radio, with no result. The 191st Infantry Division was attacked last night by heavy forces of unknown identity. They sustained heavy losses due to artillery and aircraft, but two of their regiments report that they are holding their positions. The

735th Guards Infantry Regiment evidently took the brunt of the attack, and reports from there are fragmentary.

'The most serious news is from Harbin and Bei'an. Enemy aircraft attacked all of the railroad bridges in both cities, and all of them took damage. Rail traffic north has been interrupted. We're trying now to determine how quickly it might be reestablished.'

'Is there any good news?' Marshal Luo asked.

'Yes, Comrade Minister. General Peng and his forces are getting ready now to resume their attack. We expect to have the Russian gold field in our control by midday,' Wei answered, inwardly glad that he didn't have to say what had happened to the logistical train behind Peng and his 34th Shock Army. Too much bad news could get the messenger killed, and *he* was the messenger.

'I want to talk to Peng. Get him on the phone,' Luo ordered.

'Telephone lines have been interrupted briefly, but we do have radio contact with him,' Wei told his superior.

'Then get me Peng on the radio,' Luo repeated his order.

*   *   *

'What is it, Wa?' Peng asked. Couldn't he even take a piss without interruption?

'Radio, it's the Defense Minister,' his operations officer told him.

'Wonderful,' the general groused, heading back to his command track as he buttoned his fly. He ducked to get inside and lifted the microphone.

'This is General Peng.'

'This is Marshal Luo. What is your situation?' the voice asked through the static.

'Comrade Marshal, we will be setting off in ten minutes. We have still not made contact with the enemy, and our reconnaissance has seen no sizable enemy formations in our area. Have you developed any intelligence we can use?'

'Be advised we have aerial photography of Russian mechanized units to your west, probably division strength. I would advise you to keep your mechanized forces together, and guard your left flank.'

'Yes, Comrade Marshal, I am doing that,' Peng assured him. The real reason he stopped every day was to allow his divisions to close up, keeping his fist tight. Better yet, 29th Type A Group Army was right behind his if he needed support. 'I recommend that 43rd Army be tasked to flank guard.'

'I will give the order,' Luo promised. 'How far will you go today?'

'Comrade Marshal, I will send a truckload of gold back to you this very evening. Question: What is this I've heard about damage to our line of supply?'

'There was an attack last night on some railroad bridges in Harbin and Bei'an, but nothing we can't fix.'

'Very well. Comrade Marshal, I must see to my dispositions.'

'Carry on, then. Out.'

Peng set the microphone back in its holder. 'Nothing he can't fix, he says.'

'You know what those bridges are like. You'd

need a nuclear weapon to hurt them,' Colonel Wa Cheng-Gong observed confidently.

'Yes, I would agree with that.' Peng stood, buttoned his tunic, and reached for a mug of morning tea. 'Tell the advance guard to prepare to move out. I'm going up front this morning, Wa. I want to see this gold mine for myself.'

'How far up front?' the operations officer asked.

'With the lead elements. A good officer leads from the front, and I want to see how our people move. Our reconnaissance screen hasn't detected anything, has it?'

'Well, no, Comrade General, but—'

'But what?' Peng demanded.

'But a prudent commander leaves leading to lieutenants and captains,' Wa pointed out.

'Wa, sometimes you talk like an old woman,' Peng chided.

*   *   *

'There,' Yefremov said. 'They took the bait.'

It was just after midnight in Moscow, and the embassy of the People's Republic of China had most of its lights off, but not all; more to the point, three windows had their lights on, and their shades fully open, and they were all in a row. It was just as perfect as what the Americans called a 'sting' operation. He'd stood over Suvorov's shoulder as he'd typed the message: *I have the pieces in place now. If you wish for me to carry out the operation, leave three windows in a row with the lights on and the windows fully open.* Yefremov had even had a television camera record the event, down to the point where the traitor Suvarov had tapped the

ENTER key to send the letter to his Chink controller. And he'd gotten a TV news crew to record the event as well, because the Russian people seemed to trust the semi-independent media more than their government now, for some reason or other. Good, now they had proof positive that the Chinese government was conspiring to kill President Grushavoy. That would play well in the international press. And it wasn't an accident. The windows all belonged to the Chief of Mission in the PRC Embassy, and he was, right now, asleep in his bed. They'd made sure of that by calling him on the phone ten minutes earlier.

'So, what do we do now?'

'We tell the President, and then, I expect, we tell the TV news people. And we probably spare Suvarov's life. I hope he likes it in the labor camp.'

'What about the killings?'

Yefremov shrugged. 'He only killed a pimp and a whore. No great loss, is it?'

*   *   *

Senior Lieutenant Komanov had not exactly enjoyed his last four days, but at least they'd been spent profitably, training his men to shoot. The reservists, now known as BOYAR FORCE, had spent them doing gunnery, and they'd fired four basic loads of shells over that time, more than any of them had ever shot on active duty, but the Never Depot had been well stocked with shells. Officers assigned to the formation by Far East Command told them that the Americans had moved by to their south the previous day, and that their mission was to slide north of them, and do it today. Only

644

thirty kilometers stood between them and the Chinese, and he and his men were ready to pay them a visit. The throaty rumble of his own diesel engine was answered by the thunder of two hundred others, and BOYAR started moving northeast through the hills.

*   *   *

Peng and his command section raced forward, calling ahead on their radios to clear the way, and the military-police troops doing traffic control waved them through. Soon they reached the command section of the 302nd Armored, his leading 'fist' formation, commanded by Major General Ge Li, a squat officer whose incipient corpulence made him look rather like one of his tanks.

'Are you ready, Ge?' Peng asked. The man was well-named for his task. 'Ge' had the primary meaning of 'spear'.

'We are ready,' the tanker replied. 'My leading regiments are turning over and straining at the leash.'

'Well, shall we observe from the front together?'

'Yes!' Ge jumped aboard his own command tank—he preferred this to a personnel carrier, despite the poorer radios, and led the way forward. Peng immediately established a direct radio connection with his subordinate.

'How far to the front?'

'Three kilometers. The reconnaissance people are moving now, and they are another two kilometers ahead.'

'Lead on, Ge,' Peng urged. 'I want to see that

gold mine.'

*   *   *

It was a good spot, Aleksandrov thought, *unless the enemy got his artillery set up sooner than expected* and he hadn't seen or heard Chinese artillery yet. He was on the fairly steep reverse side of an open slope that faced south, rather like a lengthy ramp, perhaps three kilometers in length, not unlike a practice shooting range at a regimental base. The sun was starting to crest the eastern horizon, and they could see now, which always made soldiers happy. Pasha had stolen a spare coat and laid his rifle across it, standing in the open top hatch of the BRM, looking through the telescopic sight of his rifle.

'So, what was it like to be a sniper against the Germans?' Aleksandrov asked once he'd settled himself in.

'It was good hunting. I tried to stick to killing officers. You have more effect on them that way,' Gogol explained. 'A German private—well, he was just a man—an enemy, of course, but he probably had no more wish to be on a battlefield than I did. But an officer, those were the ones who directed the killing of my comrades, and when you got one of them, you confused the enemy.'

'How many?'

'Lieutenants, eighteen. Captains, twelve. Only three majors, but nine colonels. I decapitated nine Fritz regiments. Then, of course, sergeants and machine-gun crews, but I don't remember them as well as the colonels. I can still see every one of those, my boy,' Gogol said, tapping the side of his

646

head.

'Did they ever try to shoot at you?'

'Mainly with artillery,' Pasha answered. 'A sniper affects the morale of a unit. Men do not like being hunted like game. But the Germans didn't use snipers as skillfully as we did, and so they answered me with field guns. That,' he admitted, 'could be frightening, but it really told me how much the Fritzes feared me,' Pavel Petrovich concluded with a cruel smile.

'There!' Buikov pointed. just off the trees to the left.

'Ahh,' Gogol said, looking through his gunsight. 'Ahh, yes.'

Aleksandrov laid his binoculars on the fleeting shape. It was the vertical steel side on a Chinese infantry carrier, one of those he'd been watching for some days now. He lifted his radio. 'This is GREEN WOLF ONE. Enemy in sight, map reference two-eight-five, nine-zero-six. One infantry track coming north. Will advise.'

'Understood, GREEN WOLF,' the radio crackled back.

'Now, we must just be patient,' Fedor Il'ych said. He stretched, touching the camouflage net that he'd ordered set up the moment they'd arrived in this place. To anyone more than three hundred meters away, he and his men were just part of the hill crest. Next to him, Sergeant Buikov lit a cigarette, blowing out the smoke.

'That is bad for us,' Gogol advised. 'It alerts the game.'

'They have little noses,' Buikov replied.

'Yes, and the wind is in our favor,' the old hunter conceded.

Lordy, Lordy,' Major Tucker observed. 'They've bunched up some.' It was Grace Kelly again, looking down on the battlefield-to-be like Pallas Athena looking down on the plains of Troy. And about as pitilessly. The ground had opened up a little, and the corridor they moved across was a good three kilometers wide, enough for a battalion of tanks to travel line-abreast, a regiment in columns of battalions, three lines of thirty-five tanks each with tracked infantry carriers interspersed with them. Colonels Aliyev and Tolkunov stood behind him, speaking in Russian over their individual telephones to the 265th Motor Rifle's command post. In the night, the entire 201st had finally arrived, plus leading elements of the 80th and 44th. There were now nearly three divisions to meet the advancing Chinese, and included in that were three full divisional artillery sets, plus, Tucker saw for the first time, a shitload of attack helicopters sitting on the ground thirty kilometers back from the point of expected contact. Joe Chink was driving into a motherfucker of an ambush. Then a shadow crossed under Grace Kelly, out of focus, but something moving fast.

*   *   *

It was two squadrons of F-16C fighter-bombers, and they were armed with Smart Pigs.

That was the nickname for J-SOW, the Joint Stand-Off Weapon. The night before, other F-16s, the CG version, the new and somewhat downsized version of the F-4G Wild Weasel, had gone into China and struck at the line of border radar transmitters, hitting them with HARM antiradar missiles and knocking most of them off the air. That denied the Chinese foreknowledge of the inbound strike. They had been guided by two E-3B Sentry aircraft, and protected by three squadrons of F-15C Eagle air-superiority fighters in the event some Chinese fighters appeared again to die, but there had been little such fighter activity in the past thirty-six hours. The Chinese fighter regiments had paid a bloody price for their pride, and were staying close to home in what appeared to be a defense mode—on the principle that if you weren't attacking, then you were defending. In fact they were doing little but flying standing patrols over their own bases—that's how thoroughly they had been whipped by American and Russian fighters—and that left the air in American and Russian control, which was going to be bad news for the People's Liberation Army.

The F-16s were at thirty thousand feet, holding to the east. They were several minutes early for the mission, and circled while awaiting word to attack. Some concertmaster was stage-managing this, they all thought. They hoped he didn't break his little baton-stick-thing.

*   *   *

'Getting closer,' Pasha observed with studied nonchalance.

'Range?' Aleksandrov asked the men down below in the track.

'Twenty-one hundred meters, within range,'

Buikov reported from inside the gun turret. 'The fox and the gardener approach, Comrade Captain.'

'Leave them be for the moment, Boris Yevgeniyevich.'

'As you say, Comrade Captain.' Buikov was comfortable with the no-shoot rule, for once.

*   *   *

'How much farther to the reconnaissance screen?' Peng asked.

'Two more kilometers,' Ge replied over the radio. 'But that might not be a good idea.'

'Ge, have you turned into an old woman?' Peng asked lightly.

'Comrade, it is the job of lieutenants to find the enemy, not the job of senior generals,' the division commander replied in a reasonable voice.

'Is there any reason to believe the enemy is nearby?'

'We are in Russia, Peng. They're here somewhere.'

'He is correct, Comrade General,' Colonel Wa Cheng-gong pointed out to his commander.

'Rubbish. Go forward. Tell the reconnaissance element to stop and await us,' Peng ordered. 'A good commander leads from the front!' he announced over the radio.

'Oh, shit,' Ge observed in his tank. 'Peng wants to show off his *ji-ji*. Move out,' he ordered his driver, a captain (his entire crew was made of officers). 'Let's lead the emperor to the recon screen.'

The brand-new T-98 tank surged forward, throwing up two rooster tails of dirt as it accelerated. General Ge was in the commander's hatch, with a major acting as gunner, a duty he practiced diligently because it was his job to keep his general alive in the event of contact with the enemy. For the moment, it meant going ahead of the senior general with blood in his eye.

*   *   *

'Why did they stop?' Buikov asked. The PLA tracks had suddenly halted nine hundred meters off, all five of them, and now the crews dismounted, manifestly to take a stretch, and five of them lit up smokes.

'They must be waiting for something,' the captain thought aloud. Then he got on the radio. 'GREEN WOLF here, the enemy has halted about a kilometer south of us. They're just sitting still.'

'Have they seen you?'

'No, they've dismounted to take a piss, looks like, just standing there. We have them in range, but I don't want to shoot until they're closer,' Aleksandrov reported.

'Very well, take your time. There's no hurry here. They're walking into the parlor very nicely.'

'Understood. Out.' He set the mike down. 'Is it time for morning break?'

'They haven't been doing that the last four days, Comrade Captain,' Buikov reminded his boss.

'They appear relaxed enough.'

'I could kill any of them now,' Gogol said, 'but they're all privates, except for that one . . .'

'That's the fox. He's a lieutenant, likes to run around a lot. The other officer's the gardener. He likes playing with plants,' Buikov told the old man.

651

'Killing a lieutenant's not much better than killing a corporal,' Gogol observed. 'There's too many of them.'

'What's this?' Buikov said from his gunner's seat. 'Tank, enemy tank coming around the left edge, range five thousand.'

'I see it!' Aleksandrov reported. '. . . Just one? Only one tank—oh, all right, there's a carrier with it—'

'It's a command track, look at all those antennas!' Buikov called.

The gunner's sight was more powerful than Aleksandrov's binoculars. The captain couldn't confirm that for another minute or so. 'Oh, yes, that's a command track, all right. I wonder who's in it . . .'

*   *   *

'There they are,' the driver called back. 'The reconnaissance section, two kilometers ahead, Comrade General.'

'Excellent,' Peng observed. Standing up to look out of the top of his command track with his binoculars, good Japanese ones from Nikon. There was Ge in his command tank, thirty meters off to the right, protecting him as though he were a good dog outside the palace of some ancient nobleman. Peng couldn't see anything to be concerned about. It was a clear day, with some puffy white clouds at three thousand meters or so. If there were American fighters up there, he wasn't going to worry about them. Besides, they'd done no ground-attacking that he'd heard about, except to hit those bridges back at Harbin, and one might as well attack a mountain as those things, Peng was sure. He had to hold on to the sill of the hatch lest the pitching of the vehicle smash him against it—it *was a track specially modified for senior officers, but no one had thought to make it safer to stand in,* he thought sourly. He wasn't some peasant-private who could smash his head with no consequence . . . Well, in any case, it was a good day to be a soldier, in the field leading his men. A fair day, and no enemy in sight.

'Pull up alongside the reconnaissance track,' he ordered his driver.

*　　　*　　　*

'Who the hell is this?' Captain Aleksandrov wondered aloud. 'Four big antennas, at least a division commander,' Bulkov thought aloud. 'My thirty will settle his hash.'

'No, no, let's let Pasha have him if he gets out.'

Gogol had anticipated that. He was resting his arms on the steel top of the BRM, tucking the rifle in tight to his shoulder. The only thing in his way was the loose weave of the camouflage netting, and that wasn't an obstacle to worry about, the old marksman was sure.

'Stopping to see the fox?' Buikov said next.

'Looks that way,' the captain agreed.

*　　　*　　　*

'Comrade General!' the young lieutenant called in surprise. 'Where's the enemy, Boy?' Peng asked loudly in return.

'General, we haven't seen much this morning.

653

Some tracks in the ground, but not even any of that for the past two hours.'

'Nothing at all?'

'Not a thing,' the lieutenant replied.

'Well, I thought there'd be something around.' Peng put his foot in the leather stirrup and climbed to the top of his command vehicle.

* * *

'It's a general, has to be, look at that clean uniform!' Buikov told the others as he slewed his turret around to center his sight on the man eight hundred meters away. It was the same in any army. Generals never got dirty.

'Pasha,' Aleksandrov asked, 'ever kill an enemy general before?'

'No,' Gogol admitted, drawing the rifle in very tight and allowing for the range . . .

* * *

'Better to go to that ridgeline, but our orders were to stop at once,' the lieutenant told the general.

'That's right,' Peng agreed. He took out his Nikon binoculars and trained them on the ridge, perhaps eight hundred meters off. Nothing to see except for that one bush . . .

Then there was a flash—

'Yes!' Gogol said the moment the trigger broke. Two seconds, about, for the bullet to—

* * *

They'd never hear the report of the shot over the

sound of their diesel engines, but Colonel Wa heard the strange, wet thud, and his head turned to see General Peng's face twist into surprise rather than pain, and Peng grunted from the sharp blow to the center of his chest, and then his hands started coming down, pulled by the additional weight of the binoculars—and then his body started down, falling off the top of the command track through the hatch into the radio-filled interior.

*   *   *

'That got him,' Gogol said positively. 'He's dead.' He almost added that it might be fun to skin him and lay his hide in the river for a final swim and a gold coating, but, no, you only did that to wolves, not people—not even Chinese.

'Buikov, take those tracks!'

'Gladly, Comrade Captain,' and the sergeant squeezed the trigger, and the big machine gun spoke.

*   *   *

They hadn't seen or heard the shot that had killed Peng, but there was no mistaking the machine cannon that fired now. Two of the reconnaissance tracks exploded at once, but then everything started moving, and fire was returned.

'Major!' General Ge called.

'Loading HEAT!' The gunner punched the right button, but the autoloader, never as fast as a person, took its time to ram the projectile and then the propellant case into the breech.

'Back us up!' Aleksandrov ordered loudly. The diesel engine was already running, and the BRM's transmission set in reverse. The corporal in the driver's seat floored the pedal and the carrier jerked backward. The suddenness of it nearly lost Gogol over the side, but Aleksandrov grabbed his arm and dragged him down inside, tearing his skin in the process. 'Go north!' the captain ordered next.

'I got three of the bastards!' Buikov said. Then the sky was rent by a crash overhead. Something had gone by too fast to see, but not too fast to hear.

'That tank gunner knows his business,' Aleksandrov observed. 'Corporal, get us out of here!'

'Working on it, Comrade Captain.'

'GREEN WOLF to command!' the captain said next into the radio.

'Yes, GREEN WOLF, report.'

'We just killed three enemy tracks, and I think we got a senior officer. Pasha, Sergeant Gogol, that is, killed a Chinese general officer, or so it appeared.'

'He was a general, all right,' Buikov agreed. 'The shoulder boards were pure gold, and that was a command track with four big radio antennas.'

'Understood. What are you doing now, GREEN WOLF?'

'We're getting the fuck away. I think we'll be seeing more Chinks soon.'

'Agreed, GREEN WOLF. Proceed to divisional CP. Out.'

'Yuriy Andreyevich, you will have heavy contact

in a few minutes. What is your plan?'

'I want to volley-fire my tanks before firing my artillery. Why spoil the surprise, Gennady?' Sinyavskiy asked cruelly. 'We are ready for them here.'

'Understood. Good luck, Yuriy'

'And what of the other missions?'

'BOYAR is moving now, and the Americans are about to deploy their magical pigs. If you can handle the leading Chinese elements, those behind ought to be roughly handled.'

'You can rape their daughters for all I care, Gennady.'

'That is *nekulturniy*, Yuriy. Perhaps their wives,' he suggested, adding, 'We are watching you on the television now.'

'Then I will smile for the cameras,' Sinyavskiy promised.

*   *   *

The orbiting F-16 fighters were under the tactical command of Major General Gus Wallace, but he, at the moment, was under the command—or at least operating under the direction—of a Russian, General—Colonel Gennady Bondarenko, who was in turn guided by the action of this skinny young Major Tucker and Grace Kelly, a soulless drone hovering over the battlefield.

'There they go, General,' Tucker said, as the leading Chinese echelons resumed their drive north.

'I think it is time, then.' He looked to Colonel Aliyev, who nodded agreement.

Bondarenko lifted the satellite phone. 'General

Wallace?'

'I'm here.'

'Please release your aircraft.'

'Roger that. Out.' And Wallace shifted phone receivers. 'EAGLE ONE, this is ROUGHRIDER. Execute, execute, execute. Acknowledge.'

'Roger that, sir, copy your order to execute. Executing now. Out.' And the colonel on the lead AWACS shifted to a different frequency: 'CADILLAC LEAD, this is EAGLE ONE. Execute your attack. Over.'

'Roger that,' the colonel heard. 'Going down now. Out.'

*　　　*　　　*

The F-16s had been circling above the isolated clouds. Their threat receivers chirped a little bit, reporting the emissions of SAM radars somewhere down there, but the types indicated couldn't reach this high, and their jammer pods were all on anyway. On command, the sleek fighters changed course for the battlefield far below and to their west. Their GPS locators told them exactly where they were, and they also knew where their targets were, and the mission became a strictly technical exercise.

Under the wings of each aircraft were the Smart Pigs, four to the fighter, and with forty-eight fighters, that came to 192 J-SOWs. Each of these was a canister thirteen feet long and not quite two feet wide, filled with BLU-108 submunitions, twenty per container. The fighter pilots punched the release triggers, dropped their bombs, and then angled for home, letting the robots do the rest of the work. The Dark Star tapes would later tell them how they'd done.

The Smart Pigs separated from the fighters, extended their own little wings to guide themselves the rest of the way to the target area. They knew this information, having been programmed by the fighters and were now able to follow guidance from their own GPS receivers. This they did, acting in accordance with their own onboard mini-computers, until each reached a spot five thousand feet over their designated segment of the battlefield. They didn't know that this was directly over the real estate occupied by the Chinese 29th Type A Group Army and its three heavy divisions, which included nearly seven hundred main-battle tanks, three hundred armored personnel carriers, and a hundred mobile guns. That made a total of roughly a thousand targets for the nearly four thousand descending submunitions. But the falling bomblets were guided, too, and each had a seeker looking for heat of the sort radiated by an operating tank, personnel carrier, self-propelled gun, or truck. There were a lot of them to look for.

No one saw them coming. They were small, no larger, really, than a common crow, and falling rapidly; they were also painted white, which helped them blend in to the morning sky. Each had a rudimentary steering mechanism, and at an altitude of two thousand feet they started looking for and homing in on targets. Their downward speed was such that a minor deflection of their control vanes was sufficient to get them close, and close meant straight down.

They exploded in bunches, almost in the same instant. Each contained a pound and a half of high-

659

explosive, the heat from which melted the metal casing, which then turned into a projectile—the process was called 'self-forging'—which blazed downward at a speed of ten thousand feet per second. The armor on the top of a tank is always the thinnest, and five times the thickness would have made no difference. Of the 921 tanks on the field, 762 took hits, and the least of these destroyed the vehicles' diesel engine. Those less fortunate took hits through the turret, which killed the crews at once and/or ignited the ammunition storage, converting each armored vehicle into a small man-fabricated volcano. Just that quickly, three mechanized divisions were changed into one badly shaken and disorganized brigade. The infantry carriers fared no better, and it was worst of all for the trucks, most of them carrying ammunition or other flammable supplies.

All in all, it took less than ninety seconds to turn 29th Type A Group Army into a thinly spread junkyard and funeral pyre.

*   *   *

'Holy God,' Ryan said. 'Is this for-real?'

'Seeing is believing. Jack, when they came to me with the idea for J-SOW, I thought it had to be something from a science-fiction book. Then they demo'd the submunitions out at China Lake, and I thought, Jesus, we don't need the Army or the Marines anymore. Just send over some F-18s and then a brigade of trucks full of body bags and some ministers to pray over them. Eh, Mickey?'

'It's some capability,' General Moore agreed. He shook his head. 'Damn, just like the tests.'

'Okay, what's happening next?'

*   *   *

'Next' was just off the coast near Guangszhou. Two Aegis cruisers, *Mobile Bay* and *Princeton*, plus the destroyers *Fletcher, Fife*, and *John Young*, steamed in line-ahead formation out of the morning fog and turned broadside to the shore. There was actually a decent beach at this spot. There was nothing much behind it, just a coastal-defense missile battery that the fighter-bombers had immolated a few hours before. To finish that job, the ships trained their guns to port and let loose a barrage of five-inch shells. The crack and thunder of the gunfire could be heard on shore, as was the shriek of the shells passing overhead, and the explosions of the detonations. That included one missile that the bombs of the previous night had missed, plus the crew getting it ready for launch. People living nearby saw the gray silhouettes against the morning sky, and many of them got on the telephone to report what they saw, but being civilians, they reported the wrong thing, of course.

*   *   *

It was just after nine in the morning in Beijing when the Politburo began its emergency session. Some of those present had enjoyed a restful night's sleep, and then been disturbed by the news that came over the phone at breakfast. Those better informed had hardly slept at all past three in the morning and, though more awake than their colleagues, were not in a happier mood.

661

'Well, Luo, what is happening?' Interior Minister Tong Jie asked.

'Our enemies counterattacked last night. This sort of thing we must expect, of course,' he admitted in as low-key a voice as circumstances permitted.

'How serious were these counterattacks?' Tong asked.

'The most serious involved some damage to railroad bridges in Harbin and Bei'an, but repairs are under way.'

'I hope so. The repair effort will require some months,' Qian Kun interjected.

'Who said that?' Luo demanded harshly.

'Marshal, I supervised the construction of two of those bridges. This morning I called the division superintendent for our state railroad in Harbin. All six of them have been destroyed—the piers on both sides of the river are totally wrecked; it will take over a month just to clear the debris. I admit this surprised me. Those bridges were very sturdily built, but the division superintendent tells me they are quite beyond repair.'

'And who is this defeatist?' Luo demanded.

'He is a loyal party member of long standing and a very competent engineer whom you will *not* threaten in my presence!' Qian shot back. 'There is room in this building for many things, but there is *not* room here for a *lie*!'

'Come now, Qian,' Zhang Han Sen soothed. 'We need not have that sort of language here. Now, Luo, how bad is it really?'

'I have army engineers heading there now to make a full assessment of the damage and to commence repairs. I am confident that we can restore service shortly. We have skilled bridging engineers, you know.'

'Luo,' Qian said, 'your magic army bridges can support a tank or a truck, yes, but not a locomotive that weighs two hundred tons pulling a train weighing four thousand. Now, what else has gone wrong with your Siberian adventure?'

'It is foolish to think that the other side will simply lie down and die. Of course they fight back. But we have superior forces in theater, and we will smash them. We will have that new gold mine in our pocket before this meeting is over,' the Defense Minister promised. But the pledge seemed hollow to some of those around the table.

'What else?' Qian persisted.

'The American naval air forces attacked last night and succeeded in sinking some of our South Sea Fleet units.'

'Which units?'

'Well, we have no word from our missile submarine, and—'

'They sank our only missile submarine?' Premier Xu asked. 'How is this possible? Was it sitting in harbor?'

'No,' Luo admitted. 'It was at sea, in company with another nuclear submarine, and that one is also possibly lost.'

'Marvelous!' Tong Jie observed. 'Now the Americans strike at our strategic assets! That's half our nuclear deterrent gone, and that was the *safe* half of it. What goes on, Luo? What is happening now?'

At his seat, Fang Gan took note of the fact that Zhang was strangely subdued. Ordinarily he would have leaped to Luo's defense, but except for the one conciliatory comment, he was leaving the Defense Minister to flap in the wind. What might that mean?

'What do we tell the people?' Fang asked, trying to center the meeting on something important.

'The people will believe what they are told,' Luo said.

And everyone nodded nervous agreement on that one. They *did* control the media. The American CNN news service had been turned off all over the People's Republic, along with all Western news services, even in Hong Kong, which usually enjoyed much looser reins than the rest of the country. But the thing no one addressed, but everyone knew to worry about, was that every soldier had a mother and a father who'd notice when the mail home stopped coming. Even in a nation as tightly controlled as the PRC, you couldn't stop the Truth from getting out—or rumors, which, though false, could be even worse than an adverse Truth. People *would* believe things other than those they were told to believe, if those other things made more sense than the Official Truth proclaimed by their government in Beijing.

Truth was something so often feared in this room, Fang realized, and for the first time in his life he wondered why that had to be. If the Truth was something to fear, might that mean they were doing something wrong in here? But, no, that couldn't be true, could it? Didn't they have a perfect political model for reality? Wasn't that Mao's bequest to their country?

But if that were true, why did they fear having the people find out what was really happening?

Could it be that they, the Politburo members,

664

could handle the Truth and the peasantry could not?

But then, if they feared having the peasantry get hold of the Truth, didn't that have to mean that the Truth was harmful to the people sitting in this room? And if the Truth was a danger to the peasants and workers, then didn't *they* have to be wrong?

Fang suddenly realized how dangerous was the thought that had just entered his mind.

'Luo, what does it mean to us strategically,' the Interior Minister asked, 'if the Americans remove half of our strategic weapons? Was that done deliberately? If so, for what cause?'

'Tong, you do not sink a ship by accident, and so, yes, the attack on our missile submarine must have been a deliberate act,' Luo answered.

'So, the Americans deliberately removed from the table one of our only methods for attacking them directly? Why? Was that not a political act, not just a military one?'

The Defense Minister nodded. 'Yes, you could see it that way.'

'Can we expect the Americans to strike at us directly? To this date they have struck some bridges, but what about our government and vital industries? Might they strike directly at *us*?' Tong went on.

'That would be unwise. We have missiles targeted at their principal cities. They know this. Since they disarmed themselves of nuclear missiles some years ago—well, they still have nuclear bombs that can be delivered by bombers and tactical aircraft, of course, but not the ability to strike at us in the way that we could strike at them—and the Russians, of course.'

'How sure are we that they are disarmed?' Tong persisted.

'If they have ballistic arms, they've concealed it from everyone,' Tan Deshi told them all. Then he shook his head decisively. 'No, they have no more.'

'And that gives us an advantage, doesn't it?' Zhong asked, with a ghoulish smile.

*   *   *

USS *Gettysburg* was alongside the floating pier in the York River. Once the warheads for Trident missiles had been stored here, and there must still have been some awaiting dismantlement, because there were Marines to be seen, and only Marines were entrusted to guard the Navy's nuclear weapons. But none of those were on the pier. No, the trucks that rolled out from the weapons depot were carrying long square-cross-sectioned boxes that contained SM-2 ER Block-IVD surface-to-air missiles. When the trucks got to the cruiser, a traveling crane lifted them up to the foredeck of the ship, where, with the assistance of some strong-backed sailors, the boxes were rapidly lowered into the vertical launch cells of the forward missile launcher. It took about four minutes per box, Gregory saw, with the captain pacing his wheelhouse all the while. Gregory knew why. He had an order to take his cruiser right to Washington, D.C., and the order had the word 'expedite' on it. Evidently, 'expedite' was a word with special meaning for the United States Navy, like having your wife call for you from the baby's room at two in the morning. The tenth box was duly lowered, and the crane swung clear of the ship.

'Mr. Richardson,' Captain Blandy said to the Officer of the Deck.

'Yes, sir,' the lieutenant answered.

'Let's get under way.'

Gregory walked out on the bridge wing to watch. The Special Sea Detail cast off the six-inch hawsers, and scarcely had they fallen clear of the cleats on the main deck when the cruiser's auxiliary power unit started pushing the ten thousand tons of gray steel away from the floating pier. And the ship was for sure in a hurry. She was not fifteen feet away when the main engines started turning, and less than a minute after that, Gregory heard the *WHOOSH* of the four jet-turbines taking a big gulp of air, and he could *feel* the ship accelerate for the Chesapeake Bay, almost like being on a city transit bus.

'Dr. Gregory?' Captain Blandy had stuck his head out the pilothouse door.

'Yeah, Captain?'

'You want to get below and do your software magic on our birds?'

'You bet.' He knew the way, and in three minutes was at the computer terminal which handled that task.

'Hey, Doc,' Senior Chief Leek said, sitting down next to him. 'All ready? I'm supposed to help.'

'Okay, you can watch, I suppose.' The only problem was that it was a clunky system, about as user-friendly as a chain saw, but as Leek had told him a week before, this was the flower of 1975 technology, back when an Apple-II with 64K of RAM was the cat's own ass. Now he had more computing power in his wristwatch. Each missile had to be upgraded separately, and each was a seven-step process.

'Hey, wait a minute,' Gregory objected. The screen wasn't right.

'Doc, we loaded six Block-IVD. The other two are stock SM-2 ER Block IIIC radar-homers. What can I tell you, Cap'n Blandy's conservative.'

'So I only do the upgrade on holes one through six?'

'No, do 'em all. It'll just ignore the changes you made to the infrared homing code. The chips on the birds can handle the extra code, no sweat, right, Mr. Olson?'

'Correct, Senior Chief,' Lieutenant Olson confirmed. 'The missiles are current technology even if the computer system isn't. It probably costs more to make missile seeker-heads with current technology that can talk to this old kludge than it would to buy a new Gateway to upgrade the whole system, not to mention having a more reliable system overall, but you'll have to talk to NAVSEA about that.'

'Who?' Gregory asked.

'Naval Sea Systems Command. They're the technical geniuses who won't put stabilizers on these cruisers. They think it's good for us to puke in a seaway.'

'Feathermerchants,' Leek explained. 'Navy's full of 'em—on land, anyway.' The ship heeled strongly to starboard.

'Cap'n's in a hurry, ain't he?' Gregory observed. *Gettysburg* was making a full-speed right-angle turn to port.

'Well, SACLANT said it's the SecDef's idea. I

guess that makes it important,' Mr. Olson told their guest.

*   *   *

'I think this is imprudent,' Fang told them all. 'Why is that?' Luo asked.

'Is fueling the missiles necessary? Is there not a danger of provocation?'

'I suppose this is a technical matter,' Qian said. 'As I recall, once you fuel them, you cannot keep them fueled for more than—what? Twelve hours?'

The technocrat caught the Defense Minister off guard with that question. He didn't know the answer. 'I will have to consult with Second Artillery for that,' he admitted.

'So, then, you will not prepare them for launch until we have a chance to consider the matter?' Qian asked.

'Why—of course not,' Luo promised.

'And so the real problem is, how do we tell the people what has transpired in Siberia?'

'The people will believe what we tell them to believe!' Luo said yet again.

'Comrades,' Qian said, struggling to keep his voice reasonable, 'we cannot conceal the rising of the sun. Neither can we conceal the loss of our rail-transport system. Nor can we conceal the large-scale loss of life. Every soldier has parents, and when enough of them realize their son is lost, they will speak of it, and the word will get out. We must face facts here. It is better, I think, to tell the people that there is a major battle going on, and there has been loss of life. To proclaim that we are winning when we may not be is dangerous for all of us.'

'You say the people will rise up?' Tong Jie asked.

'No, but I say there could be dissatisfaction and unrest, and it is in our collective interest to avoid that, is it not?' Qian asked the assembly.

'How will adverse information get out?' Luo asked.

'It frequently does,' Qian told them. 'We can prepare for it, and mitigate the effect of adverse information, or we can try to withstand it. The former offers mild embarrassment to us. The latter, if it fails, could be more serious.'

'The TV will show what we wish them to show, and the people will see nothing else. Besides, General Peng and his army group are advancing even as we speak.'

*   *   *

'What do they call it?'

'This one's Grace Kelly. The other two are Marilyn Monroe and—can't remember,' General Moore said. 'Anyway, they named 'em for movie stars.'

'And how do they transmit?'

'The Dark Star uploads directly to a communications satellite, encrypted, of course, and we distribute it out of Fort Belvoir.'

'So, we can send it out any way we want?'

'Yes, sir.'

'Okay, Ed, the Chinese are telling their people what?'

'They started off by saying the Russians committed a border intrusion and they counterattacked. They're also saying that they're

670

kicking Ivan's ass.'

'Well, that's not true, and it'll be especially untrue when they reach the Russian stop-line. That Bondareriko guy's really played his cards beautifully. They're pretty strung out. We've chopped their supply line for fair, and they're heading into a real motherfucker of an ambush,' the DCI told them. 'How about it, General?'

'The Chinese just don't know what's ahead of them. You know, out at the NTC we keep teaching people that he who wins the reconnaissance battle wins the war. The Russians know what's happening. The Chinese do not. My God, this Dark Star has really exceeded our expectations.

'It's some shiny new toy, Mickey,' Jackson agreed. 'Like going to a Vegas casino when you're able to read the cards halfway through the deck. You just can't hardly lose this way.'

The President leaned forward. 'You know, one of the reasons we took it on the chin with Vietnam is how the people got to see the war every night on Huntley-Brinkley. How will it affect the Chinese if their people see the war the same way, but *live* this time?'

'The battle that's coming? It'll shake them up a lot,' Ed Foley thought. 'But how do we—oh, oh, yeah . . . Holy shit, Jack, are you serious?'

'Can we do it?' Ryan asked.

'Technically? It's child's play. My only beef is that it really lets people know one of our capabilities. This is sensitive stuff, I mean, right up there with the performance of our reconnaissance satellites. It's not the sort of thing you just let out.'

'Why not? Hell, couldn't some university duplicate the optics?' the President asked.

'Well, yeah, I guess. The imagery systems are good, but they're not all that new a development, except some of the thermal systems, but even so—

'Ed, let's say we can shock them into stopping the war. How many lives would it save?'

'Quite a few,' the DCI admitted. 'Thousands. Maybe tens of thousands.'

'Including some of our people?'

'Yes, Jack, including some of ours.'

'And from a technical point of view, it's really child's play?'

'Yes, it's not technically demanding at all.'

'Then turn the children loose, Ed. Right now,' Ryan ordered.

'Yes, Mr. President.'

CHAPTER FIFTY-NINE

LOSS OF CONTROL

With the death of General Peng, command of 34th Shock Army devolved to Major General Ge Li, CG also of 302nd Armored. His first task was to get himself clear, and this he did, ordering his tank off the long gun-range slope while one of the surviving reconnaissance tracks recovered Peng's body. All of those tracked vehicles also pulled back, as Ge figured his first task was to determine what had happened, rather then to avenge the death of his army commander. It took him twenty minutes to motor back to his own command section, where he had a command track identical to the one Peng had driven about in. He needed the radios, since he knew the field phones were down, for whatever reason he didn't know.

'I need to talk to Marshal Luo,' he said over the command frequency, which was relayed back to Beijing via several repeater stations. It took another ten minutes because the Defense Minister, he was told, was in a Politburo meeting. Finally, the familiar voice came over the radio.

'This is Marshal Luo.'

'This is Major General Ge Li, commanding Three-Oh-Second Armored. General Peng Xi-Wang is dead,' he announced.

'What happened?'

'He went forward to join the reconnaissance section to see the front, and he was killed by a sniper bullet. The recon section ran into a small ambush, looked like a single Russian personnel carrier. I drove it off with my own tank,' Ge went on. It was fairly true, and it seemed like the sort of thing he was supposed to say.

'I see. What is the overall situation?' the Defense Minister asked.

'Thirty-fourth Shock Army is advancing—well, it was. I paused the advance to reorganize the command group. I request instructions, Comrade Minister.'

'You will advance and capture the Russian gold mine, secure it, and then continue north for the oil field.'

'Very well, Comrade Minister, but I must advise you that Twenty-ninth Army, right behind us, sustained a serious attack an hour ago, and was reportedly badly hit.'

'How badly?'

'I do not know. Reports are sketchy, but it

673

doesn't sound good.'

'What sort of attack was it?'

'An air attack, origin unknown. As I said, reports are very sketchy at this time. Twenty-ninth seems very disorganized at the moment,' Ge reported.

'Very well. You will continue the attack. Forty-third Army is behind Twenty-ninth and will support you. Watch your left flank—'

'I know of the reports of Russian units to my west,' Ge said. 'I will orient a mechanized division to deal with that, but . . .'

'But what?' Luo asked.

'But, Comrade Marshal, we have no reconnaissance information on what lies before us. I need such information in order to advance safely.'

'You will find your safety in advancing rapidly into enemy territory and destroying whatever formations you find,' Luo told him forcefully. 'Continue your advance!'

'By your command, Comrade Minister.' There wasn't much else he could say to that.

'Report back to me as necessary.'

'I will do that,' Ge promised.

'Very well. Out.' Static replaced the voice.

'You heard him,' Ge said to Colonel Wa Cheng-gong, whom he'd just inherited as army operations officer. 'Now what, Colonel?'

'We continue the advance, Comrade General.'

Ge nodded to the logic of the situation. 'Give the order.'

It took hold four minutes later, when the radio commands filtered down to battalion level and the units started moving.

They didn't need reconnaissance information now, Colonel Wa reasoned. They knew that there had to be some light Russian units just beyond the ridgeline where Peng had met his foolish death. *Didn't I warn him?* Wa raged to himself. *Didn't Ge warn him?* For a general to die in battle was not unexpected. But to die from a single bullet fired by some lone rifleman was worse than foolish. Thirty years of training and experience wasted, lost to a single rifleman!

*   *   *

'There they go again,' Major Tucker said, seeing the plume of diesel exhaust followed by the lurching of numerous armored vehicles. 'About six kilometers from your first line of tanks.'

'A pity we can't get one of these terminals to Sinyavskiy,' Bondarenko said.

'Not that many of them, sir,' Tucker told him. 'Sun Micro Systems is still building them for us.'

*   *   *

'That was General Ge Li,' Luo told the Politburo. 'We've had some bad luck. General Peng is dead, killed by a sniper bullet, I just learned.'

'How did that happen?' Premier Xu asked.

'Peng had gone forward, as a good general should, and there was a lucky Russian out there with a rifle,' the Defense Minister explained. Then one of his aides appeared and walked to the marshal's seat, handing him a slip of paper. He scanned it. 'This is confirmed?'

'Yes, Comrade Marshal. I requested and got confirmation myself. The ships are in sight of land even now.'

'What ships? What land?' Xu asked. It was unusual for him to take an active part in these meetings. Usually he let the others talk, listened passively, and then announced the consensus conclusions reached by the others.

'Comrade,' Luo answered. 'It seems some American warships are bombarding our coast near Guangszhou.'

'Bombarding?' Xu asked. 'You mean with guns?'

'That's what the report says, yes.'

'Why would they do that?' the Premier asked, somewhat nonplussed by this bit of information.

'To destroy shore emplacements, and—'

'Isn't that what one does prior to invading, a preparation to putting troops on the beach?' Foreign Minister Shen asked.

'Well, yes, it could be that, I suppose,' Luo replied, 'but—'

'Invasion?' Xu asked. 'A direct attack on our own soil?'

'Such a thing is most unlikely,' Luo told them. 'They lack the ability to put troops ashore in sufficiently large numbers. America simply doesn't have the troops to do such a—'

'What if they get assistance from Taiwan? How many troops do the bandits have?' Tong Jie asked.

'Well, they have some land forces,' Luo allowed. 'But we have ample ability to—'

'You told us a week ago that we had all the forces required to defeat the Russians, even if they got some aid from America,' Qian observed, becoming agitated. 'What fiction do you have for us now, Luo?'

'*Fiction!*' the marshal's voice boomed. 'I tell you the facts, but now you accuse me of that?'

676

'What have you *not* told us, Luo?' Qian asked harshly. 'We are not peasants here to be told what to believe.'

'The Russians are making a stand. They have fought back. I told you that, and I told you this sort of thing is to be expected—and it is. We fight a war with the Russians. It's not a burglary in an unoccupied house. This is an armed contest between two major powers and we will win because we have more and better troops. They do not fight well. We swept aside their border defenses, and we've pursued their army north, and they didn't have the manhood to stand and fight for their own land! We will *smash* them. Yes, they will fight back. We must expect that, but it won't matter. We will *smash* them, I tell you!' he insisted.

'Is there any information which you have not told us to this point?' Interior Minister Tong asked, in a voice more reasonable than the question itself.

'I have appointed Major General Ge to assume command of the Thirty-fourth Shock Army. He reported to me that Twenty-ninth Army sustained a serious air attack earlier today. The effects of this attack are not clear, probably they managed to damage communications—and an air attack cannot seriously hurt a large mechanized *land* force. The tools of war do not permit such a thing.'

'Now what?' Premier Xu asked.

'I propose that we adjourn the meeting and allow Minister Luo to return to his task of managing our armed forces,' Zhang Han Sen proposed. 'And that we reconvene, say, at sixteen hours.'

There were nods around the table. Everyone wanted the time to consider the things that they'd

677

heard this morning—and perhaps to give the Defense Minister the chance to make good his words. Xu did a head count and stood.

'Very well. We adjourn until this afternoon.' The meeting broke up in an unusually subdued manner, without the usual pairing off and pleasantries between old comrades. Outside the conference room, Qian buttonholed Fang again.

'Something is going badly wrong. I can feel it.'

'How sure are you of that?'

'Fang, I don't know what the Americans have done to my railroad bridges, but I assure you that to destroy them as I was informed earlier this morning is no small thing. Moreover, the destruction inflicted was deliberately systematic. The Americans—it must have been the Americans—deliberately crippled our ability to supply our field armies. You only do such a thing in preparation to smashing them. And now the commanding general of our advancing armies is suddenly killed—stray bullet, my ass! That *tset ha tset ha* Luo leads us to disaster, Fang.'

'We'll know more this afternoon,' Fang suggested, leaving his colleague and going to his office. Arriving there, he dictated another segment for his daily journal. For the first time, he wondered if it might turn out to be his testament.

*   *   *

For her part, Ming was disturbed by her minister's demeanor. An elderly man, he'd always nonetheless been a calm and optimistic one for the most part. His mannerisms were those of a grandfatherly gentleman even when taking her or

678

one of the other office girls to his bed. It was an endearing quality, one of the reasons the office staff didn't resist his advances more vigorously—and besides, he *did* take care of those who took care of *his* needs. This time she took her dictation quietly, while he leaned back in his chair, his eyes closed, and his voice a monotone. It took half an hour, and she went out to her desk to do the transcription. It was time for the midday meal by the time she was done, and she went out to lunch with her co-worker, Chai.

'What is the matter with him?' she asked Ming.

'The meeting this morning did not go well. Fang is concerned with the war.'

'But isn't it going well? Isn't that what they say on TV?'

'It seems there have been some setbacks. This morning they argued about how serious they were. Qian was especially exercised about it, because the Americans attacked our rail bridges in Harbin and Bei'an.'

'Ah.' Chai shoveled some rice into her mouth with her chopsticks. 'How is Fang taking it?'

'He seems very tense. Perhaps he will need some comfort this evening.'

'Oh? Well, I can take care of him. I need a new office chair anyway,' she added with a giggle.

Lunch dragged on longer than usual. Clearly their minister didn't need any of them for the moment, and Ming took the time to walk about on the street to gauge the mood of the people there. The feeling was strangely neutral. She was out just long enough to trigger her computer's downtime activation, and though the screen was blank, in the auto-sleep mode, the hard drive started turning, and silently activated the onboard modem.

*   *   *

Mary Pat Foley was in her office, though it was past midnight, and she was logging onto her mail account every fifteen minutes, hoping for something new from SORGE.

'You've got mail!' the mechanical voice told her.

'Yes!' she said back to it, downloading the document at once. Then she lifted the phone. 'Get Sears up here.'

With that done, Mrs. Foley looked at the time entry on the e-mail. It had gone out in the early afternoon in Beijing . . . what might that mean? she wondered, afraid that any irregularity could spell the death of SONGBIRD, and the loss of the SORGE documents.

'Working late?' Sears asked on entering.

'Who isn't?' MP responded. She held out the latest printout. 'Read.'

'Politburo meeting, in the morning for a change,' Sears said, scanning the first page. 'Looks a little raucous. This Qian guy is raising a little hell—oh, okay, he chatted with Fang after it and expressed serious concerns . . . agreed to meet later in the day and—oh, shit!'

'What's that?'

'They discussed increasing the readiness of their ICBM force . . . let's see . . . nothing firm was decided for technical reasons, they weren't sure how long they could keep the missiles fueled, but they were shook by our takeout of their missile submarine . . .'

'Write that up. I'm going to hang a CRITIC on it,'

the DDO announced.

CRITIC—shorthand for 'critical'—is the highest priority in the United States government for message traffic. A CRITIC-flagged document must be in the President's hands no less than fifteen minutes after being generated. That meant that Joshua Sears had to get it drafted just as quickly as he could type in his keyboard, and that made for errors in translation.

*   *   *

Ryan had been asleep for maybe forty minutes when the phone next to his bed went off.

'Yeah?'

'Mr. President,' some faceless voice announced in the White House Office of Signals, 'we have CRITIC traffic for you.'

'All right. Bring it up.' Jack swung his body across the bed and planted his feet on the rug. As a normal human being living in his home, he wasn't a bathrobe person. Ordinarily he'd just pad around his house barefoot in his underwear, but that wasn't allowed anymore, and he always kept a long blue robe handy now. It was a gift from long ago, when he'd taught history at the Naval Academy—a gift from the students there—and bore on the sleeves the one wide and four narrow stripes of a Fleet Admiral. So dressed, and wearing leather slippers that also came with the new job, he walked out into the upstairs corridor. The Secret Service night team was already up and moving. Joe Hilton came to him first.

'We heard, sir. It's on the way up now.'

Ryan, who'd been existing on less than five hours

681

of sleep per night for the past week, had an urgent need to lash out and rip the face off someone—anyone—but, of course, he couldn't do that to men who were just doing their job, with miserable hours of their own.

Special Agent Charlie Malone was at the elevator. He took the folder from the messenger and trotted over to Ryan.

'Hmm.' Ryan rubbed his hand over his face as he flipped the folder open. The first three lines jumped into his consciousness. 'Oh, shit.'

'Anything wrong?' Hilton asked.

'Phone,' Ryan said.

'This way, sir.' Hilton led him to the Secret Service upstairs cubbyhole office.

Ryan lifted the phone and said, 'Mary Pat at Langley.' It didn't take long. 'MP, Jack here. What gives?'

'It's just what you see. They're talking about fueling their intercontinental missiles. At least two of them are aimed at Washington.'

'Great. Now what?'

'I just tasked a KH-11 to give their launch sites a close look. There's two of them, Jack. The one we need to look at is Xuanhua. That's at about forty degrees, thirty-eight minutes north, one hundred fifteen degrees, six minutes east. Twelve silos with CCC-4 missiles inside. This is one of the newer ones, and it replaced older sites that stored the missiles in caves or tunnels. Straight, vertical, in-the-ground silos. The entire missile field is about six miles by six miles. The silos are well separated so that a single nuclear impact can't take out any two missiles,' MP explained, manifestly looking at overheads of the place as she spoke.

'How serious is this?'

A new voice came on the line. 'Jack, it's Ed. We have to take this one seriously. The naval bombardment on their coast might have set them off. The damned fools think we might be attempting a no-shit invasion.

'What? What with?' the President demanded.

'They can be very insular thinkers, Jack, and they're not always logical by our rules,' Ed Foley told him.

'Great. Okay. You two come on down here. Bring your best China guy with you.'

'On the way,' the DCI replied.

Ryan hung up and looked at Joe Hilton. 'Wake everybody up. The Chinese may be going squirrelly on us.'

*   *   *

The drive up the Potomac River hadn't been easy. Captain Blandy hadn't wanted to wait for a river pilot to help guide him up the river—naval officers tend to be overly proud when it comes to navigating their ships—and that had made it quite tense for the bridge watch. Rarely was the channel more than a few hundred yards wide, and cruisers are deepwater ships, not riverboats. Once they came within a few yards of a mudbank, but the navigator got them clear of it with a timely rudder order. The ship's radar was up and running— people were actually afraid to turn off the billboard system because it, like most mechanical contrivances, preferred operation to idleness, and switching it off might have broken something. As it was, the RF energy radiating from the four

683

huge billboard transmitters on *Gettysburg*'s superstructure had played hell with numerous television sets on the way northwest, but that couldn't be helped, and probably nobody noticed the cruiser in the river anyway, not at this time of night. Finally, *Gettysburg* glided to a halt within sight of the Woodrow Wilson bridge, and had to wait for traffic to be halted on the D.C. Beltway. This resulted in the usual road rage, but at this time of night there weren't that many people to be outraged, though one or two did honk their horns when the ship passed through the open drawbridge span. Perhaps they were New Yorkers, Captain Blandy thought. From there it was another turn to starboard into the Anacostia River, through another drawbridge, this one named for John Philip Sousa—accompanied by more surprised looks from the few drivers out—and then a gentle docking alongside the pier that was also home to USS *Barry*, a retired destroyer relegated to museum status.

The line handlers on the pier, Captain Blandy saw, were mainly civilians. Wasn't that a hell of a thing?

The 'evolution'—that, Gregory had learned, was what the Navy called parking a boat—had been interesting but unremarkable to observe, though the skipper looked quite relieved to have it all behind him.

'Finished with engines,' the CO told the engine room, and let out a long breath, shared, Gregory could see, by the entire bridge crew.

'Captain?' the retired Army officer asked.

'Yes?'

'What is this all about, exactly?'

'Well, isn't it kinda obvious?' Blandy responded. 'We have a shooting war with the Chinese. They have ICBMs, and I suppose the SecDef wants to be able to shoot them down if they loft one at Washington. SACLANT is also sending an Aegis to New York, and I'd bet Pacific Fleet has some looking out for Los Angeles and San Francisco. Probably Seattle, too. There's a lot of ships there anyway, and a good weapons locker. Do you have spare copies of your software?'

'Sure.'

'Well, we'll have a phone line from the dock in a few minutes. We'll see if there's a way for you to upload it to other interested parties.'

'Oh,' Dr. Gregory observed quietly. He really should have thought that one all the way through.

*   *   *

'This is RED WOLF FOUR. I have visual contact with the Chinese advance guard,' the regimental commander called on the radio. 'About ten kilometers south of us.'

'Very well,' Sinyavskiy replied. Just where Bondarenko and his American helpers said they were. Good. There were two other general officers in his command post, the CGs of 201st and 80th Motor Rifle divisions, and the commander of the 34th was supposed to be on his way as well, though 94th had turned and reoriented itself to attack east from a point about thirty kilometers to the south.

Sinyavskiy took the old, sodden cigar from his mouth and tossed it out into the grass, pulling another from his tunic pocket and lighting it. It was a Cuban cigar, and superb in its mildness. His artillery commander was on the other side of the map table—just a couple of planks on sawhorses, which was perfect for the moment. Close by were holes dug should the Chinese send some artillery fire their way, and most important of all, the wires which led to his communications station, set a full kilometer to the west—that was the first thing the Chinese would try to shoot at, because they'd expect him to be there. In fact the only humans present were four officers and seven sergeants, in armored personnel carriers dug into the ground for safety. It was their job to repair anything the Chinese might manage to break.

'So, comrades, they come right into our parlor, eh?' he said for those around him. Sinyavskiy had been a soldier for twenty-six years. Oddly, he was not the son of a soldier. His father was an instructor in geology at Moscow State University, but ever since the first war movie he'd seen, this was the profession he'd craved to join. He'd done all the work, attended all the schools, studied history with the manic attention common in the Russian army, and the Red Army before it. This would be his Battle of the Kursk Bulge, remembering the battle where Vatutin and Rokossovskiy had smashed Hitler's last attempt to retake the offensive in Russia—where his mother country had begun the long march that had ended at the Reich Chancellery in Berlin. There, too, the Red Army had been the recipient of brilliant intelligence information, letting them know the time, place, and character of the German attack, and so allowing them to prepare so well that even the best of the German field commanders, Erich von Manstein, could do no more than break his teeth on the Russian steel.

And so it will be here, Sinyavskiy promised himself. The only unsatisfactory part was that he was stuck here in this camouflaged tent instead of in the line with his men, but, no, he wasn't a captain anymore, and his place was here, to fight the battle on a goddamned printed map.

'RED WOLF, you will commence firing when the advance guard gets to within eight hundred meters.'

'Eight hundred meters, Comrade General,' the commander of his tank regiment acknowledged. 'I can see them quite clearly now.'

'What exactly can you see?'

'It appears to be a battalion-strength formation, principally Type 90 tanks, some Type 98s but not too many of those, spread out as though they went to sub-unit commanders. Numerous tracked personnel carriers. I do not see any artillery-spotting vehicles, however. What do we know of their artillery?'

'It's rolling, not set up for firing. We're watching them,' Sinyavskiy assured him.

'Excellent. They are now two kilometers off by my range finder.'

'Stand by.'

'I will do that, Command.'

'I hate waiting,' Sinyavskiy commented to the officers around him. They all nodded, having the same prejudice. He hadn't seen Afghanistan in his younger years, having served mainly in 1st and 2nd Guards Tank armies in Germany back then, preparing to fight against NATO, an event which blessedly had never taken place. This was his very first experience with real combat, and it hadn't really started yet, and he was ready for it to start.

*   *   *

'Okay, if they light those missiles up, what can we do about it?' Ryan asked.

'If they launch 'em, there's not a goddamned thing but run for cover,' Secretary Bretano said.

'That's good for us. We'll all get away. What about the people who live in Washington, New York, and all the other supposed targets?' POTUS asked.

'I've ordered some Aegis cruisers to the likely targets that are near the water,' THUNDER went on. 'I had one of my people from TRW look at the possibility of upgrading the missile systems to see if they might do an intercept. He's done the theoretical work, and he says it looks good on the simulators, but that's a ways from a practical test, of course. It's better than nothing, though.'

'Okay, where are the ships?'

'There's one here now,' Bretano answered.

'Oh? When did that happen?' Robby Jackson asked.

'Less than an hour ago. *Gettysburg.* There's another one going to New York—and San Francisco and Los Angeles. Also Seattle, though that's not really a target as far as we know. The software upgrade is going out to them to get their missiles reprogrammed.'

'Okay, that's something. What about taking those missiles out, before they can launch?' Ryan asked next.

'The Chinese silos have recently been upgraded in protection, steel armor on the concrete covers—

shaped like a Chinese coolie hat, it will probably deflect most bombs, but not the deep penetrators, the GBU-27s we used on the railroad bridges—'

'If they have any left over there. Better ask Gus Wallace,' the Vice President warned.

'What do you mean?' Bretano asked.

'I mean we never made all that many of them, and the Air Force must have dropped about forty last night.'

'I'll check that,' SecDef promised.

'What if he doesn't?' Jack asked.

'Then either we get some more in one big hurry, or we think up something else,' TOMCAT replied.

'Like what, Robby?'

'Hell, send in a special-operations team and blow them the fuck up,' the former fighter pilot suggested.

'I wouldn't much want to try that myself,' Mickey Moore observed.

'Beats the hell out of a five-megaton bomb going off on Capitol Hill, Mickey,' Jackson shot back. 'Look, the preferred thing to do is find out if Gus Wallace has the right bombs. It's a long stretch for the Black Jets, but you can tank them going and coming—and put fighters up to protect the tankers. It's complicated, but we practice that sort of thing. If he doesn't have the goddamned bombs, we fly them to him, assuming there are any. You know, weapons storage isn't a cornucopia, guys. There's a finite, discrete number for every item in the inventory.'

'General Moore,' Ryan said, 'call General Wallace and find out, right now, if you would.'

'Yes, sir.' Moore stood and left the Situation Room.

689

'Look,' Ed Foley said, pointing to the TV 'It's started.'

* * *

The wood line erupted in a sheet of flame two kilometers across. The sight caused the eyes of the Chinese tankers to flare, but most of the front rank of tank crews didn't have time for much more than that. Of the thirty tanks in that line, only three escaped immediate destruction. It was little better for the personnel carriers interspersed with them.

'You may commence firing, Colonel,' Sinyavskiy told his artillery commander.

The command was relayed at once, and the ground shook beneath their feet.

* * *

It was spectacular to see on the computer terminal. The Chinese had walked straight into the ambush, and the effect of the Russian opening volley was ghastly to behold.

Major Tucker took in a deep breath as he saw several hundred men lose their lives.

'Back to their artillery,' Bondarenko ordered.

'Yes, sir.' Tucker complied at once, altering the focus of the high-altitude camera and finding the Chinese artillery. It was mainly of the towed sort, being pulled behind trucks and tractors. They were a little slow getting the word. The first Russian shells were falling around them before any effort was made to stop the trucks and lift the limbers off the towing hooks, and for all that the Chinese gunners worked rapidly.

690

But theirs was a race against Death, and Death had a head start. Tucker watched one gun crew struggle to manhandle their 122-mm gun into a firing position. The gunners were loading the weapon when three shells landed close enough to upset the weapon and kill more than half their number. Zooming in the camera, he could see one private writing on the ground, and there was no one close by to offer him assistance.

'It is a miserable business, isn't it?' Bondarenko observed quietly.

'Yeah,' Tucker agreed. When a tank blew up it was easy to tell yourself that a tank was just a *thing*. Even though you knew that three or four human beings were inside, you couldn't see them. As a fighter pilot never killed a fellow pilot, but only shot down his aircraft, so Tucker adhered to the Air Force ethos that death was something that happened to objects rather than people. Well, that poor bastard with blood on his shirt wasn't a *thing*, was he? He backed off the camera, taking a wider field that permitted godlike distancing from the up-close-and-personal aspects of the observation.

'Better that they should have remained in their own country, Major,' the Russian explained to him.

*   *   *

'Jesus, what a mess,' Ryan said. He'd seen death up-close-and-personal himself in his time having shot people who had at the time been quite willing to shoot him, but that didn't make this imagery any the more palatable. Not by a long fucking shot. The President turned. 'Is this going out, Ed?' he asked the DCI. 'Ought to be,' Foley replied.

And it was, on a URL—'Uniform Resource Locator' in 'Netspeak—called http://www. darkstarfeed.cia.gov/siberiabattle/realtime.ram. It didn't even have to be advertised. Some 'Net crawlers stumbled onto it in the first five minutes, and the 'hits' from people looking at the 'streaming video' site climbed up from 0 to 10 in a matter of three minutes. Then some of them must have ducked into chat rooms to spread the word. The monitoring program for the URL at CIA headquarters also kept track of the locations of the people logging into it. The first Asian country, not unexpectedly, was Japan, and the fascination of the people there in military operations guaranteed a rising number of hits. The video also included audio, the real-time comments of Air Force personnel giving some perverse color-commentary back to their comrades in uniform. It was sufficiently colorful that Ryan commented on it.

'It's not meant for anyone much over the age of thirty to hear,' General Moore said, coming back into the room.

'What's the story on the bombs?' Jackson asked at once.

'He's only got two of them,' Moore replied. 'The nearest others are at the factory, Lockheed-Martin, Sunnyvale. They're just doing a production run right now.'

'Uh-oh,' Robby observed. 'Back to Plan B.'

'It might have to be a special operation, then, unless, Mr. President, that is, you are willing to authorize a strike with cruise missiles.'

'What kind of cruise missiles?' Ryan asked, knowing the answer even so.

'Well, we have twenty-eight of them on Guam with W-80 warheads. They're little ones, only about three hundred pounds. It has two settings, one-fifty or one-seventy kilotons.'

'Thermonuclear weapons, you mean?'

General Moore let out a breath before replying. 'Yes, Mr. President.'

'That's the only option we have for taking those missiles out?' He didn't have to say that he would not voluntarily launch a nuclear strike.

'We could go in with conventional smart bombs—GBU-10s and -15s. Gus has enough of those, but not deep penetrators, and the protection on the silos would have a fair chance at deflecting the weapon away from the target. Now, that might not matter. The CSS-4 missiles are delicate bastards, and the impact even of a miss could scramble their guidance systems . . . but we couldn't be sure.'

'I'd prefer that those things not fly.'

'Jack, nobody wants them to fly,' the Vice President said. 'Mickey, put together a plan. We need *something* to take them out, and we need it in one big fuckin' hurry.'

'I'll call SOCOM about it, but, hell, they're down in Tampa.'

'Do the Russians have special-operations people?' Ryan asked.

'Sure, it's called Spetsnaz.'

'And some of these missiles are targeted on Russia?'

'It certainly appears so, yes, sir,' the Chairman of the Joint Chiefs confirmed.

'Then they owe us one, and they damned well owe it to themselves,' Jack said, reaching for a phone. 'I need to talk to Sergey Golovko in Moscow,' he told the operator.

*   *   *

'The American President,' his secretary said.

'Ivan Emmetovich!' Golovko said in hearty greeting. 'The reports from Siberia are good.'

'I know, Sergey, I'm watching it live now myself. Want to do it yourself?'

'It is possible?'

'You have a computer with a modem?'

'One cannot exist without the damned things,' the Russian replied.

Ryan read off the URL identifier. 'Just log onto that. We're putting the feed from our Dark Star drones onto the Internet.'

'Why is that, Jack?' Golovko asked at once.

'Because as of two minutes ago, one thousand six hundred and fifty Chinese citizens are watching it, and the number is going up fast.'

'A political operation against them, yes? You wish to destabilize their government?'

'Well, it won't hurt our purposes if their citizens find out what's happening, will it?'

'The virtues of a free press. I must study this. Very clever, Ivan Emmetovich.'

'That's not why I called.'

'Why is that, *Tovarisch Prezidyent*?' the SVR chairman asked, with sudden concern at the change in his tone. Ryan was not one to conceal his feelings well.

'Sergey, we have a very adverse indication from

694

their Politburo. I'm faxing it to you now,' he heard. 'I'll stay on the line while you read it.'

Golovko wasn't surprised to see the pages arrive on his personal fax machine. He had Ryan's personal numbers, and the Americans had his. It was just one way for an intelligence service to demonstrate its prowess in a harmless way. The first sheets to come across were the English translation of the Chinese ideographs that came through immediately thereafter.

*   *   *

'Sergey, I sent you our original feed in case your linguists or psychologists are better than ours,' the President said, with an apologetic glance at Dr. Sears. The CIA analyst waved it off. 'They have twelve CSS-4 missiles, half aimed at you, half at us. I think we need to do something about those things. They may not be entirely rational, the way things are going now.'

'And your shore bombardment might have pushed them to the edge, Mr. President,' the Russian said over the speakerphone. 'I agree, this is a matter of some concern. Why don't you bomb the things with your brilliant bombs from your magical invisible bombers.'

'Because we're out of bombs, Sergey. They ran out of the sort they need.'

'Nichevo' was the reaction.

'You should see it from my side. My people are thinking about a commando-type operation.'

'I see. Let me consult with some of my people. Give me twenty minutes, Mr. President.'

'Okay, you know where to reach me.' Ryan

punched the kill button on the phone and looked sourly at the tray of coffee things. 'One more cup of this shit and I'm going to turn into an urn myself.'

*　　　*　　　*

The only reason he was alive now, he was sure, was that he'd withdrawn to the command section for 34th Army. His tank division was being roughly handled. One of his battalions had been immolated in the first minute of the battle. Another was now trying to maneuver east, trying to draw the Russians out into a running battle for which his men were trained. The division's artillery had been halved at best by Russian massed fire, and 34th Army's advance was now a thing of the past. His current task was to try and use his two mechanized divisions to establish a base of fire from which he could try to wrest back control of the battle. But every time he tried to move a unit, something happened to it, as though the Russians were reading his mind.

'Wa, pull what's left of Three-Oh-Second back to the ten o'clock start-line, and do it now!' he ordered.

'But Marshal Luo won't—'

'And if he wishes to relieve me, he can, but he isn't here *now*, is he?' Ge snarled back. 'Give the order!'

'Yes, Comrade General.'

*　　　*　　　*

'With this toy in our hands, the Germans would not

have made it as far as Minsk,' Bondarenko said.

'Yeah, it helps to know what the other guy's doing, doesn't it?'

'It's like being a god on Mount Olympus. Who thought this thing up?'

'Oh, a couple of people at Northrop started the idea, with an airplane called Tacit Rainbow, looked like a cross between a snow shovel and a French baguette, but it was manned, and the endurance wasn't so good.'

'Whoever it is, I would like to buy him a bottle of good vodka,' the Russian general said. 'This is saving the lives of my soldiers.'

And beating the living shit out of the Chinese, Tucker didn't add. But combat was that sort of game, wasn't it?

'Do you have any other aircraft up?'

'Yes, sir. Grace Kelly's back up to cover First Armored.'

'Show me.'

Tucker used his mouse to shrink one video window and then opened another. General Diggs had a second terminal up and running, and Tucker just stole its take. There were what looked like two brigades operating, moving north at a measured pace and wrecking every Chinese truck and track they could find. The battlefield, if you could call it that, was a mass of smoke columns from shot-up trucks, reminding Tucker of the vandalized Kuwaiti oil fields of 1991. He zoomed in to see that most of the work was being done by the Bradleys. What targets there were simply were not worthy of a main-gun round from the tanks. The Abrams just rode herd on the lighter infantry carriers, doing protective overwatch as they ground mercilessly forward. The major slaved one camera to his terminal and went scouting around for more action . . .

'Who's this?' Tucker asked.

'That must be BOYAR,' Bondarenko said.

It was what looked like twenty-five T-55 tanks advancing on line, and these tanks were using their main guns . . . against trucks and some infantry carriers . . .

*　　　*　　　*

'Load HEAT,' Lieutenant Komanov ordered. 'Target track, one o'clock! Range two thousand.'

'I have him,' the gunner said a second later.

'Fire!'

'Firing,' the gunner said, squeezing the trigger. The old tank rocked backwards from the shot. Gunner and commander watched the tracer arcing out . . .

'Over, damn it, too high. Load another HEAT.'

The loader slammed another round into the breech in a second: 'Loaded!'

'I'll get the bastard this time,' the gunner promised, adjusting his sights down a hair. The poor bastard out there didn't even know he'd been shot at the first time . . .

'Fire!'

'Firing . . .'

Yet another recoil, and . . .

'Hit! Good shooting Vanya!'

Three Company was doing well. The time spent in gunnery practice was paying off handsomely, Komanov thought. This was much better than sitting in a damned bunker and waiting for them to come to you . . .

*   *   *

'What is that?' Marshal Luo asked.

'Comrade Marshal, come here and see,' the young lieutenant colonel urged.

'What is this?' the Defense Minister asked with a trailing-off voice . . . *'Cao ni ma,'* he breathed. Then he thundered: *'What the hell is this?'*

'Comrade Marshal, this is a web site, from the Internet. It purports to be a live television program from the battlefield in Siberia.' The young field-grade officer was almost breathless. 'It shows the Russians fighting Thirty-fourth Shock Army . . .'

'And?'

'And they're slaughtering our men, according to this,' the lieutenant colonel went on.

'Wait a minute—what—how is this possible?' Luo demanded.

'Comrade, this heading here says *darkstar.* 'Dark Star' is the name of an American unmanned aerial vehicle, a reconnaissance drone, reported to be a stealth aircraft used to collect tactical intelligence. Thus, it appears that they are using this to feed information, and putting the information on the Internet as a propaganda tool.' He had to say it that way, and it was, in fact, the way he thought about it.

'Tell me more.'

The officer was an intelligence specialist. 'This explains the success they've had against us, Comrade Marshal. They can see everything we do, almost before we do it. It's as though they listen to our command circuit, or even listen into our staff

699

and planning meetings. There is no defense against this,' the staff officer concluded.

'You young defeatist!' the marshal raged.

'Perhaps there is a way to overcome this advantage, but I do not know what it is. Systems like this can see in the dark as well as they can in the sunlight. Do you understand, Comrade Marshal? With this tool they can see everything we do, see it long before we approach their formations. It eliminates any possibility of surprise . . . see here,' he said, pointing at the screen. 'One of Thirty-fourth Army's mechanized divisions is maneuvering east. They are here—' he pointed to a printer map on the table— 'and the enemy is here. If our troops get to this point unseen, then perhaps they can hit the Russians on their left flank, but it will take two hours to get there. For the Russians to get one of their units to a blocking position will take but one hour. That is the advantage,' he concluded.

'The Americans do that to us?'

'Clearly, the feed on the Internet is from America, from their CIA.'

'This is how the Russians have countered us, then?'

'Clearly. They've outguessed us at every turn today. This must be how they do it.'

'Why do the Americans put this information out where everyone can see it?' Luo wondered. The obvious answer didn't occur to him. Information given out to the public had to be carefully measured and flavored for the peasants and workers to draw the proper conclusions from it.

'Comrade, it will be difficult to say on state television that things are going well when this is available to anyone with a computer.'

'Ahh.' Less a sound of satisfaction than one of sudden dread. 'Anyone can see this?'

'Anyone with a computer and a telephone line.' The young lieutenant colonel looked up, only to see Luo's receding form.

'I'm surprised he didn't shoot me,' the officer observed.

'He still might,' a full colonel told him. 'But I think you frightened him.' He looked at the wall clock. It was sixteen hours, four in the afternoon.

'Well, it is a concern.'

'You young fool. Don't you see? Now he can't even conceal the truth from the Politburo.'

*   *   *

'Hello, Yuri,' Clark said. It was different to be in Moscow in time of war. The mood of the people on the street was unlike anything he'd ever seen. They were concerned and serious—you didn't go to Russia to see the smiling people any more than you went to England for the coffee—but there was something else, too. Indignation. Anger . . . determination? Television coverage of the war was not as strident and defiant as he'd expected. The new Russian news media were trying to be even-handed and professional. There was commentary to the effect that the army's inability to stop the Chinese cold spoke ill of their country's national cohesion. Others lamented the demise of the Soviet Union, whom China would not have dared to threaten, much less attack. More asked what the hell was the use of being in NATO if none of the other countries came to the aid of their supposed

701

new ally.

'We told the television people that if they told anyone of the American division now in Siberia, we'd shoot them, and of course they believed us,' Lt. Gen. Kirillin said with a smile. That was something new for Clark and Chavez to see. He hadn't smiled much in the past week.

'Things looking up?' Chavez inquired.

'Bondarenko has stopped them at the gold mine. They will not even see that, if my information is correct. But there is something else,' he added seriously.

'What's that, Yuriy?' Clark asked.

'We are concerned that they might launch their nuclear weapons.'

'Oh, shit,' Ding observed. 'How serious is that?'

'It comes from your President. Golovko is speaking with President Grushavoy right now.'

'And? How do they plan to go about it? Smart bombs?' John asked.

'No, Washington has asked us to go in with a special-operations team,' Kirillin said.

'What the hell?' John gasped. He pulled his satellite phone out of his pocket and looked for the door. 'Excuse me, General. E.T. phone home.'

*   *   *

'You want to say that again, Ed?' Foley heard.

'You heard me. They've run out of the bombs they need. Evidently, it's a pain in the ass to fly bombs to where the bombers are.'

'Fuck!' the CIA officer observed, out in the parking lot of this Russian army officers' club. The encryption on his phone didn't affect the emotion in his voice. 'Don't tell me, since RAINBOW is a NATO asset, and Russia's part of NATO now, and since you're going to be asking the fucking Russians to front this operation, in the interest of North Atlantic solidarity, we're going to get to go and play, too, right?'

'Unless you choose not to, John. I know you can't go yourself. Combat's a kid's game, but you have some good kids working for you.'

'Ed, you expect me to send my people in on something like that and I stay home and fucking knit socks?' Clark demanded heatedly.

'That's your call to make. You're the RAINBOW commander.'

'How is this supposed to work? You expect us to jump in?'

'Helicopters—'

'Russian helicopters. No thanks, buddy, I—'

'Our choppers, John. First Armored Division had enough and they're the right kind . . .'

*   *   *

'They want me to do *what*?' Dick Boyle asked.

'You heard me.'

'What about fuel?'

'Your fueling point's right about here,' Colonel Masterman said, holding the just-downloaded satellite photo. 'Hilltop west of a place called Chicheng. Nobody lives there, and the numbers work out.'

'Yeah, except out flight path takes us within ten miles of this fighter base.'

'Eight F-111s are going to hit it while you're on the way in. Ought to close down their runways for a good three days, they figure.'

'Dick,' Diggs said, 'I don't know what the problem is exactly, but Washington is really worried that Joe is going to launch his ICBMs at us at home, and Gus Wallace doesn't have the right bombs to take them out reliably. That means a special-ops force, down and dirty. It's a strategic mission, Dick. Can you do it?'

Colonel Boyle looked at the map, measuring distance in his mind . . . 'Yeah, we'll have to mount the outrigger wings on the Blackhawks and load up to the max on gas, but, yeah, we got the range to get there. Have to refuel on the way back, though.'

'Okay, can you use your other birds to ferry the fuel out?'

Boyle nodded. 'Barely.'

'If necessary, the Russians can land a Spetsnaz force anywhere through here with additional fuel, so they tell me. This part of China is essentially unoccupied, according to the maps.'

'What about opposition on the ground?'

'There is a security force in the area. We figure maybe a hundred people on duty, total, say a squad at each silo. Can you get some Apaches out there to run interference?'

'Yeah, they can get that far, if they travel light.' *Just cannon rounds and 2.75-inch rockets*, he thought.

'Then get me your mission requirements,' General Diggs said. It wasn't quite an order. If he said it was impossible, then Diggs couldn't make him do it. But Boyle couldn't let his people go out and do something like this without being there to command them.

704

The MI-24s finished things off. The Russian doctrine for their attack helicopters wasn't too different from how they used their tanks. Indeed, the MI-24—called the Hind by NATO, but strangely unnamed by the Russians themselves—was referred to as a flying tank. Using AT-6 Spiral missiles, they finished off a Chinese tank battalion in twenty minutes of jump and shoot, sustaining only two losses in the process. The sun was setting now, and what had been Thirty-fourth Shock Army was wreckage. What few vehicles had survived the day were pulling back, usually with wounded men clinging to their decks.

In his command post, General Sinyavskiy was all smiles. Vodka was snorted by all. His 265th Motor Rifle Division had halted and thrown back a force more than double its size, suffering fewer than three hundred dead in the process. The TV news crews were finally allowed out to where the soldiers were, and he delivered the briefing, paying frequent compliments to his theater commander, Gennady Iosefovich Bondarenko, for his cool head and faith in his subordinates. 'He never lost his nerve,' Sinyavskiy said soberly. 'And he allowed us to keep ours for when the time came. He is a Hero of Russia,' the division commander concluded. 'And so are many of my men!'

*   *   *

'Thank you for that, Yuriy Andreyevich, and, yes, for that you will get your next star,' the theater commander told the television screen. Then he turned to his staff. 'Andrey Petrovich, what do we do tomorrow?'

'I think we will let Two-Six-Five start moving south. We will be the hammer, and Diggs will be the anvil. They still have a Type A Group army largely intact to the south, the Forty-third. We will smash it starting day after tomorrow, but first we will maneuver it into a place of our choosing.'

Bondarenko nodded. 'Show me a plan, but first, I am going to sleep for a few hours.'

'Yes, Comrade General.'

CHAPTER SIXTY

SKYROCKETS IN FLIGHT

It was the same Spetsnaz people they'd trained for the past month or so. Nearly everyone on the transport aircraft was a commissioned officer, doing sergeants' work, which had its good points and its bad ones. The really good thing was that they all spoke passable English. Of the RAINBOW troopers, only Ding Chavez and John Clark spoke conversational Russian.

The maps and photos came from SRV and CIA, the latter transmitted to the American Embassy in Moscow and messengered to the military airfield out of which they'd flown. They were in an Aeroflot airliner, fairly full with over a hundred passengers, all of them soldiers.

'I propose that we divide by nationalities,' Kirillin said. 'Vanya, you and your RAINBOW men take this one here. My men and I will divide the

706

rest among us, using our existing squad structures.'

'Looks okay, Yuriy. One target's pretty much as good as another. When will we be going in?'

'Just before dawn. Your helicopters must have good range to take us all the way down, then back with only one refueling.'

'Well, that'll be the safe part of the mission.'

'Except this fighter base at Anshan,' Kirillin said. 'We pass within twenty kilometers of it.'

'Air Force is going to hit that, they tell me, Stealth fighters with smart bombs, they're gonna post-hole the runways before we drive past.'

'Ah, that is a fine idea,' Kirillin said.

'Kinda like that myself,' Chavez said. 'Well, Mr. C, looks like I get to be a soldier again. It's been a while.'

'What fun,' Clark observed. Oh, yeah, sitting in the back of a helicopter, going deep into Indian Country, where there were sure to be people with guns. Well, could be worse. Going in at dawn, at least the gomers on duty would be partly asleep, unless their boss was a real prick. *How tough was discipline in the People's Liberation Army?* John wondered. Probably pretty tough. Communist governments didn't encourage back talk.

'How, exactly, are we supposed to disable the missiles?' Ding asked.

'They're fueled by a ten-centimeter pipe—two of them, actually—from underground fueling tanks adjacent to the launch silo. First, we destroy the pipes,' Kirillin said. 'Then we look for some way to access the missile silo itself. A simple hand grenade will suffice. These are delicate objects. They will not sustain much damage,' the general said confidently.

'What if the warhead goes off?' Ding asked.

Kirillin actually laughed at that. 'They will not, Domingo Stepanovich. These items are very secure in their arming procedures, for all the obvious reasons. And the sites themselves will not be designed to protect against a direct assault. They are designed to protect against nuclear blast, not a squad of engineer-soldiers. You can be sure of that.'

Hope you're right on that one, fella, Chavez didn't say aloud.

'You seem knowledgeable on this subject, Yuriy'

'Vanya, this mission is one Spetsnaz has practiced more than once. We Russians have thought from time to time about taking these missiles—how you say? Take them out of play, yes?'

'Not a bad idea at all, Yuriy. Not my kind of weapons,' Clark said. He really did prefer to do his killing close enough to see the bastard's face. Old habits died hard, and a telescopic sight was just as good as a knife in that respect. Much better. A rifle bullet didn't make people flop around and make noise the way a knife across the throat did. But death was supposed to be administered one at a time, not whole cities at once. It just wasn't tidy or selective enough.

Chavez looked at his Team-2 troopers. They didn't look overtly tense, but good soldiers did their best to hide such feelings. Of their number, only Ettore Falcone wasn't a career soldier, but instead a cop from the Italian Carabinieri, which was about halfway between military and police. Chavez went over to see him.

'How you doing, BIG BIRD?' Ding asked.

'It is tense, this mission, no?' Falcone replied.

'It might be. You never really know until you get there.'

The Italian shrugged. 'As with raids on mafiosi, sometimes you kick the door and there is nothing but men drinking wine and playing cards. Sometimes they have *machinapistoli*, but you must kick the door to find out.'

'You do a lot of those?'

'Eight,' Falcone replied. 'I am usually the first one through the door because I am usually the best shot. But we have good men on the team there, and we have good men on the team here. It should go well, Domingo. I am tense, yes, but I will be all right. You will see,' BIG BIRD ended. Chavez clapped him on the shoulder and went off to see Sergeant-Major Price.

'Hey, Eddie.'

'Do we have a better idea for the mission yet?'

'Getting there. Looks like mainly a job for Paddy, blowing things up.

'Connolly's the best explosives man I've ever seen,' Price observed. 'But don't tell him that. His head's swollen enough already.'

'What about Falcone?'

'Ettore?' Price shook his head. 'I will be very surprised if he puts a foot wrong. He's a very good man, Ding, bloody machine—a robot with a pistol. That sort of confidence rarely goes bad. Things are too automatic for him.'

'Okay, well, we've picked our target. It's the north- and east-most silo. Looks like it's on fairly flat ground, two four-inch pipes running to it. Paddy'll blow those, and then try to find a way to pop the cover off the silo or otherwise find an access door—there's one on the overhead. Then get inside, toss a grenade to break the missile, and we get the hell out of Dodge City.'

'Usual division of the squad?' Price asked. It had to be, but there was no harm in making sure.

Chavez nodded. 'You take Paddy, Louis, Hank, and Dieter, and your team handles the actual destruction of the missile. I take the rest to do security and overwatch.' Price nodded as Paddy Connolly came over.

'Are we getting chemical gear?'

'What?' Chavez asked.

'Ding, if we're going to be playing with bloody liquid-fueled missiles, we need chemical-warfare gear. The fuels for these things—you don't want to breathe the vapor, trust me. Red-fuming nitric acid, nitrogen tetroxide, hydrazine, that sort of thing. Those are bloody corrosive chemicals they use to power rockets, not like a pint of bitter at the Green Dragon, I promise you. And if the missiles are fueled and we blow them, well, you don't want to be close, and you *definitely* don't want to be downwind. The gas cloud will be bloody lethal, like what you chaps use in America to execute murderers, but rather less pleasant.'

'I'll talk to John about that.' Chavez made his way back forward.

*   *   *

'Oh, shit,' Ed Foley observed when he took the call. 'Okay, John, I'll get hold of the Army on that one. How long 'til you're there?'

'Hour and a half to the airfield.'

'You okay?'

'Yeah, sure, Ed, never been better.'

Foley was struck by the tone. Clark had been CIA's official iceman for close to twenty years. He'd gone out on all manner of field operations without so much as a blink. But being over fifty—had it changed him, or did he just have a better appreciation of his own mortality now? The DCI figured that sort of thing came to everybody. 'Okay, I'll get back to you.' He switched phones. 'I need General Moore.'

'Yes, Director?' the Chairman of the Joint Chiefs said in greeting. 'What can I do for you?'

'Our special-operations people say they need chemical-warfare gear for their mission and—'

'Way ahead of you, Ed. SOCOM told us the same thing. First Armored's got the right stuff, and it'll be waiting for them at the field.'

'Thanks, Mickey.'

'How secure are those silos?'

'The fueling pipes are right in the open. Blowing them up ought not to be a problem. Also, every silo has a metal access door for the maintenance people, and again, getting into it ought not to be a problem. My only concern is the site security force; there may be as much as a whole infantry battalion spread out down there. We're waiting for a KH-11 to overfly the site now for a final check.'

'Well, Diggs is sending Apaches down to escort the raiding force. That'll be an equalizer,' Moore promised. 'What about the command bunker?'

'It's centrally located, looks pretty secure, entirely underground, but we have a rough idea of the configuration from penetrating radar.' Foley referred to the KH-14 Lacrosse satellite. NASA had once published radar photos that had shown

711

underground tributaries of the Nile that emptied into the Mediterranean Sea at Alexandria. But the capability hadn't been developed for hydrologists. It had also spotted Soviet missile silos that the Russians had thought to be well camouflaged, and other sensitive facilities, and America had wanted to let the Russians know that the locations were not the least bit secret. 'Mickey, how do you feel about the mission?'

'I wish we had enough bombs to do it,' General Moore replied honestly.

'Yeah,' the DCI agreed.

*   *   *

The Politburo meeting had gone past midnight.

'So, Marshal Luo,' Qian said, 'things went badly yesterday. How badly? We need the truth here,' he concluded roughly. If nothing else, Qian Kun had made his name in the past few days, as the only Politburo member with the courage to take on the ruling clique, expressing openly the misgivings that they'd all felt. Depending on who won, it could mean his downfall, either all the way to death or simply to mere obscurity, but it seemed he didn't care. That made him unusual among the men in the room, Fang Gan thought, and it made him a man to be respected.

'There was a major battle yesterday between 34th Shock Army and the Russians. It appears to have been a draw, and we are now maneuvering to press our advantage,' the Defense Minister told them. They were all suffering from fatigue in the room, and again the Finance Minister was the only one to rise to his words.

'In other words, a battle was fought, and we lost it,' Qian shot back.

'I didn't say that!' Luo responded angrily.

'But it is the truth, is it not?' Qian pressed the point.

'I told you the truth, Qian!' was the thundering reply.

'Comrade Marshal,' the Finance Minister said in a reasonable tone, 'you must forgive me for my skepticism. You see, much of what you've said in this room has turned out to be less than completely accurate. Now, I do not blame you for this. Perhaps you have been misinformed by some of your subordinates. All of us are vulnerable to that, are we not? But now is the time for a careful examination of objective realities. I am developing the impression that objective reality may be adverse to the economic and political objectives on whose pursuit this body has sent our country and its people. Therefore, we must *now* know what the facts are, and what also are the dangers facing us. So, Comrade Marshal, now, what is the military situation in Siberia?'

'It has changed somewhat,' Luo admitted. 'Not entirely to our benefit, but the situation is by no means lost.' He'd chosen his words a little too carefully.

By no means lost, everyone around the table knew, was a delicate way of saying that a disaster had taken place. As in any society, if you knew the aphorisms, you could break the code. Success here was always proclaimed in the most positive terms. Setbacks were brushed aside without admission as something less than a stunning success. Failure was something to be blamed on individuals who'd failed in their duty—often to their great misfortune. But a real policy disaster was invariably explained as a situation that could yet be restored.

'Comrades, we still have our strengths,' Zhang told them all. 'Of all the great powers of the world, only we have intercontinental missiles, and no one will dare strike us hard while we do.'

'Comrade, two days ago the Americans totally destroyed bridges so stout that one would have thought that only an angry deity could so much as scratch them. How secure can those missiles be, when we face a foe with invisible aircraft and magical weapons?' Qian asked. 'I think we may be approaching the time when Shen might wish to approach America and Russia to propose an end to hostilities,' he concluded.

'You mean surrender?' Zhang asked angrily. *'Never.'*

*　　　*　　　*

It had already started, though the Politburo members didn't know it yet. All over China, but especially in Beijing, people owning computers had logged onto the Internet. This was especially true of young people, and university students most of all.

The CIA feed, http://www.darkstarfeed. cia.gov/siberiabattle/realtime.ram, had attracted a global audience, catching even the international news organizations by surprise. CNN, Fox, and Europe's SkyNews had immediately pirated it, and then called in their expert commentators to explain things to their viewers in the first continuous news coverage of an event since February of 1991. CIA

714

had taken to pirating CNN in turn, and now available on the CIA website were live interviews from Chinese prisoners. They spoke freely, they were so shocked at their fates—stunned at how near they'd come to death, and so buoyantly elated at their equally amazing survival when so many of their colleagues had been less fortunate. That made for great verbosity, and it was also something that couldn't be faked. Any Chinese citizen could have spotted false propaganda, but equally, any could discern this sort of truth from what he saw and heard.

The strange part was that Luo hadn't commented on the Internet phenomenon, thinking it irrelevant to the political facts of life in the PRC, but in that decision he'd made the greatest political misapprehension of his life.

They met in college dorm rooms first of all, amid clouds of cigarette smoke, chattering animatedly among themselves as students do, and like students everywhere they combined idealism with passion. That passion soon turned to resolve. By midnight, they were meeting in larger groups. Some leaders emerged, and, being leaders, they felt the need to take their associates somewhere. When the crowds mingled outside, the individual leaders of smaller groups met and started talking, and superleaders emerged, rather like an instant military or political hierarchy, absorbing other groups into their own, until there were six principal leaders of a group of about fifteen hundred students. The larger group developed and then fed upon its own energy. Students everywhere are well supplied with piss and vinegar, and these Chinese students were no different. Some of the boys were there hoping to score with girls—another universal motivation for students—but the unifying factor here was rage at what had happened to their soldiers and their country, and even more rage at the lies that had gone out over State TV, lies so clearly and utterly refuted by the reality they saw over the Internet, a source they'd learned to trust.

There was only one place for them to go, Tian'anmen Square, the 'Square of Heavenly Peace', the psychological center of their country, and they were drawn there like iron filings to a magnet. The time of day worked for them. The police in Beijing, like police everywhere, worked twenty-four-hour days divided into three unequal shifts, and the shift most lightly manned was that from 2300 to 0700. Most people were asleep then, and as a direct result there was little crime to suppress, and so this shift was the smallest in terms of manning, and also composed of those officers loved the least by their commanders, because no man in his right mind prefers the vampire life of wakefulness in darkness to that in the light of day. And so the few police on duty were those who had failed to distinguish themselves in their professional skills, or were disliked by their captains, and returned the compliment by not taking their duties with sufficient gravity.

The appearance of the first students in the square was barely noted by the two policemen there. Their main duties involved directing traffic and/or telling (frequently inebriated) foreign tourists how to stumble back to their hotels, and the only danger they faced was usually that of being blinded by the flashes of foreign cameras held by oafishly pleasant but drunken *gwai*.

This new situation took them totally by surprise, and their first reaction was to do nothing but watch. The presence of so many young people in the square *was* unusual, but they weren't *doing* anything overtly unlawful at the moment, and so the police just looked on in a state of bemusement. They didn't even report what was going on because the watch captain was an ass who wouldn't have known what to do about it anyway.

*　　　　*　　　　*

'What if they strike at our nuclear arms?' Interior Minister Tong Jie asked.

'They already have,' Zhang reminded them. 'They sank our missile submarine, you will recall. If they also strike at our land-based missiles, then it would mean they plan to attack us as a nation, not just our armed forces, for then they would have nothing to hold them back. It would be a grave and deliberate provocation, is that not so, Shen?'

The Foreign Minister nodded. 'It would be an unfriendly act.'

'How do we defend against it?' Tan Deshi asked.

'The missile field is located far from the borders. Each is in a heavily constructed concrete silo,' Defense Minister Luo explained. 'Moreover, we have recently fortified them further with steel armor to deflect bombs that might fall on them. The best way to add to their defense would be to deploy surface-to-air missiles.'

'And if the Americans use their stealthy bombers, then what?' Tan asked.

'The defense against that is passive, the steel hats we put on the silos. We have troops there—

717

security personnel of Second Artillery Command—but they are there only for site security against intruders on the ground. If such an attack should be made, we should launch them. The principle is to use them or lose them. An attack against our strategic weapons would have to be a precursor to an attack against our nationhood. That is our one trump card,' Luo explained. 'The one thing that even the Americans truly fear.'

'Well, it should be,' Zhang Han Sen agreed. 'That is how we tell the Americans where they must stop and what they must do. In fact, it might now be a good time to tell the Americans that we have those missiles, and the willingness to use them if they press us too hard.'

'Threaten the Americans with nuclear arms?' Fang asked. 'Is that wise? They know of our weapons, surely. An overt threat against a powerful nation is most unwise.'

'They must know that there are lines they may not cross,' Zhang insisted. 'They can hurt us, yes, but we can hurt them, and this is one weapon against which they have no defense, and their sentimentality for their people works for us, not them. It is time for America to regard us as an equal, not a minor country whose power they can blithely ignore.'

'I repeat, Comrade,' Fang said, 'that would be a most unwise act. When someone points a gun at your head, you do not try to frighten him.'

'Fang, you have been my friend for many years, but in this you are wrong. It is *we* who hold that pistol now. The Americans only respect strength controlled by resolve. This will make them think. Luo, are the missiles ready for launch?'

The Defense Minister shook his head. 'No, yesterday we did not agree to ready them. To do so takes about two hours—to load them with fuel. After that, they can be kept in a ready condition for about forty-eight hours. Then you defuel them, service them—it takes about four hours to do that—and you can refuel them again. We could easily maintain half of them in a ready-launch condition indefinitely.'

'Comrades, I think it is in our interest to ready the missiles for flight.'

'No!' Fang countered. 'That will be seen by the Americans as a dangerous provocation, and provoking them this way is madness!'

'And we should have Shen remind the Americans that we have such weapons, and they do not,' Zhang went on.

'That invites an attack on us!' Fang nearly shouted. 'They do not have rockets, yes, but they have other ways of attacking us, and if we do that now, when a war is already under way, we guarantee a response.'

'I think not, Fang,' Zhang replied. 'They will not gamble millions of their citizens against all of ours. They have not the strength for such gambling.'

'Gambling, you say. Do we gamble with the life of our country? Zhang, you are mad. This is lunacy,' Fang insisted.

'I do not have a vote at this table,' Qian observed. 'But I have been a Party member all of my adult life, and I have served the People's Republic well, I think. It is our job here to build a country, not destroy it. What have we done here? We've turned China into a thief, a highway robber—and a *failed* highway robber at that! Luo

719

has said it. We have lost our play for riches, and now we must adjust to that. We can recover from the damage we have done to our country and its people. That recovery will require humility on our part, not blustering defiance. To threaten the Americans now is an act of weakness, not strength. It's the act of an impotent man trying to show off his *gau*. It will be seen by them as a foolish and reckless act.'

'If we are to survive as a nation—if *we* are to survive as the rulers of a powerful China,' Zhang countered, 'we must let the Americans know that they cannot push us farther. Comrades, make no mistake. Our lives lie on this table.' And that focused the discussion. 'I do not suggest that we launch a nuclear strike on America. I propose that we demonstrate to America our resolve, and if they press us too far, then we will punish them—and the Russians. Comrades, I propose that we fuel up our missiles, to place them in a ready posture, and then have Shen tell the Americans that there are limits beyond which we cannot be pushed without the gravest possible consequences.'

'No!' Fang retorted. 'That is tantamount to the threat of nuclear war. *We must not do such a thing!*'

'If we do not, then we are all doomed,' said Tan Deshi of the Ministry of State Security. 'I am sorry, Fang, but Zhang is correct here. Those are the only weapons with which we can hold the Americans back. They will be tempted to strike at them—and if they do . . .'

'If they do, then we must use them, because if they take those weapons away from us, then they can strike us at will, and destroy all we have built in sixty years,' Zhang concluded. 'I call a vote.'

Suddenly and irrationally, Fang thought, the meeting had struck out on a path with no logic or direction, leading to disaster. But he was the only one who saw this, as for the first time in his life he took a stand against the others. The meeting finally broke up. The Politburo members drove directly home. None of them passed through Tiananmen Square on the way, and all of them fell rapidly asleep.

*　　　*　　　*

There were twenty-five UH-60A Blackhawks and fifteen Apaches on the ramp. Every one had stubby wings affixed to the fuselage. Those on the Blackhawks were occupied with fuel tanks. The Apaches had both fuel and rockets. The flight crews were grouped together, looking at maps.

Clark took the lead. He was dressed in his black Ninja gear, and a soldier directed him and Kirillin—he was in the snowflake camouflage used by Russian airborne troops—to Colonel Boyle.

'Howdy, Dick Boyle.'

'I'm John Clark, and this is Lieutenant General Yuriy Kirillin. I'm RAINBOW,' John explained. 'He's Spetsnaz.'

Boyle saluted. 'Well, I'm your driver, gentlemen. The objective is seven hundred sixteen miles away. We can just about make it with the fuel we're carrying, but we're going to have to tank up on the way back. We're doing that right here'—he pointed to a spot on the navigation chart—'hilltop west of this little town named Chicheng. We got lucky. Two C-130s are going to do bladder drops for us. There will be a fighter escort for top cover, F-15s, plus some F-16s to go after any radars along the way, and when we get to about here, eight F-117s are going to trash this fighter base at Anshan. That should take care of any Chinese fighter interference. Now, this missile base has an associated security force, supposed to be battalion strength, in barracks located here'—this time it was a satellite photo—'and five of my Apaches are going to take that place down with rockets. The others will be flying direct support. The only other question is, how close do you want us to put you on these missile silos?'

'Land right on top of the bastards,' Clark told him, looking over at Kirillin.

'I agree, the closer the better.'

Boyle nodded. 'Fair enough. The helicopters all have numbers on them indicating the silo they're flying for. I'm flying lead, and I'm going right to this one here.'

'That means I go with you,' Clark told him.

'How many?'

'Ten plus me.'

'Okay, your chem gear's in the aircraft. Suit up, and we go. Latrine's that way,' Boyle pointed. It would be better for every man to take a piss before the flight began. 'Fifteen minutes.'

Clark went that way, and so did Kirillin. Both old soldiers knew what they needed to do in most respects, and this one was as vital as loading a weapon.

'Have you been to China before, John?'

'Nope. Taiwan once, long ago, to get screwed, blued, and tattooed.'

'No chance for that on this trip. We are both too old for this, you know.'

'I know,' Clark said, zipping himself up. 'But you're not going to sit back here, are you?'

'A leader must be with his men, Ivan Timofeyevich.'

'That is true, Yuriy. Good luck.'

'They will not launch a nuclear attack on my country, or on yours,' Kirillin promised. 'Not while I live.'

'You know, Yuriy, you might have been a good guy to have in 3rd SOG.'

'And what is that, John?'

'When we get back and have a few drinks, I will tell you.'

The troops suited up outside their designated helicopters. The U.S. Army chemical gear was bulky, but not grossly so. Like many American-issue items, it was an evolutionary development of a British idea, with charcoal inside the lining to absorb and neutralize toxic gas, and a hood that—

'We can't use our radios with this,' Mike Pierce noted. 'Screws up the antenna.'

'Try this,' Homer Johnston suggested, disconnecting the antenna and tucking it into the helmet cover.

'Good one, Homer,' Eddie Price said, watching what he did and trying it himself. The American-pattern Kevlar helmet fit nicely into the hoods, which they left off in any case as too uncomfortable until they really needed it. That done, they loaded into their helicopters, and the flight crews spooled up the General Electric turboshaft engines. The Blackhawks lifted off. The special-operations troops were set in what were—for military aircraft—comfortable seats, held in place with fourpoint safety belts. Clark took the jump seat, aft and between the two pilots, and tied into the intercom.

'Who, exactly, are you?' Boyle asked.

'Well, I have to kill you after I tell you, but I'm CIA. Before that, Navy.'

'SEAL?' Boyle asked.

'Budweiser badge and all. Couple years ago we set up this group, called RAINBOW, special operations, counter-terror, that sort of thing.'

'The amusement park job?'

'That's us.'

'You had a -60 supporting you for that. Who's the driver?'

'Dan Malloy. Goes by "BEAR" when he's driving. Know him?'

'Marine, right?'

'Yep.' Clark nodded.

'Never met him, heard about him a little. I think he's in D.C. now.'

'Yeah, when he left us he took over VMH-1.'

'Flies the President?'

'Correct.'

'Bummer,' Boyle observed.

'How long you been doing this?'

'Flying choppers? Oh, eighteen years. Four thousand hours. I was born in the Huey, and grew up into these. Qualified in the Apache, too.

'What do you think of the mission?' John asked.

'Long' was the reply, and Clark hoped that was the only cause for concern. A sore ass you could recover from quickly enough.

*　　　*　　　*

'I wish there was another way to do this one,

724

Robby,' Ryan said over lunch. It seemed utterly horrid to be sitting here m the White House Mess, eating a cheeseburger with his best friend, while others—including two people he knew well, Jack had learned—were heading into harm's way. It was enough to kill his appetite as dead as the low-cholesterol beef in the bun. He set it down and sipped at his Coke.

'Well, there is—if you want to wait the two days it's going to take Lockheed-Martin to assemble the bombs, then a day to fly them to Siberia, and another twelve hours to fly the mission. Maybe longer. The Black Jet only flies at night, remember?' the Vice President pointed out.

'You're handling it better than I am.'

'Jack, I don't like it any more than you do, okay? But after twenty years of flying off carriers, you learn to handle the stress of having friends in tight corners. If you don't, might as well turn in your wings. Eat, man, you need your strength. How's Andrea doing?'

That generated an ironic smile. 'Puked her guts out this morning. Had her use my own crapper. It's killing her, she was embarrassed as a guy caught naked in Times Square.'

'Well, she's in a man's job, and she doesn't want to be seen as a wimp,' Robby explained. 'Hard to be one of the boys when you don't have a dick, but she tries real hard. I'll give her that.'

'Cathy says it passes, but it isn't passing fast enough for her.' He looked over to see Andrea standing in the doorway, always the watchful protector of her President.

'She's a good troop,' Jackson agreed.

'How's your dad doing?'

'Not too bad. Some TV ministry agency wants him and Gerry Patterson to do some more salt-and-pepper shows on Sunday mornings. He's thinking about it. The money could dress up the church some.

'They were impressive together.'

'Yeah, Gerry didn't do bad for a white boy—and he's actually a pretty good guy, Pap says. I'm not sure of this TV ministry stuff, though. Too easy to go Hollywood and start playing to the audience instead of being a shepherd to your flock.'

'Your father's a pretty impressive gent, Robby.'

Jackson looked up. 'I'm glad you think so. He raised us pretty good, and it was pretty tough on him after Mom died. But he can be a real sundowner. Gets all pissy when he sees me drink a beer. But, what the hell, it's his job to yell at people, I suppose.'

'Tell him that Jesus played bartender once. It was his first public miracle.'

'I've pointed that out, and then he says, if Jesus wants to do it, that's okay for Jesus, boy, but *you* ain't Jesus.' The Vice President had a good chuckle. 'Eat, Jack.'

'Yes, Mom.'

*　　　*　　　*

'This food isn't half bad,' Al Gregory said, two miles away in the wardroom of USS *Gettysburg*.

'Well, no women and no booze on a ship of war,' Captain Blandy pointed out. 'Not this one yet, anyway. You have to have some diversion. So, how are the missiles?'

'The software is fully loaded, and I e-mailed the

upgrade like you said. So all the other Aegis ships ought to have it.'

'Just heard this morning that the Aegis office in the Pentagon is having a bit of a conniption fit over this. They didn't approve the software.'

'Tell 'em to take it up with Tony Bretano,' Gregory suggested.

'Explain to me again, what exactly did you upgrade?'

'The seeker software on the missile warhead. I cut down the lines of code so it can recycle more quickly. And I reprogrammed the nutation rate on the laser on the fusing system so that I can handle a higher rate of closure. It should obviate the problem the Patriots had with the Scuds back in '91—I helped with that software fix, too, back then, but this one's about half an order of magnitude faster.'

'Without a hardware fix?' the skipper asked.

'It *would* be better to increase the range of the laser, yes, but you can get away without it—at least it worked okay on the computer simulations.'

'Hope to hell we don't need to prove it.'

'Oh, yeah, Captain. A nuke headed for a city is a *bad* thing.'

'Amen.'

*   *   *

There were five thousand of them now, with more coming, summoned by the cell phones that they all seemed to have. Some even had portable computers tied into cellular phones so that they could tap into the Internet site out here in the open. It was a clear night, with no rain to wreck a computer. The leaders of the crowd—they now thought of it as a demonstration—huddled around them to see more, and then relayed it to their friends. The first big student uprising in Tiananmen Square had been fueled by faxes. This one had taken a leap forward in technology. Mainly they milled around, talking excitedly with one another, and summoning more help. The first such demonstration had failed, but they'd all been toddlers then and their memory of it was sketchy at best. They were all old and educated enough to know what needed changing, but not yet old and experienced enough to know that change in their society was impossible. And they didn't know what a dangerous combination that could be.

*   *   *

The ground below was dark and unlit. Even their night-vision goggles didn't help much, showing only rough terrain features, mainly the tops of hills and ridges. There were few lights below. There were some houses and other buildings, but at this time of night few people were awake, and all of the lights were turned off.

The only moving light sources they could see were the rotor tips of the helicopters, heated by air friction to the point that they would be painful to touch, and hot enough to glow in the infrared spectrum that the night goggles could detect. Mainly the troops were lulled into stuporous lassitude by the unchanging vibration of the aircraft, and the semi-dreaming state that came with it helped to pass the time.

That was not true of Clark, who sat in the jump

728

seat, looking down at the satellite photos of the missile base at Xuanhua, studying by the illumination of the IR light on his goggles, looking for information he might have missed on first and twenty-first inspection. He was confident in his men. Chavez had turned into a fine tactical leader, and the troops, experienced sergeants all, would do what they were told to the extent of their considerable abilities.

The Russians in the other helicopters would do okay, too, he thought. Younger—by eight years on average—than the RAINBOW troopers, they were all commissioned officers, mainly lieutenants and captains with a leavening of a few majors, and all were university graduates, well educated, and that was almost as good as five years in uniform. Better yet, they were well motivated young professional soldiers, smart enough to think on their feet, and proficient in their weapons.

The mission should work, John thought. He leaned to check the clock on the helicopter's instrument panel. Forty minutes and they'd find out. Turning around, he noticed the eastern sky was lightening, according to his goggles. They'd hit the missile field just before dawn.

*   *   *

It was a stupidly easy mission for the Black Jets. Arriving overhead singly, about thirty seconds apart, each opened its bomb bay doors and dropped two weapons, ten seconds apart. Each pilot, his plane controlled by its automatic cruising system, put his laser dot on a preplanned section of the runway. The bombs were the earliest Paveway-

II guidance packages bolted to Mark-84 2,000-pound bombs with cheap—$7.95 each, in fact—M905 fuses set to go off a hundredth of a second after impact, so as to make a hole in the concrete about twenty feet across by nine feet deep. And this all sixteen of them did, to the shocked surprise of the sleepy tower crew, and with enough noise to wake up every person within a five-mile radius—and just that fast, Anshan fighter base was closed, and would remain so for at least a week. The eight F-117s turned singly and made their way back to their base at Zhigansk. Flying the Black Jet wasn't supposed to be any more exciting than driving a 737 for Southwest Airlines, and for the most part it wasn't.

*   *   *

'Why he hell didn't they send one of those Dark Stars down to cover the mission?' Jack asked.

'I suppose it never occurred to anybody,' Jackson said. They were back in the situation room.

'What about satellite overheads?'

'Not this time,' Ed Foley advised. 'Next pass over is in about four hours. Clark has a satellite phone. He'll clue us in.'

'Great.' Ryan leaned back in a chair that suddenly wasn't terribly comfortable.

*   *   *

'Objective in sight,' Boyle said over the intercom. Then the radio. 'BANDIT SIX to chicks, objective in sight. Check in, over.'

'Two.' 'Three.' 'Four.' 'Five.' 'Six.' 'Seven.' 'Eight.' 'Nine.' 'Ten.'

'COCHISE, check in.'

'This is COCHISE LEADER with five, we have the objective.'

'Crook with five, objective in sight,' the second attack—helicopter team reported.

'Okay, move in as briefed. Execute, execute, execute!'

Clark was perked up now, as were the troops in the back. Sleep was shaken off, and adrenaline flooded into their bloodstreams. He saw them shake their heads and flex their jaws. Weapons were tucked in tight, and every man moved his left hand to the twist-dial release fitting on the belt buckle.

COCHISE flight went in first, heading for the barracks of the security battalion tasked to guard the missile base. The building could have been transported bodily from any WWII American army base—a two-story wood-frame construction, with a pitched roof, and painted white. There was a guard shack outside, also painted white, and it glowed in the thermal sights of the Apache gunners. They could even see the two soldiers there, doubtless approaching the end of their duty tour, standing slackly, their weapons slung over their shoulders, because *nobody* ever came out here, rarely enough during the day, and never in living memory at night—unless you counted the battalion commander coming back drunk from a command-staff meeting.

Their heads twisted slightly when they thought they heard something strange, but the four-bladed rotor on the Apache was also designed for sound suppression, and so they were still looking when they saw the first flash—

—the weapons selected were the 2.75-inch-diameter free-flight rockets, carried in pods on the Apaches' stub wings. Three of the section of five handled the initial firing run, with two in reserve should the unexpected develop. They burned in low, so as to conceal their silhouettes in the hills behind them, and opened up at two hundred meters. The first salvo of four blew up the guard shack and its two sleepy guards. The noise would have been enough to awaken those in the barracks building, but the second salvo of rockets, this time fifteen of them, got there before anyone inside could do more than blink his eyes open. Both floors of the two-story structure were hit, and most of those inside died without waking, caught in the middle of dreams. The Apaches hesitated then, still having weapons to fire. There was a subsidiary guard post on the other side of the building; COCHISE LEADER looped around the barracks and spotted it. The two soldiers there had their rifles up and fired blindly into the air, but his gunner selected his 20-mm cannon and swept them aside as though with a broom. Then the Apache pivoted in the air and he salvoed his remaining rockets into the barracks, and it was immediately apparent that if anyone was alive in there, it was by the grace of God Himself, and whoever it was would not be a danger to the mission.

'COCHISE Four and Five, Lead. Go back up Crook, we don't need you here.'

'Roger, Lead,' they both replied. The two attack helicopters moved off, leaving the first three to look for and erase any signs of life.

*   *   *

Crook flight, also of five Apaches, smoked in just ahead of the Blackhawks. It turned out that each silo had a small guard post, each for two men, and those were disposed of in a matter of seconds with cannon fire. Then the Apaches climbed to higher altitude and circled slowly, each over a pair of missile silos, looking for anything moving, but seeing nothing.

BANDIT SIX, Colonel Dick Boyle, flared his Blackhawk three feet over Silo #1, as it was marked on his satellite photo.

'Go!' the co-pilot shouted over the intercom. The RAINBOW troopers jumped down just to the east of the actual hole itself; the 'Chinese hat' steel structure, which looked like an inverted blunt ice cream cone, prohibited dropping right down on the door itself.

*   *   *

The base command post was the best-protected structure on the entire post. It was buried ten meters underground, and the ten meters was solid reinforced concrete, so as to survive a nuclear bomb's exploding within a hundred meters, or so the design supposedly promised. Inside was a staff of ten, commanded by Major General Xun Qing-Nian. He'd been a Second Artillery (the Chinese name for their strategic missile troops) officer since graduating from university with an engineering degree. Only three hours before, he'd supervised the fueling of all twelve of his CSS-4 intercontinental ballistic missiles, which had never happened before in his memory. No explanation had come with that order, though it didn't take a rocket scientist—which he was, by profession—to connect it with the war under way against Russia.

Like all members of the People's Liberation Army, he was a highly disciplined man, and always mindful of the fact that he had his country's most valuable military assets under his personal control. The alarm had been raised by one of the silo-guard posts, and his staff switched on the television cameras used for site inspection and surveillance. They were old cameras, and needed lights, which were switched on as well.

*   *   *

'What the fuck!' Chavez shouted. 'Turn the lights off!' he ordered over his radio.

It wasn't demanding. The light standards weren't very tall, nor were they very far away. Chavez hosed one with his MP-10, and the lights went out, thank you. No other lasted for more than five seconds at any of the silos.

*   *   *

'We are under attack,' General Xun said in a quiet and disbelieving voice. 'We are under attack,' he repeated. But he had a drill for this. 'Alert the guard force,' he told one NCO. 'Get me Beijing,' he ordered another.

*   *   *

At Silo #1, Paddy Connolly ran to the pipes that led to the top of the concrete box that marked the top of the silo. To each he stuck a block of Composition B, his explosive of choice. Into each block he inserted a blasting cap. Two men, Eddie Price and Hank Patterson, knelt close by with their weapons ready for a response force that was nowhere to be seen.

'Fire in the hole!' Patterson shouted, running back to the other two. There he skidded down to the ground, sheltered behind the concrete, and twisted the handle on his detonator. The two pipes were blown apart a millisecond later.

'Masks!' he told everyone on the radio . . . but there was no vapor coming off the fueling pipes. That was good news, wasn't it?

'Come on!' Eddie Price yelled at him. The three men, guarded now by two others, looked for the metal door into the maintenance entrance for the silo.

'Ed, we're on the ground, we're on the ground,' Clark was saying into his satellite phone, fifty yards away. 'The barracks are gone, and there's no opposition on the ground here. Doing our blasting now. Back to you soon. Out.'

* * *

'Well, shit,' Ed Foley said in his office, but the line was now dead.

* * *

'What?' It was an hour later in Beijing, and the sun was up. Marshal Luo, having just woken up after not enough sleep following the worst day he'd known since the Cultural Revolution, had a telephone thrust into his hands. 'What is this?' he demanded of the phone.

'This is Major General Xun Qing-Nian at Xuanhua missile base. We are under attack here. There is a force of men on the ground over our heads trying to destroy our missiles. I require instructions!'

'Fight them off!' was the first idea Luo had.

'The defense battalion is dead, they do not respond. Comrade Minister, what do I do?'

'Are your missiles fueled and ready for launch?'

'Yes!'

Luo looked around his bedroom, but there was no one to advise him. His country's most priceless assets were now about to be ripped from his control. His command wasn't automatic. He actually thought first, but in the end, it wouldn't matter how considered his decision was.

'Launch your missiles,' he told the distant general officer.

'Repeat your command,' Luo heard.

'*Launch your missiles!*' his voice boomed. '*Launch your missiles NOW!*'

'By your command,' the voice replied.

*   *   *

'Fuck,' Sergeant Connolly said. 'This is some bloody door!' The first explosive block had done nothing more than scorch the paint. This time he attached a hollow-charge to the upper and lower hinges and backed off again. 'This one will do it,' he promised as he trailed the wires back.

The crash that followed gave proof to his words. When next they looked in, the door was gone. It had been hurled inward, must have flown into the silo like a bat out of—

—'Bloody hell!' Connolly turned. 'Run! *RUN!*'

Price and Patterson needed no encouragement. They ran for their lives. Connolly caught them reaching for his protective hood as he did so, not stopping until he was over a hundred yards away.

'The bloody missile's fueled. The door ruptured the upper tank. It's going to blow!'

'Shit! Team, this is Price, the missiles are fueled, I repeat the missiles are fueled. Get the fucking hell away from the silo!'

*   *   *

The proof of that came from Silo #8, off to Price's south. The concrete structure that sat atop it surged into the air, and under it was a volcanic blast of fire and smoke. Silo #1, theirs, did the same, a gout of flame going sideways out of the open service door.

*   *   *

The infrared signature was impossible to miss. Over the equator, a DSP satellite focused in on the thermal bloom and cross-loaded the signal to Sunnyvale, California. From there it went to NORAD, the North American Aerospace Defense Command, dug into the subbasement level of Cheyenne Mountain, Colorado.

'Launch! Possible launch at Xuanhua!'

'What's that?' asked CINC–NORAD.

'We got a bloom, a huge—*two* huge ones at Xuanhua,' the female captain announced. 'Fuck, there's another one.'

'Okay, Captain, settle down,' the four-star told her. 'There's a special op taking that base down right now. Settle down, girl.'

*　　*　　*

In the control bunker, men were turning keys. The general in command had never really expected to do this. Sure, it was a possibility, the thing he'd trained his entire career for, but, no, not this. No. Not a chance.

But someone was trying to destroy his command—and he did have his orders, and like the automaton he'd been trained to be, he gave the orders and turned his command key.

*　　*　　*

The Spetsnaz people were doing well. Four silos were now disabled. One of the Russian teams managed to crack the maintenance door on their first try. This team, General Kirillin's own, sent its technical genius inside, and he found the missile's guidance module and blew it apart with gunfire. It would take a week at least to fix this missile, and just to make sure *that* didn't happen, he affixed an explosive charge to the stainless steel body and set the timer for fifteen minutes. 'Done!' he called.

'Out!' Kirillin ordered. The lieutenant general, now feeling like a new cadet in parachute school, gathered his team and ran to the pickup point. As guilty as any man would be of mission focus, he

738

looked around, surprised by the fire and flame to his north—

—but more surprised to see three silo covers moving. The nearest was only three hundred meters away, and there he saw one of his Spetsnaz troopers walk right to the suddenly open silo and toss something in—then he ran like a rabbit—

—because three seconds later, the hand grenade he'd tossed in exploded, and took the entire missile up with it. The Spetsnaz soldier disappeared in the fireball he'd caused, and would not be seen again—

—but then something worse happened. From exhaust vents set left and right of Silos #5 and #7 came two vertical fountains of solid white-yellow flame, and less than two seconds later appeared the blunt, black shape of a missile's nosecone.

*   *   *

'Fuck,' breathed the Apache pilot coded CROOK TWO. He was circling a kilometer away, and without any conscious thought at all lowered his nose, twisted throttle, and pulled collective to jerk his attack helicopter at the rising missile.

'Got it,' the gunner called. He selected his 20-mm cannon and held down the trigger. The tracers blazed out like laser beams. The first set missed, but the gunner adjusted his lead and walked them into the missile's upper half—

—the resulting explosion threw CROOK TWO out of control, rolling it over on its back. The pilot threw his cyclic to the left, continuing the roll before he stopped it, barely, a quarter of the way through the second one, and then he saw the fireball rising, and the burning missile fuel falling back to the ground, atop Silo #9, and on all the men there who'd disabled that bird.

$$* \qquad * \qquad *$$

The last missile cleared its silo before the soldiers there could do much about it. Two tried to shoot at it with their personal weapons, but the flaming exhaust incinerated them in less time than it takes to pull a trigger. Another Apache swept in, having seen what CROOK TWO had accomplished, but its rounds fell short, so rapidly the CSS-4 climbed into the air.

$$* \qquad * \qquad *$$

'Oh, fuck,' Clark heard in his radio earpiece. It was Ding's voice. 'Oh, fuck.'

John got back on his satellite phone.

'Yeah, how's it going?' Ed Foley asked.

'One got off, one got away, man.'

'What?'

'You heard me. We killed all but one, but that one got off . . . going north, but leaning east some. Sorry, Ed. We tried.'

It took Foley a few seconds to gather his thought and reply. 'Thanks, John. I guess I have some things to do here.'

$$* \qquad * \qquad *$$

'There's another one,' the captain said.

CINC–NORAD was trying to play this one as cool as he could. Yes, there was a spec-op laid on to take this Chinese missile farm down, and so he

740

expected to see some hot flashes on the screen, and okay, all of them so far had been on the ground.

'That should be all of them,' the general announced.

'Sir, this one's moving. This one's a launch.'

'Are you sure?'

'Look, sir, the bloom is moving off the site,' she said urgently. 'Valid launch, valid launch—valid threat!' she concluded. 'Oh, my God . . .'

'Oh, shit,' CINC–NORAD said. He took one breath and lifted the Gold Phone. No, first he'd call the NMCC.

The senior watch officer in the National Military Command Center was a Marine one-star named Sullivan. The NORAD phone didn't ring very often.

'NMCC, Brigadier General Sullivan speaking.'

'This is CINC–NORAD. We have a valid launch, valid threat from Xuanhua missile base in China. I say again, we have a valid launch, valid threat from China. It's angling east, coming to North America.'

'Fuck,' the Marine observed.

'Tell me about it.'

The procedures were all written down. His first call went to the White House military office.

*   *   *

Ryan was setting down to dinner with the family. An unusual night, he had nothing scheduled, no speeches to give, and that was good, because reporters always showed up and asked questions, and lately—

'Say that again?' Andrea Price-O'Day said into her sleeve microphone. 'What?'

741

Then another Secret Service agent bashed into the room. '*Marching Order!*' he proclaimed. It was a code phrase often practiced but never spoken in reality.

'What?' Jack said, half a second before his wife could make the same sound.

'Mr. President, we have to get you and your family out of here,' Andrea said. 'The Marines have the helicopters on the way.'

'What's happening?'

'Sir, NORAD reports an inbound ballistic threat.'

'What? China?'

'That's all I know. Let's go, right now,' Andrea said forcefully.

'*Jack*,' Cathy said in alarm.

'Okay, Andrea.' The President turned. 'Time to go, honey. Right now.'

'But—what's happening?'

He got her to her feet first, and walked to the door. The corridor was full of agents. Trenton Kelly was holding Kyle Daniel—the lionesses were nowhere in sight—and the principal agents for all the other kids were there. In a moment, they saw that there was not enough room in the elevator. The Ryan family rode. The agents mainly ran down the wide, white marble steps to the ground level.

'*Wait!*' another agent called, holding his left hand up. His pistol was in his right hand, and none of them had seen *that* very often. They halted as commanded—even the President doesn't often argue with a person holding a gun.

Ryan was thinking as fast as he knew how: 'Andrea, where do I go?'

'You go to KNEECAP. Vice President Jackson will

join you there. The family goes to Air Force One.'

*   *   *

At Andrews Air Force base, just outside Washington, the pilots of First Heli the USAF 1st Helicopter Squadron, were sprinting to their Bell Hueys. Each had an assignment, and each knew where his Principal was, because the security detail of each was reporting in constantly. Their job was to collect the cabinet members and spirit them away from Washington to preselected places of supposed safety. Their choppers were off the ground in less than three minutes, scattering off to different preselected pickup points.

*   *   *

'Jack, what is this?' It took a lot to make his wife afraid, but this one had done it.

'Honey, we have a report that a ballistic missile is flying toward America, and the safest place for us to be is in the air. So, they're getting you and the kids to Air Force One. Robby and I will be on KNEECAP. Okay?'

'Okay? Okay? What is this?'

'It's bad, but that's all I know.'

*   *   *

On the Aleutian island of Shemya, the huge Cobra Dane radar scanned the sky to the north and west. It frequently detected satellites, which mainly fly lower than ICBM warheads, but the computer that analyzed the tracks of everything that came into the system's view categorized this contact as exactly what it was, too high to be a low-orbit satellite, and too slow to be a launch vehicle.

'What's the track?' a major asked a sergeant.

'Computer says East Coast of the United States. In a few minutes we'll know more . . . for now, somewhere between Buffalo and Atlanta.' That information was relayed automatically to NORAD and the Pentagon.

*　　　*　　　*

The entire structure of the United States military went into hyperdrive, one segment at a time, as the information reached it. That included USS *Gettysburg*, alongside the pier in the Washington Navy Yard.

Captain Blandy was in his in-port cabin when the growler phone went off. 'Captain speaking . . . go to general quarters, Mr. Gibson,' he ordered, far more calmly than he felt.

Throughout the ship, the electronic gonging started, followed by a human voice: 'General Quarters—General Quarters—all hands man your battle stations.'

Gregory was in CIC, running another simulation. 'What's that mean?'

Senior Chief Leek shook his head. 'Sir, that means something ain't no simulation no more.' *Battle stations alongside the fucking pier?* 'Okay, people, let's start lighting it all up!' he ordered his sailors.

*　　　*　　　*

The regular Presidential helicopter muttered down on the South Lawn and the Secret Service agent at the door turned and yelled: *'COME ON!'*

Cathy turned. 'Jack, you coming with us?'

'No, Cath, I have to go to Kneecap. Now, get along. I'll see you later tonight, okay?' He gave her a kiss, and all the kids got a hug, except for Kyle, whom the President took from Kelley's arms for a quick hold before giving him back. 'Take care of him,' he told the agent.

'Yes, sir. Good luck.' Ryan watched his family run up the steps into the chopper, and the Sikorsky lurched off before they could have had a chance to sit and strap down.

Then another Marine helicopter appeared, this one with Colonel Dan Malloy at the controls. This one was a VH-60, whose doors slid open. Ryan walked quickly to it, with Andrea Price-O'Day at his side. They sat and strapped down before it lumbered back into the air.

'What about everybody else?' Ryan asked.

'There's a shelter under the East Wing for some . . .' she said. Then her voice trailed off and she shrugged.

'Oh, shit, what about everybody else?' Ryan demanded.

'Sir, I have to look after *you*.'

'But—what—'

Then Special Agent Price-O'Day started retching. Ryan saw and pulled out a barf bag, one with a very nice Presidential logo printed on it, and handed it to her. They were over the Mall now, just passing the George Washington Monument. Off to the right was southwest Washington, filled with the working- and middle-class homes of regular people who drove cabs or cleaned up offices, tens of thousands of them . . . there were people visible in the Mall, on the grass, just enjoying a walk in the falling darkness, just being people . . .

And you just left behind a hundred or so. Maybe twenty will fit in the shelter under the East Wing . . . what about the rest, the ones who make your bed and fold your socks and shine your shoes and serve dinner and pick up after the kids—what about them, *Jack?* A small voice asked. *Who flies* them *off to safety?*

He turned his head to see the Washington Monument, and beyond that the reflecting pool and the Lincoln Memorial. He was in the same line as those men, in the city named for one, and saved in time of war by another . . . and he was running away from danger . . . the Capital Building, home of the Congress. The light was on atop the dome. Congress was in session, doing the country's work, or trying to, as they did . . . but he was running away . . . eastern Washington, mainly black, working-class people who did the menial jobs for the most part, and had hopes to send their kids to college so that they could make out a little better than their parents had . . . eating their dinner, watching TV, maybe going out to a movie tonight or just sitting on their porches and shooting the bull with their neighbors—

—Ryan's head turned again, and he saw the two gray shapes at the Navy Yard, one familiar, one not, because Tony Bretano had—

Ryan flipped the belt buckle in his lap and lurched forward, knocking into the Marine sergeant in the jump seat. Colonel Malloy was in the right-front seat, doing his job, flying the chopper. Ryan grabbed his left shoulder. The head came around.

'Yes, sir, what is it?'

'See that cruiser down there?'

'Yes, sir.'

'Land on it.'

'Sir, I—'

'Land on it, that's an order!' Ryan shouted at him.

'Aye aye,' Malloy said like a good Marine.

The Blackhawk turned, arcing down the Anacostia River, and flaring as Malloy judged the wind. The Marine hesitated, looking back one more time. Ryan insistently jerked his hand at the ship.

The Blackhawk approached cautiously.

'What are you doing?' Andrea demanded.

'I'm getting off here. You're going to KNEECAP.'

'*NO!*' she shouted back. 'I stay with you!'

'Not this time. Have your baby. If this doesn't work out, I hope the kid turns out like you and Pat.' Ryan moved to open the door. The Marine sergeant got there first. Andrea moved to follow.

'Keep her aboard, Marine!' Ryan told the crew chief. 'She goes with you!'

'*NO!*' Price-O'Day screamed.

'Yes, sir,' the sergeant acknowledged, wrapping his arms around her.

President Ryan jumped to the nonskid decking of the cruiser's landing area and ducked as the chopper pulled back into the sky. Andrea's face was the last thing he saw. The rotor wash nearly knocked him down, but going to one knee prevented that. Then he stood up and looked around.

'What the hell is—Jesus, sir!' the young petty

officer blurted, recognizing him.

'Where's the captain?'

'Captain's in CIC, sir.'

'Show me!'

The petty officer led him into a door, then a passageway that led forward. A few twists and turns later, he was in a darkened room that seemed to be set sideways in the body of the ship. It was cool in here. Ryan just walked in, figuring he was President of the United States, Commander-in-Chief of the Army and Navy, and the ship belonged to him anyway. It took a stretch to make his limbs feel as though they were a real part of his body, and then he looked around, trying to orient himself. First he turned to the sailor who'd brought him here.

'Thanks, son. You can go back to your place now.'

'Aye, sir.' He turned away as though from a dream/nightmare and resumed his duties as a sailor.

Okay, Jack thought, now what? He could see the big radar displays set fore and aft, and the people sitting sideways to look at it. He headed that way, bumping into a cheap aluminum chair on the way, and looked down to see what looked like a Navy chief petty officer in a khaki shirt whose pocket— well, damn—Ryan exercised his command prerogative and reached down to steal the sailor's cigarette pack. He lifted one out, and lit it with a butane lighter. Then he walked to look at the radar display.

'Jesus, sir,' the chief said belatedly.

'Not quite. Thanks for the smoke.' Two more steps and he was behind a guy with silver eagles on his collar. That would be the captain of USS

Gettysburg. Ryan took a long and comforting drag on the smoke.

'God damn it! There's no smoking in my CIC!' the captain snarled.

'Good evening, Captain,' Ryan replied. 'I think at this moment we have a ballistic warhead inbound on Washington, presumably with a thermonuclear device inside. Can we set aside your concerns about secondhand smoke for a moment?'

Captain Blandy turned around and looked up. His mouth opened as wide as a U.S. Navy ashtray. 'How—who—what?'

'Captain, let's ride this one out together, shall we?'

'Captain Blandy, sir,' the man said, snapping to his feet.

'Jack Ryan, Captain.' Ryan shook his hand and bade him sit back down. 'What's happening now?'

'Sir, the NMCC tells us that there's a ballistic inbound for the East Coast. I've got the ship at battle stations. Radar's up. Chip inserted?' he asked.

'The chip is in, sir,' Senior Chief Leek confirmed.

'Chip?'

'Just our term for it. It's really a software thing,' Blandy explained.

*　　　*　　　*

Cathy and the kids were pulled up the steps and hustled into the forward cabin. The colonel at the controls was in an understandable hurry. With Three and Four already turning, he started engines One and Two, and the VC-25 started rolling the

749

instant the truck with the steps pulled away, making one right-angle turn, and then lumbering down Runway One-Nine, right into the southerly wind. Immediately below him, Secret Service and Air Force personnel got the First Family strapped in, and for the first time in fifteen minutes, the Secret Service people allowed themselves to breathe normally. Not thirty seconds later, Vice President Jackson's helicopter landed next to the E-4B National Emergency Airborne Command Post, whose pilot was as anxious to get off the ground as the driver of the VC-25. That was accomplished in less than ninety seconds. Jackson had never strapped in, and stood to look around. 'Where's Jack?' the Vice President asked. Then he saw Andrea, who looked as though she just miscarried her pregnancy.

'He stayed, sir. He had the pilot drop him on the cruiser in the Navy Yard.'

'He did *what*?'

'You heard me, sir.'

'Get him on the radio—*right now*!' Jackson ordered.

*   *   *

Ryan was actually feeling somewhat relaxed. No more rushing about, here he was, surrounded by people calmly and quietly going about their jobs—outwardly so, anyway. The captain looked a little tense, but captains were supposed to, Ryan figured, being responsible in this case for a billion dollars' worth of warship and computers.

'Okay, how are we doing?'

'Sir, the inbound, if it's aimed at us, is not on the

scope yet.'

'Can you shoot it down?'

'That's the idea, Mr. President,' Blandy replied. 'Is Dr. Gregory around?'

'Here, Captain,' a voice answered. A shape came closer. 'Jesus!'

'That's not my name—I know you!' Ryan said in considerable surprise 'Major—Major . . .'

'Gregory, sir. I ended up a half a colonel before I pulled the plug. SDIO. Secretary Bretano had me look into upgrading the missiles for the Aegis system,' the physicist explained. 'I guess we're going to see if it works or not.'

'What do you think?' Ryan asked.

'It worked fine on the simulations,' was the best answer available.

'Radar contact. We got us a bogie,' a petty officer said. 'Bearing three-four-niner, range nine hundred miles, speed—that's the one, sir. Speed is one thousand four hundred knots—I mean fourteen *thousand* knots, sir.' *Damn*, he didn't have to add.

'Four and a half minutes out,' Gregory said.

'Do the math in your head?' Ryan asked.

'Sir, I've been in the business since I got out of West Point.'

Ryan finished his cigarette and looked around for—

'Here, sir.' It was the friendly chief with an ashtray that had magically appeared in CIC. 'Want another one?'

'Why not?' the President reasoned. He took a second one, and the senior chief lit it up for him. 'Thanks.'

'Gee, Captain Blandy, maybe you're declaring a

751

blanket amnesty?'

'If he isn't, I am,' Ryan said.

'Smoking lamp is lit, people,' Senior Chief Leek announced, an odd satisfaction in his voice.

The captain looked around in annoyance, but dismissed it.

'Four minutes, it might not matter a whole lot,' Ryan observed as coolly as the cigarette allowed. Health hazard or not, they had their uses.

'Captain, I have a radio call for the President, sir.'

'Where do I take it?' Jack asked.

'Right here, sir,' yet another chief said, lifting a phone-type receiver and pushing a button.

'Ryan.'

'Jack, it's Robby.'

'My family get off okay?'

'Yeah, Jack, they're fine. Hey, what the hell are you doing down there?'

'Riding it out. Robby, I can't run away, pal. I just can't.'

'Jack if this thing goes off—'

'Then you get promoted,' Ryan cut him off.

'You know what I'll have to do?' the Vice President demanded.

'Yeah, Robby, you'll have to play catch-up. God help you if you do.' *But it won't be* my *problem*, Ryan thought. There was some consolation in that. Killing some guy with a gun was one thing. Killing a million with a nuke . . . no, he just couldn't do that without eating a gun afterward. *You're just too Catholic, Jack, my boy.*

'Jesus, Jack,' his old friend said over the digital, encrypted radio link. Clearly thinking about what horrors he'd have to commit, son of a preacher—

752

man or not . . .

'Robby, you're the best friend any man could hope to have. If this doesn't work out, look after Cathy and the kids for me, will ya?'

'You know it.'

'We'll know in about three minutes, Rob. Get back to me then, okay?'

'Roger,' the former Tomcat driver replied. 'Out.'

'Dr. Gregory, what can you tell me?'

'Sir, the inbound is probably their equivalent of one of our old W-51s. Five megatons, thereabouts. It'll do Washington, and everything within ten miles—hell, it'll break windows in Baltimore.'

'What about us, here?'

'No chance. Figure it'll be targeted inside a triangle defined by the White House, the Capitol Building, and the Pentagon. The ship's keel might survive, only because it's under water. No people. Oh, maybe some really lucky folks in the D.C. subway. That's pretty far underground. But the fires will suck all the air out of the tunnels, probably.' He shrugged. 'This sort of thing's never happened before. You can't say for sure until it does.'

'What chances that it'll be a dud?'

'The Pakistanis have had some failed detonations. We had fizzles once, mainly from helium contamination in the secondary. That's why the terrorist bomb at Denver fizzled—'

'I remember.'

'Okay,' Gregory said. 'It's over Buffalo now. Now it's reentering the atmosphere. That'll slow it down a little.'

'Sir, the track is definitely on us, the NMCC says,' a voice said.

753

'Agreed,' Captain Blandy said.

'Is there a civilian alert?' Ryan asked.

'It's on the radio, sir,' a sailor said. 'It's on CNN, too.'

'People will be panicking out there,' Ryan murmured, taking another drag.

Probably not. Most people don't really know what the sirens mean, and the rest won't believe the radio, Gregory thought. 'Captain, we're getting close.' The track crossed over the Pennsylvania/New York border—

'System up?' Blandy asked.

'We are fully on line, sir,' the Weapons Officer answered. 'We are ready to fire from the forward magazine. Firing order is selected, all Block IVs.'

'Very well.' The captain leaned forward and turned his key in the lock. 'System is fully enabled. Special-Auto.' He turned. 'Sir, that means the computer will handle it from here.'

'Target range is now three hundred miles,' a kid's voice announced.

They're so cool about this, Ryan thought. *Maybe they just don't believe it's real . . . hell, it's hard enough for me . . .* He took another drag on the cigarette, watching the blip come down, following its computer-produced velocity vector right for Washington, D.C.

'Any time now,' the Weapons Officer said.

He wasn't far off. *Gettysburg* shuddered with the launch of the first missile.

'One away!' a sailor said off to the right. 'One is away clean.'

'Okay.'

The SM2-ER missile had two stages. The short booster kicked the assembly out of its silo-type hole

754

in the forward magazine, trailing an opaque column of gray smoke.

'The idea is to intercept at a range of two hundred miles,' Gregory explained. 'The interceptor and the inbound will rendezvous at the same spot, and—zap!'

'Mainly farmland there, place you go to shoot pheasants,' Ryan said, remembering hunting trips there in his youth.

'Hey, I got a visual on the fucker,' another voice called. There was a TV camera with a ten-power lens slaved into the fire-control radar, and it showed the inbound warhead, just a featureless white blob now, like a meteor, Ryan thought.

'Intercept in four—three—two—one—'

The missile came close, but exploded behind the target.

'Firing Two!' *Gettysburg* shook again.

'Two away clean!' the same voice as before announced.

It was over Harrisburg, Pennsylvania, now, its speed 'down' to thirteen thousand miles per hour . . .

Then a third missile launched, followed a second later by a fourth. In the 'Special-Auto' setting, the computer was expending missiles until it saw a dead target. That was just fine with everyone aboard.

'Only two Block IVs left,' Weps said.

'They're cheap,' Captain Blandy observed. 'Come on, baby!'

Number Two also exploded behind the target, the TV picture showed.

'Three—two—one—now!'

So did Number Three.

755

'Oh, shit, oh, my God!' Gregory exclaimed. That caused heads to snap around.

'What?' Blandy demanded.

The IR seekers, they're going for the centroid of the infrared source, and that's *behind* the inbound.'

'What?' Ryan asked, his stomach in an instant knot.

'The brightest part of the target is *behind* the target. The missiles are going for *that!* Oh, fuck!' Dr. Gregory explained.

'Five away . . . Six away . . . both got off clean,' the voice to the right announced again.

The inbound was over Frederick, Maryland, now, doing twelve thousand knots . . .

'That's it, we're out of Block IVs.'

'Light up the Block IIIs,' Blandy ordered at once.

The next two interceptors did the same as the first two, coming within mere feet of the target, but exploding just behind it, and the inbound was traveling faster than the burn rate of explosive in the Standard-2-ER missile warheads. The lethal fragments couldn't catch up—

'Firing Seven! Clean.' *Gettysburg* shook yet again.

'That one's a radar homer,' Blandy said, clenching his fist before his chest.

Five and Six performed exactly as the four preceding them, missing by mere yards, but a miss in this case *was* as good as a mile.

Another shudder.

'Eight! Clean!'

'We have to get it before it gets to five or six thousand feet. That's optimal burst height,' Gregory said.

'At that range, I can engage it with my five-inch forward,' Blandy said, some fear in his voice now.

For his part, Ryan wondered why he wasn't shaking. Death had reached its cold hand out for him more than once . . . the Mall in London . . . his own home . . . *Red October* . . . some nameless hill in Colombia. Someday it would touch him. Was this the day? He took a last drag on the smoke and stabbed it out in the aluminum ashtray.

'Okay, here comes seven—six—five—four—three—two—one—now!'

'Miss! *Fuck!*'

'Nine away—Ten away, both clean! We're out of missiles,' the distant chief called out. 'This is it, guys.'

The inbound crossed over the D.C. Beltway, Interstate Highway 695, now at an altitude of less than twenty thousand feet, streaking across the night sky like a meteor, and so some people thought it was, pointing and calling out to those nearby. If they continued to look at it until detonation, their eyes would explode, and they would then die blind . . .

'Eight missed! Missed by a cunt hair!' a voice announced angrily. Clear on the TV, the puff of the explosion appeared mere inches from the target.

'Two more to go,' the Weapons Officer told them.

Aloft, the forward port-side SPG-62 radar was pouring out X-band radiation at the target. The rising SM-2 missile, its rocket motor still burning, homed in on the reflected signal, focusing, closing, seeing the source of the reflected energy that drew it as a moth to a flame, a kamikaze robot the size of a small car, going at nearly two thousand miles per hour, seeking an object going six times faster . . . two miles . . . one mile . . . a thousand yards . . . five hundred, one hun—

—On the TV screen the RV meteor changed to a shower of sparks and fire—

'*Yeah!*' twenty voices called as one.

The TV camera followed the descending sparks. The adjacent radar display showed them falling within the city of Washington.

'You're going to want to get people to collect those fragments. Some of them are going to be plutonium. Not real healthy to handle,' Gregory said, leaning against a stanchion. 'Looked like a skin-skin kill. Oh, God, how did I fuck up my programming like that?' he wondered aloud.

'I wouldn't sweat it too bad, Dr. Gregory,' Senior Chief Leek observed. 'Your code also helped the last one home in more efficient-like. I think I might want to buy you a beer, fella.'

CHAPTER SIXTY-ONE

REVOLUTION

As usual, the news didn't get back quickly to the place where it had actually started. Having given the launch order, Defense Minister Luo had little clue what to do next. Clearly, he couldn't go back to sleep. America might well answer his action with a nuclear strike of its own, and therefore his first rational thought was that it might be a good idea for him to get the hell out of Beijing. He rose, made normal use of his bathroom, and splashed

758

water on his face, but then again his mind hit a brick wall. What to do? The one name he knew to call was Zhang Han Sen. Once connected, he spoke very quickly indeed.

'You did—*what* happened, Luo?' the senior Minister Without Portfolio asked with genuine alarm.

'Someone—Russians or Americans, I'm not sure which—struck at our missile base at Xuanhua, attempting to destroy our nuclear deterrent. I ordered the base commander to fire them off, of course,' Luo told his associate minister, in a voice that was both defiant and defensive. 'We agreed on this in our last meeting, did we not?'

'Luo, yes, we discussed the possibility. But *you fired them without consulting with us?*' Zhang demanded. Such decisions were always collegial, never unilateral.

'What choice did I have, Zhang?' Marshal Luo asked in reply. 'Had I hesitated a moment, there would have been none left to fire.'

'I see,' the voice on the phone said. 'What is happening now?'

'The missiles are flying. The first should hit their first targets, Moscow and Leningrad, in about ten minutes. I had no choice, Zhang. I could not allow them to disarm us completely.'

Zhang could have sworn and screamed at the man, but there was no point in that. What had happened had happened, and there was no sense expending intellectual or emotional energy on something he could not alter. 'Very well. We need to meet. I will assemble the Politburo. Come to the Council of Ministers Building at once. Will the Americans or Russians retaliate?'

'They cannot strike back in kind. They have no nuclear missiles. An attack by bombers would take some hours,' Luo advised, trying to make it sound like good news.

*　　　*　　　*

At his end of the connection, Zhang felt a chill in his stomach that rivaled liquid helium. As with many things in life, this one—contemplated theoretically in a comfortable conference room—was something very different now that it had turned into a most uncomfortable reality. And yet—was it? It was a thing too difficult to believe. It was too unreal. There were no outward signs—you'd at least expect thunder and lightning outside the windows to accompany news like this, even a major earthquake, but it was merely early morning, not yet seven o'clock. Could this be real?

Zhang padded across his bedroom, switched on his television, and turned it to CNN—it had been turned off for most of the country, but not *here*, of course. His English skills were insufficient to translate the rapid-fire words coming over the screen now. They were showing Washington, D.C., with a camera evidently atop the CNN building there—wherever that was, he had not the faintest idea. It was a black American speaking. The camera showed him standing atop a building, microphone in hand like black plastic ice cream, speaking very, very rapidly—so much so that Zhang was catching only one word in three, and looking off to the camera's left with wide, frightened eyes.

So, he knows what is coming there, doesn't he? Zhang thought, then wondered if he would see the

760

destruction of the American capital via American news television. That, he thought, would have *some* entertainment value.

'Look!' the reporter said, and the camera twisted to see a smoke trail race across the sky—

—*What the hell is that?* Zhang wondered. Then there was another . . . and more besides . . . and the reporter was showing real fear now . . .

. . . it was good for his heart to see such feelings on the face of an American, especially a black American *reporter.* Another one of those *monkeys* had caused his country such great harm, after all . . .

So, now he'd get to see one incinerated . . . or maybe not. The camera and the transmitter would go, too, wouldn't they? So, just a flash of light, maybe, and a blank screen that would be replaced by CNN headquarters in Atlanta . . .

. . . more smoke trails. Ah, yes, they were surface-to-air missiles . . . could such things intercept a nuclear missile? *Probably not*, Zhang judged. He checked his watch. The sweep hand seemed determined to let the snail win this race, it jumped so slowly from one second to the next, and Zhang felt himself watching the display on the TV screen with anticipation he knew to be perverse. But America had been his country's principal enemy for so many years, had thwarted two of his best and most skillfully laid plans—and now he'd see its destruction by means of one of its very own agencies, this cursed medium of television news, and though Tan Deshi claimed that it was not an organ of the American government, surely that could not be the case. The Ryan regime in Washington must have a very cordial relationship with those minstrels, they followed the party line of the Western governments so fawningly . . .

. . . two more smoke trails . . . the camera followed them and . . . what was that? Like a meteor, or the landing light of a commercial aircraft, a bright light, seemingly still in the sky—no, it was moving, unless that was the fear of the cameraman showing—oh, yes, that was it, because the smoke trails seemed to seek it out . . . but not quite closely enough, it would seem . . . *and so, farewell, Washington*, Zhang Han Sen thought. Perhaps there'd be adverse consequences for the People's Republic, but he'd have the satisfaction of seeing the death of—

—what was that? Like a bursting firework in the sky, a shower of sparks, mainly heading down . . . what did *that* mean . . . ?

It was clear sixty seconds later. Washington had not been blotted from the map. *Such a pity*, Zhang thought . . . *especially since there would be consequences* . . . With that, he washed and dressed and left for the Council of Ministers Building.

*   *   *

'Dear God,' Ryan breathed. The initial emotions of denial and elation were passing now. The feelings were not unlike those following an auto accident. First was disbelief, then remedial action that was more automatic than considered, then when the danger was past came the whiplash after—fear, when the psyche started to examine what had passed, and what had almost been, and fear after survival, fear *after* the danger was past, brought on the real shakes. Ryan remembered that Winston

Churchill had remarked that there was nothing more elating than rifle fire that had missed—'to be shot at without result' was the exact quote the President remembered. If so, Winston Spencer Churchill must have had ice water in his cardiovascular system, or lie enjoyed braggadocio more than this American President did.

'Well, I hope that was the only one,' Captain Blandy observed.

'Better be, Cap'n. We be out of missiles,' Chief Leek said, lighting up another smoke in accordance with the Presidential amnesty.

'Captain,' Jack said when he was able to, 'every man on this ship gets promoted one step by Presidential Order, and USS *Gettysburg* gets a Presidential Unit Citation. That's just for starters, of course. Where's a radio? I need to talk to KNEECAP.'

'Here, sir.' A sailor handed him a phone receiver. 'The line's open, sir.

'Robby?'

'Jack?'

'You're still Vice President,' SWORDSMAN told TOMCAT.

'For now, I suppose. Christ, Jack, what the hell were you trying to do?'

'I'm not sure. It seemed like the right idea at the time.' Jack was seated now, both holding the phone in his hand and cradling it between cheek and shoulder, lest he drop it on the deck. 'Is there anything else coming in?'

'NORAD says the sky is clear—only one bird got off. Targeted on us. Shit, the Russians still have dedicated ABM batteries all around Moscow. *They* probably could have handled it better than us.'

Jackson paused. 'We're calling in the Nuclear Emergency Search Team from Rocky Mountain Arsenal to look for hot spots. DOD has people coordinating with the D.C. police . . . Jesus, Jack, that was just a little intense, y'know?'

'Yeah, it was that way here, too. Now what?' the President asked.

'You mean with China? Part of me says, load up the B-2 bombers on Guam with the B-61 gravity bombs and send them to Beijing, but I suppose that's a little bit of an overreaction.'

'I think some kind of public statement—not sure what kind yet. What are you gonna be doing?'

'I asked. The drill is for us to stay up for four hours before we come back to Andrews. Same for Cathy and the kids. You might want to call them, too.'

'Roger. Okay, Robby, sit tight. See you in a few hours. I think I'm going to have a stiff one or two.'

'I hear that, buddy.'

'Okay, POTUS out.' Ryan handed the phone back. 'Captain?'

'Yes, Mr. President?'

'Your entire ship's crew is invited to the White House, right now, for some drinks on the house. I think we all need it.'

'Sir, I will not disagree with that.'

'And those who stay aboard, if they feel the need to bend an elbow, as Commander-in-Chief, I waive Navy Regulations on that subject for twenty-four hours.'

'Aye, aye, sir.'

'Chief?' Jack said next.

'Here, sir.' He handed his pack and lighter over. 'I got more in my locker, sir.'

Just then two men in civilian clothes entered CIC. It was Hilton and Malone from the night crew.

'How'd you guys get here so fast?' Ryan asked.

'Andrea called us, sir—did what we think happened just happen?'

'Yep, and your President needs a bottle and a soft chair, gentlemen.

'We have a car on the pier, sir. You want to come with us?'

'Okay—Captain, you get buses or something, and come to the White House right away. If it means locking the ship up and leaving her without anyone aboard, that's just fine with me. Call the Marine Barracks at Eighth and I for security if you need to.'

'Aye, aye, Mr. President. We'll be along shortly.'

I might be drunk before you get there, the President thought.

The car Hilton and Malone had brought down was one of the black armored Chevy Suburbans that followed the President everywhere he went. This one just drove back to the White House. The streets were suddenly filled with people simply standing and looking up—it struck Ryan as odd. The thing was no longer in the sky, and whatever pieces were on the ground were too dangerous to touch. In any case, the drive back to the White House was uneventful, and Ryan ended up in the Situation Room, strangely alone. The uniformed people from the White House Military Office—called Wham-O by the staff, which seemed particularly inappropriate at the moment—were all in a state somewhere between bemused and stunned. And the immediate consequence of the great effort to whisk senior government officials out of town—the scheme was officially called the Continuation of Government—had had the reverse effect. The government was at the moment still fragmented in twenty or so helicopters and one E-4B, and quite unable to coordinate itself. Ryan figured that the emergency was better designed to withstand a nuclear attack than to avoid one, and that, at the moment, seemed very strange.

Indeed, the big question for the moment was *What the hell do we do now?* And Ryan didn't have much of a clue. But then a phone rang to help him.

'This is President Ryan.'

'Sir, this is General Dan Liggett at Strike Command in Omaha. Mr. President, I gather we just dodged a major bullet.'

'Yeah, I think you can say that, General.'

'Sir, do you have any orders for us?'

'Like what?'

'Well, sir, one option would be retaliation, and—'

'Oh, you mean because they blew a chance to nuke us, we should take the opportunity to nuke them for real?'

'Sir, it's my job to present options, not to advocate any,' Liggett told his Commander-in-Chief.

'General, do you know where I was during the attack?'

'Yes, sir. Gutsy call, Mr. President.'

'Well, I am now trying to deal with my own restored life, and I don't have a clue what I ought to do about the big picture, whatever the hell that is. In another two hours or so, maybe we can think of something, but at the moment I have no idea at all. And you know, I'm not sure I want to have any such idea. So, for the moment, General, we do nothing at all. Are we clear on that?'

'Yes, Mr. President. Nothing at all happens with Strike Command.'

'I'll get back to you.'

'Jack?' a familiar voice called from the door.

'Arnie, I hate drinking alone—except when there's nobody else around. How about you and me drain a bottle of something? Tell the usher to bring down a bottle of Midleton, and, you know, have him bring a glass for himself.'

'Is it true you rode it out on the ship down at the Navy Yard?'

'Yep.' Ryan bobbed his head.

'Why?'

'I couldn't run away, Arnie. I couldn't run off to safety and leave a couple of million people to fry. Call it brave. Call it stupid. I just couldn't bug out that way.'

Van Damm leaned into the corridor and made the drink order to someone Jack couldn't see, and then he came back in. 'I was just starting dinner at my place in Georgetown when CNN ran the flash. Figured I might as well come here—didn't really believe it like I should have, I suppose.'

'It was somewhat difficult to swallow. I suppose I ought to ask myself if it was our fault, sending the special-operations people in. Why is it that people second-guess everything we do here?'

'Jack, the world is full of people who can only feel big by making other people look small, and the bigger the target, the better they feel about it. And reporters love to get their opinions, because it makes a good story to say you're wrong about anything. The media prefers a good story to a good truth most of the time. It's just the nature of the business they're in.'

'That's not fair, you know,' Ryan observed, when the head usher arrived with a silver tray, a bottle of Irish whiskey, and some glasses with ice already in them. 'Charlie, you pour yourself one, too,' the President told him.

'Mr. President, I'm not supposed—'

'Today the rules changed, Mr. Pemberton. If you get too swacked to drive home, I'll have the Secret Service take you. Have I ever told you what a good guy you are, Charlie? My kids just plain love you.'

Charles Pemberton, son and grandson of ushers at the White House, poured three drinks, just a light one for himself, and handed the glasses over with the grace of a neurosurgeon.

'Sit down and relax, Charlie. I have a question for you.'

'Yes, Mr. President?'

'Where did you ride it out? Where did you stay when that H-bomb was coming down on Washington?'

'I didn't go to the shelter in the East Wing, figured that was best for the womenfolk. I—well, sir, I took the elevator up to the roof and figured I'd just watch.'

'Arnie, there sits a brave man,' Jack said, saluting with his glass.

'Where were you, Mr. President?' Pemberton asked, breaking the etiquette rules because of pure curiosity.

'I was on the ship that shot the damned thing down, watching our boys do their job. That reminds me, this Gregory guy, the scientist that Tony Bretano got involved. We look after him,

768

Arnie. He's one of the people who saved the day.'

'Duly noted, Mr. President.' Van Damm took a big pull on his glass. 'What else?'

'I don't *have* a what-else right now,' SWORDSMAN admitted.

*   *   *

Neither did anyone in Beijing, where it was now eight in the morning, and the ministers were filing into their conference room like sleepwalkers, and the question on everyone's lips was 'What happened?'

Premier Xu called the meeting to order and ordered the Defense Minister to make his report, which he did in the monotone voice of a phone recording.

'You ordered the launch?' Foreign Minister Shen asked, aghast.

'What else was I to do? General Xun told me his base was under attack. They were trying to take our assets away—we spoke of this possibility, did we not?'

'We spoke of it, yes,' Qian agreed. 'But to do such a thing without our approval? That was a political action without reflection, Luo. What new dangers have you brought on us?'

'And what resulted from it?' Fang asked next.

'Evidently, the warhead either malfunctioned or was somehow intercepted and destroyed by the Americans. The only missile that launched successfully was targeted on Washington. The city was not, I regret to say, destroyed.'

'You regret to say—you *regret* to say?' Fang's voice spoke more loudly than anyone at the table

769

could ever remember. 'You fool! If you had succeeded, *we would be facing national death now!* You *regret?*'

*   *   *

At about that time in Washington, a mid-level CIA bureaucrat had an idea. They were feeding live and taped coverage from the Siberian battlefield over the Internet, because independent news coverage wasn't getting into the People's Republic. 'Why not,' he asked his supervisor, 'send them CNN as well?' That decision was made instantaneously, though it was possibly illegal, maybe a violation of copyright laws. But on this occasion, common sense took precedence over bureaucratic caution. CNN, they decided quickly, could bill them later.

And so, an hour and twenty minutes after the event, http://www.darkstarfeed.cia.gov/siberiabattle/realtime.ram began to cover the coverage of the near-destruction of Washington, D.C. The news that a nuclear war had been begun but aborted stunned the students in Tiananmen Square. The collective realization that they themselves might be the targets of a retaliatory strike did not put fear so much as rage into their young hearts. There were about ten thousand of them now, many with their portable laptop computers, and many of those hooked into cell phones for Internet access. From overhead you could tell their positions just by the tiny knots of pressed-together bodies. Then the leaders of the demonstration got together and started talking fast among themselves. They knew they had to do something, they just didn't know exactly what. For all they knew, they might well all be facing death.

The ardor was increased by the commentators CNN had hurriedly rushed into their studios in Atlanta and New York, many of whom opined that the only likely action for America was to reply in kind to the Chinese attack, and when the reporter acting as moderator asked what 'in kind' meant, the reply was predictable.

For the students, the question now was not so much life and death as saving their nation—the thirteen hundred *million* citizens whose lives had been made forfeit by the madmen of the Politburo. The Council of Ministers Building was not all that far away, and the crowd started heading that way.

By this time, there was a police presence in the Square of Heavenly Peace. The morning watch replaced the night team and saw the mass of young people—to their considerable surprise, since this had not been a part of their morning briefing. The men going off duty explained that nothing had happened at all that was contrary to the law, and for all they knew, it was a spontaneous demonstration of solidarity and support for the brave PLA soldiers in Siberia. So, there were few of them about, and fewer still of the People's Armed Police. It would probably not have mattered in any case. The body of students coalesced, and marched with remarkable discipline to the seat of their country's government. When they got close, there were armed men there. These police officers were not prepared to see so many people coming toward theirs. The senior of their number, a captain, walked out alone and demanded to know who was in charge of this group, only to be brushed aside by a twenty-two-year-old engineering student.

Again, it was a case of a police officer totally unaccustomed to having his words disregarded, and totally nonplussed when it took place. Suddenly, he was looking at the back of a young man who was supposed to have stopped dead in his tracks when he was challenged. The security policeman had actually expected the students to stop as a body at his command, for such was the power of law in the People's Republic, but strong as the force of law was, it was also brittle, and when broken, there was nothing behind it. There were also only forty armed men in the building, and all of them were on the first floor in the rear, kept out of the way because the ministers wanted the armed peasants out of sight, except in ones and twos. The four officers on duty at the main entrance were just swept aside as the crowd thundered in through the double doors. All drew their pistols, but only one fired, wounding three students before being knocked down and kicked into senselessness. The other three just ran to the main post to find the reserve force. By the time they got there, the students were running up the wide, ceremonial stairs to the second floor.

The meeting room was well soundproofed, a security measure to prevent eavesdropping. But soundproofing worked in both directions, and so the men sitting around the table did not hear anything until the corridor was filled with students only fifty meters away, and even then the ministers just turned about in nothing more than annoyance—

—the armed guard force deployed in two groups, one running to the front of the building on the first floor, the other coming up the back on the second, led by a major who thought to evacuate the ministers. The entire thing had developed much too quickly, with virtually no warning, because the city police had dropped the ball rather badly, and there was no time to call in armed reinforcements. As it played out, the first-floor team ran into a wall of students, and while the captain in command had twenty men armed with automatic rifles, he hesitated to order opening fire because there were more students in view than he had cartridges in his rifles, and in hesitating, he lost the initiative. A number of students approached the armed men, their hands raised, and began to engage them in reasonable tones that belied the wild-eyed throng behind them.

It was different on the second floor. The major there didn't hesitate at all. He had his men level their rifles and fire one volley high, just to scare them off. But these students didn't scare. Many of them crashed through doors off the main corridor, and one of these was the room in which the Politburo was sitting.

The sudden entrance of fifteen young people got every minister's attention.

'*What is this!*' Zhang Han Sen thundered. 'Who are you?'

'And who are you?' the engineering student sneered back. 'Are you the maniac who started a nuclear war?'

'There is no such war—who told you such nonsense?' Marshal Luo demanded. His uniform told them who he was.

'And you are the one who sent our soldiers to their death in Russia!'

'What is this?' the Minister Without Portfolio

asked.

'I think these are the people, Zhang,' Qian Kun observed. '*Our* people, Comrade,' he added coldly.

Into the vacuum of power and direction, more of the students forced their way into the room, and now the guard force couldn't risk shooting—too many of their country's leadership was right there, right in the field of fire.

'Grab them, grab them! They will not shoot these men!' one student shouted. Pairs and trios of students raced around the table, each to a separate seat.

'Tell me, boy,' Fang said gently to the one closest to him, 'how did you learn all this?'

'Over our computers, of course,' the youngster replied, a little impolitely, but not grossly so.

'Well, one finds truth where one can,' the grandfatherly minister observed.

'So, Grandfather, is it true?'

'Yes, I regret to say it is,' Fang told him, not quite knowing what he was agreeing to.

Just then, the troops appeared, their officer in the lead with a pistol in his hand, forging their way into the conference room, wide-eyed at what they saw. The students were not armed, but to start a gunfight in this room would kill the very people he was trying to safeguard, and now it was his turn to hesitate.

'Now, everyone be at ease,' Fang said, pushing his seat gently back from the table. 'You, Comrade Major, do you know who I am?'

'Yes, Minister—but—'

'Good, Comrade Major. First, you will have your men stand down. We need no killing here. There has been enough of that.'

The officer looked around the room. No one else seemed to be speaking just yet, and into that vacuum had come words which, if not exactly what he wanted to hear, at least had some weight in them. He turned and without words—waving his hands—had his men relax a little.

'Very good. Now, comrades,' Fang said, turning back to his colleagues. 'I propose that some changes are needed here. First of all, we need Foreign Minister Shen to contact America and tell them that a horible accident has occurred, and that we rejoice that no lives were lost as a result, and that those responsible for that mistake will be handled by us. To that end, I demand the immediate arrest of Premier Xu, Defense Minister Luo, and Minister Zhang. It is they who caused us to embark on the foolish adventure in Russia that threatens to bring ruin to us all. You three have endangered our country, and for this crime against the people, you must pay.'

'Comrades, what is your vote?' Fang demanded.

There were no dissents; even Tan and Interior Minister Tong nodded their assent.

'Next, Shen, you will immediately propose an end to hostilities with Russia and America, telling them also that those responsible for this ruinous adventure will be punished. Are we agreed on that, comrades?'

They were.

'For myself, I think we ought all to give thanks to Heaven that we may be able to put an end to this madness. Let us make this happen quickly. For now, I will meet with these young people to see what other things are of interest to them. You, Comrade Major, will conduct the three prisoners to a place of confinement. Qian, will you remain with me and speak to the students as well?'

'Yes, Fang,' the Finance Minister said. 'I will be pleased to.'

'So, young man,' Fang said to the one who'd seemed to act like a leader. 'What is it you wish to discuss?'

*   *   *

The Blackhawks were long on their return flight. The refueling went off without a hitch but it was soon apparent that almost thirty men, all Russians, had been lost in the attack on Xuanhua. It wasn't the first time Clark had seen good men lost, and as before, the determining factor was nothing more than luck, but that was a lousy explanation to have to give to a new widow. The other thing eating at him was the missile that had gotten away. He'd seen it lean to the east. It hadn't gone to Moscow, and that was all he knew right now. The flight back was bleakly silent the whole way, and he couldn't fix it by calling in on his satellite phone because he'd taken a fall at some point and broken the antenna off the top of the damned thing. He'd failed. That was all he knew, and the consequences of this kind of failure surpassed his imagination. The only good news he could come up with was that no one in his family lived close to any likely target, but lots of other people did. Finally the chopper touched down, and the doors were opened for the troopers to get out. Clark saw General Diggs there and went over to him.

'How bad?'

'The Navy shot it down over Washington.'

'What?'

'General Moore told me. Some cruiser— *Gettysburg*, I think he said—shot the bastard down right over the middle of D.C. We got lucky, Mr. Clark.'

John's legs almost buckled at that news. For the past five hours, he'd been imagining a mushroom cloud with his name on it over some American city, but God, luck, or the Great Pumpkin had intervened, and he'd settle for that.

'What gives, Mr. C?' Chavez asked, with considerable worry in his voice. Diggs gave him the word, too.

'The Navy? The fuckin' Navy? Well, I'll be damned. They are good for something, eh?'

*　　*　　*

Jack Ryan was about half in the bag by this time, and if the media found out about it the hell with them. The cabinet was back in town, but he'd put off the meeting until the following morning. It would take time to consider what had to be done. The most obvious response, the one talking heads were proclaiming on the various TV stations, was one he could not even contemplate, much less order. They'd have to find something better than wholesale slaughter. He wouldn't order that, though some special operation to take out the Chinese Politburo certainly appealed to his current state of mind. A lot of blood had been spilled, and there would be some more, too. To think it had all begun with an Italian cardinal and a Baptist preacher, killed by some trigger-happy cop. Did the world really turn on so perverse an axis as that?

That, Ryan thought, *calls for another drink.*

But some good had to come from this. You had to learn lessons from this sort of thing. But what was there to learn? It was too confusing for the American President. Things had happened too fast. He'd gone to the brink of something so deep and so dreadful that the vast maw of it still filled his eyes, and it was just too much for one man to handle. He'd bounced back from facing imminent death himself, but not the deaths of millions, not as directly as this. The truth of the matter was that his mind was blanked out by it all, unable to analyze, unable to correlate the information in a way that would help him take a step forward, and all he really wanted and needed to do was to embrace his family, to be certain that the world still had the shape he wanted it to have.

People somehow expected him to be a superman, to be some godlike being who handled things that others could not handle—*well*, *yeah*, Jack admitted to himself. Maybe he had shown courage by remaining in Washington, but after courage came deflation, and he needed something outside himself to restore his manhood. The well he'd tapped wasn't bottomless at all, and this time the bucket was clunking down on rocks . . .

The phone rang. Arnie got it. 'Jack? It's Scott Adler.'

Ryan reached for it. 'Yeah, Scott, what is it?'

'Just got a call from Bill Kilmer, the DCM in Beijing. Seems that Foreign Minister Shen was just over to the embassy. They have apologized for launching the missile. They say it was a horrible accident and they're glad the thing didn't go off—'

'That's fucking nice of them,' Ryan observed.

'Well, whoever gave the order to launch is under arrest. They request our assistance in bringing an end to hostilities. Shen said they'd take any reasonable action to bring that about. He said they're willing to declare a unilateral cease-fire and withdraw all their forces back to their own borders, and to consider reparations to Russia. They're surrendering, Jack.'

'Really? Why?'

'There appears to have been some sort of riot in Beijing. Reports are very sketchy, but it seems that their government has fallen. Minister Fang Gan seems to be the interim leader. That's all I know, Jack, but it looks like a decent beginning. With your permission, and with the concurrence of the Russians, I think we ought to agree to this.'

'Approved,' the President said, without much in the way of consideration. *Hell*, he told himself, *you don't have to dwell too much on* ending *a war, do you?* 'Now what?'

'Well, I want to talk to the Russians to make sure they'll go along. I think they will. Then we can negotiate the details. As a practical matter, we hold all the cards, Jack. The other side is folding.'

'Just like that? We end it all just like that?' Ryan asked.

'It doesn't have to be Michelangelo and the Sistine Chapel, Jack. It just has to work.'

'Will it work?'

'Yes, Jack, it ought to.'

'Okay, get hold of the Russians,' Ryan said, setting his glass down.

Maybe this was the end of the last war, Jack thought. If so, no, it didn't have to be pretty.

It was a good dawn for General Bondarenko, and was about to get better. Colonel Tolkunov came running into his command center holding a sheet of paper.

'We just copied this off the Chinese radio, military and civilian. They are ordering their forces to cease fire in place and to prepare to withdraw from our territory.'

'Oh? What makes them think we will let them go?' the Russian commander asked.

'It's a beginning, Comrade General. If this is accompanied by a diplomatic approach to Moscow, then the war will soon be over. You have won,' the colonel added.

'Have I?' Gennady Iosifovich asked. He stretched. It felt good this morning, looking at his maps, seeing the deployments, and knowing that he held the upper hand. If this was the end of the war, and he was the winner, then that was sufficient to the moment, wasn't it? 'Very well. Confirm this with Moscow.'

It wasn't that easy, of course. Units in contact continued to trade shots for some hours until the orders reached them, but then the firing died down, and the invading troops withdrew away from their enemies, and the Russians, with orders of their own, didn't follow. By sunset, the shooting and the killing had stopped, pending final disposition. Church bells rang all over Russia.

*   *   *

Golovko took note of the bells and the people in the streets, swigging their vodka and celebrating their country's victory. Russia felt like a great power again, and that was good for the morale of the people. Better yet, in another few years they'd start reaping the harvest of their resources—and before that would come bridge loans of enormous size . . . and maybe, just maybe, Russia would turn the corner, finally, and begin a new century well, after wasting most of the previous one.

*   *   *

It was nightfall before the word got out from Beijing to the rest of China. The end of the war so recently started came as a shock to those who'd never really understood the reasons or the facts in the first place. Then came word that the government had changed, and that was also a puzzling development for which explanations would have to wait. The interim Premier was Fang Gan, a name known from pictures rather than words or deeds, but he looked old and wise, and China was a country of great momentum rather than great thoughts, and though the course of the country would change, it would change slowly so far as its people were concerned. People shrugged, and discussed the puzzling new developments in quiet and measured words.

For one particular person in Beijing, the changes meant that her job would change somewhat in importance if not in actual duties. Ming went out to

781

dinner—the restaurants hadn't closed—with her foreign lover, gushing over drinks and noodles with the extraordinary events of the day, then walked off to his apartment for a dessert of Japanese sausage.